EIGHT WORKS FROM TODAY'S MOST EXCITING NEW PLAYWRIGHTS

David Rabe's **STREAMERS,** set in a U.S. Army post in Virginia, is a scathing indictment of the military—and modern American society.

MARCO POLO SINGS A SOLO is John Guare's "brilliantly absurdist comedy of ideas" (*The New York Times*) set on an iceberg off the coast of Norway.

Arthur Kopit's **WINGS,** called "wise, magical, and shattering" by *The New York Times*, explores the tormented mind of a former aviatrix who has suffered a stroke.

Christopher Durang's **SISTER MARY IGNATIUS EXPLAINS IT ALL FOR YOU** brings together an unbending, pathological Catholic school nun and four of her former students in a work that is "ferociously unique" (*The New York Times*).

CRIMES OF THE HEART, Beth Henley's Pulitzer Prize-winning play, is written with "a daffy complexity of plot that old pros like Kaufman and Hart would have envied" (*The New Yorker*), and depicts three wacky sisters on a series of "bad days" in Hazlehurst, Mississippi.

In **THE DINING ROOM,** New York Drama Desk Award-winner A. R. Gurney offers a changing tableau of characters connected to each other only through the room itself.

In **PAINTING CHURCHES,** Tina Howe crafts a "radiant, loving, zestfully humorous play" (*Time*) about a portrait painter and her aging parents.

MA RAINEY'S BLACK BOTTOM, by Pulitzer Prize-winner August Wilson, "a major find for the American theater" (*The New York Times*), is a devastating exploration of the destruction of black lives and black identity.

MENTOR Books of Plays   (0451)

☐ **EIGHT GREAT TRAGEDIES edited by Sylvan Barnet, Morton Berman and William Burto.** The great dramatic literature of the ages. Eight memorable tragedies by Aeschylus, Euripides, Sophocles, Shakespeare, Ibsen, Strindberg, Yeats, and O'Neill. With essays on tragedy by Aristotle, Emerson and others.   (626788—$4.95)

☐ **EIGHT GREAT COMEDIES edited by Sylvan Barnet, Morton Berman and William Burto.** Complete texts of eight masterpieces of comic drama by Aristophanes, Machiavelli, Shakespeare, Molière, John Gay, Wilde, Chekhov, and Shaw. Includes essays on comedy by four distinguished critics and scholars.   (623649—$4.95)

☐ **THE GENIUS OF THE EARLY ENGLISH THEATRE edited by Sylvan Barnet, Morton Berman and William Burto.** Complete plays including three anonymous plays—"Abraham and Isaac," "The Second Shepherd's Play," and "Everyman," and Marlowe's "Doctor Faustus," Shakespeare's "Macbeth," Jonson's "Volpone," and Milton's "Samson Agonistes," with critical essays.   (624432—$4.95)*

☐ **THE MENTOR BOOK OF SHORT PLAYS edited by Richard Goldstone and Abraham H. Lass.** Introduction and "On Reading Plays" by the editors. Includes works of Granberry, Inge, Synge, Vidal, Chayefsky, Rose, Gregory, Wilde, Williams, Chekhov, Rostand, and Rattigan.   (626311—$4.95)

☐ **SCENES AND MONOLOGUES FROM THE NEW AMERICAN THEATER Edited by Frank Pike and Thomas G. Dunn.** A collection of exciting, playable new scenes for two men, two women, or a man-woman team, plus 19 outstanding monologues. Fresh material from America's dynamic young playwrights. An essential book for every actor. (625471—$4.95)

☐ **PLAYS FROM THE CONTEMPORARY AMERICAN THEATER, edited and with an introduction by Brooks McNamara.** Modern American drama from the pens of eight noted playwrights: David Rabe, Arthur Kopit, A.R. Gurney, Christopher Durang, John Guare, Beth Henley, August Wilson, and Tina Howe.   (625803—$6.95)

*Prices slightly higher in Canada

PLAYS FROM THE CONTEMPORARY AMERICAN THEATER

Edited and
with an Introduction by

Brooks McNamara

A MENTOR BOOK

NEW AMERICAN LIBRARY

NEW YORK AND SCARBOROUGH, ONTARIO

NAL BOOKS ARE AVAILABLE AT QUANTITY DISCOUNTS
WHEN USED TO PROMOTE PRODUCTS OR SERVICES.
FOR INFORMATION PLEASE WRITE TO PREMIUM MARKETING DIVISION.
NEW AMERICAN LIBRARY, 1633 BROADWAY,
NEW YORK, NEW YORK 10019.

ACKNOWLEDGMENTS
Streamers by David Rabe. Copyright as an unpublished work 1970,
1975 by David William Rabe. Copyright © 1976, 1977 by David
William Rabe. Reprinted by permission of Alfred A. Knopf, Inc.
Marco Polo Sings a Solo by John Guare. Copyright © 1977 by St. Jude
Productions, Inc. Reprinted by permission of St. Jude Productions,
Inc.
Wings by Arthur Kopit. Copyright © 1978 by Arthur Kopit. Reprinted by
permission of Farrar, Straus and Giroux, Inc. and International
Creative Management, Inc.

(The Following page constitutes an extension of this copyright page.)

MENTOR TRADEMARK REG. U.S. PAT. OFF. AND FOREIGN COUNTRIES

REGISTERED TRADEMARK—MARCA REGISTRADA

HECHO EN CHICAGO, U.S.A.

SIGNET, SIGNET CLASSIC, MENTOR, ONYX, PLUME, MERIDIAN and NAL
BOOKS are published *in the United States* by NAL PENGUIN INC.,
1633 Broadway, New York, New York 10019,
in Canada by The New American Library of Canada Limited,
81 Mack Avenue, Scarborough, Ontario M1L 1M8

Library of Congress Catalog Card Number: 87–63517

First Printing, June, 1988

1 2 3 4 5 6 7 8 9

PRINTED IN THE UNITED STATES OF AMERICA

To Nan

Contents

ACKNOWLEDGMENTS

With special thank to four friends whose generosity and support helped to make this anthology possible: Diane Cleaver, Eileen Blumenthal, Cynthia Jenner, and Andrea Stulman Dennett.

Introduction

The eight plays in this anthology, all produced between 1976 and 1984, reflect the tremendous changes that have overtaken American theatre in recent years. Not so long ago, their authors could have expected to see these plays presented on Broadway. Yet, by the mid-seventies this was no longer the case: some of the plays began and ended their runs in off-Broadway theatres; others originated off-off-Broadway or in university or regional companies. Although several of the plays ultimately wound up on Broadway, not one of them got its start there.

But the altered circumstances of production tell only part of the story. Since the sixties there have been landmark changes in both the form and content of American playwriting. Although one or two of the plays presented here have the kind of traditional cause-and-effect structure typical of most American plays before the sixties, the majority are far looser and more episodic. And, for the most part, the subjects the playwrights address, the behavior they catalogue, and the language their characters speak are light-years away from anything to be found on the American stage even a quarter century ago. The story of these changes represents an important background to the eight plays presented here.

In 1961, Robert Corrigan, the editor of *The Tulane Drama Review,* wrote an editorial about the new Absurdist writers of Europe. Their radical plays, he argued, offered a "vitality we have missed" in the American theatre. At the time there were those who vehemently disputed his conclusions. But in retrospect it is clear that American playwriting of the forties and fifties had indeed lacked a certain kind of essential vitality. Besides Tennessee Williams and Arthur Miller, few American writers for the theatre seemed much interested in experimenting with either form or content.

By the late fifties, however, as Corrigan would note, a new

and freer approach to playwriting had already started to de-velop in America as the Absurdist plays of Jean Genet, Eu-gene Ionesco, and Samuel Beckett began to be seen and imitated here. Such works as Beckett's *Waiting for Godot*, Ionesco's *The Bald Soprano*, and Genet's *The Balcony* had been, in effect, attempts to demonstrate the absurdity of existence and the treacherousness of language. They reflected that same absurdity in new dramatic forms that challenged the traditional organization of incidents (exposition, complication, crisis, and resolution) that had been the standard of most plays up to their time. At the end of the decade, the important influence of the Absurdists was seen here in such plays as Edward Albee's *The Sand Box* (1959), *The Zoo Story* (1960), and *The American Dream* (1961), and in Arthur Kopit's *Oh, Dad, Poor Dad, Mama's Hung You in the Closet and I'm Feeling So Sad* (1960).

The venue for many of these European and American Ab-surdist plays was off-Broadway. Begun in the 1950s as a reac-tion against the so-called commercialization of Broadway and its rapidly rising production costs, such groups as the Circle in the Square and the Phoenix Theatre were attempts to bring first-rate "non-commercial" plays to discerning audiences. Sim-ilarly progressive theatres were being founded outside New York City by such regional producers as Margo Jones, Nina Vance, Zelda Fichandler, Jules Irving, and Herbert Blau.

By the sixties, however, off-Broadway was increasingly being forced to respond to many of the same economic pressures that had shaped Broadway producing for so many years. And with somewhat similar results; in many theatres play selection be-came safer and less challenging. As a result, New York's center of creative experiment in playwriting and production began to shift to the still newer theatres which, in 1969, the *Village Voice* labeled "off-off-Broadway."

It was in these theatres that the whole nature of playwriting was being most seriously and hotly debated during the sixties and early seventies. The convictions about experiment being put into practice off-off-Broadway would have a profound influ-ence on the whole course of writing for the American theatre. Some of the new breed of directors and producers were com-mitted both to a revolutionary political stance and to an ex-treme reshaping of the play in production. They were influenced by Julian Beck and Judith Malina's anarchist Living Theatre and by the theories of Bertold Brecht and Antonin Artaud. They were inspired by the so-called "Happenings" movement from the art world, and by the work of such prominent Eastern

European directors as Jerzy Grotowski. Many of them abandoned conventional theatres, performing in parks, on street corners, and in "environments" where actors and spectators shared the same space. In the most radical of these companies, the creative process and the actual performance would come to assume far greater importance than the play text.

For example, in the Open Theatre, founded in 1963 by Joseph Chaiken and Peter Feldman, the playwright developed the script in conjunction with the company, using improvisation, game theory, role playing, and other devices. Perhaps the Open Theatre's best known and most praised effort was *The Serpent* (1969), in which playwright Jean Claude van Itallie and the actors mixed biblical material with current politics in a highly abstract and unorthodox form.

The most extreme American avant-gardists of the day would declare playwriting officially dead. But such attacks during the late sixties and early seventies seem simply to have freed writers to work in increasingly non-traditional ways. By this period, a number of institutions—both off-off Broadway and outside New York—had begun actively promoting the work of these new playwrights. As early as 1961, for example, Joe Cino had begun to produce experimental plays in his Caffe Cino coffee house in Greenwich Village, and by the middle of the decade he had staged the work of some two hundred writers.

Ellen Stewart's venerable Cafe La Mama, founded in 1961, produced hundreds of experimental plays. The Judson Poets Theatre, also created in 1961, became the home of a number of small, experimental musicals, many of which were written by the theatre's founder, Al Carmines. Three years later the American Place Theatre would be established specifically as a venue for new American writers. Other producing groups with an interest in new plays gradually appeared, among them the Manhattan Theatre Club, Playwrights Horizons, Circle Rep, and the Ensemble Studio Theatre.

In addition, such agencies as the Ford, Rockefeller, and Shubert Foundations and the National Endowment for the Arts had come to recognize the importance of playwriting and were now directly subsidizing the work of promising American dramatists. Beyond this, from the late fifties onward, major grants began to become available to support resident companies. As a result, by the seventies, there were more potential homes for new plays outside New York and a growing regional interest in developing new playwriting talent.

A number of regional companies, among them the Mark

Taper Forum in Los Angeles, the Tyrone Guthrie Theatre in Minneapolis, and the Dallas Theatre Center, developed new play projects and playwright-in-residence programs, as did several major universities. New writers could also now receive financial assistance, criticism, and exposure for their plays at the New Dramatists Committee in New York and the National Playwrights Conference at the Eugene O'Neill Center in Waterford, Connecticut. During the seventies and eighties, the route taken by a new play has often led from one of these institutions to another—or to several others—through a mixture of readings, workshops, small showcase productions, and full-scale presentations. Broadway production has become increasingly less of an issue.

Sometimes—although less and less frequently—the path has led ultimately to Broadway. But the examples are few and far between. The economics of professional theatre in New York City has made the straight play an endangered species in Broadway houses. The problem is a complex one, but ultimately it seems to come down to the fact that Broadway audiences seem disinclined to support straight plays in sufficient numbers to interest commercial producers and theatre owners in the playwrights' products. There are exceptions, of course; as Robert Anderson suggested, a playwright can make a killing on Broadway even though he or she can't make a living there. But many producers feel, on the basis of bitter experience, that a straight play—especially one with a large cast and more than a single set—is unlikely to show a profit on Broadway. They are probably correct.

Joseph Papp's Public Theatre, however, has become an especially important pipeline to Broadway for both straight plays and musicals. In 1967, Papp, who had worked with the New York Shakespeare Festival since the fifties, acquired the old Astor Library in Greenwich Village, which he turned into a striking performing arts complex. The new complex opened with a production of the radical rock musical, *Hair. Hair* went on to Broadway to become a smash hit, as did a number of other Public Theatre shows, including the legendary *Chorus Line* (1975) and such important straight plays as Charles Gordone's *No Place to Be Somebody* (1969) and Jason Miller's *That Championship Season* (1971). In recent years also, the Yale School of Drama has managed to move several prestigious plays to Broadway, including most recently August Wilson's 1987 hit, *Fences.*

Out of this complicated web of organizations has come a

number of significant new writers for the theatre, among them Sam Shepard, Lanford Wilson, Irene Fornes, Israel Horowitz, Ed Bullins, Rochelle Owens, Paul Foster, Miguel Pinero, Adrienne Kennedy, David Mamet, Amiri Baraka, Albert Innaurato, Richard Wesley, Charles Gordone, Terence McNally, Romulus Linney, and Ronald Ribman, as well as such playwright-directors as Richard Foreman, Charles Ludlam, Lee Breuer, JoAnne Akalaitis, and Robert Wilson. And, of course, the eight writers included in this anthology: Christopher Durang, John Guare, A. R. Gurney, Beth Henley, Tina Howe, Arthur Kopit, David Rabe, and August Wilson.

It is impossible to generalize about the work of America's new playwrights. But it is important to emphasize once again that, for the most part, their work is very different from anything seen in America before the 1960s. For one thing, the "demographics" of playwriting have radically changed. Not only do plays now routinely originate all over America, but also, for the first time in our history, there is a growing—and increasingly articulate—body of women, blacks, Hispanics, and Asians writing for the theatre.

Moreover, the grammar of contemporary playwriting is by no means that of the previous generation. Probably there is a debt to the structural principles of film and television among these writers. In any case, many of them clearly organize their material in ways that are far more cinematic than traditionally theatrical. There is also a new kind of fragmentation and abstraction behind the structure of these contemporary plays which apparently derives from the radical avant-garde of the late sixties and early seventies. In addition, there seems to be a debt to the earlier avant-gardists in the new writers' frank, often brutal language, their candid view of sexuality, their bizarre comedy, and their commitment to candid treatments of such subjects as war, politics, race relations, religion, and homosexuality. Such candor would have been unthinkable not so long ago.

The eight plays collected here suggest some of the broad range of American playwriting in the last dozen years or so. David Rabe's *Streamers* is the earliest of the plays, produced first at the Long Wharf Theatre in New Haven in January 1976, and later that year by Joseph Papp at the Mitzi Newhouse Theatre at Lincoln Center. Rabe, a Vietnam veteran, had previously written two shattering and controversial indictments of the war, *The Basic Training of Pavlo Hummel* and *Sticks and*

Bones, both of which were produced by Papp at the Public Theatre in 1971. *Pavlo Hummel* examined the effect of the Vietnam war on both soldiers and noncombatants, while *Sticks and Bones* centered on the tragic aftermath of Vietnam and its effect on a Middle American family. *Streamers,* in a sense, formed the third part of this Vietnam war trilogy in which Rabe, as he said, attempted "to define the event for myself and for other people."

Streamers is set in a single grim room in a Virginia army barracks in 1965. The characters are soldiers, among them a middle-class homosexual, a pair of drunken, over-the-hill sergeants, one of whom is dying of leukemia, and an unbalanced young black man, who sets in motion the play's terrifying and bloody climax. Rabe's play, although realistic in its approach, is structurally unconventional. For example, relatively little happens before that climax. We simply learn about the characters and their relationship, as the pain, futility, and horror of war and the military gradually permeate the dismal room. The inevitable end is murder: that is all there is.

The play was received with great enthusiasm by the majority of critics, although most of them seemed a bit wary about the play's meaning and whether it was, in fact, even a war play in the conventional sense. For Julius Novick of the *Village Voice,* *Streamers* was "not fundamentally about 'Vietnam,' or about the army, but about how people's needs and wants and fears and ways of being impinge on other people, and about how people deal with these impingements." *The New York Times* critic Walter Kerr arrived at a somewhat similar view. Kerr wrote that the play's "actual message, if I read it correctly, is this. We are all—black, white, straight, queer, parents, children, friends, foes, stable, unstable—living together in the same 'house.' And we can't do it."

John Guare's futuristic comedy, *Marco Polo Sings a Solo,* strikes a very different theatrical note. Guare, the author of the well-known and much praised *The House of Blue Leaves* (1971), has been described by Lloyd Rose in *Atlantic Monthly* as "cerebral, a little abstract." His plays, Rose suggests, "feel like librettos set to some manic melody he can't get out of his head. Certainly they give the sense, as John Stuart Mill wrote of poetry, of having been overheard. Guare is in love with language, and the American dreamers of his plays revel in talk. They tell long, marvelous stories. They give long, impassioned monologues. And they never really listen to one another."

The American dreamers of *Marco Polo Sings a Solo* are a

curious lot. The play, which was first produced at the Nantucket Stage Company in 1973, opened in a drastically rewritten version at the Public Theatre in 1977, with an extraordinary cast which included Madeline Kahn, Chris Sarandon, Joel Grey, and Anne Jackson. Clearly Absurdist in its orientation, *Marco Polo* is set in 1999 on an iceberg off the coast of Norway. The central character, Stony McBride, is making a movie about Marco Polo, while his wife engages in an affair with a statesman who has found a cure for cancer. The film stars McBride's father who is really his mother, and the action of the play includes an earthquake, the discovery of an uncharted planet, astral impregnation by an astronaut, and the birth of a new hero at a moment when McBride and his entourage teeter on the brink of some ghastly new reality.

In one sense Guare's bizarre adventure is a kind of vaudeville— an anthology of traditional comedy devices. But the comedy material is used with a reverse English that turns *Marco Polo* finally into a study in isolation and despair. As Guare himself phrased it: "Everyone in the play is Marco Polo, travelling out of himself, herself, or both selves as in the case of one character. The people's very freedom makes them terrified. All walls are down. They are by themselves."

Arthur Kopit's *Wings* eventually reached Broadway by a circuitous route. Written originally in 1976 for National Public Radio's "Earplay" series, it was heard by Robert Brustein, then Dean of the Yale School of Drama, who commissioned a stage version of the script for the Yale Repertory Theatre in New Haven. The Yale Rep brought the play to the Public Theatre for a limited run in 1978. It was produced by Roger Stevens for the Kennedy Center at Broadway's Lyceum Theatre in 1979.

Kopit is probably the most widely produced of the playwrights represented here, and several of his plays are American standards, among them the early *Oh, Dad Poor Dad . . .* (1960), and *Indians* (1968). *Wings* is both a brilliant summary of Kopit's twenty-year exploration of playwriting technique and an intensely personal and private play. In 1976 Kopit's father suffered a stroke which left him incapable of speech. *Wings* came about as a result of his son's attempt to deal with puzzling and frustrating questions about his father's infirmity: "To what extent was he still intact?" Kopit asked himself. "To what extent was he aware of what had befallen him? *What was it like inside?*"

At one level, the play—almost a monologue—is about a former aviatrix, Emily Stilson (played by Constance Cummings) who suffers a stroke and loses her powers of speech. Throughout the play she struggles to regain it, and, to a limited extent, she does so, only to be imprisoned anew by a second stroke at the end of the play. In a larger sense, however, *Wings* is about a human being attempting to re-establish her connections with a lost reality, once again to communicate. As Richard Eder of the *Times* phrased it, the play "presents a mind whose language has been knocked out from under it; one that struggles blindly, with alternating grace and terror, to regain its footing."

What is perhaps most powerful and most remarkable about *Wings* is that the movement of the play seems to take place within Emily's tortured mind. As Kopit suggests in his notes on producing the play: "No attempt should be made to create a literal representation of Mrs. Stilson's world, especially since Mrs. Stilson's world is no longer in any way literal. The scenes should blend. No clear boundaries or domains in time or space for Mrs. Stilson any more." Once again, in her torment, the old aviatrix flies free, and the audience flies with her. Gerald Rabkin of the *SoHo Weekly News* caught the experience this way: "With her we soar far above the ground. With her we fight free of the physical pain and limitations of the human body. We float to the ceiling and beyond. It is exhilarating but also terrifying for there is no place to land."

In Christopher Durang's *Sister Mary Ignatius Explains It All for You* there is no place to hide. Your sins will find you out in the person of Durang's engagingly homicidal nun. Durang, a product of Harvard and the Yale Drama School, is perhaps the most consciously comic of the new American playwrights, although his comedy takes on a macabre cutting edge in such works as *The Marriage of Bette and Boo* (1973) and *A History of the American Film* (1976). And especially in *Sister Mary Ignatius*. First produced off-off-Broadway at the Ensemble Studio Theatre in 1980, it was seen again a year later at Playwrights Horizons, along with another Durang one-act, *The Actor's Nightmare*.

Durang is a wicked parodist. In *American Film,* for example, he dissected the central clichés of our motion-picture industry; in *Nightmare* he brought together and annihilated an unlikely quartet of playwrights: Noel Coward, Shakespeare, Samuel Beckett, and Robert Bolt. With *Sister Mary Ignatius,* Durang turned a blinding comic spotlight on a far more controversial subject, the Catholic Church in America. Like Kopit's *Wings, Sister Mary Ignatius* is basically a monologue with additional characters; also like *Wings* it stems from catastrophic events in the writer's life and the questions which resulted from them. Durang began his play as his mother, a devout Catholic, was dying of cancer, and finished it a few months after her death. "The play," Durang says, "was in no way written 'because' my mother died. It was written partly in giddy recall (who can believe we once believed in limbo?), and partially in anger (the Church's teachings on sex have done nobody any good). And it's also written from a basic, and disappointed, non-belief. . . ."

The play begins as a bizarre moral lecture by Sister, assisted by a seven-year-old boy who serves as a kind of stooge and acolyte. As the lecture progresses, four of Sister's former students enter to present a Christmas pageant, disguised as Mary, Joseph, and the front and rear halves of a camel. The students, we discover, have not turned out quite as Sister would have hoped: one is an alcoholic, another a homosexual, a third has had numerous abortions, and the fourth has had an illegitimate child. The play now turns in a different—and murderous—direction. As Frank Rich of the *Times* noted, the comedic confrontation escalates "to a literally violent climax that strips the nun's moral authority bare even as it allows her to retain her crippling psychological power over her students, past and present."

Sister Mary Ignatius has been an immense success—and immensely controversial. But, as Durang suggested in the *Times* about his title character, "She's not the entire Catholic church any more than Medea was every mother who ever lived. . . . Further, my play attacks ideas taught by the conservative Church to me and to countless others—that any sex whatsoever outside of marriage sends you to burn in hell everlastingly, for instance. If we are not allowed to criticize ideas, I don't know what the use of free speech is."

Murder—or at least the attempt—is also on the minds of a number of characters in Beth Henley's Pulitzer Prize-winning *Crimes of the Heart*. Henley, a Mississippian, is the author of several other plays, among them *The Miss Firecracker Contest,* a recent off-Broadway production, and, like *Crimes of the Heart,* a study in Southern Gothic comedy. First presented at the Actor's Theatre of Louisville in 1979, Henley's *Crimes* made its New York debut at the Manhattan Theatre Club the following year and moved to the Golden Theatre on Broadway in 1981. The play has been made into a film starring Sissy Spacek, Jessica Lang, Diane Keaton, and Sam Shepard.

Crimes of the Heart is a pitch-black comedy about the lives of three sisters in a small Mississippi town. It is a town that would have endeared itself to Chekhov or Tennessee Williams: Lenny is approaching spinsterhood with a "shrunken ovary" and no gentleman callers; Meg, who escaped the town for a singing career that never happened, has returned after a period in a psychiatric ward; Babe has shot her husband in the stomach and is not much interested in whether he lives or dies. Meanwhile, Babe's husband has come up with a set of highly inflammatory photographs of her affair with a fifteen-year-old black boy, Lenny's pet horse has died, and their grandfather has suffered a stroke and lies comatose in the hospital. It is, as Babe points out, a "bad day" in Hazlehurst, Mississippi.

In a sense, *Crimes of the Heart* is the most traditionally structured of the plays in this anthology. Still, nothing very conclusive happens in the two days during which the play takes place. As Stanley Kauffman noted in *Saturday Review,* the heart of Henley's play is "the tension between the fierce lurking lunacy underlying the small-town life she knows so well and the sunny surface that tries to accommodate it. *Crimes* moves to no real resolution, but this is part of its power. It presents a condition that, in miniscule, implies much about the state of the world, as well as the state of Mississippi, and about human chaos; it says, 'Resolution is not my business. Ludicrously horrifying honesty is.' "

A. R. Gurney's *The Dining Room* and Tina Howe's *Painting Churches* both examine another slice of Americana—what an anthropology student in *The Dining Room* refers to with clinical precision as "the WASPS of the Northeastern United States." Both plays are basically comedy, but their moods and emphases are very different. Gurney (St. Paul's School, Williams, Yale Drama School) is clearly the product of the world about which he writes—a "protected, genteel, in many ways warm, civilized, and fundamentally innocent world," which, he says, "didn't seem in any way to prepare me for the late twentieth century." In such plays as *Scenes from American Life* (1970), *The Middle Ages* (1977) and the recent *The Perfect Party* (1986), Gurney says, he writes about "people who are operating under these old assumptions, but are confronting an entirely different system of values."

In *The Dining Room,* first produced at Playwrights Horizons in 1981, the old assumptions and the new values confront each other in an archetypal WASP setting. The dining room is occupied during the course of the play by six actors who play several dozen different people of all ages, who are glimpsed on various private and public occasions. Each scene is a separate entity, connected to the others only through the room itself and the shared conventions of those who love it—or who flee from it.

We eavesdrop on a quarrel between a brother and sister over who will inherit the dining room table, a senile matriarch at Thanksgiving dinner, an old man dictating his funeral arrangements, the student anthropologist interviewing his aunt about "the eating habits of various vanishing cultures." Finally, *The Dining Room* is less a play than a kind of revue, made up of sketches and vignettes around a central theme which Julius Novick of the *Village Voice* defines as "the dying life-style of wealthy WASPdom."

Novick's comment is perhaps an even more accurate description of Tina Howe's *Painting Churches*. Howe comes from a distinguished Boston family and is well qualified to examine the folkways of the Eastern Establishment. She is the author of two other well received plays, *Museum* (1977) and *The Art of Dining* (1979), and the recent Broadway success, *Coastal Disturbances* (1987). *Painting Churches*, which featured Marian Seldes, was produced initially by the Second Stage at New York's South Street Theatre in 1983; it moved the next year to the off-Broadway Lambs Theatre.

Although richly comic in its way, *Painting Churches* is also a very serious study in the fading of cultures, and families and individuals. The plot—more a situation, really—involves Mags Church, a New York artist who returns to her Boston home to paint a picture of her parents just as they are about to retire and move permanently to their summer cottage in Cotuit. Her father is a distinguished poet who has become distinctly vague in old age, and her mother is an outlandish Brahmin whose life has come to little or nothing.

Mags's painting provides the real core of the action. As it progresses, the grand Beacon Hill drawing room is gradually emptied of its contents and the lives of Gardner and Fanny Church seem to waste away moment by moment on the stage. We soon see, too, that Mags, the painter, is every bit as mad and lost as the father and mother whom she is recording on canvas. As Ross Wetzsteon suggests in *New York Magazine,* this inevitable ebbing away reveals "the two emotions one always feels at a Tina Howe play—delight at the eccentricity of the world she presents and pain at the sudden shafts of recognition."

August Wilson's *Ma Rainey's Black Bottom* explores another sort of ebbing away—the destruction of black lives and black identity in a white racist society. Workshopped at the Eugene

O'Neill Theatre Center and first produced at the Yale Rep in New Haven in 1984, the play moved to Broadway's Cort Theatre later the same year. Its author, a poet and playwright, has also written the Pulitzer Prize-winning *Fences* (1987).

Ma Rainey is loosely based on a historical figure, the famous blues singer Gertrude "Ma" Rainey, and is set at a recording session for one of her songs, from which the title of the play is taken. At the session we see that Ma Rainey, like other black artists of her day, is grossly exploited by white recording entrepreneurs. In fact, she has been turned into a kind of grotesque parody of these powerful influences. As Frank Rich suggested in the *Times:* "We soon realize that, while Ma's music is from the heart, her life has become a sad, ludicrous 'imitation' of white stardom."

The play, however, is not really centered on the old singer at all, but on the four backup musicians who are working with her that day. The action of *Ma Rainey* takes on a kind of musical structure as it plumbs their lives and personalities through the music and the increasingly volatile talk in the shabby bandroom next door to the recording studio. Finally, one of the musicians, Levee, is driven to a murderous rage as white exploitation of him and his people hits home. Levee's rage creates a terrifying and bloody climax for *Ma Rainey's Black Bottom.* As Michael Feingold noted in the *Village Voice,* however, the "white exploitation of black artists is only one ongoing theme of *Ma Rainey.*" That theme, Feingold suggests, is mirrored by a second one: "the inability of blacks—and of artists—to make common cause in the face of the exploiters."

These are the eight plays. I have tried to suggest the common theatrical heritage which stands behind them all and at least some sense of what makes each distinctive and an important artistic document. The rest is up to the reader.

—Brooks McNamara
NEW YORK UNIVERSITY

STREAMERS

A DRAMA IN TWO ACTS

by
David Rabe

Streamers was produced by the Long Wharf Theater on January 30, 1976 under the direction of Mike Nichols with the following cast:

MARTIN	*Michael-Raymond O'Keefe*
RICHIE	*Peter Evans*
CARLYLE	*Joe Fields*
BILLY	*John Heard*
ROGER	*Herbert Jefferson Jr.*
COKES	*Dolph Sweet*
ROONEY	*Kenneth McMillan*
M.P. LIEUTENANT	*Stephen Mendillo*
PFC HINSON (M.P.)	*Ron Siebert*
PFC CLARK (M.P.)	*Michael Kell*

Set by Tony Walton; costumes by Bill Walker; lighting by Ronald Wallace; stage manager Nina Seely.

Streamers was produced in New York by Joseph Papp on April 21, 1976 at the Mitzi Newhouse Theater at Lincoln Center under the direction of Mike Nichols with the following cast:

MARTIN	*Michael Kell*
RICHIE	*Peter Evans*
CARLYLE	*Dorian Harewood*
BILLY	*Paul Rudd*
ROGER	*Terry Alexander*

COKES ....*Dolph Sweet*

ROONEY ....*Kenneth McMillan*

M.P. LIEUTENANT ....*Arlen Dean Snyder*

PFC HINSON (M.P.) ....*Les Roberts*

PFC CLARK (M.P.) ....*Mark Metcalf*

FOURTH M.P. ....*Miklos Horvath*

Associate Producer, Bernard Gersten; set by Tony Walton; costumes by Bill Walker; lighting by Ronald Wallace; stage manager Nina Seely.

ACT I

The set is a large Cadre Room thrusting angularly toward the audience. The floor is wooden and brown. Brightly waxed in places, it is worn and dull in other sections. The back wall is brown and angled. There are two hanging lights at the center of the room. They hang covered by green metal shades. Against the back wall and to the stage right side are three wall lockers side by side. Stage center in the back wall is the door, the only entrance to the room. It opens onto a hallway that runs off to the latrines, showers, other cadre rooms and larger barracks rooms. There are three bunks. BILLY'S bunk is parallel to ROGER'S bunk. They are upstage and on either side of the room, and face downstage. RICHIE'S bunk is downstage and at a right angle to BILLY'S bunk. At the foot of each bunk is a green, wooden footlocker. There is a floor plug near ROGER'S bunk. He uses it for his radio. A reading lamp is clamped onto the metal piping at the head of RICHIE'S bunk. A wooden chair stands beside the wall lockers. Two mops hang in the stage left corner near a trash can.

It is dusk as the lights rise on the room. RICHIE is seated and bowed forward wearily on his bunk. He wears his long sleeved, Khaki summer dress uniform. Upstage behind him is MARTIN, a thin, dark young man, pacing, worried. A white towel stained red with blood is wrapped across his wrist. He paces several steps and falters, stops. He stands there.

RICHIE. Honest to god, Martin, I don't know what to say anymore. I don't know what to tell you.
MARTIN. (Beginning to pace again.) I mean it. I just can't stand it. Look at me.
RICHIE. I know.
MARTIN. I hate it.
RICHIE. We've got to make up a story. They'll ask you a hundred questions.

17

MARTIN. Do you know how I hate it?

RICHIE. Everybody does. Don't you think I hate it, too?

MARTIN. I enlisted, though. I enlisted and I hate it.

RICHIE. I enlisted, too.

MARTIN. I vomit every morning. I get the dry heaves. In the middle of every night. (*He flops down on the corner of* BILLY'S *bed and sits there, slumped forward, shaking his head.*)

RICHIE. You can stop that. You can.

MARTIN. No.

RICHIE. You're just scared. It's just fear.

MARTIN. They're all so mean; they're all so awful. I've got two years to go. Just thinking about it is going to make me sick. I thought it would be different from the way it is.

RICHIE. But you could have died, for god's sake. (*He has turned now; he is facing* MARTIN.)

MARTIN. I just wanted out.

RICHIE. I might not have found you, though. I might not have come up here.

MARTIN. I don't care. I'd be out.

(*The door opens and a black man in filthy fatigues—they are grease-stained and dark with sweat—stands there. He is* CARLYLE, *looking about.* RICHIE, *seeing him, rises and moves toward him.*)

RICHIE. No. Roger isn't here right now.

CARLYLE. Who isn't?

RICHIE. He isn't here.

CARLYLE. They tole me a black boy livin' in here. I don't see him. (*He looks suspiciously about the room.*)

RICHIE. That's what I'm saying. He isn't here. He'll be back later. You can come back later. His name is Roger.

MARTIN. I slit my wrist. (*Thrusting out the bloody towel-wrapped wrist.*)

RICHIE. Martin! Jesus!

MARTIN. I did.

RICHIE. He's kidding. He's kidding.

CARLYLE. What was his name? Martin? (*He is confused and the confusion has made him angry. He moves toward* MARTIN.) You Martin?

MARTIN. Yes.

(*As* BILLY, *a white in his mid-twenties, blonde and trim, appears in the door, whistling, carrying a slice of pie on a paper napkin. Sensing something, he falters, looks at* CARLYLE, *then* RICHIE.)

BILLY. Hey, what's goin' on?

CARLYLE. (*Turning, leaving.*) Nothin', man. Not a thing.

(BILLY *looks questioningly at* RICHIE. *Then, after placing piece of pie on the chair beside the door, he crosses to his footlocker.*)

RICHIE. He came in looking for Roger, but he didn't even know his name.

BILLY. (*Sitting on his footlocker, he starts taking off his shoes.*) How come you weren't at dinner, Rich? I brought you a piece of pie. Hey, Martin.

MARTIN. (*Thrust out his wrist and towel.*) I cut my wrist, Billy.

RICHIE. Oh, for god's sake, Martin! (*He whirls away.*)

BILLY. Huh?

MARTIN. I did.

RICHIE. You are disgusting, Martin.

MARTIN. No. It's the truth, I did. I am not disgusting.

RICHIE. Well, maybe it isn't disgusting, but it certainly is disappointing.

BILLY. What are you guys talking about? (*Sitting there, he really doesn't know what is going on.*)

MARTIN. I cut my wrists, I slashed them, and Richie is pretending I didn't.

RICHIE. I am not. And you only cut one wrist and you didn't slash it.

MARTIN. I can't stand the army anymore, Billy. (*He is moving now to petition* BILLY, *and* RICHIE *steps between them.*)

RICHIE. Billy, listen to me. This is between Martin and me.

MARTIN. It's between me and the army, Richie.

RICHIE. (*Taking* MARTIN *by the shoulders as* BILLY *is now trying to get near* MARTIN.) Let's just go outside and talk, Martin. You don't know what you're saying.

BILLY. Can I see? I mean, did he really do it?

RICHIE. No!

MARTIN. I did.

BILLY. That's awful. Jesus. Maybe you should go to the infirmary.

RICHIE. I washed it with peroxide. It's not deep. Just let us be. Please. He just needs to straighten out his thinking a little, that's all.

BILLY. Well, maybe I could help him?

MARTIN. Maybe he could.

RICHIE. (*Suddenly pushing at* MARTIN, RICHIE *is angry and exasperated. He wants* MARTIN *out of the room.*) Get out of here, Martin. Billy, you do some pushups or something. (*Having been pushed toward the door,* MARTIN *wanders out.*)

BILLY. No.

RICHIE. I know what Martin needs. (RICHIE *whirls and rushes into the hall after* MARTIN, *leaving* BILLY *scrambling to get his shoes on.*)

BILLY. You're no doctor, are you? I just want to make sure he doesn't have to go to the infirmary, then I'll leave you alone. (*One shoe on, he grabs up the second and runs out the door into the hall after them.*) Martin! Martin, wait up!

(*Silence. The door has been left open. Fifteen or twenty seconds pass. Then someone is heard coming down the hall. He is singing "Get a Job" and trying to do the voices and harmonies of a vocal group.* ROGER, *a tall, well-built black in long sleeved Khakis, comes in the door. He has a laundry bag over his shoulder, a pair of clean civilian trousers and a shirt on a hanger in his other hand. After dropping the bag on the bed, he goes to his wall locker, where he carefully hangs up the civilian clothes. Returning to the bed he picks up the laundry and then, as if struck, he throws the bag down on the bed, he tears off his tie and sits angrily down on the bed. For a moment, with his head in his hands, he sits there. Then, willfully, he rises, takes up the position of attention, and simply topples forward, his hands leaping out to break his fall at the last instant to put him into the pushup position. Counting in a hissing, whispering voice, he does ten pushups before simply giving up and flopping onto his belly. He simply does not have the will to do any more. Lying there, he counts rapidly on.*)

ROGER. . . . fourteen, fifteen, twenty, twenty-five. (BILLY, *shuffling dejectedly back in, sees* ROGER *lying there.* ROGER *springs to his feet, heads toward his footlocker out of which he takes an ashtray and a pack of cigarettes.*) You come in this area, you come in here marchin', boy; standin' tall. (BILLY, *having gone to his wall locker, is tossing a Playboy Magazine onto his bunk. He will also remove a towel, a Dopp Kit and can of foot powder.*)

BILLY. I was marchin'.

ROGER. You call that marchin'?

BILLY. I was as tall as I am; I was marchin'—what do you want?

ROGER. Outa here, man; outa this goddamn typin' terrors outfit and into some kinda real army. Or else out and free.

BILLY. So go; who's stoppin' you; get out. Go on.

ROGER. Ain't you a bitch.

BILLY. You and me more regular army than the goddamn sergeants around this place, you know that?

ROGER. I was you, Billy, boy, I wouldn't be talkin' so sacrilegious so loud, or they be doin' you like they did the ole Sarge.

BILLY. He'll get off.

ROGER. Sheee-it, he'll get off. (*Sitting down on the side of his bed and facing* BILLY, ROGER *lights up a cigarette.* BILLY *has arranged the towel, Dopp Kit and foot powder on his own bed.*) Don't you think L.B.J. want to have some sergeants in that Vietnam, man. In Disneyland, baby? Lord have mercy on the ole Sarge. He goin' over there to be Mickey Mouse.

BILLY. Do him a lot of good. Make a man outa him.

ROGER. That's right, that's right. He said the same damn thing about himself and you, too, I do believe. You know what's the ole boy's MOS? His Military Occupation Specialty? Demolitions, baby. Expert is his name.

BILLY. (*Taking off his shoes and beginning to work on a sore toe,* BILLY *hardly looks up.*) You're kiddin' me.

ROGER. Do I jive?

BILLY. You mean that poor ole bastard who cannot light his own cigar for shakin' is supposed to go over there blowin' up bridges and shit? Do they wanna win this war or not, man?

ROGER. Ole Sarge was over in Europe in the big one, Billy. Did all kindsa bad things.

BILLY. (*Swinging his feet up onto the bed,* BILLY *sits, filing the cuticles of his toes, powdering his feet.*) Was he drinkin' since he got the word?

ROGER. Was he breathin', Billy? Was he breathin'?

BILLY. Well, at least he ain't cuttin' his fuckin' wrists. (*Silence.* ROGER *looks at* BILLY, *who keeps on working.*) Man, that's the real damn army over there, ain't it. That ain't shinin' your belt buckle and standin' tall. And we might end up in it, man. (*Silence.* ROGER, *rising, begins to sort his laundry.*) Roger. You ever ask yourself if you'd rather fight in a war where it was freezin' cold or one where there was awful snakes? You ever ask that question?

ROGER. Can't say I ever did.

BILLY. We used to ask it all the time. All the time. I mean, us kids sittin' out on the back porch tellin' ghost stories at night. 'Cause it was Korea time and the newspapers were fulla

pictures of soldiers in snow with white frozen beards—they got
these rags tied around their feet. And snakes. We hated snakes.
Hated 'em. I mean, it's bad enough to be in the jungle duckin'
bullets, but then you crawl right into a goddamn snake. That's
awful. That's awful.

ROGER. It don't sound none too good.

BILLY. I got my draft notice, goddamn Vietnam didn't even
exist. I mean, it existed, but not as in a war we might be in. I
started crawlin' around the floor a this house where I was
stayin' 'cause I'd dropped outa school and I was goin', "Bang,
bang," pretendin'. Jesus.

ROGER. (*Continuing with his laundry, he tries to joke.*) My
first goddamn formation in basic, Billy, this NCO's up there
jammin' away about how some a us are goin' to be dyin' in the
war. I'm sayin', "What war? What that crazy man talkin' about?"

BILLY. Us too. I couldn't believe it. I couldn't believe it. And
now we got three people goin' from here.

ROGER. Five. (*They look at each other, and then turn away,
each returning to his task.*)

BILLY. It don't seem possible. I mean, people shootin' at
you. Shootin' at you to kill you. (*Slight pause.*) It's somethin'.

ROGER. What did you decide your preferred?

BILLY. Huh?

ROGER. Did you decide you would prefer the snakes or
would you prefer the snow. 'Cause it look like it is going to be
the snakes.

BILLY. I think I had pretty much made my mind up on the
snow.

ROGER. Well, you just let 'em know that, Billy. Maybe they
get one goin' special just for you up in Alaska. You can go to
the Klondike. Fightin' some snowmen.

(RICHIE *bounds into the room and shuts the door as if to keep
out something dreadful. He looks at* ROGER *and* BILLY *and
crosses to his wall locker, pulling off his tie as he moves. Tossing
the tie into the locker, he begins unbuttoning the cuffs of his
shirt.*)

RICHIE. Hi, hi, hi, everybody. Billy, hello.

BILLY. Hey.

ROGER. What's happenin', Rich? (*Moving to the chair beside
the door, he picks up the pie* BILLY *left there. He will place the
pie atop the locker, and then, sitting, he will remove his shoes
and socks.*)

RICHIE. I simply did this rather wonderful thing for a friend of mine, helped him see himself in a clearer, more hopeful light—little room in his life for hope? And I feel very good. Didn't Billy tell you?

ROGER. About what?

RICHIE. About Martin.

ROGER. No.

BILLY. (*Looking up and speaking pointedly.*) No. (RICHIE *looks at* BILLY *and then at* ROGER. RICHIE *is truly confused.*)

RICHIE. No? No?

BILLY. What do I wanna gossip about Martin for?

RICHIE. (*He really can't figure out what is going on with* BILLY. *Shoes and socks in hand, he heads for his wall locker.*) Who was planning to gossip? I mean, it did happen. We could talk about it. I mean, I wasn't hearing his goddamn confession. Oh, my sister told me Catholics were boring.

BILLY. Good thing I ain't one anymore.

RICHIE. (*Taking off his shirt, he moves toward* ROGER.) It really wasn't anything, Roger, except Martin made this rather desperate, pathetic gesture for attention that seems to have brought to the surface Billy's more humane and protective side. (*Reaching out, he tousles* BILLY'S *hair.*)

BILLY. Man, I am gonna have to obliterate you.

RICHIE. (*Tossing his shirt into his locker.*) I don't know what you're so embarrassed about.

BILLY. I just think Martin's got enough trouble without me yappin' to everybody. (RICHIE *has moved nearer* BILLY, *his manner playful and teasing.*)

RICHIE. "Obliterate?" "Obliterate?" did you say? Oh, Billy, you better say "shit," "ain't" and "mother-fucker" real quick now or we'll all know just how far beyond the fourth grade you went.

ROGER. (*Having moved to his locker into which he is placing his folded clothes.*) You hear about the ole Sarge, Richard?

BILLY. (*Grinning.*) You ain't . . . shit . . . , mother-fucker.

ROGER. (*Laughing.*) All right.

RICHIE. (*Moving center and beginning to remove his trousers.*) Billy, no, no. Wit is my domain. You're in charge of sweat and running around the block.

ROGER. You hear about the ole Sarge?

RICHIE. What about the ole Sarge? Oh, who cares. Let's go to a movie. Billy, wanna? Let's go. C'mon. (*Trousers off, he hurries to his locker.*)

BILLY. Sure. What's playin'?

RICHIE. I don't know. Can't remember. Something good, though.

(*With a* Playboy *magazine he has taken from his locker,* ROGER *is sitting down on his bunk, his back toward both* ROGER *and* RICHIE.)

BILLY. You wanna go, Rog?

RICHIE. (*In mock irritation.*) Don't ask Roger! How are we going to kiss and hug and stuff if he's there?

BILLY. That ain't funny, man. (*He is stretched out on his bunk, and* RICHIE *comes bounding over to flop down and lie beside him.*)

RICHIE. And what time will you pick me up?

BILLY. (*He pushes at* RICHIE, *knocking him off the bed and onto the floor.*) Well, you just fall down and wait, all right?

RICHIE. Can I help it if I love you? (*Leaping to his feet, he will head to his locker, removes his shorts, put on a robe.*)

ROGER. You gonna take a shower, Richard?

RICHIE. Cleanliness is nakedness, Roger.

ROGER. Is that right? I didn't know that. Not too many people know that. You may be the only person in the world who know that.

RICHIE. And godliness is in there somewhere, of course. (*Putting a towel around his neck, he is gathering toiletries to carry to the shower.*)

ROGER. You got your own way a lookin' at things, man. You cute.

RICHIE. That's right.

ROGER. You go'wan, have a good time in that shower.

RICHIE. Oh, I will.

BILLY. (*Without looking up from his feet which he is powdering.*) And don't drop your soap.

RICHIE. I will if I want to. (*Already out the door, he slams it shut with a flourish.*)

BILLY. Can you imagine bein' in combat with Richie—people blastin' away at you—he'd probably want to hold your hand.

ROGER. Ain't he somethin'.

BILLY. Who's zat?

ROGER. He's all right.

BILLY. (*Rising, he heads toward his wall locker, where he will put the powder and Dopp Kit.*) Sure he is except he's livin' underwater. (*Looking at* BILLY, ROGER *senses something unnerving: it makes* ROGER *rise, and return his magazine to his footlocker.*)

ROGER. I think we oughta do this area, man. I think we oughta do our area. Mop and buff this floor.

BILLY. You really don't think he means that shit he talks, do you?

ROGER. Huh? Awwww, man; Billy, no.

BILLY. I'd put money on it, Roger, and I ain't got much money.

ROGER. Man, no, no. I'm tellin' you, lad, you listen to the ole Rog. You seen that picture a that little dollie he's got in his locker? He ain't swish, man, believe me, he's cool.

BILLY. It's just that ever since we been in this room, he's been different somehow. Somethin'.

ROGER. No, he ain't. (BILLY *turns to his bed, where he carefully starts folding the towel. Then he looks at* ROGER.)

BILLY. You ever talk to any a these guys—queers, I mean; you ever sit down, just rap with one of 'em?

ROGER. Hell, no; what I wanna do that for? Shit, no.

BILLY. (*Crossing to the trash can in the corner where he will shake the towel empty.*) I mean, some of 'em are okay guys, just way up this bad alley and you say to 'em, "I'm straight, be cool," they go their own way. But then there's these other ones, these bitches, man, and they're so crazy they think anybody can be had. Because they been had themselves. So you tell 'em you're straight and they just nod and smile. You ain't real to 'em. They can't see nothin' but themselves and these goddamn games they're always playin'. (*Having returned to his bunk, he is putting on his shoes.*) I mean, you can be decent about anything, Roger, you see what I'm sayin'? We're all just people, man, and some of us are hardly that. That's all I'm sayin'. (*There is a slight pause as he sits there thinking. Then he gets to his feet.*) I'll go get some buckets and stuff so we can clean up, okay? This area's a mess. This area ain't standin' tall.

ROGER. That's good talk, lad; this area a midget you put it next to an area standin' tall.

BILLY. Got to be good fuckin' troopers.

ROGER. That's right, that's right. I know the meanin' of the words.

BILLY. I mean, I just think we all got to be honest with each other, you understand me?

ROGER. No, I don't understand you; one stupid fuckin' nigger like me—how's that gonna be?

BILLY. That's right; mock me, man. That's what I need. I'll go get the wax. (*Out the door he goes, talking to himself and leaving the door open. For a moment,* ROGER *sits, thinking, and then he looks at* RICHIE'S *locker and then he gets to his feet and walks to the locker. He opens it and looks at the pin-up hanging on the wall. He takes a step backward.*)

ROGER. Sheee-it.

(*Through the open door comes* CARLYLE. ROGER *doesn't see him. And* CARLYLE *stands there looking at* ROGER *and the picture in the locker.*)

CARLYLE. Boy . . . , whose locker you lookin' into?

ROGER. (*He is startled; recovers.*) Hey, baby, what's happenin'?

CARLYLE. That ain't your locker is what I'm askin', Nigger. I mean, you ain't got no white goddamn woman hangin' on your wall.

ROGER. Oh, no; no, no.

CARLYLE. You don't wanna be lyin' to me 'cause I got to turn you in you lyin', and you do got the body a some white goddamn woman hangin' there for you to peek at nobody around but you—you can be thinkin' about that sweet wet pussy an' maybe it hot an' maybe it cool.

ROGER. I could be thinkin' all that, except I know the penalty for lyin'.

CARLYLE. Thank god for that. (*Extending his hand, palm up.*)

ROGER. That's right. This here the locker of a faggot.

CARLYLE. 'Course it is; I see that; any damn body know that. (ROGER *crosses toward his bunk and* CARLYLE *swaggers about, pulling a pint of whiskey from his hip pocket.*) You want a shot? Have you a little taste, my man.

ROGER. Naw.

CARLYLE. C'mon. C'mon. I think you a Tom you don't drink outa my bottle. (*He thrusts the bottle toward* ROGER *and wipes a sweat- and grease-stained sleeve across his mouth.*)

ROGER. (*Taking the bottle.*) Shit.

CARLYLE. That right. How do I know? I just got in. New boy in town. Somewhere over there; I dunno. They dump me in amongst a whole bunch a pale boring motherfuckers. (*He is exploring the room. Finding* BILLY'S *Playboy, he edges onto* BILLY'S *bed and leafs nervously through the pages.*) I just come in from P Company. Man, and I been all over this place, don't see too damn many of us. This outfit look like it a little short on soul. I been walkin' all around, I tell you, and the number is small. Like one hand you can tabulate the lot of 'em. We got few brothers I been able to see, is what I'm sayin'. You and me and two cats down in the small bay. That's all I found. (*As* ROGER *is about to hand the bottle back,* CARLYLE, *almost angrily, waves him off.*) No, no, you take another; take you a real taste.

ROGER. It ain't so bad here. We do all right.

CARLYLE. (*He moves, shutting the door. Suspiciously, he approaches* ROGER.) How about the white guys? They give you any sweat? What's the situation? No jive. I like to know what is goin' on within the situation before that situation get a chance to be closin' in on me.

ROGER. (*Putting the bottle on the footlocker, he sits down.*) Man, I'm tellin' you, it ain't bad. They're just pale, most of 'em, you know. They can't help it; how they gonna help it? Some of 'em got little bit a soul, couple real good boys around this way. Get 'em little bit of copper-tone, they be straight, man.

CARLYLE. How about the NCO's. We got any brother NCO watchin' out for us or they all white, like I goddamn well KNOW all the officers are. Fuckin' officers always white; man, fuckin' snow cones and bars everywhere you look. (*He cannot stay still; he moves to his right, his left, he sits, he stands.*)

ROGER. First Sergeant's a black man.

CARLYLE. All right; good news. Hey, hey, you wanna go over the club with me, or maybe downtown? I got wheels. Let's be free. (*Now he rushes at* ROGER.) Let's be free.

ROGER. Naw . . .

CARLYLE. Ohhh, baby . . . ! (*He is wildly pulling at* ROGER *to get him to the door.*)

ROGER. Some other time. I gotta get the area straight. Me and the guy sleeps in here too are gonna shape the place up a little. (*He has pulled free, and* CARLYLE *cannot understand. It hurts him, depresses him.*)

CARLYLE. You got a sweet deal here an' you wanna keep it, that right? (*He paces about the room, he opens a footlocker, looks inside.*) How you rate you get a room like this for yourself— you and a couple guys?

ROGER. Spec 4. The three of us in here Spec 4.

CARLYLE. You get a room then, huh? (*And suddenly, without warning he is angry.*) Oh, man, I hate this goddamn army. I hate this bastard army. I mean, I just got outa basic—off leave—you know? Back on the block for two weeks . . . and now here. They don't pull any a that petty shit, now, do they—that goddamn petty basic training bullshit? They do and I'm gonna be bustin' some head—my hand is gonna be upside all kindsa heads, 'cause I ain't gonna be able to endure it man, not that kinda crap, understand? (*And again, he is rushing at* ROGER.)

Hey, hey, oh, c'mon, let's get my wheels and make it, man, do me the favor.

ROGER. How'm I gonna, I got my obligations. (*And* CARLYLE *spins away in anger.*)

CARLYLE. Jesus, baby, can't you remember the outside? How long it been since you been on leave? It is so sweet out there, Nigger; you got it all forgot. I had such a sweet, sweet time. They doin' dances, baby, make you wanna cry. I hate this damn army. (*The anger overwhelms him.*) All these mother actin' jacks givin' you jive about what you gotta do and what you can't do. I had a bad scene in basic—up the hill and down the hill; it ain't somethin' I enjoyed even a little. So they do me wrong here, Jim, they gonna be sorry. Some-damn-body! And this whole Vietnam—THING—I do not dig it. (*He falls onto his knees before* ROGER. *It is a gesture that begins as a joke, a mockery. And then a real fear pulses through him to nearly fill the pose he has taken.*) Lord, Lord, don't let 'em touch me. Christ, what will I do, they DO! Whoooooooooooo! And they pullin' guys outa here, too, ain't they? Pullin' 'em like weeds, man; throwin' 'em into the fire. It's shit, man.

ROGER. They got this ole Sarge sleeps down the hall—just today, they got him.

CARLYLE. Which ole Sarge?

ROGER. He sleeps just down the hall; little guy.

CARLYLE. Wino, right?

ROGER. Booze hound.

CARLYLE. Yeh; I seen him. They got him, huh?

ROGER. He's goin'; gotta be packin' his bags. And three other guys two days ago. And two guys last week.

CARLYLE. (*Leaping up from* BILLY'S *bed.*) Ohhh, them bastards. Them bastards. And everybody just takes it. It ain't our war, brother. I'm tellin' you. That's what gets me, Nigger, it ain't our war no how because it ain't our country and that's what burns my ass—that and everybody just sittin' and takin' it. They gonna be bustin' balls, man—kickin' and stompin' —everybody here maybe one week from shippin' out to get blown clean away and man, whata they doin'? They doin' what they told. That what they doin'. Like you? Shit! You gonna straighten up your goddamn area! Well, that ain't for me; I'm gettin' hat, and makin' it out where it's sweet and the people's livin'. I can't cut this jive here, man. I'm tellin' you. I can't cut it. (*He has moved toward* ROGER *and behind him now* RICHIE *enters, running, his hair wet, traces of shaving cream on his face. Toweling his hair, he falters, seeing* CARLYLE. *Then he crosses to his locker.* CARLYLE *grins at* ROGER, *looks at* RICHIE, *steps toward him and gives a little bow.*) My name is Carlyle; what is yours?

RICHIE. Richie.

CARLYLE. (*He turns toward* ROGER *to share his joke.*) Hello. Where is Martin? That cute little Martin. (*And* RICHIE *has just taken off his robe as* CARLYLE *turns back.*) You cute, too, Richie.

RICHIE. Martin doesn't live here. (*Hurriedly putting on underpants to cover his nakedness.*)

CARLYLE. (*Watching* RICHIE, *he slowly turns toward* ROGER.) You ain't gonna make it with me, man?

ROGER. Naw . . . , like I tole you. I'll catch you later.

CARLYLE. That's sad, man; make me cry in my heart.

ROGER. You go'wan, get your head smokin'—stop on back.

CARLYLE. Okay, okay, got to be one man one more time. (*On the move for the door, his hand extended palm up behind him, demanding the appropriate response.*) Baby! Gimme! Gimme! (*Lunging,* ROGER *slaps the hand.*)

ROGER. Go'wan home! Go'wan home.

CARLYLE. You gonna hear from me. (*And he is gone out the door and down the hallway.*)

ROGER. I can . . . , and do . . . , believe . . . that.

(RICHIE, *putting on his T shirt, watches* ROGER *who stubs out his cigarette, then crosses to the trash can to empty the ashtray.*)

RICHIE. Who was that?

ROGER. Man's new, Rich. Dunno his name more than that "Carlyle" he said. He's new—just outa basic.

RICHIE. (*Powdering his thighs, and under his arms.*) Oh . . . my god . . . (*As* BILLY *enters pushing a mop bucket with a wringer attached and carrying a container of wax.*)

ROGER. Me and Billy's gonna straighten up the area; you wanna help?

RICHIE. Sure, sure, help, help.

BILLY. (*Talking to* ROGER, *but turning to look at* RICHIE *who is still putting powder under his arms.*) I hadda steal the wax from third platoon.

ROGER. Good man.

BILLY. (*Moving to* RICHIE, *joking, yet really irritated in some strange way.*) What? Whata you doin', singin'? Look at that, Rog. He's got enough jazz there for an entire beauty parlor. (*Grabbing the can from* RICHIE'S *hand.*) What is this? BABY POWDER! BABY POWDER!

RICHIE. I get rashes.

BILLY. Okay, okay, you get rashes, so what? They got powder for rashes that isn't baby powder.

RICHIE. It doesn't work as good. I've tried it. Have you tried it? (*Grabbing* BILLY'S *waist,* RICHIE *pulls him close.*)

BILLY. Man, I wish you could get yourself straight. I'll mop, too, Roger, okay? Then I'll put down the wax and you can spread it? (*He has walked away from* RICHIE.)

RICHIE. What about buffing?

ROGER. In the morning. (*He is already busy mopping up near the door.*)

RICHIE. What do you want me to do?

BILLY. (*Grabbing up a mop, he heads downstage to work.*) Get inside your locker and shut the door and don't holler for help. Nobody'll know you're there; you'll stay there.

RICHIE. But I'm so pretty.

BILLY. NOW! (*Pointing to* ROGER. *He wants to get this clear.*) Tell that man you mean what you're sayin', Richie.

RICHIE. Mean what?

BILLY. That you really think you're pretty. .

RICHIE. Of course I do; I am. Don't you think I am? Don't *you* think I am, Roger?

ROGER. I tole you—you fulla shit and you cute, man. Carlyle just tole me you cute, too.

RICHIE. Don't you think it's true, Billy?

BILLY. It's like I tole you, Rog.

RICHIE. What did you tell him?

BILLY. That you go down; that you go up and down like a yo-yo and you go blowin' all the trees like the wind.

(RICHIE *is stunned. He looks at* ROGER, *and then he turns and stares into his own locker. The others keep mopping.* RICHIE *takes out a towel, and putting it around his neck, he walks to where* BILLY *is working. He stands there, hurt, looking at* BILLY.)

RICHIE. What the hell made you tell him I been down, Billy?

BILLY. (*Still mopping.*) It's in your eyes; I seen it.

RICHIE. What?

BILLY. You.

RICHIE. What is it, Billy, you think you're trying to say—you and all your wit and intelligence—your *humanity.*

BILLY. I said it, Rich; I said what I was tryin' to say.

RICHIE. *Did* you?

BILLY. I think I did.

RICHIE. *Do* you?

BILLY. Loud and clear, baby. (*Still mopping.*)

ROGER. They got to put me in with the weirdo's—why is

that, huh? How come the *army hate me,* do this shit to me—
know what to do. (*Whimsical and then suddenly loud, angered,
violent.*) Now you guys put socks in your mouths, right now—
get shut up—or I am gonna beat you to death with each other.
Roger got work to do. To be doin' it!

RICHIE. (*Turning to his bed, he kneels upon it.*) Roger, I
think you're so innocent, sometimes. Honestly, it's not such a
terrible thing. Is it, Billy?

BILLY. How would I know? (*He slams his mop into the
bucket.*) Oh, go fuck yourself.

RICHIE. Well, I can give it a try, if that's what you want. Can
I think of you as I do?

BILLY. (*Throwing down his mop.*) GODDAMNIT! That's it!
IT! (*He exits, rushing into the hall and slamming the door
behind him.* ROGER *looks at* RICHIE. *Neither quite knows what
is going on. Suddenly, the door bursts open and* BILLY *storms
straight over to* RICHIE *who still kneels on the bed.*) Now I am
gonna level with you. Are you gonna listen? You gonna hear
what I say, Rich; and not what you think I'm sayin'? (RICHIE
turns away as if to rise, his manner flippant, disdainful.) No!
Don't get cute; don't turn away cute. I wanna say somethin'
straight out to you and I want you to hear it!

RICHIE. I'm all ears, goddamnit! For what, however, I do not
know, except some boring evasion.

BILLY. At least wait the hell till you hear me!

RICHIE. (*In irritation.*) Okay, okay! What?

BILLY. Now this is level, Rich; this is straight talk. (*He is
quiet, intense. This is difficult for him. He seeks the exactly
appropriate words of explanation.*) No B.S. No tricks. What
you do on the side, that's your business and I don't care about
it. But if you don't cut the cute shit with me, I'm gonna turn
you off. Completely. You ain't gonna get a good mornin' outa
me, you understand, because it's gettin' bad around here. I
mean, I know how you think—how you keep lookin' out and
seein' yourself and that's what I'm tryin' to tell you because
that's all that's happenin', Rich. That's all there is to it when
you look out at me and think there's some kind of approval or
whatever you see in my eyes—you're just seein' yourself. And
I'm talkin' the simple quiet truth to you, Rich, I swear I am.
(*He looks away from* RICHIE *now and tries to go back to the
mopping. It is embarrassing for them all.* ROGER *has watched,
has tried to keep working.* RICHIE *has flopped back on his bunk.
There is a silence.*)

RICHIE. How . . . do . . . you want me to be? I don't know how else to be.

BILLY. Ohhh, man, that ain't any part of it. (*The mop is clenched in his hands.*)

RICHIE. Well, I don't come from the same kind of world as you do.

BILLY. Damn, Richie, you think Roger and I come off the same street?

ROGER. Shit . . .

RICHIE. All right. Okay. But I've just done what I wanted all of my life. If I wanted to do something, I just did it. Honestly. I've never had to work or anything like that and I've always had nice clothing and money for cab fare. Money for whatever I wanted. Always. I'm not like you are.

ROGER. You ain't sayin' you really done that stuff, though, Rich.

RICHIE. What?

ROGER. That fag stuff.

RICHIE. (*He continues looking at* ROGER *and then he looks away.*) Yes.

ROGER. Do you even know what you're sayin', Richie? Do you even know what it means to be a fag?

RICHIE. Roger, of course I know what it is. I just told you I've done it. I thought you black people were supposed to understand all about suffering and human strangeness. I thought you had depth and vision from all your suffering. Has someone been misleading me? I just told you I did it. I know all about it. Everything. All the various positions.

ROGER. Yeh, so maybe you think you've tried it, but that don't make you it. I mean, we used to . . . in the old neighborhood . . . man, we had a couple dudes swung that way. But they was weird, man. There was this one little fella, he was a screamin' goddamn faggot . . . uh . . . (*He considers* RICHIE, *wondering if perhaps he has offended him.*) Ohhh, ohhh, you ain't no screamin' goddamn faggot, Richie, no matter what you say. And the baddest man on the block was my boy Jerry Lemon. So one day, Jerry's got the faggot in one a them ole deserted stairways and he's bouncin' him off the walls. I'm just a little fella, see, and I'm watchin' the baddest man on the block do this thing. So he come bouncin' back into me instead of Jerry, and just when he hit, he gave his ass this little twitch, man, like he thought he was gonna turn me on. I'd never a thought that was possible, man, for a man to be twitchin' his ass on me, just like he thought he was a broad. Scared me to death. I took off runnin'. Oh, oh, that ole neighborhood put me into all kindsa crap. I did some sufferin' just like Richie says. Like this once, I'm swingin' on up the street after school, and outa this phone booth comes this man with a goddamned knife stickin' outa his gut. So he sees me and starts tryin' to pull his motherfuckin' coat out over the handle, like he's worried about how he looks, man. "I didn't know this was gonna happen," he says. And then he falls over. He was just all of a sudden dead, man; just all of a sudden dead. You ever seen anything like that, Billy? Any crap like that? (BILLY *sitting on* ROGER'S *bunk, is staring at* ROGER.)

BILLY. You really seen that?

ROGER. Richie's a big city boy.

RICHIE. Oh, no; never anything like that.

ROGER. "Momma, help me," I am screamin', "Jesus, momma help me." Little fella, he don't know how to act, he sees somethin' like that. (*For a moment they are silent, each thinking.*)

BILLY. How long you think we got?

ROGER. What do you mean? (*He is hanging up the mops.* BILLY *is kneeling on* ROGER'S *bunk.*)

BILLY. Till they pack us up, man, ship us out.

ROGER. To the war, you mean? To Disneyland? Man, I dunno; that up to them I.B.M.'s. Them machines is figurin' that. Maybe tomorrow, maybe next week, maybe never. (*The war—the threat of it—is the one thing they share.*)

RICHIE. I was reading they're planning to build it all up to more than five hundred thousand men over there. Americans. And they're going to keep it that way until they win.

BILLY. Be a great place to come back from, man, you know? I keep thinkin' about that. To have gone there, to have been there, to have seen it and lived.

ROGER. (*Settling onto* BILLY'S *bunk,* ROGER *lights a cigarette.*) Well, what we got right here is a fool, gonna probably be one of them five hundred thousand. Do you know this fool cry at the goddamn anthem yet? The flag is flyin' at a ball game, the ole Roger gets all wet in the eye. After all the shit been done to his black ass. But I don't know what I think about this war. I do not know.

BILLY. I'm tellin' you, Rog; I've been doin' alot a readin' and I think it's right we go. I mean, it's just like when North Korea invaded South Korea or when Hitler invaded Poland and all those other countries. He just kept testin' everybody and when nobody said "no" to him, he got so committed he couldn't back up even if he wanted. And that's what this Ho Chi Minh is doin'. And all those other Communists. If we let 'em know somebody is gonna stand up against 'em, they'll back off, just like Hitler would have.

ROGER. There is folks, you know, who are sayin' L.B.J. is the Hitler, and not ole Ho Chi Minh at all.

RICHIE. (*Talking as if this is the best news he's heard in years.*) Well, I don't know anything at all about all that—but I am certain I don't want to go—whatever is going on. I mean, those Viet Cong don't just shoot you and blow you up, you know. My god, they've got those other awful things they do—putting elephant shit on these stakes in the ground and then you step on 'em and you got elephant shit in a wound in your foot. The infection is horrendous. And then there's these caves they hide in and when you go in after 'em, they've got the snakes that they've tied by their tails to the ceiling—so it's dark and the snake is furious from having been hung by its tail and you crawl right into them—your face. My god.

BILLY. They do not. (*He knows he has been caught; they all know it.*)

RICHIE. I read it, Billy. They do.

BILLY. (*Completely facetious, yet the fear is real.*) That's bullshit, Richie.

ROGER. That's right—Richie, they maybe do that stuff with the elephant shit, but nobody's gonna tie a snake by its tail, let ole Billy walk into it.

BILLY. That's disgusting, man.

ROGER. Guess you better get ready for the Klondike, my man.

BILLY. That is probably the most disgusting thing I ever heard of. I DO NOT WANT TO GO! NOT TO NOWHERE WHERE THAT KINDA SHIT IS GOIN' ON! L.B.J. is Hitler; suddenly I see it all very clearly.

ROGER. Billy got him a hatred for snakes.

RICHIE. I hate them, too. They're hideous.

BILLY. (*And now, as a kind of apology to* RICHIE, BILLY *continues his self-ridicule far into the extreme.*) I mean, that is one of the most awful things I ever heard of any person doing. I mean, any person who would hang a snake by its tail in the dark of a cave in the hope that some other person might crawl into it and get bitten to death, that first person is somebody who oughta be shot. And I hope the five hundred thousand other guys that get sent over there kill 'em all—all them gooks— get 'em all driven back into Germany where they belong. And in the meantime, I'll be holding the northern border against the snowmen.

ROGER. (*Rising from* BILLY'S *bed.*) And in the meantime before that, we better be gettin' at the ole area here. Got to be strike troopers.

BILLY. Right.

RICHIE. Can I help?

ROGER. Sure. Be good. (*And he crosses to his footlocker and takes out a radio.*) Think maybe I put on a little music, though it's gettin' late. We got time, Billy, you think?

BILLY. Sure. (*Getting nervously to his feet.*)

ROGER. Sure. All right. We can be doin' it to the music. (*He plugs the radio into the floor plug as* BILLY *bolts for the door.*)

BILLY. I gotta go pee.

ROGER. You watch out for the snakes.

BILLY. It's the snowmen, man; the snowmen. (*He is gone and a recording, preferably by Ray Charles, comes from the radio. For a moment, as the music plays,* ROGER *watches* RICHIE *wander about the room, pouring little splashes of wax onto the floor. Then* RICHIE *moves to his bed and lies down, and* RO-GER, *shaking his head, starts to leisurely spread the wax with* RICHIE *watching.*)

RICHIE. How come you and Billy take all this so seriously? You know.

ROGER. What?

RICHIE. This army nonsense; you're always shining your brass and keeping your footlocker neat and your locker so neat. There's no point to any of it.

ROGER. We here, ain't we, Richie; we in the army. (*Still working the wax.*)

RICHIE. There's no point to any of it. And doing those pushups, the two of you.

ROGER. We just see a lot a things the same way is all. Army ought to be a serious business, even if sometimes it ain't.

RICHIE. You're lucky, you know; the two of you. Having each other for friends the way you do. I never had that kind of friend ever. Not even when I was little.

ROGER. (*After a pause, during which* ROGER, *working, sort of peeks at* RICHIE *every now and then.*) You ain't really inta that stuff, are you, Richie? (*It is a question that is a statement.*)

RICHIE. (*Coyly,* RICHIE *looks at* ROGER.) What stuff is that, Roger?

ROGER. That fag stuff, man. You know. You ain't really into it, are you? You maybe messed in it a little is all, am I right?

RICHIE. I'm very weak, Roger. And by that I simply mean that if I have an impulse to do something, I don't know how to deny myself. If I feel like doing something, I just do it. I . . . will . . . admit to sometimes wishing I . . . was a little more like you . . . and Billy, even, but not to any severe extent.

ROGER. But that's such a bad scene, Rich. You don't want that. Nobody wants that. Nobody wants to be a punk. Not nobody. You wanna know what I think it is? You just got in with the wrong bunch. Am I right? You just got in with a bad bunch, that can happen. And that's what I think happened to you. I bet you never had a chance to really run with the boys before. I mean, regular normal guys like Billy and me. How'd you come in the army, huh, Richie? You get drafted?

RICHIE. No.

ROGER. That's my point, see. (*He has stopped working. He stands, leaning on the mop, looking at* RICHIE.)

RICHIE. About four years ago, I went to this party. I was very young, and I went to this party with a friend who was older and . . . this "fag stuff," as you call it, was going on . . . so I did it.

ROGER. And then you come in the army to get away from it, right? Huh?

RICHIE. I don't know.

ROGER. Sure.

RICHIE. I don't know, Roger.

ROGER. Sure; sure; and now you're gettin' a chance to run with the boys for a little; you'll get yourself straightened around. I know it for a *fact; I know that thing*.

(*From off there is the sudden loud bellowing sound of* SERGEANT ROONEY.)

ROONEY. THERE AIN'T BEEN NO SOLDIERS IN THIS CAMP BUT ME. I BEEN THE ONLY ONE—I BEEN THE ONLY ME! (*And* BILLY *comes dashing into the room.*)

BILLY. Oh, boy.

ROGER. Guess who?

ROONEY. FOR SO LONG I BEEN THE ONLY GOD-DAMN ONE!

BILLY. (*Leaping onto his bed and covering his face with a* Playboy *magazine as* RICHIE *is trying to disappear under his sheets and blankets and* ROGER *is trying to get the wax put away so he can get into his own bunk.*) Hut who hee whor—he's got some yo-yo with him, Rog!

ROGER. Huh?

(*As* COKES *and* ROONEY *enter. Both are in fatigues and drunk and big-bellied. They are in their fifties, their hair whitish and cut short. Both men carry whiskey bottles, beer bottles.* COKES *is a little neater than* ROONEY, *his fatigue jacket tucked in and not so rumpled and he wears canvas-sided jungle boots.* ROONEY, *very disheveled, chomps on a stub of a big cigar. They swagger in looking for fun and stand there side by side.*)

ROONEY. What kinda platoon I got here? You buncha shit-sacks. Everybody look sharp. (*The three boys lay there, unmoving.*) Off and on!

COKES. OFF AND ON! (*He seems barely conscious, wavering as he stands.*)

ROGER. What's happenin', Sergeant?

ROONEY. (*Shoving his bottle of whiskey at* ROGER, *who is sitting up.*) Shut up, Moore! You want a belt? (*Splashing whiskey on* ROGER'S *chest.*)

ROGER. How can I say no?

COKES. My name is Cokes!

BILLY. (*Rising to sit on the side of his bed.*) How about me, too?

COKES. You wait your turn.

ROONEY. (*He looks at the three of them as if they are fools. He indicates* COKES *with a gesture.*) Don't you see what I got here?

BILLY. Who do I follow for my turn?

ROONEY. (*Suddenly, crazily, petulant.*) Don't you see what I got here? Everybody on their feet and at attention! (BILLY *and* ROGER *climb from their bunks and stand at attention. They don't know what* ROONEY *is mad at.*) I mean it! (RICHIE *bounds to the position of attention.*) This here is my friend, who in addition just come back from the war! The goddamn war! He been to it and he come back. (ROONEY *is patting* COKES *gently, proudly.*) The man's a fuckin' hero! (ROONEY *hugs* COKES, *almost kissing him on the cheek.*) He's always been a fuckin' hero. (COKES, *embarrassed in his stupor, kind of wobbles a little from side to side.*)

COKES. Nooooo . . . (*And* ROONEY *grabs him, starts pushing him toward* BILLY'S *footlocker.*)

ROONEY. Show 'em your boots, Cokes. Show 'em your jungle boots. (*With a long, clumsy step,* COKES *climbs onto the footlocker,* ROONEY *supporting him from behind and then bending to lift one of* COKES'S *booted feet and display it for the boys.*) Lookee that boot. That ain't no everyday goddamn army boot.

That is a goddamn jungle boot! That green canvas is a jungle boot 'cause a the heat, and them little holes in the bottom are so the water can run out when you been walkin' in a lotta water like in a jungle swamp. (*He is extremely proud of all this; he looks at them.*) The army ain't no goddamn fool. You see a man wearin' boots like that you might as well see he's got a chestful of medals, 'cause he been to the war. He don't have no boots like that unless he been to the war! Which is where I'm goin' and all you slap-happy mother-fuckers, too. Got to go kill some gooks. (*He is nodding at them, smiling.*) That's right.

COKES. (*Bursting loudly from his stupor.*) Gonna piss on 'em. Old booze. At's what I did. Piss in the rivers. Goddamn G.I.'s secret weapon is old booze and he's pissin' it in all their runnin' water. Makes 'em yellow. Ahhhha, ha, hah, ha! (*He laughs and laughs, and* ROONEY *laughs, too, hugging* COKES.)

ROONEY. Me and Cokesie been in so much shit together we oughta be brown. (*And then he catches himself, looks at* ROGER.) Don't take no offense at that, Moore. We been swimmin' in it. One hundred and first airborne, together. One-Oh-One. Screamin' goddamn eagles! (*Looking at each other, face to face, eyes glinting, they make sudden loud screaming eagle sounds.*) This ain't the army, you punks ain't in the army. You ain't ever seen the army. The army is airborne! Airborne!

COKES. (*Beginning to stomp his feet.*) Airborne, airborne! ALL THE WAY! (*As* RICHIE, *amused and hoping for a drink, too, reaches out toward* ROONEY.)

RICHIE. Sergeant, Sergeant, I can have a little drink, too. (ROONEY *looks at him and clutches the bottle.*)

ROONEY. Are you kiddin' me? You gotta be kiddin' me. (*He looks to* ROGER.) He's kiddin' me, ain't he, Moore? (*And then to* BILLY *and then to* COKES.) Ain't he, Cokesie? (COKES *steps forward and down with a thump, taking charge for his bewildered friend.*)

COKES. Don't you know you are tryin' to take the booze from the hand a the future goddamn congressional honor winner . . . medal . . . ? (*And he looks lovingly at* ROONEY. *He beams.*) Ole Rooney, ole Rooney. (*He hugs* ROONEY'S *head*). He almost done it already. (*And* ROONEY, *overwhelmed, starts screaming "Agggggghhhhhhhhhh," a screaming eagle sound and making clawing eagle gestures at the air. He jumps up and down, stomping his feet.* COKES *instantly joins in, stomping and jumping and yelling.*)

ROONEY. Let's show these shit-sacks how men are men jumpin' outa planes. Agggggggghhhhhhhhhhhhh. (*Stomping and yelling, they move in a circle,* ROONEY *followed by* COKES.) A plane fulla yellin' stompin' men!

COKES. All yellin stompin' men! (*They yell and stomp, making eagle sounds and then* ROONEY *leaps up on* BILLY'S *bed and runs the length of it until he is on the footlocker,* COKES *still on the floor, stomping.* ROONEY *makes a gesture of hooking his ripcord to the line inside the plane. They yell louder and louder and* ROONEY *leaps high into the air, yelling "GEERRONI-MOOOO!" as* COKES *leaps onto the locker and then high into the air, bellowing "GEERRONIMOOOO!" They stand side by side, their arms held up in the air as if grasping the shroud lines of open chutes. They seem to float there in silence.*) Whata feelin'. . . .

ROONEY. Beautiful feelin'. . . . (*For a moment more, they float there, adrift in the room, the sky, their memory.* COKES *smiles at* ROONEY.)

COKES. Remember that one guy. O'Flannigan—

ROONEY. (*Nodding, smiling, remembering.*) —O'Flannigan—

COKES. —he was this one guy—O'Flannigan— (*He moves now toward the boys,* BILLY, ROGER *and* RICHIE, *who have gathered on* ROGER'S *bed and footlocker.* ROONEY *follows several steps, then drifts backward onto* BILLY'S *bed, where he sits and then lies back, listening to* COKES. We was testing chutes where you could just pull a lever by your ribs here when you hit the ground . . . see . . . and the chute would come off you, because it was just after a whole bunch a guys had been dragged to death in an unexpected and terrible wind at Fort Bragg. So they wanted you to be able to release the chute when you hit if there was a bad wind when you hit. So O'Flannigan was this kinda joker who had the goddamn sense a humor of a clown and nerves I tell you of steel, and he says he's gonna release the lever midair, then reach up, grab the lines, and float on down, hanging. (*His hand paws at the air, seeking a rope that isn't there.*) So I seen him pull the lever at five hundred feet and he reaches up to two fistfuls a air, the chute's twenty feet above him, and he went into the ground like a knife. (*The bottle held high over his head falls through the air to the bed, all watching it.*)

BILLY. Geezus.

ROONEY. (*Nodding gently.*) Didn't get to sing the song, I bet.

COKES. (*Standing, staring at the fallen bottle.*) No way.

RICHIE. What song?

ROONEY. (*He rises up, mysteriously angry.*) Shit-sack! Shit-sack!

RICHIE. What song, Sergeant Rooney?

ROONEY. Beautiful Streamer, Shit-sack. (COKES, *gone into another reverie, is staring skyward.*)

COKES. I saw this one guy—never forget it. Never.

BILLY. That's Richie, Sergeant Rooney. He's a beautiful screamer.

RICHIE. He said, "Streamer," not "screamer," asshole. (COKES *is still in his reverie.*)

COKES. This guy with his chute goin' straight up above him in a streamer, like a tulip only white, you know. All twisted and never gonna open. Like a big icicle sticking straight up above him. He went right by me. We met eyes sort of. He was lookin' real puzzled. He looks right at me. Then he looks up in the air at the chute, then down at the ground.

ROONEY. Did *he* sing it?

COKES. He didn't sing it. He started going like this. (*He reaches desperately upward with both hands and begins to claw at the sky while his legs pump up and down.*) Like he was gonna climb right up the air.

RICHIE. Ohhhhh, Geezus.

BILLY. God. (ROONEY *has collapsed again backwards on* BILLY'S *bed and he lies there and then he rises.*)

ROONEY. Cokes got the silver star for rollin' a barrel a oil down a hill in Korea into forty-seven chinky dinky Chinese gooks who were climbin' up the hill and when he shot into it with his machine gun, it blew them all to grape jelly.

COKES. (*Rocking a little on his feet, begins to hum and then sing "Beautiful Streamer" to the tune of Stephen Foster's "Beautiful Dreamer."*) "Beautiful Streamer, open for me . . . the sky is . . . above . . . me . . . ." (*And then the singing stops.*) But the one I remember is this little guy in his spider hole which is a hole in the ground with a lid over it. (*And he is using* RICHIE'S *footlocker before him as the spider hole. He has fixed on it, is moving toward it.*) And he shot me in the ass as I was runnin' by, but the bullet hit me so hard— (*His body kind of jerks and he runs several steps.*) —it knocked me into this ditch where he couldn't see me, I got behind him. (*Now at the head of* RICHIE'S *bed, he begins to creep along the side of the bed as if sneaking up on the footlocker.*) Crawlin'. And I dropped a grenade into his hole. (*He jams a whiskey bottle into the footlocker, then slams down the lid.*) Then sat on the lid, him bouncin' and yellin' under me. Bouncin' and yellin' under the lid. I could hear him. Feel him. I just sat there. (*Silence.*)

ROONEY. (*Waits, thinking, then leaning forward.*) He was probably singin' it.

COKES. (*Sitting there.*) I think so.

ROONEY. You think we should let 'em hear it?

BILLY. We're good boys. We're good ole boys.

COKES. (*Jerking himself to his feet,* COKES *staggers sideways to join* ROONEY *on* BILLY'S *bed.*) I don't care who hears it. I just wanna be singin' it.

ROONEY. (*Rises; he goes to the boys on* ROGER'S *bed and speaks to them carefully, as if lecturing people on something of great importance.*) You listen up; you just be listenin' up, 'cause if you hear it right you can maybe stop bein' shit-sacks. This is what a man sings, he's goin' down through the air, his chute don't open. (*Flopping back down on the bunk beside* COKES, ROONEY *looks at* COKES *and then at the boys. The two old men put their arms around each other and they begin to sing.*)

COKES and ROONEY. (*Singing.*)
Beautiful Streamer
Open for me,
The sky is above me,
But no canopy.

BILLY. (*Murmuring.*) I don't believe it.

COKES and ROONEY.
Counted ten thousand,
Pulled on the cord.
My chute didn't open,
I shouted "Dear Lord."

Beautiful Streamer,
This looks like the end,
The earth is below me,
My body won't bend.

Just like a mother,
Watching o'er me.
     Beautiful Streamer
Ohhhhhh, open for me.

ROGER. Unfuckin' believable.

ROONEY. (*Beaming with pride.*) Ain't that a beauty.

(*And then,* COKES *topples forward onto his face and flops limply to his side. The three boys leap to their feet,* ROONEY *lunges toward* COKES.)

RICHIE. Sergeant!

ROONEY. Cokie! Cokie!

BILLY. Jesus.

ROGER. Hey!

COKES. Huh? Huh? (*He sits up;* ROONEY *is kneeling beside him.*)

ROONEY. Jesus, Cokie.

COKES. I been doin' that; I been doin' that. It don't mean nothin'.

ROONEY. No, no.

COKES. (*Pushing at* ROONEY, *who is trying to help him get back to the bed.* ROONEY *agrees with everything* COKES *is now saying and the noises he makes are little animal noises.*) I told 'em when they wanted to send me back I ain't got no leukemia, they wanna check it. They think I got it. I don't think I got it. Rooney? Whata you think?

ROONEY. No.

COKES. My mother had it. She had it. Just 'cause she did and I been fallin' down.

ROONEY. It don't mean nothin'.

COKES. (*He lunges back and up onto the bed.*) I tole 'em I fall down 'cause I'm drunk. I'm drunk all the time.

ROONEY. You'll be goin' back over there with me is what I know, Cokie. (*He is patting* COKES, *nodding, dusting him off.*) That's what I know. (*As* BILLY *comes up to them, almost seeming to want to be a part of the intimacy they are sharing.*)

BILLY. That was somethin', Sergeant Cokes; Jesus.

ROONEY. (*Whirls on him, ferocious, pushing him.*) Get the fuck away, Wilson! Whata you know? Get the fuck away. You don't know shit. Get away! You don't know shit. (*And he turns to* COKES *who is standing up from the bed.*) Me and Cokes are goin' to the war zone like we oughta. Gonna blow it to shit. (*He is grabbing at* COKES *who is laughing. They are both laughing.* ROONEY *whirls on the boys.*) Ohhh, I'm gonna be so happy to be away from you assholes; you pussies. Not one regular army people among you possible. I swear it to my mother who is holy. You just be watchin' the papers for Cokes and Rooney doin' darin' brave deeds. 'Cause we're old hands at it. Makin' shit disappear. Goddamn-woosh!

COKES. Whoosh!

ROONEY. Demnalitions. Me and . . . (*And he knows he hasn't said it right.*) Me and Cokie. . . . Demnal . . . Demnali. . . .

RICHIE. (*Still sitting on* ROGER'S *bed.*) You can do it, Sergeant.

BILLY. Get it. (*He stands by the lockers and* ROONEY *glares at him.*)

ROGER. 'Cause you're cool with dynamite is what you're tryin' to say.

ROONEY. (*Charging at* ROGER, *bellowing.*) Shut the fuck up, that's what you can do; and go to goddamn sleep. You buncha shit . . . sacks. Buncha mothers—know it all motherin' shit-sacks, that's what you are.

COKES. (*Shoulders back, he is taking charge.*) Just goin' to sleep is what you can do, 'cause Rooney and me fought it through two wars already and we can make it through this one more and leukemia that comes or doesn't come, who gives a shit, not guys like us. We're goin' just pretty as pie. And it's lights out time, ain't it, Rooney?

ROONEY. Past it, goddamnit. So the lights are goin' out. (*There is fear in the room, and the three boys rush to their wall lockers, where they start to strip to their underwear, preparing for bed.* ROONEY *paces the room, watching them, glaring.*) Somebody's gotta teach you soldierin'. You hear me? Or you wanna go outside and march around a while, huh? We can do that if you wanna. Huh? You tell me? Marchin' or sleepin'? What's it gonna be?

RICHIE. (*Rushing to get into bed.*) Flick out the ole lights, Sergeant, that's what we say.

BILLY. (*Climbing into bed.*) Put out the ole lights.

ROGER. (*In bed and pulling up the covers.*) Do it.

COKES. Shut up. (*He rocks, forward and back, trying to stand at attention. He is saying goodnight.*) And that's an order. Just shut up. I got grenades down the hall. . . . I got a pistol, I know where to get nitro—you don't shut up, I'll blow . . . you . . . to . . . fuck. (*Making a military left face, he stalks to the wall switch and turns the lights out.* ROONEY *is watching proudly, as* COKES *faces the boys again. He looks at them.*) That's right. (*In the dark, there is only a spill of light from the hall coming in the open door.* COKES *and* ROONEY *put their arms around each other and go out the door.* RICHIE, ROGER, *and* BILLY *lie in their bunks, staring. They do not move. They lay there. The* SERGANTS *seem to have vanished soundlessly once they went out the door. Light touches each of the boys as they lie there.*)

ROGER. Lord have mercy, if that ain't a pair. If that ain't one pair of beauties.

BILLY. Oh, yeh. (*He does not move.*)

ROGER. Too much. Man, too, too much.

RICHIE. They made me sad; but I loved them, sort of. Better than movies.

ROGER. Too much. Too, too much. (*Silence.*)

BILLY. What time is it?

ROGER. Sleep time, men. Sleep time. (*Silence.*)

BILLY. Right.

ROGER. They were somethin'. Too much.

BILLY. Too much.

RICHIE. Night.

ROGER. Night. (*Silence.*) Night, Billy.

BILLY. Night. (RICHIE stirs in his bed. ROGER *turns onto his side.* BILLY *is motionless.*) I . . . had a buddy, Rog . . . and this is the whole thing, this is the whole point, a kid I grew up with, played ball with in high school, and he was a tough little cat, a real bad man sometimes. Used to have gangster pictures, up in his room. Anyway, we got into this deal, where we'd drive on down to the big city, man, you know, hit the bad spots, let some queer pick us up . . . sort of . . . long enough to buy us some good stuff. It was kinda the thing to do for a while, and we all did it, the whole gang of us. So we'd let these cats pick us up, most of 'em old guys, and they were hurtin' and happy as hell to have us, and we'd get alot of free booze, maybe a meal and we'd turn 'em on. Then pretty soon, they'd ask us—did we want to go over to their place. "Sure," we'd say and order one more drink, and then when we hit the street, we'd tell 'em to kiss off. We'd call 'em fag and queer and jazz like that and tell 'em to kiss off. And Frankie, the kid I'm tellin' you about, he had a mean streak in him and if they gave us a bad time at all, he'd put 'em down. That's the way he was. So that kinda jazz went on and on for sort of a long time and it was a good deal if we were low on cash or needed a laugh and it went on for a while. And then Frankie—one day he come up to me—and he says he was goin' home with the guy he was with. He said, "What the hell, what did it matter?" And he's sayin', Frankie's sayin'— Why don't I tag along? "What the hell," he's sayin', "what does it matter who does it to you, some broad or some old guy, you close your eyes, a mouth's a mouth, it don't matter"—that's what he's sayin'. I tried to talk him out of it but he wasn't hearin' anything I was sayin'. So, the next day, see, he calls me up to tell me about it. "Okay, okay," he says, it was a cool scene, he says; they played poker— a buck minimum and he made a fortune. Frankie was eatin' it up, man. It was a pretty way to live, he says. So he

stayed at it, and he had this nice little girl he was goin'
with at the time—you know the way a real bad cat can sometimes do that, have a good little girl who's crazy about him
and he is for her, too, and he's a different cat when he's
with her?

ROGER. Uh-huh. (*The hall light slants across* BILLY'S *face.*)

BILLY. Well, that was him and Linda, and then one day
he dropped her, he cut her loose. He was hooked, man.
He was into it with no way he knew out—you understand
what I'm sayin'? He had got his ass hooked. He had never
thought he would and then one day he woke up and he was
on it. He just hadn't been told, that's the way I figure it;
somebody didn't tell him somethin' he shoulda been told
and he come to me wailin' one day, man, all broke up and
wailin', my boy Frankie, my main man, and he was a fag. He
was a faggot, black Roger, and I'm not lyin'. I am not lyin'
to you.

ROGER. Damn.

BILLY. So that's the whole thing, man; that's the whole thing.
(*Silence. They lie there.*)

ROGER. Holy . . . Christ, Richie . . . , you hear him? You
hear what he said.

RICHIE. He's a story teller.

ROGER. Whata you mean?

RICHIE. I mean, he's a story teller, all right, he tells stories,
all right.

ROGER. What are we in to now? You wanna end up like that
friend of his, or you don't believe what he said? Which are you
sayin'? (*The door bursts open; the sounds of machine guns
and cannon are being made by someone, and* CARLYLE,
drunk and playing, comes crawling in. ROGER. RICHIE *and*
BILLY *all pop up, startled, to look at him.*) Hey, hey, what's
happenin'?

BILLY. Who's happenin'?

ROGER. You attackin' or you retreatin', man?

CARLYLE. (*Looking up; big grin.*) Hey, baby . . . ? (*Continues shooting, crawling. The three boys look at each other.*)

ROGER. What's happenin', man; whatcha doin'?

CARLYLE. I dunno, Soul; I dunno. Practicin' my duties, my
new abilities. (*Half sitting, he flops onto his side, starts to
crawl.*) The low crawl, man; like I was taught in basic, that's
what I'm doin'. You gotta know your shit, man, else you get
your ass blown so far away you don't ever see it again. Oh, sure,
you guys don't care. I know it. You got it made. You got it

made. I don't got it made. You got a little home here, got friends. People to talk to. I got nothin'. You got jobs, they probably ain't ever gonna ship you out, you got so important jobs. I got no job. They don't even wanna give me a job. I know it. They are gonna kill me. They are gonna send me over there to get me killed, *goddamnit. Whatsamatter with all you people?* (*The anger explodes out of the grieving and* ROGER *rushes to kneel beside* CARLYLE. *He speaks gently, firmly.*)

ROGER. Hey, man, get cool, get some cool; purchase some cool, man.

CARLYLE. Awwwww . . . (*Clumsily, he turns away.*)

ROGER. Just hang in there.

CARLYLE. I don't wanna be no *dead* man. I don't wanna be the one they all thinkin' is so stupid he's the only one'll go they tell him, they don't even have to give him a job. I got thoughts, man; in my head; alla time, burnin', burnin' thoughts a understandin'.

ROGER. Don't you think we know that, man? It ain't the way you're sayin' it.

CARLYLE. It is.

ROGER. No. I mean, we all probably gonna go. We all probably gonna have to go.

CARLYLE. Nooooo.

ROGER. I mean it.

CARLYLE. (*Suddenly, he nearly topples over.*) I am very drunk. (*And he looks up at* ROGER.) You think so?

ROGER. I'm sayin' so. And I am sayin', "No sweat." No point.

CARLYLE. (*Angrily pushes at* ROGER, *knocking him backwards.*) Awwwww, damnit, damnit, mother . . . shit . . . it . . . ohhhhhhh. (*Sliding to the floor, the rage and anguish softening into only breathing.*) I mean it. I mean it. (*Silence. He lies there.*)

ROGER. What . . . a you doin' . . . ?

CARLYLE. Huh?

ROGER. I don't know what you're up to on our freshly mopped floor.

CARLYLE. Gonna go sleep, okay? No sweat . . . (*Suddenly very polite, he is looking up.*) Can I, Soul? Izzit all right?

ROGER. Sure, man, sure, if you wanna, but why don't you go where you got a bed. Don't you like beds?

CARLYLE. Dunno where's zat. My bed, I can' fin' it, I can' fin' my own bed. I looked all over, but I can' fin' it, anywhere.

GONE! (*Slipping back down now, he squirms to make a nest; he hugs his bottle.*)

ROGER. (*Moving to his bunk where he grabs a blanket.*) Okay, okay, man. But get on top a this, man. (*He is spreading the blanket on the floor, trying to help* CARLYLE *get on it.*) Make it softer. C'mon, c'mon . . . get on this.

(BILLY *has risen with his own blanket, and is moving now to hand it to* ROGER.)

BILLY. Cat's hurtin', Rog.

ROGER. Ohhhhh, yeh.

CARLYLE. Ohhhhh . . . it was so sweet at home . . . , it was so sweet. Baby; sooo good . . . ; they doin' dances make you wanna cry. . . . (*Hugging the blankets now, he drifts in a kind of dream.*)

ROGER. I know, man.

CARLYLE. So sweet . . . !

(BILLY *is moving back to his own bed where, quietly, he sits.*)

ROGER. I know, man.

CARLYLE. So sweet . . . !

ROGER. Yeh.

CARLYLE. How come I gotta be here? (*On his way to the door to close it,* ROGER *falters, looks at* CARLYLE, *then moves on toward the door.*)

ROGER. I dunno, Jim. (BILLY *is sitting and watching, as* ROGER *goes on to the door, gently closes it, and returns to his bed.*)

BILLY. I know why he's gotta be here, Roger, you wanna know? Why don't you ask me?

ROGER. Okay. How come he gotta be here?

BILLY. (*Smiling.*) Freedom's frontier, man. That's why.

ROGER. (*Settled on the edge of his bed and about to lie back.*) Oh . . . , yeh. . . . (*As a distant bugle begins to play* TAPS *and* RICHIE, *carrying a blanket, is nearing* CARLYLE. ROGER *settles back;* BILLY *is staring at* RICHIE; CARLYLE *does not stir; the bugle plays.*) Bet that ole Sarge don't live a year, Billy. Fuckin' blow his own ass sky high. (RICHIE *has covered* CARLYLE. *He pats* CARLYLE'S *arm, and then straightens in order to return to his bed.*)

BILLY. Richie . . . ! (*His hissing voice freezes* RICHIE *who stands, and then starts again to move and* BILLY'S *voice comes again and* RICHIE *cannot move.*) Richie . . . how . . . come you gotta keep doin' that stuff? (ROGER *looks at* BILLY, *staring at* RICHIE, *who stands still as a stone over the sleeping* CARLYLE.) How come?

ROGER. He dunno, man. Do you? You dunno, do you, Rich?
RICHIE. No.
CARLYLE. (*From deep in his sleep and grieving.*) It . . .
was . . . so . . . pretty . . . !
RICHIE. No.

(*The LIGHTS fade to black with the last soft notes of TAPS.*)

ACT II

SCENE 1

Lights come up on the Cadre Room. It is late afternoon and BILLY *is lying on his bed on his stomach, his head at the foot of the bed, his chin resting on his hands. He wears gym shorts and sweat socks; his T shirt lies on the bed and sneakers are on the floor.* ROGER *is at his footlocker taking out a pair of sweat socks. His sneakers and his basketball are on his bed. He is wearing his Khakis.*

A silence passes, and then ROGER *closes his footlocker and sits on his bed, where he starts lacing his sneakers, holding them in his hands.*

BILLY. Rog . . . , you think I'm a busybody? In any way? (*Silence.* ROGER *laces his sneakers.*) Roger?

ROGER. Huh? Uh-uh.

BILLY. Some people do. I mean back home. (*He rolls slightly to look at* ROGER.) Or that I didn't know how to behave. Sort of.

ROGER. It's time we maybe get changed, don't you think? (*He rises and goes to his locker. He takes off his trousers, shoes and socks.*)

BILLY. Yeh. I guess. I don't feel like it, though. I don't feel good, don't know why.

ROGER. Be good for you, man; be good for you. (*Pulling on his gym shorts,* ROGER *returns to his bed, carrying his shoes and socks.*)

BILLY. Yeh. (*He sits up on the edge of his bed.* ROGER, *sitting, is bowed over, putting on his socks.*) I mean, a lot of people thought like I didn't know how to behave in a simple way. You know? That I over complicated everything. I didn't think so. Don't think so. I just thought I was seein' complications that were there but nobody else saw. (*He is struggling now to put on his T shirt. He seems weary, almost weak.*) I mean, Wisconsin's a funny place. All those clear-eyed people sayin'

49

"Hello" and lookin' you straight in the eye. Everybody's good you think and happy and honest. And then there's all of a sudden a neighbor who goes mad as a hatter. I had a neighbor who came out of his house one morning with axes in both hands. He started *then* attackin' the cars that were driving up and down in front of his house. An' we all knew why he did it, sorta. (*He pauses, he thinks.*) It made me wanna be a priest. I wanted to be a priest then. I was sixteen. Priests could help people. Could take away what hurt 'em. I wanted that, I thought. Somethin', huh?

ROGER. (*He has the basketball in his hands.*) Yeh. But everybody's got feelin's like that sometimes.

BILLY. I don't know.

ROGER. You know, you oughta work on a little jump shot, my man. Get you some kinda fall away jumper to go with that beauty of a hook. Make you tough out there.

BILLY. Can't fuckin' do it. Not my game. I mean, like that bar we go to. You think I could get a job there bartendin', maybe. I could learn the ropes. (*He is watching* ROGER *who has risen to walk to his locker.*) You think I could get a job there off duty hours?

ROGER. (*Pulling his locker open to display the pin-up on the wall.*) You don't want no job. It's that little black-haired waitress you wantin' to know.

BILLY. No, man. Not really.

ROGER. It's okay. She tough, man. (*He begins to remove his uniform shirt. He will put on an O.D. T shirt to go to the gym.*)

BILLY. I mean, not the way you're sayin' it, is all. Sure, there's somethin' about her. I don't know what. I ain't even spoke to her yet. But somethin'. I mean, what's she doin' there? When she's dancin', it's like she knows somethin'. She's degradin' herself, I sometimes feel. You think she is?

ROGER. Man, you don't even know the girl. She's workin'.

BILLY. I'd like to talk to her. Tell her stuff. Find out about her. Sometimes I'm thinkin' about her and it and I got a there, I get to know her and she and I get to be real tight, man; close, you know. Maybe we scream, maybe we don't. It's nice . . . whatever.

ROGER. Sure. She a real fine lookin' Chippie, Billy. Got nice cakes. Nice little titties.

BILLY. I think she's smart, too. (ROGER *starts laughing so hard he almost falls into his locker.*) Oh, all I do is talk. "Yabba-yabba." I mean, my mom and dad are really terrific people. How'd they ever end up with somebody so weird as me? (ROGER *moves to him, jostles him.*)

ROGER. I'm tellin' you, the gym and a little ball is what you need. Little exercise. Little bumpin' into people. The Soul is tellin' you.

BILLY. (*Rises and goes to his locker where he starts putting on his sweat clothes.*) I mean, Roger, you remember how we met in P Company. Both of us brand new. You started talkin' to me and you didn't stop.

ROGER. (*Hardly looking up.*) Yeh.

BILLY. Did you see somethin' in me made you pick me?

ROGER. I was talkin' to everybody, man. For that whole day. Two whole days. You was just the first one to talk back friendly. Though you didn't say much, as I recall.

BILLY. The first white person, you mean. (*Wearing his sweat pants,* BILLY *is now at his bed putting on his sneakers.*)

ROGER. Yeh. I was tryin' to come outa myself a little. Do like the fuckin' headshrinker been tellin' me to stop them fuckin' headaches I was havin', you know. Now, let us do fifteen or twenty pushups and get over to that gymnasium, like I been sayin'. Then we can take our civvies with us—we can shower and change at the gym. (*He crosses to* BILLY *who flops down on his belly on the bed.*)

BILLY. I don't know; I don't know . . . what it is I'm feelin'. Sick like. (ROGER *forces* BILLY *up onto his feet and shoves him playfully downstage where they both fall forward into the pushup position, side by side.*)

ROGER. Do 'em, Trooper. Do 'em. Get it.

(ROGER *starts.* BILLY *joins in. After five* ROGER *realizes that* BILLY *has his knees on the floor. They start again. This time,* BILLY *counts in double time. They start again. At about "seven"* RICHIE *enters. Neither* BILLY *nor* ROGER *see him. They keep going.*)

ROGER and BILLY. Seven, eight, nine, ten. . . .

RICHIE. No, no; no, no; no, no, no. That's not it, that's not it. (*They keep going, yelling the numbers louder and louder.*)

ROGER and BILLY. . . . eleven, twelve, thirteen. . . . (RICHIE crosses to his locker and gets his bottle of cologne, and then returning to the center of the room to stare at them, he stands there dabbing cologne onto his face.*) . . . fourteen . . . , fifteen.

RICHIE. You'll never get it like that. You're so far apart and you're both humping at the same time. And all that counting. It's so unromantic.

ROGER. (*Rising and moving to his bed to pick up the basketball.*) We was exercisin', Richard. You heard a that?

RICHIE. Call it what you will, Roger. (*With a flick of his wrist,* ROGER *tosses the basketball to* BILLY.) Everybody has their own cute little pet names for it.

BILLY. Hey! (*And he tosses the ball at* RICHIE, *hitting him in the chest, sending the cologne bottle flying.* RICHIE *yelps, as* BILLY *retrieves the ball and grabbing up his sweat jacket from the bed, heads for the door.* ROGER, *at his own locker, has taken out his suitbag of civilian clothes.*) You missed.

RICHIE. Billy, Billy, Billy, please, please, the ruffian approach will not work with me. It impresses me not even one tiny little bit. All you've done is spill my cologne. (*He bends to pick the cologne from the floor.*)

BILLY. That was my aim.

ROGER. See you. (BILLY *is passing* RICHIE. *Suddenly,* RICHIE *sprays* BILLY *with cologne, some of it getting on* ROGER, *as* ROGER *and* BILLY, *groaning and cursing at* RICHIE, *rush out the door.*)

RICHIE. Try the more delicate approach next time, Bill. (*Having crossed to the door, he stands a moment, leaning against the frame. Then, he bounces to* BILLY'S *bed, sings, "He's just my Bill," and squirts cologne on the pillow. At his locker, he deposits the cologne, takes off his shirt, shoes and socks. Removing a hardcover copy of Pauline Kael's "I Lost It at the Movies" from the top shelf of the locker, he bounds to the center of the room and tosses the book the rest of the way to the bed. Quite pleased with himself, he fidgets, pats his stomach, then lowers himself into the pushup position, goes to his knees and stands up.*) Am I out of my fucking mind? Those two are crazy. I'm not crazy. (*He pivots and strides to his locker. With an ashtray, pack of matches and pack of cigarettes, he hurries to his bed and makes himself comfortable to read, his head propped up on a pillow. Settling himself, he opens the book, finds his place, thinks a little, starts to read. For a moment, he lies there. And then* CARLYLE *steps into the room. He comes through the doorway, looking to his left and right. He comes several steps into the room and looks at* RICHIE. RICHIE *see him. They look at each other.*)

CARLYLE. Ain't nobody here, man?

RICHIE. Hello, Carlyle. How are you today?

CARLYLE. Ain't nobody here? (*He is nervous and angrily disappointed.*)

RICHIE. Who do you want?

CARLYLE. Where's the black boy?

RICHIE. Roger? My god, why do you keep calling him that? Don't you know his name yet? Roger. Roger. (*He thickens his voice at this, imitating someone very stupid.* CARLYLE *stares at him.*)

CARLYLE. Yeh. Where is he?

RICHIE. I am not his keeper, you know. I am not his private secretary, you know.

CARLYLE. I do not know. I do not know. That is why I am asking. I come to see him. You are here. I ask you. I don't know. I mean, Carlyle made a fool out a himself comin' in here the other night, talkin' on and on like how he did. Lay on the floor. He remember. You remember? It all one hype, man; that all one hype. You know what I mean. That ain't the real Carlyle was in here. This one here and now the real Carlyle. Who the real Richie?

RICHIE. Well . . . the real Richie . . . has gone home. To Manhattan. I, however, am about to read this book. (*Which he again starts to try to do.*)

CARLYLE. Oh. Shit. Jus' you the only one here, then, huh?

RICHIE. So it would seem. (*He looks at the air and then under the bed as if to find someone.*) So it would seem. Did you hear about Martin?

CARLYLE. What happened to Martin? I ain't seen him.

RICHIE. They are shipping him home. Someone told about what he did to himself. I don't know who.

CARLYLE. Wasn't me. Not me. I keep that secret.

RICHIE. I'm sure you did. (*Rising, walking toward* CARLYLE *and the door, cigarette pack in hand.*) You want a cigarette? Or don't you smoke. Or do you have to go right away. (*Closing the door.*) There's a chill sometimes coming down the hall, I don't know from where. (*Crossing back to his bed and climbing in.*) And I think I've got the start of a little cold. Did you want the cigarette?

CARLYLE. (*Stares at him. Then he examines the door and looks again at* RICHIE. *He stares at* RICHIE, *thinking, and then he walks toward him.*) You know what I bet. I been lookin' at you real close. It just a way I got about me. And I bet if I was to hang my boy out in front of you, my big boy, man, you'd start wantin' to touch him. Be beggin' and talkin' sweet to ole

Carlyle. Am I right or wrong? (*He leans over* RICHIE.) What do you say?

RICHIE. Pardon?

CARLYLE. You heard me. Ohhh, I am so restless, I don't even understand it. My big black boy is what I was talkin' about. My thing, man; my rope, Jim. HEY RICHIE! (*And he lunges, then moves his fingers through* RICHIE'S *hair.*) How long you been a punk? Can you hear me? Am I clear? Do I talk funny? (*He is leaning closer.*) Can you smell the gin on my mouth?

RICHIE. I mean, if you really came looking for Roger, he and Billy are gone to the gymnasium. They were—

CARLYLE. No. (*He slides down on the bed, his arm placed over* RICHIE'S *legs.*) I got no athletic abilities. I got none. No moves. I don't know. HEY RICHIE! (*Leaning close again.*) I just got this question I asked, I got no answer.

RICHIE. I don't know . . . what . . . you mean.

CARLYLE. I heard me. I understand me. "How long you been a punk?" is the question I asked—have you got a reply?

RICHIE. (*Confused, irritated, but fascinated.*) Not to that question.

CARLYLE. Who do if you don't? I don't. How'm I gonna? (*Suddenly there is whistling in the hall, as if someone might enter, footsteps approaching, and* RICHIE *leaps to his feet and scurries away toward the door, tucking his shirt in as he goes.*) Man, don't you wanna talk to me? Don't you wanna talk to ole Carlyle?

RICHIE. Not at the moment.

CARLYLE. (*He is rising, starting after* RICHIE *who stands nervously near* ROGER'S *bed.*) I want to talk to you, man; why don't you want to talk to me? We can be friends. Talkin' back and forth, sharin' thoughts and bein' happy.

RICHIE. I don't think that's what you want.

CARLYLE. (*He is very near to* RICHIE.) What do I want?

RICHIE. I mean, to talk to me. (*As if repulsed, he crosses away.*)

CARLYLE. What am I doin'? I am talkin'. DON'T YOU TELL ME I AIN'T TALKIN' WHEN I AM TALKIN'! 'COURSE I AM. Bendin' over backwards. Do you know they still got me in that goddamn P Company. That goddamn transient company. It like they think I ain't got no notion what a home is. No nose for no home—like I ain't never had no home. I had a home. IT LIKE THEY THINK THERE AIN'T NO PLACE FOR ME IN THIS MOTHER ARMY BUT K.P.

ALL SUDSY AND WRINKLED AND SWEATIN'. EVERY
DAY SINCE I GOT TO THIS SHIT HOUSE, MISTER!
HOW MANY TIMES YOU BEEN ON K.P.? WHEN'S THE
LAST TIME YOU PULLED K.P.? (*He has roared down to
where* RICHIE *had moved, the rage possessing him.*)

RICHIE. I'm E.D.

CARLYLE. You E.D.? You E.D.? You Edie, are you? I
didn't ask you what you friends call you, I asked you when's the
last time you had K.P.?

RICHIE. (*Edging toward his bed. He will go there, get and
light a cigarette.*) E.D. is exempt from duty.

CARLYLE. (*Moving after* RICHIE.) You ain't got no duties?
What shit you talkin' about? Everybody in this fuckin' army got
duties? That what the fuckin' army all about. You ain't got no
duties, who got 'em?

RICHIE. Because of my job, Carlyle. I have a very special
job. And my friends don't call me Edie. (*Big smile.*) They call
me Irene.

CARLYLE. That mean what you sayin' is you kiss ass for
somebody, don't it? Good for you. Good for you. (*Seemingly
relaxed and gentle, he settles down on* RICHIE'S *bed. He seems
playful and charming.*) You know the other night I was sleepin'
there. You know.

RICHIE. Yes.

CARLYLE. (*Gleefully, enormously pleased.*) You remember
that? How come you remember that? You sweet.

RICHIE. We don't have people sleeping on our floor that
often, Carlyle.

CARLYLE. But the way you crawl over in the night, gimme a
big kiss on my joint. That nice.

RICHIE. (*He is shocked. He blinks.*) What?

CARLYLE. Or did I dream that?

RICHIE. (*Laughing in spite of himself.*) My god, you're
outrageous!

CARLYLE. Maybe you dreamed it.

RICHIE. What . . . ? No. I don't know.

CARLYLE. Maybe you did it, then, you didn't dream it.

RICHIE. How come you talk so much?

CARLYLE. I don't talk, man, who's gonna talk? YOU?
(*He is laughing and amused, but there is an anger near the
surface now, an ugliness.*) That bore me to death. I don't like
nobody's voice but my own. I am so pretty. Don't like nobody
else face. (*And then viciously, he spits out at* RICHIE.) You
goddamn face ugly fuckin' queer punk!

RICHIE. (*Jumps in confusion.*) What's the matter with you?

CARLYLE. You goddamn ugly punk face. YOU UGLY!

RICHIE. Nice mouth.

CARLYLE. That's right. That's right. And you got a weird mouth. Like to suck joints. (*As* RICHIE *storms to his locker, throwing the book inside. He pivots, grabbing a towel, marching toward the door.*) Hey, you gonna jus' walk out on me? Where you goin'? You c'mon back. Hear?

RICHIE. That's my bed, for chrissake. (*He lunges into the hall.*)

CARLYLE. You'd best. (*Lying there, he makes himself comfortable. He takes a pint bottle from his back pocket.*) You come back, Richie. I tell you a good joke. Make you laugh, make you cry. (*He takes a big drink.*) That's right, ole Frank and Jessie, they got the stagecoach stopped, all the people's lined up—Frank say, "All right, peoples, we gonna rape all the men and rob all the women." Jessie say, "Frank, no, no—that ain't it—we gonna—" And this one little man yell real loud— "You shut up, Jessie; Frank knows what he's doin'." (*Loudly, he laughs and laughs.* BILLY *enters.* CARLYLE *is laughing.* BILLY *is startled at the sight of* CARLYLE *there in* RICHIE'S *bed and he falters, as* CARLYLE *gestures toward him.*) Hey, man . . . ! Hey, you know, they send me over to that Vietnam, I be cool, 'cause I been dodgin' bullets and shit since I been old enough to get on pussy make it happy to know me. I can get on, I can do my job. (BILLY *looks weary and depressed. Languidly he crosses to his bed. He still wears his sweat clothes.* CARLYLE *studies him, then stares at the ceiling.*) Yeah. I was just layin' there thinkin' that and you come in and out it come, words to say my feelin'. That my problem. That the black man's problem all together. You ever considered that? Too much feelin'. He too close to everything. He is, man; too close to his blood, to his body. It ain't that he don't have no good mind, but he BELIEVE in his body. Is . . . that Richie the only punk in this room, or is there more?

BILLY. What?

CARLYLE. The punk; is he the only punk? (*Carefully, he takes one of* RICHIE'S *cigarettes and lights it.*)

BILLY. He's all right.

CARLYLE. I ain't askin' about the quality of his talent, but is he the only one is my question?

BILLY. (*He does not want to deal with this. He sits there.*) You get orders yet?

CARLYLE. Orders for what?

BILLY. To tell you where you work.

CARLYLE. I'm P Company, man. I work in P Company. I do K.P. That all. Don't deserve no more. Do you know I been in this army three months and ten days and everybody still doin' the same shit and sayin' the same shit and wearin' the same green shitty clothes? I ain't been happy one day and that a lotta goddamn misery back-to-back in this ole boy. Is that Richie a good punk? Huh? Is he? He takes care of you and Roger, that how come you in this room, the three of you.

BILLY. What?

CARLYLE. (*Emphatically.*) You and Roger are hittin' on Richie, right?

BILLY. He's no queer if that's what you're sayin'. A little effeminate but that's all, no more; if that's what you're sayin'.

CARLYLE. I'd like to get some of him myself if he a good punk is what I'm sayin'. That's what I'm sayin'! You don't got no understandin' how a man can maybe be a little diplomatic about what he's sayin' sorta sideways, do you. Jesus.

BILLY. He don't do that stuff.

CARLYLE. (*Lying there.*) What stuff?

BILLY. Listen, man; I don't feel too good, you don't mind.

CARLYLE. What stuff?

BILLY. What you're thinkin'.

CARLYLE. What . . . am I thinkin'?

BILLY. You . . . know . . .

CARLYLE. Yes, I do. It in my head, that how come I know. But how do you know? I can see your heart, Billy, boy, but you cannot see mine. I am unknown. YOU . . . are known.

BILLY. (*As if he is about to vomit, and fighting it.*) You just . . . talk fast and keep movin', don't you? Don't ever stay still.

CARLYLE. Words to say my feelin', Billy, boy. (RICHIE *steps into the room. He sees* BILLY *and* CARLYLE *and freezes.*) There he is. There he be.

RICHIE. (*Moves to his locker to put away the towel.*) He's one of them who hasn't come down far out of the trees, yet, Billy; believe me.

CARLYLE. You got rudeness in your voice, Richie—you got meanness I can hear about ole Carlyle. You tellin' me I oughta leave, is that what you think you're doin'? You don't want me here?

RICHIE. You come to see Roger who isn't here, right? Man, like you must have important matters to take care of all over the quad; I can't imagine a man like you not having extremely

important things to do all over the world, as a matter of fact,
Carlyle.

CARLYLE. (*He rises. He begins to smooth the sheets and
straighten the pillow. He will put the pint bottle in his back pocket
and cross near to* RICHIE.) Ohhh, listen, don't mind all the shit
I say. I just talk bad is all I do, I don't do bad. I got to have
friends just like anybody else. I'm just bored and restless, that
all; takin' it out on you two. I mean, I know Richie here ain't
really no punk, not really. I was just talkin', just jivin' and
entertainin' my own self. Don't take me serious, not ever. I get
on out and see you all later. (*He moves for the door,* RICHIE
right behind him, almost ushering him.) You be cool, hear?
Man don't do the jivin', he the one gettin' jived. That what my
little brother Henry tell me and tell me. (*Moving leisurely, he
backs out the door and is gone.* RICHIE *shuts the door. There is
a silence as* RICHIE *stands by the door.* BILLY *looks at him and
then looks away.*)

BILLY. I am gonna have to move myself outa here, Roger
decides to adopt that sonofabitch.

RICHIE. He's an animal.

BILLY. Yeh, and on top a that, he's a rotten person.

RICHIE. (*He laughs nervously, crossing nearer to* BILLY.) I
think you're probably right. (*Still laughing a little, he pats* BIL-
LY'S *shoulder and* BILLY *freezes at the touch. Awkwardly,* RICHIE
*removes his hand and crosses to his bed. When he has lain
down,* BILLY *bends to take off his sneakers, then lies back on his
pillow staring, thinking, and there is a silence.* RICHIE *does not
move. He lies there, struggling to prepare himself for something.*)
Hey . . . , Billy? (*Very slight pause.*) Billy?

BILLY. Yeah.

RICHIE. You know that story you told the other night.

BILLY. Yeh . . . ?

RICHIE. You know.

BILLY. What . . . about it?

RICHIE. Well, was it . . . about you? (*Pause.*) I mean, was it
. . about you? Were you Frankie? (*This is difficult for him.*)
Are . . . you Frankie? Billy? (BILLY *is slowly sitting up.*)

BILLY. You sonofabitch . . . !

RICHIE. Or was it really about somebody you knew . . . !

BILLY. (*Sitting, outraged and glaring.*) You didn't hear me at
all!

RICHIE. I'm just askin' a simple question, Billy, that's all I'm
doing.

BILLY. You are really sick. You know that? Your brain is

really, truly rancid! Do you know there's a theory now, it's genetic? That it's all a matter of genes and shit like that?

RICHIE. Everything is not so ungodly cryptic, Billy.

BILLY. You. You, man, and the rot it's makin' outa your feeble fuckin' brain. (ROGER, *dressed in civilian clothes, bursts in and* BILLY *leaps to his feet.*)

ROGER. Hey, hey, anyone got a couple bucks he can loan me?

BILLY. Rog, where you been?

ROGER. (*Throwing the basketball and his sweat clothes into his locker.*) I need five. C'mon.

BILLY. Where you been? That asshole friend a yours was here.

ROGER. I know, I know. Can you gimme five?

RICHIE. (*He jumps to the floor and heads for his locker.*) You want five, I got it. You want ten or more, even? (BILLY, *watching* RICHIE, *turns, and nervously paces down right where he moves about, worried.*)

BILLY. I mean, we gotta talk about him, man; we gotta talk about him.

ROGER. (*As* RICHIE *is handing him two fives.*) 'Cause we goin' to town together. I jus' run into him out on the quad, man, and he was feelin' real bad 'bout the way he acted, how you guys done him, he was fallin' down apologizin' all over the place.

BILLY. (*As* RICHIE *marches back to his bed and sits down.*) I mean, he's got a lot a weird ideas about us; I'm tellin' you.

ROGER. He's just a little fucked up in his head is all, but he ain't trouble. (*He takes a pair of sunglasses from the locker and puts them on.*)

BILLY. Who needs him? I mean, we don't need him.

ROGER. You gettin' too nervous, man. Nobody said anything about anybody needin' anybody. I been on the street all my life; he brings back home. I played me a little ball, Billy; took me a shower. I'm feelin' good! (*He has moved down to* BILLY.)

BILLY. I'm tellin' you there's somethin' wrong with him, though.

ROGER. (*Face to face with* BILLY, ROGER *is a little irritated.*) Every black man in the world ain't like me, man; you get used to that idea. You get to know him, and you gonna like him. I'm tellin' you. You get to be laughin' just like me to hear him talk his shit. But you gotta relax.

RICHIE. I agree with Billy, Roger.

ROGER. Well, you guys got it all worked out and that's good, but I am goin' to town with him. Man's got wheels. Got a good head. You got any sense you'll come with us.

BILLY. What are you talkin' about come with you—I just tole you he's crazy.

ROGER. And I tole you you're wrong.

RICHIE. We weren't invited.

ROGER. I'm invitin' you.

RICHIE. No, I don't wanna.

ROGER. (*He moves to* RICHIE; *it seems he really wants* RICHIE *to go.*) You sure, Richie? C'mon.

RICHIE. No.

ROGER. Billy? He got wheels, we goin' in drinkin', see if gettin' our heads real bad don't make us feel real good. You know what I mean. I got him right, you got him wrong.

BILLY. But what if I'm right?

ROGER. Billy, Billy, the man is waitin' on me. You know you wanna. Jesus. Bad cat like that gotta know the way. He been to D.C. before. Got cousins here. Got wheels for the weekend. You always talkin' how you don't do nothin'—you just talk it—let's do it tonight—stop talkin'—be cruisin' up and down the strip, leanin' out the window, bad as we wanna be. True cool is a car—we can flip us cigarettes out the window—we can watch it bounce. Get us some chippies. You know we can. And if we don't he knows a cat house, it fulla cats.

BILLY. You serious?

RICHIE. You mean you're going to a whorehouse? That's disgusting.

BILLY. Listen who's talkin'. What do you want me to do? Stay here with you?

RICHIE. We could go to a movie or something.

ROGER. I am done with this talkin'—you goin', you stayin'? (*He crosses to his locker, pulls into view a wide-brimmed black and shiny hat and puts it on, cocking it at a sharp angle.*)

BILLY. I don't know.

ROGER. (*Stepping for the door.*) I am goin'.

BILLY. (*Turning,* BILLY *sees the hat.*) I'm going. Okay! I'm going! Going, going, going! (*And he runs to his locker.*)

RICHIE. Oh, Billy, you'll be scared to death in a cat house and you know it.

BILLY. BULLSHIT! (*He is removing his sweat pants and putting on a pair of gray corduroy trousers.*)

ROGER. Billy got him a lion tamer 'tween his legs!

(*The door bangs open and* CARLYLE *is there still clad in his filthy fatigues but wearing a going-to-town black knit cap on his head and carrying a bottle.*)

CARLYLE. Man, what's goin' on? I been waitin' like through-out my fuckin' life?

ROGER. Billy's goin' too. He's gotta change.

CARLYLE. He goin', too! Hey! Beautiful! That beautiful! (*His grin is large, his laugh is loud.*)

ROGER. Didn't I tell you, Billy?

CARLYLE. That beautiful, man; we all goin' to be friends!

RICHIE. (*Sitting on his bed.*) What about me, Carlyle?

(CARLYLE *looks at* RICHIE *and then at* ROGER *and then he and* ROGER *begin to laugh.* CARLYLE *pokes* ROGER *and they laugh as they are leaving.* BILLY, *grabbing up his sneakers to follow, stops at the door, looking only briefly at* RICHIE. *Then* BILLY *goes and shuts the door. The LIGHTS are fading to black. Bugle sounds TAPS*).

SCENE 2

(*In the dark, TAPS begins to play. And then slowly the lights rise, but the room remains dim. Only the lamp attached to* RICHIE'S *bed burns and there is the glow and spill of the hallway coming through the transom.* BILLY, CARLYLE, ROGER, *and* RICHIE *are sprawled about the room.* BILLY, *lying on his stomach, has his head at the foot of his bed, a half-empty bottle of beer dangling in his hand. He wears a blue oxford cloth shirt and his sneakers lie beside his bed.* ROGER, *collapsed in his own bed, lies upon his back, his head also at the foot, a Playboy magazine covering his face and a half-bottle of beer in his hands folded on his belly. Having removed his civilian shirt, he wears a white T shirt.* CARLYLE *is lying on his belly on* RICHIE'S *bed, his head at the foot and he is facing out.* RICHIE *is sitting on the floor, resting against* ROGER'S *footlocker. He is wrapped in a blanket. Beside him is an unopened bottle of beer and a bottle opener.*

They are all dreamy in the dimness as TAPS plays sadly on and then fades into silence. No one moves.)

RICHIE. I don't now where it was, but it wasn't here. And we were all in it—it felt like—but we all had different faces. After you guys left, I only dozed for a few minutes so it couldn't have been long. Roger laughed a lot and Billy was taller. I don't remember all the details exactly, and even though we were the

ones in it, I know it was about my father. He was a big man. I
was six. He was a very big man when I was six and he went
away, but I remember him. He started drinking and staying
home making model airplanes and boats and paintings by the
numbers. We had money from mom's family so he was just
home all the time. And then one day I was coming home from
kindergarten and as I was starting up the front walk, he came
out the door and he had these suitcases in his hands. He was
leaving, see, sneaking out and I'd caught him. We looked at
each other and I just knew and I started crying. He yelled at me:
"Don't you cry; don't you start crying." I tried to grab him and
he pushed me down in the grass. And then he was G.O.N.E.

BILLY. And that was it? That was it?

RICHIE. I remember hiding my eyes. I lay in the grass and hid
my eyes and waited.

BILLY. He never came back?

RICHIE. No.

CARLYLE. Ain't that some shit. Now I'm a goddamn jive-
time street nigger. I knew where my daddy was all the while.
He workin' in this butcher shop two blocks up the street. Ole
Mom used to point him out. "There he go. That him, that your
daddy." We'd see him on the street; "there he go."

ROGER. Man couldn't see his way to livin' with you, that
what you're sayin'?

CARLYLE. Never saw the day.

ROGER. And still couldn't get his ass outa the neighborhood
. . . ? (RICHIE begins trying to open his bottle of beer.)

CARLYLE. Ain't that a bitch; poor ole bastard just duck his
head—Mom pointin' at him—he git this real goddamn hang-
dog look like he don't know who we talkin' about and he walk
a little faster. Why the hell he never move away I don't know,
unless he was crazy. But I don't think so. He come up to me
once—I was playin'—"Boy," he says, "I ain't your daddy. I
ain't. Your momma's crazy." "Don't you be callin' Momma
crazy, Daddy," I tole him. Poor ole thing didn't know what to
do.

RICHIE. (Giving up; he can't get the beer open.) Somebody
open this for me? I can't get this open. (BILLY seems about to
move to help, but CARLYLE is quicker, rising a little on the bunk
and reaching.)

CARLYLE. Ole Carlyle get it.

RICHIE. (Slides along the floor until he can place the bottle in
CARLYLE'S outstretched hand.) Then there was this once, there
was this TV documentary about these bums in San Francisco,

this TV guy interviewing all these bums and just for maybe ten seconds while he was talkin' . . . (*Smiling,* CARLYLE *hands* RICHIE *the opened bottle.*) . . . to this one bum, there was this other one in the background jumpin' around like he thought he was dancin', and wavin' his hat and even though there wasn't anything about him like my father and I didn't really ever see his face at all, I just kept thinkin', "That's him. My dad. He thinks he's dancin'." (*They lie there in silence and suddenly, softly,* BILLY *giggles, and then he giggles a little more and louder.*)

BILLY. Jesus!

RICHIE. What?

BILLY. That's ridiculous, Richie; sayin' that, thinkin' that. If it didn't look like him it wasn't him, but you gotta be makin' up a story.

CARLYLE. (*Shifting now for a more comfortable position,* CARLYLE *moves his head to the pillow at the top of the bed.*) Richie first saw me, he didn't like me much no how, but he thought it over now, he changed his way a thinkin'. I can see that clear. We gonna be one big happy family.

RICHIE. Carlyle likes me, Billy; he thinks I'm pretty.

CARLYLE. (*Sitting up a little to make his point clear.*) No, I don't think you pretty. A broad is pretty. Punks ain't pretty. Punk—if he good lookin'—is cute. You cute.

RICHIE. He's gonna steal me right away, Little Billy. You're so slow, Bill. I prefer a man who's decisive. (*He is lying down now on the floor at the foot of his bed.*)

BILLY. You just keep at it you're gonna have us believin' you are just what you say you are.

RICHIE. Which is more than we can say for you.

(*Now* ROGER *rises on his elbow to light a cigarette.*)

BILLY. Jive, jive.

RICHIE. You're arrogant, Billy. So arrogant.

BILLY. What are you—on the rag?

RICHIE. Wouldn't it just bang your little balls if I were!

ROGER. (*To* RICHIE.) Hey, man. What's with you?

RICHIE. Stupidity offends me; lies and ignorance offend me.

BILLY. You know where we was? The three of us? All three of us—earlier on—to the wrong side of the tracks, Richard. One good black upside down whorehouse where you get what you buy, no jive along with it—so if it's a lay you want and need, you go! Or don't they have faggot whorehouses?

ROGER. IF YOU GUYS DON'T CUT THIS SHIT OUT I'M

GONNA BUST SOMEBODY'S HEAD! (*Angrily, he flops on his bed. There is a silence as they all lie there.*)

RICHIE. "Where we *was*," he says. Listen to him. "Where we *was*." And he's got more school, Carlyle, than you have fingers . . . and . . . (*He has lifted his foot onto the bed; it touches, presses* CARLYLE'S *foot.*) toes. It's this pseudo-earthy quality he feigns—but inside he's all cashmere.

BILLY. That's a lie. (*Giggling, he is staring at the floor.*) I'm polyester, worsted and mohair.

RICHIE. You have a lot of school, Billy, don't say you don't.

BILLY. You said "fingers and toes," you didn't say "alot."

CARLYLE. I think people get dumber the more they put their butts into some schoolhouse door.

BILLY. It depends on what the hell you're talkin' about. (*Now he looks at* CARLYLE, *and sees the feet, touching.*)

CARLYLE. I seen cats back on the block, they knew what was shakin'—then they got into all this school jive and man, every year they went they come back they didn't know nothin'.

(BILLY *is staring at* RICHIE'S *foot pressed and rubbing* CARLYLE'S *foot.* RICHIE *sees* BILLY *looking.* BILLY *cannot believe what he is seeing. It fills him with fear. The silence goes on and on.*)

RICHIE. Billy, why don't you and Roger go for a walk?

BILLY. What? (*He bolts to his knees. He is frozen on his knees on the bed.*)

RICHIE. Roger asked you to go downtown, you went, you had fun.

ROGER. (*Having turned, he knows almost instantly what is going on.*) I asked you, too.

RICHIE. You asked me; you *begged* Billy. I said "no." Billy said "no." You took my ten dollars. You begged Billy. I'm asking you a favor now—go for a walk—let Carlyle and me have some time. (*Silence.*)

CARLYLE. (*He sits up, uneasy and wary.*) That how you work it?

ROGER. Work what?

CARLYLE. Whosever turn it be.

BILLY. No, no, that ain't the way we work it because *we* don't work it.

CARLYLE. See? See? There it is—that goddamn education showin' through. All them years in school. Man, didn't we have a good time tonight? You rode in my car. I showed you a good cat house, all that sweet black pussy. Ain't we friends? Richie likes me. How come you don't like me?

BILLY. 'Cause if you really are doin' what I think you're doin', you're a fuckin' animal!

(CARLYLE *leaps to his feet, hand snaking to his pocket to draw a weapon.*)

ROGER. Billy, no.

BILLY. NO, WHAT?!

ROGER. Relax, man; no need. (*He turns to* CARLYLE; *patiently, wearily, he speaks.*) Man, I tole you it ain't goin' on here. We both told you it ain't goin' on here.

CARLYLE. Don't you jive me, Nigger. You goin' for a walk like I'm askin' or not? I wanna get this clear.

ROGER. Man, we live here.

RICHIE. It's my house, too, Roger; I live here, too. (*He bounds to his feet, flinging the blanket that has been covering him so it flies and lands on the floor near* ROGER'S *footlocker.*)

ROGER. Don't I know that? Did I say somethin' to make you think I didn't know that?

RICHIE. (*Standing, is removing his trousers and throwing them down on his footlocker.*) Carlyle is my guest. (*Sitting down on the side of his bed, and facing out, he puts his arms around* CARLYLE'S *thigh.* ROGER *jumps to his feet and grabs the blanket from the foot of his bed. Shaking it open, he drops onto the bed, his head at the foot of the bed and facing off as he covers himself.*)

ROGER. Fine. He your friend. This your home. So that mean he can stay. It don't mean, I gotta leave. I'll catch you all in the mornin'.

BILLY. Roger, what the hell are you doin'?

ROGER. What you better do, Billy. It's gettin' late. I'm goin' to sleep.

BILLY. What?

ROGER. Go to fucking bed, Billy. Get up in the rack, turn your back and look at the wall.

BILLY. You gotta be kiddin'.

ROGER. DO IT!

BILLY. Man . . . !

ROGER. Yeah . . . !

BILLY. You mean just. . . .

ROGER. It been goin' on a long damn time, man, you ain't gonna put no stop to it.

CARLYLE. You . . . ain't . . . serious.

RICHIE. (*Both he and* CARLYLE *are staring at* ROGER *and then* BILLY *who is staring at* ROGER.) Well, I don't believe it. Of all the childish . . . infantile. . . .

CARLYLE. Hey! (*Silence.*) HEY! Even I got to say this is a little weird, but if this the way you do it . . . (*And he turns toward* RICHIE *below him.*) . . . it the way I do it. I don't know.

RICHIE. With them right there? Are you kidding? My god, Carlyle, that'd be obscene. (*Pulling slightly away from* CARLYLE.)

CARLYLE. Ohhh, man . . . they backs turned.

RICHIE. No.

CARLYLE. What I'm gonna do? (*Silence. He looks at them, all three of them.*) Don't you got no feelin' for how a man feel? I don't understand you two boys. Unless you a pair of motherfuckers. That what you are, you a pair of motherfuckers? You slits, man. DON'T YOU HEAR ME!? I DON'T UN-DERSTAND THIS SITUATION HERE. I THOUGHT WE MADE A DEAL! (RICHIE *rises, starts to pull on his trousers.* CARLYLE *grabs him.*) YOU GET ON YOUR KNEES, YOU PUNK, I MEAN, NOW, AND YOU GONNA BE ON MY JOINT FAST OR YOU GONNA BE ONE BUSTED PUNK. AM I UNDERSTOOD? (*He hurls* RICHIE *down onto the floor.*)

BILLY. I ain't gonna have this going on here; Roger, I can't.

ROGER. I been turnin' my back on one thing or another all my life.

RICHIE. Jealous, Billy?

BILLY. (*Getting to his feet.*) Just go out that door—the two of you. Go. Go on out in the bushes or out in some field. See if I follow you. See if I care. I'll be right here and I'll be sleepin', but it ain't gonna be done in my house. I don't have much in this goddamn army, but *here* is mine. (*He stands beside his bed.*)

CARLYLE. I WANT MY FUCKIN' NUT! HOW COME YOU SO UPTIGHT? HE WANTS ME! THIS BOY HERE WANTS ME! WHO YOU TO STOP IT?

ROGER. (*Spinning to face* CARLYLE *and* RICHIE.) That's right, Billy. Richie one a those people want to get fucked by niggers, man. It what he know was gonna happen all his life—can be his dream come true. Ain't that right, Richie! (*Jumping to his feet,* RICHIE *starts putting on his trousers.*) Want to make it real in the world, how a nigger is an animal. Give 'em an inch, gonna take a mile. Ain't you some kinda fool, Richie? Hear me, Carlyle.

CARLYLE. Man, don't make me no never-mind what he think he's provin' an' shit, long as I get my nut, I KNOW I ain't no animal, don't have to prove it.

RICHIE. (*Pulling at* CARLYLE'S *arm, wanting to move him toward the door.*) Let's go. Let's go outside, the hell with it.

(*But* CARLYLE *tears himself free; he squats furiously down on the bunk, his hands seizing it, his back to all of them.*)

CARLYLE. Bullshit. Bullshit! I ain't goin' no fuckin' where—this jive ass ain't runnin' me. Is this you house or not? (*He doesn't know what is going on; he can hardy look at any of them.*)

ROGER. (*Bounding out of bed, hurling his pillow across the room.*) I'm goin' to the fuckin' john, Billy. Hang it up, man; let 'em be.

BILLY. No.

ROGER. I'm smarter than you—do like I'm sayin'.

BILLY. It ain't right.

ROGER. Who gives a big rat's ass!

CARLYLE. Right on, Bro! That boy know; he do. (*He is circling the bed toward them.*) Hear him. Look into his eyes.

BILLY. This fuckin' army takin' everything else away from me, they ain't takin' more than they got—I see what I see—I don't run, don't hide.

ROGER. (*Turning away from* BILLY, *he stomps out the door, slamming it.*) You fuckin' well better learn.

CARLYLE. That right. Time for more schoolin'. Lesson number one. (*Stealthily, he steps and snaps out the only light, the lamp clamped to* RICHIE'S *bed.* (You don't see what you see so well in the dark. It dark in the night. Black man got a black body—he disappear. (*The darkness is so total they are all no more than shadows.*)

RICHIE. Not to the hands; not to the fingers. (*Moving from across the room toward* CARLYLE.)

CARLYLE. You do like you talk, boy, you gonna make me happy. (*As* BILLY, *nervously clutching his sneaker, is moving backward.*)

BILLY. Who says the lights go out? Nobody goddamn asked me if the lights go out. (*He lunges to the wall switch, throws it. The overhead lights flash on, flooding the room with light.* CARLYLE *is seated on the edge of* RICHIE'S *bed,* RICHIE *kneeling before him.*)

CARLYLE. I DO, MOTHERFUCKER, I SAY! (*And the switchblade seems to leap from his pocket to his hand.*) I SAY! CAN'T YOU LET PEOPLE BE? (BILLY *hurls his shoe at the floor at* CARLYLE'S *feet. Instantly,* CARLYLE *is across the room, blocking* BILLY'S *escape out the door.*) Goddamn you, boy! I'm gonna cut your ass—just to show you how it feel . . . and cuttin' can happen—this knife true.

RICHIE. Carlyle, now c'mon.

CARLYLE. Shut up, Pussy.

RICHIE. Don't hurt him, for crissake.

CARLYLE. Goddamn man throw a shoe at me, he don't walk around clean in the world thinkin' he can throw another. He get some shit comin' back at him. (BILLY *doesn't know which way to go, and then* CARLYLE, *jabbing the knife at the air before* BILLY'S *chest, has* BILLY *running backward, his eyes fixed on the moving blade. He stumbles, having run into* RICHIE'S *bed. He sprawls backward and* CARLYLE *is over him.*) No, no; no, no. Put you hand out there. Put it out. (*Slight pause;* BILLY *is terrified.*) DO THE THING I'M TELLIN'! (BILLY *lets his hand rise in the air and* CARLYLE *grabs it, holds it.*) That's it. That's good. See? See?

(*The knife flashes across* BILLY'S *palm; the blood flows.* BILLY *winces, recoils, but* CARLYLE'S *hand still clenches and holds.*)

BILLY. Motherfucker.

(*Again the knife darts, cutting, and* BILLY *yelps.* RICHIE, *on his knees beside them, turns away.*)

RICHIE. Oh, my god, what are you—

CARLYLE. (*In his own sudden distress,* CARLYLE *flings the hand away.*) That you blood. The blood inside you, you don't ever see it there—take a look how easy it come out—and enough of it come out, you in the middle of the worst goddamn trouble you ever gonna see. And know I'm the man can deal that kinda trouble, easy as I smile. And I smile . . . easy. Yeah. (BILLY *is curled in upon himself, holding the hand to his stomach as* RICHIE *now reaches tentatively and shyly out as if to console* BILLY, *who repulses the gesture.* CARLYLE *is angry and strangely depressed. Forlornly, he slumps onto* BILLY'S *footlocker as* BILLY *staggers up to his wall locker and takes out a towel.*) Bastard ruin my mood, Richie. He ruin my mood. Fightin' and lovin' real different in the feelin's I got. I see blood come outa somebody like that it don't make me feel good— hurt me—hurt on somebody I thought was my friend. But I ain't supposed to see. One dumb nigger. No mind, he thinks, no heart, no feelings a gentleness. You see how that ain't true, Richie. Goddamn man threw a shoe at me, a lotta people woulda cut his heart out. I gotta make him know he throw shit, he get shit. But I don't hurt him bad, you see what I mean?

BILLY. (*Back to them, he stands hunched at his locker and suddenly, his voice, hissing, erupts.*) Jesus H. . . . . Christ . . . ! Do you know what I'm doin'? Do you know what I'm standin' here doin'? (*He whirls now; he holds a straight razor in his hand. A bloody towel is wrapped around the hurt hand.* CARLYLE *tenses, rises, seeing the razor.*) I'm a twenty-four-year-old-goddamn college graduate—intellectual goddamn scholar-type, and I got a razor in my hand, I'm thinkin' about comin' up behind one black human being and I'm thinkin' nigger-this and nigger-that—I wanna cut his throat. THAT IS RIDICULOUS. I NEVER FACED ANYBODY IN MY LIFE WITH ANYTHING TO KILL THEM. YOU UNDERSTAND ME? I DON'T HAVE A GODDAMN THING ON THE LINE HERE! (*The door opens, and* ROGER *rushes in, having heard the yelling.* BILLY *flings the razor into his locker.*) Look at me, Roger, look at me. I got a cut palm, I don't know what happened. Jesus Christ, I got sweat all over me when I think a what I was near to doin'. I swear it, I mean, do I think I need a reputation as a killer, a bad man with a knife? (*He is wild with the energy of feeling free and with the anger at what those others almost made him do.* CARLYLE *slumps down on the footlocker; he sits there.*) Bullshit! I need shit! I got sweat all over me. I got the mile record in my home town. I did 4:42 in high school and that's the goddamn record in Windsor County, I don't need approval from either one of the pair of you. (*And he rushes at* RICHIE.) You wanna be a goddamn swish—a goddamn faggot-queer—GO! Suckin' cocks and takin' it in the ass, the thing of which you dream, GO! AND YOU— (*Whirling on* CARLYLE.) You wanna be a bad-assed animal, man, get it on—go—but I wash my hands—I am not human as you are. I put you down, I put you down (*He almost hurls himself at* RICHIE.), you gay little piece a shit-cake—SHIT-CAKE—AND YOU— (*Hurt, confused,* RICHIE *turns away, nearly pressing his face into the bed beside which he kneels, as* BILLY *has spun back to tower over the pulsing, weary* CARLYLE.) —you are your own goddamn fault, SAMBO! SAMBO! (*And the knife flashes up in* CARLYLE'S *hand into* BILLY'S *stomach, and* BILLY *yelps.*) Ahhhhhhhhh. (*And pushes at the hand.* RICHIE *is still turned away.*)

RICHIE. Well, fuck you, Billy.

BILLY. (*He backs off the knife.*) Get away, get away.

RICHIE. (*As* ROGER, *who could not see because of* BILLY'S *back to him, is approaching* CARLYLE *and* BILLY *goes walking up toward the lockers as if he knows where he is going, as if he is going to go out the door and to a movie, his hands holding his belly.*) You're so messed up.

ROGER. (*To* CARLYLE.) Man, what's the matter with you?

CARLYLE. Don't nobody talk that weird shit to me, you understand?

ROGER. You jive, man. That's all you do, jive!

(BILLY, *striding swiftly, walks flat into the wall lockers; he bounces, turns. They are all looking at him.*)

RICHIE. Billy! Oh, Billy! (ROGER *looks at* RICHIE.)

BILLY. Ahhhhhhh. Ahhhhhhh. (ROGER *looks at* CARLYLE *as if he is about to scream, and beyond him,* BILLY *turns from the lockers, starts to walk again, now staggering and moving toward them.*)

RICHIE. I think . . . he stabbed him. I think Carlyle stabbed Billy. Roger!

(ROGER *whirls to go to* BILLY, *who is staggering down and angled away, hands clenched over his belly.*)

BILLY. Shut up! It's just a cut, it's just a cut. He cut my hand, he cut gut. (*He collapses onto his knees just beyond* ROGER'S *footlocker.*) It took the wind out of me, scared me, that's all. (*Fiercely, he tries to hide the wound and remain calm.*)

ROGER. Man, you all right? (*He moves to* BILLY, *who turns to hide the wound. Till now no one is sure what happened.* RICHIE *only "thinks"* BILLY'S *been stabbed,* BILLY *is pretending he isn't hurt. As* BILLY *turns from* ROGER, *he turns toward* RICHIE *and* RICHIE *sees the blood.*)

CARLYLE. You know what I was learnin', he was learnin' to talk all that weird shit, cuttin', baby, cuttin', the ways and means a shit, man razors.

RICHIE. Carlyle, you stabbed him; you stabbed him.

ROGER. You all right? Or what? He slit you?

BILLY. Just took the wind outa me, scared me.

CARLYLE. Ohhhh, pussy, pussy, pussy, Carlyle know what he do.

ROGER. (*Trying to lift* BILLY.) Get up, okay? Get up on the bed.

BILLY. (*Irritated, pulling free.*) I am on the bed.

ROGER. What?

RICHIE. No, Billy, no, you're not.

BILLY. Shut up!

RICHIE. You're on the floor.

BILLY. I'm on the bed. I'm on the bed. (*Emphatically. And then he looks at the floor.*) What?

ROGER. Let me see what he did. (BILLY'S *hands are clenched on the wound.*) Billy, let me see where he got you.

BILLY. (*Recoiling.*) NOOOOOOO, you nigger!

ROGER. (*He leaps at* CARLYLE.) What did you do?

CARLYLE. (*Hunching his shoulders, ducking his head.*) Shut up.

ROGER. What did you do, Nigger, you slit him or stick him? (*And then he tries to get back to* BILLY.) Billy, let me see.

BILLY. (*Doubling over till his head hits the floor.*) Noooooo! Shit, shit, shit.

RICHIE. (*Suddenly sobbing and yelling.*) Oh, my god, my god, ohhhh, ohhhh, ohhhh. (*Bouncing on his knees on the bed.*)

CARLYLE. FUCK IT, FUCK IT, I STUCK HIM. I TURNED IT. This mother army break my heart, I can't be out there where it pretty, don't wanna live! Wash me clean, shit-face!

RICHIE. Ohhhh, ohhhhh, ohhhhhhhhhh. Carlyle stabbed Billy, oh, ohhhhh, I never saw such a thing in my life. Ohhhhhhh. (*As* ROGER *is trying gently, fearfully to straighten* BILLY *up.*) Don't die, Billy; don't die.

ROGER. Shut up and go find somebody to help. Richie, go!

RICHIE. Who? I'll go. I'll go. (*Scrambling off the bed.*)

ROGER. I don't know. JESUS CHRIST! DO IT!

RICHIE. O.K. O.K. Billy, don't die. Don't die. (*Backing for the door, he turns and runs.*)

ROGER. The Sarge, or C.Q.

BILLY. (*Suddenly doubling over, vomiting blood.* RICHIE *is gone.*) Ohhhhhhhhhh. Blood. Blood.

ROGER. Be still, be still.

BILLY. (*Pulling at a blanket on the floor beside him.*) I want to stand up. I'm—vomiting— (*Making no move to stand, only covers himself.*) blood. What does that mean?

ROGER. I don't know. (*Slowly, standing.*)

BILLY. Yes, yes, I want to stand up. Give me blanket, blanket. (*He rolls back and forth, fighting to get the blanket over him.*)

ROGER. RIICCHHHIIEEEE! (*As* BILLY *is furiously grappling with the blanket.*) No, no. (*He looks at* CARLYLE *who is slumped over muttering to himself.* ROGER *runs for the door.*) Wait on, be tight, be cool.

BILLY. Cover me. Cover me. (*At last, he gets the blanket over his face. The dark makes him grow still. He lies there beneath his blanket. Silence. No one moves. And then* CARLYLE *senses the quiet, he turns, looks. Slowly, wearily, he rises and walks to where* BILLY *lies. He stands over him, the knife hanging loosely from his left hand as he reaches with his right to gently take the blanket and lift it slowly from off* BILLY'S *face. They look at each other.* BILLY *reaches up and pats* CARLYLE'S *hand holding the blanket.*) I don't want to talk to you right now, Carlyle. All right? Where's Roger? Do you know where he is? (*Slight pause.*) Don't stab me anymore, Carlyle, okay? I was dead wrong doin' what I did. I know that now. Carlyle, promise me you won't stab me anymore. I couldn't take it . . . okay? I'm cold . . . , my blood . . . is . . .

(*From off comes a voice.*)

ROONEY. Cokesie? Coksie-woksie? (*And he staggers into the doorway, very drunk, a beer bottle in his hand.*) Ollie-ollie ach-shon-freee. (*He looks at them.* CARLYLE *quickly, secretly, slips the knife into his pocket.*) How you all doin'? Everybody drunk, huh? I los' my friend. (*He is staggering sideways toward* BILLY'S *bunk, where he finally drops down, sitting.*) How are you, Soldier? (CARLYLE *has straightened, his head ducked down as he is edging for the door.*) Who are you, Soldier?

(RICHIE, *running, comes roaring into the room. He looks at* ROONEY *and cannot understand what is going on.* CARLYLE *is standing.* ROONEY *is just sitting there.* RICHIE *moves along the lockers, trying to get behind* ROONEY, *his eyes never off* CARLYLE.)

RICHIE. Ohhhhhhh, Sergeant Rooney, I've been looking for you everywhere—where have you been? Carlyle stabbed Billy, he stabbed him.

ROONEY. (*Sitting there.*) What?

RICHIE. Carlyle stabbed Billy.

ROONEY. Who's Carlyle?

RICHIE. He's Carlyle. (*As* CARLYLE *seems about to advance, the knife again showing in his hand.*) Carlyle, don't hurt anybody more!

ROONEY. (*On his feet, he is staggering toward the door.*) You got a knife there? What's with the knife? What's goin' on HERE? (CARLYLE *steps as if to bolt for the door, but* ROONEY *is in the way, having inserted himself between* CARLYLE *and* RICHIE *who has backed into the doorway.*) Wait! Now wait!

RICHIE. (*As* CARLYLE *raises the knife.*) Carlyle, don't! (RICHIE *runs from the room.*)

ROONEY. You watch your step, you understand. You see what I got here? (*He lifts the beer bottle, waves it threateningly.*) You watch your step, motherfucker. Relax. I mean, we can straighten all this out—we— (CARLYLE *lunges at* ROONEY, *who tenses.*) I'm just askin' what's goin' on, that's all I'm doin'. No need to get all— (*And* CARLYLE *swipes at the air again;* ROONEY *recoils.*) Motherfucker. Motherfucker. (*He seems to be tensing, his body gathering itself for some mighty effort. And he throws his head back and gives the eagle yell.*) Eeeeeeeeeeeeeaaaa-aaaaahhhhhhhh! Eeeeeaaaaaaaaaahhhhhhhhhh! (CARLYLE *jumps, he looks left and right.*) Goddamnit, I'll cut you good. (*He lunges to break the bottle on the edge of the wall lockers. The bottle shatters and he yelps, dropping everything.*) Ohhhhhhhh! Ohhhhhhhhhhhhh! (CARLYLE *bolts, running from the room.*) I hurt myself, I cut myself. I hurt my hand. (*Holding the wounded hand, he scurries to* BILLY'S *bed where he sits on the edge, trying to wipe the blood away so he can see the wound.*) I cut— (*Hearing a noise, he whirls, looks;* CARLYLE *is plummeting in the door and toward him.* ROONEY *stands.*) I hurt my hand, goddamnit! (*The knife goes into* ROONEY'S *belly. He flails at* CARLYLE.) I HURT MY HAND! WHAT ARE YOU DOING? WHAT ARE YOU DOING? WAIT! WAIT! (*He turns away falling to his knees, and the knife goes into him again and again.*) No fair. No fair! (ROGER, *running, skids into the room headed for* BILLY *and then he sees* CARLYLE *on* ROONEY, *the knife.* ROGER *lunges, grabbing* CARLYLE, *pulling him to get him off* ROONEY. CARLYLE *leaps free of* ROGER, *sending* ROGER *flying backwards. And then* CARLYLE *begins to circle* ROGER'S *bed. He is whimpering, wiping at the blood on his shirt as if to wipe it away.* ROGER *backs away as* CARLYLE *keeps waving the knife at him.* ROONEY *is crawling along the floor under* BILLY'S *bed and then he stops crawling, lies there.*)

CARLYLE. You don't tell nobody on me you saw me do this, I let you go, okay? Ohhhhhhhhh. (*Rubbing, rubbing at the shirt.*) Ohhhhhh, how'm I gonna get back to the world now, I got all this mess to—

ROGER. What happened? That you—I don't understand that you did this! That you did—

CARLYLE. YOU SHUT UP! Don't be talkin' all that weird shit to me—don't you go talkin' all that weird shit!

ROGER. Noooooooooooo!

CARLYLE. I'm Carlyle, man. You know me. You know me. (*He turns, he flees out the door.* ROGER, *alone, looks about the room.* BILLY *is there.* ROGER *moves toward* BILLY *who is shifting, undulating on his back.*)

BILLY. Carlyle, no; oh, Christ, don't stab me anymore. I'll die. I will, I'll die. Don't make me die. I'll get my dog after you. I'LL GET MY DOG AFTER YOU! (ROGER *is saying "Oh, Billy, man, Billy." He is trying to hold* BILLY. *Now he lifts* BILLY *into his arms.*)

ROGER. Oh, Billy; oh, man. GODDAMNIT, BILLY! (*As a* MILITARY POLICE LIEUTENANT *comes running in the door, his .45 automatic drawn and he levels it at* ROGER.)

LIEUTENANT. Freeze, Soldier! Not a quick move out of you. Just real slow, straighten your ass up. (ROGER *has gone rigid;*

the LIEUTENANT *is advancing on him. Tentatively,* ROGER *turns, looks.*)

ROGER. Huh? No.

LIEUTENANT. Get your ass against the lockers.

ROGER. Sir, no. I—

LIEUTENANT. (*Hurling* ROGER *away toward the wall lockers.*) MOVE! (*As another M.P.,* PFC HINSON, *comes in, followed by* RICHIE, *flushed and breathless.*) Hinson, cover this bastard.

HINSON. (*Drawing his .45 automatic moving on* ROGER.) Yes, sir. (*The* LIEUTENANT *frisks* ROGER *who is spread-eagled at the lockers.*)

RICHIE. What? Oh, sir, no, no. Roger, what's going on?

LIEUTENANT. I'll straighten this shit out.

ROGER. Tell 'em to get the gun off me, Richie.

LIEUTENANT. SHUT UP!

RICHIE. But, sir, sir, he didn't do it. Not him.

LIEUTENANT. (*Fiercely, he shoves* RICHIE *out of the way.*) I told you all of you to shut up. (*He moves to* ROONEY'S *body.*) Jesus, god, this SFC is cut to shit. He's cut awful. (*He hurries to* BILLY'S *body.*) This man too. Awful.

(*A SIREN is heard through the following. As* CARLYLE *appears in the doorway, his hands cuffed behind him, a third M.P.,* PFC CLARK, *shoves him forward.* CARLYLE *seems shocked and cunning, his mind whirring.*)

CLARK. Sir, I got this guy on the street runnin' like a streak a shit. (*He hurls the struggling* CARLYLE *forward and* CARLYLE *stumbles toward the head of* RICHIE'S *bed as* RICHIE, *seeing him coming, hurries away along* BILLY'S *bed and toward the wall lockers.*)

RICHIE. He did it! Him, him!

CARLYLE. What is going on here? I don't know what is going on here!

CLARK. (*Club at the ready, he stations himself beside* CARLYLE.) He's got blood all over him, sir. All over him.

LIEUTENANT. What about the knife?

CLARK. No, sir. He must have thrown it away.

(*As a fourth M.P. has entered to stand in the doorway, and* HINSON, *leaving* ROGER, *bends to examine* ROONEY. *He will also kneel and look for life in* BILLY.)

LIEUTENANT. You throw it away, Soldier?

CARLYLE. Oh, you thinkin' about how my sister got happened, too. Oh, you ain't so smart as you think you are! No way!

ROGER. Jesus God Almighty.

LIEUTENANT. What happened here? I want to know what happened here.

HINSON. (*Rising from* BILLY'S *body.*) They're both dead, sir. Both of them.

LIEUTENANT. (*Confidential, almost whispering.*) I know they're both dead. That's what I'm talkin' about.

CARLYLE. Chicken blood, sir. Chicken blood and chicken hearts is what all over me. I was goin' on my way, these people jump out the bushes be pourin' it all over me. Chicken blood and chicken hearts. (*Thrusting his hands out at* CLARK.) You goin' take these cuffs off me, boy.

LIEUTENANT. Sit him down, Clark. Sit him down and shut him up.

CARLYLE. This my house, sir. This my goddamn house. (CLARK *grabs him, begins to move him.*)

LIEUTENANT. I said to shut him up.

CLARK. Move it; move! (*Struggling to get* CARLYLE *over to* ROGER'S *footlocker as* HINSON *and the other M.P. exit.*)

CARLYLE. I want these cuffs taken off my hands.

CLARK. You better do like you been told. You better sit and shut up!

CARLYLE. I'm gonna be thinkin' over here. I'm gonna be thinkin' it all over. I got plannin' to do. I'm gonna be thinkin' in my quietness, don't you be makin' no mistake. (*He slumps over, muttering to himself.* HINSON *and the other M.P. return, carrying a stretcher. They cross to* BILLY, *chatting with each other about how to go about the lift. They will lift him; they will carry him out.*)

LIEUTENANT. (*To* RICHIE.) You're Wilson?

RICHIE. No, sir. (*Indicating* BILLY.) That's Wilson. I'm Douglas.

LIEUTENANT. (*To* ROGER.) And you're Moore. And you sleep here.

ROGER. Yes, sir.

RICHIE. Yes, sir. And Billy slept here and Sergeant Rooney was our platoon sergeant and Carlyle was a transient, sir. He was a transient from "P" Company.

LIEUTENANT. (*Scrutinizing* ROGER.) And you had nothing to do with this? (*To* RICHIE.) He had nothing to do with this?

ROGER. No, sir, I didn't.

RICHIE. No, sir, he didn't. I didn't either. Carlyle went crazy and Billy and he got into a fight and it was awful. I didn't even know what it was about exactly.

LIEUTENANT. How'd the SFC get involved?

RICHIE. Well, he came in, sir.

ROGER. I had to run off to call you, sir. I wasn't here.

RICHIE. Sergeant Rooney just came in—I don't now why—he heard all the yelling, I guess, and Carlyle went after him. Billy was already stabbed.

CARLYLE. (*Rising, his manner that of a man who is taking charge.*) All right, now, you gotta be gettin' the fuck outa here. All of you. I have decided enough of the shit has been goin' on around here and I am tellin' you to be gettin' these motherfuckin' cuffs off me and you be gettin' me a bus ticket home. I am quittin' this jive-time army.

LIEUTENANT. You are doin' what?

CARLYLE. No, I ain't gonna be quiet. No way. I am quittin' this goddamn—

LIEUTENANT. You shut the hell up, Soldier. I am ordering you.

CARLYLE. I don't understand you people! Don't you people understand when a man be talkin' English at you to say his mind. I have quit the army!

LIEUTENANT. Get him outa here!

RICHIE. What's the matter with him?

LIEUTENANT. Hinson! Clark! (*They move, grabbing him. They drag him struggling toward the door.*)

CARLYLE. Oh, no. Oh, no. You ain't gonna be doin' me no more. I been tellin' you. To get away from me. I am stayin' here. This my place, not your place. You take these cuffs off me like I been tellin' you! My poor little sister, Lin Sue, understood what was goin' on here! She tole me! She knew! (*He is howling in the hallway now.*) You better be gettin' these cuffs off me!

(*Silence.* ROGER, RICHIE *and the* LIEUTENANT *are all staring at the door. The* LIEUTENANT *turns, crosses to the foot of* ROGER'S *bed.*)

LIEUTENANT. All right now. I will be getting to the bottom of this. You know I will be getting to the bottom of this. (*He is taking two forms from his clipboard.*)

RICHIE. Yes, sir.

(HINSON *and the fourth M.P. return with another stretcher. They walk to* ROONEY, *talking to one another about how to lift him. They drag him from under the bed. They will roll him onto the stretcher, lift him, and walk out.* ROGER *moves, watching them, down along the edge of* BILLY'S *bed.*)

LIEUTENANT. Fill out these forms. I want your serial number, rank, your MOS, the NCOIC of your work. Any leave coming up will be cancelled. Tomorrow at 0800 you will report to my office at the Provost Marshall's Headquarters. You know where that is?

ROGER. (*As they are leaving with the stretcher and* ROONEY'S *body.*) Yes, sir.

RICHIE. Yes, sir.

LIEUTENANT. (*Crossing to* ROGER, *he hands him the two forms.*) Be prepared to do some talking. Two perfectly trained and primed, strong pieces of U.S. Army property got cut to shit up here. We are going to find out how and why. Is that clear?

RICHIE. Yes, sir.

ROGER. Yes, sir. (*The* LIEUTENANT *looks at each of them. He surveys the room. He marches out.*

RICHIE. Oh, my god. Oh. Oh. (*He runs to his bed and collapses, sitting, hunched down at the foot. He holds himself and rocks as if very cold.* ROGER, *quietly, is weeping. He stands and then walks to his bed. He puts down the two forms. He moves purposefully up to the mops hanging on the wall in the corner. He takes one down. He moves with the mop and the bucket to* BILLY'S *bed where* ROONEY'S *blood stains the floor. He mops.* RICHIE, *in horror, is watching.*) What . . . are you doing?

ROGER. This area a mess, man. (*Dragging the bucket, carrying the mop, he moves to the spot where* BILLY *had lain. He begins to mop.*)

RICHIE. That's Billy's blood, Roger. His blood.

ROGER. Is it?

RICHIE. I feel awful.

ROGER. (*He keeps mopping.*) How come you made me waste all that time talkin' shit to you, Richie? All my time, talkin' shit, and all the time you was a faggot, man; you really was. You shoulda jus' tole ole Roger. He don't care. All you gotta do is tell me.

RICHIE. I've been telling you. I did.

ROGER. Jive, man, jive!

RICHIE. No!

ROGER. You did bullshit all over us! ALL OVER US!

RICHIE. I just wanted to hold his hand, Billy's hand, to talk

to him, go to the movies hand in hand like he would with a girl
or I would with someone back home.

ROGER. But he didn't wanna; *he* didn't wanna. (*Finished
now, dragging the mop and bucket back toward the corner.*
RICHIE *is sobbing, he is at the edge of hysteria.*)

RICHIE. He did.

ROGER. No, man.

RICHIE. He did. He did. It's my fault. (ROGER *slams the
bucket into the corner and rams the mop into the bucket. Furious, he marches down to* RICHIE. *Behind him* SERGEANT COKES,
grinning and lofting a wine bottle, appears in the doorway.)

ROGER. You know what you oughta do? Get yourself a little
mustache, get you some hair around your mouth—make it look
like what you think it is—you do that!

COKES. Hey! (RICHIE, *in despair, rolls onto his belly.* COKES *is
very, very happy.*) Hey! What a day. Gen'lmen. How you all
doin'?

ROGER. (*Crossing up near the head of his own bed.*) Hello,
Sergeant Cokes.

COKES. (*Affectionate and casual, he moves near to* ROGER.)
How you all doin'? Where's ole Rooney? I lost him.

ROGER. What?

COKES. We had a hell of a day, ole Rooney and me, lemme
tell you. We been playin' hide and go seek, and I was hidin'
and now I think maybe he started hidin' without tellin' me he
was gonna and I can't find him and I thought maybe he was
hidin' up here.

RICHIE. Sergeant, he—

ROGER. No. No, we ain't seen him.

COKES. I gotta find him. He knows how to react in a tough
situation. He didn't come up here looking for me?

ROGER. (*Moves around to the far side of his bed, turning his
back to* COKES. *Sitting,* ROGER *takes out a cigarette, but he does
not light it.*) We was goin' to sleep, Sarge, got to get up early.
You know the way this mother army is.

COKES. (*Nodding, drifting backwards, he sits down on* BILLY'S
bed.) You don't mind if I sit here a little. Wait on him. Got a
little wine. You can have some. (*Tilting his head way back, he
takes a big drink and then looking straight ahead, corks the
bottle with a whack of his hand.*) We got back into the area, we
had been downtown, he wanted to play hide and go seek. I tole
him okay, I was ready for that. He hid his eyes. So I run and
hid in the bushes and then under this jeep. 'Cause I thought it
was better. I hid and I hid and I hid. He never did come. So

finally, I got tired—I figured I'd give up, come lookin' for him. I was way over by the movie theater. I don't know how I got there. Anyway, I got back here and I figured maybe he come up here lookin' for me, figurin' I was hidin' up with you guys. You ain't seen him, huh?

ROGER. No, we ain't seen him. I tole you that, Sarge. We ain't seen him.

COKES. Oh.

RICHIE. Roger!

ROGER. He's drunk, Richie! He's blasted drunk. Got a brain turned to mush!

COKES. (*In deep agreement.*) That ain't no lie.

ROGER. Let it be for the night, Richie. Let him be for the night.

COKES. I still know what's goin' on, though. Never no worry about that. I always know what's goin' on. I always know. Don't matter what I drink or how much I drink. I always still know what's goin' on. But . . . I'll be goin' maybe and look for Rooney. (*But rising, he wanders down center.*) But. . . . I mean, we could be doin' that forever. Him and me. Me under the jeep. He wants to find me, he goes to the jeep, I'm over here. He comes here. I'm gone. You know, maybe I'll just wait a little while more I'm here. He'll find me then if he comes here. You guys want another drink. (*Turning, he goes to* BILLY'S *footlocker, where he sits and takes another enormous guzzle of wine.*) Jesus, what a goddamn day we had. Me and Rooney started drivin' and we was comin' to this intersection and out comes this goddamn Chevy. I try to get around her, but no dice, BINGO! I hit her in the left rear. She was furious. I didn't care. I gave her my name and number. My car had a headlight out, the fender bashed in. Rooney wouldn't stop laughin'. I didn't' know what to do. So we went to D.C. to this private club I know. Had ten or more snorts and decided to get back here after playin' some snooker. That was fun. On the way, we picked up this kid from the engineering unit, hitch-hiking. I'm starting to feel real clear-headed now. So I'm comin' around this corner and all of a sudden there's this car stopped dead in front of me. He's not blinkin' to turn or anything. I slam on the brakes but it's like puddin' the way I slide into him. There's a big noise, and we yell. Rooney starts laughin' like crazy and the kid jumps outa the back and says he's gonna take a fuckin' bus. The guy from the other car is swearin' at me. My car's still workin' fine so I move it off to the side and tell him to do the same, while we wait for the cops. He says he wants his car right

where it is and he had the right of way 'cause he was makin' a
legal turn. So we're waitin' for the cops. Some cars go by. The
guy's car is this big fuckin' Buick. Around the corner comes this
little red Triumph. The driver's this blonde kid, got this blonde
girl next to him. You can see what's gonna happen. There's this
fuckin' car sittin' there, nobody in it. So the Triumph goes
crashin' into the back of the Buick with nobody in it. BIFF-
BANG-BOOM. And everything stops. We're staring. It's all
still. And then that fuckin' Buick kinda shudders and starts to
move. With nobody in it. It starts to roll from the impact. And
it rolls just far enough to get where the road starts a downgrade.
It's driftin' to the right. It's driftin' to the shoulder and over it
and onto this hill where it's pickin' up speed 'cause the hill is
steep and then it disappears over the side, and into the dark,
just rollin' real quiet. Rooney falls over he's laughin' so hard. I
don't know what to do. In a minute the cops come and in
another minute some guy comes runnin' up over the hill to tell
us some other guy had got run over by this car with nobody in
it. We didn't know what to think. This was fuckin' unbelievable
to us. But we found out later from the cops that this wasn't true
and some guy had got hit over the head with a bottle in a bar
and when he staggered out the door it was just at the instant
that this fuckin' Buick with nobody in it went by. Seein' this,
the guy stops cold and turns around and just goes back into the
bar. Rooney is screamin' at me how we been in four goddamn
accidents and fights and how we have got out clean. So then we
got everything all straightened out and we come back here, to
play hide and seek cause that's what ole Rooney wanted. (*He is
taking another drink, but finding the bottle empty.*) Only now I
can't find him. (*Near* RICHIE'S *footlocker, stands a beer bottle
and* COKES *begins to move toward it. Slowly, he bends and
grasps the bottle; he straightens, looking at it. He drinks. And
settles down on* RICHIE'S *footlocker.*) I'll just sit a little. (RICHIE,
*lying on his belly, shudders. The sobs burst out of him. He is
shaking.* COKES, *blinking, turns to study* RICHIE.) What's up?
Hey, what're you cryin' about, Soldier? Hey? (RICHIE *cannot
help himself.*) What's he cryin' about?

ROGER. (*Disgustedly. He sits there.*) He's cryin' 'cause he's a
queer.

COKES. Oh. You a queer, boy?

RICHIE. Yes, Sergeant.

COKES. Oh. (*Pause.*) How long you been a queer?

ROGER. All his fuckin' life.

RICHIE. I don't know.

COKES. (*Turning to scold* ROGER.) Don't be yellin' mean at
him. Boy, I tell you it's a real strange thing the way havin'
leukemia gives you a lotta funny thoughts about things. Two
months ago—or maybe even yesterday—I'da called a boy who
was a queer a lotta awful names. But now I just wanna be
figurin' things out. I mean, you ain't kiddin' me out about ole
Rooney, are you boys, 'cause of how I'm a Sergeant and you're
enlisted men so you got some idea a vengeance on me. You
ain't doin' that are you, boys?

ROGER. No.

RICHIE. Ohhhh. Jesus. Ohhhh. I don't know what's hurtin' in
me.

COKE. No, no, boy. You listen to me. You gonna be okay.
There's a lotta worse things in this world than bein' a queer. I
seen a lot of 'em, too. I mean, you could have leukemia. That's
worse. That can kill you. I mean, it's okay. You listen to the ole
Sarge. I mean, maybe I was a queer I wouldn't have leukemia.
Who's to say? Lived a whole different life. Who's to say? I
keep thinkin' there was maybe somethin' I coulda done different. Maybe not drunk so much. Or if I'd killed more gooks, or
more Krauts or more dinks. I was kind-hearted sometimes. Or
if I'd had a wife and I had some kids. Never had any. But my
mother did and she died of it anyway. Gives you a whole funny
different way a lookin' at things, I'll tell you. Ohhhhhh, Rooney,
Rooney. (*Slight pause.*) Or if I'd let that little gook outa that
spider hole he was in, I was sittin' on it. I'd let him out now if
he was in there. (*He rattles the footlocker lid under him.*) But he
ain't. Oh, how'm I ever gonna forget it? That funny little guy.
I'm runnin' along, he pops up outa that hole—I'm never gonna
forget him—how'm I ever gonna forget him?—I see him and
dive—goddamn bullet hits me in the side, I'm mid-air, everything's turnin' around. I go over the edge of this ditch and I'm
crawlin' real fast. I lost my rifle. Can't find it. Then I come up
behind him. He's half out of the hole. I bang him on top of his
head, stuff him back into the hole with a grenade for company.
Then I'm sittin' on the lid and it's made outa steel. I can feel
him in there, though, bangin' and yellin' under me, and his
yelling I can hear is beggin' for me to let him out. It was like a
goddamn Charlie Chaplin movie, everybody fallin' down and
clumsy, and him in there yellin' and bangin' away, and I'm just
sittin' there lookin' around. And he was Charlie Chaplin. I
don't know who I was. And then he blew up. (*Pause.*) Maybe
I'll just get a little shut-eye right sittin' here while I'm waitin'

for ole Rooney. We figure it out. All of it. You don't mind I
just doze a little here, you boys.

ROGER. No.

RICHIE. No.

(ROGER *rises and walks to the door. He switches off the light
and gently closes the door. The transom glows.* COKES *sits in a
flower of light.* ROGER *crosses back to his bunk and settles in,
sitting.*)

COKES. 'Night, boys.

RICHIE. 'Night, Sergeant. (*He sits there, fingers entwined,
trying to sleep.*)

COKES. I mean, he was like Charlie Chaplin. And then he
blew up.

ROGER. (*Suddenly feeling very sad for this old man.*) Sergeant. Maybe you was Charlie Chaplin, too.

COKES. No. No. (*Pause.*) No. I don't know who I was.
'Night.

ROGER. You think he was singin' it?

COKES. What?

ROGER. You think he was singin' it?

COKES. Oh, yeah. Oh, yeah; he was singin' it. (*Slight pause.*
COKES *sitting on the footlocker, begins to sing a makeshift
language imitating Korean, to the tune of "Beautiful Streamer."
He begins with an angry, mocking energy that slowly becomes
a dream, a lullaby, a farewell, a lament.*)

Yo no som lo no.
Ung toe lo knee
Ra so me la lo
la see see oh doe

Doe no tee ta ta
too low see see
Ra mae me lo lo
Ah boo boo boo eee

Boo boo eee boo eeee
La so lee lem
Lem lo lee da ung
Uhhh so ba booooo ohhhh.

Boo booo ee ung ba
eee eee la looo
Lem lo le la la
Eeee oohhh ohhh ohhh ohhhhh.

(*In the silence, he makes the soft, whispering sound of a child imitating an explosion, and his entwined fingers come apart. The dark figures of* RICHIE *and* ROGER *are near. The lingering light fades.*)

MARCO POLO SINGS A SOLO

by
John Guare

AUTHOR'S NOTE

"House of Blue Leaves" had been a play about limits: people limited by a lack of talent, limited economically, limited emotionally, limited geographically. At one point in the play, the lead character called his best friend in California, a man who had immense power to create possibilities and to actuate them into reality, the only place where dreams make any sense and can't lash around and destroy us. That point fascinated me: people living without traditional limits. People who had all the money in the world, who had all the talent they needed to turn those dreams into reality, who had mobility, who had everything. Except limits. What do you hang onto in a limitless world? The answer seemed to be obvious: yourself. Each character in "Marco Polo Sings a Solo" is yearning for an even greater glory, an ever greater beauty, a greater power, a greater love, a greater truth, and moving into such intense territory by yourself, that very same self becomes all the more important. Everyone in the play is a Marco Polo, travelling out by himself, herself or both selves as in the case of one character. The people's very freedom makes them terrified. All walls are down. They are by themselves. They are terrified. They each are forced to search out for some kind of structure, whether it be a chemical formula to end cancer or a film to ennoble the world or a love to hang onto at night. How to play the play? The play is a comedy, the comedy coming out of each character's complete obsession with self, the ultimate structure, the ultimate source of the need. The "Notice Me" becomes as powerful in a world without limits as it did in a world walled only with limits. The play is a high comedy, played very grandly and confidently as if it were some 21st century reworking of *The Philadelphia Story* with all kinds of Katherine Hepburns and Cary Grants littering the stage. The people want the most, need the most, have to have the best, have the most, and in their own way, are the best of their time. Their problem is they know it and congratulate themselves on it a lot. Again, why it's a comedy. The bolts from heaven come down to wake these people up, to purify them, to restore nature to some kind of balance before this new century comes into being. One of them makes it. The others are too frightened to let go of themselves ultimately, in spite of the massacres and demolition. If they stopped listening to their solo, they might die. Stony McBride takes that risk and therefore can live.

The end of a century is traditionally a time of despair and soul-searching and in the middle ages a new century would provoke waves of suicides. These people are at a brink. What makes them noble is they really do want the best. What makes this a comedy is how lazy and satisfied they are.

J.G.

ACT ONE

A galaxy of stars. A man in a silver space suit appears floating in space. He takes off his helmet: STONY MCBRIDE. *He is absolutely amazed. He talks to us.*

STONY. I feel myself changing. I twist the gauge. I lift up. Is change this easy? Through stratospheres. Dodging quasars. I will get to you, Frank Schaeffer. You are the best part of me! This is the me I always wanted to be! To think! I woke up this morning a vegetable and here I am by nightfall a new sign of the zodiac! Stony McBride! Children born under this sign can change their lives at will. I've done it. How did I do it? Was change all this easy? Remembry. Dismember. Membrotic. Membrosis. A new word for the neurotic and panic-stricken act of obsessive memory. I, membrotic. How did I get here? How did I make the change? Did it begin only this morning? Membrosis. Membrotic. A man. A woman. A Norwegian breakfast. Napkins strewn between them like rumpled bedsheets. Membrosis. Membrotic. Remembry. Dismembry. Dismember. Remembry. Changing. I heard. I did not speak. I saw. I did not act. I watched. I did not move. Only this morning . . . only today . . .

(STONY *fades into dark as the lights reveal an iceberg. Some genius has carved a flat plane out of this great, Titanic-killer of an iceberg floating in the Norwegian sea. It's the time of year when the Arctic sun never rises, but high-tech heat lamps provide the necessary light and warmth to make this space more than livable. The dining table is set quite elegantly, a baby carriage is off to one side, and, of all things, a Baroque grand piano is tied with an enormous pink bow on its leg and an extravagant bouquet of lush flowers set on its closed lid. Outside the area of light, the ice makes chaotic shapes. At the moment, in the light, two extraordinarily attractive people are at the table finishing a breakfast.*

89

DIANE MCBRIDE *is a lush, indolent beauty in her thirties. This is the year 1999 and the clothes that year you'll remember were reminiscent of 1940s erotic glamor with a good old-fashioned self-aware salute to Buck Rogers and Flash Gordon. A century was ending. People were very cheery.*

Across from her, as crazy about her as she is about him, sits TOM WINTERMOUTH, *late thirties. Yes, the one the evening news is about. The one on the front page of the morning papers. He's handsome. He's beautifully tailored. The 1990s were a lucky time to contain such a confident leader.*

They are served by FREYDIS, *a spunky Norwegian country girl who looks like an escapee from a Brueghel painting. She's very clean, pours wine for them both and steps back to a respectful distance. TOM and DIANE clink their glasses . . .)*

DIANE. You said the Sandstones? That's fine, Freydis.

TOM. The Shootselfs. I said about the Shootselfs.

DIANE. Keep it coming, Tom. Oink is right into the trough. I am starved for every syllable that's happening down there in the real world.

TOM. Bob and Stephanie Shootself—

DIANE. We're up here in Reality Heights.

TOM. —flew to Idaho, right to a mountaintop, and repeated their marriage vows.

DIANE. But Tom, they had to. In their ten years together, between them, they've suffered so many nose jobs, chin jobs, eye lifts, ass lifts, breast lifts, name changes, I don't think there's any of the original bride and groom left.

TOM. I'm all for change.

DIANE. But they take it too far. Last year, didn't Stephanie have her entire body relifted? Flying from Palm Springs to Palm Beach, the altitude unravelled the stitches. The silicone zinged out. The whole new ass falls off. Broke the stewardess's foot. They had to turn the plane back. Put her ass in intensive care. I've heard of having your ass in a sling, but in this year of 1999, Stephanie carried it a little too far.

TOM. That space between your eyes and your ears. Blind people can see there. Facial vision they call it.

DIANE. Fryedis, that's enough. Eeenooof. *Prego. Prosit. Skol! Exit.* (FREYDIS *leaves. Diane's manner changes. She leans forward urgently, passionately.*) Why didn't you write? I thought you had died. I thought you were dead. I thought you'd forgotten me. I heard a commotion. A delivery being made. A piano being lowered down out of a helicopter.

TOM. Not just a piano. Edvard Grieg's piano.

DIANE. As if the piano had flown here under its own steam. Pursuing me. Had Pegasus been transformed into a piano? It's my wedding anniversary. My fifth wedding anniversary. I go back to my room. Why is there a piano here? I look in mirror getting ready for a party.

TOM. Your thighs. Your skin. The way your hair grows out of your skull.

DIANE. A party in the Arctic Circle. I see my life with such a sudden clarity, the precision of it kicked the air out of my lungs. I said: "No, it's not oxygen there's a shortage of in Norway. It's light. Remember light? Six months of no oxygen?" Wanting to call you. Not knowing where you are. Paris? Washington? Have you died? Have you forgotten me? Is there somebody new? (*They kiss. The baby cries.* DIANE *goes to comfort the baby. The baby is quiet.* DIANE *is in emotional turmoil.*) I sit in the mirror getting ready for a party and look at this portrait of myself trying to guess what those eyes are thinking. What holiday that face is a mask for.

TOM. I flew to Bergen.

DIANE. A hand appears on my breast.

TOM. I rented a boat.

DIANE. I cannot see beyond the horizon of the frame—

TOM. A hydrofoil.

DIANE. —to see who the hand belongs to.

TOM. I sailed up.

DIANE. The hand on my breast speaks.

TOM. The first time we made love.

DIANE. The face moves into the frame.

TOM. You had just had a child.

DIANE. The face speaks.

TOM. *His* child.

DIANE. Have I gone crazy?

TOM. Your breasts were filled with milk.

DIANE. Tom?

TOM. I pressed you to me.

DIANE. Tom Wintermouth?

TOM. The milk spilled over us. I was in Washington. That's all I could think of. The purity of that first fabulous time. We made love. Your legs. Your ass. I love the way your lips join the line under your nose. (*They embrace.*)

STONY. (*Offstage.*) Diane?

(TOM *and* DIANE *break apart.* STONY *comes into the light from out of the darkness. We see him now as he generally is; a man who appears to have at least five radios going on in his head at once, who valiantly tries to give the impression of control and serenity. His clothes suggest speed, a combination of jogging-racing-cycling-skating. You feel in his happy calm he might just explode.*)

STONY. I did it. On the spur of the moment I just shot the last scene of the film. Was it the light? The look on my father's face? Inspiration.

TOM. You finished the picture? You shot the last scene?

DIANE. They don't shoot films in order.

STONY. Marco Polo has been sidestepping death. Wandering through all these new worlds. He's seen so much. He's witnessed so much. But he has nothing of his own. He wants to change his life. Twenty-four years have gone by. Marco Polo comes home to Venice. To be recognized. And this is the scene. No one in Venice believes his life. His family thinks he's a beggar. He slashes open his ragged cloak and this proof of rubies and diamonds and pearls and emeralds spill out of him. This weary traveler with this waterfall of hidden treasures pouring out of him. Giving his life credence. He stands there emptied. Home. Changed. Ready to begin again. Hello.

DIANE. Brilliant. Absolutely brilliant.

TOM. Marco Polo in Norway?

STONY. It's fantastic for filming. The light's always the same. The control it allows you. The security it gives you. The dependability of the dark. Plus you can save a lot of money. You want the Great Wall of China? Carve it out of ice. Venice in the thirteenth century? We just carve the icebergs into any shape you want. (*To* DIANE.) Oh, I bet you thought I'd forgotten. (*Hands her a script.*) Happy anniversary, darling.

DIANE. (*Looking at the script.*) You've dedicated the film to me?

STONY. History may have supplied the facts, but this woman supplied the spirit. My wife is my life.

(LUSTY MCBRIDE *enters in a rage.* LUSTY *is a great Hollywood star in his sixties. The last time anyone looked like this in a movie— try to find a still of John Wayne in* Barbarian and the Geisha.)

LUSTY. False pretenses!!!! (LUSTY *rages off into the dark. He is gone.*)

STONY. No false pretenses, Dad. (STONY *follows* LUSTY *off.*)
TOM. (*To* DIANE.) Your wrists. Your teeth.

(LUSTY *rages back on, followed by* STONY *and* MRS. MCBRIDE
—*late fifties, she's dressed as a Renaissance Italian princess.*)

LUSTY. I left California for this? The house is damp. I'm
freezing. Standing there in the water up to my ass in Mongolian
hordes. Wearing this costume.
STONY. Tom, Diane, I'll be right with you.
TOM. (*To* DIANE.) Your skull. Your skin.
LUSTY. He says Dad, change your ways of working. Dad,
treat it as a musical experience. Dad, open yourself up. I've
learned one thing in my life, son, it's easier to open yourself
when you're sitting around a pool in Palm Springs.
STONY. Dad, it's 1999. I want to help the audience recuperate
from the entire twentieth century. Marco Polo sailing out for
new worlds. Always enriching. Never destroying. He always
took what he needed and gave what he had.
LUSTY. Spaghetti and gunpowder. I'll give you one hour to
give me heroic stature and three good laughs. Or you'll find me
back at that pool in Palm Springs. Don't think because we
adopted you, don't think I'd hurl you back into the abyss. I
wouldn't do that, boy! You're my son. But there are priorities.
(LUSTY *leaves.*)
MRS. MCBRIDE. Stony, I have a wonderful present for you
that will make you feel so much better.
STONY. Mom . . .
MRS. MCBRIDE. Stony, don't let him make you crazy.
STONY. To be a father figure to my own father.
TOM. (*To* DIANE.) The way your shadow moves after you.
(MRS. MCBRIDE *tries to embrace* STONY.)
STONY. Mom, please. We have guests.
MRS. MCBRIDE. Don't I see—
STONY. Mother, have you met . . . (*Starts to introduce* TOM.)
MRS.. MCBRIDE. No names, please. I know how it is with you
great men. Being married to one myself. I know how you
treasure your anonymity.
TOM. I know who you are.
MRS. MCBRIDE. Who am I? I won't look. Should I guess?
TOM. When I was a kid, I had that picture of you over my
bed, you burning the American flag, singing "The Ending of
the Age of Pisces." I nearly wore that record out. You were the
first naked woman I ever saw.

MRS. MCBRIDE. Well, I hope you've seen more since.

STONY. Mom, go rehearse your scene.

MRS. MCBRIDE. You try to give somebody a present. A pleasure. (*Sings*.) "It's the ending of the Age of Pisces/Some call it Piskus/My blood boils and freezes/At people who say Pieces/It's Pisces! Pisces! Pisces!" (MRS. MCBRIDE *stumbles out*.)

STONY. Mom's been taking tranquilizers.

DIANE. Not nearly enough, I'm afraid.

STONY. It seems you've come in the middle of a little artistic crisis. What were you saying?

TOM. Let me bathe in this atmosphere. The wild Arctic raging right out there. The house so cold and damp. Yet under these heat lamps, it's so serene. How absolutely brilliant to force the Arctic to accommodate you, Diane. Feel this heat. My body feels so alive. You've heard the grape about Skippy Schaeffer.

STONY. I'm afraid we don't get much grape in Norway. Working around the clock—

TOM *whispers in* DIANE'S *ear and begins fondling her blatantly*.)

DIANE. What? Skippy Schaeffer kidnapped from the White House? Frank Schaeffer in outer space?

STONY. What are you saying?

TOM. Excellent authority. Privileged source.

STONY. What about Frank Schaeffer? I am consumed by Frank Schaeffer. I think about him. I dream about him. This hero out there in space. Giving us legends. What are you telling her?

DIANE. Go on. Go on. Don't get him started on Frank Schaeffer. Yes. Go on. What!? Thrown down on a bed in the Lincoln Room??? Frank Schaeffer's wife, Skippy, has been kidnapped and taken to the White House??? They've inserted a metal disc into a transformer that will transform as transformers do transform that semen into nuclear bolts that will travel through space to find their destination, the metal disc with Skippy?

STONY. Let me get this right. Nuclear bolts traveling through space to find a metal disc within Skippy?!

TOM. Yes, from an impeccable source.

DIANE. Well! That's a brilliant public relations job, correct?

TOM. Perfect! Frank Schaeffer will impregnant Skippy through space. The theory that all the knowledge of the world, the truth, all that's best, rises and actually lives in outer space.

DIANE. Not another investigation on Hegel. Why can't they leave poor Hegel alone?

STONY. Hegel?

DIANE. George Wilhelm. The spirit constantly maturing. Constantly evolving. Thesis. Synthesis. Antithesis.

TOM. Of course. Hegel.

DIANE. But not in that order. Hegel puts it so hauntingly. Desire transforms being.

STONY. Man as an individual trapped by his structure.

DIANE. Freydis?

FREYDIS. (*Appears.*) Ya?

DIANE. Is there a diet fudge? A diet soda? Anything so long as it has diet in the title.

FREYDIS. Ya? (*She curtsies and goes.*)

TOM. They won't even bother with an election. The world will drag Frank Schaeffer out of that spacecraft when he returns and crown him king of the world.

DIANE. Brilliant. Absolutely brilliant.

TOM. With what's left of the world. Poor Italy. Shaped like a boot.

STONY. Tom!

TOM. The heel fell off.

DIANE. What are you saying?

STONY. Don't tell her.

TOM. This morning.

DIANE. No!

TOM. Twenty million dead.

STONY. I wasn't going to tell her. An earthquake. Italy's gone.

DIANE. (*Desperate.*) Gian-Carlo? I have to get through to Gian-Carlo?

STONY. You can't get through.

DIANE. Yes, I will. Adriadne? I need to talk to Adriadne. Freydis?

FREYDIS. (*Appearing.*) Ya?

DIANE. Get my address book.

STONY. Calm, calm!

FREYDIS. Add-Dress-Buk?

DIANE. Do you understand me? Call. Quick. Pronto. Dial. Telephone. Somehow get through to Italy.

FREYDIS. Eee-Tall-Lee. (*She curtsies and goes.*)

DIANE. (*Calls after.*) Keep calling every name in the Italian section until you find a friend who answers. A friend who's survived.

STONY. I tried. We won't know who survived for days. (STONY *goes to* DIANE, *trying to comfort her. She backs off.*)

DIANE. Italy gone. *All* of Italy? Not some of Italy?

STONY. Gone.

TOM. I'm sorry. I didn't mean to be the one to tell you.

DIANE. No. I do not want to be touched. I'm just going off from under these heat lamps and lie down in the snow for a bit. (*She goes into the dark and lies in the snow.*)

STONY. (*Calls after her.*) Diane? It will be the same as when Hawaii went. The good thing about earthquakes is it gets rid of the people you wanted to get rid of anyway. It cleans out your address book. Everything will be all right.

TOM. Diane, are you safe out there?

STONY. (*Takes* TOM *by the arm.*) She'll be fine. When I came downstairs before and saw this man talking to my wife, I thought it was a holograph. An astral projection. Tom Wintermouth here? I knew my wife had a chum named Tom but I never knew that her Tom was that Tom. *The* Tom. Why don't *you* run for President, Tom? With Adalbert in Washington and Frank Schaeffer up there in big Frank Schaeffer country, you could just walk in and pick up the marbles. I mean, you'd split the votes in this house. I have to go with Frank. Is that what you're planning?

TOM. No, I'm only the power behind. Adalbert or Schaeffer. It makes no difference to me. I work behind whoever can give me what I want. The power to wage peace. Anonymous. Never up front. Not like you. The artist. Your name plastered everywhere.

(LARRY ROCKWELL, *thirties, comes into the light. Even though his legs have been mangled sometime in the past, he moves with incredible speed thanks to his silver canes. He is in a constant state of rage.* FREYDIS *follows carrying a birthday cake.*)

LARRY. "Happy anniversary to you/Happy anniversary to you/Happy anniversary dear Stony and Diane/Happy anniversary to you."

FREYDIS. "Hippy. Hippy. Anna-vish-new."

LARRY. (*Finishes singing.* FREYDIS *continues.*) Thank you, Freydis.

FREYDIS. Yer velcome. (FREYDIS *curtsies and leaves.*)

LARRY. If the two of you don't recognize the fact, I do. You've been married five years today. Do I have to remember everything? Diane, will you get out of that snowbank. I brought you a present. Not one of the new books. I mean, Caroline

Kennedy's *Memoirs* are a toilet. This is a very old book, long out of print. I went to a great deal of pain and trouble and difficulty in locating it, but it's all for you, Diane and Stony. Diane! (DIANE *comes into the light.* LARRY *blows out the candles.*)

STONY. (*Opens the gift and reads the title.*) "Living Well Is the Best Revenge."

LARRY. By Calvin Tomkins.

DIANE. The one about Gerald and Sara Murphy?

TOM. Gerald Murphy, wasn't he . . .

LARRY. They were only Scott Fitzgerald's models for Dick and Nicole Diver in *Tender Is the Night.* She had an affair with Hemingway . . . he with Cole Porter. Together they dug out the legendary beach at La Garoupe with their own hands and invented the twenties.

STONY. Larry, have you met our friend, Diane's friend really. This is—

LARRY. I am perfectly aware of who this person is. Jung says the only sin is to be unconscious. I have committed no Jungian crimes. I am perfectly aware of *who* this person is. But *why* this person is.

STONY. Tom, have you met our friend Larry Rockwell? He's head of the five thousand Chinese extras.

TOM. What an extraordinary job description.

STONY. Tom's a friend of Diane's too.

LARRY. Don't you think every golden age has an inseparable couple that sums up that age? Gerald and Sara Murphy the twenties. Fred and Ginger the thirties. Jack and Jackie the sixties. John and Yoko the seventies. Bob and Stephanie Shootself the eighties. Stony and Diane the nineties. "Hippie Anna Vish-New." To quote the domestics.

STONY. Think of it, darling. We're the nineties.

DIANE. Well, if we stay together into the next decade, will we be the nothings? the zeros? I don't know, what do they call the first ten years of the new century?

LARRY. I don't want you lending this book. This book is intended only for the two of you to read. In your bed. In your room. The two of you. I mean you're really cleaning up today. A rare book from me. A piano from whoosi—

TOM. This is not just a piano. This is the piano Grieg composed the concerto and "Peer Gynt" on.

STONY. Two pieces she always said made her seasick.

DIANE. That is so hardly the point.

TOM. Thank you, darling.

STONY. Do people confiscate pianos as presents if they don't expect something in return?

TOM. No, they don't. Quid pro quid. (FREYDIS *enters with a tray and a glass of cola.*)

FREYDIS. Diet.

TOM. Du lingner Skippy Schaeffer.

FREYDIS. I want to learn your English.

TOM. Ah, yes. You look very much like Skippy Schaeffer.

FREYDIS. Skee Pee? I not Skee Pee. I Freydis. I clean. I am gut. I am gut.

TOM. Yes, yes, you're very gut. In this strange, artificial light, she almost looks like a version of Skippy Schaeffer. You don't suppose Skippy Schaeffer came up here to change her life.

DIANE. Freydis? Could you bring out some of those diet hors d'oeuvres? Those little Norwegian meatballs you make with the Kleenex and the snow?

FREYDIS. Ya. (FREYDIS *goes out.*)

DIANE. What would I have done if any of you had been in Italy? It would have been so easy for any of you to be in Italy. I don't know what I would have done. I feel so whole now. All the parts of my life together. (DIANE *kisses* LARRY, *then* STONY. *She approaches* TOM, *who shakes her hand tenderly.*)

TOM. All that I told you about Frank Schaeffer. Skippy Schaeffer. All that was classified information.

DIANE. Who are we going to tell? Donder? Blitzen?

LARRY. Diane, don't forget we have theater tickets tonight. We're flying to Oslo to see that production of *A Doll House.* Don't you dare forget. Do you hear me? You do not forget. (LARRY *goes into the dark.*)

DIANE. Anyway, I say good for Frank Schaeffer, in any case. If it takes all that for him to get it up, for him to father a child, then I say Go to it. Poor grotesque sad Frank.

TOM. Not like us.

STONY. Five years ago today, Frank Schaeffer stepped into his spacecraft vowing to bring back to earth that new planet strapped over the fender of his spacecraft like a deer at the height of hunting season. I had become separated from my father in the rush of people there at Cape Kissinger. And there in the cool, in the shade, sitting at a piano, waiting for a concert to begin, sat Diane. We met. We talked. She gave me peace. She gave me comfort. And the sudden harmony of Frank Schaeffer in space, Diane in the cool, Dad looking for me, pulled us together in this chemical equation. The four of us in this perfect emulsion. This divine parallelogram. All the parts of *my* life together. My wife is my life. Tom, why are you here? Are we the new chic? Christ, I am so vain. Thinking you've come to see us. Scandinavia. Sweden. The Nobel Prize. How many Nobels is that you've won now? And the Peace work. I mean, Saudi–Israel. What a brilliant solution to a previously tragic impasse.

TOM. Actually, I've come to see your wife. The first time we made love, she had just had a child. Your child.

DIANE. Could we at least start considering dinner?

TOM. Her breasts were filled with milk. I pressed her to me. The milk ran out of her breasts down my chest down our sides. We drank it.

DIANE. Or is it time for breakfast?

TOM. During certain hearings at the UN last summer . . .

STONY. The Wintermouth hearings! Do you hear that? He calls his own hearings "certain hearings." She always had fabulous friends. All her men friends.

DIANE. (*Calls off.*) Freydis?

TOM. A message was sent to my table. It said: "If you look up, you will see a woman in a flagrant red dress standing by the exit door."

DIANE. Is there any of that reindeer bacon left?

TOM. Was it an assassin? Was it my savior?

DIANE. Let's just call it six P.M. Okay? That's a good sturdy time.

TOM. I stood up. There she was. "Exit" over her head.

DIANE. We'll send for take-out. That's what we'll do.

TOM. I took this woman in her fragrant, flagrant red dress.

STONY. Peking has the best take-out. They can jet it here in two hours. Would you like that?

TOM. I took her from under that exit sign into a cloakroom deep within the United Nations.

DIANE. What do you think about paella? We could call Madrid. Order it al presto.

TOM. Our clothes vanished like anger at the end of a war.

DIANE. Or there's that wonderful trattoria in Rome.

STONY. No, no, no, the mozzarella always came cold.

TOM. Sex is sex only with you.

DIANE. (*In despair.*) I forgot Rome, I forgot Italy. Oh God.

TOM. With anyone else, you say let's make love. Have an affair. Tender raindrop walks on a beach.

DIANE. Twenty million dead?

TOM. With you it's all hot and scorching and fierce and hungry.

STONY. Twenty million dead. At least.

DIANE. I don't see how we can ever eat pasta again.

TOM. —And our mutual orgasms hurl us out of time and space—

DIANE. Hawaii lost into the sea . . . And now Italy . . . Oh God . . .

TOM. —And when we finish and check that we're still alive we crawl up out of the ocean of ourselves gasping for air onto the beach of reality.

DIANE. (*Anguished.*) ROMA! FIRENZE! MILANO! SIENA! The entire RENAISSANCE gone. No!

TOM. Sex with you is lurid and gaudy and hot and brazen . . .

DIANE. Sometimes we just have to say no to Mother Nature.

TOM. My lungs can't get enough air.

DIANE. I will not eat again until Mother Nature straightens herself out.

TOM. Your eyes. Your skull. The roof of your mouth.

DIANE. Dinner. Dinner. We'll eat one last dinner tonight and that's it.

TOM. I won't say your wife brought peace to the world.

DIANE. One feels so powerless in this vast universe.

TOM. But after our fabulous commission of love in the UN dashiki-filled cloakroom, I saw a way out after many years of not seeing a way out.

DIANE. Man stumbling into the new century.

TOM. Without dressing, I drew up a document. I created Saudi–Israel. I took her naked hand.

DIANE. Changing. Yearning.

TOM. I guided it with mine over the newborn treaty. My signature. Our signature. Brought peace, at least to one part of the world.

DIANE. It's our only salvation.

TOM. We dressed and stepped out into a world, that your wife, as simple as this, had made a little bit better. (TOM *takes* DIANE *into his arms and kisses her deeply.*)

STONY. Well, I hope you let her keep the pen. (*Singing.*) "I'd like to see that midnight sun come up . . ." This has got to be our best anniversary yet. We weren't in Italy. We have a visitor. Frank Schaeffer is in that sky. I think we need a little celebration. (*Calls off.*) Freydis? Could you bring some of that veal wine out here?

TOM. Veal wine?

STONY. Do you think I'd crush a grape to make a sip of wine for my own pleasure? But take one live juicy living veal. Ground it into a fluid. Ferment it. Two or three days. Perfect. Grape wine takes years. Why? The grape is fighting off death. The grape wants to live. But animals want to die. If we don't kill them, they think we're bored with them. Not being killed is the same as not being noticed. They die from boredom.

TOM. An interesting theory.

STONY. Theory? You call scientific fact theory? It's mankind's problem in a nutshell. We never go far enough. We have to keep pushing ourselves further and further to recognizing the needs of others. I recognize the needs of the grape. The grape wants to live. The veal wants to die. Why should I stand in the way of the veal? Deny the grape. So locked off from life with your peace work. Don't you know anything? Next life around, I'm coming back as a vegetable researcher. I'm committed to being an artist in this life. But one feels so inadequate when I compare the work I'm doing to the work they're doing on vegetables. Have you ever heard the cries of the asparagus? (STONY *takes out a pocket cassette and presses a button. Agonizing screams are heard.*) Granted, zucchinis are dumb. (*Moans are heard.*) But radishes are brilliant. (*More squeals.*) If we could just break the code . . . All the money wasted trying to break the language of the dolphin. They finally do. What are the dolphins saying to us? These high, reedy, squeaky voices singing: "Sun goes down, tide goes out, darkies gather round and dey all begin to shout." I have no sympathy for mammals. Meat can run away. Meat has wings. Meat has gills. Meat has hooves. Meat can escape. Meat can change. Meat can die. Meat wants to die. But plants have roots. Plants are trapped. Plants are dependent. Plants know about survival. Plants have to stay there. One of the great fallacies of science is aligning man with the mammals. Man is a plant. We may look like meat, but we're not meat. We can never escape. Nor change. We are planted firmly in the ground. We are what we grow out of. My plant nature. I celebrate that. (FREYDIS *enters with wine.*) Ahhhh, veal wine. Thank you, Freydis. You certainly have fabulous friends, darling. Tom Wintermouth himself flying up from Washington? The world of politics! Tom, why *is* New Zealand bombing the hell out of Toronto? Explain New Zealand's anger? I mean, what happened to negotiations?

TOM (*Fierce.*) Let me explain negotiations. I. WANT. YOUR. WIFE.

(STONY *suddenly breaks away from* TOM. *A spotlight comes down on* STONY.)

STONY. Frank. Schaeffer. Has. Found. The. New. Planet. He

flies beyond the third moon of Venus. A green shadow blurs
that part of the galaxy. This planet is on no map. A green
planet so fertile it looks like a ball of manure popped out of a
black hole in space. Frank Schaeffer lands on the new planet.
The earth will never go hungry again. He is elated. Immortality
guaranteed. He toasts the plants that live on this planet with
powdered champagne. One special plant dances by. Frank
Schaeffer is aroused. Frank Schaeffer is lonely. Frank Schaeffer
has been without contact for five years. This plant may not
be human but it beckons to him, waving its leaves. Frank
Schaeffer risks death. He takes off his space suit. He stands
naked. He stands erect. The green plant wraps its tendrils
around him. Frank Schaeffer forces the green plant down.
The green plant tilts Frank over. The plant overpowers Frank.
Pistils. Stamens enter Frank. Green sap spills. Bursts. I've
lost contact. My head is dead. (*The lights come back up.*
DIANE *comforts* STONY.) I can't go into the new century this
frightened.

DIANE. You're not frightened. You're brave.

STONY. Insignificant. No air. No breath. All my life I've lived
in my father's shadow. The great Lusty McBride.

DIANE. You're not the son of Lusty McBride. You're adopted.
You have to say that over and over, and know it.

STONY. I'm adopted. I'm adopted.

DIANE. You have no share in his genes. He didn't pass on any
worn-out genes to you. You are not his son.

STONY. I am not his son.

DIANE. No blood to live up to.

STONY. No past. No heredity.

DIANE. You can invent yourself.

STONY. I can invent myself. I am Frank Schaeffer.

DIANE. No, you are not. Frank Schaeffer is up there in space
finding a new planet that will feed the world. You're here in
Norway making a film about the life of Marco Polo that will—I
don't know what it will do.

TOM. You're in touch with Frank Schaeffer?

DIANE. No, he's not in touch with Frank Schaeffer. Stony
projects his life onto the life of Frank Schaeffer the way you
would project a film onto a screen to give himself size. To give
himself shape.

STONY. I used to get us all mixed up. I got Diane mixed up
with me. I've got that straightened out now. She's Diane. I'm
Stony. That's Frank Schaeffer up there. (*To* TOM.) I'm not too
sure about you.

DIANE. I hate this year. 1999. All those nines. So negative. *Nein. Nein. Nein.*

TOM. Diane. Diane. I went into a record store in Rio and there in a discontinued bin were all the recordings you had made. All your smiling faces beaming up at me with a promise of what your future could be. Before you married this man. Before he got you pregnant. Before he brought you to the Arctic. Before. Before. (TOM *gets album covers from his brief-case.*) Look at yourself. Look at what you could have been. Look at your past! Before you married this man and he scooped your insides out. (TOM *holds several album covers with* DIANE's *face on them.*)

STONY. She doesn't play anymore.

TOM. This is you, Diane.

STONY. She let her fingernails grow.

TOM. This is the best part of you.

DIANE. If I played now, it'd all sound like Carmen. My fingernails castanetting against the keys. Click. Click. Click.

TOM. I've just come from South America.

DIANE. Is there someone else? Who is she? Don't betray me.

TOM. (*Extracts a small piece of paper from a cylinder that is handcuffed to his wrist under his jacket.*) A lone doctor in a jungle outpost hospital in South America has discovered the cure for cancer.

DIANE. My God! Let me see that!

TOM. This lone doctor contacted me. I flew down there with a battery of physicians from Columbia-Presbyterian. They were overwhelmed by the beauty and ease, by the architectonics of the cure. On their way back to New York, the plane crashed. They were all killed. This is the only copy extant of the cure for cancer. I'm on my way to the UN to deliver it. I want you to be at my side when I deliver it. Already hospitals are closing entire wings. Patients who were considering suicide are signing up for dancing lessons. Pain is about to be stopped. The world will be at peace. (*Music begins playing in the distance: shepherd's pipes and drums. The sun is rising. Colors play against the sky.*) Diane! See that! That yellow! That blue! That gold! That red! The winter's over. The summer can begin. And change is coming into our lives as surely as the light gathering strength to appear. Day and night. Light and dark Indian wrestling on the edge of the universe. Diane, are you with me? You have no choice. Hear the bells ringing? Diane, are you with me? The fish have leapt out of the sea. The snakes sprout feathers. The birds test the air. Diane, a fuse lights beneath the present. Now becomes a Hiroshima. Diane, pack your bags! Cancer is cured and we're in love! (*TOM and DIANE embrace. The sound of an air taxi is heard. LARRY enters dressed for evening.*)

LARRY. It's the air taxi, Diane. I called the air taxi.

STONY. What are you talking about? We have work to do on that other island.

LARRY. Diane and I have a date in Oslo.

TOM. Oslo! You're leaving with me!

DIANE. Tom, we have theater tickets.

TOM. Theater tickets?!?!?!

LARRY. Diane, you promised. I'm in pain. I hurt. I have an extra ticket. (*DIANE, TOM, and LARRY go off. We hear the air taxi taking off as LUSTY comes on.*)

LUSTY. Stony! Do I have to wear this goddam hat? Did you get me three laughs? Don't forget I'm photographed from the left side only.

STONY. I've got it all right here, Dad. We've got the light. We're going to be all right. It's day. It's finally day! (*STONY and LUSTY go off. FREYDIS comes on to clean. MRS. MCBRIDE comes on.*)

MRS. MCBRIDE. Stony? Does any women go off to see forty-one different productions of *A Doll's House* if she's not trying to tell her husband something? Stony?

(*MRS. MCBRIDE goes off. The air taxi is gone. Silence. Then a beeping noise begins. FREYDIS looks up from her scrubbing to locate this mysterious piercing noise. She stands up. She realizes that the beeps seem to be coming from her. She hears a great Whoooosh from above. A man in a silver space suit descends to earth. He takes off his helmet. He is FRANK SCHAEFFER, in his thirties.*)

FRANK. Hello, Skippy. Guess who's back?

FREYDIS. (*Drops her accent.*) What are these beeps? What have you done?

FRANK. I have come the distance of forty moons to tell you the good news. We're going to have a baby.

FREYDIS. What are these beeps?

FRANK. Come back to Washington and we'll talk.

FREYDIS. No babies. No Washington. I have a life here. I'm very happy.

FRANK. This is no job. Honey, you've been elected the Fourth Most Admired Woman in the World, thanks to me. Looking up in the heavens waiting for me these past five years.

FREYDIS. I have a stiff neck and a broken heart and I want to be left alone. Don't even talk to me. Two months ago I went into the White House to accept that award and instead was dragged into a dark passage, thrown down on a bed in the Lincoln Room . . .

FRANK. How do you think this job makes me look?

FREYDIS. Rude hands spread my legs and inserted into me, Skippy Schaeffer, a disc. A metal disc that is burning in me right this moment.

FRANK. If you'd stop being hysterical and let me explain—

FREYDIS. I was held prisoner in the White House. I'm not talking about Tijuana, Mexico. I'm talking about the White House.

FRANK. Our new address if you don't go humiliating me.

FREYDIS. A marine guard played the cello while they tied me down on Lincoln's bed.

FRANK. So you wouldn't be frightened when the bolts came.

FREYDIS. I waited till she dozed.

FRANK. The cello was to wile away the terror.

FREYDIS. I picked up that bow and plunged it through her heart. I ran out of the White House. I got to a heliport where I commandeered a helicopter. Get me out of light. Get me to darkness. This burning within me. My helicopter exploded. I Icarus through the sky. Land in the North Sea. Eliza across ice floes. Dolphins take me on their backs to Oslo. I go to the Oslo Employment Agency. I want to be pure. I want to be clean. They say Ahhh, you want to *clean*. They give me job. I sail forty miles out to sea. To this iceberg. (*She resumes her Norwegian accent.*) I Fredyis. I cook. I clean.

FRANK. The child was supposed to be born in the White House. You're so goddam selfish. I'd splash down New Year's Eve as 1999 becomes 2000. You'd present me with the perfect child. Give the world a new legend.

FREYDIS. (*Begins scrubbing the ice with a vengeance. The beeps grow louder.* FREYDIS *is terrified.*) I have burned my house. I am cleaning the world. I am trying to be a Saint, in the church of life. I am trying to purify myself.

FRANK. (*Unzips his space suit and steps out of it, now in his NASA long johns.*) Okay, Skippy. Deny the world dreams. Deny the world legends. I'm sorry, but my kid is going to be born in the White House or not at all. Skippy, put on the suit. It's the only thing that can block those bolts that are coming down on you.

FREYDIS. I not Skippy. I Freydis. You leave me alone. The woman you married no longer exists. I have changed myself. I am a brand-new person. Oh God, re-invent fire and burn Frank Schaeffer in his spacecraft. I am no longer married to you. I have changed myself. I am happy! So happy!

FRANK. Honey, I found the new planet and I took the liberty of naming it after you. There's Saturn, Uranus, Pluto, Neptune, Earth, Venus, Mars, Jupiter, Mercury, and now Skippy!

(MRS. MCBRIDE, LUSTY, *and* STONY *come on.* MRS. MCBRIDE *is soaking wet and wrapped in a polar bear blanket.* FRANK *hears them coming and hides behind an iceberg in the darkness.*)

LUSTY. Give my boy a break. It worked once for Walter Huston being directed by his son John in *Treasure of the Sierra Madre.* But they were real father and son. That must be the ticket.

STONY. Dad, *Treasure of the Sierra Madre* was an adaptation. *Marco Polo* is an original.

LUSTY. Well, I'm going to be an original postage stamp. The United States Post Office has picked me to be a commemorative stamp for the end of the twentieth century. I got the six-cent slot. Beat out Paul Newman. Beat out Gary Cooper. How come the United States government can see the ache in my eyes that the prairie is dead and my son can't.

STONY. You'll love being a postage stamp. You've always wanted people licking your backside.

LUSTY. Did I hear right?

STONY. I'm sorry. It just popped out!

LUSTY. You be careful the way you address an actual commemorative stamp.

MRS. MCBRIDE. Stony? Did you like the way I played my scene? That was my idea to jump into the Arctic with my clothes on. I jumped into the Arctic all for the sake of art and my son's film.

LUSTY. You're disgusting. You never were any good with your clothes on anyway. Here! (*Hands her papers.*)

MRS. MCBRIDE. What are these?

LUSTY. Divorce papers. I want my girlfriend Bonnie by my side. I need my Bonnie. You get me Bonnie. (LUSTY *goes off.*)

MRS. MCBRIDE. Why didn't Dad talk to me? Tell me he was unhappy with me? You're not unhappy with me?

STONY. Mom, you have a little problem that makes it difficult sometimes to talk to you.

MRS. MCBRIDE. You call a little grass, you call a few vitamins, a problem?

STONY. Let's not have any pretenses. They're not vitamins. Just leave me alone. I look at you and I don't know who I am.

MRS MCBRIDE. But Stony, you're the most wonderful extraordinary person in the whole wide world.

STONY. Sure, Mom. The best. Mom, I'm nothing.

MRS. MCBRIDE. I have a little anniversary present for you, my darling. Along with the pianos and the books, I have a wonderful anniversary present for you. (*She hands* STONY *a paper.*) You're hardly nothing.

STONY. It's a birth certificate.

MRS. MCBRIDE. Of course it's a birth certificate.

STONY. But it says here Stony McBride, born January 1, 1965, New York Hospital. It says here Mother: Debbie-Lisa Dempsey. That's you. It says here Father: Philip McBride. That's Dad. This is not my birth certificate. On the birth certificate I used all my life, it said Parents Unknown.

MRS. MCBRIDE. That was a forgery.

STONY. Then this is real? You're my real parents?

MRS. MCBRIDE. Are you embarrassed?

STONY. Why did you tell me I was adopted?

MRS. MCBRIDE. Your father's name was Elliott.

STONY. Wait a minute. My father's name was Philip. Changed to Lusty.

MRS. MCBRIDE. As I was saying, your dad, your pop, your father's name was Elliot. And Elliot fell in love with a man named Philip McBride, whose stage name was Lusty, and Lusty was the word for Elliot's feelings, for the feelings that lived in his heart. He followed Lusty across country. He followed him every minute. He captured his garbage that Lusty would throw away and the edges of the half-eaten lamb chops, pork chops that Lusty would eat for breakfast. And all the time, Elliot was blocked from Lusty by the rows, lines, hordes, of girls that continually surround the great, the growing greater, the soon-to-be-a-star, soon-to-be-a-legend, the great Lusty McBride. And Elliot would hear the groupies talking, how great Lusty was, how each of them balled him, how beautiful Lusty's body was inside them. Elliot looked at his body in the mirror and was consumed with hatred for the appendages that dangled off it and blocked him by a simple biological, physiological fact from knowing the warmth of Lusty McBride. So Elliot, being the ultimate fan, the ultimate worshiper, removed himself from the sight of Lusty and went on a little trip to Johns Hopkins Hospital in Baltimore, Maryland, and stayed there a year, like a virgin preparing for her marriage, a nun in a convent of silence preparing for Jesus to come to her. And Elliot left Maryland for New York where Lusty was starting auditions for his new musical, "Skin," and the new Elliot auditioned and Lusty McBride in the dark audience out there said, "Nudity is required for this role." Ahh, yes. "Would you take off your clothes so we may see your body, ahh yes." Drums fanfared in Elliot's head. Elliot removed his clothes and like Venus on the half shell wept as Botticelli must have the first time he realized what his painting "The Birth of Venus" was turning into. Elliot stood naked and everyone came near respectfully, hushed, a sound I've only heard at the feet of the Winged Victory in the Louvre Museum since. They came to me. Touched me with their eyes. Asked me my name. I said, "I am Debbie Lisa." They said the part was mine but Lusty's eyes said I want you. As they say, the rest was show biz history. On opening night in front of fifteen hundred people we made love and sang "It's the Ending of the Age of Pisces" and had simultaneous orgasms and the critics ran out of their seats and the reviews were all on the front page. We married at the opening night party. We flew to Woodstock where we would have a cottage. I changed into a nightgown. Lusty's naked body came through the door. He throws me violently on the bed. Ahh, life. Ahh, love. Those were my words. I opened my eyes. Lusty held out the telephone. He threw the phone on the bed. "Dial him," he commanded. "Dial who," I said. "Dial your brother." I said, "I don't have a brother." He said, "Don't give me that. Why do you think I hired you? Why do you think I married you? You are the spitting image of your brother. The only man I ever loved that I could never have. Your brother followed me for two years, always on the outskirts of the crowds of worshipers. I would play for him. I would leave half-eaten chops in the trash and watch behind curtains as he would go through my trash and munch on them and I could feel my lips receive his bites and munches through the glass. He never spoke to me. I tried to catch his eye. Nothing. I've been able to ball everyone I wanted in my life. Except him. He knew the groupie girls. I'd ball them so they might tell him that I was available. That I wanted him. That part of me that wanted him would stick onto those young groupies' voices and he would hear me through them like some celestial ventriloquist act. Then he vanished for a year. I went crazy. Where was he? I couldn't play Madison Square Garden. I could play nowhere. Where was his face? I learned his name. I sent detectives. Find me Elliot. No Elliot. Vanished. I would perform no more. I would become an actor and lose my identity. I invented the role of Ulysses. Searching. Searching. Then you appeared. Elliot's face. But the body of the enemy. I checked into you. You and Elliot had the same last name. You and Elliot lived at the same address. You and Elliot had the same birthday. Elliot's twin sister. I loved you. You and Elliot have been conceived at the same moment. Floated in the same womb. The same face. Even though I hate women, you were different. You were a link. Call him. Call your brother. Bring Elliot over here." Well, I didn't want to tell him I was the brother, I mean it was his wedding night too. So I dialed a number and then said, "Hi, Elliot!" All the while the weather report is going in my ear. Sunny in the afternoon. Winds at twelve degrees from the North. Barometer's falling. "Hi, Elliot, it's your sister, Debbie. Debbie Lisa. Can you come over? You'll never guess who I married. Lusty McBride. Come on over and help us celebrate." So here I am. Spending my wedding night with the man I love. Locked in passion? Oh no. Talking to my former self. Lusty's eyes were filled with tears. "What is he saying? What is Elliot saying?" I can't tell him Elliot is saying ten percent chance of showers in the afternoon. I said, "Lusty, Elliot doesn't want to come." Lusty says, "Let me talk to him. I love him. I love him. I'll give him money. I'll kill myself. I'll kill you." I held the phone away from my ear. I said, "Elliot has hung up." Lusty wept in floods in spite of the ten percent chance of showers. I comforted Lusty. Held him. Touched him. I was finally where I wanted to be. "Elliot will come for Christmas." Lusty looked up like a baby. "You promise?" I kissed him all over. "Mommy promises." That was our married life. Elliot held us together. And Lusty would say, "When is Elliot coming?" And I'd be in the tub washing the body I had built for Lusty and I'd say "Godot will show up before Elliot." And Lusty would say, "What did you say?" I'd call out, "I talked to Elliot today." Lusty opened the bathroom door. "He said he didn't want to see you, Lusty. He didn't even watch your TV show. He threw his TV out the window so he wouldn't have to watch you." And Lusty wept these great Garden of Gethsemane tears and would run out of the house, our mansion, our estate, and I would leap out of the tub, let the wind dry me off, hide in the back seat of his Maserati while he drove to the more unsavory sections of whatever city we were in, and the car would stop, but the motor kept running and Lusty would mention money and a young man would get in the front seat and they would drive off to Mulholland Drive or some enchanted vista and I would lay there in the back seat in a puddle of bath water, listening to my husband and a stranger make love and my husband cry out the name Elliot. "Elliot." I grew to love Elliot so much that I became insanely jealous of him, passionate about him, thought every moment of Elliot. I traveled back to Baltimore, Maryland. I went to Johns Hopkins. Before my change, I had made a deposit in the sperm bank. The doctors were only too happy to transplant the first womb into my body. They inserted my deposit. Elliot entered me on the operating table. I became pregnant. You were born. Named Stony after Dr. Stevens and Dr. Antonacci who had created my life. They found the truth of me. I wanted you to have that truth. Your real name is Stoneyacci. You were a love child, Stony, with all the love in the world because I loved myself when you were born. And you're famous. I gave you that much. You're in all the medical books. I tried to shield you from the truth. I didn't do wrong. You're making a wonderful movie. You've got a wonderful wife. Have good friends. Given me grandchildren. And you're all me. Everything about you is me. I filled your head with great men because you are like the first person born out of twenty-first century technology. I filled your head with heroes because I think I was a hero. Or a heroine. And if you ever read in any of those books written about the sixties that someone else claims to be the First Flower Child, you tell me and I'll sue because your Mom, right here, little Debbie-Lisa, right here, can produce interviews on old yellow pieces of paper that prove she was the first flower child of the whole wonderful sixties.

STONY. (*Looks at her and begins screaming. He runs in an ever-widening circle until he's lost in the dark. He screams and screams. He returns and sits by her side. He is very still. A spotlight appears on* STONY.) Constellations of stars have fallen out of another galaxy. They hurtle towards earth. Frank Schaeffer steers his spacecraft into the eye of the lost constellation. He destroys it. Star shards sprinkle down on us. Order is restored. Frank Schaeffer is victorious again. (*The lights return to their normal state.*) I am not you. My parents were teen sweethearts in Idaho. Iowa. Wisconsin. No, no, no, no, I am not you. I am so happy. I am Frank Schaeffer. I am in space. I am anybody in the world but you.

MRS. MCBRIDE. Don't try to escape emotional family traditions. This is a beginning. My friend. My son. My self. Man to man. I'll pass on the only bit of wisdom I ever picked up in my entire life. We were born for chaos. That's our natural state. Chaos comes natural. Give in to it. Serenity you got to bust your ass for. Go through hell for. I look back on those days of my torment and yearning and anguish and I say That was the happy time. That was life.

STONY. I am anybody in the world but you.

(*His scream is drowned out by the sound of the air taxi descending. Enter* LARRY. TOM, *and* DIANE.)

LARRY. Ibsen knew everything. Even though you know the plot of this play, you lean forward, Ibsen makes you lean forward. Perhaps tonight will be different. Tonight the play that insures Ibsen's place in world drama will change and Nora might not leave.

TOM. Yes, for a play that was written a hundred years ago . . .

LARRY. 1879. 1879. *A Doll House* was written one hundred twenty years ago. Didn't you read your playbill?

TOM. Freydis? (*Calls off.*) Would you begin packing Mrs. McBride's clothes? She'll need the barest minimum down there at the Equator. Freydis? Where is she?

LARRY. And it's not *A Doll's House*. The accurate translation is *A Doll House*. Not the house of the doll, but the house itself.

DIANE. Stony, I brought you a little present. God, the production was incredible. They sold video cassettes of the production in the lobby right next to the orange drink. I brought it home to show you. Larry, flash it against that iceberg over there, please.

(LARRY *takes a video projector from under the dining table and inserts the cassette into it.*)

TOM. I think Ibsen would be very happy to know his play had caused a woman to walk out on her life.

DIANE. Her alleged life.

TOM. And in leaving that life, find a better life. A truer life.

DIANE. The actors played *Doll House* entirely on trampolines. Nora doesn't just walk out the door, she leaps this incredible bounce into freedom. Into infinity. Stony, it was done by Ingmar Bergman's son and I thought of all these great men surpassing their fathers.

TOM. I'll set up the video, Diane.

LARRY. *I've* set up the video, Diane.

(LARRY *projects the image against an iceberg. A video shows a man and woman in dour nineteenth-century dress bouncing up and down wildly on trampolines, flipping over as they recite Ibsen's closing lines:*

HELMER.   Men jeg vil tro pa det
           Nevn det! Forvandee oss salede at—?
           (HELMER *does a back flip.*)
NORA.   If Samliv mellow oss to Kunne
           Ble et ektestap. Farvel.
           (*She flips and tumbles out of sight.*)
HELMER.   Nora! Nora! Tomt. Hun en her
           ikke mer. Det vid underligste.
           (*He laughs and bounces high. A door slams.
           Freeze frame on his bouncing.*)

STONY. Isn't it incredible. Here it is 1999 and people still miss the point of that play.

TOM. And what is the point of the play?

STONY. Nora never left.

TOM. Pardon me while I laugh, but the entire point of the play is . . .

STONY. Nora never left. Ibsen's entire point is Nora's husband knew she was leaving and, quick as a shooting star, he constructed a new living room that enclosed the outside of the front door. So when Nora left, she found herself not in the outside world, but in another, a newer, a stranger room. And since there was no door in that room, she drew a window and quickly climbed out of it. But her brilliant, heroic husband built a new room off that window. And she beat down the walls of that new room and the walls crumbled and her hands bled and the dust cleared and she found herself in a newer room still damp from construction. And she crawled through the ceiling, gnawing, and her husband dropped a new room on top of that escape hatch. So the wife invented fire and burned down all the rooms and her skin blistered but she smiled, for she knew she would soon be free. And the smoke cleared and an enormous igloo domed the sky and she ripped out her heart and intestines and forged them into an ice pick and chopped her way out through the sky and she opened the ice door that would lead her into the nebula, the Milky Way, heaven, freedom, but no, she chopped back the door to heaven and was warmed by the glow of a cozy room, her Christmas card list, a lifetime subscription to a glossy magazine called *Me*, her children, her closet crammed with clothes, her possessions, her life sat waiting for her in a rocking chair.

MRS. MCBRIDE. Stony, can't you see anything? Your wife is pulling the big ankle like little Nora in the *Valley of the Dolls* playing against that iceberg over there. Your little wife is leaving you.

STONY. She's right here, Mom.

DIANE. Debbie-Lisa, could you please not butt in—

MRS. MCBRIDE. My life is here screaming in front of you. Can't you hear me? Can't you acknowledge what I've just told you? (MRS. MCBRIDE *goes off.*)

DIANE. Listen to that bell on the mainland. It rings all night. I hate that damn church bell ringing all night.

STONY. Why didn't you say so, Diane? I have a horde of five thousand Mongolians at my command. You just have to tell me what you want. You want that bell stopped? I'll stop it. I take my directions from you. You are my life. My wife is my life. (STONY *runs off.* TOM *rewinds the video and plays it again.*)

TOM. Watch Nora bounce. Watch Nora leap.

DIANE. Oh, God, to be that free.

TOM. (*Snaps the video off.*) But you've been that free. That's what keeps us in common. You're no stranger either to the icy blasts of greatness. Tchaikovsky competition. Gold Medal. Moscow 1992. Monte Carlo Music Festival 1993. Juilliard Great Alumnae Performers, 1994. Carnegie Hall, 1993. Requiem for poor dead King Charles, Westminster Abbey, 1994. I bought the records. I play them. You know what's amazing?

DIANE. Everything.

TOM. Your unerring sense of the inner . . .

DIANE. . . . structure.

TOM. Structure. Exactly.

DIANE. You're not the first to say that.

TOM. Your way of leaning on the inner structure so as to reveal the composer's secret intention.

DIANE. It's all in the structure.

TOM. (*Spreads the tapes and record jackets in front of her.*) This is you, Diane. This is the best part of you. This is the you I want to give back to you. Diane de la Nova. Metropolitan Opera House: Great Solo Performers Series, 1994. Your last concert. Your last program. Bach. Beethoven. Schoenberg. Schubert. Schumann. Satie. Ravel. What a program. (TOM *picks a tape at random and inserts it into a cassette that he carries in his pocket. Piano music flows out, Satie's "Gymnopedie."*)

DIANE. I recorded this three times. Once when I was twenty-eight. Then again when I was eighteen. Then again when I was eight.

TOM. Which is this?

DIANE. (*Listens.*) Eight.

TOM. Eight! Eight years old! Do you realize how small an eight year old's hands are?

DIANE. I really started cookin' when I was eight. I sat down at the piano as I had every day since I could walk, threw back the lid of the Knabe-Bechstein-Steinway and there on the keys was Mozart. I was never lonely playing the piano. Brahms was always there. Bach. Chopin. And here was Mozart. Hi, Mozart! Only this time he had a raincoat on. A little raincoat. Now I had been told to beware of men in raincoats, but after all, it was Mozart. Mozart's no degenerate. Mozart's no creep. You can trust Mozart. The cool water of Mozart. He says, "Hello, little girl. You gonna bring me back to La Vie?" I said, "Golly, I'll try." And I began playing that Kochel listing I had been practicing for a year with that magical imitative brilliance that children can have. The technical mastery and total non-comprehension that children can have. I lifted my hands, dug them into the eighty-eights and Mozart says: "Yeah. Give it to me." I looked down. Mozart. The raincoat. Opened. The keys became erect. Black. White. I became terrified. Mozart! This isn't a school yard. This is a hall named after Mr. Andrew Carnegie and I'm only eight years old and what the hell are you doing??? "More. More. More," says Mozart and he throws back his head. "Dig those digits into these eighty-eights. Bring me back to life. Bring me back to life." Mother??? Dad?? They're in the wings blowing kisses at me. Holding up signs. "You've never played better." Mozart moans. It's a short piece. It ends. Mozart spurts all over me. I'm wet. Mozart wet. Frightened. The audience roars. This child prodigy. Can't they see what's happened? I look down and hear a chorus of "yeahs" coming from all those little dead men in raincoats. There's a scuffle and Brahms leaps on the keys. "Me next! Me next! Bring me back to life." My fingers dig into Brahms. Well, I started to like it. Mozart lives. Brahms lives. For the next twenty years that was my life. Diane de la Nova and her circus of Music. Diane de la Nova and her Massage Parlor of Melody.

TOM. You were brilliant.

DIANE. It's so easy to get brilliant reviews. You simply sit at the piano every day for twenty years with the moss growing up your legs, sparrows nesting in your hair, bringing dead men in raincoats back to life.

TOM. (*Reads a jacket.*) "Diane de la Nova has reached a pinnacle of perfection."

DIANE. That was the day I called Uncle. Closed the lid on all those dead men who had shot their wad all over me for twenty years. Used me. I dried myself off . . . Went to a tattooist. Had a life line inserted on my palm. Said: "Where does life begin?" Stony come into view. The day of my last concert. The day Frank Schaeffer shot into space. I closed one door. Opened another. Now I close that door and open yet another.

TOM. Nora slammed the door behind her and Modern Drama was born.

LARRY. Don't you love people who manage to squeeze, to actually use, the phrase "the birth of Modern Drama" in everyday conversation?

TOM. Where did you say you met this man?

LARRY. She ran over me in a car crash, Wintermouth, and you know what? It's still the luckiest thing that ever happened to me.

DIANE. Let's not play this record over again please.

(LARRY *turns on the video for its last moments.*)

TOM. That's the end of the film. Nora leaves.

DIANE. Run it again.

LARRY. (*Stands in front of the projector blocking the image.*) But this is a warning. If she does leave him, you cannot lock me out.

DIANE. Nor will we. No one's locking you out. Move out of the way—

TOM. Exactly. Open door policy. Christ, a key. You can have a key. Dinner anytime you want. Dinner or lunch or breakfast. A plate. A permanent plate nailed on the table.

LARRY. I'm not sucking around for dinner invites. I have credit cards. I have dozens of credit cards. I have a very high credit rating. I have all the major credit cards. I can eat at any restaurant in the world and take anyone I want with me. I am included in the structure of their lives. Her life. She can leave him. I don't mind. She can go anywhere she wants, but she can't lock me out of the structure of her life. When her kid was born, I went to the hospital secretly and picked up the still damp child, still damp from birth, and screamed at the child: "Don't think you can lock me out!!!" I come in the package. I am in the bloodstream. I am in the bones. I am in the marrow.

DIANE. Freydis? Would you bring down Mr. Rockwell's suitcase? Larry, you've carried your new legs with you long enough. You must be used to them now. Get those useless pins sawed off. The new legs . . . the doctors just screw them on.

(FREYDIS *comes on dragging* LARRY'S *suitcase. She tries to pay no attention to the beeps.*)

FREYDIS. Ting a ling a.

LARRY. I am not a prejudiced person but I think I hate the Norewegian language more than . . .

FREYDIS. Ting a ling a.

LARRY. Hoona Hoona Hoona.

FREYDIS. Ting a ling a Him. (*Points to* TOM. *She goes off.*)

LARRY. I think there's a phone call for you, Tom. That's all it sounds like to me. Hoona, Hoona, Hoona.

TOM. No one knows I'm here. (TOM *leaves.*)

LARRY. Is that all you want from me, Diane? Why didn't you say that's all you wanted? (*Opens the suitcase to reveal a pair of new plastic pink legs.*)

DIANE. Put those away! I want to see them under your trousers, not in a box.

LARRY. Between the plastic legs and the new medical shoes, I'll be much taller.

DIANE. Larry, I am not going in the house until you apologize to me for this unapologizable outburst. Put those legs away! I thought you were—

LARRY. Were? Were?

DIANE. Are my friend, my ally.

LARRY. You I thought told me I had to be more curious about life. You ran over me and pulled me out of that wreckage. You gave me mouth to mouth. You gave me ear to ear. Hummed me love themes from operas. Told me what it was like for a man and a woman to be in love. What they did. The secrets that happened between men and women. And then the ambulance came and you got in with me. I could be the world's richest cripple from the way you ran over me, but instead I kiss these limbs because you brought me home with you. You told me I could have life any way I wanted. You told me . . . you told me. . . . (*He cries.*)

DIANE. Now, Larry.

LARRY. Yes?

DIANE. Could you have electricity put in the legs so you could receive phone calls and I could always call you?

LARRY. I could have hot plates on the knee caps. Whip up a soufflé. Plug in for a cup of coffee. Hot and cold running water.

DIANE. A little drawer here for your valuables.

LARRY. So there won't be any unsightly bulge in my trousers.

DIANE. So you can stand up straight and tall and be presentable and attractive and meet people and lead your own life?

LARRY. I'm doing a good job on the movie.

DIANE. Larry, training five thousand Chinese not to look in the camera as they run by screaming is not a life's work.

LARRY. When you two leave, I'll leave with you. You can drop me off at Helsinki. That's where they do the operation. That's the least you can do.

DIANE. The least. Hurry.

LARRY. Is this all you wanted from me? Why didn't you say? Freydis? Freydis? Help me with this. (LARRY *goes off with his suitcase.* TOM *comes out of the house, highly upset.*)

TOM. Mxmmmmamfmatmaffsssfmmm.

DIANE. Tom? What happened?

TOM. Adalbert. Stroke.

(FREYDIS *runs past. Her beeps louder, more insistent.*)

DIANE. Freydis, please. Tom, look at me. Stop shaking.

(LARRY *rushes on with a radio. He listens to it.*)

LARRY. Listen, everybody! President Adalbert has had a stroke. The Vice President has committed suicide. The government is in chaos. Military rule in Washington.

TOM. They want me to go back. President.

DIANE. President!

TOM. This cure for cancer makes me a very powerful man.

LARRY. (*Quoting radio.*) "Thomas Wintermouth is mentioned to be interim President. Plans made to find Frank Schaeffer in space and bring him back from wherever he is in space."

TOM. I'm afraid! I said it. Oh God.

DIANE. This is not the Thomas Wintermouth I know. Larry would you go in the house and find Tom? This isn't Tom. This must be an astral projection.

(LARRY *goes back into the house.*)

TOM. I . . . afraid . . . I say I don't know . . .

DIANE. It's your time in history, Tom. It's our time.

TOM. What an incredible turn of events. Did you think this morning when you woke up you'd be the wife of the President of the United States? Before night fell?

DIANE. I take strength from the words Bob Dylan wrote so many years ago: "Take what you have gathered from coincidence."

TOM. And I strength from you.

DIANE. Call Washington.

TOM. Washington.

DIANE. Tell them you accept.

TOM. I don't have to call. I left them on hold.

DIANE. I love you.

TOM. And I you. Oh, I you.

DIANE. I want you.

TOM. And I you.

DIANE. Strong.

TOM. Your mouth.

DIANE. Powerful.

TOM. Your breasts.

DIANE. Loving.

TOM. Your eyes.

DIANE. Tasteful.

TOM. Let me kiss your breast. Just for a moment. (TOM *buries his head in* DIANE's *breast*. STONY *comes on carrying a large bell.*)

STONY. I took the motorboat over to the mainland. I found the bell. I bought it.

DIANE. I don't care. It's too late.

STONY. Too late?

DIANE. Too late too late too late.

TOM. Too late?

DIANE. Not you. Strong. Powerful. Loving. The best.

TOM. Just for a moment there I had a lapse. Never again. I apologize. I don't know what came over me. President. Lean on me. Depend on me. (TOM *goes into the house.*)

STONY So.

DIANE. So.

STONY. I have my film.

DIANE. I have my life.

STONY. My life is starting.

DIANE. Ditto.

STONY. My father and I finish this picture. My life begins.

DIANE. Ditto the dittoes.

STONY. Frank Schaeffer's in that sky. Soon you'll be in that sky. The sky's the place to be.

DIANE. Tom has a friend who's lending us his ranch in South America. He raises leopards. Lobotomizes them. Takes out their vocal cords. Grafts on the vocal cords of humming-birds. Amputates their tails. Grafts on coral snakes. Quite striking.

STONY. Why?

DIANE. When evolution takes a turn, beauty must be included.

STONY. I'm not asking why some South American asshole is grafting snakes onto leopards. I'm asking the larger Why. The cosmic Why. The reason why Why was invented. Why didn't you leave me before. Why when I was a wreck. Why when I was falling apart. That kind of Why.

DIANE. I don't leave wreckage behind. I don't desert sinking ships. When five thousand extras arrived last week to be citizens of Venice and Mongolian hordes, you had them line up on the decks of this flotilla of Venetian gondolas carved out of ice. High noon. Pitch black. You sailed between them, a spotlight on your face. The only lighted thing around. You introduced yourself. Welcomed them. Told them how much this film meant to you. Five years of work beginning to culminate. Your father playing the lead. How much that meant to you. And I looked at you and said Yes. Here is a man I can leave. You see, I only leave the best for the best. Tom is the best. Now you're the best. I can leave.

STONY. Did you tell him you were pregnant?

DIANE. I shall.

STONY. Is it mine?

DIANE. Of course it's mine. It's yours. None of your business. It's mine. It's yours. Yes.

STONY. Why did you get pregnant if you were leaving me?

DIANE. I wasn't leaving. I hadn't heard from Tom. I thought he'd forgotten me. You're up here filming over on that other iceberg all the time. No sunshine. I don't even cast a shadow. Who needs me? I wanted something in me so I wouldn't float away.

STONY. I'm glad I could be of service. The worst of a kid. Joined at the hip whether you like it or not. Never really separate.

DIANE. I really hate the weight of this child already beginning to claw its way out of me . . .

STONY. The child will be born. You'll have to tell me. I'll have to see it. Visitation rights.

DIANE. Second month. Fingernails starting. Like I'm trying to claw my way out of you.

STONY. Custody battles. Sicknesses. Christmases. Graduations. Weddings.

DIANE. Let its eyes develop so it can see you for the fool you are. Let its sex develop into a man so you can see the man you should be. Let its ears develop so it can hear the shit I have to contend with. Let his feet form so he can run away from you. Let his spine develop so he can stand up straight. He'll be born in the year 2000. He's due to be born in the last week of December 1999, but I'm holding him in. I don't want this kid born in any century that contained you.

STONY. What am I supposed to do? Nail your shoes to the floor? Tie your hair to the trees? Drop you in a block of ice and freeze you here?

DIANE. I want more.

STONY. I want more.

DIANE. You have your film. Your film will be great.

STONY. I've already started on my next project.

DIANE. That's wonderful. What's it about?

STONY. You.

DIANE. Really? What is it called?

STONY. Whore. Slut. Pig. Death. Die. Go.

DIANE. I must look for it. (DIANE starts to leave.)

STONY. Diane? Don't leave me. (STONY *runs after* DIANE *as* LUSTY *comes on with his luggage.*)

LUSTY. Son, Bonnie's waiting for me. I'm going to go see her.

STONY. What are you talking about? We still have to film the key scene. Diane, wait— (*She's gone.*)

LUSTY. You've got enough footage. End the picture now.

STONY. Marco Polo has to sail out for new worlds. Diane!

LUSTY. What new world? Looks like the same old world to me. Mother shooting up. You ranting and raving.

STONY. Dad, I have a new project. There's a lot of money in it—for you. (*Pause.*)

LUSTY. What kind of project?

STONY. (*Improvising wildly.*) I've—I've—I've negotiated for the rights to the new Marcel Proust western. *Kill My Palomino.*

LUSTY. Marcel Proust western? Are we talking about the same Marcel Proust?

STONY. People think he spent all his time in his room writing *Remembrance of Things Past.* He wrote that on a bet to show anything could sell. What he thought he'd be remembered for were these four hundred really first-rate Western novels he wrote under his real name: Pancho Diehard. You know all that faggola stuff??? Asthmatic? That was all publicity. He was Jewish. That much is true.

(MRS. MCBRIDE *wanders on.*)

MRS. MCBRIDE. Stony? Lusty? Did you see my little yellow case? It has some needles, in it, some white powder, a rubber hose and a spoon. Have you seen it? I need my little yellow case. (MRS. MCBRIDE *wanders off.*)

LUSTY. I want Bonnie. I want all this insanity out of my life.

STONY. (*Tries to block* LUSTY's *way.*) Dad, I'm remembering a time. I've never told you this. You took me for a walk. And then there was the time. Well, I don't have to tell you. And then I'm remembering the time. The emotional shorthand. An eyebrow tilt. A shoulder shrug. More weight that the entire works of Balzac. And what about the time! And don't forget the time! Are you remembering the same time too? This is ESP. Wasn't that a time!

LUSTY. Let me go!!!!! (LUSTY *throws* STONY *aside into a snowbank and is gone.* DIANE *comes on with her suitcase. We hear the sound of very loud beeps.* FREYDIS *crawls on in pain.*)

DIANE. Freydis, where are my traveling shoes? I can't travel in these shoes. I can't travel in this dress.

FREYDIS. Madam, I am in pain.

DIANE. What? Shall we put handkerchiefs over everyone's pain and clap for our favorite? I am on my way to the White House. I'm going to send for you and the baby in about a month. You like that? Big trip across ocean? I'd like the baby to lose about five pounds. Never too early to start slimming. Willpower. Freydis? You hear me? Willpower. Those beeps? What are those beeps? (DIANE *goes off into the house.* STONY *crawls out of the snow into the light.*)

STONY. Frank Schaeffer, who art in heaven, keep my family here. You have your structure. You have your life-support suit that controls you and feeds you and keeps you alive. Keep me alive. Keep my wife here and my father here and my son here. Help me, Frank. Bring something down. Give me a sign. What do you want in exchange? Take anything of mine you want. I sent my dreams up to you like incense. Help me.

FREYDIS. (*Crawls after* STONY.) Master, I am in pain.

(STONY *looks up as he hears* FRANK's *voice boom out of* FREYDIS's *body.*)

FRANK'S VOICE. Skippy? Tonight's the night. I hope you're all cozy there in the White House.

STONY. Did I do it? Did I contact Frank Schaeffer? There is a Frank Schaeffer who hears my prayers? The powers in my mind. The untapped powers. Diane? Diane?

(STONY *goes off.* FRANK *runs into* FREYDIS. *He carries his space suit in his hand. He places his space suit beside her. Overhead, the sky begins to change with strange swirling streaks of violent color.*)

FRANK. Okay. Now, Skippy. Listen to me because in a few moments, very colorful bolts containing my semen will zap down on you. I know you're going to say Why. Well, blame it on the media. They wanted your impregnation to be this physical Fourth of July. Right now, these bolts containing my semen are gathering force to zap down on you, change you into a pregnant woman with the twenty-first century man. You'll be hearing my voice. Oh, it's the big production. You'll be a technological madonna. Me, Frank Schaeffer, I'll be a technological messiah. Don't be afraid when the bolts come down. You'll put on my suit. Nothing can hurt you. If we can't do something right, we won't do it at all. You'll put on the suit and we'll sit back and laugh.

FRANK'S VOICE. I hope you're feeling as romantic as I am, little missy. (*Lights start flashing under* FREYDIS's *skirt.*)

FRANK. That's my voice, darling. Broadcasting out of that little disc. Now put on the silver suit. It's the only thing that can stop the bolts.

(DIANE *comes into the light.*)

DIANE. What is that little voice? Why are we having ventriloquism at this point in my life? And why is your lap doing imitations of Times Square at New Year's Eve—

FRANK. Will somebody help me put the suit on her? (FREYDIS *knocks* FRANK *down and runs off. He dashes after her.*) Wait a minute. Skippy!! Please??? (LARRY *comes on.*)

LARRY. What's going on? The sky is swirling with light like some terrible Van Gogh—

DIANE. Stop it with the artistic analogies!!

(FRANK *and* FREYDIS *dash past* LARRY *and* DIANE *and run off.*)

LARRY. (*As* FRANK *runs by.*) You're Frank Schaeffer!! It's Frank Schaeffer!

FRANK. Write NASA. They'll send you an autographed picture. (FRANK *runs off after* FREYDIS. MRS. MCBRIDE *wanders on, happily.*)

MRS. MCBRIDE. Fillmore East. That's what the sky looks like. Fillmore East. Does that mean anything to anybody? Back in the sixties when psychedelic was a brand-new word.

(STONY *comes back on and sees* FRANK's *space suit lying on the ground.* STONY *picks it up.*)

STONY. Is that a sign? Frank Schaeffer wants me. Frank Schaeffer is sending me transportation. Frank Schaeffer wants me! (STONY *rushes off with the space suit in his hands.* FREYDIS *and* FRANK *run on and off.*)

FRANK'S VOICE. Do you have your little government-issue negligee on? Are you all hot and sexy?

MRS. MCBRIDE. Hey Hey LBJ How Many Kids Did You Kill Today!!

(TOM *comes on.*)

TOM. (*To* DIANE. *Very formal.*) Darling, how to put this. I have to fly to Washington immediately. I said I'd be bringing my new bride. They said she's still married. Give her up. They said this is no time for a new President to be breaking up homes. It's really outrageous, but what I will do is send for you in about three months. (DIANE *faints.*) Just let me get the world in order. Get the President and the Vice-President swept under the couch with all the other dustballs of history. Diane. Get up. Please. Diane.

MRS. MCBRIDE. HO Ho Ho Chi Minh. N.L.F. Is Gonna Win!!!

(FRANK *comes back with* FREYDIS *in his arms.*)

TOM. Hello, Frank.

FRANK. Hello, Tom.

TOM. Frank Schaeffer!?! (*The bolts begin.*)

(*ZAP!*)

FRANK. Where's the suit? Who has the suit? Skippy, dodge those bolts!!!

(ZAP!)

(*A bolt hits* LARRY'*s suitcase. Flames!*)

LARRY. My legs!!!

(ZAP! *A bolts hits the piano. It begins playing a Grieg concerto. ZAP! A bolt hits the carriage. ZAP! A bolt hits the cure for cancer in* TOM'*s hand. ZAP! A bolt hits* FREYDIS. *Everyone is in a daze.* FREYDIS *is lying against a wall of snow, knocked out, smoke steams around her.*)

FRANK. Skippy, tell me you like it. Oh, God, Skippy, I'm sorry. It was all supposed to be in Washington. Skippy? I meant well.

MRS. MCBRIDE. (*Begins ringing the bell that* STONY *brought from the mainland.*) Relax. The chaos won. Give into it. The chaos won. We're home!

(STONY *comes on, wearing* FRANK'*s space suit.*)

STONY. This is the me I always wanted to be! I'm on my way, Frank! (STONY *begins to ascend into space, into the light.* FRANK'*s* VOICE *comes out of* FREYDIS.)

FRANK'S VOICE. Hail Skippy full of grace. Now you're filled with the twenty-first-century man.

MRS. MCBRIDE. LBJ pull down your pants!

All we are saying is give peace a chance. (MRS. MCBRIDE *sees smoke coming out of the baby carriage. She hears the baby*

crying. The carriage begins shaking. She looks into the burned carriage.) Kid, make it a learning experience. (*She rocks the burned carriage and sings.*)
    "It's the ending of the Age of Pisces/
    Some call it Piskus/
    My blood boils and freezes/
    At people who say Pieces/
    It's Pisces! Pisces! Pisces!"
    (STONY *ascends and is gone.*)

CURTAIN

ACT II

A few moments later. The baby carriage, burned, glows. All the furniture is burned and scattered. Grieg's piano lies on its side. Larry's legs gape out of his scorched and battered suitcase. Everyone lies in a daze. FREYDIS is already at least nine months pregnant. We hear one final rumble in the sky. The sky is clear. Everyone slowly revives.

MRS. MCBRIDE. Stony? Wasn't there another iceberg over there? Wasn't there a big white cube with the Great Wall of China carved out of ice on it? Wasn't there a film a man put five years of his life into? Wasn't Dad having a comeback in it? Wasn't I an Italian princess? Wasn't life over there? (MRS. MCBRIDE *wanders off.* TOM *shakes the container holding the cure for cancer. Ashes fall out of it.*)

TOM. The cure for cancer? Where is it? It was right here. (TOM *begins searching frantically for the cure.*)

DIANE. The carriage containing our child has been hit. Why am I afraid to look in the carriage? Stony?

LARRY. Look at my luggage! What was in those bolts?

FRANK. I am truly, truly sorry.

LARRY. Forty-five alligators did not give up their lives so you could say I'm truly sorry. Stony? (LARRY *stuffs his new legs into the ruined suitcase and goes off looking for* STONY.) Stony? Stony?

(DIANE *crawls with great trepidation to the glowing baby carriage. She looks in it. She screams.*)

DIANE. The baby's been burned! It's been hit. Get a doctor! Stony? Help!

FRANK. (*Looks in the carriage.*) The baby's fine. I think. Yes, he's fine. What a fine little boy. He's just a little dusty.

(DIANE *takes the child out of the carriage and begins bathing him. The baby cries.* DIANE *sings a lullaby.* MRS. MCBRIDE *comes on. She holds a piece of fruit in her hand.* FRANK *goes to her.*)

MRS. MCBRIDE. Have I gone bonkers? On my way up from the beach, I slip. Reach out in the dark to regain my balance. Squish. Have I squeezed a pair of polar bear's nuts?

FRANK. It's a mango.

MRS. MCBRIDE. A mango, he says. And what are those flashes of pink in the sky?

FRANK. Those are flamingoes.

MRS. MCBRIDE. Flamingoes?

FRANK. Hawaii fell into the sea. The entire pineapple industry lost. I negotiated for Norway to buy the rights to the Gulf Stream before I left for space. The Gulf Stream is on its way up here now. Nuclear re-routing. I guess the bolts made it all happen sooner. Oh God.

MRS. MCBRIDE. Norway. The pineapple capital of the world. (MRS. MCBRIDE *goes off.*)

TOM. (*To* FRANK.) Pardon me. You haven't seen a piece of white paper in your travels? Have you? Rectangular? White. Official looking. Lots of C's I remember. Lots of CH's. Square roots growing off into hexagonal shapes? It was in my hand for a second. Then it wasn't there. It was in a lead container. A lead asbestos flame-proof container. It's not important. It's just the cure for cancer and the UN general assembly is waiting for me and I'm supposed to be President of the— (FRANK *buries his head in his hands.*) oh well. Nothing really out of the ord. Nothing really spesh. Take over the shards of government. Cure the world. It was right here. The piece of paper. In this hand. It was right here. (TOM *continues searching.*)

FRANK. (*To* FREYDIS.) Darling, I didn't mean it to be this way. There's a perfect child in you right this moment, but it's not in Washington. It wasn't filmed. This will be our Bethlehem. Come back to D.C. At least. The child will be born there.

FREYDIS. The child will be born of Freydis. In the woods. On the cliff. Overlooking the sea. Private. Quiet. I do not know the father. This sometimes happens to country girls. Men from other farms attack us on spring evenings and fill us full of baby.

FRANK. You're my wife.

FREYDIS. Naughty Freydis. No ring on any finger.

FRANK. Skippy. Give me a hold. I'm so lonely. It's not like there's any USO in outer space.

FREYDIS. Skippy was your wife. When Skippy was your wife, Skippy would hold you. I no Skippy. (*She contracts with labor pains.*) Mrs. McBride, please forgive. Dinner be slightly late this evening. (FREYDIS *and* FRANK *go off.* DIANE *puts the quiet child back into his carriage and rocks it gently.* TOM *crawls by on his search. He looks up at her.*)

TOM. It might have seemed back there as if I didn't.

DIANE. Didn't? Didn't what?

TOM. You know.

DIANE. Yes?

TOM. Love you.

DIANE. Oh, no.

TOM. Us leaving together. It was just inopportune.

DIANE. Of course.

TOM. With the new developments.

DIANE. History in the making.

TOM. The President's stroke.

DIANE. Vice-President's suicide.

TOM. Moral tone. Me. Provide.

DIANE. Moral leadership.

TOM. Exactly. I couldn't break up a home at this moment.

DIANE. Wouldn't look right.

TOM. Hold the world together.

DIANE. You must.

TOM. You understand.

DIANE. Always.

TOM. I'll send for you.

DIANE. Never.

TOM. But if I can't find the paper and lose the Presidency and Frank Schaeffer goes to Washington instead of me plus I can't find the cure for cancer plus all the peace work goes to hell, we can start up again? I can't lose everything plus you. You have to stay with me.

DIANE. I loved you.

TOM. And I you.

DIANE. Can't you even squeeze out the verb? You come all the way up to Norway and you can't even squeeze out the verb?

TOM. Your breasts. Your eyes.

(DIANE *looks at* TOM *and goes off.* TOM *continues to search for the cure.* FRANK *comes back on.*)

FRANK. The baby's dead. The baby ran out of her. A boy. Skippy was only pregnant hardly any time, but the nuclear transformers sped the gestation. Our child would be the Twenty-First Century man. That's what I was promised. Conceived from space. I felt like God the father. Skippy ran to a cave. Opened her legs. Did you hear her scream? Tropical birds looked down from the sky. Our child was not delivered. He strode out of her womb. Enormous. Tall. Golden. Wet. I went

up to him. "I am your father. Hi!" He looked in my eyes and
said "You are not pure. You are corrupt." At that very moment a group of unsuccessful lemmings crawled up out of the
sea and ran up the cliff to make the leap again. My son looked
around at the world and looked at me. He joined the lemmings.
He leaped over the cliff. They were all successful this time.

(MRS. MCBRIDE *comes on carrying a frozen flamingo.*)

MRS. MCBRIDE. I don't know much about symbols, but I'd
say when frozen flamingoes fall out of the sky, good times are
not in store.

(DIANE *comes back into the light carrying her suitcase and
wearing a traveling cloak.*)

DIANE. (*To* MRS. MCBRIDE.) Could you look after your grand-
child just for a bit? I have to go over to the mainland.

TOM. (*Leaps up in exaltation, waving a piece of paper.*) I
found it! I found the cure! "Dimethylene carbonitrate square
acetycyclic bionic methyldratic acid benzoid!"

DIANE. (*Reads it.*) This is the label for my diet pepsi. (DIANE
*goes. There is sudden darkness. The darkness of outer space.
Comets, asteroids, novas swirl by.* STONY *appears in space.*)

STONY. Bolts came. I was on earth. Now I am here. I dodge
quasars. I am not hallucinating. Hallucinations never bring
peace. This is real. Glass-of-milk real. I ascend through space
twisting, turning, to show gravity does not apply. I am being
carried home. Frank Schaeffer waits for me on the new planet.
We shall re-enact some primitive conception. Become true father and son. The answer to some prophecy at last. I count the
one moon we know. Two moons. Three moons. Four. Forty
moons! The silver suit knows the way to its rightful owner. We
pass a third moon of Venus. There it is. The new planet. I see
Frank Schaeffer's space craft on it. Sending out beeps. I land
on the planet. So green. (*The light around* STONY *becomes lush
and green. He takes off his helmet.*) Hellooo?? Frank Schaeffer???
Anybody home? Am I alone on the planet? A light rain falls. I
hear a music like two crystal glasses rubbing together. I feel
around. A green plant dances by, its tendrils reaching out to
me. It must recognize my plant nature. I want union with this
green plant. I want to set roots down here. I risk death. I take
off my suit. I stand naked. I stand erect. I take the plant and
hold it to me. We breathe. The plant shudders with delight. In
an instant, I see little images of me run up the stem, fill up
the stamen. These perfect representations of me pop out of the
petals. I take another plant. That plant becomes pregnant,
wrapping its leaves around me. More mes pop out of the petals.

This is the world I want! A world populated by only me. I hear a scream. One me hits another me. Is that rape? One of the mes rapes another me? More mes now march out of more petals. Mes fill the horizon. Downtown India is a ghost town compared to all the mes screaming in fear. Me! Me! Notice me! Each me screaming to be heard. Me! Me! Each one moaning, whining Me! This is not the me I had planned to be. I came up here to find Frank Schaeffer. My true self. My true father. My true son. All I see are these mes. I take an axe. I slash the plants. I stomp the roots. I take a gun. I shoot all the mes. I take flame. I burn the planet. Flames in space. I burn the new planet. I don't care. I want these mes out of me. I have killed a planet. (*The planet turns bright red and then disappears. The blackness of outer space. Stars. Comets. Earth comes into view.*) I put my suit on. I twist a gauge. I plunge down toward earth. Is the fear out of me? I am so quiet. I have killed me. I want no more solos. I crave duets. The joy of a trio. The harmony of a quartet. The totality of an orchestra. Home. I head for home! Duets! Trios! A quartet! Yes, even an orchestra. Make some music out of my life. I descend on my garden. I am home.

(*The clear light returns to our iceberg. Everything is as it was before.* FRANK *is alone picking out a simple melody on Grieg's tilted piano.* STONY *descends, enters.*)

STONY. Hello? Hello? Where is the other iceberg? Where is the Great Wall of China? Where is my film?
FRANK. Gone.
STONY. The crew?
FRANK. Gone.
STONY. There were five thousand Chinese extras.
FRANK. Gone.
STONY. Diane?
FRANK. (*Stops playing the piano.*) Gone.
STONY. Larry?
FRANK. Gone.
STONY. All dead?
FRANK. Not dead. Just gone.
STONY. I can't tell if you look familiar or not.
FRANK. I'm nobody. Who are you. Are you nobody, too?
STONY. Are you Emily Dickinson?
FRANK. I have other news for you. Your father.
STONY. Gone?
FRANK. He wouldn't wait for anyone. He took off in the

air taxi. Bolts hit the helicopter. It exploded. Your father's dead.

STONY. What a rotten comeback he's having. Oh boy. Oh God. All those years trying to connect with him. I'm remembering a time. No, I'm not. Nothing ever happened between us. My father's dead. My film is gone. My wife is gone. I've killed a planet. On top of everything, I killed a planet that was supposed to feed the world.

FRANK. Oh, you found that planet too? You saw yourself? All the versions of yourself screaming Me Me? I found that planet. I killed it. It grows back. Don't worry. You didn't kill it. You only saw yourself.

STONY. Why is it that all the things that should hold us together, help us change—love, creativity, sex, talent, dreams—those are the very elements that drive us apart and the things that you think would separate us—hate, fear, meanness—those are the very things that bind us together and keep us from growing. Keep us from changing.

FRANK. By the way . . . your son.

STONY. My son. Nothing's happened to my son.

FRANK. *He's* not dead. The bolts hit your son's carriage.

STONY. What are you saying?

FRANK. The bolts that so speeded up my own wife's gestation so that the greatest creation known to man was accomplished in a matter of a few moments . . . Those bolts hit your son.

STONY. Why am I afraid to look in the carriage?

FRANK. After your wife left, we thought everything was all right. But as you can see, I guess it's not.

STONY. (*Looks in the carriage. The carriage begins to glow. He's shocked.*) I've seen my life. I don't want . . . (STONY *runs into the darkness and scales an iceberg.*)

FRANK. (*Yells after him.*) You can't run away from it. You can't hide from it. Open your eyes to it. You can't close your eyes to it. (FRANK *is left alone.*) Now let me see, what are my choices? Should I go back into space and become a hero or stay here and try to win Skippy back? The world on one hand. Me on the other. (FRANK *takes a burned flower from the bouquet and begins plucking the singed petals to make his choice.*) The world. Me. The world. Me. (FRANK *wanders off.*)

(*In the distance* TOM *calls to* STONY. *The carriage glows and begins to shake violently. A large hand appears over the edge of the baby carriage. Then a large leg follows. The baby emerges. He looks exactly like* STONY. *He is wearing "Doctor Denton"*

*pajamas and is sucking a juice bottle. The baby walks unsteadily
over to the table and pulls at the tablecloth until it comes off,
spilling the dishes onto the floor. The baby sticks his head
through one of the holes burnt in the tablecloth and crawls
around the ice dragging it behind him.* TOM *runs into the light.)*

TOM. *(To the baby.)* Stony! God, where have you been?
Everybody's vanished off this island. I felt like Robinson Crusoe
all of a sudden. My man Friday! (TOM *slaps the baby in an
attempt at good humor. The baby cries.)* Oh, Christ. I'm
sorry. Did you get a vaccination? I hate it when people do that.
Hit you in the arm right after you've been shot up with . . .
Stony, you've got to help me. I have to come right out and say
it. Hide me out just for a while? Let me work on the film. Stop
crying, Stony. Let me work on the film. I've been impressive.
Been referred to as impressive and even felt impressive. But
now maybe it's time for a change. A change of direction. Time
for, say, Art. I've been in the library in your house dipping
into, God, like Chekhov while I was waiting for your wife
to leave you. And by the way, I hope that silly misunderstanding
is over. Please say something to me? Please? This is no time for
vindictiveness. What I'm asking for is a job. Anything where
my face won't be seen. Where I can work with the creative
sides of my personality. I'm not going to trod on your toes. On
your territory. I've got—it seems I've got the entire UN waiting for me. It seems I had announced the cure for cancer all
ready, that I held it in my possession. Thousands of people
have swarmed out of hospitals and are waiting at airports for
me to return. I have to—vanish seems melodramatic a word,
using a word like vanish at a time when ironically I feel so
present, when I feel so there. You see, I feel my soul has
moved finally into my body and I could be such a good helper
on your film. Carry the film to the drugstore or wherever you
go to have it developed. I could get coffee. I could work on the
costumes. Stony, wait till you see what I found. *(He takes a
rusty tin box out of his jacket breast pocket.)* I was down at
Flamingo Beach and saw a flamingo pawing the sand. The sun
glinted. What was buried there? I pushed the flamingo away
and dug this up with my bare hands. (TOM *opens the box. He
takes out a pile of letters.)* Wait till you see what this is. (TOM
reads the letter.) "Mein Liebstram Eva . . . Die Lieblich, Adolf."
Yes! Can you believe it? Hitler's love letters! This place was
built as a summer house for Hitler when the war would be over
and he and Eva could come up here and relax. Isn't it extraordi-

nary? You decide to make a film about heroes and about men
who wanted to change history and, my God, you move inadver-
tently into Hitler's hideaway. The world of Art! My God! Does
it always create this chain on which every event fits in some
crazy exact magical pattern? The World of Art? Let me move
into it. I'll hide anywhere. Hear the exclamation points I'm
talking in. My mind makes spears out of exclamation points and
nails me right onto the world of Art. Right onto your life. Let
me stay. I can't go back. I am a laughingstock, Stony. I heard
on the radio that my name has passed in the vocabulary. Not
since Wrong Way Corrigan. As sure as Benedict Arnold is a
synonym for traitor so will Tom Wintermouth pass into everyday speech as a byword for asshole. For one who promises and
cannot deliver. For one who has a smugness and a self-pleasure.
For one who . . . Stony, say something. Help me? Let me stay?

BABY. Ga ga splee do. Juice. Up! Up! (*The baby holds up
his arms.* TOM *picks him up and carries the baby to the couch.*)

TOM. Stony, you want juice. Anything you want, you can
have. I wish you'd get that tablecloth off your back. I'm not
much into fashion, but I don't think tablecloths are in anybody's fashion forecast. You're impressive. You're the director.
Stony, while we're having this heart-to-heart, let me tell you an
idea I had. After I found Hitler's love letters which I just leave
with you as a bread and butter gift, look what else I found.
(TOM *unfurls a giant painted map of the world. It covers the
entire garden floor.*) Isn't that something??? A map of the
world circa 1935. Hitler's map! Showing what he hoped the
world would look like after the war was over. Forget that. I use
the map as a prop to tell you my idea. Why start with Marco
Polo? The world needs heroes or at least people who dare
dream beyond themselves. It'll soon be the new century. Take
a hero—representative—from each of the last ten centuries.
Leif Ericson here in Norway—man going out to search for New
Worlds. Then the twelfth century. Abelard, down here in France!
Abelard! Man moving into his mind. New World's within. Man
thinking for himself! Then we leap to Italy and look all the way
to China. Marco Polo is a wonderful idea!! Thirteenth-century
man going into New Worlds and taking from them what he
needs and giving what he has. Mutual enrichment. Stony, don't
turn away. Hear me out? Please? Next century: Francis Bacon,
I thought. Science is born. Man learning to use this world. Next
century—I don't know—Rembrandt! Man trying to capture this
world on canvas. Eighteenth century we leap from Holland to
America because you have to do George Washington. I could

even play George Washington. I mean, I've had experience in front of the TV cameras. The Wintermouth Hearings. I've had my own hearings. And your wife who is the smartest person in the whole wide world said I have dreams where other people have pupils. My eyes alone. Destroy my face. I don't care. Look, Stony, your wife sleeps with me and that gives me some rights around here. For the nineteenth century I haven't decided fully on Marx or Freud. Then for the Twentieth Century Man, we could— (TOM *leaps across the "ocean" again and plunges through the map. Vanishes. The baby looks up at the sounds of an air taxi landing.* DIANE *comes on carrying her suitcase. The baby toddles to her. She sits beside the baby.*)

DIANE. I called my old piano teacher in Paris. Could I see her? I flew there. Such a lovely day in Paris. April. I went into her studio and lifted the lid of the old Knabe-Bechstein-Steinway and Mozart and Brahms were there in their little raincoats and if they didn't exactly break out into "Hello Dolly it's so nice to have you back . . ." I got through the Mozart-Köchel listing 453A. Started in on the Brahms. She stopped me. My old—my very old—piano teacher said if I practiced two years, three years, eight hours a day, then perhaps she could begin with me again. But really I was too old to think of starting a career again. I was a child prodigy and I'll always stay alive in the history books, but I had stayed away too long to resume an adult career. She said, "You have a nice husband. A child." I said, "I hate my husband. I'm having an affair." She said, "Stages. Compromises. Phases. Settle." I said, "But I want to keep my lover and have my marriage and resume my career." And she said, "Yes, and I wish it were 1938 again and World War Two hadn't happened and I still lived in Vienna." Stony, I sleep with Tom.

BABY. Go da splee do.

DIANE. I know you know. I want to continue. Darling, what did you spill that you're all wet? Poor Stony. Trying to find life-size. Is that why we're all so afraid? It used to worry me that I gave you nothing. That you got nothing from me. It used to hurt me that I wanted nothing from you. That you had nothing to give me. I see now, darling, that's our secret weapon. We can be together and always leave each other alone. Darling, I got frightened after I left. I got rid of the baby. I wanted to start all over again. I'm not pregnant. It was easy. I feel fine. I feel great. (*The baby tries to nurse.*) No, darling, don't think you have to compete with Tom. No! Don't kiss me with so much passion. I don't want that. I want you to go out and do

what you have to do and I'll go out and do what I have to do
and then we'll come home and beg forgiveness and we'll both
swear we'll be different and both swear we'll change but our
secret that holds us together is that we secretly love and adore
the way we are. I don't want you to change. But we'll keep the
promise of change. Let's just hold each other and heal our
wounds and call that growing.

(*The baby cries.*) What? You don't believe me? You think
I'm going to leave you? What do you want? Silence? You want
silence? You never lied to me. I certainly don't want to lie to
you. (*She turns on a cassette tape of a piano recording.*) One of
my best pieces. "The reason the piano was invented." I was the
best. I thought if I were the best in music . . . (*She goes to the
piano and slams the lid on her hand.*) I was then the best in it
all. (*Slam.*) I see. (*Slam.*) I see. (*Slam. She cries in pain. She
holds up her hands. They are bleeding.*) See what I've done for
you, darling? Music with anyone, but silences with you. Where
is Tom? I want Tom. Freydis? Somebody? Could I have a
valium and some gauze? Are you in there? (FRANK *appears
dressed as a Norwegian peasant. He carries a glass of water and
some bandages.*)

FRANK. I am Einar.

DIANE. Anything you want to be. (*He bandages her hand.*
MRS. MCBRIDE *comes out.*) Debbie-Lisa? Were you ever happy?

MRS. MCBRIDE. Only once really. On my way to Johns
Hopkins. It was my last day as a man. I took a walk before the
operation. I had made a choice. There was a beautiful little girl
playing in a field. I would soon be like her. But I also felt a
strong feeling for her I suppose was sexual. Pre-sexual, if there's
such a thing. And I did something I never did before or since. I
opened my raincoat to her. I exposed myself to her. She was so
beautiful. I wanted myself with her. I probably frightened her. I
don't care. I don't think it was sick. I wanted somebody to see
me as a man. I was proud at that moment to be a man. I was
proud I would be a woman. I was proud I had made a choice.
She was such a beautiful little girl.

(FREYDIS *appears in tatters.*)

FREYDIS. Was that in Baltimore? Baltimore, Maryland? 1965?
I don't think I ever saw a happier human being. I followed you
to the door of the hospital. I waited for you to come out. You
never did. All my life I have dreamed of those eyes. I married
Frank because I thought the joy I saw in his eyes was the joy of
a man who has made a choice and revels in it. Let me look in
your eyes. Yes. Those are the eyes.

MRS. MCBRIDE. It is you!

FREYDIS. Let me sit on your lap.

MRS. MCBRIDE. Of course. You come sit in my lap.

FREYDIS. (*Sits in* MRS. MCBRIDE'*s lap.*) I need a comfort zone.

MRS. MCBRIDE. Of course you do.

FREYDIS. There's a little cottage at the far end of this island that's filled with food and chintz curtains. Come live with me and I'll take care of you. I grow you poppies. I'll make you drugs. I'll grow you hash. It'll be a wonderful new century. I want to get back to what I am.

MRS. MCBRIDE. I'll walk you there, but it's too late for me to get back to anywhere near where I was.

(*The sound of the air taxi descending.* MRS. MCBRIDE *and* FREYDIS *go off together.* FRANK/EINAR *picks up the baby and carries him out.* LARRY *enters very happy.*)

LARRY. So. I go to Helsinki, say: I lost my legs. Got a spare pair? They say "sure." I see my new legs waiting for me. Beautiful. Shining my legs. And I thought, I can go anywhere I want to. I am free. And I thought, "But the only place I want to go is here." Isn't that a hoot and a howl???? The doctors . . . they were surprised. I mean I left a lot of dislocated jaws in that hospital. "But your new legs," they said. "You're in a great deal of pain," they said. I tipped my hat, picked up my old kit bag, turned to the doctors and said, "Doctors, why go anywhere when you're where you want to be. After all, pain isn't the worst thing in the world." Isn't that a brilliant choice? Absolutely brilliant? I'm home. I came home. Diane, did you see there's another production of *Doll House* in Oslo? This time on roller skates and surfboards! Why not? (TOM *pushes himself up through a hole in the ice, supporting himself on his elbows.*) Tom, if I were you, I'd get out of that water as quickly and as quietly as I could. On my way back here, with all the tropical waters coming up here, for the first time in Norway, there's a piranha scare. *"Peerannnaskeeren,"* I believe, is the latest addition to the Norwegian dictionary.

DIANE. Piranhas? Tom? Get out of the water!

TOM. I *am* out of the water. This is all there is. They already, it would appear, have got to me. I have read how your body produces morphine to deaden pain at times of great shock and loss. It's really not so bad . . . I want to cry. But it's really not so bad . . .

DIANE. (*Kneels beside* TOM.) I've made bargains with Stony, Tom. We can make love anytime we want to. It's all arranged.

We have no illusions about what we need from each other. It's all worked out, Tom. You can fill me. What do you mean this is all there is of you? Tom, get out of the water. Tom, come into me. Tom, I need you. Just for a moment. Tom, it is very undignified to beg for comfort.

TOM. I've been reading Chekhov. *Three Sisters.* Those poor girls, all the time trying to get to Moscow. I looked at this map before I went through it. The town they lived in was only forty-eight miles from Moscow. In 1999 that town is probably part of Greater Downtown Moscow. They were in Moscow all the time. Those three dumb broads. There all the time. We spend all this time talking about the future. We're here. Baby, we are the future.

(*The sky begins to darken.*)

DIANE. No. This is not my life. The clock has not yet started ticking on my life. I'll let life know when I'm ready for it to begin. My parents told me I could have life anyway I wanted it. When I have a life, it's going to be a wonderful thing. A treasure you can put on a shelf. Warmth. Passion. Golden. Light. Freedom.

(FRANK/EINAR *comes on carrying a door.*)

FRANK/EINAR. (*In a bad Norwegian accent.*) I am not ready to go through any doors, but what I will do is fix this door so when I am ready to go through a door, I will have the door with me. (*He leans the door against an iceberg and begins fixing it.* MRS. MCBRIDE *and* FREYDIS *come on.* FREYDIS *carries a tray of champagne and glasses. She hands glasses to everyone.* MRS. MCBRIDE *takes out a cassette and puts it in the player: Guy Lombardo's recording of* Auld Lang Syne.)

MRS. MCBRIDE. Now, it's not too late to start planning for a New Century party. Oh, I know you're going to say the new century doesn't start till 2001, but as far as this little girl's concerned, when that taxi meter of time goes click click click and tumbles into two oh oh oh, that's the new century and 2001 is just a darling sweet old movie I saw in a museum just before I came here. Stanley Kubrick hobbled out. So charming. We must have him. And Guy Lombardo if they can unfreeze him in time. And we'll have the powdered champagne—I'm sorry, but I love it—and midnight will come and we'll all toast so quietly so we won't frighten the new century away and we'll all whisper: Happy New Year.

(*They all freeze in the midst of their toast with their champagne glasses.* STONY *comes on holding his space suit in his hands. The lights slowly dim until only* STONY *is illuminated by a single spotlight. He talks to us.*)

STONY. I looked at all these people waiting for a future that would never come and when it did come, when the new century finally did arrive, they would wait another hundred for yet another century and then a hundred years for another, waiting, waiting, always for rebirth. Should I reveal myself to them and explain and cry and he saids and she saids and forgives and forgets and going backs and resumes? Or should I simply twist the gauge again, lift up there in space, spend years ruminating about the events of these days, holding them to me until they finally cripple me.

Remembry.

Dismember.

Membrotic.

Membrosis.

A new word for the panic-stricken act of obsessive memory?

And I realized what I would have to do. Draw the curtain. Say goodbye forever. Take my son. Go out into the now. Out there where you live. Into the present. Out there where you are. Grow. Change. My plant nature. Our plant nature. To celebrate that. (STONY *holds up his hands. Two green plants appear in them.*)

CURTAIN

WINGS

A DRAMA

by

Arthur Kopit

To George Kopit, my father
1913–1977

CAST

EMILY STILSON .... *Constance Cummings*
AMY .... *Mary-Joan Negro*
DOCTORS .... *Roy Steinberg, Ross Petty*
NURSES .... *Gina Franz, Mary Michelle Rutherfurd*
BILLY .... *James Tolkan*
MR. BROWNSTEIN .... *Carl Don*
MRS. TIMMINS .... *Betty Pelzer*

WINGS was given its first stage performance at the Yale Repertory Theatre in New Haven, Connecticut, on March 3, 1978, with the following cast:

EMILY .... *Constance Cummings*
AMY .... *Marianne Owen*
DOCTORS .... *Geoffrey Pierson, Roy Steinberg*
NURSES .... *Caris Corfman, Carol Ostrow*
BILLY .... *Richard Grusin*
MR. BROWNSTEIN .... *Ira Bernstein*
MRS. TIMMINS .... *Betty Pelzer*

Directed by JOHN MADDEN
Designed by ANDREW JACKNESS
Costumes by JEANNE BUTTON
Lighting by TOM SCHRAEDER
Sound by TOM VOEGELI
Music by HERB PILHOFER

PREFACE

In the fall of 1976, I was commissioned to write an original radio play for Earplay, the drama project of National Public Radio. They did not stipulate what the play should be about, only that it should not last longer than an hour. *Wings* was the result. It has since, of course, been altered and expanded, mainly to accommodate the visual components of my central character's condition. But the play was, and still remains, essentially about language disorder and its implications. For that reason, radio was the perfect initial medium; it did not permit me to get lost in the myriad and always fascinating perceptual aberrations that can accompany any severe damage to the brain. I now believe that if I had conceived *Wings* directly for the stage instead, I would have inevitably found myself seduced by the stage's greater freedom into investigating at length these astonishing but ultimately peripheral aspects of aphasia. Most likely, more characters would have been introduced, a welter of extraordinary syndromes revealed and examined. If brain damage is terrifying to behold, it is also alluring. One feels the need to avert one's eyes and hide, and the equal if not greater need to keep looking. It is a very scary business, this job of exploring who we are. Very quickly, I suspect, my focus would have vanished. All of which is to say that if *Wings* exhibits in its present form any excellence of vision and craft, that excellence is without question a direct function of the rigor imposed on it by its initial incarnation. For that reason, I must express a deep debt of gratitude to Earplay for having commissioned this play, and particularly to the man who directed both its initial version and its first production on the stage at Yale, John Madden.

There is a question which I suspect must arise inevitably in the mind of anyone who reads or sees this play: to what degree is *Wings* faithful to fact, to what degree sheer speculation.

In the spring of 1976, seven months before Earplay was to commission me to write on a subject of my choosing, my father suffered a major stroke which rendered him incapable of speech. Furthermore, because of certain other complications, all related to his aphasia, and all typical of stroke, it was impossible to know how much he comprehended. Certainly there was no doubt that his capacity to comprehend had been dramatically impaired and reduced. As best I could, I tried to understand what he was going through. It seemed to me that, regardless of how reduced his senses were, the isolation he was being forced to endure had to verge on the intolerable; clearly, he had not lost all comprehension—the look of terror in his eyes was unmistakable. Yet, not only did he tolerate this state; every now and then, if one watched carefully enough, something escaped from this shell that was his body and his prison, something almost but not quite palpable, something not readily brought to the attention of a nurse (I tried it once but she saw nothing), something which I felt possessed a kind of glow or flicker, rather like a lamp way off in the dark, something only barely perceptible. I took these faint flashes to be him signaling. And although I allowed for the possibility that what I was perceiving was nothing but mirage, or the mirrored reflections of my own hopeful and constant signalings to him, nonetheless, it seemed to me (indeed, seemed irrefutable) that in some ineffably essential way, reduced as he was, he was still the same person he had been. This thought was both heartening and frightful. To what extent was he still intact? To what extent was he aware of what had befallen him? *What was it like inside?*

And then Earplay came along. By its very nature, radio seemed to offer an especially appropriate means of exploring these particular questions.

I recognized at once that I could not deal directly with my father. For one thing, I was too close to him to hold any hope of objectivity. For another, his case was too severe, too grim, my audience would turn away. So I looked elsewhere for a model. The questions would remain the same, of course, and just as valid; my understanding of my father's world would have to come—if indeed it could at all—through analogy. I decided to focus on two patients I had met at the Burke Rehabilitation Center in White Plains, New York, where my father had been transferred after his stay in the hospital. Both were women: one was old, in her late seventies, perhaps older; the other, not quite thirty. Like my father, both had suffered major strokes, though neither was as incapacitated as he; both at least could talk. Certainly they could not talk well.

The speech of the younger woman was fluent and possessed normal intonations, cadence, and syntactical structure—in fact, to such an extent that anyone who did not understand English would have sworn she was making sense. Nonetheless, her sentences were laced with a kind of babbled jargon so that, by and large, she made no sense at all. In her early stages, she seemed unaware of this appalling deficit.* In contrast, the older woman's words had no fluency, no melodic inflection, no syntactical richness. Her words emerged with difficulty and sounded like something composed for a telegram. Modifiers and conjunctions for the most part were absent. But at least her words made sense. The problem was, as often as not, the sense they conveyed was not the sense she intended. Though she usually was aware of these "mistakes," or at least could be made aware of them, she could not prevent them from occurring. Neither could she readily correct them. Aside from her aphasia, each woman was relatively free of other symptoms.

I had met the older woman while accompanying my father one afternoon on his rounds. When he went down for speech therapy, she was one of the three other patients in the room. I had never observed a speech therapy session before and was nervous. The day, I recall vividly, was warm, humid. The windows of the room were open. A scent of flowers suffused the air. To get the session started, the therapist asked the older woman if she could name the seasons of the year. With much effort, she did, though not in proper order. She seemed annoyed with herself for having any difficulty at all with such a task. The therapist then asked her which of these seasons corresponded to the present. The woman turned at once to the window. She could see the garden, the flowers. Her eyes were clear, alert; there was no question but that she understood what was wanted. I cannot remember having ever witnessed such an intense struggle. At first, she did nothing but sit calmly and wait for the word to arrive on its own. When it didn't, she tried to force the word out by herself, through thinking; as if to assist what clearly was a process of expulsion, she scrunched her face up, squeezed her eyelids shut. But no word emerged. Physically drained, her face drenched with sweat, she tried another trick: she cocked her head and listened to the birds, whose sound was incessant. When this too led to nothing, she sniffed the air. When nothing came of this strategy either, she turned her attention to what she was wearing, a light cotton dress; she even touched the fabric. Finally, something connected. Her lips began to form a word. She shut her eyes. The word emerged. *Winter*.

---

* This particular kind of speech, typical of a certain form of aphasia, is characterized by neologisms, and sounds very much like double talk or gibberish. The word *gibberish*, however, suggests psychosis and dementia, and is therefore inappropriate for describing an effect of organic brain disease; the term *jargonaphasia* is used instead.

When informed that it was summer she seemed astonished, how was it possible? . . . a mistake like that . . . obviously she knew what season it was, anyone with eyes could tell at once what season it was! . . . and yet . . . She looked over at where I sat and shook her head in dismay, then laughed and said, "This is really nuts, isn't it!"

I sat there, stunned. I could not believe that anyone making a mistake of such gross proportions and with such catastrophic implications could laugh at it.

So there would be no misunderstanding, the therapist quickly pointed out that this mistake stemmed completely from her stroke; in no way was she demented. The woman smiled (she knew all that) and turned away, stared back out of the window at the garden. *This is really nuts, isn't it!*—I could not get her phrase from my mind. In its intonation, it had conveyed no feeling of anger, resignation, or despair. Rather, it had conveyed amazement, and in that amazement, a trace (incredible as it seemed) of delight. This is not to suggest that anyone witnessing this incident could, even for an instant, have imagined that she was in any sense pleased with her condition. The amazement, and its concomitant delight, seemed to me to reflect only an acknowledgment that her condition was extraordinary, and in no way denied or obviated the terror or the horror that were at its core. By some (I supposed) nourishing spring of inner strength and light, of whose source I had no idea, she had come to a station in her life from which she could perceive in what was happening something that bore the aspect of adventure, and it was through this perhaps innate capacity to perceive and appreciate adventures, and perhaps in this sense only, that she found some remaining modicum of delight, which I suspect kept her going. Of course, all this was speculation. As I said, I was stunned. The therapist asked her to try again and she did. And she got it—summer! With great excitement, she tried once again. Same result. She had it! Summer! She tried again. *Winter*. It was lost. She heard but could do nothing. She shook her head in consternation. Smiled in wonderment. In the course of the session, I discovered we shared the same birthday.

Later that afternoon, I inquired as to who she was, and was told she was a former aviatrix and wing-walker. I believe my response to this news was *"What?"*—although I think I may have said, *"Wing-walker?"* Either way, my composure was slipping. I felt decidedly inadequate.

A nurse brought me to her room (she was out, gone down to dinner) and showed me a photograph pinned up on her wall; it had been taken when she was in her twenties. In the photograph, a biplane sits on a large grassy field, a crowded grandstand in the distance, its front railing draped with flags. The plane is a Curtiss Jenny. A pilot sits in the rearmost of its two open cockpits; she is standing out on its lower wing, white silk scarf around her neck, goggles set back on top of her leather helmet. She wears jodhpurs, boots, a leather jacket. Her face is lean and handsome and imperious. The same noble and slightly quizzical smile I'd seen that afternoon is there. Her right hand is holding on to the wire stays behind her. The propeller is spinning; apparently, her plane is about to take off. Several nurses come in and join us in staring at the photograph. Her eyes seem on fire; they were filled with an unquenchable eager passion. Her left hand is waving toward the camera and the unseen throng.

Needless to say, had I invented her, the invention would have been excessive, would have strained credulity—only in dreams and fiction did one meet persons such as this. Yet, here she was, she existed. Everyone at Burke who knew her agreed that the fortitude and *esprit* I'd seen that afternoon in the therapy session were no aberration. By nature she was one of the bravest, most extraordinary persons they had ever met. There was no other choice: she was my model.

With that decision, a task that might otherwise have been little more than grim took on the aspects of an adventure. As scrupulously as possible, I would try to explore, through her mind, this terrible and awesome realm of being. Surely, that realm bore resemblance to my father's. Courage was not her quality alone.

The title came at once. Also, with it, two recognitions: if *Wings* was to be effective, it would have to deal specifically with its central character and not with some general condition called stroke; at the same time, to be effective, it would have to possess an absolutely solid clinical accuracy.

To these ends, I began an exhaustive study of airplanes and brain damage—unquestionably a weird conjunction of subjects. The study of airplanes was simple. Libraries provided everything I had to know about early aviation—how the old biplanes were flown, who flew them, what their cockpits looked like, felt like; and especially about that remarkable post-World War I phenomenon known as barnstorming, when pilots (many of them women) toured the country, thrilling crowds with exhibitions of their marvelous, death-defying daring and skill. Burke was where I went to study brain damage and rehabilitation.

It quickly became clear that, for my purposes at least, the

speech patterns of this older woman (due to the nature of her stroke) were not as varied and therefore not as interesting as the speech patterns of many other patients.

For greater linguistic richness, I turned to the patient in her late twenties as the principal model for my central character's speech. In her own right, this young woman was as exceptional as the older. Certainly she was no less brave. When I met her, she was able to acknowledge the gravity of her condition, and fought all tendencies to self-pity and despair. With as much cheerfulness as she could muster (her capacity for hope seemed limitless), she worked every moment that she could at the one task in her life that mattered: the reassembling of her shattered world. But there was yet another exceptional aspect to this young woman, and in truth it was this that made me turn to her as the model not only for my central character's patterns of speech but, in fact, ultimately, her very processes of thought: *she was left-handed*. From this one seemingly insignificant trait, many remarkable abilities derived.

In a right-handed person, the left hemisphere of the cerebral cortex is dominant and controls all activities connected with speech and analytic consciousness. However, for persons who are by nature left-handed, some of the left hemisphere's usual functions are taken over by the normally nonverbal and intuitive right. Should such a person suffer a stroke or injury to the left cerebral hemisphere, he stands a good chance of retaining a degree of verbal lucidity and insight inaccessible to those whose left hemisphere maintains sole dominance. This was the case with the young woman I met at Burke. Because of her left-handedness, she possessed the rare ability to recognize and articulate, to a slight but still significant extent, her own patterns of thought. Repeatedly, she would describe a certain dividedness within her head, as if she literally sensed the separate hemispheres at work, usually in contradiction to each other. In such instances, she would actually refer to her mind's "two sides," and frequently accompany this description with a slicing gesture of her hand, clearly suggestive of a vertically symmetrical division of her entire body. Once, she described coming to a large puddle. With great amusement she recounted how one side of her head told her to go left, while the other side told her to go right, to end the controversy and resolve the debate, she walked through the middle.

At Burke, I studied her attempts at keeping a journal, listened to hours of taped interviews between her and her speech therapist, and of course, as often as possible, talked directly to her myself. She seemed to understand something of my project and its purposes, and seemed pleased that somehow she could be of help. Gradually, an image of a remarkable and quite vivid interior landscape began to form in my mind, frightening and awesome in its details, its blatant gaps, its implications.

But there was still another person crucial to my research: her therapist, Jacqueline Doolittle. Her knowledge of aphasia was my touchstone. At all hours of the day and sometimes night, I would call Mrs. Doolittle with some generally naïve question about the brain, and she, with limitless good humor, would set me straight. It is both astonishing and humbling the number of assumptions one can make in this field which are absolutely wrong. Nonetheless, I kept phoning and, if not phoning, stopping by her office, usually unannounced. To her credit, and perhaps to mine, she never threw me out. Gradually, things became clearer. I should point out, Mrs. Doolittle's understanding of aphasia went far beyond the clinical: Jacqueline Doolittle had herself been aphasic once.

Her aphasia had resulted from a head injury sustained in an auto accident. Eventually she recovered, and her recollections of this period are like visions of a sojourn in another realm: vivid and detailed. Without a doubt, it was this experience that lay at the root of her exceptional empathic abilities as a therapist.

What she described was a world of fragments, a world without dimension, a world where time meant nothing constant, and from which there seemed no method of escape. She thought she had either gone mad or been captured by an unknown enemy for purposes she could not fathom, and in fact took the hospital she was in to be a farmhouse in disguise, controlled by her captors. For a long time, she was unable to distinguish that the words she spoke were jargon, and wondered why everyone she saw spoke to her in a foreign tongue. Her state was one of utter isolation, confusion, terror, and disarray. She wondered if perhaps she was dreaming. Sometimes the thought occurred to her that she was dead. Then, very gradually, the swelling in her head subsided, and little by little the cells in her left cerebral hemisphere began to make their proper neural connections. She began to understand what people said. When she spoke, the right words, as if by magic, started flowing. She returned to the world she knew. *Wings* owes much of its structure and detail to these recollections.

How much of this play, then, is speculation?

Wings is a play about a woman whom I have called Emily Stilson. Though she suffers a stroke, in no way is it a case study, and in its execution I have assiduously avoided any kind of clinical or documentary approach. Indeed, it has been so conceived and constructed that its audience can, for the most part, observe this realm that she is in only through her own consciousness. In short, *Wings* is a work of speculation informed by fact.

But any attempt to render a person's consciousness through words, even autobiography, must be speculative. Where thoughts are concerned, there are no infallible reporters. What we remember of our pasts is filtered by our sensibilities and predilections, and can as easily be imaginary as real. To what extent did Jacqui Doolittle remember only what she wanted to? To what extent did her mind, in its damaged state, withhold from her consciousness something essential to her experience? Given that she was suffering a severe language deficit, how much can we trust her verbal recollections? In this arena, hard facts do not exist. Yet, if we cannot hope for what is provable, we at least can strive for what is plausible. By any criteria, Jacqui Doolittle's account has emotional validity. The same holds true for the young left-handed woman's. It was this emotional truth, informed by fact, that I was after. So far as I was able, I have avoided in this play any colorations of my own and, as far as I know, have attributed to Emily Stilson no symptoms that are unlikely or impossible. Though Emily Stilson is a composite of many persons, and derives finally from my imagination, I have worked as if in fact she existed, and in this light, and within the limitations of this form, have felt myself obliged to render her condition as it was, not as I might have preferred it.

There are two books whose influence on me I would like to acknowledge, and which I strongly recommend to anyone interested in further explorations of this subject: Howard Gardner's *The Shattered Mind,* and A. R. Luria's *The Man with a Shattered World*.

I would also like to acknowledge the crucial role of Robert Brustein, as Dean of the Yale School of Drama, in the evolution of this play. Mr. Brustein had heard the radio play performed, and had expressed his admiration of the work. In November of 1977, he called me to say that he had been thinking about the play, and had come to believe it could be even more effective on the stage. A slot had opened in the Yale Rep's spring schedule. Was I interested?

Not only was I interested, I was flabbergasted. Since summer, when I had first heard *Wings* performed, I had been trying to figure out if it was possible to adapt it to the stage. The problems, it turned out, were considerable, both structurally and thematically. That afternoon, indeed less than an hour before the call came in, I had suddenly realized how to do it.

For those who may have missed the issue, *Forbes Magazine* ranks playwriting extremely low on the list of Easy Ways to Earn One's Fortune. In fact, it is no simple matter to earn one's living at its practice. I would therefore like to express both my family's and my deep gratitude to the Rockefeller Foundation for a generous and timely grant, which alone enabled me to devote, with ease of mind, the enormous time and energy that I soon found the work demanded, both in the writing and in the research.

For their extensive and always generous assistance in that research, I am profoundly indebted and grateful to the Burke Rehabilitation Center; and especially to Jacqueline Doolittle.

A.L.K.

I weave in and out of the strange clouds, hidden in my tiny cockpit, submerged, alone, on the magnitude of this weird, unhuman space, venturing where man has never been, perhaps never meant to go. Am I myself a living, breathing, earth-bound body, or is this a dream of death I'm passing through? Am I alive, or am I really dead, a spirit in a spirit world. Am I actually in a plane, or have I crashed on some worldly mountain, and is this the afterlife?

Charles Lindbergh,
The Spirit of St. Louis.

NOTES ON OTHER PRODUCTIONS
OF *WINGS*

I cannot emphasize strongly enough how crucial it is that any-one directing WINGS do some homework first. The production must be grounded in a thorough clinical authenticity. This is not that hard to come by. Several books will help, and are a good preliminary step. *The Shattered Mind* by Howard Gardner is a first-rate introduction to the brain and brain damage; A. R. Luria's *The Man with a Shattered World* is another fine and very helpful book, though the damage suffered by the man in Luria's study differs significantly in his symptoms from anyone in WINGS. Still, the Luria book communicates an extraordinary sense of what the world is like for someone whose mind has been drastically and permanently altered, and it cannot help but prove useful to a director of WINGS.

I also strongly suggest that the director, designer, and cast visit a first-rate rehabilitation center. It is vital, particularly for the director, that there be real-life models to draw upon. I don't think, for example, that the group therapy scene can work unless the director is personally aware of the relaxed atmosphere in which such a session can be conducted in (that phase again) "real life." And while the director and performers will inevitably and rightly create their own interpretations, they must know what it is they are interpreting.

As for the style of the production itself, one can stage the play as it was staged in New York, which is to say, for a proscenium or thrust, with full and quite elaborate lights and set, seemingly simple in execution but not in their detail, or one can do the play environmentally. During rehearsal of WINGS for New York, it quickly became apparent to its director, John Madden, and to me, that the play could be very effectively staged with no light and sound changes at all! The key to all productions, it seems to me, is the eliciting of the audience's imaginative participation. And this can be done through lights and sound, in a traditional mode, or by very baldly announcing that no quasi-realistic devises will be used at all. Mrs. Stilson's terrible isolation can be conveyed in many ways, and done skillfully and carefully, an audience will give its faith and attention to all of them.

Therefore, I urge the director to attend carefully to the play's stage directions and suggestions, but to trust his own theatrical instincts in production. The actors, theater, design limitations, all will suggest a mode of production. But while the play can be done many ways, I think it must always be done with great rigor and precision.

The basic step in designing a production is to find the appropriate theatrical analogs to Mrs. Stilson's condition; the script suggests one approach. There are others.

About the characters. Billy should not seem demented or in any way sinister. He is suffering from brain damage caused by an operation to remove a brain tumor; he is *almost* all right, and must appear likeable, jovial, and *almost normal.*

The patients in the speech therapy session are all happy to be there. Their rapport with Amy is profound and immediately apparent. Amy is intuitive.

About wheelchairs. In rehearsal, we found that putting Mrs. Stilson in a wheelchair (during her early convalescence) caused the audience to worry more about her ambulatory disabilities than her aphasia. For some reason, a wheelchair on stage is a mightier symbol than one in real life. We quickly abandoned it. (Perhaps, in an environmental production, the effect would be different. I pass this information on only so the director may be forewarned and prepared.)

—Arthur Kopit
September 1979

CHARACTERS

EMILY STILSON
AMY, a therapist
DOCTORS
NURSES
BILLY, a patient
MR. BROWNSTEIN, a patient
MRS. TIMMINS, a patient

The play takes place over a period of two years; it should be performed without intermission.

NOTES ON THE PRODUCTION
OF THIS PLAY

The stage as a void.

System of black scrim panels that can move silently and easily, creating the impression of featureless, labyrinthine corridors.

Some panels mirrored so they can fracture light, create the impression of endlessness, even airiness, multiply and confuse images, confound one's sense of space.

Sound both live and pre-recorded, amplified; speakers all around the theater.

No attempt should be made to create a literal representation of Mrs. Stilson's world, especially since Mrs. Stilson's world is no longer in any way literal.

The scenes should blend. No clear boundaries or domains in time or space for Mrs. Stilson any more.

It is posited by this play that the woman we see in the center of the void is the intact inner self of Mrs. Stilson. This inner self does not need to move physically when her external body (which we cannot see) moves. Thus, we infer movement from the context; from whatever clues we can obtain. It is the same for her, of course. She learns as best she can.

And yet, sometimes, the conditions change; then the woman we observe is Mrs. Stilson as others see her. We thus infer who it is we are seeing from the context, too. Sometimes we see both the inner and outer self at once.

Nothing about her world is predictable or consistent. This fact is its essence.

The progression of the play is from fragmentation to integration. By the end, boundaries have become somewhat clearer. But she remains always in another realm from us.

PRELUDE

As audience enters, a cozy armchair visible Downstage in a pool of light, darkness surrounding it. A clock heard ticking in the dark. Lights to black. Hold.

When the lights come back, EMILY STILSON, *a woman well into her seventies, is sitting in the armchair reading a book. Some distance away, a floor lamp glows dimly. On the other side of her chair, also some distance away, a small table with a clock. The chair, the lamp, and the table with the clock all sit isolated in narrow pools of light, darkness between and around them. The clock seems to be ticking a trifle louder than normal.*

MRS. STILSON, *enjoying her book and the pleasant evening, reads on serenely. And then she looks up. The lamp disappears into the darkness. But she turns back to her book as if nothing odd has happened; resumes reading. And then, a moment later, she looks up again, an expression of slight perplexity on her face. For no discernible reason, she turns toward the clock. The clock and the table it is sitting on disappear into the darkness. She turns front. Stares out into space. Then she turns back to her book. Resumes reading. But the reading seems an effort; her mind is on other things. The clock skips a beat. Only after the clock has resumed its normal rhythm does she look up. It is as if the skipped beat has only just then registered. For the first time, she displays what one might call concern. And then the clock stops again. This time the interval lasts longer. The book slips out of* MRS. STILSON's *hands; she stares out in terror. Blackout. Noise.*

The moment of a stroke, even a relatively minor one, and its immediate aftermath, are an experience in chaos. Nothing at all makes sense. Nothing except perhaps this overwhelming disorientation will be remembered by the victim. The stroke usually happens suddenly. It is a catastrophe.

155

It is my intention that the audience recognize that some real event is occurring; that real information is being received by the victim, but that it is coming in too scrambled and too fast to be properly decoded. Systems overload.

And so this section must not seem like utter "noise," though certainly it must be more noisy than intelligible. I do not believe there is any way to be true to this material if it is not finally "composed" in rehearsal, on stage, by "feel." Theoretically, any sound or image herein described can occur anywhere in this section. The victim cannot process. Her familiar world has been rearranged. The puzzle is in pieces. All at once, and with no time to prepare, she has been picked up and dropped into another realm.

In order that this section may be put together in rehearsal (there being no one true "final order" to the images and sounds she perceives), I have divided this section into three discrete parts with the understanding that in performance these parts will blend together to form one cohesive whole.

The first group consists of the visual images Mrs. Stilson perceives.

The second group consists of those sounds emanating outside herself. Since these sounds are all filtered by her mind, and since her mind has been drastically altered, the question of whether we in the audience are hearing what is actually occurring or only hearing what she believes is occurring is unanswerable.

The third group contains Mrs. Stilson's words: the words she thinks and the words she speaks. Since we are perceiving the world through Mrs. Stilson's senses, there is no sure way for us to know whether she is actually saying any of these words aloud.

Since the experience we are exploring is not one of logic but its opposite, there is no logical reason for these groupings to occur in the order in which I have presented them. These are but components, building blocks, and can therefore be repeated, spliced, reversed, filtered, speeded up or slowed down. What should determine their final sequence and juxtaposition, tempi, intensity, is the "musical" sense of this section as a whole; it must pulse and build. An explosion quite literally is occurring in her brain, or rather, a series of explosions: the victim's mind, her sense of time and place, her sense of self, all are being shattered if not annihilated. Fortunately, finally, she will pass out. Were her head a pinball game it would register TILT—game over—stop. Silence. And resume again. Only now the victim is in yet another realm. The Catastrophe section is the journey or the fall into this strange and dreadful realm.

In the world into which Mrs. Stilson has been so violently and suddenly transposed, time and place are without definition. The distance from her old familiar world is immense. For all she knows, she could as well be on another planet.

In this new world, she moves from one space or thought or concept to another without willing or sometimes even knowing it. Indeed, when she moves in this maze-like place, it is as if the world around her and not she were doing all the moving. To her, there is nothing any more that is commonplace or predictable. Nothing is as it was. Everything comes as a surprise. Something has relieved her of command. Something beyond her comprehension has her in its grip.

In the staging of this play, the sense should therefore be conveyed of physical and emotional separation (by the use, for example, of the dark transparent screens through which her surrounding world can be only dimly and partly seen, or by alteration of external sound) and of total immersion in strangeness.

Because our focus is on Mrs. Stilson's inner self, it is important that she exhibit no particular overt physical disabilities. Furthermore, we should never see her in a wheelchair, even though, were we able to observe her through the doctors' eyes, a wheelchair is probably what she would, more often than not, be in.

One further note: because Mrs. Stilson now processes information at a different rate from us, there is no reason that what we see going on around her has to be the visual equivalent of what we hear.

CATASTROPHE

IMAGES	SOUNDS OUTSIDE HERSELF
	(SOUNDS *live or on tape, altered or unadorned.*)
	Of wind.
Mostly, it is whiteness. Dazzling, blinding.	
	Of someone breathing with effort, unevenly.
	Of something ripping like a sheet.
Occasionally, there are brief rhombs of color, explosions of color, the color red being dominant.	*Of something flapping, the sound suggestive of an old screen door perhaps, or a sheet or sail in the wind. It is a rapid fibrillation. And it is used mostly to mark transitions. It can seem ominous or not.*
The mirrors, of course, reflect infinitely. Sense of endless space, endless corridors.	*Of a woman's scream (though this sound should be altered by filters so it resembles other things, such as sirens.)*
Nothing seen that is not a fragment. Every aspect of her world has been shattered.	*Of random noises recorded in a busy city hospital, then altered so as to be only minimally recognizable.*
	Of a car's engine at full speed.
	Of a siren (altered to resemble a woman screaming).
Utter isolation.	*Of an airplane coming closer thundering overhead, then zooming off into silence.*

MRS. STILSON'S VOICE.

(VOICE *live or on tape, altered or unadorned.*)

Oh my God oh my God oh
my God—

—trees clouds houses mostly
planes flashing past, images
without words, utter disarray disbelief, never seen this
kind of thing before!

Where am I? How'd I get here?

My leg (What's my leg?)
feels wet arms . . . wet too,
belly same chin nose everything (Where are they taking
me?) something sticky (What
has happened to my plane?)
feel something sticky.

Doors! Too many doors!

                    Must
have . . . fallen cannot . . .
move at all sky . . . (Gliding!)
dark cannot . . . talk (Feel
as if I'm gliding!).

MAGES

SOUNDS OUTSIDE HERSELF01

In this vast whiteness, like apparitions, partial glimpses of doctors and nurses can be seen. They appear and disappear like a pulse. They are never in one place for long. The mirrors multiply their incomprehensibility.

Of random crowd noises, the crowd greatly agitated. In the crowd, people can be heard calling for help, a doctor, an ambulance. But all the sounds are garbled.

Of people whispering.

Of many people asking questions simultaneously, no question comprehensible.

Of doors opening, closing, opening, closing.

Sometimes the dark panels are opaque, sometimes transparent. Always, they convey a sense of layers, multiplicity, separation. Sense constantly of doors opening, closing, opening, closing.

Of someone breathing oxygen through a mask.

VOICES. (*Garbled.*) Just relax. /No one's going to hurt you. /Can you hear us?

Fragments of hospital equipment appear out of nowhere and disappear just as suddenly. Glimpse always too brief to enable us to identify what this equipment is, or what its purpose.

/Be careful! /You're hurting her!/No, we're not. /Don't lift her, leave her where she is! Someone call an ambulance!/I don't think she can hear.

MALE VOICE. Have you any idea—

OTHER VOICES. (*Garbled.*) Do you know your name?/Do you know where you are?/What year is this?/If I say the tiger has been killed by the lion, which animal is dead?

Mrs. Stilson's movements seem random. She is a person wandering through space, lost.

A hospital paging system heard.

Finally, Mrs. Stilson is led by attendants downstage, to a chair. Then left alone.

Equipment being moved through stone corridors, vast vaulting space. Endless echoing.

MRS. STILSON'S VOICE.

Yes, feels cool, nice . . .
Yes, this is the life all right!

My plane! What has hap-
pened to my plane!

Help . . .

—all around faces of which
nothing known no sense ever
all wiped out blank like ice
I think saw it once flying over
something some place all
was white sky and sea clouds
ice almost crashed couldn't
tell where I was heading right
side up topsy-turvy under over
I was flying actually if I can
I do yes do recall was upside
down can you believe it almost scraped my head on the
ice caps couldn't tell which
way was up wasn't even dizzy
strange things happen to me
that they do!

What's my name? I don't
know my name!

Where's my arm? I don't
have an arm!

What's an arm?

AB-ABC-ABC123DE4512
12 what? 123—1234567897 2357
better yes no problem I'm
okay soon be out soon be
over storm . . . will pass I'm
sure. Always has.

AWAKENING

In performance, the end of the Catastrophe section should blend, without interruption, into the beginning of this.

MRS. STILSON *Downstage on a chair in a pool of light, darkness all around her. In the distance behind her, muffled sounds of a hospital. Vague images of* DOCTORS, NURSES *attending to someone we cannot see. One of the* DOCTORS *calls* MRS. STILSON'S *name. Downstage,* MRS. STILSON *shows no trace of recognition. The* DOCTOR *calls her name again. Again no response. One of the* DOCTORS *says, "It's possible she may hear us but be unable to respond."*

One of the NURSES *tries calling out her name. Still no response. The* DOCTOR *leaves. The remaining* DOCTORS *and* NURSES *fade into the darkness. Only* MRS. STILSON *can be seen. Pause.*

MRS. STILSON. Still . . . sun moon too or . . . three times happened maybe globbidged rubbidged uff and firded-forded me to nothing there try again (*We hear a window being raised somewhere behind her.*) window! up and heard (*Sounds of birds.*) known them know I know them once upon a birds! that's it better getting better soon be out of this. (*Pause.*) Out of . . . what? (*Pause.*) Dark . . . space vast of . . . in I am or so it seems feels no real clues to speak of. (*Behind her, brief image of a* DOCTOR *passing.*) Something tells me I am not alone. Once! Lost it. No here back thanks work fast now, yes empty vast reach of space desert think they call it I'll come back to that anyhow down I . . . something what (*Brief image of a* NURSE.) it's SOMETHING ELSE IS ENTERING MY!— no wait got it crashing OH MY GOD! CRASHING! deadstick dead-of-night thought the stars were airport lights upside down was I what a way to land glad no one there to see it, anyhow tubbish blaxed and vinkled I commenshed to uh-oh where's it gone to somewhere flubbished what? with (*Brief images of hospital staff on the move.*) images are SOMETHING ODD IS!

. . . yes, then there I thank you crawling sands and knees
still can feel it hear the wind all alone somehow wasn't scared
why a mystery, vast dark track of space, we've all got to
die that I know, anyhow then day came light came with it
so with this you'd think you'd hope just hold on they will
find me I am . . . still intact. (*Pause.*) In here. (*Long silence.*)
Seem to be the word removed. (Long silence.) How long have I
been here? . . . And wrapped in dark. (*Pause.*) Can remember
nothing.

(*Outside sounds begin to impinge; same for images. In the
distance, an attendant dimly seen pushing a floor polisher. Its
noise resembles an animal's growl.*)

MRS. STILSON. (*Trying hard to be cheery.*) No, definitely I
am not alone! (*The sound of the polisher grows louder, seems
more bestial, voracious; it overwhelms everything. Explosion!
She gasps. Rapidly and in panic, sense of great commotion
behind her. A crisis has occurred.*) There I go there I go hallway
now it's screaming crowded pokes me then the coolbreeze
needle scent of sweetness can see palms flowers flummers couldn't
fix the leaking sprouting everywhere to save me help me CUTS
UP THROUGH to something movement I am something moving without movement!

(*Sound of a woman's muffled scream from behind her. The
scream grows louder.*)

MRS. STILSON. (*With delight.*) What a strange adventure I am
having!

(*Lights to black on everything. In the dark, a pause. When her
voice is heard again, it is heard first from all the speakers. Her
voice sounds groggy, slurred. No longer any sense of panic discernible. A few moments after her voice is heard, the lights come
up slowly on her. Soon, only she is speaking; the voice from the
speakers has disappeared.*)

MRS. STILSON. Hapst aporkship fleetish yes of course it's
yes the good ol' times when we would mollis I mean collis
all around still what my son's name is cannot for the life
of me yet face gleams smiles as he tells them what I did but
what his name is cannot see it pleasant anyway yes palms now
ocean sea breeze wafting floating up and lifting holding

weightless and goes swooooping down with me least I . . . think
it's me.

(*Sound of something flapping rapidly open and closed, open
and closed. Sound of wind. Lights change into a cool and airy
blue. Sense of weightlessness, serenity. In another realm now.*)

MRS. STILSON. Yes, out there walking not holding even
danger ever-present how I loved it love it still no doubt will
again hear them cheering wisht or waltz away to some place
like Rumania . . . (*The wind disappears.*) Nothing . . . (*The
serene blue light begins to fade away. Some place else now that
she is going.*) Of course beyond that yet 1, 2 came before the
yeast rose bubbled and MY CHUTE DIDN'T OPEN PROP-
ERLY! Still for a girl did wonders getting down and it was
Charles! no Charlie, who is Charlie? see him smiling as they tell
him what I—

(*Outside world begins to impinge. Lights are changing, growing brighter, something odd is happening. Sense of imminence.
She notices.*)

MRS. STINSON. (*Breathless with excitement.*) Stop hold cut
stop wait stop come-out-break-out light can see it ready heart
can yes can feel it pounding something underway here light is
getting brighter lids I think the word is that's it lifting of their
own but slowly knew I should be patient should be what? wait
hold on steady now it's spreading no no question something
underway here spreading brighter rising lifting light almost yes
can almost there a little more now yes can almost see this . . .
place I'm . . . in and . . . (*Look of horror.*) Oh my God! Now
I understand! THEY'VE GOT ME!

(*For first time doctors, nurses, hospital equipment all clearly
visible behind her. All are gathered around someone we cannot
see. From the way they are all bending over, we surmise this
person we cannot see is lying in a bed. Lights drop on MRS.
STILSON, Downstage.*)

NURSE. (*Talking to the person Upstage we cannot see.*) Mrs.
Stilson, can you open your eyes? (*Pause.*)
MRS. STILSON. (*Separated from her questioners by great dis-
tance.*) Don't know how.
DOCTOR. Mrs. Stilson, you just opened your eyes. We

saw you. Can you open them again? (*No response.*) Mrs. Stilson . . . ?

MRS. STILSON. (*Proudly, triumphantly.*) My name then—Mrs. Stilson!

VOICE ON P.A. SYSTEM. Mrs. Howard, call on three! Mrs. Howard . . . !

MRS. STILSON. My name then—Mrs. Howard?

(*Lights fade to black on hospital staff. Sound of wind, sense of time passing. Lights come up on* MRS. STILSON. *The wind disappears.*)

MRS. STILSON. The room that I am in is large, square. What does large mean? (*Pause.*) The way I'm turned I can see a window. When I'm on my back the window isn't there.

DOCTOR. (*In the distance, at best only dimly seen.*) Mrs. Stilson, can you hear me?

MRS. STILSON. Yes.

SECOND DOCTOR. Mrs. Stilson, can you hear me?

MRS. STILSON. Yes! I said yes! What's wrong with you?

FIRST DOCTOR. Mrs. Stilson, CAN YOU HEAR ME!

MRS. STILSON. Don't believe this—I've been put in with the deaf!

SECOND DOCTOR. Mrs. Stilson, if you can hear us, nod your head.

MRS. STILSON. All right, fine, that's how you want to play it—there! (*She nods. The* DOCTORS *exchange glances.*)

FIRST DOCTOR. Mrs. Stilson, if you can hear us, NOD YOUR HEAD!

MRS. STILSON. Oh my God, this is grotesque!

(*Cacophony of sounds heard from all around, both live and from the speakers. Images suggesting sensation of assault as well. Implication of all these sounds and images is that* MRS. STILSON *is being moved through the hospital for purposes of examination, perhaps even torture. The information we receive comes in too fast and distorted for rational comprehension. The realm she is in is terrifying. Fortunately, she is not in it long. As long as she is, however, the sense should be conveyed that her world moves around her more than she through it. What we hear.*)

THE COMPONENTS. Are we moving you too fast? /Mustlian pottid or blastigrate, no not that way this, that's fletchit gottit careful now. / Now put your nose here on this line, would you?

That's it, thank you, well done, well done. / How are the
wickets today? / (*Sound of a cough.*) / Now close your— / Is my
finger going up or— / Can you feel this? / Can you feel this? /
Name something that grows on trees. / Who fixes teeth? / What
room do you cook in? / What year is this? / How long have you
been here? / Are we being too rippled shotgun? / Would you
like a cup of tea? / What is Jim short for? / Point to your
shoulder. / No, your shoulder. / What do you do with a book? /
Don't worry, the water's warm. We're holding you, don't worry.
In we go, that's a girl!

(*And then, as suddenly as the assault began, it is over. Once
again, MRS. STILSON all alone on stage, darkness all around her,
no sense of walls or furniture. Utter isolation.*)

MRS. STILSON. (*Trying hard to keep smiling.*) Yes, all in all
I'd say while things could be better could be worse, far worse,
how? Not quite sure. Just a sense I have. The sort of sense that
only great experience can mallees or rake, plake I mean, flake
. . . Drake! That's it. (*She stares into space. Silence. In the
distance behind her, two DOCTORS appear.*)

FIRST DOCTOR. Mrs. Stilson, who was the first President of
the United States?

MRS. STILSON. Washington. (*Pause.*)

SECOND DOCTOR. (*Speaking more slowly than the FIRST
DOCTOR did; perhaps she simply didn't hear the question.*) Mrs.
Stilson, who was the first President of the United States?

MRS. STILSON. Washington!

SECOND DOCTOR. (*To first.*) I don't think she hears herself.

FIRST DOCTOR. No, I don't think she hears herself.

(*The two DOCTORS emerge from the shadows, approach MRS.
STILSON. She looks up in terror. This should be the first time
that the woman on stage has been directly faced or confronted by
the hospital staff. Her inner and outer worlds are beginning to
come together.*)

FIRST DOCTOR. Mrs. Stilson, makey your naming powers?

MRS. STILSON. What?

SECOND DOCTOR. Canju spokeme?

MRS. STILSON. Can I what?

FIRST DOCTOR. Can do peerperear?

MRS. STILSON. Don't believe what's going on!

SECOND DOCTOR. Ahwill.

FIRST DOCTOR. Pollycadjis.

SECOND DOCTOR. Sewyladda?

FIRST DOCTOR. (*With a nod.*) Hm-hm. (*Exit* DOCTORS.)

MRS. STILSON. (*Alone again.*) How it came to pass that I was captured! (*She ponders.*) Hard to say really. I'll come back to that. (*Pause.*) The room that I've been put in this time is quite small, square, what does square mean? . . . Means . . . (*Sense of time passing. The lights shift. The space she is in begins to change its shape.*) Of course morning comes I think . . . (*She ponders.*) Yes, and night of course comes . . . (*Ponders more.*) Though sometimes . . . (MRS. STILSON *some place else now. And she is aware of it.*) Yes, the way the walls choose to move around me . . . Yes, I've noticed that, I'm no fool! (*A* NURSE *appears carrying a dazzling bouquet of flowers. This bouquet is the first real color we have seen.*)

NURSE. Good morning! Look what somebody's just sent you! (*She sets them on a table.*) Wish I had as many admirers as you.

(*Exit* NURSE, *smiling warmly.* MRS. STILSON'*s eyes are drawn to the flowers. And something about them apparently renders it impossible for her to shift her gaze away. Something about these flowers has her in their thrall. What it is is their color. It is as if she has never experienced color before. And the experience is so overwhelming, both physiologically and psychologically, that her brain cannot process all the information. Her circuitry is over-loaded. It is too much sensory input for her to handle. An explosion is imminent. If something does not intervene to divert her attention,* MRS. STILSON *will very likely faint, perhaps even suffer a seizure. A narrow beam of light, growing steadily in intensity, falls upon the bouquet of flowers, causing their colors to take on an intensity themselves that they otherwise would lack. At the same time, a single musical tone is heard, volume increasing. A* NURSE *enters the room.*)

NURSE. May I get you something?

MRS. STILSON. (*Abstracted, eyes remaining on the flowers.*) Yes, a sweater.

NURSE. Yes, of course. Think we have one here. (*The* NURSE *opens a drawer, takes out a pillow, hands the pillow to* MRS. STILSON.) Here.

(MRS. STILSON *accepts the pillow unquestioningly, eyes never leaving the flowers. She lays the pillow on her lap, promptly forgets about it. The musical tone and the beam of light continue relentlessly toward their peak. The* NURSE, *oblivious of any crisis, exits. The single tone and the beam of light crest together. Silence follows. The beam disappears. The flowers seem normal. The lights around* MRS. STILSON *return to the way they were before the gift of flowers was brought in.*)

MRS. STILSON. (*Shaken.*) This is not a hospital of course, and I know it! What it is is a farmhouse made up to look like a hospital. Why? I'll come back to that. (*Enter another* NURSE.)

NURSE. Hi! Haven't seen you in a while. Have you missed me?

MRS. STILSON. (*No hint of recognition visible.*) What?

NURSE. (*Warmly.*) They say you didn't touch your dinner. Would you like some pudding?

MRS. STILSON. No.

NURSE. Good, I'll go get you some. (*Exit* NURSE, *very cheerfully.*)

MRS. STILSON. Yes no question they have got me I've been what that word was captured is it? No it's—Yes, it's captured how? Near as it can figure. I was in my prane and crashed, not unusual, still in all not too common. Neither is it very grub. Plexit rather or I'd say propopic. Well that's that, jungdaball! Anyhow to resume, what I had for lunch? That's not it, good books I have read, good what, done what? Whaaaaat? Do the busy here! Get inside this, rubbidge all around let the vontul do some yes off or it of above semilacrum pwooosh! what with noddygobbit nip-n-crashing inside outside witsit watchit funnel vortex sucking into backlash watchit get-out caught-in spinning ring-grab grobbit help woooosh! cannot stoppit on its own has me where it wants. (*And suddenly she is in another realm. Lights transformed into weightless blue. Sense of ease and serenity.*) Plane! See it thanks, okay, onto back we were and here it is. Slow down easy now. Captured. After crashing, that is what we said or was about to, think it so, cannot tell for sure, slow it slow it, okay here we go . . . (*Speaking slower now.*) captured after crashing by the enemy and brought here to this farm masquerading as a hospital. Why? For I would say offhand information. Of what sort though hard to tell. For example, questions such as can I raise my fingers, what's an overcoat, how many nickels in a rhyme, questions such as these. To what use can they be to the enemy? Hard to tell from here. Nonetheless, I would say must be certain information I possess that they want well I won't give it I'll escape! Strange things happen to me that they do! Good thing I'm all right! Must be in Rumania.

Just a hunch of course. (*The serene blue light starts to fade.*)
Ssssh, someone's coming.

(A NURSE *has entered. The* NURSE *guides* MRS. STILSON *to a*
DOCTOR. *The blue light is gone. The* NURSE *leaves. The space*
MRS. STILSON *now is in appears much more "real" and less*
fragmentary than what we have so far been observing. We see
MRS. STILSON *here as others see her.*)

DOCTOR. Mrs. Stilson, if you don't mind, I'd like to ask you
some questions. Some will be easy, some will be hard. Is that
all right?

MRS. STILSON. Oh yes I'd say oh well yes that's the twither of
it.

DOCTOR. Good. Okay. Where were you born?

MRS. STILSON. Never. Not at all. Here the match wundles up
you know and drats flames fires I keep careful always—

DOCTOR. Right . . . (*Speaking very slowly, precise enuncia-*
tion.) Where were you born?

MRS. STILSON. Well now well now that's a good thing knowing yushof course wouldn't call it such as I did andinjurations or
aplovia could it? No I wouldn't think so. Next? (*Pause.*)

DOCTOR. Mrs. Stilson, are there seven days in a week?

MRS. STILSON. . . . Seven . . . Yes.

DOCTOR. Are there five days in a week? (*Pause.*)

MRS. STILSON. (*After much pondering.*) No.

DOCTOR. Can a stone float on water? (*Long pause.*)

MRS. STILSON. No.

DOCTOR. Mrs. Stilson, can you cough?

MRS. STILSON. Somewhat.

DOCTOR. Well, would you show me how you cough?

MRS. STILSON. Well now well now not so easy what you
cromplie is to put these bushes open and—

DOCTOR. No no, Mrs. Stilson, I'm sorry—I would like to
hear you cough.

MRS. STILSON. Well I'm not bort you know with plajits or
we'd see it wencherday she brings its pillow with the fistils-
opening I'd say outward always outward never stopping it.
(*Long silence.*)

DOCTOR. Mrs. Stilson, I have some objects here. (*He takes a*
comb, a toothbrush, a pack of matches, and a key from his
pocket, sets them down where she can see.) Could you point to
the object you would use for cleaning your teeth? (*Very long*
silence. Finally she picks up the comb and shows it to him. Then

she puts it down. Waits.) Mrs. Stilson, here, take this object in your hand. (*He hands her the toothbrush.*) Do you know what this object is called?

MRS. STILSON. (*With great difficulty.*) Toooooooooovvvv . . . bbbrum?

DOCTOR. Very good. Now put it down. (*She puts it down.*) Now, pretend you have it in your hand. Show me what you'd do with it. (*She does nothing.*) What does one do with an object such as that, MRS. STILSON? (*No response.*) MRS. STILSON, what is the name of the object you are looking at?

MRS. STILSON. Well it's . . . wombly and not at all . . . rigged or tuned like we might twunter or toring to work the clambness out of it or—

DOCTOR. Pick it up.

MRS. STILSON. (*As soon as she's picked it up.*) Tooovebram, tooove-britch bratch brush bridge, two-bridge.

DOCTOR. Show me what you do with it. (*For several moments she does nothing, then she puts it to her lips, holds it there motionless.*) Very good. Thank you.

(*She sighed heavily, puts it down. The* DOCTOR *gathers up his objects, leaves. Once again* MRS. STILSON *all alone. She stares into space. Then her voice is heard coming from all around; she herself does not speak.*)

HER VOICE. Dark now again out the window on my side lying here all alone . . . (*Very long silence.*)

MRS. STILSON. Yesterday my children came to see me. (*Pause.*) Or at least, I was told they were my children. Never saw them before in my life. (*She stares out, motionless. No expression. Then after a while she looks around. Studies the dark for clues.*) Time has become peculiar.

(*And she continues this scrutiny of the dark. But if this activity stems from curiosity, it is a mild curiosity at most. No longer does she convey or probably even experience the extreme, disoriented dread we saw earlier when she first arrived in this new realm. Her sense of urgency is gone. Indeed, were we able to observe* MRS. STILSON *constantly, we would inevitably conclude that her curiosity is now only minimally purposeful; that, in fact, more likely her investigations are the actions, possibly merely the reflex actions, of someone with little or nothing else to do. This is not to deny that she is desperately trying to piece her shattered world together. Undoubtedly, it is the dominant motif in her mind. But it is a motif probably more absent from her consciousness than present, and the quest it inspires is intermittent at best. Her mental abilities have not only been severely altered, they have been diminished: that is the terrible fact one cannot deny. And then suddenly she is agitated.*)

MRS. STILSON. Mother! . . . didn't say as she usually . . . (*Pause.*) And I thought late enough or early rather first light coming so when didn't move I poked her then with shoving but she didn't even eyes or giggle when I tickled. (*Pause.*) What it was was not a trick as I at first had— (*Pause.*) Well I couldn't figure, he had never lied, tried to get her hold me couldn't it was useless. Then his face was, I had never known a face could . . . It was like a mask then like sirens it was bursting open it was him then I too joining it was useless. Can still feel what it was like when she held me. (*Pause.*) So then well I was on my own. He was all destroyed, had I think they say no strength for this. (*Then she's silent. No expression. Stares into space. Enter a* DOCTOR *and a* NURSE.)

DOCTOR. (*Warmly.*) Hello, Mrs. Stilson. (*He comes over next to her. We cannot tell if she notices him or not. The* NURSE, *chart in hand, stands a slight distance away.*) You're looking much, much better. (*He smiles and sits down next to her. He watches her for several moments, searching for signs of recognition.*) Mrs. Stilson, do you know why you're here?

MRS. STILSON. Well now well now . . . (*She gives it up. Silence.*)

DOCTOR. You have had an accident—

MRS. STILSON.

(*Her words over-powering his.*) I don't trust him, don't trust anyone. Must get word out, send a message where I am. Like a wall between me and others. No one ever gets it right even though I tell them right. They are playing tricks on me, two sides, both not my friends, goes in goes out too fast too fast hurts do the busy I'm all right I talk right why acting all these others like I don't, what's he marking, what's he writing?

DOCTOR.

(*To all intents and purposes, what he says is lost.*) At home. Not in an airplane. It's called a stroke. This means that your brain has been injured and brain tissue destroyed, though we are not certain of the cause. You could get better, and you're certainly making progress. But it's still too soon to give any sort of exact prognosis. (*He studies her. Then he rises and marks something on his clipboard.*)

(*Exit* DOCTOR *and* NURSE.)

MRS. STILSON. I am doing well of course! (*Pause. Secretive tone.*) They still pretend they do not understand me. I believe they may be mad. (*Pause.*) No they're not mad, I am mad. Today I heard it. Everything I speak is wronged. SOMETHING HAS BEEN DONE TO ME!

DOCTOR. (*Barely visible in the distance.*) Mrs. Stilson, can you repeat this phrase: "We live across the street from the school." (*She ponders.*)

MRS. STILSON. "Malacats on the forturay are the kesterfats of the romancers."

(*Look of horror comes across her face; the* DOCTOR *vanishes. Through the screens, Upstage, we see a* NURSE *bringing on a tray of food.*)

NURSE. (*Brightly.*) Okay ups-a-girl, ups-a-baby, dinnertime! Open wide now, mustn't go dribble-dribble—at's-a-way!

MRS. STILSON. (*Screams, swings her arms in fury. In the distance, Upstage, the tray of food goes flying.*) Out! Get out! Take this shit away, I don't want it! Someone get me out of here!

NURSE. (*While* MRS. STILSON *continues shouting.*) Help, someone, come quick! She's talking! Good as you or me! It's a miracle! Help! Somebody! Come quick!

(*While* MRS. STILSON *continues to scream and flail her arms,* NURSES *and* DOCTORS *rush on Upstage and surround the patient we never see. And although* MRS. STILSON *continues to scream coherently, in fact she isn't any better, no miracle has occurred. Her ability to articulate with apparent normalcy has been brought on by extreme agitation and in no way implies that she could produce these sounds again "if she only wanted"; will power has nothing to do with what we hear. Her language, as it must, soon slips back into jargon. She continues to flail her arms. In the background, we can see a* NURSE *preparing a hypodermic.*)

MRS. STILSON. (*Struggling.*) —flubdgy please no-mommy-callming holdmeplease to sleeEEEEP SHOOOOP shop shnoper CRROOOOOCK SNANNING wuduitcoldly should I gobbin flutter truly HELP ME yessisnofun, snofun, wishes awhin dahd killminsilf if . . . could. (*In the distance, we see the needle given.*) OW! . . . would I but . . . (*She's becoming drowsy.*)

awful to me him as well moas of all no cantduit . . . jusscant-
duit . . .

(*Head drops. Into sleep she goes. Exit* DOCTORS, NURSES.
Sound of a gentle wind is heard. Lights fade to black on MRS.
STILSON. *Darkness everywhere; the sound of the wind fades
away. Silence. Lights up on* AMY, *Downstage Right. Then lights
up on* MRS. STILSON *staring into space.*)

AMY. Mrs. Stilson? (MRS. STILSON *turns toward the sound,
sees* AMY.) You have had what's called a stroke. (*Change of
lights and panels open. Sense of terrible enclosure gone. Birds
heard. We are outside now.* AMY *puts a shawl around* MRS.
STILSON's *shoulders.*) Are you sure that will be enough?

MRS. STILSON. Oh yes . . . thhhankyou. (*She tucks the shawl
around herself. Then* AMY *guides her through the panels as if
through corridors; no rush, slow gentle stroll. They emerge other
side of stage. Warm light.* AMY *takes in the view.* MRS. STILSON
appears indifferent.)
AMY. Nice to be outside, isn't it? . . . Nice view.
MRS. STILSON. (*Still with indifference.*) Yes indeed. (*There
are two chairs nearby, and they sit. Silence for a time.*)
AMY. Are you feeling any better today? (*But she gets no
response. Then, a moment later,* MRS. STILSON *turns to* AMY; *it
is as if* AMY's *question has not been heard.*)
MRS. STILSON. The thing is . . . (*But the statement trails off
into nothingness. She stares out, no expression.*)
AMY. Yes? What? (*Long silence.*)
MRS. STILSON. I can't make it do it like it used to.
AMY. Yes, I know. That's because of the accident.
MRS. STILSON. (*Seemingly oblivious of* AMY's *words.*) The
words, they go in sometimes then out they go, I can't stop them
here inside or make maybe globbidge to the tubberway or—
AMY. Emily. Emily!
MRS. STILSON. (*Shaken out of herself.*) . . . What?
AMY. Did you hear what you just said?
MRS. STILSON. . . . Why?
AMY. (*Speaking slowly.*) You must listen to what you're
saying.
MRS. STILSON. Did I . . . do . . .
AMY. (*Nodding, smiling; clearly no reproach intended.*) Slow
down. Listen to what you're saying. (*Silence.*)
MRS. STILSON. (*Slower.*) The thing is . . . doing all this busy

in here gets, you know with the talking it's like . . . sometimes when I hear here (*She touches her head.*) . . . but when I start to . . . kind more what kind of voice should . . . it's like pfffft!" (*She makes a gesture with her hand of something flying away.*)

AMY. (*Smiling.*) Yes, I know. It's hard to find the words for what you're thinking of.

MRS. STILSON. Well yes. (*Long pause.*) And then these people, they keep waiting . . . And I see they're smiling and . . . they keep . . . waiting . . . (*Faint smile, helpless gesture. She stares off. Long silence.*)

AMY. Emily. (MRS. STILSON *looks up.*) Can you remember anything about your life . . . before the accident?

MRS. STILSON. Not sometimes, some days it goes better if I see a thing or smell . . . it . . . remembers me back, you see? And I see things that maybe they were me and maybe they were just some things you know that happens in the night when you . . . (*Struggling visibly.*) have your things closed, eyes.

AMY. A dream you mean.

MRS. STILSON. (*With relief.*) Yes. So I don't know for sure. (*Pause.*) If it was really me. (*Long silence.*)

AMY. Your son is bringing a picture of you when you were younger. We thought you might like that. (*No visible response. Long silence.*) You used to fly, didn't you?

MRS. STILSON. (*Brightly.*) Oh yes indeed! Very much! I walked . . . out . . . (*Pause. Softly, proudly.*) I walked out on wings. (*Lights fade on* AMY. MRS. STILSON *alone again.*) Sitting here on my bed I can close my eyes shut out all that I can't do with, hearing my own talking, others, names that used to well just be there when I wanted now all somewhere else. No control. Close my eyes then, go to— (*Sound of something flapping rapidly. A fibrillation. Lights become blue. Sense of weightlessness, serenity.*) Here I go. No one talks here. Images coming I seem feel it feels better this way here is how it goes: this time I am still in the middle Stilson in the middle going out walking out wind feels good hold the wires feel the hum down below far there they are now we turn it bank it now we spin! Looks more bad than really is, still needs good balance and those nerves and that thing that courage thing don't fall off! . . . And now I'm out . . . and back and . . . (*With surprise.*) there's the window. (*Lights have returned to normal. She is back where she started.* AMY *enters.*)

AMY. Hello, Emily.

MRS. STILSON. Oh, Amy! . . . Didn't hear what you was . . . coming here to . . . Oh!

AMY. What is it?

MRS. STILSON. Something . . . wet.

AMY. Do you know what it is?

MRS. STILSON. Don't . . . can't say find it word.

AMY. Try. You can find it.

MRS. STILSON. Wet . . . thing, many, both sides yes.

AMY. Can you name them? What they are? You do know what they are. (*Pause.*)

MRS. STILSON. . . . Tears?

AMY. That's right, very good. Those are tears. And do you know what that means?

MRS. STILSON. . . . Sad?

AMY. Yes, right, well done, it seems . . . that you are sad.

EXPLORATIONS

Stage dark. In the dark, a piano heard: someone fooling around on the keyboard, brief halting snatches of old songs emerging as the product; would constitute a medley were the segments only longer, more cohesive. As it is, suspicion aroused that what we hear is all the pianist can remember. Sound of general laughter, hubbub. Lights rise.

What we see is a rec room, in some places clearly, in others not (the room being observed partly through the dark scrim panels). Upstage Right, an upright piano, players and friends gathered round. Doctors, therapists, nurses, attendants, patients, visitors certainly are not all seen, but those we do see come from such a group. We are in the rec room of a rehabilitation center. Some patients in wheelchairs. The room itself has bright comfortable chairs, perhaps a card table, magazine rack, certainly a TV set. Someone now turns on the TV.

What emerges is the sound of Ella Fitzgerald in live performance. She sings scat: mellow, upbeat. The patients and staff persuade the pianist to cease. Ella's riffs of scat cast something like a spell.

MRS. STILSON *wanders through the space. The rec room, it should be stressed, shows more detail and color than any space we've so far seen. Perhaps a vase of flowers helps to signal that* MRS. STILSON'S *world is becoming fuller, more integrated. Movements too seem normal, same for conversations that go on during all of this, though too softly for us to comprehend. The music of course sets the tone. All who listen are in its thrall.*

New time sense here, a languor almost. The dread MRS. STILSON *felt has been replaced by an acknowledgment of her condition, though not an understanding. In this time before she speaks, and in fact during, we observe the life of the rec room behind and around her. This is not a hospital any more, and a kind of normalcy prevails. The sense should be conveyed of corridors leading to and from this room.*

Then the music and the rec room sounds grow dim; MRS.
STILSON *comes forward, lost in the drifts of a thought.*

MRS. STILSON. (*Relaxed, mellow.*) Wonder . . . what's inside of
it . . . ? (*Pause.*) I mean, how does it work? What's inside that
. . . makes it work? (*Long pause. She ponders.*) I mean when
you . . . think about it all . . . (*Pause.*) And when you think
that it could . . . ever have been . . . possible to . . . be another
way . . . (*She ponders. But it's hard for her to keep in mind
what she's been thinking of, and she has to fight the noise of the
rec room, its intrusive presence. Like a novice juggler,* MRS.
STILSON *is unable to keep outside images and inner thoughts
going simultaneously. When she's with her thoughts, the outside
world fades away. When the outside world is with her, her
thoughts fade away. But she fights her way through it, and keeps
the thought in mind. The rec room, whose noise has just in-
creased, grows quiet.*) Maybe . . . if somehow I could—(*She
searches for the words that match her concept.*)—get inside . . .
(*Pause. Sounds of the rec room pulse louder. She fights against
it. The rec room sounds diminish.*) Prob'ly . . . very dark inside
. . . (*She ponders; tries to picture what she's thinking.*) Yes . . .
twisting kind of place I bet . . . (*Ponders more.*) With lots of
. . . (*She searches for the proper word; finds it.*) passageways
that . . . lead to . . . (*Again, she searches for the word. The
outside world rushes in.*)

PATIENT IN A WHEELCHAIR. (*Only barely audible.*) My foot
feels sour. (*An attendant puts a lap rug over the patient's limbs.
Then the rec room, once again, fades away.*)

MRS. STILSON. (*Fighting on.*) . . . lead to . . . something . . .
Door! Yes . . . closed off now I . . . guess possib . . . ly for
good I mean . . . forever, what does that mean? (*She ponders.*)

ATTENDANT. Would you like some candy?

MRS. STILSON. No.

ATTENDANT. Billy made it.

MRS. STILSON. No! (*The* ATTENDANT *moves back into the
shadows.*) Where was I? (*She looks around.*) Why can't they
just . . . let me . . . be when I'm . . . (*Lights start to change.
Her world suddenly in flux. The rec room fades from view.
Sounds of birds heard, dimly at first. Aware of the change as it is
occurring.*) okay. Slipping out of . . . it and . . . (MRS. STILSON
in a different place.) Outside now! How . . . did I do that?

AMY. (*Emerging from the shadows.*) Do you like this new
place better?

MRS. STILSON. Oh well oh well yes, much, all . . . nice flowers here, people seem . . . more like me. Thank you. (AMY *moves back toward the shadows.*) And then I see it happen once again . . . (AMY *gone from sight.*) Amy kisses me. Puts her—what thing is it, arm! yes, arm, puts her arm around my . . . (*Pause.*) shoulder, turns her head away so I can't . . (*Pause.*) Well, it knows what she's doing. May not get much better even though I'm here. No, I know that. I know that. No real need for her to . . . (*Long pause.*) Then she kisses me again. (*Pause.*) Walks away . . .

(*Pause. Lights change again, world again in flux. Noises of the building's interior can be heard like a babel, only fleetingly coherent. The rec room seen dissolving.*)

MRS. STILSON. Where am I? (*She begins to wander through a maze of passageways. The mirrors multiply her image, create a sense of endlessness.*)

(*NOTE. The following blocks of sound, which accompany her expedition, are meant to blend and overlap in performance and, to that end, can be used in any order and combined in any way desired, except for the last five blocks, numbers 12-16, which must be performed in their given sequence and in a way that is comprehensible. The sounds themselves may be live or prerecorded; those which are pre-recorded should emanate from all parts of the theater and in no predictable pattern. The effect should be exhilarating and disorienting. An adventure. With terrifying aspects to be sure. But the sense of mystery and adventure must never be so overwhelmed by the terror that it is either lost altogether or submerged to the point of insignificance. MRS. STILSON may be frightened here, but the fear does not prevent her from exploring. She wanders through the labyrinth of dark panels as if they were so many doors, each door leading into yet another realm.*)

BLOCK 1. It was but a few years later that Fritsch and Hitzig stimulated the cortex of a dog with an electric current. Here at last was dramatic and indisputable evidence that—

BLOCK 2. Would you like me to change the channel?

BLOCK 3. . . . presented, I would say, essentially similar conclusions on the behavioral correlates of each cerebral convolution.

BLOCK 4. (*Being the deep male voice, speaking slowly,*

*enunciating carefully, that one hears on the speech-therapy
machine known as "The Language Master."*) Mother led Bud to
the bed.

BLOCK 5. . . . In the laboratory then, through electrical stim-
ulation of neural centers or excisions of areas of the brain,
scientists acquired information about the organization of mental
activities in the monkey, the dog, the cat, and the rat. The
discovery of certain peculiar clinical pictures, reminiscent of
bizarre human syndromes, proved of special interest.

BLOCK 6. Can you tell me what this object's called?

BLOCK 7. Ella's riffs of scat, as if we were still in the rec
room after all.

BLOCK 8. One has only to glance through the writings of this
period to sense the heightened excitement attendant upon these
discoveries!

BLOCK 9. Possibly some diaschisis, which would of course
help account for the apparent mirroring. And then, of course,
we must not overlook the fact that she's left-handed.

BLOCK 10. Of course, you understand, these theories may all
be wrong! (*Sound of laughter from an audience.*) Any other
questions? Yes, over there, in the corner.

BLOCK 11. Mrs. Stilson, this is Dr. Rogans. Dr. Rogans, this
is Emily Stilson.

BLOCK 12. (*Male voice.*)—definite possibility I would say of a
tiny subclinical infarct in Penfield's area. Yes? (*Female Voice.*)
Are you sure there is a Penfield's area? (*Male Voice.*) No.
(*Laughter from his audience. Male Voice again, itself on the
verge of laughter.*) But *something* is wrong with her! (*Raucous
laughter from his audience.*)

NOTE. Emerging out of the laughter in BLOCK *12, a single
musical TONE. This tone increases in intensity. It should carry
through* BLOCK *16 and into* MRS. STILSON's *emergence from the
maze of panels, helping to propel her into the realm and the
memory to which this expedition has been leading.*)

BLOCK 13. The controversy, of course, is that some feel
it's language without thought, and others, thought without
language . . .

BLOCK 14. What it is, of course, is the symbol system. Their
symbol system's shot. They can't make analogies.

BLOCK 15. You see, it's all so unpredictable. There are no
fixed posts, no clear boundaries. The victim, you could say, has
been cut adrift . . .

BLOCK 16. Ah, now you're really flying blind there!

* * *

(MRS. STILSON *emerges from the maze of corridors. Sound perhaps of wind, or bells. Lights blue, sense again of weightlessness, airiness.*)

MRS. STILSON. (*In awe and ecstasy.*) As I see it now, the plane was flying BACKWARDS! Really, wind that strong, didn't know it could be! Yet the sky was clear, not a cloud, crystal blue, gorgeous, angels could've lived in the sky like that . . . I think the cyclone must've blown in on the Andes from the sea . . . (*Blue light fades. Wind gone, bells gone, musical tone is gone. Coming out of it.*) Yes . . . (*She looks around; gets her bearings.*) Yes, no question, this . . . place better. (*And now she's landed.*) All these people just . . . like me, I guess. (*She takes in where she is, seems slightly stunned to be back where she started. Sense of wonderment apparent. An attendant approaches.*)

ATTENDANT. Mrs. Stilson?
MRS. STILSON. (*Startled.*) Oh!
ATTENDANT. Sorry to—
MRS. STILSON. Is it . . . ?
ATTENDANT. Yes.
MRS. STILSON. Did I . . . ?
ATTENDANT. No, no need to worry. Here, I'll take you. (*The* ATTENDANT *guides* MRS. STILSON *to a therapy room, though, in fact, more likely [on the stage] the room assembles around her. In the room are* AMY, BILLY *[a man in his middle thirties],* MRS. TIMMINS *[elderly, in a wheelchair], and* MR. BROWNSTEIN *[also elderly and in a wheelchair]. The* ATTENDANT *leaves.*)

AMY. Well! Now that we're all here on this lovely afternoon, I thought that maybe—
BILLY. She looks really good.
AMY. What?
BILLY. This new lady here, can't remember what her name is, no bother, anyhow, she looks really nice all dressed like this, an' I jus' wanna extent a nice welcome here on behalf o' all of us. (*The other patients mumble their assent.*)
AMY. Well, that is very nice, Billy, very nice. Can any of the rest of you remember this woman's name?
BILLY. I seen her I think when it is, yesterday, how's that?
AMY. Very good, that's right, you met her for the first time yesterday. Now, can any of you remember her name?

BILLY. Dolores.

AMY. (*Laughing slightly.*) No, not Dolores.

MR. BROWNSTEIN. She vas, I caught sight ya know, jussa-minute, flahtied or vhat, vhere, midda (*He hums a note.*)—

AMY. Music.

MR. BROWNSTEIN. Yeah right goodgirlie right she vas lissning, I caught slight, saw her vooding bockstond tipping-n-topping de foot vas jussnow like dis. (*He starts to stamp his foot.*)

AMY. Mrs. Stilson, were you inside listening to some music just now?

MRS. STILSON. Well . . . (*Pause. Very fast.*) Well now I was yes in the what in-the-in-the where the—

AMY. (*Cheerfully.*) Sssssllllow dowwwwn. (*The other patients laugh; MRS. TIMMINS softly echoes the phrase "slow down." Speaking very slowly.*) Listen to yourself talking.

MRS. STILSON. (*Speaking slowly.*) Well yes, I was . . . listen-ing and it was it was going in . . . good I think, I'd say, very good yes I liked it very nice it made it very nice inside.

AMY. Well, good.

MRS. TIMMINS. Applawdgia!

AMY. Ah, Mrs. Timmins! You heard the music, too?

MRS. TIMMINS. (*With a laugh.*) Ohshorrrrrrn. Yossssssso, TV.

AMY. Well, good for you! Anyway, I'd like you all to know that this new person in our group is named Mrs. Stilson.

MR. BROWNSTEIN. Sssssstaa-illlllsssim.

AMY. Right! Well done, Mr. Brownstein!

MR. BROWNSTEIN. (*Laughing proudly.*) It's vurk-tiddiDIN-Gobitch!

AMY. That's right it's working, I told you it would.

BILLY. Hey! Wait, hold on here—jus' remembered!

AMY. What's that, Billy?

BILLY. You've been holdin' out pay up where is it?

AMY. Where . . . is what?

BILLY. Where is for all what I did all that time labor which you—don't kid me, I see you grinning back there ate up (*He makes munching sounds.*) so where is it, where's the loot?

AMY. For the cheesecake.

BILLY. That's right you know it for the cheesecape, own recipe, extra-special, pay up.

AMY. (*To MRS. STILSON.*) Billy is a terrific cook.

MRS. STILSON. (*Delighted.*) Oh!

BILLY. Well used t' be, not now much what they say, any-how, hah-hah! see? look, laughing, giggles, tries t' hide it, she knows she knows, scoundrel, thief, can't sleep nights can you, people give their arms whatnots recipe like that one is. Cheap-skate. Come on fork over hand it over, don't be chief.

AMY. . . . What?

BILLY. Don't be chief. (*Pause.*) You know, when someone don' pay, you say he's chief.

AMY. . . . What?

BILLY. Don't be chief. (*Pause.*) You know, when someone don' pay, you say he's chief.

AMY. (*Warmly, nearly laughing.*) Billy, you're not listening.

BILLY. Okay not the word not the right word what's the word? I'll take any help you can give me. (*He laughs.*)

AMY. Cheap.

BILLY. That's it that's the word that's what you are, from now on I'm gonna sell my recipes somewhere else.

AMY. Billy, say cheap. (*He sighs mightily.*)

BILLY. . . . Chief. (*Her expression tells him everything.*) Not right okay, try again this thing we can, what's it, lessee okay here we go CHARF! Nope. Not right. Ya know really, this could take all day.

AMY. Well then, the sooner you do it, the sooner we can go on to what I've planned.

BILLY. You've got somethin' planned? You've never got somethin' planned.

AMY. I've *always* got something planned.

BILLY. Oh come on don' gimme that, you're jus' tryin' to impress this new lady, really nice new lady, Mrs. . . .

AMY. Stilson.

BILLY. Yeah her, you're jus' tryin'—what's that word again?

AMY. Cheap.

BILLY. Cheap right okay lessee now—

AMY. Billy! You jus' said it!

BILLY. Did I? Good. Then maybe we can go on to somethin' else, such as when you're gonna fork over for the cheesecake, I could be a rich man now.

AMY. Billy, I never made the cheesecake.

BILLY. I'll bet you've gone sold the recipe to all the stores the whatnot everywhere fancy bigdeal places made a fortune, gonna retire any day t' your farm in New Jersey.

AMY. I don't have a farm in New Jersey, *you* have a farm in New Jersey!

BILLY. Oh? Then what were you doin' on my farm then?

AMY. I wasn't on your farm, Billy, I've been here! (BILLY *starts arguing about something incomprehensible and seemingly unrelated to farm life, the argument consisting mostly of the recitation of a convoluted string of numbers;* AMY *cuts him short before he goes too far astray.*) Billy, cheap, say cheap! (*Long silence.*)

BILLY. (*Simply and without effort.*) Cheap. (AMY *cheers. Overjoyed.*) Cheap!—cheap-cheap-cheap-cheap!

MR. BROWNSTEIN. I vas hoping you could polsya and git vid mustard all dis out of dis you gottit right good I say hutchit and congratulupsy!

AMY. Congratu*lations*.

MR. BROWNSTEIN. Yeah right dassit goodgirlie, phhhhew! fin'lly!

(*Lights fade to black all around* MRS. STILSON. *Nothing seen but her. Silence for a time.*)

MRS. STILSON. What it was . . . how I heard it how I said it not the same, you would think so but it's not. Sometimes . . . well it just goes in so fast, in-and-out all the sounds. I know they mean— (*Pause.*) I mean I know they're . . . well like with me, helping, as their at their in their best way knowing how I guess they practice all the time so I'd say must be good or even better, helps me get the dark out just by going you know ssssslowww and thinking smiling . . . it's not easy. (*Pause.*) Sometimes . . . how can . . . well it's just I think these death things, end it, stuff like sort of may be better not to listen anything no more at all or trying even talking cause what good's it, I'm so far away! Well it's crazy I don't mean it I don't think, still it's just like clouds that you can push through. Still you do it, still you try to. I can't hear things same as others say them. (*Pause.*) So the death thing, it comes in, I don't ask it, it just comes in, plays around in there, I can't get it out till it's ready, goes out on its own. Same I guess for coming. I don't open up the door.

(*Silence. Lights up on a chair, small table. On the table, a cassette recorder.* MRS. STILSON *goes to the chair. Sits. Stares at the recorder. A few moments later,* BILLY *and a* DOCTOR *enter.*)

BILLY. Oh, I'm sorry, I didn't know you was in . . . here or . . .

MRS. STILSON. Dr. Freedman said I could . . . use room and his . . . this . . . (*She gestures toward the recorder.*)

DOCTOR. No problem, we'll use another room. (*He smiles.*

Exit BILLY *and* DOCTOR. MRS. STILSON *turns back to the machine. Stares at it. Then she reaches out, presses a button.*)

DOCTOR'S VOICE. (*From cassette recorder.*) All right, essentially, a stroke occurs when there's a stoppage . . . When blood flow ceases in one part of the brain . . . And that brain can no longer get oxygen . . . And subsequently dies. Okay? Now, depending upon which part of the brain is affected by the stroke, you'll see differences in symptoms. Now what you've had is a left cerebral infarction. Oh, by the way, you're doing much, much better. We were very worried when you first arrived . . . (*Silence. She clicks off the recording machine. Does nothing, stares at nothing. Then she reaches out and pushes the rewind button. The machine rewinds to start of tape. Stops automatically. She stares at the machine. Deep breath. Reaches out again. Presses the playback button.*) DOCTOR'S VOICE. All right, essentially, a stroke occurs when there's a stoppage . . . When blood flow ceases in one part of the brain . . . And that brain can no long— (*She shuts it off. Stares into space. Silence.*)

(MRS. STILSON *with* AMY *sitting next to her on another chair.*)

MRS. STILSON. (*Still staring into space.*) "Memory" . . . (*Pause.*)

AMY. Yes, come on, "memory" . . . (*No response.*) Anything. (*Still no response. Warmly.*) Oh, come on, I bet there are lots of things you can talk about . . . You've been going out a lot lately . . . With your son . . . With your niece . . . (*Pause.*) What about Rhinebeck? Tell me about Rhinebeck. (*Pause.*)

MRS. STILSON. On . . . Saturday . . . (*She ponders.*) On . . . Sunday my . . . son . . . (*Ponders again.*) On Saturday my son . . . took me to see them out at Rhinebeck.

AMY. See what?

MRS. STILSON. What I used to . . . fly in.

AMY. Can you think of the word?

MRS. STILSON. . . . . What word?

AMY. For what you used to fly in. (*Long pause.*)

MRS. STILSON. Planes!

AMY. Very good!

MRS. STILSON. Old . . . planes.

AMY. That is very good. Really!

MRS. STILSON. I sat . . . inside one of them. He said it was

like the kind I used to . . . fly in and walk . . . out on wings in.
I couldn't believe I could have ever done this. (*Pause.*) But he
said I did, I had. He was very . . . proud. (*Pause.*) Then . . . I
saw my hand was pushing on this . . . stick . . . Then my hand
was . . . pulling. Well I hadn't you know asked my hand to do
this, it just went and did it on its own. So I said okay Emily, if
this is how it wants to do it you sit back here and watch . . . But
. . . my head, it was really . . . hurting bad. And I was up here
both . . sides, you know . . .

AMY. Crying.

MRS. STILSON. (*With effort.*) Yeah. (*Long pause.*) And then
all at once—it remembered everything! (*Long pause.*) But now
it doesn't. (*Silence.*)

(*Faint sound of wind. Hint of bells. The screens open. We are
outside. Sense of distance, openness. All feeling of constraint is
gone.* AMY *helps* MRS. STILSON *into an overcoat;* AMY *is in an
overcoat already.*)

AMY. Are you sure you'll be warm enough?

MRS. STILSON. Oh yes . . . (*And they start to walk—a leisurely stroll through a park or meadow, sense of whiteness
everywhere. They head toward a bench with snow on its slats.
The sound of wind grows stronger. Faint sound of an airplane
overhead, the sound quickly disappearing.*) This is winter, isn't
it?

AMY. Yes.

MRS. STILSON. That was just a guess, you know.

AMY. (*With a warm, easy laugh.*) Well, it was a good one,
keep it up! (MRS. STILSON *laughs.* AMY *stops by the bench.*) Do
you know what this is called?

MRS. STILSON. Bench!

AMY. Very good! No, I mean what's on top of it. (*No
response.*) What I'm brushing off . . . (*Still no response.*) What's
falling from the sky . . . (*Long silence.*)

MRS. STILSON. Where do you get names from?

AMY. I? From in here, same as you.

MRS. STILSON. Do you know how you do it?

AMY. No.

MRS. STILSON. Then how am I supposed . . . to learn?

AMY. (*Softly.*) I don't really know.

MRS. STILSON. (*Stares at* AMY. *Then she points at her and
laughs. At first,* AMY *doesn't understand. Then she does. And
then both of them are laughing.*) Look. You see? (*She scoops*

some snow off the bench.) If I pick this . . . stuff up in my hand, then . . . I know its name. I didn't have to pick it up to know . . . what it *was*.

AMY. No . . .

MRS. STILSON. But to find its name . . . (*She stares at what is in her hand*.) I had to pick it up.

AMY. What's its name?

MRS. STILSON. Snow. It's really nuts, isn't it!

AMY. It's peculiar! (*They laugh. Then, laughter gone, they sit; stare out. Silence for a time*.)

MRS. STILSON. A strange thing happened to me . . . (*Pause*.) I think last night.

AMY. Can you remember it?

MRS. STILSON. Perfectly.

AMY. Ah!

MRS. STILSON. I think it may have been . . . you know, when you sleep . . .

AMY. A dream.

MRS. STILSON. Yes, one of those, but I'm not . . . sure that it was . . . that. (*Pause. Then she notices the snow in her hand*.) Is it all right if I . . . eat this?

AMY. Yes! We used to make a ball of it, then pour maple syrup on top. Did you ever do that?

MRS. STILSON. I don't know. (*Pause*.) No, I remember— I did! (*She tastes the snow. Smiles. After a time, the smile vanishes. She turns back to* AMY.) Who was that man yesterday?

AMY. What man?

MRS. STILSON. In our group. He seemed all right.

AMY. Oh, that was last week.

MRS. STILSON. I thought for sure he was all right! I thought he was maybe, you know, a doctor.

AMY. Yes, I know.

MRS. STILSON. (*Searching her memory*.) And you asked him to show you where his . . . hand was.

AMY. And he knew.

MRS. STILSON. That's right, he raised his hand, he knew. So I thought, why is Amy joking? (*She ponders*.) Then you asked him . . . (*She tries to remember*.) where . . . (*She turns to* AMY.)

AMY. His elbow was.

MRS. STILSON. Yes! And he . . . (*She struggles to find the word*.)

AMY. (*Helping*.) Pointed—

MRS. STILSON. (*At the same time.*) Pointed! to . . . (*But the struggle's getting harder.*)

AMY. The corner of the room.

MRS. STILSON. Yes. (*Pause. Softly.*) That was very . . . scary.

AMY. Yes. (MRS. STILSON *stares into space. Silence.*) What is it that happened to you last night?

MRS. STILSON. Oh yes! Well, this . . . *person* . . . came into my room. I couldn't tell if it was a man or woman or . . . young or old. I was in my bed and it came. Didn't seem to have to walk just . . . came over to my . . . bed and . . . smiled at where I was. (*Pause.*) And then it said . . . (*In a whisper.*) "Emily . . . we're glad you changed your mind." (*Pause.*) And then . . . it turned and left.

AMY. Was it a doctor? (MRS. STILSON *shakes her head.*) One of the staff? (MRS. STILSON *shakes her head.*) How do you know?

MRS. STILSON. I just know. (*Pause.*) Then . . . I left my body.

AMY. *What?*

MRS. STILSON. (*With great excitement.*) I was on the . . . what's the name over me—

AMY. Ceiling?

MRS. STILSON. Yes! I was floating like a . . .

AMY. Cloud? (MRS. STILSON *shakes her head.*) Bird?

MRS. STILSON. Yes, up there at the— (*She searches for the word; finds it.*) ceiling, and I looked down and I was still there in my bed! Wasn't even scared, which you'd think I would be . . . And I thought, wow! this is the life isn't it? (*Sound of wind. Lights begin to change.* AMY *recedes into the darkness.*) It comes now without my asking . . . Amy is still beside me but I am somewhere else. I'm not scared. It has taken me, and it's clear again. Something is about to happen. (*Pause.* AMY *now completely gone.* MRS. STILSON *in a narrow spot of light, darkness all around.*) I am in a plane, a Curtiss Jenny, and it's night. Winter. Snow is falling. Feel the tremble of the wings! How I used to walk out on them! Could I have really done—Yes. What I'd do, I'd strap myself with a tether to the stays, couldn't see the tether from below, then out I'd climb! Oh my, but it was wonderful! I could feel the wind! shut my eyes, all alone— FEEL THE SOARING! (*The wind grows stronger. Then the wind dies away. Silence. She notices the change.*) But this is in another time. Where I've been also . . . It is night and no one else is in the plane. Is it . . . remembering? (*Pause.*) No . . . No,

I'm simply there again! (*Pause.*) And I'm lost . . . I am lost, completely lost, have to get to . . . somewhere, Omaha I think. The radio is out, or rather for some reasons picks up only Bucharest. Clouds all around, no stars only snow, don't possess a clue to where I am, flying blind, soon be out of gas . . . And then the clouds open up a bit, just a bit, and lights appear below, faint, a hint, like torches. Down I drop! heart pounding with relief, with joy, hoping for a landing place, I'll take anything—a field, a street, and down I drop! No place to land . . . It's a town but the smallest—one tiny street is all, three street lamps, no one on the street, all deserted . . . just a street and some faint light in the middle of darkness. Nothing. Still, down I go! Maybe I can find a name on a railroad station, find out where I am! . . . But I see nothing I can read . . . So I begin to circle, though I know I'm wasting fuel and I'll crash if I keep this up! But somehow, I just can't tear myself away! Though I know I should pull back on the stick, get the nose up, head north into darkness—Omaha must be north! But no, I keep circling this one small silly street in this one small town . . . I'm scared to leave it, that's what, as if I guess once away from it I'll be inside something empty, black, and endless . . . (*Pause.*) So I keep circling—madness!—but I love it, what I see below! And I just can't bring myself to give it up, it's that simple—just can't bring myself to give it up! (*Pause.*) Then I know I have to. It's a luxury I can't afford. Fuel is running low, almost gone, may be too late anyway, so— (*Pause.*) I pull the nose up, kick the rudder, bank, and head out into darkness all in terror! GOD, BUT IT TAKES EFFORT! JUST DON'T WANT TO DO IT! . . . But I do. (*Pause. Suddenly calm.*) Actually, odd thing, once I did, broke free, got into the dark, found I wasn't even scared . . . Or was I? (*Slight laugh.*) Can't remember . . . Wonder where that town was . . . ? (*Pause.*) Got to Omaha all right. (*Pause.*) Was it Omaha . . . ? (*Pause.*) Yes, I think so . . . Yes, Topeka, that was it! (*Pause.*) God, but it was wonderful! (*Slight laugh.*) Awful scary sometimes, though!

(AMY *seen in the distance.*)

AMY. Emily! Emily, are you all right? (*Sudden, sharp, terrifying, flapping sound.* MRS. STILSON *gasps,* AMY *disappears.*)

MRS. STILSON. (*Rapidly.*) Around! There here spins saw it rumple chumps and jumps outgoes inside up and . . . takes it, gives it, okay . . . (*Pause. Easier.*) Touch her for me, would you? (*Pause. Even easier.*) Oh my, yes, and here it goes then out . . . there I think on . . . wings? Yes . . . (*Pause. Softly, faint smile.*) Thank you. (*No trace of terror. Music. Hint of bells. Lights to black. Silence.*)

SISTER MARY IGNATIUS EXPLAINS IT ALL FOR YOU

---

by
Christopher Durang

SISTER MARY IGNATIUS EXPLAINS IT ALL FOR YOU was first presented by the Ensemble Studio Theatre, in New York City, on a bill with one-act plays by David Mamet, Marsha Norman, and Tennessee Williams, on December 14, 1979. The production was directed by Jerry Zaks; set design by Brian Martin; light design by Marie Louise Moreto; costume design by Madeline Cohen. The cast was as follows:

SISTER MARY IGNATIUS. .... Elizabeth Franz
THOMAS .... Mark Stefan
GARY SULLAVAN .... Gregory Grove
DIANE SYMONDS .... Ann McDonough
PHILOMENA ROSTOVICH ...... Prudence Wright Holmes
ALOYSIUS BUSICCIO .... Don Marino

SISTER MARY IGNATIUS EXPLAINS IT ALL FOR YOU was then presented off-Broadway by Playwrights Horizons, in New York City, on a double-bill with "The Actor's Nightmare" on October 14, 1981. The production was directed by Jerry Zaks; set design by Karen Schulz; costume design by William Ivey Long; lighting design by Paul Gallo; sound design by Aural Fixation; production stage manager was Esther Cohen. The cast was as follows:

SISTER MARY IGNATIUS .... Elizabeth Franz
THOMAS .... Mark Stefan
GARY SULLAVAN .... Timothy Landfield
DIANE SYMONDS .... Polly Draper
PHILOMENA ROSTOVICH .... Mary Catherine Wright
ALOYSIUS BENHEIM .... Jeff Brooks

Enter SISTER MARY IGNATIUS, *dressed in an old-fashioned nun's habit. The stage is fairly simple. There should be a lectern, a potted palm, a few chairs. There is also an easel, or some sort of stand, on which are several drawings made on cardboard, the only one we can see at the top of the play is either blank or is a simple cross. Sister looks at the audience until she has their attention, then smiles, albeit somewhat wearily. She then begins her lecture, addressing the audience directly.*

SISTER. (*Crossing herself.*) In the name of the Father, and of the Son, and of the Holy Ghost, Amen. (*Shows the next drawing on the easel, which is a neat if childlike picture of the planet earth, the sun, and moon.*) First there is the earth. Near the earth is the sun, and also nearby is the moon. (*Goes to next picture which, split in three, shows the gates of heaven amid clouds, some sort of murky area of paths, or some other image that might suggest waiting, wandering, and a third area of people burning up in flames, with little devils with little pitchforks, poking them.*) Outside the universe, where we go after death, is heaven, hell, and purgatory. Heaven is where we live in eternal bliss with out Lord Jesus Christ. (*Bows her head.*) Hell is where we are eternally deprived of the presence of our Lord Jesus Christ (*Bows her head.*), and are thus miserable. This is the greatest agony of hell, but there are also unspeakable physical torments, which we shall nonetheless speak of later. Purgatory is the middle area where we go after death to suffer if we have not been perfect in our lives and are thus not ready for heaven, or if we have not received the sacraments and made a good confession to a priest right before our death. Purgatory, depending on our sins, can go on for a very, *very* long time and is fairly unpleasant. Though we do not yet know whether there is any physical torment in purgatory, we do know that there is much psychological torment because we are being delayed from being in the presence of our Lord Jesus Christ. (*Bows her head.*) For those non-Catholics present, I bow my head to show respect for our Savior when I say His Name, Our Lord Jesus Christ. (*Bows head.*) Our Lord Jesus Christ. (*Bows head.*) Our Lord Jesus Christ. (*Bows head.*) You can expect to be in purgatory for anywhere from 300 years to 700 billion years. This may sound like forever, but don't forget in terms of eternity 700 billion years does come to an end. All things come to an end except our Lord Jesus Christ. (*Bows head. Points to the drawing again, reviewing her point.*) Heaven, hell, purgatory. (*Smiles. Goes to the next drawing which, like that of purgatory, is of a murky area, perhaps with a prison-like fence, and which has unhappy baby-like creatures floating about in it.*) There is also limbo, which is where unbaptized babies were sent for eternity before the Ecumenical Council and Pope John XXIII. The unbaptized babies sent to limbo never leave limbo and so never get to heaven. *Now* unbaptized babies are sent straight to purgatory where, presumably, someone baptizes them and then they are sent to heaven. The unbaptized babies who died before the Ecumenical Council, however, remain in limbo and will never be admitted to heaven. Limbo is not all that unpleasant, it's just that it isn't heaven and you never leave there. I want to be very clear about the Immaculate Conception. It does not mean that the Blessed Mother gave birth to Christ without the prior unpleasantness of physical intimacy. That is true but is not called the Immaculate Conception; that is called the Virgin Birth. The Immaculate Conception means that the Blessed Mother was herself born without original sin. Everyone makes this error, it makes me lose my patience. That Mary's conception was immaculate is an infallible statement. A lot of fault-finding non-Catholics run around saying that Catholics believe that the Pope is infallible whenever he speaks. This is untrue. The Pope is infallible only on certain occasions, when he speaks "ex cathedra," which is Latin for "out of the cathedral." When he speaks ex cathedra, we must accept what he says at that moment as dogma, or risk hell fire; or, now that things are becoming more liberal, many, many years in purgatory. I would now like a glass of water. Thomas. (*Enter* THOMAS *dressed as a parochial school boy with tie and blazer. It would be nice if he could look age seven.*) This is Thomas, he is seven years old and in the second grade of Our Lady of Perpetual Sorrow School. Seven is the age of reason, so now that Thomas has turned seven he is capable of choosing to commit sin or not to commit sin, and God will hold him accountable for whatever he does. Isn't that so, Thomas?

THOMAS. Yes, Sister.

SISTER. Before we turn seven, God tends to pay no attention to the bad things we do because He knows we can know no better. Once we turn seven, He feels we are capable of knowing. Thomas, who made you?

THOMAS. God made me.

SISTER. Why did God make you?

THOMAS. God made me to show forth His goodness and share with us His happiness.

SISTER. What is the sixth commandment?

THOMAS. The sixth commandment is thou shalt not commit adultery.

SISTER. What is forbidden by the sixth commandment?

THOMAS. The sixth commandment forbids all impurities in thought, word or deed, whether alone or with others.

SISTER. That's correct, Thomas. (*Gives him a cookie.*) Thomas has a lovely soprano voice which the Church used to preserve by creating castrati. Thomas unfortunately will lose his soprano voice in a few years and will receive facial hair and psychological difficulties in its place. To me, it is not a worthwhile exchange. You may go now, Thomas. What is the fourth commandment?

THOMAS. The fourth commandment is honor thy mother and thy father.

SISTER. Very good. (*Gives him a cookie. He exits.*) Sometimes in the mornings I look at all the children lining up in front of school, and I'm overwhelmed by a sense of sadness and exhaustion thinking of all the pain and suffering and personal unhappiness they're going to face in their lives. (*Looks sad, eats a cookie.*) But can their suffering compare with Christ's on the cross? Let us think of Christ on the cross for a moment. Try to feel the nails ripping through His hands and feet. Some experts say that the nails actually went through His wrists, which was better for keeping Him up on the cross, though of course most of the statues have the nails going right through His palms. Imagine those nails being driven through: pound, pound, pound, rip, rip, rip. Think of the crown of thorns eating into His skull, and the sense of infection that He must have felt in His brain and near His eyes. Imagine blood from His brain spurting forth through His eyes, imagine His vision squinting through a veil of red liquid. Imagine these things, and then just *dare* to feel sorry for the children lining up outside of school. We dare not; His suffering was greater than ours. He died for our sins! Yours and mine. We put Him up there, you did, all you people sitting out there. He loved us so much that He came all the way down to earth just so He could be nailed painfully to a cross and hang there for three hours. Who else has loved us as much as that? I come from a large family. My father was big and ugly, my mother had a nasty disposition and didn't like me, and there were twenty-six of us. It took three hours just to wash the dishes, but Christ hung on that cross for three hours and *He* never complained. We lived in a small, ugly house, and I shared a room with all my sisters. My father would bring home drunken bums off the street, and let them stay in the same room as himself and my mother. "Whatever you do to the least of these, you do also to Me," Christ said. Sometimes these bums would make my mother hysterical, and we'd have to throw water on her. Thomas, could I have some more water please? And some chocolates? (*Enter* THOMAS.) Who made you?

THOMAS. God made me.

SISTER. What is the ninth commandment?

THOMAS. The ninth commandment is thou shalt not covet they neighbor's wife.

SISTER. What is forbidden by the ninth commandment?

THOMAS. The ninth commandment forbids all indecency in thought, word and deed, whether alone or with thy neighbor's wife.

SISTER. Thank you. Go away again. (*He exits*.) Bring the little children unto me, Our Lord said. I don't remember in reference to what. I have your questions here on little file cards. (*Reads*.) If God is all powerful, why does He allow evil in the world? (*Goes to next card with no reaction. Reads*.) Tell us some more about your family. (*Smiles*.) We said grace before every meal. My mother was a terrible cook. She used to boil chopped meat. She hated little children, but they couldn't use birth control. Let me explain this one more time. Birth control is wrong because God, whatever you may think about the wisdom involved, created sex for the purpose of procreation, *not* recreation. Everything in this world has a purpose. We eat food to feed our bodies. We don't eat and then make ourselves throw up immediately afterward, do we? So it should be with sex. Either it is done for its proper purpose, or it is just so much throwing up, morally speaking. Next question. (*Reads*.) Do nuns go to the bathroom? Yes. (*Reads*.) Was Jesus effeminate? Yes. (*Reads*.) I have a brain tumor and am afraid of dying. What should I do? Now I thought I had explained what happens after death to you already. There is heaven, hell and purgatory. What is the problem? Oh ye of little faith, Christ said to someone. All right. As any seven-year-old knows, there are two kinds of sin: mortal sin and venial sin. Venial sin is the less serious kind, like if you tell a small lie to your parents, or when you kick a barking dog. If you die with any venial sins on your conscience, no matter how many of them there are, you can eventually work it all out in purgatory. However—mortal sin, on the other hand, is the most serious kind of sin you can do—murder, sex outside of marriage, hijacking a plane, masturbation—and if you die with any of these sins on your soul, even just one, you will go straight to hell and burn for all of eternity. Now to rid yourself of mortal sins, you must go make a good confession and vow never to do it again. If, as many of you know, you are on your way to confession to confess a mortal sin and you are struck by a car or bus before you get there, God may forgive you without confession if before you die you manage to say a good act of contrition. If you die instantaneously and are unable to say a good act of contrition, you will go straight to hell. Thomas, come read this partial list of those who are going to burn in hell. (*Enter* THOMAS.)

THOMAS. (*Reads.*) Christine Keeler, Roman Polanski, Zsa Zsa Gabor, the editors of *After Dark* magazine, Linda Lovelace, Georgina Spelvin, Big John Holmes, Brooke Shields, David Bowie, Mick Jagger, Patty Hearst, Betty Comden, Adolph Green.

SISTER. This is just a partial list. It is added to constantly. Thomas, how can we best keep from going to hell?

THOMAS. By not committing a mortal sin, by keeping close to the sacraments, especially going to confession and receiving communion, and by obeying our parents. (*She gives him a cookie.*)

SISTER. Good boy. Do you love our Lord, Thomas?

THOMAS. Yes, Sister.

SISTER. How much?

THOMAS. This much. (*Holds arms out wide.*)

SISTER. Well, that's very nice, but Christ loves us an infinite amount. How do we know that, Thomas?

THOMAS. Because you tell us.

SISTER. That's right. And by His actions. He died on the cross for us to make up for our sins. Wasn't that nice of Him?

THOMAS. Very nice.

SISTER. And shouldn't we be grateful?

THOMAS. Yes we should.

SISTER. That's right, we should. (*Gives him a cookie.*) How do you spell cookie?

THOMAS. C-o-o-k-i-e.

SISTER. Very good. (*Give him a cookie.*) Mary has had an argument with her parents and has shot and killed them. Is that a venial sin or a mortal sin?

THOMAS. That's a mortal sin.

SISTER. If she dies with this mortal sin on her soul, will she go to heaven or to hell?

THOMAS. She will go to hell.

SISTER. Very good. How do you spell ecumenical?

THOMAS. (*Sounding it out.*) Eck—e-c-k; you—u; men—m-e-n; ical—i-c-k-l-e.

SISTER. Very good. (*Gives him a cookie.*) What's two plus two?

THOMAS. Four.

SISTER. What's one and one and one and one and one and one and one and one and one?

THOMAS. Nine.

SISTER. Very good. (*Gives him a cookie.*) Because she is afraid to show her parents her bad report card, Susan goes to the top of a tall building and jumps off. Is this a venial sin or a mortal sin?

THOMAS. Mortal sin.

SISTER. And where will she go?

THOMAS. Hell.

SISTER. Sit on my lap. (*He does.*) Would you like to keep your pretty soprano voice forever?

THOMAS. Yes, Sister.

SISTER. Well, we'll see what we can do about it (*Sings.*)

Cookies in the morning, cookies in the evening,
Cookies in the summertime,
Be my little cookie.
And love me all the time.

God, I've done so much talking, I've got to rest. Here, you take care of some of these questions, Thomas, and I'll sleep a little. (*To audience.*) I'll just be a minute. (*Closes her eyes, he looks at cards.*)

THOMAS. (*Reads.*) How do we know there is a God? We know that there is a God because the Church tells us so. And also because everything has a primary cause. Dinner is put on the table because the primary cause, our mother, has put it in the oven and cooked it. (*Reads.*) If God is all powerful, why does He allow evil? (*Skips that one, next one.*) What does God look like? God the father looks like an old man with a long white beard.

SISTER. I'll take the next one. (*Reads.*) Are you ever sorry you became a nun? I am never sorry I became a nun. (*Reads.*) It used to be a mortal sin to eat meat on Fridays, and now it isn't. Does that mean that people who ate meat on Fridays back when it was a sin are in hell? Or what? People who ate meat on Fridays back when it was a mortal sin are indeed in hell if they did not confess the sin before they died. If they confessed it, they are not in hell, unless they did not confess some other mortal sin they committed. People who would eat meat on Fridays back in the fifties tended to be the sort who would commit other mortal sins, so on a guess, I bet many of them *are* in hell for other sins, even if they did confess the eating of meat. (*Reads.*) What exactly went on in Sodom? (*Irritated.*) Who asked me this question? (*Reads.*) I am an Aries. Is it a sin to follow your horoscope? It is a sin to follow your horoscope because only God knows the future and He won't tell us. Also, we can tell that horoscopes are false because according to astrology Christ would be a Capricorn, and Capricorn people are cold, ambitious and attracted to Scorpio and Virgo, and we know that Christ was warm, loving, and not attracted to anybody. Give me a cookie, Thomas (*He does.*) I'm going to talk about Sodom a bit. Thomas, please leave the stage. (*He does. She talks softer.*) To answer your question, Sodom is where they committed acts of homosexuality and bestiality in the Old Testament, and God, infuriated by this, destroyed them all in one fell swoop. Modern day Sodoms are New York City, San Francisco, Amsterdam, Los Angeles. . . . well, basically anywhere where the population is over 50,000. The only reason that God has not destroyed these modern-day Sodoms is that Catholic nuns and priests live in these cities, and God does not wish to destroy them. He does, however, give these people body lice and hepatitis. It's so hard to know why God allows wickedness to flourish. I guess it's because God wants man to choose goodness freely of his own free will; sometimes one wonders if free will is worth all the trouble if there's going to be so much evil and unhappiness, but God knows best, presumably. If it were up to me, I might be tempted to wipe out cities and civilizations, but luckily for New York and Amsterdam, I'm not God. (*Reads.*) Why is St. Christopher no longer a saint, and did anyone listen to the prayers I prayed to him before they decided he didn't exist? The name Christopher means Christ-bearer and we used to believe that he carried the Christ child across a river on his shoulders. Then sometime around Pope John XXIII, the Catholic Church decided that this was just a story and didn't really happen. I am not convinced that when we get to heaven we may not find that St. Christopher *does* indeed exist and that he dislikes Pope John XXIII; however, if he does not exist, then the prayers you prayed to him would have been picked up by St. Jude. St. Jude is the patron saint of hopeless causes. When you have a particularly terrible problem that has little hope of being solved, you pray to St. Jude. When you lose or misplace something, you pray to St. Anthony. (*Reads.*) Tell us some more about your family. (*Smiles, pleased.*) I had twenty-six brothers and sisters. From my family five became priests, seven became nuns, three became brothers, and the rest of them were institutionalized. My mother was also institutionalized shortly after she started thinking my father was Satan. Some days when we were little, we'd come home and not be able to find our mother and we'd pray to St. Anthony to help us find her. Then when we'd find her with her head in the oven, we would pray to St. Jude to make her sane again. Are all our prayers answered? Yes, they are; what people who ask that question often don't realize is that sometimes the answer to our prayer is "no." Dear God, please make my mother not be crazy. God's answer: no. Dear God, please let me recover from cancer. God's answer: no. Dear God, please take away this toothache. God's answer: alright, but you're going to be run over by a car. But every bad thing that happens to us, God has a special reason for. God is the good shepherd, we are His flock. And if God is grouchy or busy with more important matters, His beloved mother Mary is always there to intercede for us. I shall now sing the Hail Mary in Latin. (SISTER *motions to the lighting booth, and the lights change to an apparently pre-arranged special spotlight for her, atmospheric with blue spill and back lighting, the rest of the stage becomes fairly dim. Sings.*)

Ave Maria,
Gratia plena,
Maria, gratia plena,
Maria, gratia plena,
Ave, Ave! . . . (etc.)

(*As* SISTER *sings, enter four people, ages twenty-eight–thirty; they are a woman dressed as the Blessed Mother, a man dressed as St. Joseph, and two people, a man and a women, dressed as a camel. The Blessed Mother sits on the back of the camel, which is led in by St. Joseph. Because of the dim lighting, we don't see them too clearly at first. Sister, either sensing something happening due to the audience or else just by turning her head, suddenly sees them and is terribly startled and confused.)*

ST. JOSEPH. We're sorry we're late.

SISTER. Oh dear God. (*Kneels.*)

ST. JOSEPH. Sister, what are you doing?

SISTER. You look so real.

ST. JOSEPH. Sister, I'm Gary Sullavan, and (*Pointing to the Blessed Mother.*) this is Diane Symonds. We were in your fifth grade class in 1959, and you asked us to come today. Don't you remember?

SISTER. 1959?

GARY. Don't you remember asking us?

SISTER. Not very distinctly. (*Louder, to lighting booth.*) Could I have some lights please? (*Lights come back up to where they were before. To* GARY.) What did I want you to do?

GARY. You wanted us to put on a pageant.

SISTER. That camel looks false to me.

PHILOMENA. Hello, Sister. (*She's the front of the camel.*)

SISTER. I thought so.

PHILOMENA. It's Philomena, Sister. Philomena Rostovitch.

ALOYSIUS. And Aloysius Benheim.* (*He's the back of the camel.*)

SISTER. I don't really recognize any of you. Of course, you're not in your school uniforms.

DIANE. 1959.

SISTER. What?

DIANE. You taught us in 1959.

SISTER. I recognize you. Mary Jean Mahoney?

DIANE. I'm not Mary Jean Mahoney. I'm Diane Symonds.

SISTER. This is all so confusing.

GARY. Don't you want to see the pageant?

SISTER. What pageant is it?

GARY. We used to perform it at Christmas in your class; every class did. You said it was written in 1948 by Mary Jean Mahoney, who was your best student, you said.

DIANE. You said she was very elevated, and that when she was in the seventh grade she didn't have her first period, she had a stigmata.

SISTER. Oh yes. They discovered it in gym class. Mary Jean

*See Author's Note, at end of play.

Mahoney. She entered a cloistered order of nuns upon her graduation from twelfth grade. Sometimes late at night I can hear her praying. Mary Jean Mahoney. Yes, let's see her pageant again. (*To audience.*) She was such a bright student. (*Vague.*) I remember asking them to come now, I think. I wanted to tell you about Mary Jean Mahoney, and the perfect faith of a child. Yes, the pageant, please. Thomas, come watch with me. (THOMAS *enters and sits on* SISTER's *lap.*)

GARY. (*Announcing.*) The pageant of the birth and death of Our Beloved Saviour Jesus Christ, by Mary Jean Mahoney as told to Mrs. Robert J. Mahoney. The setting: a desert near Bethlehem. St. Joseph and the Virgin Mary and their trusty camel must flee from the wicked King Herod.

DIANE. (*Sings; to tune of "We Gather Together to Ask the Lord's Blessings."*)
Hello, my name's Mary,
And his name is Joseph,
We're parents of Jesus,
Who's not been born yet,

We're fleeing from Herod,
And nobody knows if,
We'll make it to the town,
But we'll try, you can bet.

And I'm still a virgin,
And he's not the father,
The father descended
From heaven above,

And this is our camel,
He's really not much bother,
We're off to Bethlehem,
Because God is love.

GARY. Here's an Inn, Mary. But there doesn't look like there's any room.

DIANE. Well ask them, Joseph.

GARY. (*Knocks on imaginary door.*) Excuse me, you don't have room at this Inn, do you? (*Listens.*) He said they don't, Mary.

DIANE. Oh dear. Well let's try another Inn.

GARY. (*Knocks.*) Excuse me, you don't have room at this Inn, do you? (*Listens.*) He says they don't allow camels.

DIANE. Let's try the third Inn.

GARY. (*Knocks.*) Excuse me, you don't have room at your

Inn, do you? (*Listens.*) I thought not . . . what? You would? Oh, Mary, this kind Innkeeper says that even though he has no room at the Inn, we can sleep in his stable.

DIANE. Do I look like a barn animal?

GARY. Mary, we really haven't any choice.

DIANE. Yes we do. Sister says we have choice over everything, because God gave us free will to decide between good and evil. And so I choose to stay in the stable.

GARY. Well here it is.

DIANE. Pew. It smells just like the zoo Mommy took me and Cynthia to visit last summer. We liked to look at the animals, but we didn't like to smell them.

GARY. I don't think there are any sheets.

DIANE. I don't need sheets, I'm so tired, I could sleep anywhere.

GARY. Well, that's good. Goodnight, Mary.

DIANE. But I do need pillows.

GARY. Mary, what can I do? We don't have any pillows.

DIANE. I can't sleep without pillows.

GARY. Let's pray to God then. If you just pray, he answers your prayers.

DIANE. Sometimes he says no, Joseph.

GARY. I know, but let's try. Dear God, we beseech thee, hear our prayer.

DIANE. Pillows! Pillows! Pillows!

GARY. And behold God answered their prayers.

CAMEL. (PHILOMENA.) We have an idea, Mary and Joseph. We have two humps, and you can use them as pillows.

DIANE. Thank you, God! Come on, Joseph. Let's go to sleep.

CAMEL. (As MARY *and* JOSEPH *start to sleep, sings a lullaby:*)
Rockaby, and good night,
May God keep you and watch you,
Rockabye, and good night, (etc.)

(*They sleep.* ALOYSIUS *makes baby crying noises, tosses out a doll onto the floor.*)

DIANE. (*Seeing the doll.*) Joseph, He's born, Jesus is born.

GARY, DIANE, and CAMEL. (*Sing.*)
Joy to the world, the Saviour's come.
Let earth receive her king,
La la la la la la la la,
La la la la la la la la,
Let heaven and nature sing,
Let heaven and nature sing,
Let heaven, and heaven, and nature sing!

GARY. (*To doll.*) Can you say Poppa, Jesus? Can you say Momma?

DIANE. He's not that kind of child, Joseph. He was born without original sin like me. This is called my Immaculate Conception, which is not to be confused with my Virgin Birth. Everyone makes this error, it makes me lose my patience. *We* must learn from *him*, Joseph.

GARY. (*To audience.*) And so Jesus instructed His parents, and the priests in the Temple, and He said many unusual things, many of them irritating to parents. Things like "Before Abraham was, I am." And "Do you not know that I must go about my father's business?" after we'd been worried to death and unable to find Him for hours and hours. And He performed many miracles.

DIANE. He turned water into wine.

GARY. He made cripples walk.

DIANE. He walked on the water.

GARY. And then came the time for His crucifixion. And His mother said to him:

DIANE. (*To doll.*) But why, Jesus, why? Why must you be crucified? And what do you mean by "I must die so that others may know eternal life"?

GARY. And Jesus explained that because Adam and Eve, especially Eve, had sinned that mankind was cursed until Jesus could redeem us by dying on the cross.

DIANE. But that sounds silly. Why can't God just forgive us? And it's Adam and Eve anyway, not us.

GARY. But Jesus laughed at her and He said, "Yours is not to reason why, yours is but to do and die." And then He said, "But seriously, Mother, it is not up to God to justify His ways to man; rather man must have total and complete faith in God's wisdom, he must accept and not question, just like an innocent babe accepts and doesn't question his parents." And then Mary said:

DIANE. I understand. Or rather, I understand that I am not supposed to understand. Come, let us go to Golgotha and watch you be crucified.

GARY. And Mary and the apostles and the faithful camel, whose name was Misty, followed Jesus to the rock of Golgotha and watched Him be nailed to a cross. (GARY *has a hammer and nails, and nails the doll to the cross; then stands it up that way.*)

DIANE. And Jesus looked at the two thieves crucified on either side of him, and He said to one:

GARY. Thou art saved; and to the other, He said:

DIANE. Thou art condemned for all eternity.

GARY. And then He hung there for three hours in terrible agony.

DIANE. Imagine the agony. Try to feel the nails ripping through His hands and feet. Pound, pound, pound, rip, rip, rip. Washing the dishes for three hours is nothing compared to hanging on a cross.

GARY. And then He died. He's dead now, Mary.

DIANE. (*Sad, lost*) Oh.

GARY. Let's go for a long walk.

DIANE. Oh, Joseph, I feel so alone.

GARY. So do I, Mary.

DIANE. (*Truly wondering.*) Do you think He was just a nut? Do you think maybe the Holy Ghost isn't His Father at all, that I made it all up? Maybe I'm not a virgin . . . Maybe . . .

GARY. But then Misty said . . .

CAMEL. (PHILOMENA.) Do not despair, Mary and Joseph. Of course, He is God, He'll rise again in three days.

DIANE. If only I could believe you. But why should I listen to a dumb animal?

CAMEL. (PHILOMENA.) O ye, of little faith.

DIANE. (*Sad.*) Oh, Joseph, I'm losing my mind.

GARY. And so Mary and Joseph and the camel hid for three days and three nights, and on Sunday morning they got up and went to the Tomb where Christ was buried. And when they got there, standing by the Tomb was an angel. And the angel spoke.

ALOYSIUS. (*Back of camel.*) Mary and Joseph, your son has risen from the dead, just like your dumb animal Misty told you He would.

DIANE. I can't see the angel, can you, Joseph?

ALOYSIUS. O doubting Thomases of the world, must you see and touch everything in order to believe? Mary and Joseph! Your son Jesus wishes you to go out into the world and tell the people that unless they have the faith of the dumb animal Misty they shall not enter the Kingdom of Heaven. For, yea I say to you, at the end of the world the first in the class will be the last in the class, the boy with A in arithmetic will get F, the girl with F in geography will graduate with honors, and those with brains will be cast down in favor of those who are like dumb animals. For thus are the ways of the Lord.

GARY. And then Mary and Joseph, realizing their lack of faith, thanked Misty and made a good Act of Contrition. And then Jesus came out from behind the tree where He was hiding, they spent forty days on earth enjoying themselves and setting the groundwork for the Catholic Church, and then Jesus, Mary, Joseph and Misty ascended into heaven and lived happily ever after. (DIANE *and* GARY, *holding the doll between them, stand in front of the camel. All sing the final jubilant phrase of "Angels We Have Heard on High" Christmas carol, as* DIANE *and* GARY *mime ascension by waving their arms in a flying motion.*)

ALL. (*Singing.*) Glor-or-or-or-ia! In Excelsis Deo!

(*All four bow.* SISTER *applauds enthusiastically. After their bow, the four quickly get out of their costumes, continuing to do so during some of* SISTER's *next speech if necessary. Their "regular" clothes are indeed regular and not too noteworthy:* DIANE *might wear slacks or jeans but with an attractive sweater or blouse and with a blazer,* GARY *might wear chinos, a nice shirt with even a tie, or a vest—casual but neat, pleasant,* PHILOMENA *might wear a dress,* ALOYSIUS *a short and slacks [or, if played as a bit formal, even a suit.*])

SISTER. Oh, thank you, children. That was lovely. Thank you. (*To audience.*) The old stories really are the best, aren't they? Mary Jean Mahoney. What a good child. And what a nice reunion *we're* having. What year did you say you were in my class again?

GARY. 1959.

SISTER. 1959. Oh, those were happy years. Eisenhower, Pope Pius still alive, then the first Catholic president. And so now you've all grown up. Let's do some of the old questions, shall we? (*To* ALOYSIUS.) Who made you?

ALOYSIUS. God made me.

SISTER. Quite correct. What is the seventh commandment?

PHILOMENA. The seventh commandment is thou shalt not steal.

SISTER. Very good. (*To* DIANE) What is contrition? You.

DIANE. Uh . . . being sorry for sin?

SISTER. (*Cheerfully chastising.*) That's not how we answer questions here, young lady. Thomas?

THOMAS. Contrition is sincere sorrow for having offended God, and hatred for the sins we have committed, with a firm purpose of sinning no more.

DIANE. Oh yes. Right.

SISTER. (*Still kindly.*) For someone who's just played the Virgin, you don't know your catechism responses very well. What grade are you in?

DIANE. I'm not in a grade. I'm in life.

SISTER. Oh yes, right. Well, cookies, anyone? Thomas, go bring our nice guests some cookies. (THOMAS *exits.*) It's so nice to see you all again. You must all be married by now, I imagine. I hope you all have large families like we encouraged?

PHILOMENA. I have a little girl, age three.

SISTER. That's nice.

ALOYSIUS. I have two boys.

SISTER. I like boys. (*To* GARY.) And you?

GARY. I'm not married.

SISTER. Well, a nice-looking boy like you, it won't be long before some pretty girl snatches you up. (*To* DIANE.) And you?

DIANE. I don't have any children. But I've had two abortions. (SISTER *is stunned. Enter* THOMAS *with cookies.*)

SISTER. No cookies, Thomas. Take them away. (THOMAS *exits immediately. To* DIANE.) You are in a state of mortal sin, young woman. What is the fifth commandment?

DIANE. Thou shalt not kill.

SISTER. You are a murderer.

DIANE. (*Unemotional.*) The first one was when I was raped when I was eighteen.

SISTER. Well I am sorry to hear that. But only God has power over life and death. God might have had very special plans for your baby. Are you sure I taught you?

DIANE. Yes you taught me.

SISTER. Did I give you good grades?

DIANE. Yes. Very good.

SISTER. Have you told these sins in confession?

DIANE. What sins?

SISTER. You know very well what I mean.

DIANE. I don't go to confession.

SISTER. Well, it looks pretty clear to me, we'll just add you to the list of people going to hell. (*Calling.*) Thomas, we'll put her name right after Comden and Green. Somebody, change the subject. I don't want to hear any more about this.

GARY. (*Trying to oblige.*) Ummmm . . . it certainly is strange being able to chew the communion wafer now, isn't it?

SISTER. What?

GARY. Well, you used to tell us that because the communion wafer was really the body of Christ, if we chewed it, it might bleed.

SISTER. I was speaking metaphorically.

GARY. Oh.

SISTER. (*Pause.*) Well, I still feel shaken by that girl over there. (*Points to* DIANE.) Let's talk about something positive. You, with the little girl. Tell me about yourself.

PHILOMENA. Well my little girl is three, and her name is Wendy.

SISTER. There is no Saint Wendy.

PHILOMENA. Her middle name is Mary.

SISTER. Wendy Mary. Too many y's. I'd change it. What does your husband do?

PHILOMENA. I don't have a husband. (*Long pause.*)

SISTER. Did he die?

PHILOMENA. I don't think so. I didn't know him for very long.

SISTER. Do you sign your letters Mrs. or Miss?

PHILOMENA. I don't write letters.

SISTER. Did this person you lost track of *marry* you before he left?

PHILOMENA. (*Sad.*) No. (*Cries.*)

SISTER. Children, you are making me very sad. (*To* PHILOMENA.) Did you get good grades in my class?

PHILOMENA. No, Sister. You said I was stupid.

SISTER. Are you a prostitute?

PHILOMENA. Sister! Certainly not. I just get lonely.

SISTER. The Mother Superior of my own convent may get lonely, but does she have illegitimate children?

ALOYSIUS. There was that nun who stuffed her baby behind her dresser last year. (SISTER *stares at him.*) It was in the news.

SISTER. No one was addressing you, Aloysius. Philomena, my point is that loneliness does not excuse sin.

PHILOMENA. But there are worse sins. And I believe Jesus forgives me. After all, he didn't want them to stone the woman taken in adultery.

SISTER. That was merely a *political* gesture. In private Christ stoned *many* women taken in adultery.

DIANE. That's not in the Bible.

SISTER. (*Suddenly very angry.*) Not everything has to be in the Bible! (*To audience, trying to recoup.*) There's oral tradition within the Church. One priest tells another priest something, it gets passed down through the years.

PHILOMENA. (*Unhappy.*) But don't you believe Jesus forgives people who sin?

SISTER. Yes, of course, He forgives sin, but He's *tricky*. You have to be *truly* sorry, and you have to *truly* resolve not to sin again, or else He'll send you straight to hell just like the thief He was crucified next to.

PHILOMENA. I think Jesus forgives me.

SISTER. Well I think you're going to hell. (*To* ALOYSIUS.) And what about you? Is there anything the matter with you?

ALOYSIUS. Nothing. I'm fine.

SISTER. But are you living properly?

ALOYSIUS. Yes.

SISTER. And you're married?

ALOYSIUS. Yes.

SISTER. And you don't use birth control?

ALOYSIUS. No.

SISTER. But you only have two children. Why is that? You're not spilling your seed like Onan, are you? That's a sin, you know.

ALOYSIUS. No. It's just chance that we haven't had more.

SISTER. And you go to Mass once a week, and communion at least once a year, and confession at least once a year? Right?

ALOYSIUS. Yes.

SISTER. Well I'm very pleased then.

ALOYSIUS. I am an alcoholic, recently I've started to hit my wife, and I keep thinking about suicide.

SISTER. Within bounds, all those things are venial sins. At least one of my students turned out well. Of course, I don't know how hard you're hitting your wife; but with prayer and God's grace . . .

ALOYSIUS. My wife is very unhappy.

SISTER. Yes, but eventually there's death. And then everlasting happiness in heaven. Some days I long for heaven. (*To* GARY.) And you? Have you turned out all right?

GARY. I'm okay.

SISTER. And you don't use birth control?

GARY. Definitely not.

SISTER. That's good. (*Looks at him.*) What do you mean, "definitely not"?

GARY. I don't use it.

SISTER. And you're not married. Have you not found the right girl?

GARY. In a manner of speaking.

SISTER. (*Grim.*) Okay. You do that thing that makes Jesus puke, don't you?

GARY. Pardon?

SISTER. Drop the polite boy manners, buster. When your mother looks at you, she turns into a pillar of salt, right?

GARY. What?

SISTER. Sodom and Gomorrha, stupid. You sleep with men, don't you?

GARY. Well . . . yes.

SISTER. Jesus, Mary, and Joseph! We have a regular cross section in here.

GARY. I got seduced when I was in the seminary. I mean, I'd been denying it up to then.

SISTER. We don't want to hear about it.

GARY. And then when I left the seminary I was very upset, and then I went to New York and I slept with five hundred different people.

SISTER. Jesus is going to throw up.

GARY. But then I decided I was trashing my life, and so I only had sex with guys I had an emotional relationship with.

SISTER. That must have cut it down to about three hundred.

GARY. And now I'm living with this one guy who I'd gone to grade school with and only ran into again two years ago, and we're faithful with one another and stuff. He was in your class too. Jeff Hannigan.

SISTER. He was a bad boy. Some of them should be left on the side of a hill to die, and he was one.

GARY. You remember him?

SISTER. Not really. His type.

GARY. Anyway, when I met him again, he was still a practicing Catholic, and so now I am again too.

SISTER. I'd practice a little harder if I were you.

GARY. So I don't think I'm so bad.

SISTER. (*Vomit sound.*) Blah. You make me want to blah. Didn't any of you listen to me when I was teaching you? What were you all doing? (*Mad, trying to set the record straight again.*) There is the universe, created by God. Eve ate the apple, man got original sin, God sent down Jesus to redeem us. Jesus said to St. Peter, "Upon this rock," rock meaning Peter, "I build my Church," by which he meant that Peter was the first Pope and that he and the subsequent Popes would be infallible on matters of doctrine and morals. So your way is very clear: you have this infallible Church that tells you what is right and wrong, and you follow its teaching, and then you get to heaven. Didn't you all *hear* me say that? Did you all have wax in your ears? Did I speak in a foreign language? Or what? And you've all sinned against sex— (*To* ALOYSIUS.) not you, you're just depressed, you probably need vitamins—but the rest of you. Why this obsession with sex? The Church has been very clear setting up the guidelines for you. (*To* PHILOMENA *and*

DIANE.) For you two girls, why can't you simply marry one Catholic man and have as many babies as chance and the good Lord allows you to? Simple, easy to follow directions. (*To* GARY.) And for you, you can *force* yourself to marry and procreate with some nice Catholic girl—try it, it's not so hard—or you can be celibate for the rest of your life. Again, simple advice. (*Suddenly furious.*) Those are your options! No others. They are your direct paths to heaven and salvation, to everlasting happiness! Why aren't you following these paths? Are you insane?

DIANE. You're insane.

SISTER. You know, you're my least favorite person here today. I mean, the little effeminate one over there (*Points to* GARY.) makes me want to blah, but I can tell he once was nice, and he might get better with shock treatments and aversion therapy. But I can tell shock treatments wouldn't help you. You're fresh as paint, and you're nasty. I can see it in your face.

DIANE. You shouldn't be teaching children. You should be locked up in a convent where you can't hurt anybody.

SISTER. Me hurt someone. You're the one who runs around killing babies at the drop of a hat.

DIANE. It's a medical procedure. And even the Church admits it can't pinpoint *when* life begins in the womb. Why should you decide that the minute the sperm touches the ovum that . . .

SISTER. Don't talk filth to me, I don't want to hear it. (*Suddenly very suspicious.*) Why did you all come here today? I don't remember asking you.

GARY. It was Diane's idea.

SISTER. What? What was?

PHILOMENA. We wanted to embarrass you.

ALOYSIUS. None of us ever liked you.

SISTER. What do you mean? My students always loved me. I was the favorite.

ALOYSIUS. No. We thought you were a bully.

SISTER. I was the *favorite*.

ALOYSIUS. You never let me go to the bathroom when I needed to.

SISTER. All you had to do was raise your hand.

ALOYSIUS. There were sixty children, and I sat in the back of the room; and I did raise my hand, but you never acknowledged me. Every afternoon my bladder became very full, and I always ended up wetting my pants.

SISTER. Big deal.

ALOYSIUS. I spoke to you about recognizing me sooner, and about my problem, but all you said then was "big deal."

SISTER. I remember you. You used to make a puddle in the last row every day.

ALOYSIUS. I have bladder problems to this day.

SISTER. What a baby. You flunked. I was giving you a lesson in life, and you flunked. It was up to you to solve the problem: don't drink your little carton of milk at lunch; bring a little container with you and urinate behind your desk; or simply hold it in and offer the discomfort up to Christ. He suffered three hours of agony on the cross, surely a full bladder pales by comparison. I talk about the universe and original sin and heaven and hell, and you complain to me about bathroom privileges. You're a ridiculous crybaby. (*Cuffs him on the head.*)

PHILOMENA. You used to hit me too.

SISTER. You probably said stupid things.

PHILOMENA. I did. I told you I was stupid. That was no reason to hit me.

SISTER. It seems a very good reason to hit you. Knock some sense into you.

PHILOMENA. You used to take the point of your pencil and poke it up and down on my head when I didn't do my homework.

SISTER. You should have done your homework.

PHILOMENA. And when I didn't know how to do long division, you slammed my head against the blackboard.

SISTER. Did I ever break a bone?

PHILOMENA. No.

SISTER. There, you see! (*To* GARY.) And what about you?

GARY. You didn't do anything to me in particular. I just found you scary.

SISTER. Well I am scary.

GARY. But my lover Jeff doesn't like you cause you made him wet his pants too.

SISTER. All this obsession with the bladder. (*To* DIANE.) And you, the nasty one, why did you want to embarrass me?

DIANE. (*Said simply.*) Because I believed you. I believed how you said the world worked, and that God loved us, and the story of the Good Shepherd and the lost sheep; and I don't think you should lie to people.

SISTER. But that's how things are. I didn't lie.

DIANE. When I was sixteen, my mother got breast cancer, which spread. I prayed to God to let her suffering be small, but her suffering seemed to me quite extreme. She was in bad pain for half a year, and then terrible pain for much of a full year.

The ulcerations on her body were horrifying to her and to me. Her last few weeks she slipped into a semi-conscious state, which allowed her, unfortunately, to wake up for a few minutes at a time and to have a full awareness of her pain and her fear of death. She was able to recognize me, and she would try to cry, but she was unable to; and to speak, but she was unable to. I think she wanted me to get her new doctors; she never really accepted that her disease was going to kill her, and she thought in her panic that her doctors must be incompetent and that new ones could magically cure her. Then, thank goodness, she went into a full coma. A nurse who I knew to be Catholic assured me that everything would be done to keep her alive—a dubious comfort. Happily, the doctor was not Catholic, or if he was, not doctrinaire, and they didn't use extraordinary means to keep her alive; and she finally died after several more weeks in her coma. Now there are, I'm sure, far worse deaths—terrible burnings, tortures, plague, pestilence, famine; Christ on the cross even, as Sister likes to say. But I thought my mother's death was bad enough, and I got confused as to why I had been praying and to whom. I mean, if prayer was really this sort of button you pressed—admit you need the Lord, then He stops your suffering—then why didn't it always work? Or ever work? And when it worked, so-called, and our prayers were supposedly answered, wasn't it as likely to be chance as God? God always answers our prayers, you said, He just sometimes says no. But why would He say no to stopping my mother's suffering? I wasn't even asking that she live, just that He end her suffering. And it can't be that He was letting her suffer because she'd been bad, because she hadn't been bad and besides suffering doesn't seem to work that way, considering the suffering of children who've obviously done nothing wrong. So why was He letting her suffer? Spite? Was the Lord God actually malicious? That seemed possible, but far fetched. Maybe He had no control over it, maybe He wasn't omnipotent as you taught us He was. Maybe He created the world sort of by accident by belching one morning or getting the hiccups, and maybe He had no idea how the whole thing worked. In which case, He wouldn't be malicious, just useless. Or, of course, more likely than that, He didn't exist at all, the universe was hiccupped or belched into existence all on its own, and my mother's suffering just existed like rain or wind or humidity. I became angry at myself, and by extension at you, for ever having expected anything beyond randomness from the world. And while I was thinking these things, the day that my mother died, I was raped. Now I know that's really too much, one really loses all sympathy for me because I sound like I'm making it up or something. But bad things sometimes happen all at once, and this particular day on my return from the hospital I was raped by some maniac who broke into the house. He had a knife and cut me up some. Anyway, I don't really want to go on about the experience, but I got very depressed for about five years. Somehow the utter randomness of things—my mother's suffering, my attack by a lunatic who was either born a lunatic or made one by cruel parents or perhaps by an imbalance of hormones or whatever, etc. etc.—*this randomness seemed intolerable.* I found I grew to hate you, Sister, for making me once expect everything to be ordered and to make sense. My psychiatrist said he thought my hatred of you was obsessive, that I just was looking for someone to blame. Then he seduced me, and he was the father of my second abortion.

SISTER. I think she's making all this up.

DIANE. He said I seduced him. And maybe that's so. But he could be lying just to make himself feel better. (*To* SISTER.) And of course your idea that I should have had this baby, either baby, is preposterous. Have you any idea what a terrible mother I'd be? I'm a nervous wreck.

SISTER. God would have given you the strength.

DIANE. I suppose it is childish to look for blame, part of the randomness of things is that there is no one to blame; but basically I think everything is your fault, Sister.

SISTER. You have obviously never read the Book of Job.

DIANE. I have read it. And I think it's a nasty story.

SISTER. God explains in that story why He lets us suffer, and a very lovely explanation it is too. He likes to test us so that when we choose to love Him no matter what He does to us that proves how great and deep our love for Him is.

DIANE. That sounds like "The Story of O."

SISTER. Well there's obviously no talking to you. You don't want help or knowledge or enlightenment, so there's nothing left for you but an unhappy life, sickness, death, and hell.

DIANE. Last evening I killed my psychiatrist and now I'm going to kill you. (*Takes out a gun.*)

GARY. Oh dear. I thought we were just going to embarrass her.

SISTER. (*Stalling for time.*) And you have, very much so. So no need to kill me at all. Goodbye, Diane, Gary, Aloysius . . .

DIANE. You're insane. You shouldn't be allowed to teach

children. I see that there's that little boy here today. You're going to make him crazy.

SISTER. Thomas, stay offstage with the cookies, dear.

DIANE. I want you to admit that everything's your fault, and then I'm going to kill you.

PHILOMENA. Maybe we should all wait outside.

SISTER. Stay here. Diane, look at me. I was wrong. I admit it. I'm sorry. I thought everything made sense, but I didn't understand things properly. There's nothing I can say to make it up to you but . . . (*Seeing something awful behind* DIANE's *head.*) LOOK OUT! (DIANE *looks behind her,* SISTER *whips out her own gun and shoots* DIANE *dead.* SISTER *like a circus artist completing a stunt, hands up:*) Ta-da! For those non-Catholics present, murder is allowable in self-defense, one doesn't even have to tell it in confession. Thomas, bring me some water.

GARY. We didn't know she was bringing a gun. (THOMAS *brings water.*)

SISTER. I remember her now from class. (*Looks at her dead body.*) She had no sense of humor.

ALOYSIUS. I have to go to the bathroom.

SISTER. (*Aims gun at him.*) Stay where you are. Raise your hand if you want to go to the bathroom, Aloysius, and wait until I have acknowledged you. (*She ignores him now, though keeps gun aimed at him most of the time.*) Thomas, bring me a cookie. (*He does.*) Most of my students turned out beautifully, these are the few exceptions. But we never give up on those who've turned out badly, do we, Thomas? What is the story of the Good Shepherd and the Lost Sheep?

THOMAS. The Good Shepherd was so concerned about his Lost Sheep that he left his flock to go find the Lost Sheep, and then He found it.

SISTER. That's right. And while he was gone, a great big wolf came and killed his entire flock. No, just kidding, I'm feeling lightheaded from all this excitement. No, by the story of the Lost Sheep, Christ tells us that when a sinner strays we mustn't give up on the sinner. (SISTER *indicates for* THOMAS *to exit, he does.*) So I don't totally despair for these people standing here. Gary, I hope that you will leave your friend Jeff, don't even tell him where you're going, just disappear, and then I hope you will live your life as a celibate. Like me. Celibate rhymes with celebrate. Our Lord loves celibate people. And you, Philomena, I hope you will get married to some nice Catholic man, or if you stay unmarried then you too will become a celibate. Rhymes with celebrate.

ALOYSIUS. Sister, I have my hand up.

SISTER. Keep it up. And you, Aloysius, I hope you'll remember not to kill yourself, which is a mortal sin. For if we live by God's laws even though we are having a miserable life, remember heaven and eternal happiness are our reward.

GARY. Should we help you with the body, Sister?

SISTER. The janitor will help me later, thank you. You two may go now, so I can finish my lecture.

GARY. Why don't you let him go to the bathroom?

SISTER. Gary?

GARY. Yes, Sister?

SISTER. You still believe what you do with Jeff is wrong, don't you? I mean, you still confess it in confession, don't you?

GARY. Well I don't really think it's wrong, but I'm not sure, so I do still tell it in confession.

SISTER. When did you last go to confession?

GARY. This morning actually. I was going to be playing Saint Joseph and all.

SISTER. And you haven't sinned since then, have you?

GARY. No, Sister. (SISTER *shoots him dead.*)

SISTER. (*Triumphantly.*) I've sent him to heaven! (*To* PHILO-MENA.) Okay, you with the little girl, go home before I decide your little girl would be better off in a Catholic orphanage. (PHILOMENA *exits in terror. To audience.*) I'm not really within the letter of the law shooting Gary like this, but really if he did make a good confession I have sent him straight to heaven and eternal, blissful happiness. And I'm afraid otherwise he would have ended up in hell. I think Christ will allow me this little dispensation from the letter of the law, but I'll go to confession later today, just to be sure.

ALOYSIUS. Sister, I have to go to the bathroom.

SISTER. Wait until I recognize you, Aloysius.

ALOYSIUS. I'm going to leave now.

SISTER. (*Angry, emphasizing the gun.*) I've used this twice today, don't tempt me to use it again. Thomas! (*He enters.*) Who made you?

THOMAS. God made me.

SISTER. Why did God make you?

THOMAS. God made me to show forth his goodness and to share with us his happiness.

ALOYSIUS. If you don't let me go to the bathroom, I'm going to wet my pants.

SISTER. We have free will, Aloysius. Thomas, explain about the primary cause again.

THOMAS. Everything has a primary cause. Dinner is put on the table because the primary cause . . .

SISTER. Thomas, I'm going to nap some, I'm exhausted. (*Hands him gun.*) You keep that dangerous man over there covered, and if he moves shoot him; and also recite some nice catechism questions for us all while I rest. All right, dear?

THOMAS. Yes, Sister. (*Sister sits on a chair and naps.* THOMAS *sits on her lap, aiming the gun at* ALOYSIUS, *and recites from memory.*)

"What must we do to gain the happiness of heaven?"
   To gain the happiness of heaven, we must know, love, and serve God in this world.
   (*Lights start to dim*)
"From whom do we learn to know, love and serve God?"
   We learn to know, love, and serve God from Jesus Christ, the Son of God, who teaches us through the Catholic Church
"What are some of the perfections of God?"
   Some of the perfections of God are: God is eternal, all-good, all-knowing, all-present, and almighty.
   (*Lights have dimmed to black.*)

ADDENDUM
(Author's Notes)

Since scripts are so open to interpretations, I wanted to suggest some things to avoid, as well as to aim for, in presenting this play; and to make a few clarifications.

The casting of Sister Mary is obviously of the utmost importance. In casting for the Ensemble Studio Theatre production, we saw a great many different types for Sister; and these auditions were helpful in suggesting the various pitfalls of casting and playing the role.

For starters, it's a mistake to have an actress play (or, worse, seem to be) mean. Though a strident, bullying approach may work in an audition and even be funny, it can't really sustain for the whole play; we see Sister kill two people at the end of the play, we shouldn't expect her to do so five minutes after we first see her. (There are places, of course, where Sister *should* be strident and bullying; but it should be underneath and revealed only sometimes.) Also, perhaps more importantly, the strength and power of figures like Sister Mary (or, say, Jean Brodie) is in their charm; we believe them because they take us in. If Sister were obviously a horror, we'd know not to believe her.

In line with this, the relationship between Sister and Thomas should have warmth and even love. It's true that she presents him as one might present a dog doing tricks; and yet he does all the tricks well, and she rewards him with not only cookies but warmth, approval, bounces on the knee, etc. All this fondness and attention could easily make Thomas adore Sister.

The actress playing Sister should avoid commenting on her role. (All the actors should avoid commenting.) The humor works best when presented straight. That is, it's fine that we as an audience think it outrageous that Sister contemplates Thomas' castration to save his pretty voice; the actress should not indicate her own awareness of this outrageousness (that kind of comic-wink acting that is effective sometimes in a skit, rarely in a play). Sister thinks nothing is wrong with her contemplation, and it's only her feelings we should see.

In terms of age range for Sister, anywhere between forty and sixty seems correct to me. The over-sixty, more grandmotherly-looking actresses we auditioned seemed to throw the play out of whack: they seemed less powerful and more dotty, and also we felt bad for them when the ex-students berated them.

It is possible to consider casting someone younger as Sister, though you will lose the important theatrical fact of having three generations on stage. However, depending on your casting resources, a younger Sister Mary with comic flair and believability is, of course, preferable to an older one with neither attribute.

One other thought in terms of casting: the excellent Sister Mary at E.S.T., Elizabeth Franz, also brought to the role a delicate femininity that was true to a certain kind of real-life nun, very much added to her charm with Thomas and with the audience, and was an extremely effective starting point that nowhere tipped off Sister's potential for murderous rages.

Thomas should be seven or eight, and be smart and polite. There should be no attempt to play up his being a child (like having him not be able to read the list of names going to hell; he should read them easily). An older child could play it, but seven or eight has a genuine innocence that can't be faked—an innocence which is central to the play's meaning.

The tone of the pageant is tricky. It should be childlike, as opposed to childish. It is thirty year olds performing it, so they shouldn't pretend to be children, but they can't act like adults precisely either. They should be simple and direct, presenting the story as if we didn't know it and as if it didn't have a child's imprint on the writing. Lots of busy stage business making fun of clunky amateur productions will get in the way.

There is and enormous trap to be avoided in the playing of the four ex-students, and that centers around their apparent plot to come to Sister's lecture to "embarrass" her.

For starters, you mustn't play the plot as a subtext in the pageant or really anywhere before it's mentioned because the audience simply won't know what you're doing. Plus, there's a further trap: if you choose to play that the four have come to embarrass Sister by telling her how much they've strayed from her teaching (Philomena's illegitimate child, Gary's being gay), those revelation scenes won't work comically (as they're intended) because the comedy is based partially on Gary and Philomena not meaning to reveal what Sister drags out of them.

I think to make sense of the "plot" (happily, this is something the audience doesn't really have time to brood about) one would have to imagine Diane calling up the other three with an extremely *vague* plan: let's put on that old pageant, which is so silly and which will disrupt her lecture; then the "point" of the intrusion will be to eventually tell Sister that she's not fondly remembered (her temper, her not letting people go to the bathroom, etc.). Or maybe the plan is only to put on the pageant, just as a joke to themselves on their past. The vaguer you allow the plan to be in your head, the less saddled with unnecessary subtext you'll be and the more easily (and humorously) the various confrontations with Sister will play. (Diane's sense of the plan has to be different and darker than the others, of course, because she's packing a gun; but even she can be unsure of what she's going to do. Note: I do see the logic of Diane showing some of her bitterness and edge in the pageant, but I warn against it as confusing to the audience and as destructive to the enjoyment of the pageant.)

A final danger in playing the foursome: avoid kvetching (admittedly tricky since complaining *is* more or less what they're doing in some sections). With Philomena's complaints about being hit and with Aloysius' complaints about the bathroom, it's important to find a balance between the legitimate complaints (Sister was indeed spiteful) and the fact that Philomena and Aloysius are near thirty and that these things are in the past. Apropos of this, real horror and sense memory of what it was like not to go to the bathroom are to be avoided; if the complaints are presented too hysterically, the people will seem stupid and I don't want them to be stupid. It's difficult: I don't want them to be blasé either. It's a balance that's needed, that sense of having the character know it's childish to still be angry but to nonetheless still be angry.

A word or two about Diane's monologue. It is obviously meant very seriously, but though it has a high emotional content, the actress should be very careful in how much emotion she lets through and when. In auditions, some actresses ranted and raved and wept in the speech, and it was ungodly. Diane's speech is very verbal, and very methodically point-by-point; hysteria is an illogical interpretation of the tone and content of what she's saying.

The speech has so much charged material (the mother's death, the rape) that one must also be careful not to *ask* for sympathy.

It might be helpful in approaching the speech to remember that what she describes happened many years ago (not that she's not traumatized, it's just that time has taken some of the immediacy away at least); and also that Diane tries to *distance* herself from the pain she feels by being analytic. The tone of much of the speech, whatever underlying sadness might come through, should be factual, her attempt at distancing herself:

this happened to me, and then I thought that, but that wasn't true, so then I thought this and this, etc.

There is, though, probably a natural place (among other possibilities) for the anger and pain to break through all this distancing, and that's on "—this randomness seemed intolerable," which both follows a particularly futile attempt at reasoning things out (her run-on, off-the-point comments on what made the rapist a rapist) and is also the core of what she hates Sister for: making her expect and desire order where there doesn't seem to be any.

Some miscellaneous things:

At E.S.T. we cast Aloysius as an Italian street kid grown up, and changed his last name to Busiccio. This seemed to work fine, and is an option. The other option, I'd presume, is to present him as tense, formal, uptight, and of undetermined ancestry. (Note: with the latter option, be careful that the interpretation does not imply homosexuality in any way, which would throw the play's balance off.)

Gary is not meant to be effeminate. Sister's comment to that effect is meant to show her prejudice, not reflect any reality.

When Gary says "Definitely not" to Sister's query as to whether he uses birth control, I don't mean for him to be playing cat-and-mouse with her or to be making some smirking allusion to being gay; it's simply that he indeed doesn't use birth control and he says "definitely not" quickly, without thinking what it might imply. The scene plays comically if she draw these facts out of him unwittingly; otherwise we're back in the "revenge plot" trap again.

"Celibate" does not rhyme with "celebrate," nor (in my mind) does Sister think it does. I prefer that she pronounce both words properly and then says they rhyme because she wants them to; it sort of extends her power to say blatantly false things when she feels like it, to make a point (as when she says Christ stoned many women taken in adultery).

In production, we found having Sister's gun right in the lectern (out of sight) worked best, with Sister standing conveniently behind it. Having it in her habit seemed unworkable. Diane's gun, though, seemed to fit inside her blazer successfully.

Some extra thoughts on "Sister Mary" since I wrote the first notes.

I wish to reiterate the advice that Sister *not* be played as mean and that she show and have real affection for Thomas. I also want to urge that the actress play that Sister really *does* want the best for her students, it's just that she feels she has the infallible truth on most matters and so is understandably confused and angered when her students turn out not to have followed her teachings. Thus, she should be *really* furious during what Jerry Zaks and I call her "Blah!" speech (p.211); we often used this speech to audition understudies and replacements and found that it was important to see if the actress was willing to commit to the enormity of Sister's anger there; without Sister's out and out exploding at this point, the shape of the play goes off, and the seriousness of Diane's speech and the later killings will seem unprepared for and stylistically out of the blue.

Another stray point about Sister. Her speeches are a real mouthful; maybe it's due to all those years studying Latin, but for some reason Sister's diction is convoluted and not average. There are some actresses who have a tendency to *hold on* to the words, and to work too hard coloring each one of Sister's lines. Alas, it must be an instinctive thing because obviously I'm not asking that the actress speak in a rapid monotone. But there are two kinds of examples I can give of when it's good that the actress not *hold on* to words.

The first concerns how Sister presents all the various rules. In the first half of the play when she is making statements about "how things are"—such as "there are also unspeakable physical torments" and "Purgatory, depending on our sins, can go on for a very long time and is fairly unpleasant"—these rules can be presented in a straight-forward manner and be all the funnier for being conversational. If you drag out and color the words "unspeakable," "torments," "fairly" or "unpleasant"—or emphasize all four of them—you will probably be on the way to making Sister's diction laborious as well as lengthy.

The second kind of example occurs when Sister is basically making one point, but saying it in a long-winded fashion; it is best at those times not to break the thought up into several little beats. For instance, when Sister explains the Book of Job, she says "He likes to test us so that when we choose to love Him no matter what He does to us that proves how great and deep our love for Him is." That's not a simple sentence to memorize, but it is one complete thought, with no commas indicating "rests," so it should be said as smoothly and as uninterruptedly as possible. I heard a fine actress once play the speech instead as follows: "He likes to test us (pause), so that when we choose to love Him (pause), no matter what He does to us (pause), that proves how great (pause) and deep (pause) our love for Him is." Because the actress in question was a fine one, the moment held and we got her sincerity; but the overall pace was not helped, and actually the sense of the line itself was not helped by all those pauses either. I hope this isn't confusing; but when you're auditioning actresses, look out for those who make the speeches stop and start in ways not indicated in the script.

PACE DURING THE LAST SECTION OF THE PLAY

From the point when Sister shoots Diane, she has taken control back and can shortly return to her lecture. Sister feels exhilarated from the joy of having things in her control again and speedy from the unexpected way in which things have turned out. So be sure that from Diane's killing on, Sister is excited and exhilarated; thus most of the pace of this last section of the play should be fast.

CUTS IN THE PAGEANT

The pageant as presently in the written text seems to play as too long, especially on a double bill with "The Actor's Nightmare," so in New York and Los Angeles we made the following cuts.

On page 203, cut Gary's second line "Excuse me you don't have room at this Inn, do you? (*Listens.*) He said they don't, Mary" down through Diane's line "Let's try the third Inn." This section would now read:

DIANE. Well ask them, Joseph.
GARY. (*Knocks.*) Excuse me, you don't have room at your Inn, do you? (*Listens.*) I thought not . . . What? You would? (Etc.)

Cut Diane's line "It smells just like the zoo Mommy took me and Cynthia to visit last summer. We liked to look at the animals, but we didn't like to smell them."
Also cut Diane's "I'm so tired, I could sleep anywhere."
On page 205, cut Gary's line "and He said many unusual things, many of them irritating to parents. Things like 'Before Abraham was, I am' (etc.)" up through "to find Him for hours and hours."

Gary's newer, simpler lines after the above cut would then be: "And so Jesus instructed His parents, and the priests in the Temple. And He performed many miracles."

Same page, cut Diane's "And what do you mean by 'I must die so that others may know eternal life?' "

Same page, cut Diane's "And it's Adam and Eve anyway, not us."

Same page, cut Gary's speech from "rather man must have total and complete faith" up through "doesn't question his parents."

Same page, cut the lines about the two thieves, starting with Diane's "And Jesus looked at the two thieves . . ." up through Diane's "Thou art condemned for all eternity."

On page 206, a big cut: cut Diane's "I can't see the angel, can you, Joseph?" and *all* of Aloysius's following speech.

What remains after the above cut is as follows:

ALOYSIUS. Mary and Joseph, your son Jesus has risen from the dead just like your dumb animal Misty told you He would.

DIANE. Thank you, Misty, you were right. [new line] (*Kisses Misty.*)

GARY. And then Mary and Joseph, realizing their lack of faith, made a good act of contrition. (Etc. as written)

MISCELLANEOUS

Contrary to my earlier note, we have now found it perfectly possible to have Sister keep the gun hidden in her habit; just, of course, work it out so she doesn't have trouble getting it out of her pocket, and so no one ever notices it before it's appropriate.

That's all. I hope the notes aren't confusing.

—Christopher Durang
February, 1984

CRIMES OF
THE HEART

A PLAY

by
Beth Henley

THE CHARACTERS

LENNY MAGRATH, thirty, the oldest sister
CHICK BOYLE, twenty-nine, the sister's first cousin
DOC PORTER, thirty, Meg's old boyfriend
MEG MAGRATH, twenty-seven, the middle sister
BABE BOTRELLE, twenty-four, the youngest sister
BARNETTE LLOYD, twenty-six, Babe's lawyer

THE SETTING

The setting of the entire play is the kitchen in the MaGrath sisters' house in Hazlehurst, Mississippi, a small Southern town. The old-fashioned kitchen is unusually spacious, but there is a lived-in, cluttered look about it. There are four different entrances and exits to the kitchen: the back door, the door leading to the dining room and the front of the house, a door leading to the downstairs bedroom and a staircase leading to the upstairs room. There is a table near the center of the room, and a cot has been set up in one of the corners.

THE TIME

In the fall, five years after Hurricane Camille.

Warner Theatre Productions, Inc., Claire Nichtern, Mary Lea Johnson, Martin Richards, and Francine LeFrak presented *Crimes of the Heart* in New York City, opening November 4, 1981, at the John Golden Theatre. The production was directed by Melvin Bernhardt.

Cast
(*in order of appearance*)

LENNY MAGRATH	Lizbeth Mackay
CHICK BOYLE	Sharon Ullrick
DOC PORTER	Raymond Baker
MEG MAGRATH	Mary Beth Hurt
BABE BOTRELLE	Mia Dillion
BARNETTE LLOYD	Peter MacNicol

John Lee Beatty designed the sets. Patricia McGourty designed the costumes. Dennie Parichy designed the lighting.

Crimes of the Heart was given its New York première by the Manhattan Theatre Club in 1980. Originally produced at Actors Theatre of Louisville in February 1979.

ACT ONE

The lights go up on the empty kitchen. It is late afternoon. LENNY MAGRATH, a thirty-year-old woman with a round figure and face, enters from the back door carrying a white suitcase, a saxophone case, and a brown paper sack. She sets the suitcase and the sax case down and takes the brown sack to the kitchen table. After glancing quickly at the door, she gets the cookie jar from the kitchen counter, a box of matches from the stove, and then brings both objects back to the kitchen table. Excitedly, she reaches into the brown sack and pulls out a package of birthday candles. She quickly opens the package and removes a candle. She tries to stick the candle onto a cookie—it falls off. She sticks the candle in again, but the cookie is too hard and it crumbles. Frantically, she gets a second cookie from the jar. She strikes a match, lights the candle, and begins dripping wax onto the cookie. Just as she is beginning to smile we hear CHICK's voice from offstage.

CHICK'S VOICE: Lenny! Oh, Lenny! (LENNY *quickly blows out the candle and stuffs the cookie and candle into her dress pocket.* CHICK, *twenty-nine, enters from the back door. She is a brightly dressed matron with yellow hair and shiny red lips.*)

CHICK. Hi! I saw your car pull up.

LENNY. Hi.

CHICK. Well, did you see today's paper?

(LENNY *nods.*)

CHICK. It's just too awful! It's just way too awful! How I'm gonna continue holding my head up high in this community, I do not know. Did you remember to pick up those pantyhose for me?

LENNY. They're in the sack.

CHICK. Well, thank goodness, at least I'm not gonna have to go into town wearing holes in my stockings. (*She gets the package, tears it open, and proceeds to take off one pair of stockings and put on another throughout the following scene.*

There should be something slightly grotesque about this woman changing her stockings in the kitchen.)

LENNY. Did Uncle Watson call?

CHICK. Yes, Daddy has called me twice already. He said Babe's ready to come home. We've got to get right over and pick her up before they change their simple minds.

LENNY. (*Hesitantly.*) Oh, I know, of course, it's just—

CHICK. What?

LENNY. Well, I was hoping Meg would call.

CHICK. Meg?

LENNY. Yes, I sent her a telegram: about Babe, and—

CHICK. A telegram?! Couldn't you just phone her up?

LENNY. Well, no, 'cause her phone's . . . out of order.

CHICK. Out of order?

LENNY. Disconnected. I don't know what.

CHICK. Well, that sounds like Meg. My, these are snug. Are you sure you bought my right size?

LENNY. (*Looking at the box.*) Size extra-petite.

CHICK. Well, they're skimping on the nylon material. (*Struggling to pull up the stockings.*) That's all there is to it. Skimping on the nylon. (*She finishes one leg and starts the other.*) Now, just what all did you say in this "telegram" to Meg?

LENNY. I don't recall exactly. I, well, I just told her to come on home.

CHICK. To come on home! Why, Lenora Josephine, have you lost your only brain, or what?

LENNY. (*Nervously, as she begins to pick up the mess of dirty stockings and plastic wrappings.*) But Babe wants Meg home. She asked me to call her.

CHICK. I'm not talking about what Babe wants.

LENNY. Well, what then?

CHICK. Listen, Lenora, I think it's pretty accurate to assume that after this morning's paper, Babe's gonna be incurring some mighty negative publicity around this town. And Meg's appearance isn't gonna help out a bit.

LENNY. What's wrong with Meg?

CHICK. She had a loose reputation in high school.

LENNY. (*Weakly.*) She was popular.

CHICK. She was known all over Copiah County as cheap Christmas trash, and that was the least of it. There was that whole sordid affair with Doc Porter, leaving him a cripple.

LENNY. A cripple—he's got a limp. Just kind of, barely a limp.

CHICK. Well, his mother was going to keep *me* out of the Ladies' Social League because of it.

LENNY. What?

CHICK. That's right. I never told you, but I had to go plead with that mean old woman and convinced her that I was just as appalled with what Meg had done as she was, and that I was only a first cousin anyway and I could hardly be blamed for all the skeletons in the MaGraths' closet. It was humiliating. I tell you, she even brought up your mother's death. And that poor cat.

LENNY. Oh! Oh! Oh, please, Chick! I'm sorry. But you're in the Ladies' League now.

CHICK. Yes. That's true, I am. But frankly, if Mrs. Porter hadn't developed that tumor in her bladder, I wouldn't be in the club today, much less a committee head. (*As she brushes her hair.*) Anyway, you be a sweet potato and wait right here for Meg to call, so's you can convince her not to come back home. It would make things a whole lot easier on everybody. Don't you think it really would?

LENNY. Probably.

CHICK. Good, then suit yourself. How's my hair?

LENNY. Fine.

CHICK. Not pooching out in the back, is it?

LENNY. No.

CHICK. (*Cleaning the hair from her brush.*) All right then, I'm on my way. I've got Annie May over there keeping an eye on Peekay and Buck Jr., but I don't trust her with them for long periods of time. (*Dropping the ball of hair onto the floor.*) Her mind is like a loose sieve. Honestly, it is. (*As she puts the brush back into her purse.*) Oh! Oh! Oh! I almost forgot. Here's a present for you. Happy birthday to Lenny, from the Buck Boyles! (*She takes a wrapped package from her bag and hands it to* LENNY.)

LENNY. Why, thank you, Chick. It's so nice to have you remember my birthday every year like you do.

CHICK. (*Modestly.*) Oh, well, now, that's just the way I am, I suppose. That's just the way I was brought up to be. Well, why don't you go on and open up the present?

LENNY. All right. (*She starts to unwrap the gift.*)

CHICK. It's a box of candy—assorted crèmes.

LENNY. Candy—that's always a nice gift.

CHICK. And you have a sweet tooth, don't you?

LENNY. I guess.

CHICK. Well, I'm glad you like it.

LENNY. I do.

CHICK. Oh, speaking of which, remember that little polka-dot dress you got Peekay for her fifth birthday last month?

LENNY. The red-and-white one?

CHICK. Yes; well, the first time I put it in the washing machine, I mean the very first time, it fell all to pieces. Those little polka dots just dropped right off in the water.

LENNY. (*Crushed.*) Oh, no. Well, I'll get something else for her, then—a little toy.

CHICK. Oh, no, no, no, no, no! We wouldn't hear of it! I just wanted to let you know so you wouldn't go and waste any more of your hard-earned money on that make of dress. Those inexpensive brands just don't hold up. I'm sorry, but not in these modern washing machines.

DOC PORTER'S VOICE. Hello! Hello, Lenny!

CHICK. (*Taking over.*) Oh, look, it's Doc Porter! Come on in Doc! Please come right on in!

(DOC PORTER *enters through the back door. He is carrying a large sack of pecans.* DOC *is an attractively worn man with a slight limp that adds rather than detracts from his quiet seductive quality. He is thirty years old, but appears slightly older.*)

CHICK. Well, how are you doing? How in the world are you doing?

DOC. Just fine, Chick.

CHICK. And how are you liking it now that you're back in Hazlehurst?

DOC. Oh, I'm finding it somewhat enjoyable.

CHICK. Somewhat! Only somewhat! Will you listen to him! What a silly, silly, silly man! Well, I'm on my way. I've got some people waiting on me. (*Whispering to Doc.*) It's Babe. I'm on my way to pick her up.

DOC. Oh.

CHICK. Well, goodbye! Farewell and goodbye!

LENNY. 'Bye.

(CHICK *exits.*)

DOC. Hello.

LENNY. Hi. I guess you heard about the thing with Babe.

DOC. Yeah.

LENNY. It was in the newspaper.

DOC. Uh huh.

LENNY. What a mess.

DOC. Yeah.

LENNY. Well, come on and sit down. I'll heat us up some coffee.

DOC. That's okay. I can only stay a minute. I have to pick up Scott; he's at the dentist.

LENNY. Oh; well, I'll heat some up for myself. I'm kinda thirsty for a cup of hot coffee. (*She puts the coffeepot on the burner.*)

DOC. Lenny—

LENNY. What?

DOC. (*Not able to go on.*) Ah . . .

LENNY. Yes?

DOC. Here, some pecans for you. (*He hands her the sack.*)

LENNY. Why, thank you, Doc. I love pecans.

DOC. My wife and Scott picked them up around the yard.

LENNY. Well, I can use them to make a pie. A pecan pie.

DOC. Yeah. Look, Lenny, I've got some bad news for you.

LENNY. What?

DOC. Well, you know, you've been keeping Billy Boy out on our farm; he's been grazing out there.

LENNY. Yes—

DOC. Well, last night, Billy Boy died.

LENNY. He died?

DOC. Yeah. I'm sorry to tell you when you've got all this on you, but I thought you'd want to know.

LENNY. Well, yeah. I do. He died?

DOC. Uh huh. He was struck by lightning.

LENNY. Struck by lightning? In that storm yesterday?

DOC. That's what we think.

LENNY. Gosh, struck by lightning. I've had Billy Boy so long. You know. Ever since I was ten years old.

DOC. Yeah. He was a mighty old horse.

LENNY. (*Stung.*) Mighty old.

DOC. Almost twenty years old.

LENNY. That's right, twenty years. 'Cause; ah, I'm thirty years old today. Did you know that?

DOC. No, Lenny, I didn't know. Happy birthday.

LENNY. Thanks. (*She begins to cry.*)

DOC. Oh, come on now, Lenny. Come on. Hey, hey, now. You know I can't stand it when you MaGrath women start to cry. You know it just gets me.

LENNY. Oh ho! Sure! You mean when Meg cries! Meg's the one you could never stand to watch cry! Not me! I could fill up a pig's trough!

DOC. Now, Lenny . . . stop it. Come on. Jesus!

LENNY. Okay! Okay! I don't know what's wrong with me. I don't mean to make a scene. I've been on this crying jag. (*She blows her nose.*) All this stuff with Babe, and Old Granddaddy's gotten worse in the hospital, and I can't get in touch with Meg.

DOC. You tried calling Meggy?

LENNY. Yes.

DOC. Is she coming home?

LENNY. Who knows. She hasn't called me. That's what I'm waiting here for—hoping she'll call.

DOC. She still living in California?

LENNY. Yes; in Hollywood.

DOC. Well, give me a call if she gets in. I'd like to see her.

LENNY. Oh, you would, huh?

DOC. Yeah, Lenny, sad to say, but I would.

LENNY. It is sad. It's very sad indeed. (*They stare at each other, then look away. There is a moment of tense silence.*)

DOC. Hey, Jell-O Face, your coffee's boiling.

LENNY. (*Going to check*) Oh, it is? Thanks. (*After she checks the pot.*) Look, you'd better go on and pick Scott up. You don't want him to have to wait for you.

DOC. Yeah, you're right. Poor kid. It's his first time at the dentist.

LENNY. Poor thing.

DOC. Well, 'bye. I'm sorry to have to tell you about your horse.

LENNY. Oh, I know. Tell Joan thanks for picking up the pecans.

DOC. I will. (*He starts to leave.*)

LENNY. Oh, how's the baby?

DOC. She's fine. Real pretty. She, ah, holds your finger in her hand; like this.

LENNY. Oh, that's cute.

DOC. Yeah. 'Bye, Lenny.

LENNY. 'Bye.

(DOC *exits.* LENNY *stares after him for a moment, then goes and sits down at the kitchen table. She reaches into her pocket and pulls out a somewhat crumbled cookie and a wax candle. She lights the candle again, lets the wax drip onto the cookie, then sticks the candle on top of the cookie. She begins to sing the "Happy Birthday" song to herself. At the end of the song she pauses, silently makes a wish, and blows out the candle. She waits a moment, then relights the candle, and repeats her ac-*

tions, only this time making a different wish at the end of the song. She starts to repeat the procedure for the third time, as the phone rings. She goes to answer it.)

LENNY. Hello . . . Oh, hello, Lucille, how's Zackery? . . . Oh, no! . . . Oh, I'm so sorry. Of course, it must be grueling for you . . . Yes, I understand. Your only brother . . . No, she's not here yet. Chick just went to pick her up . . . Oh, now, Lucille, she's still his wife, I'm sure she'll be interested . . . Well, you can just tell me the information and I'll relate it all to her . . . Uh hum, his liver's saved. Oh, that's good news! . . . Well, of course, when you look at it like that . . . Breathing stabilized . . . Damage to the spinal column, not yet determined . . . Okay . . . Yes, Lucille, I've got it all down . . . Uh huh, I'll give her that message. 'Bye, 'bye. (LENNY *drops the pencil and paper. She sighs deeply, wipes her cheeks with the back of her hand, and goes to the stove to pour herself a cup of coffee. After a few moments, the front door is heard slamming.* LENNY *starts. A whistle is heard, then* MEG's *voice.)*

MEG'S VOICE. I'm home! (*She whistles the family whistle.*) Anybody home?

LENNY. Meg? Meg!

(MEG, twenty-seven, enters from the dining room. She has sad, magic eyes and wears a hat. She carries a worn-out suitcase.)

MEG. (*Dropping her suitcase, running to hug* LENNY.) Lenny—

LENNY. Well, Meg! Why, Meg! Oh, Meggy! Why didn't you call? Did you fly in? You didn't take a cab, did you? Why didn't you give us a call?

MEG. (*Overlapping.*) Oh, Lenny! Why, Lenny! Dear Lenny! (*Then she looks at Lenny's face.*) My God, we're getting so old! Oh, I called, for heaven's sake. Of course, I called!

LENNY. Well, I never talked to you—

MEG. Well, I know! I let the phone ring right off the hook!

LENNY. Well, as a matter of fact, I was out most of the morning seeing to Babe—

MEG. Now, just what's all this business about Babe? How could you send me such a telegram about Babe? And Zackery! You say somebody's shot Zackery?

LENNY. Yes, they have.

MEG. Well, good Lord! Is he dead?

LENNY. No. But he's in the hospital. He was shot in his stomach.

MEG. In his stomach! How awful! Do they know who shot him? (LENNY nods.) Well, who? Who was it? Who? Who?

LENNY. Babe! They're all saying Babe shot him! They took her to jail! And they're saying she shot him! They're all saying it! It's horrible! It's awful!

MEG. (*Overlapping.*) Jail! Good Lord, jail! Well, who? Who's saying it? Who?

LENNY. Everyone! The policemen, the sheriff, Zackery, even Babe's saying it! Even Babe herself!

MEG. Well, for God's sake. For God's sake.

LENNY. (*Overlapping as she falls apart.*) It's horrible! It's horrible! It's just horrible!

MEG. Now calm down, Lenny. Just calm down. Would you like a Coke? Here, I'll get you some Coke. (*She gets a Coke from the refrigerator. She opens it and downs a large swig.*) Why? Why would she shoot him? Why? (*She hands the Coke bottle to* LENNY.)

LENNY. I talked to her this morning and I asked her that very question. I said, "Babe, why would you shoot Zackery? He was your own husband. Why would you shoot him?" And do you know what she said? (MEG *shakes her head.*) She said, " 'Cause I didn't like his looks. I just didn't like his looks."

MEG. (*After a pause.*) Well, I don't like his looks.

LENNY. But you didn't shoot him! You wouldn't shoot a person 'cause you didn't like their looks! You wouldn't do that! Oh, I hate to say this—I do hate to say this—but I believe Babe is ill. I mean in-her-head ill.

MEG. Oh, now, Lenny, don't you say that! There're plenty of good sane reasons to shoot another person, and I'm sure that Babe had one. Now, what we've got to do is get her the best lawyer in town. Do you have any ideas on who's the best lawyer in town?

LENNY. Well, Zackery is, of course; but he's been shot!

MEG. Well, count him out! Just count him and his whole firm out!

LENNY. Anyway, you don't have to worry, she's already got her lawyer.

MEG. She does? Who?

LENNY. Barnette Lloyd. Annie Lloyd's boy. He just opened his office here in town. And Uncle Watson said we'd be doing Annie a favor by hiring him up.

MEG. Doing Annie a favor? Doing Annie a favor! Well, what about Babe? Have you thought about Babe? Do we want to do her a favor of thirty or forty years in jail? Have you thought about that?

LENNY. Now, don't snap at me! Just don't snap at me! I try to do what's right! All this responsibility keeps falling on my shoulders, and I try to do what's right!

MEG. Well, boo hoo, hoo, hoo! And how in the hell could you send me such a telegram about Babe!

LENNY. Well, if you had a phone, or if you didn't live way out there in Hollywood and not even come home for Christmas, maybe I wouldn't have to pay all that money to send you a telegram!

MEG. (*Overlapping.*) BABE'S IN TERRIBLE TROUBLE—STOP! ZACKERY'S BEEN SHOT—STOP! COME HOME IMMEDIATELY—STOP! STOP! STOP!

LENNY. And what was that you said about how old we're getting? When you looked at my face, you said. "My God, we're getting so old!" But you didn't mean we—you meant me! Didn't you? I'm thirty years old today and my face is getting all pinched up and my hair is falling out in the comb.

MEG. Why, Lenny! It's your birthday, October 23. How could I forget. Happy birthday!

LENNY. Well, it's not. I'm thirty years old and Billy Boy died last night. He was struck by lightning. He was struck dead.

MEG. (*Reaching for a cigarette.*) Struck dead. Oh, what a mess. What a mess. Are you really thirty? Then I must be twenty-seven and Babe is twenty-four. My God, we're getting so old. (*They are silent for several moments as* MEG *drags off her cigarette and* LENNY *drinks her Coke.*) What's the cot doing in the kitchen?

LENNY. Well, I rolled it out when Old Granddaddy got sick. So I could be close and hear him at night if he needed something.

MEG. (*Glancing toward the door leading to the downstairs bedroom.*) Is Old Granddaddy here?

LENNY. Why, no. Old Granddaddy's at the hospital.

MEG. Again?

LENNY. Meg!

MEG. What?

LENNY. I wrote you all about it. He's been in the hospital over three months straight.

MEG. He has?

LENNY. Don't you remember? I wrote you about all those blood vessels popping in his brain?

MEG. Popping—

LENNY. And how he was so anxious to hear from you and to

find out about your singing career. I wrote it all to you. How they have to feed him through those tubes now. Didn't you get my letters?

MEG. Oh, I don't know, Lenny. I guess I did. To tell you the truth, sometimes I kinda don't read your letters.

LENNY. What?

MEG. I'm sorry. I used to read them. It's just, since Christmas reading them gives me these slicing pains right here in my chest.

LENNY. I see. I see. Is that why you didn't use that money Old Granddaddy sent you to come home Christmas; because you hate us so much? We never did all that much to make you hate us. We didn't!

MEG. Oh, Lenny! Do you think I'd be getting slicing pains in my chest if I didn't care about you? If I hated you? Honestly, now, do you think I would?

LENNY. No.

MEG. Okay, then. Let's drop it. I'm sorry I didn't read your letters. Okay?

LENNY. Okay.

MEG. Anyway, we've got this whole thing with Babe to deal with. The first thing is to get her a good lawyer and get her out of jail.

LENNY. Well, she's out of jail.

MEG. She is?

LENNY. That young lawyer, he's gotten her out.

MEG. Oh, he has?

LENNY. Yes, on bail. Uncle Watson's put it up. Chick's bringing her back right now—she's driving her home.

MEG. Oh; well, that's a relief.

LENNY. Yes, and they're due home any minute now; so we can just wait right here for 'em.

MEG. Well, good. That's good. (As she leans against the counter.) So, Babe shot Zackery Botrelle, the richest and most powerful man in all of Hazlehurst, slap in the gut. It's hard to believe.

LENNY. It certainly is. Little Babe—shooting off a gun.

MEG. Little Babe.

LENNY. She was always the prettiest and most perfect of the three of us. Old Granddaddy used to call her his Dancing Sugar Plum. Why, remember how proud and happy he was the day she married Zackery.

MEG. Yes, I remember. It was his finest hour.

LENNY. He remarked how Babe was gonna skyrocket right to

the heights of Hazlehurst society. And how Zackery was just the right man for her whether she knew it now or not.

MEG. Oh, Lordy, Lordy. And what does Old Granddaddy say now?

LENNY. Well, I haven't had the courage to tell him all about this as yet. I thought maybe tonight we could go to visit him at the hospital, and you could talk to him and . . .

MEG. Yeah; well, we'll see. We'll see. Do we have anything to drink around here—to the tune of straight bourbon?

LENNY. No. There's no liquor.

MEG. Hell. (*She gets a Coke from the refrigerator and opens it.*)

LENNY. Then you *will* go with me to see Old Granddaddy at the hospital tonight?

MEG. Of course. (*She goes to her purse and gets out a bottle of Empirin. She takes out a tablet and puts it on her tongue.*) Brother, I know he's gonna go on about my singing career. Just like he always does.

LENNY. Well, how is your career going?

MEG. It's not.

LENNY. Why, aren't you still singing at that club down on Malibu beach?

MEG. No. Not since Christmas.

LENNY. Well, then, are you singing someplace new?

MEG. No, I'm not singing. I'm not singing at all.

LENNY. Oh. Well, what do you do then?

MEG. What I do is I pay cold-storage bills for a dog-food company. That's what I do.

LENNY. (*Trying to be helpful.*) Gosh, don't you think it'd be a good idea to stay in the show business field?

MEG. Oh, maybe.

LENNY. Like Old Granddaddy says, "With your talent, all you need is exposure. Then you can make your own breaks!" Did you hear his suggestion about getting your foot put in one of those blocks of cement they've got out there? He thinks that's real important.

MEG. Yeah. I think I've heard that. And I'll probably hear it again when I go to visit him at the hospital tonight; so let's just drop it. Okay? (*She notices the sack of pecans.*) What's this? Pecans? Great, I love pecans! (*She takes out two pecans and tries to open them by cracking them together*) Come one . . . Crack, you demons! Crack!

LENNY. We have a nutcracker!

MEG. (*Trying with her teeth.*) Ah, where's the sport in a nutcracker? Where's the challenge?

LENNY. (*Getting the nutcracker.*) It's over here in the utensil drawer. (*As* LENNY *gets the nutcracker,* MEG *opens the pecan by stepping on it with her shoe.*)

MEG. There! Open! (*She picks up the crumbled pecan and eats it.*) Mmmm, delicious. Delicious. Where'd you get the fresh pecans?

LENNY. Oh . . . I don't know.

MEG. They sure are tasty.

LENNY. Doc Porter brought them over.

MEG. Doc. What's Doc doing here in town?

LENNY. Well, his father died a couple of months ago. Now he's back home seeing to his property.

MEG. Gosh, the last I heard of Doc, he was up in the East painting the walls of houses to earn a living. (*Amused.*) Heard he was living with some Yankee woman who made clay pots.

LENNY. Joan.

MEG. What?

LENNY. Her name's Joan. She came down here with him. That's one of her pots. Doc's married to her.

MEG. Married—

LENNY. Uh huh.

MEG. Doc married a Yankee?

LENNY. That's right; and they've got two kids.

MEG. Kids—

LENNY. A boy and a girl.

MEG. God. Then his kids must be half Yankee.

LENNY. I suppose.

MEG. God. That really gets me. I don't know why, but somehow that really gets me.

LENNY. I don't know why it should.

MEG. And what a stupid-looking pot! Who'd buy it, anyway?

LENNY. Wait—I think that's them. Yeah, that's Chick's car! Oh, there's Babe! Hello, Babe! They're home, Meg! They're home.

(MEG *hides.*)

BABE'S VOICE. Lenny! I'm home! I'm free!

(BABE, twenty-four, enters exuberantly. She has an angelic face and fierce, volatile eyes. She carries a pink pocketbook.)

BABE. I'm home! (MEG *jumps out of hiding.*) Oh, Meg— Look, it's Meg! (*Running to hug her.*) Meg! When did you get home?

MEG. Just now!

BABE. Well, it's so good to see you! I'm so glad you're home! I'm so relieved.

(CHICK *enters.*)

MEG. Why, Chick; hello.

CHICK. Hello, Cousin Margaret. What brings you back to Hazlehurst?

MEG. Oh, I came on home . . . (*Turning to Babe.*) I came on home to see about Babe.

BABE. (*Running to hug* MEG.) Oh, Meg—

MEG. How are things with you, Babe?

CHICK. Well, they are dismal, if you want my opinion. She is refusing to cooperate with her lawyer, that nice-looking young Lloyd boy. She won't tell any of us why she committed this heinous crime, except to say that she didn't like Zackery's looks—

BABE. Oh, look, Lenny brought my suitcase from home! And my saxophone! Thank you! (*She runs over to the cot and gets out her saxophone.*)

CHICK. Now, that young lawyer is coming over here this afternoon, and when he gets here he expects to get some concrete answers! That's what he expects! No more of this nonsense and stubbornness from you, Rebecca MaGrath, or they'll put you in jail and throw away the key!

BABE. (*Overlapping to* MEG.) Meg, come look at my new saxophone. I went to Jackson and bought it used. Feel it. It's so heavy.

MEG. (*Overlapping* CHICK.) It's beautiful. (*The room goes silent.*)

CHICK. Isn't that right, won't they throw away the key?

LENNY. Well, honestly, I don't know about that—

CHICK. They will! And leave you there to rot. So, Rebecca, what are you going to tell Mr. Lloyd about shooting Zackery when he gets here? What are your reasons going to be?

BABE. (*Glaring.*) That I didn't like his looks! I just didn't like his stinking looks! And I don't like yours much, either, Chick the Stick! So just leave me alone! I mean it! Leave me alone! Oooh! (*She exits up the stairs. There is a long moment of silence.*)

CHICK. Well, I was only trying to warn her that she's going to have to help herself. It's just that she doesn't understand how serious the situation is. Does she? She doesn't have the vaguest idea. Does she, now?

LENNY. Well, it's true, she does seem a little confused.

CHICK. And that's putting it mildly, Lenny honey. That's putting it mighty mild. So, Margaret, how's your singing career going? We keep looking for your picture in the movie magazines. (MEG *moves to light a cigarette.*) You know, you shouldn't smoke. It causes cancer. Cancer of the lungs. They say each cigarette is just a little stick of cancer. A little death stick.

MEG. That's what I like about it, Chick—taking a drag off of death. (*She take a long, deep drag.*) Mmm! Gives me a sense of controlling my own destiny. What power! What exhilaration! Want a drag?

LENNY. (*Trying to break the tension.*) Ah, Zackery's liver's been saved! His sister called up and said his liver was saved. Isn't that good news?

MEG. Well, yes, that's fine news. Mighty fine news. Why, I've been told that the liver's a powerful important bodily organ. I believe it's used to absorb all of our excess bile.

LENNY. Yes—well—it's been saved. (*The phone rings. Lenny gets it.*)

MEG. So! Did you hear all that good news about the liver, Little Chicken?

CHICK. I heard it. And don't you call me Chicken! (MEG *clucks like a chicken.*) I've told you a hundred times if I've told you once not to call me Chicken. You cannot call me Chicken.

LENNY. . . . Oh, no! . . . Of course, we'll be right over! 'Bye! (*She hangs up the phone.*) That was Annie May—Peekay and Buck Jr. have eaten paint!

CHICK. Oh, no! Are they all right? They're not sick? They're not sick, are they?

LENNY. I don't know. I don't know. Come on. We've got to run on next door.

CHICK. (*Overlapping.*) Oh, God! Oh, please! Please let them be all right! Don't let them die! Please, don't let them die! (CHICK *runs off howling, with* LENNY *following after.* MEG *sits alone, finishing her cigarette. After a moment, BABE's voice is heard.*)

BABE'S VOICE. Pst—Psst!

(MEG *looks around.* BABE *comes tiptoeing down the stairs.*)

BABE. Has she gone?

MEG. She's gone. Peekay and Buck Jr. just ate their paints.

BABE. What idiots.

MEG. Yeah.

BABE. You know, Chick's hated us ever since we had to move here from Vicksburg to live with Old Grandmama and Old Granddaddy.

MEG. She's an idiot.

BABE. Yeah. Do you know what she told me this morning while I was still behind bars and couldn't get away?

MEG. What?

BABE. She told me how embarrassing it was for her all those years ago, you know, when Mama—

MEG. Yeah, down in the cellar.

BABE. She said our mama had shamed the entire family, and we were known notoriously all through Hazlehurst. (*About to cry.*) Then she went on to say how I would now be getting just as much bad publicity, and humiliating her and the family all over again.

MEG. Ah, forget it, Babe. Just forget it.

BABE. I told her, "Mama got national coverage! National!" And if Zackery wasn't a senator from Copiah County, I probably wouldn't even be getting statewide.

MEG. Of course you wouldn't.

BABE. (*After a pause.*) Gosh, sometimes I wonder . . .

MEG. What?

BABE. Why she did it. Why Mama hung herself.

MEG. I don't know. She had a bad day. A real bad day. You know how it feels on a real bad day.

BABE. And that old yellow cat. It was sad about that old cat.

MEG. Yeah.

BABE. I bet if Daddy hadn't of left us, they'd still be alive.

MEG. Oh, I don't know.

BABE. 'Cause it was after he left that she started spending whole days just sitting there and smoking on the back porch steps. She'd sling her ashes down onto the different bugs and ants that'd be passing by.

MEG. Yeah. Well, I'm glad he left.

BABE. That old yellow cat'd stay back there with her. I thought if she felt something for anyone it woulda been that old cat. Guess I musta been mistaken.

MEG. God, he was a bastard. Really, with his white teeth. Daddy was such a bastard.

BABE. Was he? I don't remember.

(MEG *blows out a mouthful of smoke.*)

BABE. (*After a moment, uneasily.*) I think I'm gonna make some lemonade. You want some?

MEG. Sure. (BABE *cuts lemons, dumps sugar, stirs ice cubes, etc., throughout the following exchange.*) Babe. Why won't you talk? Why won't you tell anyone about shooting Zackery?

BABE. Oooh—

MEG. Why not? You must have had a good reason. Didn't you?

BABE. I guess I did.

MEG. Well, what was it?

BABE. I . . . I can't say.

MEG. Why not? (*Pause.*) Babe, why not? You can tell me.

BABE. 'Cause . . . I'm sort of . . . protecting someone.

MEG. Protecting someone? Oh, Babe, then you really didn't shoot him! I knew you couldn't have done it! I knew it!

BABE. No, I shot him. I shot him all right. I meant to kill him. I was aiming for his heart, but I guess my hands were shaking and I—just got him in the stomach.

MEG. (*Collapsing.*) I see.

BABE. (*Stirring the lemonade.*) So I'm guilty. And I'm just gonna have to take my punishment and go on to jail.

MEG. Oh, Babe—

BABE. Don't worry, Meg, jail's gonna be a relief to me. I can learn to play my new saxophone. I won't have to live with Zackery anymore. And I won't have his snoopy old sister, Lucille, coming over and pushing me around. Jail will be a relief. Here's your lemonade.

MEG. Thanks.

BABE. It taste okay?

MEG. Perfect.

BABE. I like a lot of sugar in mine. I'm gonna add some more sugar. (BABE *goes to add more sugar to her lemonade as* LENNY *bursts through the back door in a state of excitement and confusion.*)

LENNY. Well, it looks like the paint is primarily on their arms and faces, but Chick wants me to drive them all over to Dr. Winn's just to make sure. (*She grabs her car keys from the counter, and as she does so, she notices the mess of lemons and sugar.*) Oh, now, Babe, try not to make a mess here; and be careful with this sharp knife. Honestly, all that sugar's gonna get you sick. Well 'bye, 'bye. I'll be back as soon as I can.

MEG. 'Bye, Lenny.

BABE. 'Bye.

(LENNY *exits.*)

BABE. Boy, I don't know what's happening to Lenny.

MEG. What do you mean?

BABE. "Don't make a mess; don't make yourself sick; don't cut yourself with that sharp knife." She's turning into Old Grandmama.

MEG. You think so?

BABE. More and more. Do you know she's taken to wearing Old Grandmama's torn sunhat and her green garden gloves?

MEG. Those old lime-green ones?

BABE. Yeah; she works out in the garden wearing the lime-green gloves of a dead woman. Imagine wearing those gloves on your hands.

MEG. Poor Lenny. She needs some love in her life. All she does is work out at that brick yard and take care of Old Granddaddy.

BABE. Yeah. But she's so shy with men.

MEG. (*Biting into an apple.*) Probably because of that *shrunken* ovary she has.

BABE. (*Slinging ice cubes.*) Yeah, that *deformed* ovary.

MEG. Old Granddaddy's the one who's made her feel self-conscious about it. It's his fault. The old fool.

BABE. It's so sad.

MEG. God—you know what?

BABE. What?

MEG. I bet Lenny's never even slept with a man. Just think, thirty years old and never even had it once.

BABE. (*Slyly.*) Oh, I don't know. Maybe she's . . . had it once.

MEG. She has?

BABE. Maybe. I think so.

MEG. When? When?

BABE. Well . . . maybe I shouldn't say—

MEG. Babe!

BABE. (*Rapidly telling the story.*) All right, then. It was after Old Granddaddy went back to the hospital this second time. Lenny was really in a state of deep depression, I could tell that she was. Then one day she calls me up and asks me to come over and to bring along my Polaroid camera. Well, when I arrive she's waiting for me out there in the sun parlor wearing her powder-blue Sunday dress and this old curled-up wig. She confided that she was gonna try sending in her picture to one of those lonely-hearts clubs.

MEG. Oh, my God.

BABE. Lonely Hearts of the South. She'd seen their ad in a magazine.

MEG. Jesus.

BABE. Anyway, I take some snapshots and she sends them on in to the club, and about two weeks later she receives in the mail this whole load of pictures of available men, most of 'em fairly odd-looking. But of course she doesn't call any of 'em up 'cause she's real shy. But one of 'em, this Charlie Hill from Memphis, Tennessee, he calls her.

MEG. He does?

BABE. Yeah. And time goes on and she says he's real funny on the phone, so they decide to get together to meet.

MEG. Yeah?

BABE. Well, he drives down here to Hazlehurst 'bout three or four different times and has supper with her; then one weekend she goes up to Memphis to visit him, and I think that is where it happened.

MEG. What makes you think so?

BABE. Well, when I went to pick her up from the bus depot, she ran off the bus and threw her arms around me and started crying and sobbing as though she'd like to never stop. I asked her, I said, "Lenny, what's the matter?" And she said, "I've done it, Babe! Honey, I have done it!"

MEG. (*Whispering.*) And you think she meant that she'd done *it?*

BABE. (*Whispering back, slyly.*) I think so.

MEG. Well, goddamn! (*They laugh.*)

BABE. But she didn't say anything else about it. She just went on to tell me about the boot factory where Charlie worked and what a nice city Memphis was.

MEG. So, what happened to this Charlie?

BABE. Well, he came to Hazlehurst just one more time. Lenny took him over to meet Old Granddaddy at the hospital, and after that they broke it off.

MEG. 'Cause of Old Granddaddy?

BABE. Well, she said it was on account of her missing ovary. That Charlie didn't want to marry her on account of it.

MEG. Ah, how mean. How hateful.

BABE. Oh, it was. He seemed like such a nice man, too— kinda chubby, with red hair and freckles, always telling these funny jokes.

MEG. Hmmm, that just doesn't seem right. Something about that doesn't seem exactly right. (*She paces about the kitchen and comes across the box of candy* LENNY *got for her birthday.*) Oh, God, "Happy birthday to Lenny, from the Buck Boyles."

BABE. Oh, no! Today's Lenny's birthday!

MEG. That's right.

BABE. I forgot all about it.

MEG. I know. I did, too.

BABE. Gosh, we'll have to order up a big cake for her. She always loves to make those wishes on her birthday cake.

MEG. Yeah, let's get her a big cake! A huge one! (*Suddenly noticing the plastic wrapper on the candy box.*) Oh, God, that Chick's so cheap!

BABE. What do you mean?

MEG. This plastic has poinsettias on it!

BABE. (*Running to see.*) Oh, let me see— (*She looks at the package with disgust.*) Boy, oh boy! I'm calling that bakery and ordering the very largest size cake they have! That jumbo deluxe.

MEG. Good!

BABE. Why, I imagine they can make one up to be about— *this* big. (*She demonstrates.*)

MEG. Oh, at least; at least that big. Why, maybe it'll even be *this* big. (*She makes a very, very, very large-size cake.*)

BABE. You think it could be *that* big?

MEG. Sure!

BABE. (*After a moment, getting the idea.*) Or, or what if it were *this* big? (*She maps out a cake that covers the room.*) What if we get the cake and it's *this* big? (*She gulps down a fistful of cake.*) Gulp! Gulp! Gulp! Tasty treat!

MEG. Hmmm—I'll have me some more! Give me some more of that birthday cake!

(*Suddenly there is a loud knock at the door.*)

BARNETTE'S VOICE. Hello . . . Hello! May I come in?

BABE. (*To* MEG, *in a whisper, as she takes cover.*) Who's that?

MEG. I don't know.

BARNETTE'S VOICE. (*He is still knocking.*) Hello! Hello, Mrs. Botrelle!

BABE. Oh, shoot! It's that lawyer. I don't want to see him.

MEG. Oh, Babe, come on. You've got to see him sometime.

BABE. No, I don't! (*She starts up the stairs.*) Just tell him I died. I'm going upstairs.

MEG. Oh, Babe! Will you come back here!

BABE. (*As she exits.*) You talk to him, please, Meg. Please! I just don't want to see him—

MEG. Babe—Babe! Oh, shit . . . Ah, come on in! Door's open!

(BARNETTE LLOYD, twenty-six, enters carrying a briefcase. He is a slender, intelligent young man with an almost fanatical intensity that he subdues by sheer will.)

BARNETTE. How do you do. I'm Barnette Lloyd.

MEG. Pleased to meet you. I'm Meg MaGrath, Babe's older sister.

BARNETTE. Yes, I know. You're the singer.

MEG. Well, yes . . .

BARNETTE. I came to hear you five different times when you were singing at the club in Biloxi. Greeny's I believe was the name of it.

MEG. Yes, Greeny's.

BARNETTE. You were very good. There was something sad and moving about how you sang those songs. It was like you had some sort of vision. Some special sort of vision.

MEG. Well, thank you. You're very kind. Now . . . about Babe's case—

BARNETTE. Yes?

MEG. We've just got to win it.

BARNETTE. I intend to.

MEG. Of course. But, ah . . . (*She looks at him.*) Ah, you know, you're very young.

BARNETTE. Yes. I am. I'm young.

MEG. It's just, I'm concerned, Mr. Lloyd—

BARNETTE. Barnette. Please.

MEG. Barnette; that, ah, just maybe we need someone with, well, with more experience. Someone totally familiar with all the ins and outs and the this and thats of the legal dealings and such. As that.

BARNETTE. Ah, you have reservations.

MEG. (*Relieved.*) Reservations. Yes, I have . . . reservations.

BARNETTE. Well, possibly it would help you to know that I graduated first in my class from Ole Miss Law School. I also spent three different summers taking advanced courses in criminal law at Harvard Law School. I made A's in all the given courses. I was fascinated!

MEG. I'm sure.

BARNETTE. And even now, I've just completed one year working with Jackson's top criminal law firm, Manchester and Wayne. I was invaluable to them. Indispensable. They offered to double my percentage if I'd stay on; but I refused. I wanted to return to Hazlehurst and open my own office. The reason being, and this is a key point, that I have a personal vendetta to settle with one Zackery F. Botrelle.

MEG. A personal vendetta?

BARNETTE. Yes, ma'am. You are correct. Indeed, I do.

MEG. Hmm. A personal vendetta . . . I think I like that. So you have some sort of a personal vendetta to settle with Zackery?

BARNETTE. Precisely. Just between the two of us, I not only intend to keep that sorry s.o.b. from ever being reelected to the state senate by exposing his shady, criminal dealings; but I also intend to decimate his personal credibility by exposing him as a bully, a brute, and a red-neck thug!

MEG. Well; I can see that you're—fanatical about this.

BARNETTE. Yes, I am. I'm sorry if I seem outspoken. But for some reason I feel I can talk to you . . . those songs you sang. Excuse me; I feel like a jackass.

MEG. It's all right. Relax. Relax, Barnette. Let me think this out a minute. (*She takes out a cigarette. He lights it for her.*) Now just exactly how do you intend to get Babe off? You know, keep her out of jail.

BARNETTE. It seems to me that we can get her off with a plea of self-defense, or possibly we could go with innocent by reason of temporary insanity. But basically I intend to prove that Zackery Botrelle brutalized and tormented this poor woman to such an extent that she had no recourse but to defend herself in the only way she knew how!

MEG. I like that!

BARNETTE. Then, of course, I'm hoping this will break the ice and we'll be able to go on to prove that the man's a total criminal, as well as an abusive bully and contemptible slob!

MEG. That sounds good! To me that sounds very good!

BARNETTE. It's just our basic game plan.

MEG. But now, how are you going to prove all this about Babe being brutalized? We don't want anyone perjured. I mean to commit perjury.

BARNETTE. Perjury? According to my sources, the'll be no need for perjury.

MEG. You mean it's the truth?

BARNETTE. This is a small town, Miss MaGrath. The word gets out.

MEG. It's really the truth?

BARNETTE. (*Opening his briefcase.*) Just look at this. It's a photostatic copy of Mrs. Botrelle's medical chart over the past four years. Take a good look at it, if you want your blood to boil!

MEG. (*Looking over the chart.*) What! What! This is maddening. This is madness! Did he do this to her? I'll kill him; I will—I'll fry his blood! Did he do this?

BARNETTE. (*Alarmed.*) To tell you the truth, I can't say for certain what was accidental and what was not. That's why I need to talk with Mrs. Botrelle. That's why it's very important that I see her!

MEG. (*Her eyes are wild, as she shoves him toward the door.*)

Well, look, I've got to see her first. I've got to talk to her first. What I'll do is I'll give you a call. Maybe you can come back over later on—

BARNETTE. Well, then, here's my card—

MEG. Okay. Goodbye.

BARNETTE. 'Bye!

MEG. Oh, wait! Wait! There's one problem with you.

BARNETTE. What?

MEG. What if you get so fanatically obsessed with this vendetta thing that you forget about Babe? You forget about her and sell her down the river just to get at Zackery. What about that?

BARNETTE. I—wouldn't do that.

MEG. You wouldn't?

BARNETTE. No.

MEG. Why not?

BARNETTE. Because I'm—I'm fond of her.

MEG. What do you mean you're fond of her?

BARNETTE. Well, she . . . she sold me a pound cake at a bazaar once. And I'm fond of her.

MEG. All right; I believe you. Goodbye.

BARNETTE. Goodbye. (*He exits.*)

MEG. Babe! Babe, come down here! Babe!

(BABE *comes hurrying down the stairs.*)

BABE. What? What is it? I called about the cake—

MEG. What did Zackery do to you?

BABE. They can't have it for today.

MEG. Did he hurt you? Did he? Did he do that?

BABE. Oh, Meg, please—

MEG. Did he? Goddamnit, Babe—

BABE. Yes, he did.

MEG. Why? Why?

BABE. I don't know! He started hating me, 'cause I couldn't laugh at his jokes. I just started finding it impossible to laugh at his jokes the way I used to. And then the sound of his voice got to where it tired me out awful bad to hear it. I'd fall asleep just listening to him at the dinner table. He'd say, "Hand me some of that gravy!" Or, "This roast beef is too damn bloody." And suddenly I'd be out cold like a light.

MEG. Oh, Babe. Babe, this is very important. I want you to sit down here and tell me what all happened right before you shot Zackery. That's right, just sit down and tell me.

BABE. (*After a pause.*) I told you, I can't tell you on account of I'm protecting someone.

MEG. But, Babe, you've just got to talk to someone about all this. You just do.

BABE. Why?

MEG. Because it's a human need. To talk about our lives. It's an important human need.

BABE. Oh. Well, I do feel like I want to talk to someone. I do.

MEG. Then talk to me; please.

BABE. (*Making a decision.*) All right. (*After thinking a minute.*) I don't know where to start.

MEG. Just start at the beginning. Just there at the beginning.

BABE. (*After a moment.*) Well, do you remember Willie Jay? (MEG *shakes her head.*) Cora's youngest boy?

MEG. Oh, yeah, that little kid we used to pay a nickel to, to run down to the drugstore and bring us back a cherry Coke.

BABE. Right. Well, Cora irons at my place on Wednesdays now, and she just happened to mention that Willie Jay'd picked up this old stray dog and that he'd gotten real fond of him. But now they couldn't afford to feed him anymore. So she was gonna have to tell Willie Jay to set him loose in the woods.

MEG. (*Trying to be patient.*) Uh huh.

BABE. Well, I said I liked dogs, and if he wanted to bring the dog over here, I'd take care of him. You see, I was alone by myself most of the time 'cause the senate was in session and Zackery was up in Jackson.

MEG. Uh huh. (*She reaches for* LENNY's *box of birthday candy. She takes little nibbles out of each piece throughout the rest of the scene.*)

BABE. So the next day, Willie Jay brings over this skinny old dog with these little crossed eyes. Well, I asked Willie Jay what his name was, and he said they called him Dog. Well, I liked the name, so I thought I'd keep it.

MEG. (*Getting up.*) Uh huh. I'm listening. I'm just gonna get me a glass of cold water. Do you want one?

BABE. Okay.

MEG. So you kept the name—Dog.

BABE. Yeah. Anyway, when Willie Jay was leaving he gave Dog a hug and said, "Goodbye, Dog. You're a fine ole dog." Well, I felt something for him, so I told Willie Jay he could come back and visit with Dog any time he wanted and his face just kinda lit right up.

MEG. (*Offering the candy.*) Candy—

BABE. No, thanks. Anyhow, times goes on and Willie Jay keeps coming over and over. And we talk about Dog and how fat he's getting, and then, well, you know, things start up.

MEG. No, I don't know. What things start up?

BABE. Well, things start up. Like sex. Like that.

MEG. Babe, wait a minute—Willie Jay's a boy. A small boy, about this tall. He's about this tall!

BABE. No! Oh, no! He's taller now! He's fifteen now. When you knew him he was only about seven or eight.

MEG. But even so—fifteen. And he's a black boy; a colored boy; a Negro.

BABE. (*Flustered.*) Well, I realize that, Meg. Why do you think I'm so worried about his getting public exposure? I don't want to ruin his reputation!

MEG. I'm amazed, Babe. I'm really completely amazed. I didn't even know you were a liberal.

BABE. Well, I'm not! I'm not a liberal! I'm a democratic! I was just lonely! I was so lonely. And he was good. Oh, he was so, so good. I'd never had it that good. We'd always go out into the garage and—

MEG. It's okay. I've got the picture; I've got the picture! Now, let's just get back to the story. To yesterday, when you shot Zackery.

BABE. All right, then. Let's see . . . Willie Jay was over. And it was after we'd—

MEG. Yeah! Yeah.

BABE. And we were just standing around on the back porch playing with Dog. Well, suddenly Zackery comes from around the side of the house. And he startled me 'cause he's supposed to be away at the office, and there he is coming from round the side of the house. Anyway, he says to Willie Jay, "Hey, boy, what are you doing back here?" And I say, "He's not doing anything. You just go on home, Willie Jay! You just run right on home." Well, before he can move, Zackery comes up and knocks him once right across the face and then shoves him down the porch steps, causing him to skin up his elbow real bad on that hard concrete. Then he says, "Don't you ever come around here again, or I'll have them cut out your gizzard!" Well, Willie Jay starts crying—these tears come streaming down his face—then he gets up real quick and runs away, with Dog following off after him. After that, I don't remember much too clearly; let's see . . . I went on into the living room, and I went right up to the davenport and opened the drawer where we keep the burglar gun . . . I took it out. Then I—I brought it up to my ear. That's right. I put it right inside my ear. Why, I was gonna shoot off my own head! That's what I was gonna do. Then I heard the back door slamming and suddenly, for some reason, I thought about Mama . . . how she'd hung herself. And here I was about ready to shoot myself. Then I realized— that's right, I realized how I didn't want to kill myself! And she—she probably didn't want to kill herself. She wanted to kill him, and I wanted to kill him, too. I wanted to kill Zackery, not myself. 'Cause I—I wanted to live! So I waited for him to come on into the living room. Then I held out the gun, and I pulled the trigger, aiming for his heart but getting him in the stomach. (*After a pause.*) It's funny that I really did that.

MEG. It's a good thing that you did. It's a damn good thing that you did.

BABE. It was.

MEG. Please, Babe, talk to Barnette Lloyd. Just talk to him and see if he can help.

BABE. But how about Willie Jay?

MEG. (*Starting toward the phone.*) Oh, he'll be all right. You just talk to that lawyer like you did to me. (*Looking at the number on the card, she begins dialing.*) See, 'cause he's gonna be on your side.

BABE. No! Stop, Meg, Stop! Don't call him up! Please don't call him up! You can't! It's too awful. (*She runs over and jerks the bottom half of the phone away from* MEG.)

MEG. (*Stands, holding the receiver.*) Babe!

BABE. (*Slams her half of the phone into the refrigerator.*) I just can't tell some stranger all about my personal life. I just can't.

MEG. Well, hell, Babe; you're the one who said you wanted to live.

BABE. That's right. I did. (*She takes the phone out of the refrigerator and hands it to* MEG.) Here's the other part of the phone. (*She moves to sit at the kitchen table.*)

(MEG takes the phone back to the counter.)

BABE. (*As she fishes a piece of lemon out of her glass and begins sucking on it.*) Meg.

MEG. What?

BABE. I called the bakery. They're gonna have Lenny's cake ready first thing tomorrow morning. That's the earliest they can get it.

MEG. All right.

BABE. I told them to write on it, *Happy Birthday, Lenny—A Day Late.* That sound okay?

MEG. (*At the phone.*) It sounds nice.

BABE. I ordered up the very largest size cake they have. I told them chocolate cake with white icing and red trim. Think she'll like that?

MEG. (*Dialing the phone.*) Yeah, I'm sure she will. She'll like it.

BABE. I'm hoping.

CURTAIN

ACT TWO

The lights go up on the kitchen. It is evening of the same day.
MEG's *suitcase has been moved upstairs.* BABE's *saxophone has been taken out of the case and put together.* BABE *and* BARNETTE *are sitting at the kitchen table.* BARNETTE *is writing and recheck-ing notes with explosive intensity.* BABE, *who has changed into a casual shift, sits eating a bowl of oatmeal, slowly.*

BARNETTE. (*To himself.*) Mmm huh! Yes! I see, I see! Well, we can work on that! And of course, this is mere conjecture! Difficult, if not impossible, to prove. Ha! Yes. Yes, indeed. Indeed—

BABE. Sure you don't want any oatmeal?

BARNETTE. What? Oh, no. No, thank you. Let's see; ah, where were we?

BABE. I just shot Zackery.

BARNETTE. (*Looking at his notes.*) Right. Correct. You've just pulled the trigger.

BABE. Tell me, do you think Willie Jay can stay out of all this?

BARNETTE. Believe me, it is in our interest to keep him as far out of this as possible.

BABE. Good.

BARNETTE. (*Throughout the following,* BARNETTE *stays glued to* BABE'S *every word.*) All right, you've just shot one Zackery Botrelle, as a result of his continual physical and mental abuse— what happens now?

BABE. Well, after I shot him, I put the gun down on the piano bench, and then I went out into the kitchen and made up a pitcher of lemonade.

BARNETTE. Lemonade?

BABE. Yes, I was dying of thirst. My mouth was just as dry as a bone.

BARNETTE. So in order to quench this raging thirst that was choking you dry and preventing any possibility of you uttering

257

intelligible sounds or phrases, you went out to the kitchen and made up a pitcher of lemonade?

BABE. Right. I made it just the way I like it, with lots of sugar and lots of lemon—about ten lemons in all. Then I added two trays of ice and stirred it up with my wooden stirring spoon.

BARNETTE. Then what?

BABE. Then I drank three glasses, one right after the other. They were large glasses—about this tall. Then suddenly my stomach kind of swole all up. I guess what caused it was all that sour lemon.

BARNETTE. Could be.

BABE. Then what I did was . . . I wiped my mouth off with the back of my hand, like this . . . (*She demonstrates.*)

BARNETTE. Hmmm.

BABE. I did it to clear off all those little beads of water that had settled there.

BARNETTE. I see.

BABE. Then I called out to Zackery. I said, "Zackery, I've made some lemonade. Can you use a glass?"

BARNETTE. Did he answer? Did you hear an answer?

BABE. No. He didn't answer.

BARNETTE. So what'd you do?

BABE. I poured him a glass anyway and took it out to him.

BARNETTE. You took it out to the living room?

BABE. I did. And there he was, lying on the rug. He was looking up at me trying to speak words. I said, "What? . . . Lemonade? . . . You don't want it? Would you like a Coke instead?" Then I got the idea—he was telling me to call on the phone for medical help. So I got on the phone and called up the hospital. I gave my name and address, and I told them my husband was shot and he was lying on the rug and there was plenty of blood. (*She pauses a minute, as* BARNETTE *works frantically on his notes.*) I guess that's gonna look kinda bad.

BARNETTE. What?

BABE. Me fixing that lemonade before I called the hospital.

BARNETTE. Well, not . . . necessarily.

BABE. I tell you, I think the reason I made up the lemonade, I mean besides the fact that my mouth was bone dry, was that I was afraid to call the authorities. I was afraid. I—I really think I was afraid they would see that I had tried to shoot Zackery, in fact, that I *had* shot him, and they would accuse me of possible murder and send me away to jail.

BARNETTE. Well, that's understandable.

BABE. I think so. I mean, in fact, that's what did happen.
That's what is happening—'cause here I am just about ready to
go right off to the Parchment Prison Farm. Yes, here I am just
practically on the brink of utter doom. Why, I feel so all alone.

BARNETTE. Now, now, look— Why, there's no reason for you
to get yourself so all upset and worried. Please don't. Please.
(*They look at each other for a moment.*) You just keep filling in
as much detailed information as you can about those incidents
on the medical reports. That's all you need to think about.
Don't you worry, Mrs. Botrelle, we're going to have a solid
defense.

BABE. Please don't call me Mrs. Botrelle.

BARNETTE. All right.

BABE. My name's Becky. People in the family call me Babe,
but my real name's Becky.

BARNETTE. All right, Becky. (BARNETTE *and* BABE *stare at
each other for a long moment.*)

BABE. Are you sure you didn't go to Hazlehurst High?

BARNETTE. No, I went away to a boarding school.

BABE. Gosh, you sure do look familiar. You sure do.

BARNETTE. Well, I—I doubt you'll remember, but I did meet
you once.

BABE. You did? When?

BARNETTE. At the Christmas bazaar, year before last. You
were selling cakes and cookies and . . . candy.

BABE. Oh, yes! You bought the orange pound cake!

BARNETTE. Right.

BABE. Of course, and then we talked for a while. We talked
about the Christmas angel.

BARNETTE. You do remember.

BABE. I remember it very well. You were even thinner then
than you are now.

BARNETTE. Well, I'm surprised. I'm certainly . . . surprised.
(*The phone rings.*)

BABE. (*As she goes to answer the phone.*) This is quite a
coincidence! Don't you think it is? Why, it's almost a fluke.
(*She answers the phone.*) Hello . . . Oh, hello, Lucille . . . Oh,
he is? . . . Oh, he does? . . . Okay. Oh, Lucille, wait! Has Dog
come back to the house? . . . Oh, I see . . . Okay. Okay. (*After
a brief pause.*) Hello, Zackery? How are you doing? . . . Uh
huh . . . uh huh . . . Oh, I'm sorry . . . Please don't scream . . .
Uh huh . . . uh huh . . . You want what? . . . No, I can't come
up there now . . . Well, for one thing, I don't even have the
car. Lenny and Meg are up at the hospital right now, visiting

with Old Granddaddy . . . What? . . . Oh, really? . . . Oh, really? . . . Well, I've got me a lawyer that's over here right now, and he's building me up a solid defense! . . . Wait just a minute, I'll see. (*To* BARNETTE.) He wants to talk to you. He says he's got some blackening evidence that's gonna convict me of attempting to murder him in the first degree!

BARNETTE. (*Disgustedly.*) Oh, bluff! He's bluffing! Here, hand me the phone. (*He takes the phone and becomes suddenly cool and suave.*) Hello, this is Mr. Barnette Lloyd speaking. I'm Mrs. . . . ah, Becky's attorney . . . Why, certainly, Mr. Botrelle, I'd be more than glad to check out any pertinent information that you may have . . . Fine, then I'll be right on over. Goodbye. (*He hangs up the phone.*)

BABE. What did he say?

BARNETTE. He wants me to come see him at the hospital this evening. Says he's got some sort of evidence. Sounds highly suspect to me.

BABE. Oooh! Didn't you just hate his voice? Doesn't he have the most awful voice? I just hate—I can't bear to hear it!

BARNETTE. Well, now—now, wait. Wait just a minute.

BABE. What?

BARNETTE. I have a solution. From now on, I'll handle all communications between you two. You can simply refuse to speak with him.

BABE. All right—I will. I'll do that.

BARNETTE. (*Starting to pack his briefcase.*) Well, I'd better get over there and see just what he's got up his sleeve.

BABE. (*After a pause.*) Barnette.

BARNETTE. Yes?

BABE. What's the personal vendetta about? You know, the one you have to settle with Zackery.

BARNETTE. Oh, it's—it's complicated. It's a very complicated matter.

BABE. I see.

BARNETTE. The major thing he did was to ruin my father's life. He took away his job, his home, his health, his respectability. I don't like to talk about it.

BABE. I'm sorry. I just wanted to say—I hope you win it. I hope you win your vendetta.

BARNETTE. Thank you.

BABE. I think it's an important thing that a person could win a lifelong vendetta.

BARNETTE. Yes. Well, I'd better be going.

BABE. All right. Let me know what happens.

BARNETTE. I will. I'll get back to you right away.
BABE. Thanks.
BARNETTE. Goodbye, Becky.
BABE. Goodbye, Barnette.

(BARNETTE *exits.* BABE *looks around the room for a moment, then goes over to her white suitcase and opens it up. She takes out her pink hair curlers and a brush. She begins brushing her hair.*)

BABE. Goodbye, Becky. Goodbye, Barnette. Goodbye, Becky. Oooh (LENNY *enters. She is fuming.* BABE *is rolling her hair throughout most of the following scene.*) Lenny, hi!
LENNY. Hi.
BABE. Where's Meg?
LENNY. Oh, she had to go by the store and pick some things up. I don't know what.
BABE. Well, how's Old Granddaddy?
LENNY. (*As she picks up* BABE'*s bowl of oatmeal.*) He's fine. Wonderful! Never been better!
BABE. Lenny, what's wrong? What's the matter?
LENNY. It's Meg! I could just wring her neck! I could just wring it!
BABE. Why? Wha'd she do?
LENNY. She lied! She sat in that hospital room and shamelessly lied to Old Granddaddy. She went on and on telling such untrue stories and lies.
BABE. Well, what? What did she say?
LENNY. Well, for one thing, she said she was gonna have an RCA record coming out with her picture on the cover, eating pineapples under a palm tree.
BABE. Well, gosh, Lenny, maybe she is! Don't you think she really is?
LENNY. Babe, she sat here this very afternoon and told me how all that she's done this whole year is work as a clerk for a dog-food company.
BABE. Oh, shoot. I'm disappointed.
LENNY. And then she goes on to say that she'll be appearing on the Johnny Carson show in two weeks' time. Two weeks' time! Why, Old Granddaddy's got a TV set right in his room. Imagine what a letdown it's gonna be.
BABE. Why, mercy me.
LENNY. (*Slamming the coffeepot on.*) Oh, and she told him the reason she didn't use the money he sent her to come home

Christmas was that she was right in the middle of making a huge multimillion-dollar motion picture and was just under too much pressure.

BABE. My word!

LENNY. The movie's coming out this spring. It's called, *Singing in a Shoe Factory*. But she only has a small leading role— not a large leading role.

BABE. (*Laughing.*) For heaven's sake—

LENNY. I'm sizzling. Oh, I just can't help it! I'm sizzling!

BABE. Sometimes Meg does such strange things.

LENNY. (*Slowly, as she picks up the opened box of birthday candy.*) Who ate this candy?

BABE. (*Hesitantly.*) Meg.

LENNY. My one birthday present, and look what she does! Why, she's taken one little bite out of each piece and then just put it back in! Ooh! That's just like her! That is just like her!

BABE. Lenny, please—

LENNY. I can't help it! It gets me mad! It gets me upset! Why, Meg's always run wild—she started smoking and drinking when she was fourteen years old; she never made good grades— never made her own bed! But somehow she always seemed to get what she wanted. She's the one who got singing and dancing lessons, and a store-bought dress to wear to her senior prom. Why, do you remember how Meg always got to wear twelve jingle bells on her petticoats, while we were only allowed to wear three apiece? Why?! Why should Old Grandmama let her sew twelve golden jingle bells on her petticoats and us only three!

BABE. (*Who has heard all this before.*) I don't know! Maybe she didn't jingle them as much!

LENNY. I can't help it! It gets me mad! I resent it. I do.

BABE. Oh, don't resent Meg. Things have been hard for Meg. After all, she was the one who found Mama.

LENNY. Oh, I know; she's the one who found Mama. But that's always been the excuse.

BABE. But I tell you, Lenny, after it happened, Meg started doing all sorts of these strange things.

LENNY. She did? Like what?

BABE. Like things I never even wanted to tell you about.

LENNY. What sort of things?

BABE. Well, for instance, back when we used to go over to the library, Meg would spend all her time reading and looking through this old black book called *Diseases of the Skin*. It was full of the most sickening pictures you've ever seen. Things like rotting-away noses and eyeballs drooping off down the sides of people's faces, and scabs and sores and eaten-away places all over all parts of people's bodies.

LENNY. (*Trying to pour her coffee.*) Babe, please! That's enough.

BABE. Anyway, she'd spend hours and hours just forcing herself to look through this book. Why, it was the same way she'd force herself to look at the poster of crippled children stuck up in the window at Dixieland Drugs. You know, that one where they want you to give a dime. Meg would stand there, and stare at their eyes and look at the braces on their little crippled-up legs—then she'd purposely go and spend her dime on a double-scoop ice cream cone and eat it all down. She'd say to me, "See, I can stand it. I can stand it. Just look how I'm gonna be able to stand it."

LENNY. That's awful.

BABE. She said she was afraid of being a weak person. I guess 'cause she cried in bed every night for such a long time.

LENNY. Goodness mercy. (*After a pause.*) Well, I suppose you'd have to be a pretty hard person to be able to do what she did to Doc Porter.

BABE. (*Exasperated.*) Oh, shoot! It wasn't Meg's fault that hurricane wiped Biloxi away. I never understood why people were blaming all that on Meg—just because that roof fell in and crunched Doc's leg. It wasn't her fault.

LENNY. Well, it was Meg who refused to evacuate. Jim Craig and some of Doc's other friends were all down there, and they kept trying to get everyone to evacuate. But Meg refused. She wanted to stay on because she thought a hurricane would be—oh, I don't know—a lot of fun. Then everyone says she baited Doc into staying there with her. She said she'd marry him if he'd stay.

BABE. (*Taken aback by this new information.*) Well, he has a mind of his own. He could have gone.

LENNY. But he didn't. 'Cause . . . 'cause he loved her. And then, after the roof caved in and they got Doc to the high school gym, Meg just left him there to leave for California—'cause of her career, she says. I think it was a shameful thing to do. It took almost a year for his leg to heal, and after that he gave up his medical career altogether. He said he was tired of hospitals. It's such a sad thing. Everyone always knew he was gonna be a doctor. We've called him Doc for years.

BABE. I don't know. I guess I don't have any room to talk; 'cause I just don't know. (*Pause.*) Gosh, you look so tired.

LENNY. I feel tired.

BABE. They say women need a lot of iron . . . so they won't feel tired.

LENNY. What's got iron in it? Liver?

BABE. Yeah, liver's got it. And vitamin pills.

(*After a moment,* MEG *enters. She carries a bottle of bourbon that is already minus a few slugs, and a newspaper. She is wearing black boots, a dark dress, and a hat. The room goes silent.*)

MEG. Hello.

BABE. (*Fooling with her hair.*) Hi, Meg.

(LENNY *quietly sips her coffee.*)

MEG. (*Handing the newspaper to* BABE.) Here's your paper.

BABE. Thanks. (*She opens it.*) Oh, here it is, right on the front page.

(MEG *lights a cigarette.*)

BABE. Where're the scissors, Lenny?

LENNY. Look in there in the ribbon drawer.

BABE. Okay. (*She gets the scissors and glue out of the drawer and slowly begins cutting out the newspaper article.*)

MEG. (*After a few moments, filled only with the snipping of scissors.*) All right—I lied! I lied! I couldn't help it . . . these stories just came pouring out of my mouth! When I saw how tired and sick Old Granddaddy'd gotten—they just flew out! All I wanted was to see him smiling and happy. I just wasn't going to sit there and look at him all miserable and sick and sad! I just wasn't!

BABE. Oh, Meg, he is sick, isn't he—

MEG. Why, he's gotten all white and milky—he's almost evaporated!

LENNY. (*Gasping and turning to* MEG.) But still you shouldn't have lied! It just was wrong for you to tell such lies—

MEG. Well, I know that! Don't you think I know that? I hate myself when I lie for that old man. I do. I feel so weak. And then I have to go and do at least three of four things that I know he'd despise just to get even with that miserable, old, bossy man!

LENNY. Oh, Meg, please don't talk so about Old Granddaddy! It sounds so ungrateful. Why, he went out of his way to make a home for us, to treat us like we were his very own children. All he ever wanted was the best for us. That's all he ever wanted.

MEG. Well, I guess it was; but sometimes I wonder what we wanted.

BABE. (*Taking the newspaper article and glue over to her suitcase.*) Well, one thing I wanted was a team of white horses to ride Mama's coffin to her grave. That's one thing I wanted. (LENNY *and* MEG *exchange looks.*) Lenny, did you remember to pack my photo album?

LENNY. It's down there at the bottom, under all that night stuff.

BABE. Oh, I found it.

LENNY. Really, Babe, I don't understand why you have to put in the articles that are about the unhappy things in your life. Why would you want to remember them?

BABE. (*Pasting the article in.*) I don't know. I just like to keep an accurate record, I suppose. There. (*She begins flipping through the book.*) Look, here's a picture of me when I got married.

MEG. Let's see. (*They all look at the photo album.*)

LENNY. My word, you look about twelve years old.

BABE. I was just eighteen.

MEG. You're smiling, Babe. Were you happy then?

BABE. (*Laughing.*) Well, I was drunk on champagne punch. I remember that! (*They turn the page.*)

LENNY. Oh, there's Meg singing at Greeny's!

BABE. Oooh, I wish you were still singing at Greeny's! I wish you were!

LENNY. You're so beautiful.

BABE. Yes, you are. You're beautiful.

MEG. Oh, stop! I'm not—

LENNY. Look, Meg's starting to cry.

BABE. Oh, Meg—

MEG. I'm not—

BABE. Quick, better turn the page; we don't want Meg crying—(*She flips the pages.*)

LENNY. Why, it's Daddy.

MEG. Where'd you get that picture, Babe? I thought she burned them all.

BABE. Ah, I just found it around.

LENNY. What does it say here? What's that inscription?

BABE. It says "Jimmy—clowning at the beach—1952."

LENNY. Well, will you look at that smile.

MEG. Jesus, those white teeth—turn the page, will you; we can't do any worse than this! (*They turn the page. The room goes silent.*)

BABE. It's Mama and the cat.

LENNY. Oh, turn the page—

BABE. That old yellow cat. You know, I bet if she hadn't of hung that old cat along with her, she wouldn't have gotten all that national coverage.

MEG. (*After a moment, hopelessly.*) Why are we talking about this?

LENNY. Meg's right. It was so sad. It was awfully sad. I remember how we all three just sat up on that bed the day of the service all dressed up in our black velveteen suits crying the whole morning long.

BABE. We used up one whole big box of Kleenexes.

MEG. And then Old Granddaddy came in and said he was gonna take us out to breakfast. Remember, he told us not to cry anymore 'cause he was gonna take us out to get banana splits for breakfast.

BABE. That's right—banana splits for breakfast!

MEG. Why, Lenny was fourteen years old, and he thought that would make it all better—

BABE. Oh, I remember he said for us to eat all we wanted. I think I ate about five! He kept shoving them down us!

MEG. God, we were so sick!

LENNY. Oh, we were!

MEG. (*Laughing.*) Lenny's face turned green—

LENNY. I was just as sick as a dog!

BABE. Old Grandmama was furious!

LENNY. Oh, she was!

MEG. The thing about Old Granddaddy is, he keeps trying to make us happy, and we end up getting stomachaches and turning green and throwing up in the flower arrangements.

BABE. Oh, that was me! I threw up in the flowers! Oh, no! How embarrassing!

LENNY. (*Laughing.*) Oh, Babe—

BABE. (*Hugging her sisters.*) Oh, Lenny! Oh, Meg!

MEG. Oh, Babe! Oh, Lenny! It's so good to be home!

LENNY. Hey, I have an idea—

BABE. What?

LENNY. Let's play cards!!

BABE. Oh, let's do!

MEG. All right!

LENNY. Oh, good! It'll be just like when we used to sit around the table playing hearts all night long.

BABE. I know! (*Getting up.*) I'll fix us up some popcorn and hot chocolate—

MEG. (*Getting up.*) Here, let me get out that old back popcorn pot.

LENNY. (*Getting up.*) Oh, yes! Now, let's see, I think I have a deck of cards around here somewhere.

BABE. Gosh, I hope I remember all the rules— Are hearts good or bad?

MEG. Bad, I think. Aren't they, Lenny?

LENNY. That's right. Hearts are bad, but the Black Sister is the worst of all—

MEG. Oh, that's right! And the Black Sister is the Queen of Spades.

BABE. (*Figuring it out.*) And spades are the black cards that aren't the puppy dog feet?

MEG. (*Thinking a moment.*) Right. And she counts a lot of points.

BABE. And points are bad?

MEG. Right. Here, I'll get some paper so we can keep score. (*The phone rings.*)

LENNY. Oh, here they are!

MEG. I'll get it—

LENNY. Why, look at these cards! They're years old!

BABE. Oh, let me see!

MEG. Hello . . . No, this is Meg MaGrath . . . Doc. How are you? . . . Well, good . . . You're where? . . . Well, sure. Come on over . . . All right. 'Bye. (*She hangs up.*) That was Doc Porter. He's down the street at Al's Grill. He's gonna come on over.

LENNY. He is?

MEG. He said he wanted to come see me.

LENNY. Oh. (*After a pause.*) Well, do you still want to play?

MEG. No, I don't think so.

LENNY. All right. (*She starts to shuffle the cards, as* MEG *brushes her hair.*) You know, it's really not much fun playing hearts with only two people.

MEG. I'm sorry; maybe after Doc leaves I'll join you.

LENNY. I know; maybe Doc'll want to play. Then we can have a game of bridge.

MEG. I don't think so. Doc never liked cards. Maybe we'll just go out somewhere.

LENNY. (*Putting down the cards.* BABE *picks them up.*) Meg—

MEG. What?

LENNY. Well, Doc's married now.

MEG. I know. You told me.

LENNY. Oh. Well, as long as you know that. (*Pause.*) As long as you know that.

MEG. (*Still primping.*) Yes, I know. She made the pot.

BABE. How many cards do I deal out?

LENNY. (*Leaving the table.*) Excuse me.

BABE. All of 'em, or what?

LENNY. Ah, Meg, could I—could I ask you something?

(BABE *proceeds to deal out all the cards.*)

MEG. What?

LENNY. I just wanted to ask you—

MEG. What?

LENNY. (*Unable to go on with what she really wants to say,* LENNY *runs and picks up the box of candy.*) Well, just why did you take one little bite out of each piece of candy in this box and then just put it back in?

MEG. Oh. Well, I was looking for the ones with nuts.

LENNY. The ones with nuts.

MEG. Yeah.

LENNY. But there are none with nuts. It's a box of assorted crèmes—all it has in it are crèmes!

MEG. Oh.

LENNY. Why couldn't you just read on the box? It says right here, *Assorted Crèmes,* not nuts! Besides, this was a birthday present to me! My one and only birthday present; my only one!

MEG. I'm sorry. I'll get you another box.

LENNY. I don't want another box. That's not the point!

MEG. What is the point?

LENNY. I don't know; it's—it's— You have no respect for other people's property! You just take whatever you want. You just take it! Why, remember how you had layers and layers of jingle bells sewed onto your petticoats while Babe and I only had three apiece?

MEG. Oh, God! She's starting up about those stupid jingle bells!

LENNY. Well, it's an example! A specific example of how you always got what you wanted!

MEG. Oh, come on, Lenny, you're just upset because Doc called.

LENNY. Who said anything about Doc? Do you think I'm upset about Doc? Why, I've long since given up worrying about you and all your men.

MEG. (*Turning in anger.*) Look, I know I've had too many men. Believe me, I've had way too many men. But it's not my fault you haven't had any—or maybe just that one from Memphis.

LENNY. (*Stopping.*) What one from Memphis?

MEG. (*Slowly.*) The one Babe told me about. From the— club.

LENNY. Babe!

BABE. Meg!

LENNY. How could you! I asked you not tell anyone! I'm so ashamed! How could you? Who else have you told? Did you tell anyone else?

BABE. (*Overlapping, to Meg.*) Why'd you have to open your big mouth?

MEG. (*Overlapping.*) How am I supposed to know? You never said not to tell!

BABE. Can't you use your head just for once? (*To* LENNY.) No, I never told anyone else. Somehow it just slipped out to Meg. Really, it just flew out of my mouth—

LENNY. What do you two have—wings on your tongues?

BABE. I'm sorry, Lenny. Really sorry.

LENNY. I'll just never, never, never be able to trust you again—

MEG. (*Furiously coming to* BABE'*s defense.*) Oh, for heaven's sake, Lenny, we were just worried about you! We wanted to find a way to make you happy!

LENNY. Happy! Happy! I'll never be happy!

MEG. Well, not if you keep living your life as Old Granddaddy's nursemaid—

BABE. Meg, shut up!

MEG. I can't help it! I just know that the reason you stopped seeing this man from Memphis was because of Old Granddaddy.

LENNY. What— Babe didn't tell you the rest of the story—

MEG. Oh, she said it was something about your shrunken ovary.

BABE. Meg!

LENNY. Babe!

BABE. I just mentioned it!

MEG. But I don't believe a word of that story!

LENNY. Oh, I don't care what you believe! It's so easy for you—you always have men falling in love with you! But I have this underdeveloped ovary and I can't have children and my hair is falling out in the comb—so what man can love me? What man's gonna love me?

MEG. A lot of men!

BABE. Yeah, a lot! A whole lot!

MEG. Old Granddaddy's the only one who seems to think otherwise.

LENNY. 'Cause he doesn't want to see me hurt! He doesn't want to see me rejected and humiliated.

MEG. Oh, come on now, Lenny, don't be so pathetic! God, you make me angry when you just stand there looking so pathetic! Just tell me, did you really ask the man from Memphis? Did you actually ask that man from Memphis all about it?

LENNY. (*Breaking apart.*) No, I didn't. I didn't. Because I just didn't want him not to want me—

MEG. Lenny—

LENNY. (*Furious.*) Don't talk to me anymore! Don't talk to me! I think I'm gonna vomit— I just hope all this doesn't cause me to vomit! (*She exits up the stairs sobbing.*)

MEG. See! See! She didn't even ask him about her stupid ovary! She just broke it all off 'cause of Old Granddaddy! What a jackass fool!

BABE. Oh, Meg, shut up! Why do you have to make Lenny cry? I just hate it when you make Lenny cry! (*She runs up the stairs.*) Lenny! Oh, Lenny—

MEG. (*Gives a long sigh and goes to get a cigarette and a drink.*) I feel like hell. (*She sits in despair, smoking and drinking bourbon. There is a knock at the back door. She starts. She brushes her hair out of her face and goes to answer the door. It is* DOC)

DOC. Hello, Meggy.

MEG. Well, Doc. Well, it's Doc.

DOC. (*After a pause.*) You're home, Meggy.

MEG. Yeah, I've come home. I've come on home to see about Babe.

DOC. And how's Babe?

MEG. Oh, fine. Well, fair. She's fair.

(DOC *nods.*)

MEG. Hey, do you want a drink?

DOC. Whatcha got?

MEG. Bourbon.

DOC. Oh, don't tell me Lenny's stocking bourbon.

MEG. Well, no. I've been to the store. (*She gets him a glass and pours them each a drink. They click glasses.*)

MEG. So, how's your wife?

DOC. She's fine.

MEG. I hear ya got two kids.

DOC. Yeah. Yeah, I got two kids.

MEG. A boy and a girl.

DOC. That's right, Meggy, a boy and a girl.

MEG. That's what you always said you wanted, wasn't it? A boy and a girl.

DOC. Is that what I said?

MEG. I don't know. I thought it's what you said. (*They finish their drinks in silence.*)

DOC. Whose cot?

MEG. Lenny's. She's taken to sleeping in the kitchen.

DOC. Ah. Where is Lenny?

MEG. She's in the upstairs room. I made her cry. Babe's up there seeing to her.

DOC. How'd you make her cry?

MEG. I don't know. Eating her birthday candy; talking on about her boyfriend from Memphis. I don't know. I'm upset about it. She's got a lot on her. Why can't I keep my mouth shut?

DOC. I don't know, Meggy. Maybe it's because you don't want to.

MEG. Maybe. (*They smile at each other.* MEG *pours each of them another drink.*)

DOC. Well, it's been a long time.

MEG. It has been a long time.

DOC. Let's see—when was the last time we saw each other?

MEG. I can't quite recall.

DOC. Wasn't it in Biloxi?

MEG. Ah, Biloxi. I believe so.

DOC. And wasn't there a—a hurricane going on at the time?

MEG. Was there?

DOC. Yes, there was; one hell of a hurricane. Camille, I believe they called it. Hurricane Camille.

MEG. Yes, now I remember. It was a beautiful hurricane.

DOC. We had a time down there. We had quite a time. Drinking vodka, eating oysters on the half shell, dancing all night long. And the wind was blowing.

MEG. Oh, God, was it blowing.

DOC. Goddamn, was it blowing.

MEG. There never has been such a wind blowing.

DOC. Oh, God, Meggy. Oh, God.

MEG. I know, Doc. It was my fault to leave you. I was crazy. I thought I was choking. I felt choked!

DOC. I felt like a fool.

MEG. No.

DOC. I just kept on wondering why.

MEG. I don't know why . . . 'Cause I didn't want to care. I don't know. I did care, though. I did.

DOC. (*After a pause.*) Ah, hell—(*He pours them both another drink.*) Are you still singing those sad songs?

MEG. No.

DOC. Why not?

MEG. I don't know, Doc. Things got worse for me. After a while, I just couldn't sing anymore. I tell you, I had one hell of a time over Christmas.

DOC. What do you mean?

MEG. I went nuts. I went insane. Ended up in L.A. County Hospital, Psychiatric ward.

DOC. Hell. Ah, hell, Meggy. What happened?

MEG. I don't really know. I couldn't sing anymore, so I lost my job. And I had a bad toothache. I had this incredibly painful toothache. For days I had it, but I wouldn't do anything about it. I just stayed inside my apartment. All I could do was sit around in chairs, chewing on my fingers. Then one afternoon I ran screaming out of the apartment with all my money and jewelry and valuables, and tried to stuff it all into one of those March of Dimes collection boxes. That was when they nabbed me. Sad story. Meg goes mad.

DOC. (*Stares at her for a long moment. He pours them both another drink. After quite a pause.*) There's a moon out.

MEG. Is there?

DOC. Wanna go take a ride in my truck and look out at the moon?

MEG. I don't know, Doc. I don't wanna start up. It'll be too hard if we start up.

DOC. Who says we're gonna start up? We're just gonna look at the moon. For one night just you and me are gonna go for a ride in the country and look out at the moon.

MEG. One night?

DOC. Right.

MEG. Look out at the moon?

DOC. You got it.

MEG. Well . . . all right. (*She gets up.*)

DOC. Better take your coat. (*He helps her into her coat.*) And the bottle—(*He takes the bottle.* MEG *picks up the glasses.*) Forget the glasses—

MEG. (*Laughing*) Yeah—forget the glasses. Forget the god-damn glasses. (MEG *shuts off the kitchen lights, leaving the kitchen with only a dim light over the kitchen sink.* MEG *and* DOC *leave. After a moment,* BABE *comes down the stairs in her slip.*)

BABE. Meg—Meg? (*She stands for a moment in the moon-*

light wearing only a slip. She sees her saxophone, then moves to pick it up. She plays a few shrieking notes. There is a loud knock on the back door.)

BARNETTE'S VOICE. Becky! Becky, is that you?

BABE. (*Puts down the saxophone.*) Just a minute. I'm coming. (*She puts a raincoat on over her slip and goes to answer the door.*) Hello, Barnette. Come on in.

(BARNETTE *comes in. He is troubled but is making a great effort to hide the fact.*)

BARNETTE. Thank you.

BABE. What is it?

BARNETTE. I've, ah, I've just come from seeing Zackery at the hospital.

BABE. Oh?

BARNETTE. It seems . . . Well, it seems his sister, Lucille, was somewhat suspicious.

BABE. Suspicious?

BARNETTE. About you.

BABE. Me?

BARNETTE. She hired a private detective: he took these pictures. (*He hands* BABE *a small envelope containing several photographs.* BABE *opens the envelope and begins looking at the pictures in stunned silence.*)

BARNETTE. They were taken about two week ago. It seems she wasn't going to show them to Botrelle straightaway. She, ah, wanted to wait till the time was right.

(*The phone rings one and a half times.* BARNETTE *glances uneasily toward the phone.*)

BARNETTE. Becky?

(*The phone stops ringing.*)

BABE. (*Looking up at Barnette, slowly.*) These are pictures of Willie Jay and me . . out in the garage.

BARNETTE. (*Looking away.*) I know.

BABE. You looked at these pictures?

BARNETTE. Yes—I—well . . . professionally, I looked at them.

BABE. Oh, mercy. Oh, mercy! We can burn them, can't we? Quick, we can burn them—

BARNETTE. It won't do any good. They have the negatives.

BABE. (*Holding the pictures, as she bangs herself hopelessly into the stove, table, cabinets, etc.*) Oh, no; oh, no; oh, no! Oh, no—

BARNETTE. There—there, now—there—

LENNY'S VOICE. Babe? Are you all right? Babe—

BABE. (*Hiding the pictures.*) What? I'm all right. Go on back to bed. (BABE *hides the pictures as* LENNY *comes down the stairs. She is wearing a coat and wiping white night cream off of her face with a washrag.*)

LENNY. What's the matter? What's going on down here?

BABE. Nothing! (*Then as she begins dancing ballet style around the room.*) We're—we're just dancing. We were just dancing around down here. (*Signaling to* BARNETTE *to dance.*)

LENNY. Well, you'd better get your shoes on, 'cause we've got—

BABE. All right, I will! That's a good idea! (*She goes to get her shoes.*) Now, you go on back to bed. It's pretty late and—

LENNY. Babe, will you listen a minute—

BABE. (*Holding up her shoes.*) I'm putting 'em on—

LENNY. That was the hospital that just called. We've got to get over there. Old Granddaddy's had himself another stroke.

BABE. Oh. All right. My shoes are on. (*She stands. They all look at each other as the lights black out.*)

CURTAIN

ACT THREE

The lights go up on the empty kitchen. It is the following morning. After a few moments, BABE *enters from the back door. She is carrying her hair curlers in her hands. She lies down on the cot. A few moments later,* LENNY *enters. She is tired and weary.* CHICK's *voice is heard.*

CHICK'S VOICE. Lenny! Oh, Lenny!

(LENNY *turns to the door.* CHICK *enters energetically.*)

CHICK. Well . . . how is he?

LENNY. He's stabilized; they say for now his functions are all stabilized.

CHICK. Well, is he still in the coma?

LENNY. Uh huh.

CHICK. Hmmm. So do they think he's gonna be . . . passing on?

LENNY. He may be. He doesn't look so good. They said they'd phone us if there were any sudden changes.

CHICK. Well, it seems to me we'd better get busy phoning on the phone ourselves. (*Removing a list from her pocket.*) Now, I've made out this list of all the people we need to notify about Old Granddaddy's predicament. I'll phone half, if you'll phone half.

LENNY. But—what would we say?

CHICK. Just tell them the facts: that Old Granddaddy's got himself in a coma, and it could be he doesn't have long for this world.

LENNY. I—I don't know. I don't feel like phoning.

CHICK. Why, Lenora, I'm surprised; how can you be this way? I went to all the trouble of making up the list. And I offered to phone half of the people on it, even though I'm only one-fourth of the granddaughters. I mean, I just get tired of doing more than my fair share, when people like Meg can suddenly just disappear to where they can't even be reached in case of emergency!

LENNY. All right; give me the list. I'll phone half.

CHICK. Well, don't do it just to suit me.

LENNY. (*Wearily tearing the list in half.*) I'll phone these here.

CHICK. (*Taking her half of the list.*) Fine then. Suit yourself.
Oh, wait—let me call Sally Bell. I need to talk to her, anyway.

LENNY. All right.

CHICK. So you add Great-uncle Spark Dude to your list.

LENNY. Okay.

CHICK. Fine. Well, I've got to get on back home and see to
the kids. It is gonna be an uphill struggle till I can find
someone to replace that good-for-nothing Annie May Jenkins.
Well, you let me know if you hear any more.

LENNY. All right.

CHICK. Goodbye, Rebecca. I said goodbye. (BABE *blows her
sax.* CHICK *starts to exit in a flurry, then pauses to add.*) And
you really ought to try to get that phoning done before twelve
noon. (*She exits.*)

LENNY. (*After a long pause.*) Babe, I feel bad. I feel real
bad.

BABE. Why, Lenny?

LENNY. Because yesterday I—I wished it.

BABE. You wished what?

LENNY. I wished that Old Granddaddy would be put out of
his pain. I wished it on one of my birthday candles. I did. And
now he's in this coma, and they say he's feeling no pain.

BABE. Well, when did you have a cake yesterday? I don't
remember you having any cake.

LENNY. Well, I didn't . . . have a cake. But I just blew out
the candles, anyway.

BABE. Oh. Well, those birthday wishes don't count, unless
you have a cake.

LENNY. They don't?

BABE. No. A lot of times they don't even count when you do
have a cake. It just depends.

LENNY. Depends on what?

BABE. On how deep your wish is, I suppose.

LENNY. Still, I just wish I hadn't of wished it. Gosh, I
wonder when Meg's coming home.

BABE. Should be soon.

LENNY. I just wish we wouldn't fight all the time. I don't like
it when we do.

BABE. Me, neither.

LENNY. I guess it hurts my feelings, a little, the way Old
Granddaddy's always put so much stock in Meg and all her

singing talent. I think I've been, well, envious of her 'cause I can't seem to do too much.

BABE. Why, sure you can.

LENNY. I can?

BABE. Sure. You just have to put your mind to it, that's all. It's like how I went out and bought that saxophone, just hoping I'd be able to attend music school and start up my own career. I just went out and did it. Just on hope. Of course, now it looks like . . . Well, it just doesn't look like things are gonna work out for me. But I knew they would for you.

LENNY. Well, they'll work out for you, too.

BABE. I doubt it.

LENNY. Listen, I heard up at the hospital that Zackery's already in fair condition. They say soon he'll probably be able to walk and everything.

BABE. Yeah. And life sure can be miserable.

LENNY. Well, I know, 'cause—day before yesterday, Billy Boy was struck down by lightning.

BABE. He was?

LENNY. (*Nearing sobs.*) Yeah. He was struck dead.

BABE. (*Crushed.*) Life sure can be miserable.

(*They sit together for several moments in morbid silence.* MEG *is heard singing a loud happy song. She suddenly enters through the dining room door. She is exuberant! Her hair is a mess, and the heel of one shoe has broken off. She is laughing radiantly and limping as she sings into the broken heel.*)

MEG. (*Spotting her sisters.*) Good morning! Good morning! Oh, it's a wonderful morning! I tell you, I am surprised I feel this good. I should feel like hell. By all accounts, I should feel like utter hell! (*She is looking for the glue.*) Where's that glue? This damn heel has broken off my shoe. La, la, la, la, la! Ah, here it is! Now, let me just get these shoes off. Zip, zip, zip, zip, zip! Well, what's wrong with you two? My god, you look like doom! (BABE *and* LENNY *stare helplessly at* MEG.) Oh, I know, you're mad at me 'cause I stayed out all night long. Well, I did.

LENNY. No, we're—we're not mad at you. We're just . . . depressed. (*She starts to sob.*)

MEG. Oh, Lenny, listen to me, now; everything's all right with Doc. I mean, nothing happened. Well, actually a lot did happen, but it didn't come to anything. Not because of me, I'm afraid. (*Smearing glue on her heel.*) I mean, I was out there thinking, What will I say when he begs me to run away with him? Will I have pity on his wife and those two half-Yankee children? I mean, can I sacrifice their happiness for mine? Yes! Oh, yes! Yes, I can! But . . . he didn't ask me. He didn't even want to ask me. I could tell by this certain look in his eyes that he didn't even want to ask me. Why aren't I miserable! Why aren't I morbid! I should be humiliated! Devastated! Maybe these feelings are coming—I don't know. But for now it was . . . just such fun. I'm happy. I realized I could care about someone. I could want someone. And I sang! I sang all night long! I sang right up into the trees! But not for Old Grand-daddy. None of it was to please Old Granddaddy!

(LENNY *and* BABE *look at each other.*)

BABE. Ah, Meg—

MEG. What—

BABE. Well, it's just—It's . . .

LENNY. It's about Old Granddaddy—

MEG. Oh, I know; I know. I told him all those stupid lies. Well, I'm gonna go right over there this morning and tell him the truth. I mean every horrible thing. I don't care if he wants to hear it or not. He's just gonna have to take me like I am. And if he can't take it, if it sends him into a coma, that's just too damn bad!

(BABE *and* LENNY *look at each other.* BABE *cracks a smile.* LENNY *cracks a smile.*)

BABE. You're too late—Ha, ha, ha! (*They both break up laughing.*)

LENNY. Oh, stop! Please! Ha, ha, ha!

MEG. What is it? What's so funny?

BABE. (*Still laughing.*) It's not— It's not funny!

LENNY. (*Still laughing.*) No, it's not! It's not a bit funny!

MEG. Well, what is it, then? What?

BABE. (*Trying to calm down.*) Well, it's just—it's just—

MEG. What?

BABE. Well, Old Granddaddy—he—he's in a coma! (BABE *and* LENNY *break up again.*)

MEG. He's what?

BABE. (*Shrieking.*) In a coma!

MEG. My God! That's not funny!

BABE. (*Calming down.*) I know. I know. For some reason, it just struck us as funny.

LENNY. I'm sorry. It's—it's not funny. It's sad. It's very sad. We've been up all night long.

BABE. We're really tired.

MEG. Well, my God. How is he? Is he gonna live?

(BABE *and* LENNY *look at each other*.)

BABE. They don't think so! (*They both break up again*.)

LENNY. Oh, I don't know why we're laughing like this. We're just sick! We're just awful!

BABE. We are—we're awful!

LENNY. (*As she collects herself*.) Oh, good; now I feel bad. Now I feel like crying. I do; I feel like crying.

BABE. Me, too. Me, too.

MEG. Well, you've gotten me depressed!

LENNY. I'm sorry. I'm sorry. It, ah, happened last night. He had another stroke. (*They laugh again*.)

MEG. I see.

LENNY. But he's stabilized now. (*She chokes up once more*.)

MEG. That's good. You two okay? (BABE *and* LENNY *nod*.) You look like you need some rest. (BABE *and* LENNY *nod again. Going on, about her heel*.) I hope that'll stay. (*She puts the top back on the glue. A realization*.) Oh, of course, now I won't be able to tell him the truth about all those lies I told. I mean, finally I get my wits about me, and he conks out. It's just like him. Babe, can I wear your slippers till this glue dries?

BABE. Sure.

LENNY. (*After a pause*.) Things sure are gonna be different around here . . . when Old Granddaddy dies. Well, not for you two really, but for me.

MEG. It'll work out.

BABE. (*Depressed*.) Yeah. It'll work out.

LENNY. I hope so. I'm just afraid of being here all by myself. All alone.

MEG. Well, you don't have to be alone. Maybe Babe'll move back in here.

(LENNY *looks at* BABE *hopefully*.)

BABE. No, I don't think I'll be living here.

MEG. (*Realizing her mistake*.) Well, anyway, you're your own woman. Invite some people over. Have some parties. Go out with strange men.

LENNY. I don't know any strange men.

MEG. Well . . . you know that Charlie.

LENNY. (*Shaking her head*) Not anymore.

MEG. Why not?

LENNY. (*Breaking down*) I told him we should never see each other again.

MEG. Well, if you told him, you can just untell him.

LENNY. Oh, no I couldn't. I'd feel like a fool.

MEG. Oh, that's not a good enough reason! All people in love feel like fools. Don't they, Babe?

BABE. Sure.

MEG. Look, why don't you give him a call right now? See how things stand.

LENNY. Oh, no! I'd be too scared—

MEG. But what harm could it possibly do? I mean, it's not gonna make things any worse than this never seeing him again, at all, forever.

LENNY. I suppose that's true—

MEG. Of course it is; so call him up! Take a chance, will you? Just take some sort of chance!

LENNY. You think I should?

MEG. Of course! You've got to try— You do!

(LENNY *looks over at* BABE.)

BABE. You do, Lenny—I think you do.

LENNY. Really? Really, really?

MEG. Yes! Yes!

BABE. You should!

LENNY. All right. I will! I will!

MEG. Oh, good!

BABE. Good!

LENNY. I'll call him right now, while I've got my confidence up!

MEG. Have you got the number?

LENNY. Uh huh. But, ah, I think I wanna call him upstairs. It'll be more private.

MEG. Ah, good idea.

LENNY. I'm just gonna go on and call him up and see what happens—(*She has started up the stairs.*) Wish me good luck!

MEG. Good luck!

BABE. Good luck, Lenny!

LENNY. Thanks. (LENNY *gets almost out of sight when the phone rings. She stops;* MEG *picks up the phone.*)

MEG. Hello? (*Then, in a whisper.*) Oh, thank you very much . . . Yes, I will. 'Bye, 'bye.

LENNY. Who was it?

MEG. Wrong number. They wanted Weed's Body Shop.

LENNY. Oh. Well, I'll be right back down in a minute. (*She exits.*)

MEG. (*After a moment, whispering to Babe.*) That was the bakery; Lenny's cake is ready!

BABE. (*Who has become increasingly depressed.*) Oh.

MEG. I think I'll sneak on down to the corner and pick it up. (*She starts to leave.*)

BABE. Meg—

MEG. What?

BABE. Nothing.

MEG. You okay? (BABE *shakes her head.*) What is it?

BABE. It's just—

MEG. What?

BABE. (*Gets the envelope containing the photographs.*) Here. Take a look.

MEG. (*Taking the envelope.*) What is it?

BABE. It's some evidence Zackery's collected against me. Looks like my goose is cooked.

MEG. (*Opens the envelope and looks at the photographs.*) My God, it's—it's you and . . . is *that* Willie Jay?

BABE. Yah.

MEG. Well, he certainly *has* grown. You were right about that. My, oh, my.

BABE. Please don't tell Lenny. She'd hate me.

MEG. I won't. I won't tell Lenny. (*Putting the pictures back into the envelope.*) What are you gonna do?

BABE. What can I do? (*There is a knock on the door.* BABE *grabs the envelope and hides it.*)

MEG. Who is it?

BARNETTE'S VOICE. It's Barnette Lloyd.

MEG. Oh. Come on in, Barnette.

(BARNETTE enters. His eyes are ablaze with excitement.)

BARNETTE. (*As he paces around the room.*) Well, good morning! (*Shaking* MEG's *hand.*) Good morning, Miss MaGrath. (*Touching* BABE *on the shoulder.*) Becky. (*Moving away.*) What I meant to say is, How are you doing this morning?

MEG. Ah—fine. Fine.

BARNETTE. Good. Good. I—I just had time to drop by for a minute.

MEG. Oh.

BARNETTE. So, ah, how's your granddad doing?

MEG. Well, not very, ah—ah, he's in this coma. (*She breaks up laughing.*)

BARNETTE. I see . . . I see. (*To* BABE.) Actually, the primary reason I came by was to pick up that—envelope. I left it here last night in all the confusion. (*Pause.*) You, ah, still do have it? (BABE *hands him the envelope.*) Yes. (*Taking the envelope.*) That's the one. I'm sure it'll be much better off in my office safe. (*He puts the envelope into his coat pocket.*)

MEG. I'm sure it will.

BARNETTE. Beg your pardon?

BABE. It's all right. I showed her the pictures.

BARNETTE. Ah; I see.

MEG. So what's going to happen now, Barnette? What are those pictures gonna mean?

BARNETTE. (*After pacing a moment.*) Hmmm. May I speak frankly and openly?

BABE. Uh huh.

MEG. Please do—

BARNETTE. Well, I tell you now, at first glance, I admit those pictures had me considerably perturbed and upset. Perturbed to the point that I spent most of last night going over certain suspect papers and reports that had fallen into my hands—rather recklessly.

BABE. What papers do you mean?

BARNETTE. Papers that, pending word from three varied and unbiased experts, could prove graft, fraud, forgery, as well as a history of unethical behavior.

MEG. You mean about Zackery?

BARNETTE. Exactly. You see, I now intend to make this matter just as sticky and gritty for one Z. Botrelle as it is for us. Why, with the amount of scandal I'll dig up, Botrelle will be forced to settle this affair on our own terms!

MEG. Oh, Babe! Did you hear that?

BABE. Yes! Oh, yes! So you've won it! You've won your lifelong vendetta!

BARNETTE. Well . . . well, now of course it's problematic in that, well, in that we won't be able to expose him openly in the courts. That was the original game plan.

BABE. But why not? Why?

BARNETTE. Well, it's only that if, well, if a jury were to—to get, say, a glance at these, ah, photographs, well . . . well, possibly . . .

BABE. We could be sunk.

BARNETTE. In a sense. But! On the other hand, if a newspaper were to get a hold of our little item, Mr. Zackery Botrelle could find himself boiling in some awfully hot water. So what I'm looking for, very simply, is—a deal.

BABE. A deal?

MEG. Thank you, Barnette. It's a sunny day, Babe. (*Realizing she is in the way.*) Ooh, where's that broken shoe? (*She grabs her boots and runs upstairs.*)

BABE. So, you're having to give up your vendetta?

BARNETTE. Well, in a way. For the time. It, ah, seems to me you shouldn't always let your life be ruled by such things as, ah, personal vendettas. (*Looking at* BABE *with meaning.*) Other things can be important.

BABE. I don't know, I don't exactly know. How 'bout Willie Jay? Will he be all right?

BARNETTE. Yes, it's all been taken care of. He'll be leaving incognito on the midnight bus—heading north.

BABE. North.

BARNETTE. I'm sorry, it seemed the only . . . way. (BARNETTE *moves to her; she moves away.*)

BABE. Look, you'd better be getting on back to your work.

BARNETTE. (*Awkwardly.*) Right—'cause I—I've got those important calls out. (*Full of hope for her.*) They'll be pouring in directly. (*He starts to leave, then says to her with love.*) We'll talk.

MEG. (*Reappearing in her boots.*) Oh, Barnette—

BARNETTE. Yes?

MEG. Could you give me a ride just down to the corner? I need to stop at Helen's Bakery.

BARNETTE. Be glad to.

MEG. Thanks. Listen, Babe, I'll be right back with the cake. We're gonna have the best celebration! Now, ah, if Lenny asks where I've gone, just say I'm . . . Just say, I've gone out back to, ah, pick up some pawpaws! Okay?

BABE. Okay.

MEG. Fine; I'll be back in a bit. Goodbye.

BABE. 'Bye.

BARNETTE. Goodbye, Becky.

BABE. Goodbye, Barnette. Take care. (MEG *and* BARNETTE *exit.* BABE *sits staring ahead, in a state of deep despair.*) Goodbye, Becky. Goodbye, Barnette. Goodbye, Becky. (*She stops when* LENNY *comes down the stairs in a fluster.*)

LENNY. Oh! Oh! Oh! I'm so ashamed! I'm such a coward! I'm such a yellow-bellied chicken! I'm so ashamed! Where's Meg?

BABE. (*Suddenly bright.*) She's, ah—gone out back—to pick up some pawpaws.

LENNY. Oh. Well, at least I don't have to face her! I just couldn't do it! I couldn't make the call! My heart was pounding like a hammer. Pound! Pound! Pound! Why, I looked down and I could actually see my blouse moving back and forth! Oh, Babe, you look so disappointed. Are you?

BABE. (*Despondently.*) Uh huh.

LENNY. Oh, no! I've disappointed Babe! I can't stand it! I've gone and disappointed my little sister, Babe! Oh, no! I feel like howling like a dog!

CHICK'S VOICE. Oooh, Lenny! (*She enters dramatically, dripping with sympathy.*) Well, I just don't know what to say! I'm so sorry! I am so sorry for you! And for little Babe here, too. I mean, to have such a sister as that!

LENNY. What do you mean?

CHICK. Oh, you don't need to pretend with me. I saw it all from over there in my own back yard; I saw Meg stumbling out of Doc Porter's pickup truck, not fifteen minutes ago. And her looking such a disgusting mess. You must be so ashamed! You must just want to die! Why, I always said that girl was nothing but cheap Christmas trash!

LENNY. Don't talk that way about Meg.

CHICK. Oh, come on now, Lenny honey, I know exactly how you feel about Meg. Why, Meg's a low-class tramp and you need not have one more blessed thing to do with her and her disgusting behavior.

LENNY. I said, don't you ever talk that way about my sister Meg again.

CHICK. Well, my goodness gracious, Lenora, don't be such a noodle—it's the truth!

LENNY. I don't care if it's the Ten Commandments. I don't want to hear it in my home. Not ever again.

CHICK. In your home?! Why, I never in all my life— This is my grandfather's home! And you're just living here on his charity; so don't you get high-falutin' with me, Miss Lenora Josephine MaGrath!

LENNY. Get out of here—

CHICK. Don't you tell me to get out! What makes you think you can order me around? Why, I've had just about my fill of you trashy MaGraths and your trashy ways: hanging yourselves in cellars; carrying on with married men; shooting your own husbands!

LENNY. Get out!

CHICK. (*To* BABE.) And don't you think she's not gonna end up at the state prison farm or in some—mental institution. Why, it's a clear-cut case of manslaughter with intent to kill!

LENNY. Out! Get out!

CHICK. (*Running on.*) That's what everyone's saying, deliberate intent to kill! And you'll pay for that! Do you hear me? You'll pay!

LENNY. (*Picking up a broom and threatening* CHICK *with it.*) And I'm telling you to get out!

CHICK. You—you put that down this minute— Are you a raving lunatic?

LENNY. (*Beating* CHICK *with the broom.*) I said for you to get out! That means out! And never, never, never come back!

CHICK. (*Overlapping, as she runs around the room.*) Oh! Oh! Oh! You're crazy! You're crazy!

LENNY. (*Chasing* CHICK *out the door.*) Do you hear me, Chick the Stick! This is my home! This is my house! Get out! Out!

CHICK. (*Overlapping.*) Oh! Oh! Police! Police! You're crazy! Help! Help!

(LENNY *chases* CHICK *out of the house. They are both screaming. The phone rings.* BABE *goes and picks it up.*)

BABE. Hello? . . . Oh, hello, Zackery! . . . Yes, he showed them to me! . . . You're what! . . . What do you mean? . . . What! . . . You can't put me out to Whitfield . . . 'Cause I'm not crazy . . . I'm not! I'm not! . . . She wasn't crazy, either . . . Don't you call my mother crazy! . . . No, you're not! You're not gonna. You're not! (*She slams the phone down and stares wildly ahead.*) He's not. He's not. (*As she walks over to the ribbon drawer.*) I'll do it. I will. And he won't . . . (*She opens the drawer, pulls out the rope, becomes terrified, throws the rope back in the drawer, and slams it shut.*)

(LENNY *enters from the back door swinging the broom and laughing.*)

LENNY. Oh, my! Oh, my! You should have seen us! Why, I chased Chick the Stick right up the mimosa tree. I did! I left her right up there screaming in the tree!

BABE. (*Laughing; she is insanely delighted.*) Oh, you did!

LENNY. Yes, I did! And I feel so good! I do! I feel good! I feel good!

BABE. (*Overlapping.*) Good! Good, Lenny! Good for you! (*They dance around the kitchen.*)

LENNY. (*Stopping.*) You know what—

BABE. What?

LENNY. I'm gonna call Charlie! I'm gonna call him up right now!

BABE. You are?

LENNY. Yeah, I feel like I can really do it!

BABE. You do?

LENNY. My courage is up; my heart's in it; the time is right! No more beating around the bush! Let's strike while the iron is hot!

BABE. Right! Right! No more beating around the bush! Strike while the iron is hot!

(LENNY *goes to the phone.* BABE *rushes over to the ribbon drawer. She begins tearing through it.*)

LENNY. (*With the receiver in her hands.*) I'm calling him up, Babe— I'm really gonna do it!

BABE. (*Still tearing through the drawer.*) Good! Do it! Good!

LENNY. (*As she dials.*) Look. My hands aren't even shaking.

BABE. (*Pulling out a red rope.*) Don't we have any stronger rope than this?

LENNY. I guess not. All the rope we've got's in that drawer. (*About her hands.*) Now they're shaking a little.

(BABE *takes the rope and goes up the stairs.* LENNY *finishes dialing the number. She waits for an answer.*)

LENNY. Hello? . . . Hello, Charlie. This is Lenny MaGrath . . . Well, I'm fine. I'm just fine. (*An awkward pause.*) I was, ah, just calling to see—how you're getting on . . . Well, good. Good . . . Yes, I know I said that. Now I wish I didn't say it . . . Well, the reason I said that before, about not seeing each other again, was 'cause of me, not you . . . Well, it's just I—I can't have any children. I—have this ovary problem . . . Why, Charlie, what a thing to say! . . . Well, they're not all little snot-nosed pigs! . . . You think they are! . . . Oh, Charlie, stop, stop! You're making me laugh . . . Yes, I guess I was. I can see now that I was . . . You are? . . . Well, I'm dying to see you, too . . . Well, I don't know when, Charlie . . . soon. How about, well, how about tonight? . . . You will? . . . Oh, you will! . . . All right, I'll be here. I'll be right here . . . Goodbye, then, Charlie. Goodbye for now. (*She hangs up the phone in a daze.*) Babe. Oh, Babe! He's coming. He's coming! Babe! Oh, Babe, where are you? Meg! Oh . . . out back—picking up pawpaws. (*As she exits through the back door.*) And those pawpaws are just ripe for picking up!

(*There is a moment of silence; then a loud, horrible thud is heard coming from upstairs. The telephone begins ringing immediately. It rings five times before* BABE *comes hurrying down the stairs with a broken piece of rope hanging around her neck. The phone continues to ring.*)

BABE. (*To the phone.*) Will you shut up! (*She is jerking the rope from around her neck. She grabs a knife to cut it off.*) Cheap! Miserable! I hate you! I hate you! (*She throws the rope violently across the room. The phone stops ringing.*) Thank God. (*She looks at the stove, goes over to it, and turns the gas on. The sound of gas escaping is heard. She sniffs at it.*) Come

on. Come on . . . Hurry up . . . I beg of you—hurry up!
(*Finally, she feels the oven is ready; she takes a deep breath and
opens the oven door to stick her head into it. She spots the rack
and furiously jerks it out. Taking another breath, she sticks her
head into the oven. She stands for several moments tapping her
fingers furiously on top of the stove. She speaks from inside the
oven.*) Oh, please. Please. (*After a few moments, she reaches for
the box of matches with her head still in the oven. She tries to
strike a match. It doesn't catch.*) Oh, Mama, please! (*She throws
the match away and is getting a second one.*) Mama . . . Mama
. . . So that's why you done it! (*In her excitement she starts to
get up, bangs her head, and falls back in the oven.*)

(MEG *enters from the back door, carrying a birthday cake in
a pink box.*)

MEG. Babe! (*She throws the box down and runs to pull*
BABE's *head out of the oven.*) Oh, my God! What are you
doing? What the hell are you doing?

BABE. (*Dizzily.*) Nothing. I don't know. Nothing.

MEG. (*Turns off the gas and moves* BABE *to a chair near the
open door.*) Sit down. Sit down! Will you sit down!

BABE. I'm okay. I'm okay.

MEG. Put your head between your knees and breathe deep!

BABE. Meg—

MEG. Just do it! I'll get you some water. (*She gets some water
for* BABE.) Here.

BABE. Thanks.

MEG. Are you okay?

BABE. Uh huh.

MEG. Are you sure?

BABE. Yeah, I'm sure. I'm okay.

MEG. (*Getting a damp rag and putting it over her own face.*)
Well, good. That's good.

BABE. Meg—

MEG. Yes?

BABE. I know why she did it.

MEG. What? Why who did what?

BABE. (*With joy.*) Mama. I know why she hung that cat
along with her.

MEG. You do?

BABE. (*With enlightenment.*) It's 'cause she was afraid of
dying all alone.

MEG. Was she?

BABE. She felt so unsure, you know, as to what was
coming. It seems the best thing coming up would be a lot of

angels and all of them singing. But I imagine they have high, scary voices and little gold pointed fingers that are as sharp as blades and you don't want to meet 'em all alone. You'd be afraid to meet 'em all alone. So it wasn't like what people were saying about her hating that cat. Fact is, she loved that cat. She needed him with her 'cause she felt so all alone.

MEG. Oh, Babe . . . Babe. Why, Babe? Why?

BABE. Why what?

MEG. Why did you stick your head into the oven?!

BABE. I don't know, Meg. I'm having a bad day. It's been a real bad day; those pictures, and Barnette giving up his vendetta; then Willie Jay heading north; and—and Zackery called me up. (*Trembling with terror.*) He says he's gonna have me classified insane and then send me on out to the Whitfield asylum.

MEG. What! Why, he could never do that!

BABE. Why not?

MEG. 'Cause you're not insane.

BABE. I'm not?

MEG. No! He's trying to bluff you. Don't you see it? Barnette's got him running scared.

BABE. Really?

MEG. Sure. He's scared to death—calling you insane. Ha! Why, you're just as perfectly sane as anyone walking the streets of Hazlehurst, Mississippi.

BABE. I am?

MEG. More so! A lot more so!

BABE. Good!

MEG. But, Babe, we've just got to learn how to get through these real bad days here. I mean, it's getting to be a thing in our family. (*Slight pause as she looks at* BABE.) Come on, now. Look, we've got Lenny's cake right here. I mean, don't you wanna be around to give her her cake, watch her blow out the candles?

BABE. (*Realizing how much she wants to be here.*) Yeah, I do, I do. 'Cause she always loves to make her birthday wishes on those candles.

MEG. Well, then we'll give her her cake and maybe you won't be so miserable.

BABE. Okay.

MEG. Good. Go on and take it out of the box.

BABE. Okay. (*She takes the cake out of the box. It is a magical moment.*) Gosh, it's a pretty cake.

MEG. (*Handing her some matches.*) Here now. You can go on and light up the candles.

BABE. All right. (*She starts to light the candles.*) I love to light up candles. And there are so many here. Thirty pink ones in all, plus one green one to grow on.

MEG. (*Watching her light the candles.*) They're pretty.

BABE. They are. (*She stops lighting the candles.*) And I'm not like Mama. I'm not so all alone.

MEG. You're not.

BABE.(*As she goes back to lighting candles.*) Well, you'd better keep an eye out for Lenny. She's supposed to be surprised.

MEG. All right. Do you know where she's gone?

BABE. Well, she's not here inside—so she must have gone on outside.

MEG. Oh, well, then I'd better run and find her.

BABE. Okay; 'cause these candles are gonna melt down.

MEG. (*Starts out the door.*) Wait—there she is coming. Lenny! Oh, Lenny! Come on! Hurry up!

BABE. (*Overlapping and improvising as she finishes lighting candles.*) Oh, no! No! Well, yes— Yes! No, wait! Wait! Okay! Hurry up!

(LENNY *enters.* MEG *covers* LENNY'S *eyes with her hands.*)

LENNY. (*Terrified.*) What? What is it? What?

MEG AND BABE. Surprise! Happy birthday! Happy birthday to Lenny!

LENNY. Oh, no! Oh, me! What a surprise! I could just cry! Oh, look: *Happy birthday, Lenny—A Day Late!* How cute! My! Will you look at all those candles—it's absolutely frightening.

BABE. (*A spontaneous thought.*) Oh, no, Lenny, it's good! 'Cause—'cause the more candles you have on your cake, the stronger your wish is.

LENNY. Really?

BABE. Sure!

LENNY. Mercy! (MEG *and* BABE *start to sing.*)

LENNY. (*Interrupting the song.*) Oh, but wait! I—can't think of my wish! My body's gone all nervous inside.

MEG. For God's sake, Lenny—Come on!

BABE. The wax is all melting!

LENNY. My mind is just a blank, a total blank!

MEG. Will you please just—

BABE. (*Overlapping.*) Lenny, hurry! Come on!

LENNY. Okay! Okay! Just go!

(MEG *and* BABE *burst into the "Happy Birthday" song. As it*

ends, LENNY *blows out all the candles on the cake.* MEG *and*
BABE *applaud loudly.*)

MEG. Oh, you made it!

BABE. Hurray!

LENNY. Oh, me! Oh, me! I hope that wish comes true! I
hope it does!

BABE Why? What did you wish for?

LENNY. (*As she removes the candles from the cake.*) Why, I
can't tell you that.

BABE. Oh, sure you can—

LENNY. Oh, no! Then it won't come true.

BABE. Why, that's just superstition! Of course it will, if you
made it deep enough.

MEG. Really? I didn't know that.

LENNY. Well, Babe's the regular expert on birthday wishes.

BABE. It's just I get these feelings. Now, come on and tell us.
What was it you wished for?

MEG. Yes, tell us. What was it?

LENNY. Well, I guess it wasn't really a specific wish. This—
this vision just sort of came into my mind.

BABE. A vision? What was it of?

LENNY. I don't know exactly. It was something about the
three of us smiling and laughing together.

BABE. Well, when was it? Was it far away or near?

LENNY. I'm not sure; but it wasn't forever; it wasn't for
every minute. Just this one moment and we were all laughing.

BABE. Then, what were we laughing about?

LENNY. I don't know. Just nothing, I guess.

MEG. Well, that's a nice wish to make. (LENNY *and* MEG
look at each other a moment.) Here, now, I'll get a knife so
we can go ahead and cut the cake in celebration of Lenny being
born!

BABE. Oh, yes! And give each one of us a rose. A whole rose
apiece!

LENNY. (*Cutting the cake nervously.*) Well, I'll try—I'll try!

MEG. (*Licking the icing off a candle.*) Mmmm—this icing is
delicious! Here, try some!

BABE. Mmmm! It's wonderful! Here, Lenny!

LENNY. (*Laughing joyously as she licks icing from her fingers
and cuts huge pieces of cake that her sisters bite into ravenously.*)
Oh, how I do love having birthday cake for breakfast! How I
do!

The sisters freeze for a moment laughing and catching cake. The lights change and frame them in a magical, golden, sparkling glimmer; saxophone music is heard. The lights dim to blackout, and the saxophone continues to play.

CURTAIN

THE DINING ROOM

A PLAY

by

A. R. Gurney, Jr.

THE DINING ROOM was first produced at the Studio Theatre of Playwrights Horizons, in New York City, opening January 31, 1981, with the following cast:

1st ACTOR: Remak Ramsay   1st ACTRESS: Lois de Banzie

2nd ACTOR: John Shea   2nd ACTRESS: Ann McDonough

3rd ACTOR: W.H. Macy   3rd ACTRESS: Pippa Pearthree

It was directed by David Trainer. Loren Sherman designed the set, Deborah Shaw the costumes, and Frances Aronson the lighting. The production stage manager was M. A. Howard. Eternal thanks to them all.

CASTING SUGGESTIONS:

If a cast of six is used, and there are strong arguments for using this number, the following casting of the roles has proved to be workable and successful:

1st ACTOR: Father, Michael, Brewster, Grandfather, Stuart, Gordon, David, Harvey, and Host.

2nd ACTOR: Client, Howard, Psychiatrist, Ted, Paul, Ben, Chris, Jim, Dick, and Guest

3rd ACTOR: Arthur, Boy, Architect, Billy, Nick, Fred, Tony, Standish, and Guest

1st ACTRESS: Agent, Mother, Carolyn, Sandra, Dora, Margery, Beth, Kate, Claire, Ruth

2nd ACTRESS: Annie, Grace, Peggy, Nancy, Sarah, Harriet, Emily, Annie, and Guest.

3rd ACTRESS: Sally, Girl, Ellie, Aggie, Winkie, Old Lady, Helen, Meg, Bertha, and Guest

The play takes place in a dining room—or rather, many dining rooms. The same dining room furniture serves for all: a lovely burnished, shining dining room table; two chairs, with arms, at either end; two more, armless, along each side; several additional matching chairs, placed so as to define the walls of the room. Upstage somewhere, a sideboard, with a mirror over it.

Upstage, Left, a swinging door leads to the pantry and kitchen. Upstage, Right, an archway leads to the front hall and the rest of the house. But we should see no details from these other rooms. Both entrances should be masked in such a way as to suggest a limbo outside the dining room.

There should be a good, hardwood floor, possibly parquet, covered with a good, warm oriental rug.

A sense of the void surrounds the room. It might almost seem to be surrounded by a velvet-covered low-slung chain on brass stanchions, as if it were on display in some museum, many years from now.

Since there are no walls to the dining room, windows should be suggested through lighting. The implication should be that there are large French doors Downstage, and maybe windows along another wall.

Since the play takes place during the course of a day, the light should change accordingly.

The play requires a cast of six—three men, three women—and seems to work best with this number. Conceivably it could be done with more, but it would be impossible to do with fewer. The various roles should be assigned democratically; there should be no emphasis on one particular type of role. It might be good to cast the play with people of different ages, sizes, and shapes, as long as they are all good actors.

It would seem to make sense to end the play with the same actors playing Ruth, Annie, and the Host as played Mother, Annie, and Father in the breakfast scene in Act I.

For costumes, it is suggested that the Men wear simple, conser-

vative suits, or jackets and slacks, which can be modified as required. For more informal scenes, for example, an actor might appear in shirt sleeves, or a sweater. Women's costumes might seem to pose a more complicated problem but again the best solution turns out to be the simplest: each actress may wear the same simple, classically styled dress—or skirt and blouse— throughout, with perhaps an occasional apron when she plays a maid. There is hardly enough time between scenes for actors to fuss with changes or accessories, and there is an advantage in being as simple and straightforward as possible.

The place-mats, glassware, china, and silverware used during the course of the play should be bright, clean, and tasteful. We should only see used what is absolutely necessary for a particular scene. Actual food, of course, should not be served. The thing to remember is that this is not a play about dishes, or food, or costume changes, but rather a play about people in a dining room.

The blending and overlapping of scenes have been carefully worked out to give a sense of both contrast and flow. When there is no blending of scenes, one should follow another as quickly at possible. The play should never degenerate into a series of blackouts.

ACT I

No one on stage. The dining room furniture sparkles in the early morning light. Voices from off right. Then a woman real estate AGENT *and her male* CLIENT *appear in the doorway. Both wear raincoats.*

AGENT. . . . and the dining room.

CLIENT. Oh boy.

AGENT. You see how these rooms were designed to catch the early morning light?

CLIENT. I'll say.

AGENT. French doors, lovely garden, flowering crabs. Do you like gardening?

CLIENT. Used to.

AGENT. Imagine, imagine having a long, leisurely breakfast in here.

CLIENT. As opposed to instant coffee on Eastern Airlines.

AGENT. Exactly. You know this is a room after my own heart. I grew up in a dining room like this. Same sort of furniture. Everything.

CLIENT. So did I.

AGENT. Then here we are. Welcome home. (*Pause.*)

CLIENT. What are they asking again?

AGENT. Make an offer. I think they'll come down. (*Another pause.*)

CLIENT. Trouble is, we'll never use this room.

AGENT. Oh now.

CLIENT. We won't. The last two houses we lived in, my wife used the dining room table to sort the laundry.

AGENT. Oh dear.

CLIENT. Maybe you'd better show me something more contemporary.

AGENT. That means something farther out. How long have we got to find you a home?

CLIENT. One day.

AGENT. And how long will the corporation keep you here, after you've found it?

CLIENT. Six months to a year.

AGENT. Oh then definitely we should look farther out. (*She opens the kitchen door.*) You can look at the kitchen as we leave.

CLIENT. You shouldn't have shown me this first.

AGENT. I thought it was something to go by.

CLIENT. You've spoiled everything else.

AGENT. Oh no. We'll find you something if we've got all day. But wasn't it a lovely room?

CLIENT. Let's go, or I'll buy it! (*They both exit through the kitchen door as a brother comes in from the hall, followed by his sister. Both are middle-aged. His name is* ARTHUR, *hers is* SALLY.)

ARTHER. The dining room.

SALLY. Yes . . .

ARTHUR. Notice how we gravitate right to this room.

SALLY. I know it.

ARTHUR. You sure mother doesn't want this stuff in Florida?

SALLY. She hardly has room for what she's got. She wants us to take turns. Without fighting.

ARTHUR. We'll just have to draw lots then.

SALLY. Unless one of us wants something, and one of us doesn't.

ARTHUR. We have to do it today.

SALLY. Do you think that's enough time to divide up a whole house?

ARTHUR. I have to get back, Sal. (*He looks in the sideboard.*) We'll draw lots and then go through the rooms taking turns. (*He brings out a silver spoon.*) Here. We'll use this salt spoon. (*He shifts it from hand to hand behind his back, then holds out two fists.*) Take your pick. You get the spoon, you get the dining room.

SALLY. You mean you want to start here?

ARTHUR. Got to start somewhere. (SALLY *looks at his fists.* ANNIE, *a maid, comes out from the kitchen to set the table for breakfast. She sets placemats at either end and two coffee cups, with saucers.* SALLY *and* ARTHUR *take no notice of her.* ANNIE *then leaves.*)

SALLY. (*Not choosing.*) You mean you want the dining room?

ARTHUR. Yeah.

SALLY. What happened to the stuff you had?

ARTHUR. Jane took it. It was part of the settlement.

SALLY. If you win, where will you put it?

ARTHUR. That's my problem, Sal.

SALLY. I thought you had a tiny apartment.

ARTHUR. I'll find a place.

SALLY. I mean your children won't want it.

ARTHUR. Probably not.

SALLY. Then where on earth . . . ?

ARTHUR. Come on, Sal. Choose. (*He holds out his fists again. She chooses.* ARTHUR *lowers his hands.* ANNIE *comes in from the kitchen, bringing the morning paper. She puts it at the head of the table and then leaves.*) You don't want it.

SALLY. Of course I want it!

ARTHUR. I mean you already have a perfectly good dining room.

SALLYY. Not as good as this.

ARTHUR. You mean you want two dining rooms?

SALLY. I'd give our old stuff to Debbie.

ARTHUR. To Debbie?

SALLY. She's our oldest child.

ARTHUR. Does Debbie want a dining room?

SALLY. She might.

ARTHUR. In a condominium?

SALLY. She might.

ARTHUR. In Denver?

SALLY. She just might, Arthur. (*A* FATHER *comes in from the right. He settles comfortably at the head of the table, unfolds his newspaper importantly.*)

ARTHUR. (*Shuffling the spoon behind his back again. Then holding out his fists.*) I don't want to fight. Which hand? (SALLY *starts to choose, then stops.*)

SALLY. Are you planning to put it in storage?

ARTHUR. I might.

SALLY. I checked on that. That costs an arm and a leg.

ARTHUR. So does shipping it to Denver. (*He holds out his fists.*)

FATHER. (*Calling to kitchen.*) Good morning, Annie.

SALLY. (*Almost picking a hand, then stopping.*) I know what will happen if you win.

ARTHUR. What?

SALLY. You'll end up selling it.

ARTHUR. Selling it?

SALLY. That's what will happen. It will kick around for a while, and you'll end up calling a furniture dealer. (ANNIE *comes out with a small glass of "orange juice" on a tray.*)

Arthur. I am absolutely amazed you'd say that.

Sally. I don't want to fight, Arthur.

Arthur. Neither do I. Maybe we should defer the dining room. (*He starts for door, right.*)

Sally. (*Following him.*) Maybe we should.

Arthur. Good morning, sir.

Father. Good morning, Annie.

Arthur. Selling the dining room? Is that what you told Mother I'd do?

Sally. (*Following him.*) I told her I'd give you the piano if I can have the dining room . . .

Arthur. I'll be lucky if I keep this spoon.

Sally. I'll give you the piano and the coffee table if I can have the dining room. (Arthur *and* Sally *exit into the hall.*)

Father. Annie . . . (Annie *is almost to the kitchen door.*)

Annie. Yes sir . . .

Father. Did I find a seed in my orange juice yesterday morning?

Annie. I strained it, sir.

Father. I'm sure you did, Annie. Nonetheless I think I may have detected a small seed.

Annie. I'll strain it twice, sir.

Father. Seeds can wreak havoc with the digestion, Annie.

Annie. Yes, sir.

Father. They can take root. And grow.

Annie. Yes, sir. I'm sorry, sir. (Annie *goes out.* Father *drinks his orange juice carefully, and reads his newspaper. A little* Girl *sticks her head out through the dining room door.*)

Girl. Daddy . . .

Father. Yes, good morning, Lizzie Boo.

Girl. Daddy, could Charlie and me—

Father. Charlie and I . . .

Girl. . . . . Charlie and I come out and sit with you while you have breakfast?

Father. You certainly may, Lizzikins. I'd be delighted to have the pleasure of your company, provided—

Girl. Yippee!

Father. I said, PROVIDED you sit quietly, without leaning back in your chairs, and don't fight or argue.

Girl. (*Calling off.*) He says we *can!*

Father. I said you *may,* sweetheart. (*The* Girl *comes out adoringly, followed by a little* Boy.)

Girl. (*Kissing her father.*) Good morning, Daddy.

BOY. (*Kissing him too.*) Morning, Dad. (*They settle into their seats.* ANNIE *brings out the* FATHER's *"breakfast."*)

ANNIE. Here's your cream, sir.

FATHER. Thank you Annie.

ANNIE. You're welcome, sir. (ANNIE *goes out. The children watch their father.*)

BOY. Dad . . .

FATHER. Hmmm?

BOY. When do we get to have fresh cream on our shredded wheat?

GIRL. When you grow up, that's when.

FATHER. I'll tell you one thing. If there's a war, no one gets cream. If there's a war, we'll all have to settle for top of the bottle.

GIRL. Mother said she was thinking about having us eat dinner in here with you every night.

FATHER. Yes. Your mother and I are both thinking about that. And we're both looking forward to it. As soon as you children learn to sit up straight . . . (*They quickly do.*) then I see no reason why we shouldn't all have a pleasant meal together every evening.

BOY. Could we try it tonight, Dad? Could you give us a test?

FATHER. No, Charlie. Not tonight. Because tonight we're giving a small dinner party. But I hope very much you and Liz will come down and shake hands.

GIRL. I get so shy, Dad.

FATHER. Well you'll just have to learn, sweetie pie. Half of life is learning to meet people.

BOY. What's the other half, Dad? (*Pause. The* FATHER *fixes him with a steely gaze.*)

FATHER. Was that a crack?

BOY. No, Dad . . .

FATHER. That was a crack, wasn't it?

BOY. No, Dad. Really . . .

FTHER. That sounded very much like a smart-guy wisecrack to me. And people who make cracks like that don't normally eat in dining rooms.

BOY. I didn't mean it as a crack, Dad.

FATHER. Then we'll ignore it. We'll go on with our breakfast. (ANNIE *comes in.*)

ANNIE. (*To* GIRL.) Your car's here, Lizzie. For school. (ANNIE *goes out.*)

GIRL. (*Jumping up.*) O.K.

FATHER. (*To* GIRL.) Thank you, Annie.

GIRL. Thank you, Annie . . . (*Kisses* FATHER.) Goodbye,
Daddy.

FATHER. Goodbye, darling. Don't be late. Say good morning
to the driver. Sit quietly in the car. Work hard. Run. Run.
Goodbye. (GIRL *goes off.* FATHER *returns to his paper. Pause.*
BOY *sits watching his father.*)

BOY. Dad, can I read the funnies?

FATHER. Certainly. Certainly you may. (*He carefully extracts
the second section and hands it to his son. Both read, the son
trying to imitate the father in how he does it. Finally.*) This won't
mean much to you, but the government is systematically ruining
this country.

BOY. Miss Kelly told us about the government.

FATHER. Oh really. And who is Miss Kelly, pray tell?

BOY. She's my teacher.

FATHER. I don't remember any Miss Kelly.

BOY. She's new, Dad.

FATHER. I see. And what has she been telling you?

BOY. She said there's a depression going on.

FATHER. I see.

BOY. People all over the country are standing in line for
bread.

FATHER. I see.

BOY. So the government has to step in and do something.

FATHER. (*Long pause. Then.*) Annie!

ANNIE. (*Coming out of kitchen.*) Yes, sir.

FATHER. I'd very much like some more coffee, please.

ANNIE. Yes, sir. (ANNIE *goes out.*)

FATHER. You tell Miss Kelly she's wrong.

BOY. Why?

FATHER. I'll tell you exactly why: if the government keeps on
handing out money, no one will want to work. And if no one
wants to work, there won't be anyone around to support such
things as private schools. And if no one is supporting private
schools, then Miss Kelly will be standing on the bread lines
along with everyone else. You tell Miss Kelly that, if you please.
Thank you, Annie. (ANNIE *comes in and pours coffee.* FATHER
returns to his paper. ANNIE *has retreated to the kitchen.*)

BOY. (*Reads his funnies for a moment. Then.*) Dad . . .

FATHER. (*Reading.*) Hmmm?

BOY. Could we leave a little earlier today?

FATHER. We'll leave when we always leave.

BOY. But I'm always late, Dad.

FATHER. Nonsense.

BOY. I am, Dad. Yesterday I had to walk into assembly while they were still singing the hymn.

FATHER. A minute or two late . . .

BOY. Everyone looked at me, Dad.

FATHER. You tell everyone to concentrate on that hymn.

BOY. I can't, Dad . . .

FATHER. It's that new stoplight on Richmond Avenue. It affects our timing.

BOY. It's not just the new stoplight, Dad. Sometimes I come in when they're already doing arithmetic. Miss Kelly says I should learn to be punctual.

FATHER. (*Putting down paper.*) Miss Kelly again, eh?

BOY. She said if everyone is late, no one would learn any mathematics.

FATHER. Now you listen to me, Charlie. Miss Kelly may be an excellent teacher. Her factoring may be flawless, her geography beyond question. But Miss Kelly does not teach us politics. Nor does she teach us how to run our lives. She is not going to tell you, or me, to leave in the middle of a pleasant breakfast, and get caught in the bulk of the morning traffic, just so that you can arrive in time for a silly hymn. Long after you've forgotten that hymn, long after you've forgotten how to factor, long after you've forgotten Miss Kelly, you will remember these pleasant breakfasts around this dining room table. (MOTHER *glides into the room from the right.*) And here is your mother to prove it.

MOTHER. (*Kissing* FATHER.) Good morning, dear. (*Kissing* CHARLIE.) Good morning, Charlie.

FATHER. (*Remaining seated.*) I know people who leap to their feet when a beautiful woman enters the room. (CHARLIE *jumps up.*)

MOTHER. Oh that's all right, dear.

FATHER. I also know people who rush to push in their mother's chair. (CHARLIE *does so.*)

MOTHER. Thank you, dear.

FATHER. And finally, I know people who are quick to give their mother the second section of the morning paper.

CHARLIE. Oh! Here, Mum.

MOTHER. Thank you, dear.

FATHER. Now Charlie: take a moment, if you would, just to look at your lovely mother, bathed in the morning sunlight, and reflected in the dining room table.

MOTHER. Oh Russell . . . (CHARLIE *looks at his mother.*)

FATHER. Look at her, Charlie, and then ask yourself carefully: Which is worth our ultimate attention? Your mother? Or Miss Kelly?

MOTHER. Who is Miss Kelly?

FATHER. Never mind, dear. Which, Charlie?

CHARLIE. My mother.

FATHER. Good, Charlie. Fine. (*He gets up; taking his section of the paper.*) And now, I think you and I should make a trip upstairs before we say goodbye, and are on our way. (MOTHER *smiles sweetly.* CHARLIE *gives his mother a kiss.* FATHER *and son leave the room.* ANNIE *enters, carrying coffee server.*)

MOTHER. Good morning, Annie.

ANNIE. Good morning, Mrs.

MOTHER. Tell Irma I'll have poached eggs this morning, please, Annie.

ANNIE. Yes, Mrs. (ANNIE *goes out.* MOTHER *sits sipping coffee, reading her section of the paper. A youngish woman— call her* ELLIE—*comes out of the kitchen. Her arms are stacked with a small portable typewriter, papers, several books and notebooks. She finds a place at the table and begins to spread things out around her.* MOTHER *pays no attention to her. A man called* HOWARD, *carrying a briefcase, appears at right.*)

HOWARD. Hey!

ELLIE. Ooooops. I thought you had gone.

HOWARD. I forgot my briefcase . . . What's going on?

ELLIE. I have to get this term paper done.

HOWARD. In here?

ELLIE. Where else.

HOWARD. You're going to *type?*

ELLIE. Of course I'm going to type.

HOWARD. In here? At that table?

ELLIE. Why not?

HOWARD. You're going to sit there, banging a typewriter on my family's dining room *table?*

ELLIE. Why not?

HOWARD. Because it wasn't designed for it, that's why!

ELLIE. (*Sighing.*) Oh, Howard . . .

HOWARD. Lucky I came back. Next thing you know, you'll be feeding the dog off our Lowestoft china.

ELLIE. It's got rubber pads under it. I checked. (*Gets up, goes to sideboard.*) And I'll get something else, if you want. (*She takes out a couple of place mats.*)

HOWARD. You're not going to use those place mats?

ELLIE. I thought I would. Yes.

HOWARD. Those are good place mats.

ELLIE. We haven't used them in ten years.

HOWARD. Those are extremely good place mats, Ellie. Mother got those in Italy.

ELLIE. All *right*. *(She puts the place mats back in the sideboard, rummages around, finds a couple of hot pads. He watches her carefully.)* I'll use these, then. Mind if I use these? We put pots on them. We can certainly put a typewriter. *(She carries them to the table, puts them under the typewriter, continues to get things set up.* HOWARD *watches her. Meanwhile,* MOTHER, *impatient for her poached eggs, puts down her paper and rings a little silver bell on the table in front of her.* ANNIE *comes out of the kitchen.)*

ANNIE. Yes, Mrs?

MOTHER. I wonder if anything might have happened to my poached eggs, Annie.

ANNIE. Irma's cooking two more, Mrs.

MOTHER. Two more?

ANNIE. The first ones slid off the plate while she was buttering the toast.

MOTHER. *(Standing up.)* Is she drinking again, Annie?

ANNIE. No, Mrs.

MOTHER. Tell me the truth.

ANNIE. I don't think so, Mrs.

MOTHER. I'd better go see . . . A simple question of two poached eggs. *(She starts for the kitchen.)* Honestly, Annie, sometimes I think it's almost better if we just do thing our*selves*.

ANNIE. Yes, Mrs. (MOTHER *goes out into the kitchen;* ANNIE *clears the* MOTHER's *and* FATHER's *places, leaving a glass and plate for the next scene.* ANNIE *exits.)*

ELLIE. *(To* HOWARD, *who is standing at the doorway, still watching.)* Don't you have a plane to catch? It's kind of hard to work when your husband is hovering over you, like a helicopter.

HOWARD. Well it's kind of hard to leave when your wife is systematically mutilating the dining room table.

ELLIE. I'll be careful, Howard. I swear. Now goodbye. *(She begins to hunt and peck on the typewriter.* HOWARD *starts out, then wheels on her.)*

HOWARD. Couldn't you *please* work somewhere else?

ELLIE. I'd like to know where, please.

HOWARD. What's wrong with the kitchen table?

ELLIE. It doesn't work, Howard. Last time the kids got peanut butter all over my footnotes.

HOWARD. I'll set up the bridge table in the living room.

ELLIE. I'd just have to move whenever you and the boys wanted to watch a football game.

HOWARD. You mean, you're going to leave all that stuff *there?*

ELLIE. I thought I would. Yes.

HOWARD. All that shit? All over the dining room?

ELLIE. It's a term paper, Howard. It's crucial for my degree.

HOWARD. You mean you're going to commandeer the *dining* room for the rest of the *term?*

ELLIE. It just sits here, Howard. It's never used.

HOWARD. What if we want to give a dinner party?

ELLIE. Since when have we given a dinner party?

HOWARD. What if we want to have a few people *over,* for Chrissake?

ELLIE. We can eat in the kitchen.

HOWARD. Oh Jesus.

ELLIE. Everybody does these days.

HOWARD. That doesn't make it right.

ELLIE. Let me get this done, Howard! Let me get a good grade, and my Master's degree and a good job, so I can be *out* of here every day!

HOWARD. Fine! What the hell! Then why don't I turn it into a *tool* room, every night? (*He storms out.* ELLIE *doggedly returns to her work, angrily hunting and pecking on the typewriter.* GRACE *enters from right. She sits downstage left, and begins to work on her grocery list.* CAROLYN, *a girl of fourteen, enters sleepily a moment later.*)

CAROLYN. Why did you tell Mildred to wake me up, Mother?

GRACE. Let me just finish this grocery list.

CAROLYN. I mean it's Saturday, Mother.

GRACE. (*Finishing the list with a flourish.*) Sshh . . . There. (*Puts down the list.*) I know it's Saturday, darling, and I apologize. But something has come up, and I want you to make a little decision.

CAROLYN. What decision?

GRACE. Start your breakfast, dear. No one can think on an empty stomach. (CAROLYN *sits at the table.*) Now. Guess who telephoned this morning?

CAROLYN. Who?

GRACE. Your Aunt Martha.

CAROLYN. Oh I love her.

GRACE. So do I. But the poor thing hasn't got enough to do, so she was on the telephone at the crack of dawn.

CAROLYN. What did she want?

GRACE. Well now here's the thing: she's got an extra ticket for the theatre tonight, and she wants you to join her.

CAROLYN. Sure!

GRACE. Now wait till I've finished, dear. I told her it was your decision, of course, but I thought you had other plans.

CAROLYN. What other plans?

GRACE. Now think, darling. Isn't there something rather special going on in your life this evening? (*Pause.*)

CAROLYN. Oh.

GRACE. Am I right, or am I right.

CAROLYN. (*Grimly.*) Dancing school.

ELLIE. Shit. (*She begins to gather up her materials.*)

GRACE. Not dancing school, sweetheart. The first session of the Junior Assemblies. Which are a big step beyond dancing school.

ELLIE. I can't work in this place! It's like a tomb! (*She goes out into the kitchen.*)

GRACE. I told Aunt Martha you'd call her right back, so she could drum up someone else.

CAROLYN. I thought it was my decision.

GRACE. It is, sweetheart. Of course.

CAROLYN. Then I'd like to see a play with Aunt Martha. (*Pause.*)

GRACE. Carolyn, I wonder if you're being just a little impulsive this morning. You don't even know what the play is.

CAROLYN. What is it, then?

GRACE. Well it happens to be a very talky play called *Saint Joan.*

CAROLYN. Oh we read that in school! I want to go all the more!

GRACE. It's the road company, sweetheart. It doesn't even have Katherine Cornell.

CAROLYN. I'd still like to go.

GRACE. To some endless play? With your maiden aunt?

CAROLYN. She's my favorite person.

GRACE. Well then go, if it's that important to you.

CAROLYN. (*Getting up.*) I'll call her right now. (*She starts for the door.*)

GRACE. Carolyn . . . (CAROLYN *stops.*) You realize, of course, that on the first Junior Assembly, everyone gets acquainted.

CAROLYN. Really?

GRACE. Oh heavens yes. It starts the whole thing off on the right foot.

CAROLYN. I didn't know that.

GRACE. Oh yes. It's like the first day of school. Once you miss, you never catch up.

CAROLYN. Oh gosh.

GRACE. You see? You see why we shouldn't make hasty decisions. (*Pause.*)

CAROLYN. Then maybe I won't go at all.

GRACE. What do you mean?

CAROLYN. Maybe I'll skip all the Junior Assemblies.

GRACE. Oh Carolyn.

CAROLYN. I don't like dancing school anyway.

GRACE. Don't be silly.

CAROLYN. I don't. I've never liked it. I'm bigger than half the boys, and I never know what to say, and I'm a terrible dancer. Last year I spent half the time in the ladies room.

GRACE. That's nonsense.

CAROLYN. It's true, Mother. I hate dancing school. I don't know why I have to go. Saint Joan wouldn't go to dancing school in a million years!

GRACE. Yes, and look what happened to Saint Joan!

CAROLYN. I don't care. I've made up my mind. (*Pause.*)

GRACE. Your Aunt Martha seems to have caused a little trouble around here this morning.

CAROLYN. Maybe.

GRACE. Your Aunt Martha seems to have opened up a whole can of worms.

CAROLYN. I'm glad she did.

GRACE. All right. And how do you propose to spend your other Saturday nights? I mean, when there's no Aunt Martha. And no Saint Joan? And all your friends are having the time of their life at Junior Assemblies?

CAROLYN. I'll do something.

GRACE. Such as what? Hanging around here? Listening to that stupid Hit Parade? Bothering the maids when we're planning to have a party? (AGGIE, *a maid, comes out of the kitchen, sits at the table, begins to polish some flat silver with a silver cloth.*)

CAROLYN. I'll do *some*thing, Mother.

GACE. (*Picking up* CAROLYN'S *breakfast dishes.*) Well you're obviously not old enough to make an intelligent decision.

CAROLYN. I knew you wouldn't let me decide.

GRACE. (*Wheeling on her.*) All right, then! Decide!

CAROLYN. I'd like to—

GRACE. But let me tell you a very short story before you do. About your dear Aunt Martha. Who also made a little decision when she was about your age. She decided—if you breathe a word of this, I'll strangle you—she decided she was in love with her riding master. And so she threw everything up, and ran off with him. To Taos, New Mexico. Where your father had to track her down and drag her back. But it was too late, Carolyn! She had been . . . overstimulated. And from then on in, she refused to join the workday world. Now there it is. In a nutshell. So think about it, while I'm ordering the groceries. And decide. (*She goes out left, carrying* CAROLYN's *glass and plate.* AGGIE *polishes the silver.* CAROLYN *sits and thinks. She decides.*)

CAROLYN. I've decided, Mother.

GRACE'S VOICE. (*From the kitchen.*) Good. I hope you've come to your senses.

CAROLYN. (*Getting up.*) I've decided to talk to Aunt Martha. (*She goes out.*)

GRACE. (*Bursting through the kitchen door.*) You've got a dentist appointment, Carolyn! You've got riding lessons at noon—no, no, we'll skip the riding lessons, but—Carolyn! Carolyn! (*She rushes out through the hall as* MICHAEL *comes in through the kitchen. He is about twelve.*)

MICHAEL. (*Sneaking up on her.*) Boo!

AGGIE. Michael! You scared me out of my skin!

MICHAEL. I wanted to. (*Pause. He comes a little more into the room.* AGGIE *returns to her polishing.*)

AGGIE. Your mother said you was sick this morning.

MICHAEL. I was. I am.

AGGIE. So sick you couldn't go to school.

MICHAEL. I *am*, Aggie! I upchucked! Twice!

AGGIE. Then you get right straight back to bed. (*He doesn't.*)

MICHAEL. How come you didn't do my room yet?

AGGIE. Because I thought you was sleeping.

MICHAEL. I've just been *lying* there, Ag. Waiting

AGGIE. Well I got more to do now, since Ida left. I got the silver, and the downstairs lavatory, and all the beds besides. (*He comes farther in.*)

MICHAEL. My mother says you want to leave us. (*She polishes.*)

AGGIE. When did she say that?

MICHAEL. Last Thursday. On your day off. When she was cooking dinner. She said now there's a war, you're looking for a job with more money. (AGGIE *polishes.*) Is that true, Ag?

AGGIE. Maybe.

MICHAEL. Money isn't everything, Aggie.

AGGIE. Listen to him now.

MICHAEL. You can be rich as a king and still be miserable. Look at my Uncle Paul. He's rich as Croesus and yet he's drinking himself into oblivion.

AGGIE. What do you know about all that?

MICHAEL. I know a lot. I eat dinner here in the dining room now. I listen. And I know that my Uncle Paul is drinking himself into oblivion. And Mrs. Williams has a tipped uterus.

AGGIE. Here now. You stop that talk.

MICHAEL. Well, it's *true*, Ag. And it proves that money isn't everything. So you don't have to leave us. (*Pause. She works. He drifts around the table.*)

AGGIE. It's not just the money, darlin'.

MICHAEL. Then *what*, Ag? (*No answer.*) Don't you like us any more?

AGGIE. Oh, Michael . . .

MICHAEL. Don't you like our family?

AGGIE. Oh, Mikey . . .

MICHAEL. Are you still mad at me for peeking at you in the bathtub?

AGGIE. That's enough now.

MICHAEL. Then what *is* it, Ag? How come you're just leaving? (*Pause.*)

AGGIE. Because I don't . . . (*Pause.*) I don't want to do domestic service no more.

MICHAEL. Why?

AGGIE. Because I don't like it no more, Mike. (*He thinks.*)

MICHAEL. That's because Ida left and you have too much to do, Ag.

AGGIE. No darlin' . . .

MICHAEL. (*Sitting down near her.*) I'll help you, Ag. I swear! I'll make my own bed, and pick up my towel. I'll try to be much more careful when I pee!

AGGIE. (*Laughing.*) Lord love you, lad.

MICHAEL. No, no, really. I will. And I'll tell my parents not to have so many dinner parties, Ag. I'll tell them to give you more time off. I'll tell them to give you all day Sunday.

AGGIE. No, darlin'. No.

MICHAEL. I'm *serious*, Ag.

AGGIE. I know, darlin'! I know. (*Two men come in from R.; an* ARCHITECT *and a prospective* BUYER.)

ARCHITECT. O.K. Let's measure it out then. (*The* ARCHITECT *has a large reel tape-measure and a roll of blueprints. They begin to measure the room systematically, the* ARCHITECT *reading the figures and recording them in a small notebook, the*

BUYER *holding the end of the tape. They first measure the D. length*)

MICHAEL. When will you be going then, Ag?

AGGIE. As soon as your mother finds someone else.

MICHAEL. She can't *find* anyone, Aggie.

AGGIE. She will, she will.

MICHAEL. She says she *can't*. They keep showing up with dirty fingernails and dyed hair!

ARCHITECT. (*Reading measurements, writing them down.*) Twenty-two feet, six inches.

BUYER. Fine room.

ARCHITECT. Big room.

MICHAEL. So you *got* to stay, Ag. You can't just leave people in the *lurch*.

BUYER. Look at these French doors.

ARCHITECT. I'm looking. I'm also thinking. About heat loss. (*They measure more.*)

AGGIE. I'll stay till you go away for the summer.

ARCHITECT. (*Measuring width of "French doors."*) Eight feet two inches. (MICHAEL *gets up and comes downstage, looks out through the French doors, as the* ARCHITECT *goes Upstage, to record his notes on the sideboard.*)

MICHAEL. You gonna get married, aren't you, Ag?

AGGIE. Maybe.

MICHAEL. That guy you told me about from church?

AGGIE. Maybe.

MICHAEL. You gonna have children? (AGGIE *laughs.*) You will. I know you will. You'll have a boy of your own.

ARCHITECT. Hold it tight now.

MICHAEL. Will you come back to see us?

AGGIE. Oh my yes.

MICHAEL. You won't, Ag.

AGGIE. I will surely.

MICHAEL. You'll never come back, Ag. I'll never see you again! Ever!

ARCHITECT. (*Now measuring the width.*) Twelve feet four inches . . .

AGGIE. (*Holding out her arms.*) Come here, Mike.

MICHAEL. No.

AGGIE. Come here and give Aggie a big hug!

MICHAEL. No. Why should I? No.

AGGIE. Just a squeeze, for old time's sake!

MICHAEL. No! (*Squaring his shoulders.*) Go hug your own kids, Agnes. I've got work to do. I've got a whole stack of homework to do. I'm missing a whole day of school. (*He runs out of the room.*)

AGGIE. Michael! (*She resumes polishing the last few pieces of silver.*)

ARCHITECT. (*Reeling in his tape with professional zeal.*) O.K. There's your dining room, Doctor.

BUYER. (*Who is a psychiatrist.*) There it is.

ARCHITECT. Big room . . . light room . . . commodious room . . .

PSYCHIATRIST. One of the reasons we bought the house.

ARCHITECT. And one of the reasons we should consider breaking it up.

PSYCHIATRIST. Breaking it up?

ARCHITECT. Now bear with me: What say we turn this room into an office for you, and a waiting room for your patients?

PSYCHIATRIST. I thought we planned to open up those maid's rooms on the third floor.

ARCHITECT. Hold on. Relax. (*He begins to spread a large blueprint out on the table, anchoring its corners with his tape measure and centerpiece. AGGIE has finished polishing by now. She gathers up her silver and polishing stuff and leaves.*) The patient trusts the psychiatrist, doesn't he? Why can't the psychiatrist trust the architect? (*He begins to sketch on the blueprint, with a grease pencil.*) Now here's the ground plan of your house. Here's what you're stuck with, for the moment, and here, with these approximate dimensions, is your dining room.

PSYCHIATRIST. I see.

ARCHITECT. (*Drawing with his grease pencil.*) Now suppose . . . just suppose . . . we started with a clean slate. Suppose we open this up here, slam a beam in here, break through here and here, blast out this, throw out that, and what do we have?

PSYCHIATRIST. I'm not quite sure.

ARCHITECT. Well we don't have a dining room anymore. That's what we don't have.

PSYCHIATRIST. But where would we eat?

ARCHITECT. Here. Right here. Look. I'm putting in an eating area. Here's the fridge, the cooking units, Cuisinart, butcherblock table, chrome chairs. See? Look at the space. The flow. Wife cooks, kids set the table, you stack the dishes. All right here. Democracy at work. In your own home.

PSYCHIATRIST. Hmm.

ARCHITECT. Now, let's review your day. You come down to breakfast, everybody's fixing his or her own thing. (*He goes out through the hall, reappears through the kitchen door.*) Eggs, cornflakes, pop-tarts, whatever. You eat, chat, read the paper, say goodbye, come in here to go to work. Do you have a nurse or a receptionist?

PSYCHIATRIST. No, no. I'm just a humble shrink.

ARCHITECT. (*Beginning to move around the room.*) Well, you come in here to the reception room, maybe adjust the magazines on a table, here, maybe add your newspaper to the pile, then you go through a sound-proof door into your office. You turn on your stereo-console here, maybe select a book from a wall-unit here, and then settle behind your desk module here. You read, you listen to music. Soon—buzz—a patient arrives. You turn off the music, put aside your book, and buzz him in through the sound-proof doors. He flops on the couch here (*He creates the couch with two upstage chairs.*), tells you his dream, you look out the window here, he leaves, you write him up, buzz in the next. Soon it's time for lunch. You go in here, have lunch with the wife, or one of the kids and maybe stroll back in here for a nap. More buzzes, more patients, and soon it's time for a good easy cooperative supper with your family.

PSYCHIATRIST. But not in the dining room.

ARCHITECT. No. Not in the dining room.

PSYCHIATRIST. This room has such resonance.

ARCHITECT. So does a church. That doesn't mean we have to live in it.

PSYCHIATRIST. Mmm.

ARCHITECT. Look, I know whereof I speak: I grew up in a room like this.

PSYCHIATRIST. Oh, yes?

ARCHITECT. Oh sure. This is home turf to me.

PSYCHIATRIST. Really.

ARCHITECT. Oh God yes. My father sat in a chair just like that . . .

PSYCHIATRIST. (*Beginning to look out the window.*) Mmmm.

ARCHITECT. And my mother sat here. And my sister here. And I sat right here. (*He sits.*) Oh, it all comes back . . .

PSYCHIATRIST. (*After a pause.*) Do you want to tell me about it?

ARCHITECT. It was torture, that's all. Those endless meals, waiting to begin, waiting for the dessert, waiting to be excused so they couldn't lean on you any more.

PSYCHIATRIST. (*Almost by rote.*) Was it that bad?

ARCHITECT. Man, it was brutal. I remember one time I came

to the table without washing my hands, and my father— (*He stops.*)

PSYCHIATRIST. Go on.

ARCHITECT. (*Snapping out of it, getting up.*) Never mind. The point is, Doctor, it's time to get rid of this room. (*He begins to roll up his plans.*) Tell you frankly, I'm not interested in screwing around with any more maid's rooms. I can do that in my sleep. (PEGGY *comes out of the kitchen, carrying a large tray, loaded with paper plates, napkins, hats and favors for a children's birthday party. She begins to set the table.*) What I want is the chance to get in here, so I can open up your whole ground floor! Now what do you say?

PSYCHIATRIST. I'll have to think about it.

ARCHITECT. O.K. Fine. Take your time. (*He starts out.*) Tell you what. I'll send you my bill for the work I've done so far.

PSYCHIATRIST. Good. And I'll send you mine. (*They are out. PEGGY, meanwhile, is finishing setting the birthday table. She surveys it, then goes to the doorway, right, and calls off.*)

PEGGY. All right, Children! We're ready! (*She is almost bowled over by a moiling, shrieking mob of children coming in to celebrate the birthday party. They scream, yell, scramble over chairs, grab for favors, wrestle, whatever. PEGGY claps her hands frantically.*) Children, children, CHILDREN! (*They subside a little.*) This is a *dining* room! This is *not* the monkey house at the zoo! (*They all start imitating monkeys. PEGGY shouts them down.*) All right then. I'll just have to tell Roberta in the kitchen to put away all the ice cream and cake. (*The noise subsides. There is silence.*) Good. That's much better. Now I want everyone to leave the table . . . quietly, QUIETLY . . . (*The children begin to leave.*) And go into the hall, and then come back in here in the right way. That's it. Go out. Turn around. And come in. Come in as if you were your mummies and daddies coming into a lovely dinner party. (*Children come back in much more decorously, unconsciously parodying their parents.*) No, no. Let Winkie go first, since it's her birthday and she's the hostess . . . That's it. Good. Good. You sit at the head of the table, Winkie . . . Good . . . No, no, Billy, you sit next to Winkie . . . It should be boy-girl, boy-girl . . . That's it. Yes. Very good. (*Children are making a concerted effort to be genteel, though there are occasional subversive pokings, hitting, and gigglings.*) Now what do we do with our napkins? . . . Yes. Exactly. We unfold them and tuck them under our chins . . . And then we put on our party hats . . .

A LITTLE BOY. (*Named Brewster.*) Can the boys wear their hats in the house?

PEGGY. Yes they can, Brwster, because this is a special occasion. And sometimes on special occasions, the rules can change. (*Children explode. Ray! Yippee! PEGGY has to shout them down.*) I said *some*times. And I meant some of the rules.

ANOTHER LITTLE BOY. (*Named Billy: pointing toward the hall.*) There's my Daddy.

PEGGY. (*Quickly.*) Where, Billy? (TED *comes On from the hall; she tries to be casual.*) Oh. Hi.

TED. Hi. (*Waves to son.*) Hi, Bill. (*Party activity continues, the children opening favors. PEGGY and TED move downstage to get away from the noise.*)

PEGGY. What brings you here?

TED. Have to pick up Bill.

PEGGY. I thought Judy was picking him up.

TED. She asked me to.

PEGGY. You're a little early. We haven't even had our cake.

TED. She told me to be early. (*A LITTLE GIRL calls from the table.*)

A LITTLE GIRL. (*Named Sandra: fussing with favor.*) I can't get mine to work.

PEGGY. Help her, Brewster. Little boys are supposed to help little girls.

TED. Where's Frank?

PEGGY. Playing golf. Where else?

TED. On Winkie's birthday?

PEGGY. Don't get me started. Please. (WINKIE *calls from the head of the table.*)

WINKIE. Can we have the ice cream now, please.

PEGGY. In a minute, dear. Be patient. Then you'll have something to look forward to. (*The children whisperingly begin to count to sixty.*)

TED. Judy must have known he'd be playing golf.

PEGGY. Judy knows everything.

TED. She knows about us, at least.

PEGGY. About us? How?

TED. She said she could tell by the way we behaved.

PEGGY. Behaved? Where?

TED. At the Bramwell's dinner party.

PEGGY. We hardly spoke to each other.

TED. That's how she could tell. (*The children's counting has turned into a chant: "We want ice cream! We want ice cream!"*)

PEGGY. They want ice cream. (*She starts for the kitchen.*)

TED. (*Holding her arm.*) She says she'll fight it, tooth and nail.

PEGGY. Fight *what?* We haven't done anything.

TED. She wants to nip it in the bud.

CHILDREN. Ice cream! Ice cream!

PEGGY. All right, children. You win. (*Cheers from children.*) Now Roberta is very busy in the kitchen because she also has a dinner party tonight. So who would like to help bring things out? (*Hands up, squeals: "Me! Me!"*) All right. Tell you what. Billy, you get the ice cream, and Sandra, you bring out the cake! (*"Ray! Yippee!"*) Careful, careful! Walk, don't run! And be polite to Roberta because she's working very hard. And Brewster and Winkie, you'll have other responsibilities! (SANDRA *and* BILLY *go out into the kitchen.*) For instance, Brewster: when Billy and Sandra reappear through that door, what will you do? (*Long pause.*)

BREWSTER. Sing the song.

PEGGY. Good, Brewster. Now be very quiet, and watch that door, and as soon as they come out, start singing. (*The children watch the door.* PEGGY *hurries back to* TED.) So what do we do?

TED. She says she's thinking of telling her father about us.

PEGGY. Her *father?*

TED. He'd fire me. Immediately.

PEGGY. What if he did?

TED. I'd be out of a job, Peggy.

PEGGY. You could get another.

TED. Where? Doing what? (*The dining room door opens.* BILLY *and* SANDRA *come out carefully carrying a cake platter and an ice cream bowl. Everyone starts singing a birthday song, probably out of tune.* PEGGY *helps them along.* BILLY *puts the cake down in front of* WINKIE, *who takes a deep breath to blow out the candles.*)

PEGGY. No, no, sweetheart. Wait. Always wait. Before you blow out the candles, you have to make a wish. And Mummy has to make a wish. See? Mummy is putting her wedding ring around one of the candles. Now we both close our eyes and make a wish.

WINKIE. I wish I could have—

PEGGY. No, no. Don't tell. Never tell a wish. If you do, it won't come true. All right. Now blow. (WINKIE *blows out "the candles." The children cheer.*) Now Winkie, would you cut the cake and give everyone a piece, please. And Brewster, you pass the ice cream. (*The children organize their food as* PEGGY *joins*

TED *downstage. There is a kind of cooing hum of children eating which punctuates their dialogue.*)

TED. What did you wish for?

PEGGY. Won't tell.

TED. Do you think it will come true?

PEGGY. No. (*Pause.*)

TED. She'd make it so messy. For everyone.

PEGGY. Judy.

TED. She'd make it impossible.

PEGGY. So would Frank.

TED. I thought he didn't care.

PEGGY. He'd care if it were messy. (*Pause.*)

TED. We could leave town.

PEGGY. And go where?

TED. Wherever I find another job.

PEGGY. Yes . . .

TED. I've got an uncle in Syracuse.

PEGGY. Syracuse?

TED. We could live there.

PEGGY. Is it nice? Syracuse?

TED. I think it's on some lake.

PEGGY. Syracuse . . .

TED. You'd have Winkie. I'd get Bill in the summer.

PEGGY. In Syracuse.

TED. At least we'd be free. (*They look at their children.*)

PEGGY. Winkie, wipe your mouth, please. (*She goes to* WINKIE.)

TED. Billy.

BILLY. What?

TED. Would you come here a minute, please? (BILLY *does.* TED *takes him aside.*) Do you have to go the bathroom?

BILLY. No.

TED. Then don't do that, please.

BILLY. Don't do what?

TED. You know what. Now go back and enjoy the party. (BILLY *returns to his seat.* TED *rejoins* PEGGY.) Sorry.

PEGGY. I grew up here.

TED. Who didn't?

PEGGY. To just pick up stakes . . .

TED. I know.

PEGGY. I mean, this is where I *live.*

TED. Me, too. (*Touching her.*) We'll just have to behave ourselves, then.

PEGGY. Oh Ted . . .

TED. Be good little children.

PEGGY. Oh I can't stand it. (*She takes his hand and presses it furtively to her lips.*)

TED. And if we're seated next to each other, we'll have to make a conscious effort.

PEGGY. Oh we won't be seated next to each other. Judy will see to that.

TED. For a while anyway.

PEGGY. For quite a while. (*The children are getting noisy.* WINKIE *comes up.*)

WINKIE. Everyone's finished, Mummy.

PEGGY. Thank you, sweetheart.

WINKIE. And here's your ring. From the cake.

PEGGY. Good for you, darling! I forgot all about it! (*She puts the ring back on.*)

TED. Time to go, then?

PEGGY. I've planned some games.

TED. Want me to stay?

PEGGY. It would help.

TED. Then I'll stay.

PEGGY. (*To children.*) Into the living room now, children. For some games.

BREWSTER. What games?

PEGGY. Oh all kinds of games! Blind Man's Bluff. Pin the Tail on the Donkey . . .

CHILDREN. Yippee! Yay! (*The children run noisily Off.* PEGGY *begins putting the mess back onto the tray.*)

TED. I'll get them started.

PEGGY. Would you? While I propitiate Roberta.

TED. I'll be the donkey.

PEGGY. Oh stop.

TED. I'll be the ass.

PEGGY. Stop or I'll scream. (*He is about to kiss her, over the tray, when* WINKIE *appears at the door. They break away.*)

WINKIE. Come *on*, Mummy! We're waiting!

PEGGY. We're coming, dear. (WINKIE *disappears into the hall.* TED *and* PEGGY *go off different ways as a* GRANDFATHER *enters from the hall. He is about eighty. He sits at the head of the table, as a maid,* DORA, *comes out of the kitchen and begins to set a place in front of him. After a moment, his grandson* NICK *breathlessly appears in the doorway from the hall. He is about thirteen or fourteen.*)

NICK. (Panting, frightened.) Grampa?

GRANDFATHER. (*Looking up.*) Which one are you?

NICK. I'm Nick, Gramp.

GRANDFATHER. And what do you want?

NICK. To have lunch with you, Gramp.

GRANDFATHER. Then you're late.

NICK. I went down to the club.

GRANDFATHER. Who said I'd be at the club?

NICK. My parents. My parents said you always eat there.

GRANDFATHER. Lately I've been coming home.

NICK. Yes, sir.

GRANDFATHER. Don't know half the people at the club any more. Rather be here. At my own table. Dora takes care of me, don't you Dora?

DORA. Yes, sir.

GRANDFATHER. (*To* NICK.) Well you tracked me down, anyway. That shows some enterprise. (*Indicates a place.*) Bring him some lunch, Dora.

DORA. Yes, sir. (*She goes out.*)

NICK. (*Sitting opposite him at the other end of the table.*) Thank you, Gramp.

GRANDFATHER. So you're Nick, eh?

NICK. Yes. I am.

GRANDFATHER. You the one who wants to go to Europe this summer?

NICK. No, that's Mary. That's my cousin.

GRANDFATHER. You the one who wants the automobile? Says he can't go to college without an automobile?

NICK. No, that's my brother Tony, Gramp.

GRANDFATHER. What do you want then?

NICK. Oh I don't really want . . .

GRANDFATHER. Everyone who sits down with me wants something. Usually it's money. Do you want money?

NICK. Yes, sir.

GRANDFATHER. For what?

NICK. My education, Gramp.

GRANDFATHER. Education, eh? That's a good thing. Or can be. Doesn't have to be. Can be a bad thing. Where do you want to be educated?

NICK. Saint Luke's School, in Litchfield, Connecticut.

GRANDFATHER. Never heard of it.

NICK. It's an excellent boarding school for boys.

GRANDFATHER. Is it Catholic?

NICK. I don't think so, Gramp.

GRANDFATHER. Sounds Catholic to me.

NICK. I think it's high Episcopalian, Gramp.

GRANDFATHER. Then it's expensive.

NICK. My parents think it's a first-rate school, Gramp.

GRANDFATHER. Ah. Your parents think . . .

NICK. They've discussed all the boarding schools, and decided that this is the best.

GRANDFATHER. They decided, eh?

NICK. Yes, sir.

GRANDFATHER. And then they decided you should get your grandfather to pay for it.

NICK. Yes, sir. (DORA *has returned, and set a place mat and a plate for* NICK.)

GRANDFATHER. Another one leaving the nest, Dora.

DORA. Yes, sir. (*She waits by the sideboard.*)

GRANDFATHER. And taking a piece of the nest egg.

DORA. Yes, sir. (*Pause.*)

GRANDFATHER. Why don't you stay home?

NICK. Me?

GRANDFATHER. You.

NICK. Oh. Because I want to broaden myself.

GRANDFATHER. You want to what?

NICK. I want to broaden my horizons. My horizons need broadening.

GRANDFATHER. I see.

NICK. And I'll meet interesting new friends.

GRANDFATHER. Don't you have any interesting friends here?

NICK. Oh sure, Gramp.

GRANDFATHER. I do. I have interesting friends right here. I know a man who makes boats in his basement.

NICK. But . . .

GRANDFATHER. I know a man who plays golf with his wife.

NICK. But I'll meet different types, Gramp. From all over the country. New York . . . California . . .

GRANDFATHER. Why would you want to meet anyone from New York?

NICK. Well they're more sophisticated, Gramp. They'll buff me up.

GRANDFATHER. They'll what?

NICK. My mother says I need buffing up.

GRANDFATHER. Do you think he needs buffing up, Dora?

DORA. No, sir.

GRANDFATHER. (*To* NICK.) Dora doesn't think you need buffing up. I don't think you need buffing up. You'll have to give us better reasons.

NICK. Um. Well. They have advanced Latin there . . .

GRANDFATHER. I see. And?

NICK. And an indoor hockey rink.

GRANDFATHER. Yes. And?

NICK. And beautiful grounds and surroundings.

GRANDFATHER. Don't we? Don't we have beautiful surroundings? Why do we have to go away to have beautiful surroundings?

NICK. I don't know, Gramp. All I know is everyone's going away these days.

GRANDFATHER. Everyone's going away? Hear that, Dora? Everyone's going away.

NICK. (*Desperately.*) An awful lot of people are going away! (*Pause.*)

GRANDFATHER. I didn't go away.

NICK. I know, Gramp.

GRANDFATHER. Didn't even go to Country Day. Went to the old P.S. 36 down on Huron Street.

NICK. Yes, Gramp.

GRANDFATHER. Didn't finish, either. Father died, and I had to go to work. Had to support my mother.

NICK. I know that, Gramp.

GRANDFATHER. My father didn't go to school at all. Learned Greek at the plow.

NICK. You told us, Gramp.

GRANDFATHER. Yes well I didn't do too badly. Without a high Episcopal boarding school, and an indoor hockey rink.

NICK. But you're a self-made man, Gramp.

GRANDFATHER. Oh is that what I am? And what are you? Don't you want to be self-made? Or do you want other people to make you? Hmmm? Hmmm? What've you got to say to that?

NICK. (*Squashed.*) I don't know . . .

GRANDFATHER. Everyone wants to go away. Me? I went away twice. Took two vacations in my life. First vacation, took a week off from work to marry your grandmother. Went to Hot Springs, Virginia. Bought this table. Second vacation: Europe. 1928. Again with your grandmother. Hated the place. Knew I would. Miserable meals. Took a trunkload of shredded wheat along. Came back when it ran out. Back to this table. (*Pause.*) They're all leaving us, Dora. Scattering like birds.

DORA. Yes, sir.

GRANDFATHER. We're small potatoes these days.

DORA. Yes, sir.

GRANDFATHER. This one wants to go to one of those fancy New

England boarding schools. He wants to play ice hockey indoors with that crowd from Long Island and Philadelphia. He'll come home talking with marbles in his mouth. We won't understand a word, Dora.

DORA. Yes, sir.

GRANDFATHER. And we won't see much of him, Dora. He'll go visiting in New York and Baltimore. He'll drink liquor in the afternoon and get mixed up with women who wear lipstick and trousers and whose only thought is the next dance. And he wants me to pay for it all. Am I right?

NICK. No, Gramp! No I don't! I don't want to go! Really! I never wanted to go! I want to stay home with all of you!

GRANDFATHER. Finish your greens. They're good for your lower intestine. (*They eat silently. From left a man named* PAUL *enters. He's in his mid-thirties and wears a sweater. He starts carefully examining the dining room chairs along the left wall, one by one, turning them upside down, testing their strength. Finally; with a sigh; to* NICK.) No. You go. You've got to go. I'll send you to Saint Whoozie's and Betsy to Miss Whatsie's and young Andy to whatever-it's-called. And Mary can go to Europe this summer, and Tony can have a car, and it's all fine and dandy. (*He gets slowly to his feet.* NICK *gets up too.*) Go on. Enjoy yourselves, all of you. Leave town, travel, see the world. It's bound to happen. And you know who's going to be sitting here when you get back? I'll tell you who'll be sitting right in that chair. Some Irish fella, some Jewish gentleman is going to be sitting right at this table. Saying the same thing to *his* grandson. And your grandson will be back at the *plow!* (*Starts out the door, stops, turns.*) And come to think of it, that won't be a bad thing either. Will it, Dora?

DORA. No, sir. (*He exits.* DORA *starts clearing off.* NICK *stands in the dining room.*) Well, go on. Hurry. Bring him his checkbook before he falls asleep. (NICK *hurries off right,* DORA *goes off with plates left.* PAUL *begins to check the table. A woman, about forty, call her* MARGERY, *appears in the hall doorway. She watches* PAUL.)

MARGERY. What do you think?

PAUL. (*Working over a chair.*) You're in trouble.

MARGERY. Oh dear. I knew it.

PAUL. It's becoming unglued.

MARGERY. I know the feeling.

PAUL. Coming apart at the seams.

MARGERY. Do you think it's hopeless?

PAUL. Let me check the table. (*He crawls under the table.*)

MARGERY. It shakes very badly. I had a few friends over the other night, and every time we tried to cut our chicken, our water glasses started tinkling frantically. And the chairs creaked and groaned. It was like having dinner at Pompeii.

PAUL. (*Taking out a pocket knife.*) I'm checking the joints here.

MARGERY. It's all very sad. How things run down and fall apart. I used to tell my husband—my *ex*-husband—we have such lovely old things. We should oil them, we should wax them, we should keep them up. But of course I couldn't do everything, and he wouldn't do anything, and now here you are to give us the coup de grace.

PAUL. (*Still under table.*) Hey look at this.

MARGERY. What?

PAUL. Look under here.

MARGERY. I don't dare.

PAUL. I'm serious. Look.

MARGERY. Wait till I put on my glasses. (*She puts on her glasses which are hanging from a chain around her neck; then she bends down discreetly.*) Where? I can't see.

PAUL. Under here. Look. This support. See how loose this is?

MARGERY. I can't quite . . . Wait. (*She gets down on her knees.*)

PAUL. Come on.

MARGERY. All right. (*She crawls under the table.*)

PAUL. See? Look at this support.

MARGERY. I see. It wiggles like mad. (*They are both crawling around under the table now.*)

PAUL. (*Crawling around her.*) And look over there. I'll have to put a whole new piece in over here. See? This is gone.

MARGERY. (*Looking.*) I see.

PAUL. (*Crawling back.*) And . . . excuse me, please . . . this pedestal is loose. Probably needs a new dowel. I'll have to ream it out and put in another . . .

MAARGERY. Do you think so?

PAUL. Oh sure. In fact your whole dining room needs to be re-screwed, re-glued, and re-newed. (*His little joke. He comes out from under.*)

MARGERY. Hmmmm. (*She is still under the table.*)

PAUL. What's the matter?

MARGERY. I've never been under a table before.

PAUL. Oh yeah?

MARGERY. It's all just . . . wood under here, isn't it?

PAUL. That's all it is.

MARGERY. (*Fascinated.*) I mean you'd think a dining room *table* was something special. But it isn't, underneath. It's all just . . . wood. It's just a couple of big, wide . . . boards.

PAUL. That's right.

MARGERY. (*Peering.*) What's this, here?

PAUL. What's what?

MARGERY. Well you'll have to come back under here, to see. There's some writing here, burned into the wood.

PAUL. (*Crawling under.*) Where?

MARGERY. Right here. (*She reads, carefully.*) "Freeman's Furniture. Wilkes-Barre, Pa. 1898."

PAUL. (*Under the table.*) Oh that's the manufacturer's mark.

MARGERY. 1898?

PAUL. That's what it says.

MARGERY. But that's not so old.

PAUL. Not if it was made in 1898.

MARGERY. That's not old at all. It's not even an antique. (*Pause.*) It's just . . . American.

PAUL. There's a lot of these around. They used to crank them out, at the end of the nineteenth century.

MARGERY. Now, aren't I dumb? For years, we've been thinking it's terribly valuable.

PAUL. Well it is, in a sense. It's well made. It's a solid serviceable copy. Based on the English.

MARGERY. Well I'll be darned. You learn something every day. (*They are both sitting side by side, under the table. She looks at him.*) You know a lot about furniture, don't you?

PAUL. I'm beginning to.

MARGERY. Beginning to. I'll bet your father was a cabinet maker or something.

PAUL. My father was a banker.

MARGERY. A *banker?*

PAUL. And I was a stockbroker. Until I got into this.

MARGERY. I don't believe it.

PAUL. Sure. I decided I wanted to see what I was doing. And touch it. And see the results. So I took up carpentry.

MARGERY. I am amazed. I mean, I *know* some stockbrokers. (*Embarrassed pause. She looks at the strut.*) Is this the support that's bad?

PAUL. That's the one.

MARGERY. What if you put a nail in here?

PAUL. Not a nail. A screw.

MARGERY. (*Crawling over him.*) All right. And another one over here. Or at least some household cement.

PAUL. Well, they have these epoxy glues now . . .

MARGERY. All right. And maybe cram a matchbook or something in here.

PAUL. Not a matchbook.

MARGERY. A wedge then. A wooden wedge.

PAUL. Good idea.

MARGERY. See? I can do it too. (*In her intensity, she has gotten very close to him physically. They both suddenly realize it, and move away, crawling out from under the table on either side, and brushing themselves off.*) So. Well. Will you be taking the table away? Or can you fix it here?

PAUL. I can fix it here. If you want.

MARGERY. That might make more sense. My husband used to ask for written estimates. Materials and labor.

PAUL. I'll write one up.

MARGERY. Suppose I helped. On the labor.

PAUL. I've never worked that way . . .

MARGERY. I should learn. I shouldn't be so helpless.

PAUL. O.K. Why not?

MARGERY. Besides, it's not an antique. If I make a mistake, it's not the end of the world, is it?

PAUL. Not at all.

MARGERY. When could we start?

PAUL. Today. Now, if you want.

MARGERY. Then we're a partnership, aren't we? We should have a drink, to celebrate.

PAUL. O.K. (*From off right, we hear voices singing the Thanksgiving hymn: "Come Ye Thankful People, Come."*)

MARGERY. What'll we have? Something snappy? Like a martini?

PAUL. No, I gave them up with the stock market. How about a beer?

MARGERY. Fine idea. Good, solid beer. If I've *got* it. (*They go off into the kitchen, as* NANCY, *in her thirties, comes out, carrying a stack of plates and a carving knife and fork. She calls back over her shoulder.*)

NANCY. I've got the plates, Mrs. Driscoll. You've got your hands full with that turkey. (*She sets the plates and carving utensils at the head of the table and calls toward the hall.*) We're ready, everybody! Come on in! (*The singing continues as a Family begins to come into the dining room, to celebrate Thanksgiving dinner. The oldest son* STUART *has his mother on his arm. She is a very vague, very old* OLD LADY.)

STUART. . . . Now, Mother, I want you to sit next to me, and Fred, you sit on Mother's left, and Ben, you sit opposite her where she can see you, and Nancy and Beth hold up that end of the table, and there we are. (*Genial chatter as everyone sits down. The two sons push in their mother's chair. After a moment the* OLD LADY *stands up again, looks around distractedly.*) What's the matter, Mother?

OLD LADY. I'm not quite sure where I am.

STUART. (*Expansively; arm around her; seating her again.*) You're *here*, Mother. In your own dining room. This is your table, and here are your chairs, and here is the china you got on your trip to England, and here's the silver-handled carving knife which Father used to use.

OLD LADY. Oh yes . . . (*Genial laughter; adlibbing: "She's a little tired . . . It's been a long day . . ." The* OLD LADY *gets up again.*) But who are these people? I'm not quite sure who these people are. (*She begins to wander around the room.*)

STUART. (*Following her around.*) It's me, Mother: Stuart. Your son. And here's Fred, and Ben, and Nancy, and Beth. We're all here, Mother.

NANCY. (*Going into the kitchen.*) I'll get the turkey. That might help her focus.

STUART. Yes. (*To* OLD LADY.) Mrs. Driscoll is here, Mother. Right in the kitchen, where she's always been. And your grandchildren. All your grandchildren were here. Don't you remember? They ate first, at the children's table, and now they're out in back playing touch football. You watched them, Mother. (*He indicates the French doors.*)

OLD LADY. Oh yes . . . (*She sits down again at the other end of the table.* NANCY *comes out from the kitchen, carrying a large platter. Appropriate Oh's and Ah's from Group.*)

STUART. And look, Mother. Here's Nancy with the turkey. . . . Put it right over there, Nancy . . . See, Mother? Isn't it a beautiful bird? And I'm going to carve it just the way Father did, and give you a small piece of the breast and a dab of dressing, just as always, Mother. (*He sharpens the carving knive officiously.*)

OLD LADY. (*Still staring out into the garden.*) Just as always . . .

STUART. (*As he sharpens.*) And Fred will have the drumstick—am I right, Fred?—and Beth gets the wishbone, and Ben ends up with the Pope's nose, am I right, Ben? (*Genial in-group laughter.*)

NANCY. Save some for Mrs. Driscoll.

STUART. I always do, Nancy. Mrs. Driscoll likes the second joint.

OLD LADY. This is all very nice, but I think I'd like to go home.

STUART. (*Patiently, as he carves.*) You are home, Mother. You've lived here fifty-two years.

BEN. Fifty-four.

BETH. Forever.

STUART. Ben, pass this plate down to Mother . . .

OLD LADY. (*Getting up.*) Thank you very much, but I really do think it's time to go.

NANCY. Uh-oh.

STUART. (*Going to her.*) Mother . . .

BETH. Oh dear.

OLD LADY. Will someone drive me home, please? I live at eighteen Summer Street with my mother and sisters.

BETH. What will we do?

STUART. (*Going to* OLD LADY.) It's not there now, Mother. Don't you remember? We drove down. There's a big building there now.

OLD LADY. (*Holding out her hand.*) Thank you very much for asking me . . . Thank you for having me to your house. (*She begins to go around the table, thanking people.*)

FRED. Mother! I'm Fred! Your son!

OLD LADY. Isn't that nice? Thank you. I've had a perfectly lovely time . . . Thank you . . . Thank you so much. (*She shakes hands with* NANCY.) It's been absolutely lovely . . . Thank you, thank you.

STUART. Quickly. Let's sing to her.

BETH. Sing?

STUART. She likes singing. We used to sing to her whenever she'd get upset . . . Fred, Ben. Quickly. Over here.

OLD LADY. (*Wandering distracted around.*) Now I can't find my gloves. Where would my gloves be? I can't go out without my gloves.

BEN. What song? I can't remember any of the songs.

STUART. Sure you can. Come on. Hmmmmm. (*He sounds a note. The others try to find their parts.*)

BEN & FRED. Hmmmmmmmmm.

OLD LADY. I need my gloves, I need my hat . . .

STUART. (*Singing.*)
"As the blackbird in the spring . . .

OTHERS. (*Joining in.*)

'Neath the willow tree . . .
Sat and piped, I heard him sing,
Sing of Aura Lee . . .

(*They sing in pleasant, amateurish, corny harmony. The* OLD
LADY *stops fussing, turns her head, and listens. The other women
remain at the table.*)

MEN. (*Singing.*)
Aura Lee, Aura Lee, Maid of Golden Hair . . .
Sunshine came along with thee, and swallows in the air."

OLD LADY. I love music. Every person in our family could
play a different instrument. (*She sits in a chair along the wall,
down right.*)

STUART. (*To his brothers.*) She's coming around. Quickly.
Second verse.

MEN. (*Singing with more confidence now; more daring
harmony.*)
"In thy blush the rose was born,
Music, when you spake,
Through thine azure eye the morn
Sparkling seemed to break.
Aura Lee, Aura Lee, Maid of Golden Hair,
Sunshine came along with thee, and swallows in the air."

(*They hold a long note at the end. The* OLD LADY *claps.
Everyone claps.*)

OLD LADY. That was absolutely lovely.

STUART. Thank you, Mother.

OLD LADY. But now I've simply got to go home. Would you
call my carriage, please? And someone find my hat and gloves.
It's very late, and my mother gets very nervous if I'm not home
in time for tea. (*She heads for the hall.*)

STUART. (*To no one in particular.*) Look, Fred, Ben, we'll
drive her down, and show her everything. The new office
complex where her house was. The entrance to the Thruway.
The new Howard Johnson's motel. Everything! And she'll see
that nothing's there at all.

FRED. I'll bring the car around.

STUART. I'll get her coat.

BEN. I'm coming too.

STUART. We'll just have to go through the motions. (*The
brothers hurry after their mother.* NANCY *and* BETH *are left
alone onstage. Pause. Then they begin to stack the dishes.*)

NANCY. That's scary.

BETH. I know it.

NANCY. I suddenly feel so . . . precarious.

BETH. It could happen to us all.

NANCY. No, but it's as if we didn't exist. As if we were all just . . . ghosts, or something. Even her own sons. She walked right by them.

BETH. And guess who walked right by *us*.

NANCY. (*Glancing off.*) Yes . . . (*Pause.*) Know what I'd like?

BETH. What?

NANCY. A good stiff drink.

BETH. I'm with you.

NANCY. I'll bet Mrs. Driscoll could use a drink, too.

BETH. Bet she could.

NANCY. (*Deciding.*) Let's go out and ask her!

BETH. Mrs. Driscoll?

NANCY. Let's! (*Pause.*)

BETH. All right.

NANCY. Let's go and have a drink with Mrs. Driscoll, and then dig into this turkey, and help her with the dishes, and then figure out how to get through the rest of the goddamn day! (*They go off, into the kitchen. The table is clear, the dining room is empty.*)

END OF ACT I

ACT II

The dining room is empty. The light suggests that it is about three in the afternoon.

After a moment, a girl's voice is heard off right, from the front hall.

GIRL'S VOICE. Mom? MOM? Anybody home? (*Silence; then more softly.*) See? I told you. She isn't here. (SARAH *appears in the doorway, with* HELEN *behind her.*)

HELEN. Where is she?

SARAH. She works. At a boutique. Four days a week. And my father's away on business. In Atlanta. Or Denver or somewhere. Anyway. Come on. I'll show you where they keep the liquor.

HELEN. My mom's always there when I get home from school. Always.

SARAH. Bummer.

HELEN. And if she isn't, my grandmother comes in.

SARAH. The liquor's in the pantry. (SARAH *goes out through kitchen door, left.* HELEN *stays in the dining room.*)

HELEN. (*Taking in the dining room.*) Oh. Hey. Neat-o.

SARAH'S VOICE. (*From within.*) What?

HELEN. This *room.*

SARAH'S VOICE. (*Over clinking of liquor bottles.*) That's our dining room.

HELEN. I know. But it's viciously nice.

SARAH. (*Coming out of kitchen, carrying two bottles.*) Which do you want? Gin or vodka?

HELEN. (*Wandering around the room.*) You decide.

SARAH. (*Looking at bottles.*) Well there's more gin, so it's less chance they'll notice.

HELEN. Gin, then.

SARAH. But the reason there's more gin is that I put water in it last week.

HELEN. Vodka, then.

SARAH. Tell you what. We'll mix in a little of both. (*She goes into the kitchen.*)

HELEN. O.K. . . . Do you *use* this room?

SARAH. Oh sure.

HELEN. Special occasions, huh? When the relatives come to visit?

SARAH'S VOICE. Every night.

HELEN. Every NIGHT?

SARAH'S VOICE. Well at least every night they're both home.

HELEN. Really?

SARAH. (*Coming in, carrying two glasses.*) Oh sure. Whenever they're home, my father insists that we all eat in the dining room at seven o'clock. (*Hands* HELEN *her drink.*) Here. Gin and vodka and Fresca. The boys are bringing the pot.

HELEN. (*Drinking.*) Mmmm . . . It must be nice, eating here.

SARAH. (*Slouching in a chair.*) Oh yeah sure you bet. We have to lug things out, and lug things back, and nobody can begin till everything's cold, and we're supposed to carry on a decent conversation, and everyone has to finish before anyone can get up, and it sucks, if you want to know. It sucks out loud. (*They drink.*)

HELEN. We eat in the kitchen.

SARAH. Can you watch TV while you eat?

HELEN. We used to. We used to watch the local news and weather.

SARAH. That's something. At least you don't have to talk.

HELEN. But now we can't watch it. My mother read in *Family Circle* that TV was bad at meals. So now we turn on the stereo and listen to semi-classical music.

SARAH. My parents said they tried eating in the kitchen when I went to boarding school. But when I got kicked out, they moved back in here. It's supposed to give me some sense of stability.

HELEN. Do you think it does?

SARAH. Shit no! It just makes me nervous. They take the telephone off the hook, so no one can call, and my brother gets itchy about his homework, and when my sister had anorexia, she still had to sit here and *watch,* for God's sake, and my parents spend most of the meal bitching, and the whole thing bites, Helen. It really bites. It bites the big one. Want another?

HELEN. No thanks.

SARAH. I do . . . You call the boys and tell them it's all clear. (SARAH *goes back into the kitchen.*)

HELEN. (*Calling toward kitchen.*) Sarah . . .

SARAH'S VOICE. (*Within.*) What?

HELEN. When the boys come over, can we have our drinks in here? (KATE *a woman in her mid-forties, comes out. She carries a small tray containing a teapot, two teacups, sugar and creamer. She sits at the table and watches the teapot.*)

SARAH'S VOICE. (*Within.*) In the *dining* room?

HELEN. I mean, wouldn't it be cool, sitting around this shiny table with Eddie and Duane, drinking gin and Fresca and vodka?

SARAH. (*Coming out from the kitchen.*) No way. Absolutely no way. In here? I'd get all up tight in here. (*She heads for the hall.*) Now come on. Let's *call* them. (HELEN *starts after her.*) Having *boys* in the *dining* room? Jesus, Helen. You really are a wimp sometimes. (*They go out, right,* HELEN *looking back over her shoulder at the dining room.*)

KATE. (*Calling toward hallway.*) I'm in here, Gordon. I made tea. (GORDON *comes in from the hall. He is about her age. He is buttoning his shirt, carrying his jacket and tie slung over his shoulder.*)

GORDON. Tea?

KATE. Tea.

GORDON. Why tea?

KATE. Because I like it. I love it. (*Pause.*) Or would you like a drink?

GORDON. No thanks.

KATE. Go ahead. Don't worry about me. I'm all over that. We even have it in the house, and I never touch it.

GORDON. No thanks, Kate.

KATE. Then have tea. It's very good. It's Earl Gray.

GORDON. I ought to be getting back.

KATE. Gordon, please. Have tea. (*Pause.*)

GORDON. All right.

KATE. Thank you. (*She begins to pour him a cup.*)

GORDON. (*Ironically.*) Tea in the dining room.

KATE. Where else? Should we huddle guiltily over the kitchen table?

GORDON. No.

KATE. Then tea in the dining room . . . What would you like? Lemon or milk?

GORDON. Whatever.

KATE. Gordon.

GORDON. Milk, then. No sugar.

KATE. Milk it is. (*She hands him a cup.*) Well sit down, for heaven's sake.

GORDON. (*Not sitting.*) I thought I heard a sound.

KATE. Oh really? And what sound did you hear? A distant lawn-mower? A faulty burglar alarm?

GORDON. I thought I heard a car.

KATE. What? A car? On this godforsaken street? Should we rush to the window? Cheer? Wave flags?

GORDON. Go easy, Kate.

KATE. Well I doubt very much that you heard a car.

GORDON. (*Listening.*) It stopped.

KATE. The sound?

GORDON. The *car*. The car stopped.

KATE. All right, Gordon. You heard a car stop. But it's not Ed's car, is it? Because Ed, as you and I well know, is in Amsterdam, or Rotterdam, or who-gives-a-damn until next Tuesday. (*Reaching for his hand.*) Now sit *down*. Please. Let's have tea, for heaven's sake. (*He sits on the edge of his chair.*) Now when can we meet again?

GORDON. (*Jumping up.*) I heard a car door slam.

KATE. Oh really. That's because cars have doors. And people when they get really frustrated feel like slamming them.

GORDON. I'm going.

KATE. I see how it is—a quick tumble with the bored wife of your best friend.

GORDON. Someone's at the front door.

KATE. No . . .

GORDON. Yes. Someone with a key! (KATE *jumps up, They listen.*)

KATE. (*Whispering.*) Now you've got to stay. (GORDON *quickly puts on his coat. A boy's voice is heard calling from the hall.*)

BOY'S VOICE. Mom!

KATE. Lord help us.

BOY'S VOICE. I'm home, Mom!

KATE. (*Grimly to* GORDON.) Now you've got to have tea.

BOY'S VOICE. Mom?

KATE. (*Calling out.*) We're in the dining room, dear. (CHRIS *slides into view from right. He is about seventeen, carries a dufflebag.* KATE *goes to him effusively.*) Darling! How'd you get here?

CHRIS. I took a cab from the bus station. (KATE *embraces him. He looks at* GORDON.)

KATE. You look marvelous! Taller than ever! Say hello to Uncle Gordon.

GORDON. Hi, Chris. Welcome home.

CHRIS. (*Coolly.*) Hi.

KATE. What's this? Is this what they teach you at Deerfield? Not to shake hands? Not to call people by name?

CHRIS. Hello, Uncle Gordon. (*They shake hands.*)

GORDON. Hi, Chris.

KATE. But what brings you home, my love? I expected you Saturday.

CHRIS. I got honors.

KATE. Honors?

CHRIS. You get two days early if you get an over-85 average.

KATE. But then you should have telephoned.

CHRIS. I wanted to surprise you. (*Pause.*)

GORDON. I ought to go.

KATE. Nonsense. Have more tea. Chris, would you like tea? I was taking a nap, and Gordon stopped by, and we thought we'd have tea. Have some tea, dear. Or a Coke. Have a Coke. Or shall I get you a beer? How about a beer for a big boy who gets honors?

CHRIS. No, thanks.

GORDON. I'd really better go.

KATE. You won't have more tea.

GORDON. Can't. Sorry.

KATE. All right, then. Goodbye.

GORDON. (*Shaking hands with her stiffly.*) Goodbye . . . Goodbye, Chris. (*He tries to shake hands with* CHRIS.)

CHRIS. (*Turning away.*) Goodbye. (GORDON *goes, quickly, right.* KATE *starts to put the tea things back on the tray.*)

KATE. He wanted to talk to me about stocks. I inherited some stock he thinks I should sell, and so he stopped by—

CHRIS. Where's Dad?

KATE. He's in Europe, darling. As I think I wrote you. He'll be home Tuesday. (*She starts for the kitchen with the tray.*)

CHRIS. Oh Mom.

KATE. (*Stopping, turning.*) And what does that mean, pray tell? "Oh Mom." (*He turns away.*) I'd like to know, please, what that means? (*He shakes his head.*) I happened to be having *tea*, Christopher. It happens to be a very old custom. Your grandmother used to have tea at this very table with this same china every afternoon. All sorts of people would stop by. All the time. I'd come home from school, and there she'd be. Serving tea. It's a delightful old custom, sweetheart. (*He starts for the hall.*) Where are you going? I asked you a question, please. We don't just walk away. (CHRIS *walks out of the room.* KATE *calls after* CHRIS.) Chris, I am talking to you. I am talking to you, and I am your mother, and the least you can do is . . . (*She follows him out into the hall, still carrying the tray. A young man named* TONY *comes in from the kitchen, decked out with a camera and various pieces of photographic equipment. He begins to test the room with his light meter. He finds an area by a chair which pleases him. He calls toward the kitchen.*)

TONY. Would you mind setting up over here, Aunt Harriet? I want to get you in the late afternoon light. (AUNT HARRIET, *a woman of about sixty, appears at the kitchen door, carrying another tray, glittering with old china and crystal.*)

AUNT HARRIET. (*Beaming proudly.*) Certainly, Tony. (*She goes to where he indicates, puts down her tray, and begins to set a place at the table.*) Now I thought I'd use this Irish linen place mat with matching napkin, that my husband—who was what? Your great uncle—inherited from his sister. They have to be washed and ironed by hand every time they're used. (*She places the place mat; he photographs it.*) And then of course the silver, which was given to us as a wedding present by your great-grandmother. You see? Three prong forks. Pistol-handled knives. Spoon with rat tail back. All Williamsburg pattern. This should be polished at least every two weeks. (*She sets a place as he photographs each item. She becomes more and more at home with the camera.*) And then this is Staffordshire, as is the butter plate. All of this is Bone. The wine glasses are early Steuben, but the goblets and finger bowls are both Waterford. None of this goes in the dishwasher, of course. It's all far too delicate for detergents. (*The place is all set. She surveys it proudly.*)

TONY. Finger bowls?

AUNT HARRIET. Oh yes. Our side of the family always used finger bowls between the salad and the dessert.

TONY. Would you show me how they worked?

AUNT HARRIET. Certainly, dear. (*He continues to snap pictures of her as she talks.*) You see the maid would take away the salad plate—like this— (*She puts a plate aside to her right.*) And then she'd put down the finger bowls in front of us. Like this. (*She does.*) They would be filled approximately halfway with cool water. And there might be a little rose floating in it. Or a sliver of lemon . . . Now of course, we'd have our napkins in our laps—like this. (*She sits down, shakes out her napkin, puts it discreetly in her lap.*) And then we'd dip our fingers into the finger bowl . . . gently, gently . . . and then we'd wiggle them and shake them out . . . and then dab them on our napkins . . . and then dab our lips . . . then, of course, the maids would take them away . . . (*She moves the finger bowl aside.*) And in would come a nice sherbert or chocolate mousse! (*She beams at the camera, at last used to it. He snaps her picture.*)

TONY. Thanks, Aunt Harriet. That was terrific. (*He begins to pack up his photographic gear.*)

AUNT HARRIET. You're welcome. Now, Tony, dear, tell me again what all this is for. I didn't quite understand over the telephone.

TONY. This is a classroom project. For Amherst.

AUNT HARRIET. Oh, my. A project. (*She stands up.*) In what, pray tell.

TONY. Anthropology, actually.

AUNT HARRIET. Anthro*pology*. Heavens! (*She starts to return items to her tray.*) What does that have to do with this?

TONY. Well you see we're studying the eating habits of various vanishing cultures. For example, someone is talking about the Kikuyus of Northern Kenya. And my roommate is doing the Cree Indians of Saskatchewan. And my professor suggested I do a slide show on us.

AUNT HARRIET. Us?

TONY. The Wasps. Of Northeastern United States. (*Pause.*)

AUNT HARRIET. I see.

TONY. You can learn a lot about a culture from how it eats.

AUNT HARRIET. (*With increasing coldness.*) Such as what?

TONY. Well. Consider the finger bowls, for example. There you have an almost neurotic obsession with cleanliness, reflecting the guilt which comes with the last stages of capitalism. Or notice the unnecessary accumulation of glass and china, and the compulsion to display it. Or the subtle hint of aggression in those pistol-handled knives.

AUNT HARRIET. I think I'll ask you to leave, Tony.

TONY. Aunt Harriet . . .

AUNT HARRIET. I was going to invite you to stay for a cocktail, but now I won't.

TONY. Please, Aunt Harriet . . . (*He begins to gather up his equipment.*)

AUNT HARRIET. Out! Right now! Before I telephone long distance to your mother! (TONY *backs toward the hallway.*) Vanishing culture, my eye! I forbid you to mention my name in the classroom! Or show one glimpse of my personal property! And you can tell that professor of yours, I've got a good mind to drive up to Amherst, with this pistol-handled butter knife on the seat beside me, and cut off his anthropological balls! (TONY *runs hurriedly from the room.* HARRIET *returns to her tray proudly, and carries it back into the kitchen. As she goes, an older man, called* JIM, *comes in from the hall, followed by his daughter,* MEG. *He is in his late sixties, she is about thirty.*)

MEG. Where are you going now, Daddy?

JIM. I think your mother might want a drink.

MEG. She's reading to the children.

JIM. That's why she might want one.

MEG. She wants no such thing, Dad.

JIM. Then I want one.

MEG. Now? It's not even five.

JIM. Well then let's go see how the Red Sox are doing. (*He starts back out, right.*)

MEG. Daddy, *stop!*

JIM. Stop what?

MEG. Avoiding me. Ever since I arrived, we haven't been able to talk.

JIM. Good Lord, what do you mean? Seems to me everybody's been talking continuously and simultaneously from the moment you got off the plane.

MEG. Alone, Daddy. I mean *alone*. And you *know* I mean alone.

JIM. All right. We'll talk. (*Sits down.*) Right here in the dining room. Good place to talk. Why not? Matter of fact, I'm kind of tired. It's been a long day.

MEG. I love this room. I've always loved it. Always.

JIM. Your mother and I still use it. Now and then. Once a week. Mrs. Robinson still comes in and cooks us a nice dinner and we have it in here. Still. Lamb chops. Broilers—

MEG. (*Suddenly.*) I've left him, Daddy.

JIM. Oh well now, a little vacation . . .

MEG. I've left him permanently.

JIM. Yes, well, permanently is a very long word . . .

MEG. I can't live with him, Dad. We don't get along at all.

JIM. Oh well, you may think that now . . .

MEG. Could we live here, Dad?

JIM. Here?

MEG. For a few months.

JIM. With three small children?

MEG. While I work out my life. (*Pause.*)

JIM. (*Takes out a pocket watch and looks at it.*) What time is it? A little after five. I think the sun is over the yardarm, don't you? Or if it isn't, it should be. I think it's almost permissible for you and me to have a little drink, Meg.

MEG. Can we stay here, Dad?

JIM. Make us a drink, Meggie.

MEG. All right. (*She goes into the kitchen; the door, of course, remains open.*)

JIM. (*Calling to her.*) I'd like Scotch, sweetheart. Make it reasonably strong. You'll find the silver measuring gizmo in the drawer by the trays. I want two shots and a splash of water. And I like to use that big glass with the pheasant on it. And not too much ice. (*He gets up and moves around the table.*)

MEG'S VOICE. (*Within.*) All right.

JIM. I saw Mimi Mott the other day . . . Can you hear me?

MEG'S VOICE. (*Within.*) I can hear you, Dad.

JIM. There she was, being a very good sport with her third husband. Her third. Who's deaf as a post and extremely disagreeable. So I took her aside—can you hear me?

MEG'S VOICE. (*Within.*) I'm listening, Dad.

JIM. I took her aside, and I said, "Now Mimi, tell me the truth. If you had made half as much effort with your first husband as you've made with the last two, don't you think you'd still be married to him?" I asked her that. Point blank. And you know what Mimi said? She said, "Maybe." That's exactly what she said. "Maybe." If she had made the effort.

MEG. (*Returns with two glasses. She gives one to* JIM.) That's your generation, Dad.

JIM. That's every generation.

MEG. It's not mine.

JIM. Every generation has to make an effort.

MEG. I won't go back to him, Dad. I want to be here.

JIM. (*Looking at his glass.*) I wanted the glass with the pheasant on it.

MEG. I think the kids used it.

JIM. Oh. (*Pause. He drinks, moves away from her.*)

MEG. So can we stay, Dad?

JIM. I sleep in your room now. Your mother kicked me out because I snore. And we use the boys' room now to watch TV.

MEG. I'll use the guest room.

JIM. And the children?

MEG. They can sleep on the third floor. In the maid's rooms.

JIM. We closed them off. Because of the oil bills.

MEG. I don't care, Dad. We'll work it out. Please. (*Pause.*)

JIM. (*Sits down at the other end of the table.*) Give it another try first.

MEG. No.

JIM. Another try.

MEG. He's got someone else now, Dad. She's living there right now. She's moved in.

JIM. Then fly back and kick her out.

MEG. Oh, Dad . . .

JIM. I'm serious. You don't know this, but that's what your mother did. One time I became romantically involved with Mrs. Shoemaker. We took a little trip together. To Sea Island. Your mother got wind of it, and came right down, and told Betty Shoemaker to get on the next train. That's all there was to it. Now why don't you do that? Go tell this woman to peddle her papers elsewhere. We'll sit with the children while you do.

MEG. I've got someone too, Dad. (*Pause.*)

JIM. You mean you've had a little fling.

MEG. I've been going with someone.

JIM. Where was your husband?

MEG. He stayed with his girl.

JIM. And your children?

MEG . Oh they . . . came and went.

JIM. It sounds a little . .. complicated.

MEG. It is, Dad. That's why I needed to come home. (*Pause.*)

JIM. (*Drinks.*) Now let's review the bidding, may we? Do you plan to marry this new man?

MEG. No.

JIM. You're not in love with him?

MEG. No. He's already married, anyway.

JIM. And he's decided he loves his wife.

MEG. No.

JIM. But you've decided you don't love him.

MEG. Yes.

JIM. Or your husband.

MEG. Yes.

JIM. And your husband's fallen in love with someone else.

MEG. He lives with someone else.

JIM. And your children . . . my grandchildren . . . come and go among these various households.

MEG. Yes. Sort of. Yes.

JIM. Sounds extremely complicated.

MEG. It is, Dad. It really is. (*Pause.*)

JIM. (*Drinks, thinks, gets up, paces.*) Well then it seems to me the first thing you do is simplify things. That's the first thing. You ask the man you're living with to leave, you sue your husband for divorce, you hold onto your house, you keep the children in their present schools, you—

MEG. There's someone else, Dad. (*Pause.*)

JIM. Someone else?

MEG. Someone else entirely.

JIM. A third person.

MEG. Yes.

JIM. What was that movie your mother and I liked so much? *The Third Man?* (*He sits, downstage left.*)

MEG. It's not a man, Dad. (*Pause.*)

JIM. Not a man.

MEG. It's a woman.

JIM. A woman.

MEG. I've been involved with a woman, Dad, but it's not working, and I don't know who I am, and I've got to touch *base,* Daddy. I want to be here. (*She kneels at his feet. Pause.*)

JIM. (*Gets slowly to his feet. He points to his glass.*) I think I'll get a repair. Would you like a repair? I'll take your glass. I'll get us both repairs. (*He takes her glass and goes out to the kitchen, leaving the door open.*)

MEG. (*Moving around the dining room.*) I'm all mixed up, Dad. I'm all over the ball park. I've been seeing a Crisis Counselor, and I've taken a part-time job, and I've been jogging two miles a day, and none of it's working, Dad. I want to come home. I want to take my children to the Zoo, and the Park Lake, and the Art Gallery, and do all those things you and Mother used to do with all of us. I want to start again, Dad. I want to start all over again.

JIM. (*Comes out from the kitchen, now carrying three glasses.*) I made one for your mother. And I found the glass with the pheasant on it. In the trash. Somebody broke it. (*He crosses for the doorway, right.*) So let's have a nice cocktail with your mother, and see if we can get the children to sit quietly while we do.

MEG. You don't want us here, do you, Dad?

JIM. (*Stopping.*) Of course we do, darling. A week, ten days. You're most welcome.

MEG. (*Desperately.*) I can't go back, Dad!

JIM. (*Quietly.*) Neither can I, sweetheart. Neither can I. (*He shuffles on out.* MEG *stands for a moment in the dining room, then hurries out after him as* EMILY, *a woman of about thirty-five, comes in and looks at the table.*)

EMILY. (*Distractedly.*) I don't know whether to eat, or not. (*Her son* DAVID *comes in. He's about fourteen.*)

DAVID. What's the trouble, Mother?

EMILY. I don't know whether to eat or not. Your father and I were sitting in the living room, having a perfectly pleasant cocktail together, when all of a sudden that stupid telephone rang, and now he's holed up in the bedroom, talking away. (*She closes the kitchen door.*)

DAVID. Who's he talking to?

EMILY. I don't know. I don't even know. I think it's someone from the club. (CLAIRE, *her daughter, comes on. She's about sixteen.*)

CLAIRE. Are we eating or not?

EMILY. I simply don't know. (BERTHA, *the maid, sticks her head out of the kitchen door.*) I don't know whether to go ahead or not, Bertha. Mr. Thatcher is still on the telephone.

CLAIRE. Couldn't we at least start the soup?

EMILY. I don't know. I just don't know. Oh, let's wait five more minutes, Bertha.

BERTHA. Yes, Mrs. (BERTHA *disappears.* EMILY, DAVID, *and* CLAIRE *sit down.*)

EMILY. Honestly, that telephone! I could wring its neck! It should be banned, it should be outlawed, between six and eight in the evening. (*The father comes in hurriedly from the hall. His name is* STANDISH.)

STANDISH. I've got to go.

EMILY. (*Standing up.*) Go? Go where?

STANDISH. Out. (BERTHA *comes in with the soup tureen.*)

EMILY. You mean you can't even sit down and have some of Bertha's nice celery soup?

STANDISH. I can't even finish my cocktail. Something very bad has happened.

EMILY. Bertha, would you mind very much putting the soup back in a saucepan and keeping it on a low flame. We'll call you when we're ready.

BERTHA. Yes, Mrs. (BERTHA *goes out,* STANDISH *takes* EMILY *aside, downstage left.*)

EMILY. (*Hushed tones.*) Now what on earth is the matter?

STANDISH. Henry was insulted down at the club.

EMILY. Insulted?

CLAIRE. (*From the table.*) *Uncle* Henry?

STANDISH. (*Ignoring* CLAIRE; *to* EMILY.) Binky Byers made a remark to him in the steam bath.

EMILY. Oh no!

DAVID. What did he say, Dad?

CLAIRE. Yes, what did he say?

STANDISH. I believe I was speaking to your mother. (*Pause. The children are quelled.*) Binky made a remark, and apparently a number of the newer members laughed. Poor Henry was so upset he had to put on his clothes and leave. He called me from Mother's.

EMILY. Oh no, oh no.

STANDISH. I telephoned the club. I spoke to several people who had been in the steam bath. They confirmed the incident. I asked to speak to Binky Byers. He refused to come to the phone. And so I've got to do something about it.

EMILY. Oh dear, oh dear.

DAVID. Won't you tell us what he said to Uncle Henry, Dad?

STANDISH. I will not. I will not dignify the remark by repeating it.

DAVID. Oh come on, Dad. We're not babies.

EMILY. Yes, Standish. Really.

STANDISH. He said— (*Checks himself.*) Claire, I want you to leave the room.

CLAIRE. Why? I'm older.

EMILY. Yes. She should know. Everybody should know. These are different times. (BERTHA *comes out.*) We're not quite ready yet, Bertha. (BERTHA *goes right back in.*)

EMILY. Now go on, Standish. Be frank. This is a family.

STANDISH. (*Hesitatingly; looking from one to the other.*) Mr. Byers . . . made an unfortunate remark . . . having to do with your Uncle Henry's . . . private life. (*Pause. The children don't get it.*)

EMILY. I'm afraid you'll have to be more specific, dear.

STANDISH. (*Taking a deep breath.*) Mr. Byers, who had obviously been drinking since early afternoon, approached your Uncle Henry in the steam bath, and alluded in very specific terms to his personal relationships.

CLAIRE. What personal relationships?

STANDISH. His—associations. In the outside world. (*Pause.*)

DAVID. I don't get it.

EMILY. Darling, Mr. Byers must have made some unnecessary remarks about your Uncle Henry's bachelor attachments.

DAVID. You mean Uncle Harry is a *fruit?*

STANDISH. (*Wheeling on him.*) I WON'T HAVE THAT WORD IN THIS HOUSE!

DAVID. I was just . . .

EMILY. He got it from school, dear.

STANDISH. I don't care if he got it from God! I will not have it in this house! The point is my own *brother* was wounded at his *club!* (*Pause.*)

EMILY. But what can you do, dear?

STANDISH. Go down there.

EMILY. To your mother's?

STANDISH. To the *club!* I'll demand a public apology from Binky in front of the entire grille.

EMILY. But if he won't even come to the telephone . . .

STANDISH. I'll have to fight him.

EMILY. Oh, Standish.

STANDISH. I have to.

CLAIRE. Oh, Daddy . . .

STANDISH. I can't let the remark stand.

DAVID. Can I come with you, Dad?

STANDISH. You may not. I want you home with your mother. (*He starts for the door.*)

EMILY. Standish, for heaven's sake!

STANDISH. No arguments, please.

EMILY. But Binky Byers is half your age! And twice your size!

STANDISH. It makes no difference.

EMILY. I think he was on the boxing team at Dartmouth!

STANDISH. No difference whatsoever.

EMILY. What about your bad shoulder? What about your hernia?

STANDISH. I'm sorry, I imagine I shall be seriously hurt. But I can't stand idly by.

CLAIRE. (*Tearfully.*) Oh, Daddy, please don't go. (BERTHA *comes out of the kitchen.*)

BERTHA. The lamb will be overdone, Mrs.

EMILY. And it's a beautiful *lamb*, Standish!

STANDISH. (*Shouting them down.*) Now *listen* to me! *All* of you! (BERTHA *has been heading back to the kitchen.*) And you, too, Bertha! (*He points toward a chair downstage left.* BERTHA *crosses, as everyone watches her. She sits on the edge of the chair. Everyone turns back to* STANDISH.) There is nothing, nothing I'd rather do in this world, than sit down at this table with all of you and have some of Bertha's fine celery soup, followed by a leg of lamb with mint sauce and roast potatoes. Am I right about the sauce and the potatoes, Bertha?

BERTHA. Yes, sir.

STANDISH. There is nothing I'd rather do than that. But I have to forgo it. My own brother has been publicly insulted at his club. And that means our family has been insulted. And when the family has been insulted, that means this table, these chairs, this room, and all of us in it, including you, Bertha, are being treated with scorn. And so if I stayed here, if I sat down with all of you now, I wouldn't be able to converse, I wouldn't be able to laugh, I wouldn't be able to correct your grammar, David, I wouldn't be able to enjoy your fine meal, Bertha. (*Turning to* EMILY.) I wouldn't even be able to kiss my handsome wife goodbye. (*He kisses her. It's a passionate kiss.*) Goodbye, dear.

EMILY. Goodbye, darling. (*He kisses* CLAIRE.)

STANDISH. Goodbye, Winkins.

CLAIRE. Goodbye, Daddy. (*He shakes hands with* DAVID.)

STANDISH. Goodbye, David.

DAVID. So long, Dad. Good luck.

STANDISH. Goodbye, Bertha.

BERTHA. Goodbye, sir. God bless you.

STANDISH. Thank you very much indeed. (*He goes out. Pause.*)

EMILY. (*Now all business.*) Of course we can't eat now, Bertha. Have something yourself, and let people raid the icebox later on.

BERTHA. Yes, Mrs.

EMILY. And the children can have lamb hash on Saturday.

BERTHA. Yes, Mrs. (BERTHA *goes off.*)

EMILY. David: you and I will drive down to the club, and wait for the outcome in the visitor's lounge.

DAVID. O.K., Mother.

EMILY. So get a book. Get a good book. Get *Ivanhoe*. We could be quite a while.

DAVID. O.K. (*He goes out.*)

EMILY. And Claire: I want you to stay here, and hold the fort.

CLAIRE. All right, Mother.

EMILY. Get on the telephone to Doctor Russell. I don't care whether he's having dinner or in the operating room. Tell him to be at the club to give your father first aid.

CLAIRE. All right, Mother.

EMILY. And then study your French.

CLAIRE. All right. (*She starts out, then stops.*) Mother?

EMILY. (*Impatiently in the doorway.*) What, for heaven's sake?

CLAIRE. Is it true about Uncle Henry?

EMILY. Well it may be, sweetheart. But you don't say it to *him*. And you don't say it at the *club*. And you don't say it within a ten-mile radius of your *father*. Now goodbye. (EMILY *rushes off, right, followed by* CLAIRE. *An old man and his middle-aged son come on from right. The old man is* HARVEY, *his son is* DICK. *The light is dim in the dining room now, except downstage center, by the "French windows."*)

HARVEY. (*As he enters.*) We'll talk in here. No one will disturb us. Nobody comes near a dining room anymore. The thought of sitting down with a number of intelligent, attractive people to enjoy good food well cooked and properly served . . . that apparently doesn't occur to people anymore. Nowadays people eat in kitchens, or in living rooms, standing around, balancing their plates like jugglers. Soon they'll be eating in bathrooms. Well why not? Simplify the process considerably.

DICK. Sit down somewhere, Pop.

HARVEY. (*Coming well downstage, pulling a chair down, away from the table.*) I'll sit here. We can look out. There's a purple finch who comes to the feeder every evening. Brings his young. (DICK *pulls up a chair beside him. Behind, in the dim light, three women begin to set the table, this time for an elaborate dinner. A great white tablecloth, candles, flowers, the works. The process should be reverential, quiet, and muted, not to distract from the scene downstage. Taking an envelope from his inside pocket.*) Now. I want to go over my funeral with you.

DICK. Pop—

HARVEY. I want to do it. There are only a few more apples left in the barrel for me.

DICK. You've been saying that for years, Pop.

HARVEY. Well this time it's true. So I want to go over this, please. You're my eldest son. I can't do it with anyone else. Your mother starts to cry, your brother isn't here, and your sister gets distracted. So concentrate, please, on my funeral.

DICK. All right, Pop.

HARVEY. (*Taking out a typewritten document.*) First, here is my obituary. For both newspapers. I dictated it to Miss Kovak down at the office, and I've read it over twice, and it's what I want. It's thorough without being self-congratulatory. I mention my business career, my civic commitments, and of course my family. I even touch on my recreational life. I give my lowest score in golf and the weight of the sailfish I caught off the Keys. The papers will want to cut both items, but don't you let them.

DICK. O.K., Pop.

HARVEY. I also want them to print this picture. (*He shows it.*) It was taken when I was elected to chair the Symphony drive. I think it will do. I don't look too young to die, or so old it won't make any difference.

DICK. All right, Pop.

HARVEY (*Fussing with other documents.*) Now I want the funeral service announced at the end of the obituary, and to occur three days later. That will give people time to postpone their trips and adjust their appointments. And I want it at three-thirty in the afternoon. This gives people time to digest their lunch and doesn't obligate us to feed them dinner. Notice I've underlined the word *church*. Mr. Fayerweather might try to squeeze the service into the chapel, but don't let him. I've lived in this city all my life, and know a great many people, and I want everyone to have a seat and feel comfortable. If you see people milling around the door, go right up to them and find them a place, even if you have to use folding chairs. Are we clear on that?

DICK. Yes, Pop. (*By now the table has been mostly set behind them. The women have gone.*)

HARVEY. I've listed the following works to be played by Mrs. Manchester at the organ. This Bach, this Handel, this Schubert. All lively, you'll notice. Nothing gloomy, nothing grim. I want the service to start promptly with a good rousing hymn—*Onward Christian Soldiers*—and then Fayerweather may make some brief—underlined *brief*—remarks about my life and works. Do you plan to get up and speak, by the way?

DICK. Me?

HARVEY. You. Do you plan to say anything?

DICK. I hadn't thought, Pop . . .

HARVEY. Don't, if you don't want to. There's nothing more uncomfortable than a reluctant or unwilling speaker. On the other hand, if you, as my eldest son, were to get on your feet and say a few words of farewell . . .

DICK. (*Quickly.*) Of course I will, Pop.

HARVEY. Good. Then I'll write you in. (*He writes.*) "Brief remarks by my son Richard." (*Pause; looks up.*) Any idea what you might say?

DICK. No, Pop.

HARVEY. You won't make it sentimental, will you? Brad Hoffmeister's son got up the other day and made some very sentimental remarks about Brad. I didn't like it, and I don't think Brad would have liked it.

DICK. I won't get sentimental, Pop.

HARVEY. Good. (*Pause; shuffles documents; looks up again.*) On the other hand, you won't make any wisecracks, will you?

DICK. Oh, Pop . . .

HARVEY. You have that tendency, Dick. At Marcie's wedding. And your brother's birthday. You got up and made some very flip remarks about all of us.

DICK. I'm sorry, Pop.

HARVEY. Smart-guy stuff. Too smart, in my opinion. If you plan to get into that sort of thing, perhaps you'd better not say anything at all.

2

DICK. I won't make any cracks, Pop. I promise.

HARVEY. Thank you. (*Looks at documents; looks up again.*) Because you love us, don't you?

DICK. Yes, Pop.

HARVEY. You love us. You may live a thousand miles away, you may have run off every summer, you may be a terrible letter-writer, but you love us all, just the same. Don't you? You love me.

DICK. (*Touching him.*) Oh yes, Pop! Oh yes! Really! (*Pause.*)

HARVEY. Fine. (*Puts his glasses on again; shuffles through documents.*) Now at the graveside, just the family. I want to be buried beside my brothers and below my mother and father. Leave room for your mother to lie beside me. If she marries again, still leave room. She'll come back at the end.

DICK. All right, Pop.

HARVEY. Invite people back here after the burial. Stay close to your mother. She gets nervous at any kind of gathering, and makes bad decisions. For example, don't let her serve any of the good Beefeater's gin if people simply want to mix it with tonic water. And when they're gone, sit with her. Stay in the house. Don't leave for a few days. Please.

DICK. I promise, Pop. (ANNIE, *the maid from the first scene, now quite old, adds candlesticks and a lovely flower centerpiece to the table.*)

HARVEY. (*Putting documents back in the envelope.*) And that's my funeral. I'm leaving you this room, you know. After your mother dies, the table and chairs go to you. It's the best thing I can leave you, by far.

DICK. Thanks, Pop. (ANNIE *exits into the kitchen.*)

HARVEY. Now we'll rejoin your mother. (*He gets slowly to his feet.*) I'll put this envelope in my safe deposit box, on top of my will and the stock certificates. The key will be in my left bureau drawer. (*He starts out, then stops.*) You didn't see the purple finch feeding its young.

DICK. (*Remaining in his chair.*) Yes I did, Pop.

HARVEY. You saw it while I was talking?

DICK. That's right.

HARVEY. Good. I'm glad you saw it. (*He goes out slowly.* DICK *waits a moment, lost in thought, and then replaces the chairs. The lights come up on the table, now beautifully set with white linen, crystal goblets, silver candlesticks, flowers, the works.* ANNIE *begins to set plates as a hostess—*RUTH*—comes in from right.*)

RUTH. (*Surveying the table.*) Oh Annie! It looks absolutely spectacular.

ANNIE. Thank you, Mrs.

RUTH. (*As she begins to distribute place cards carefully around the table.*) Now make sure the soup plates are hot.

ANNIE. I always do, Mrs.

RUTH. But I think we can dispense with butter-balls. Just give everyone a nice square of butter.

ANNIE. I'll do butter-balls, Mrs.

RUTH. Would you? How nice! And keep an eye on the ashtrays, Annie. Some people still smoke between courses, but they don't like to be reminded of it.

ANNIE. I know, Mrs.

RUTH. And let's see . . . Oh yes. Before people arrive, I want to pay you. (*She produces two envelopes from the sideboard.*) For you. And for Velma in the kitchen. It includes your taxi. So you can both just leave right after you've cleaned up.

ANNIE. Thank you, Mrs.

RUTH. There's a little extra in yours, Annie. Just a present. Because you've been so helpful to the family over the years.

ANNIE. Thank you, Mrs.

RUTH. And now I'd better check the living room.

ANNIE. Yes, Mrs. (RUTH *starts out right, then stops.*)

RUTH. Oh Annie. I heard some strange news through the grapevine. (ANNIE *looks at her.*) Mrs. Rellman told me that you won't be available any more.

ANNIE. No, Mrs.

RUTH. Not even for us, Annie. We've used you more than anyone.

ANNIE. I'm retiring, Mrs.

RUTH. But surely special occasions, Annie. I mean, if we're desperate. Can I still reach you at your nephew's?

ANNIE. He's moving away, Mrs.

RUTH. But then where will you go? What will you do?

ANNIE. I've got my sister in Milwaukee, Mrs.

RUTH. But we'll be lost without you, Annie.

ANNIE. You'll manage, Mrs.

RUTH. (*Indicating the table.*) But not like this. We'll never match this.

ANNIE. Thank you, Mrs.

RUITH. I think I heard the bell.

ANNIE. I'll get it, Mrs.

RUTH. Women's coats upstairs, men's in the hall closet.

ANNIE. Yes, Mrs. (ANNIE *starts out.*)

RUTH. Annie! (ANNIE *stops.* RUTH *goes to her and hugs her.* ANNIE *responds stiffly.*) Thank you, Annie. For everything.

ANNIE. You're welcome, Mrs. (ANNIE *goes off right, to answer the door.* RUTH *goes to the sideboard, gets a book of matches. She lights the two candles on the table as she speaks to the audience.*)

RUTH. Lately I've been having this recurrent dream. We're giving this perfect party. We have our dining room back, and Grandmother's silver, before it was stolen, and Charley's mother's royal blue dinner plates, before the movers dropped them, and even the finger bowls, if I knew where they were. And I've invited all our favorite people. Oh I don't mean just our old friends. I mean everyone we've ever known and liked. We'd have the man who fixes our Toyota, and that intelligent young couple who bought the Payton house, and the receptionist at the doctor's office, and the new teller at the bank. And our children would be invited, too. And they'd all come back from wherever they are. And we'd have two cocktails, and hot hors d'oeuvres, and a first-rate cook in the kitchen, and two maids to serve, and everyone would get along famously! (*The candles are lit by now.*) My husband laughs when I tell him this dream. "Do you realize," he says, "what a party like that would cost? Do you realize what we'd have to *pay* these days for a party like that?" Well, I know. I know all that. But sometimes I think it might almost be worth it. (*The rest of the cast now spills into the dining room, talking animatedly, having a wonderful time. There is the usual gallantry and jockeying around as people read the place cards and find their seats. The men pull out the women's chairs, and people sit down. The* HOST *goes to the sideboard, where* ANNIE *has left a bottle of wine in a silver bucket. He wraps a linen napkin around it, and begins to pour people's wine. The conversation flows as well. The lights begin to dim. The* HOST *reaches his own seat at the head of the table, and pours his own wine. Then he raises his glass.*)

HOST. To all of us. (*Everyone raises his or her glass. As their glasses go down, the lights fade to black. The table is bathed in its own candlelight. Then the two downstage actors unobtrusively snuff the candles, and the play is over.*)

THE END

PAINTING CHURCHES

A DRAMA IN TWO ACTS

by
Tina Howe

Aengus." These poems are in the Public Domain in the U.S., but Ms. Howe wishes to acknowledge the owner of the copyright, Miss Anne Yeats, the daughter of the poet.

PAINTING CHURCHES was first produced at The Second Stage on February 8, 1983.

CAST

Fanny Church .... MARIAN SELDES
Gardner Church .... GEORGE N. MARTIN
Margaret Church .... ELIZABETH McGOVERN

PLACE: Beacon Hill—Boston, Mass

CHARACTERS

FANNY SEDGWICK CHURCH—A Bostonian from a fine old family, in her sixties.

GARDNER CHURCH—Her husband, an eminent New England poet from a finer family, in his seventies.

MARGARET CHURCH (MAGS)—Their daughter, a painter, in her early thirties.

ACT ONE

SCENE 1

The living room of the Churchs' townhouse on Beacon Hill one week before everything will be moved to Cape Cod. Empty packing cartons line the room and all the furniture has been tagged with brightly colored markers. At first glance it looks like any discreet Boston interior, but on closer scrutiny one notices a certain flamboyance. Oddities from second hand stores are mixed in with the fine old furniture and exotic hand made curios vie with tasteful family objets d'art. What makes the room remarkable though, is the play of light that pours through three soaring arched windows. At one hour it's hard-edged and brilliant, the next, it's dappled and yielding. It transforms whatever it touches, giving the room a distinct feeling of unreality. It's several years ago, a bright spring morning.

FANNY *is sitting on the sofa wrapping a valuable old silver coffee service. She's wearing a worn bathrobe and fashionable hat. As she works, she makes a list of everything on a yellow legal pad.* GARDNER *can be heard typing in his study down the hall.*

FANNY. (*She picks up a coffee pot.*) God, this is good looking! I'd forgotten how handsome Mama's old silver was! It's probably worth a fortune. It certainly weighs enough! (*Calling out.*) GARRRRRRRRRRRRRRRRRRRRD-NERRRRRRR-RRRRRRRR . . . ? Well, it should bring us a pretty penny, that's for sure. (*Wraps it, places it in a carton and then picks up the tray that goes with it. She holds it up like a mirror and adjusts her hat; louder in another register.*) OH GARRRRRRR-RRRRRRRD-NERRRRR . . . ? (*He continues typing. She then reaches for a small box and opens it with reverence.*) Grandma's Paul Revere teaspoons . . . ! (*She takes several out and fondles them.*) I don't care how desperate things get, these will never go! One has to maintain some standards! (*She writes*

357

on her list.) "Grandma's Paul Revere teaspoons, Cotuit!" . . . WASN'T IT THE AMERICAN WING OF THE METRO-POLITAN MUSEUM OF ART THAT WANTED GRAND-MA'S PAUL REVERE TEASPOONS SO BADLY . . . ? (*She looks at her reflection in the tray again.*) This is a very good looking hat, if I do say so. I was awfully smart to grab it up. (*Silence.*) DON'T YOU REMEMBER A DISTINGUISHED-LOOKING MAN COMING TO THE HOUSE AND OFFER-ING US $50,000 FOR GRANDMA'S PAUL REVERE TEA-SPOONS . . . ? HE HAD ON THESE MARVELOUS SHOES! THEY WERE SO POINTED AT THE ENDS WE COULDN'T IMAGINE HOW HE EVER GOT THEM ON AND THEY WERE SHINED TO WITHIN AN INCH OF THEIR LIVES AND I REMEMBER HIM SAYING HE CAME FROM THE . . . AMERICAN WING OF THE METROPOLITAN MU-SEUM OF ART! . . . HELLO? . . . GARDNER . . . ? ARE YOU THERE! (*The typing stops.*) YOO HOOOOOOO . . . (*Like a fog horn.*) GARRRRRRRRRRRRRRRD-NERRRR-RRR . . . ?

GARDNER. (*Off stage; from his study.*) YES DEAR . . . IS THAT YOU . . . ?

FANNY. OF COURSE IT'S ME! WHO ELSE COULD IT POSSIBLY BE . . . ? DARLING, PLEASE COME HERE FOR A MINUTE. (*The typing resumes.*) FOR GOD'S SAKE, WILL YOU STOP THAT DREADFUL TYPING BEFORE YOU SEND ME STRAIGHT TO THE NUT HOUSE . . . ? (*In a new register.*) GARRRRRRRRRRRRRRRRRRRRD-NERRRRRRRR . . . ? (*He stops.*)

GARDNER. (*Offstage.*) WHAT'S THAT? MAGS IS BACK FROM THE NUT HOUSE . . . ? (*Brief silence.*) I'LL BE WITH YOU IN A MOMENT, I DIDN'T HEAR HER RING. (*He starts singing the refrain of "Nothing Could be Finer."**)

FANNY. I SAID . . . Lord, I hate this yelling . . . PLEASE . . . COME . . . HERE! It's a wonder I'm not in a straight jacket already. Actually, it might be rather nice for a change . . . Peace-ful. DARLING . . . I WANT TO SHOW YOU MY NEW HAT!

---

*Note: Permission to produce *Painting Churches* does not include permission to use this song, which ought to be procured from the copyright owner.

(*Silence.* GARDNER *enters, still singing. He's wearing mismatched tweeds and is holding a stack of papers which keep drifting to the floor.*)

GARDNER. Oh, don't you look nice! Very attractive, very attractive!

FANNY. But I'm still in my bathrobe.

GARDNER. (*Looking around the room, leaking more papers.*) Well, where's Mags?

FANNY. Darling, you're dropping your papers all over the floor.

GARDNER. (*Spies the silver tray.*) I remember this! Aunt Alice gave it to us, didn't she? (*He picks it up.*) Good Lord, it's heavy. What's it made of? Lead?!

FANNY. No, Aunt Alice did *not* give it to us. It was Mama's.

GARDNER. Oh yes . . . (*He starts to exit with it.*)

FANNY. Could I have it back, please?

GARDNER. (*Hands it to her, dropping more papers.*) Oh, sure thing . . . Where's Mags? I thought you said she was here.

FANNY. I didn't say Mags was here, I asked *you* to come here.

GARDNER. (*Papers spilling.*) Damned papers keep falling . . .

FANNY. I wanted to show you my new hat. I bought it in honor of Mags' visit. Isn't it marvelous?

GARDNER. (*Picking up the papers as more drop.*) Yes, yes, very nice . . .

FANNY. Gardner, you're not even looking at it!

GARDNER. Very becoming . . .

FANNY. You don't think it's too bright, do you? I don't want to look like a traffic light. Guess how much it cost?

GARDNER. (*A whole sheaf of papers slides to the floor, he dives for them.*) OH SHIT!

FANNY. (*Gets to them first.*) It's alright, I've got them, I've got them. (*She hands them to him.*)

GARDNER. You'd think they had wings on them . . .

FANNY. Here you go . . .   GARDNER. . . . . damned things
FANNY. Gar . . . ?   won't hold still!

GARDNER. (*Has become engrossed in one of the pages and is lost reading it.*) Mmmmm?

FANNY. HELLO?

GARDNER. (*Startled.*) What's that?

FANNY. (*In a whisper.*) My hat. Guess how much it cost.

GARDNER. Oh yes. Let's see . . . $10?

FANNY. $10? . . . IS THAT ALL . . . ?

GARDNER. 20?

FANNY. GARDNER, THIS HAPPENS TO BE A DE-SIGNER HAT! DESIGNER HATS START AT $50 . . . 75!

GARDNER. (*Jumps.*) Was that the door bell?

FANNY. No, it wasn't the door bell. Though it's high time Mags were here. She was probably in a train wreck!

GARDNER. (*Looking through his papers.*) I'm beginning to get fond of Wallace Stevens again.

FANNY. This damned move is going to kill me! Send me straight to my grave!

GARDNER. (*Reading from a page.*)
"The mules that angels ride come slowly down
The blazing passes, from beyond the sun.
Descensions of their tinkling bells arrive.
These muleteers are dainty of their way . . ."
(*Pause.*) Don't you love that! "These muleteers are *dainty* of their way . . . !?"

FANNY. Gar, the hat. How much? (GARDNER *sighs.*)

FANNY. Darling . . . ?

GARDNER. Oh yes. Let's see . . . $50? 75?

FANNY. It's French.

GARDNER. 300!

FANNY. (*Triumphant.*) No, 85¢.

GARDNER. 85¢! . . . I thought you said . . .

FANNY. That's right . . . eighty . . . five . . . *cents!*

GARDNER. Well, you sure had me fooled!

FANNY. I found it at the Thrift Shop.

GARDNER. I thought it cost at least $50 or 75. You know, designer hats are very expensive!

FANNY. It was on the mark-down table. (*She takes it off and shows him the label.*) See that? Lily Daché! When I saw that label, I nearly keeled over right into the fur coats!

GARDNER. (*Handling it.*) Well, what do you know, that's the same label that's in my bathrobe.

FANNY. Darling, Lily Daché designed hats, not men's bathrobes!

GARDNER. Yup . . . "Lily Daché" . . . same name . . .

FANNY. If you look again, I'm sure you'll see . . .

GARDNER. . . . same script, same color, same size. I'll show you. (*He exits.*)

FANNY. Poor lamb can't keep anything straight anymore. (*Looks at herself in the tray again.*) God, this is a good looking hat!

GARDNER. (*Returns with a nondescript plaid bathrobe; he points to the label.*) See that . . . ? What does it say?

FANNY. (*Refusing to look at it.*) Lily Daché was a *hat* designer! She designed ladies' hats!

GARDNER. What . . . does . . . it . . . say?

FANNY. Gardner, you're being ridiculous.

GARDNER. (*Forcing it on her.*) Read . . . the label!

FANNY. Lily Daché did *not* design this bathrobe, I don't care what the label says!

GARDNER. READ! (FANNY *reads it.*) ALL RIGHT, NOW WHAT DOES IT SAY . . . ?

FANNY. (*Chagrined.*) Lily Daché.

GARDNER. I told you!

FANNY. Wait a minute, let me look at that again. (*She does, then throws the robe at him in disgust.*) Gar, Lily Daché never designed a bathrobe in her life! Someone obviously ripped the label off one of her hats and then sewed it into the robe.

GARDNER. (*Puts it on over his jacket.*) It's damned good-looking. I've always loved this robe. I think you gave it to me . . . Well, I've got to get back to work. (*He abruptly exits.*)

FANNY. Where did you get that robe anyway? . . . I didn't give it to you, did I . . . ? (*Silence; he resumes typing. Holding the tray up again and admiring herself.*) You know, I think I *did* give it to him. I remember how excited I was when I found it at the Thrift Shop . . . 50¢ and never worn! *I* couldn't have sewn that label in to impress him, could I? . . . I can't be that far gone! . . . The poor lamb wouldn't even notice it, let alone understand its cachet . . . Uuuuh, this damned tray is even heavier than the coffee pot. They must have been amazons in the old days! (*Writes on her pad.*) "Empire tray, Parke Bernet Galleries," and good riddance! (*She wraps it and drops it into the carton with the coffee pot.*) Where *is* that wretched Mags? It would be just like her to get into a train wreck! She was supposed to be here hours ago. Well, if she doesn't show up soon, I'm going to drop dead of exhaustion. God, wouldn't that be wonderful? . . . Then they could just cart me off into storage with all the old chandeliers and china . . . (*The door bell rings.*)

FANNY. IT'S MAGS, IT'S MAGS! (*A pause; dashing out of the room, colliding into* GARDNER.) GOOD GOD, LOOK AT ME! I'M STILL IN MY BATHROBE!	GARDNER. (*Offstage.*) COMING, COMING . . . I'VE GOT IT . . . COMING! (*Dash into the room, colliding into* FANNY.) I'VE GOT IT . . . HOLD ON . . . COMING . . . COMING . . .

FANNY. (*Offstage.*) MAGS IS HERE! IT'S MAGS . . . SHE'S FINALLY HERE!

(GARDNER *exits to open the front door.* MAGS *comes staggering in carrying a suitcase and enormous duffle bag. She wears wonderfully distinctive clothes and has very much her own look. She's extremely out of breath and too wrought up to drop her heavy bags.*)

MAGS. I'm sorry . . . I'm sorry I'm so late . . . Everything went wrong! A passenger had a heart attack outside of New London and we had to stop . . . It was terrifying! All these medics and policemen came swarming onto the train and the conductor kept running up and down the aisles telling everyone not to leave their seats under any circumstances . . . Then the New London fire department came screeching down to the tracks, sirens blaring, lights whirling, and all these men in black rubber suits started pouring through the doors . . . *That* took two hours . . .

FANNY. (*Offstage.*) DARLING . . . DARLING . . . WHERE ARE YOU . . . ?

MAGS. *Then,* I couldn't get a cab at the station. There just weren't any! I must have circled the block 15 times. Finally I just stepped out into the traffic with my thumb out, but no one would pick me up . . . so I walked . . .

FANNY. (*Offstage.*) Damned zipper's stuck . . .

GARDNER. You walked all the way from the South Station?

MAGS. Well actually, I ran . . .

GARDNER. You had poor Mum scared to death.

MAGS. (*Finally puts the bags down with a deep sigh.*) I'm sorry . . . I'm really sorry. It was a nightmare.

FANNY. (*Re-enters the room, her dress over her head. The zipper's stuck, she staggers around blindly.*) Damned zipper! Gar, will you please help me with this?

MAGS. (*Squeezing him tight.*) Oh Daddy . . . Daddy!

GARDNER. My Mags!

MAGS. I never thought I'd get here! . . . Oh, you look wonderful!

GARDNER. Well, you don't look so bad yourself!

MAGS. I love your hair. It's gotten so . . . white!

FANNY. (*Still lost in her dress, struggling with the zipper.*) This is *so* typical . . . just as Mags arrives, my zipper has to break! (FANNY *grunts and struggles.*)

MAGS. (*Waves at her.*) Hi, Mum . . .

FANNY. Just a minute, dear, my zipper's . . .

GARDNER. (*Picks up* MAGS' *bags.*) Well, sit down and take a load off your feet . . .

MAGS. I was so afraid I'd never make it . . .

GARDNER. (*Staggering under the weight of her bags.*) What have you got in here? Lead weights?

MAGS. I can't believe you're finally letting me do you.

FANNY. (*Flings her arms around* MAGS, *practically knocking her over.*) OH, DAR-LING . . . MY PRECIOUS MAGS, YOU'RE HERE AT LAST.

GARDNER. (*Lurching around in circles.*) Now let's see . . . where should I put these . . . ?

FANNY. I was sure your train had derailed and you were lying dead in some ditch!

MAGS. (*Pulls away from* FANNY *to come to* GARDNER's *rescue.*) Daddy, please, let me . . . these are much too heavy.

FANNY. (*Finally noticing* MAGS.) GOOD LORD, WHAT HAVE YOU DONE TO YOUR HAIR?!

MAGS. (*Struggling to take the bags from* GARDNER.) Come on, give them to me . . . please? (*She sets them down by the sofa.*)

FANNY. (*As her dress starts to slide off one shoulder.*) Oh, not again! . . . Gar, would you give me a hand and see what's wrong with this zipper. One minute it's stuck, the next it's falling to pieces. (GARDNER *goes to her and starts fussing with it.*)

MAGS. (*Pacing.*) I don't know, it's been crazy all week. Monday, I forgot to keep an appointment I'd made with a new model . . . Tuesday, I overslept and stood up my advanced painting students . . . Wednesday, the day of my meeting with Max Zoll, I forgot to put on my underpants . . .

FANNY. GODDAMNIT, GAR, CAN'T YOU DO ANY-THING ABOUT THIS ZIPPER?!

MAGS. I mean, there I was, racing down Broome Street in this gauzy Tibetan skirt when I tripped and fell right at his feet . . . SPLATT! My skirt goes flying over my head and there I am . . . everything staring him in the face . . .

FANNY. COME ON, GAR, USE A LITTLE MUSCLE!

MAGS. (*Laughing.*) Oh well, all that matters is that I finally got here . . . I mean . . . there you are . . .

GARDNER. (*Struggling with the zipper.*) I can't see it, it's too small!

FANNY. (*Whirls away from* GARDNER, *pulling her dress off*

altogether.) OH FORGET IT! JUST FORGET IT! . . . The trolly's probably missing half its teeth, just like someone else I know. (*To* MAGS.) I grind my teeth in my sleep now, I've worn them all down to stubs. Look at that! (*She flings open her mouth and points*.) Nothing left but the gums!

GARDNER. I never hear you grind your teeth . . .

FANNY. That's because I'm snoring so loud. How could you hear anything through all that racket? It even wakes me up. It's no wonder poor Daddy has to sleep downstairs.

MAGS. (*Looking around*.) Jeez, look at the place! So, you're finally doing it . . . selling the house and moving to Cotuit year round. I don't believe it. I just don't believe it!

GARDNER. Well, how about a drink to celebrate Mags' arrival?

MAGS. You've been here so long. Why move now?

FANNY. Gardner, what are you wearing that bathrobe for . . . ?

MAGS. You can't move. I won't let you!

FANNY. (*Softly to* GARDNER.) Really darling, you ought to pay more attention to your appearance.

MAGS. You love this house. *I* love this house . . . This room . . . the light.

GARDNER. So, Mags, how about a little . . . (*He drinks from an imaginary glass*.) to wet your whistle?

FANNY. We can't start drinking now, it isn't even noon yet!

MAGS. I'm starving. I've got to get something to eat before I collapse! (*She exits towards the kitchen*.)

FANNY. What *have* you done to your hair, dear? The color's so queer and all your nice curl is gone.

GARDNER. It looks to me as if she dyed it.

FANNY. Yes, that's it. You're absolutely right! It's a completely different color. She dyed it bright red! (MAGS *can be heard thumping and thudding through the ice box*.) NOW MAGS, I DON'T WANT YOU FILLING UP ON SNACKS . . . I'VE MADE A PERFECTLY BEAUTIFUL LEG OF LAMB FOR LUNCH! . . . HELLO? . . . DO YOU HEAR ME . . . ? (*To* GARDNER.) No one in our family has *ever* had red hair, it's so common looking.

GARDNER. I like it. It brings out her eyes.

FANNY. WHY ON EARTH DID YOU DYE YOUR HAIR *RED*, OF ALL COLORS . . . ?!

MAGS. (*Returns, eating saltines out of the box*.) I didn't dye my hair, I just added some highlight.

FANNY. I suppose that's what your arty friends in New York do . . . dye their hair all the colors of the rainbow!

GARDNER Well, it's damned attractive if you ask me . . .

damned attractive! (MAGS *unzips her duffle bag and rummages around in it while eating the saltines.*)

FANNY. Darling, I told you not to bring a lot of stuff with you. We're trying to get rid of things.

MAGS. (*Pulls out a folding easel and starts setting it up.*) AAAAAHHHHHHH, here it is. Isn't it a beauty? I bought it just for you!

FANNY. Please don't get crumbs all over the floor. Crystal was just here yesterday. It was her last time before we move.

MAGS. (*At her easel.*) God, I can hardly wait! I can't believe you're finally letting me do you.

FANNY. "*Do*" us? . . . What *are* you talking about?

GARDNER. (*Reaching for the saltines.*) Hey, Mags, could I have a couple of those?

MAGS. (*Tosses him the box.*) Sure! (*To* FANNY.) Your portrait.

GARDNER. Thanks. (*He starts munching on a handful.*)

FANNY. You're planning to paint our portrait now? While we're trying to move . . . ?

GARDNER. (*Mouth full.*) Mmmmm, I'd forgotten just how delicious saltines are!

MAGS. It's a perfect opportunity. There'll be no distractions, you'll be completely at my mercy. Also, you promised.

FANNY. I did?

MAGS. Yes, you did.

FANNY. Well, I must have been off my rocker.

MAGS. No, you said, "You can paint us, you can dip us in concrete, you can do anything you want with us, just so long as you help us get out of here!"

GARDNER. (*Offering the box of saltines to* FANNY.) You really ought to try some of these, Fan, they're absolutely delicious!

FANNY. (*Taking a few.*) Why, thank you.

MAGS. I figure we'll pack in the morning and you'll pose in the afternoons. It'll be a nice diversion.

FANNY. These *are* good!

GARDNER. Here, dig in . . . take some more.

MAGS. I have some wonderful news . . . amazing news! I wanted to wait til I got here to tell you. (*They eat their saltines, passing the box back and forth as* MAGS *speaks.*) You'll die! Just fall over into the packing cartons and die! Are you ready . . . ? BRACE YOURSELVES . . . OK, HERE GOES . . . I'm being given a one-woman show at one of the most important galleries in New York this fall. Me, Margaret Church, exhibited at Castelli's, 420 West Broadway . . . Can you believe

it?! . . . MY PORTRAITS HANGING IN THE SAME ROOMS
THAT HAVE SHOWN RAUSCHENBURG, JOHNS, WAR-
HOL, KELLY, LICHTENSTEIN, STELLA, SERRA, ALL
THE HEAVIES . . . It's incredible, beyond belief . . . I mean,
at my age . . . Do you know how good you have to be to get in
there? It's a miracle . . . an honest-to-God, star spangled miracle! (*Pause.*)

FANNY. (*Mouth full.*) Oh,   GARDNER. (*Likewise.*) No
darling, that's wonderful.   one deserves it more, no
We're so happy for you!   one deserves it more!

MAGS. Through some fluke, some of Castelli's people showed
up at our last faculty show at Pratt and were knocked out . . .

FANNY. (*Reaching for the box of saltines.*) More, more . . .

MAGS. They said they hadn't seen anyone handle light like
me since the French Impressionists. They said I was this weird
blend of Pierre Bonnard, Mary Cassat and David Hockney . . .

GARDNER. (*Swallowing his own mouthful.*) I told you they
were good.

MAGS. Also, no one's doing portraits these days. They're
considered passé. I'm so out of it, I'm in.

GARDNER. Well, you're loaded with talent and always have
been.

FANNY. She gets it all from Mama, you know. Her miniature
of Henry James is still one of the main attractions at the
Atheneum. Of course no woman of breeding could be a professional artist in her day. It simply wasn't done. But talk about
talent . . . that woman had talent to burn!

MAGS. I want to do one of you for the show.

FANNY. Oh, do Daddy, he's the famous one.

MAGS. No, I want to do you both. I've always wanted to do
you and now I've finally got a good excuse.

FANNY. It's high time somebody painted Daddy again! I'm
sick to death of that dreadful portrait of him in the National
Gallery they keep reproducing. He looks like an undertaker!

GARDNER. Well, I think you should just do Mum. She's
never looked handsomer.

FANNY. Oh, come on, I'm a perfect fright and you know it.

MAGS. I want to do you both. Side by side. In this room.
Something really classy. You look so great. Mum with her crazy
hats and everything and you with that face. If I could just get
you to hold still long enough and actually pose.

GARDNER. (*Walking around, distracted.*) Where are those
papers I just had? God damnit, Fanny . . .

MAGS. I have the feeling it's either now or never.

GARDNER. I can't hold on to anything around here. (*He exits to his study.*)

MAGS. I've always wanted to do you. It would be such a challenge.

FANNY. (*Pulling* MAGS *next to her onto the sofa.*) I'm so glad you're finally here, Mags. I'm very worried about Daddy.

MAGS. Mummy, please. I just got here.

FANNY. He's getting quite gaga.

MAGS. Mummy . . . !

FANNY. You haven't seen him in almost a year. Two weeks ago he walked through the front door to the Codmans' house, kissed Emily on the cheek and settled down in the maid's room, thinking he was home!

MAGS. Oh come on, you're exaggerating.

FANNY. He's as mad as a hatter and getting worse every day! It's this damned new book of his. He works on it around the clock. I've read some of it, and it doesn't make one word of sense, it's all at sixes and sevens . . .

GARDNER. (*Poking his head back in the room, spies some of his papers on a table and grabs them.*) Ahhh, here they are. (*And exits.*)

FANNY. (*Voice lowered.*) Ever since this dry spell with his poetry, he's been frantic, absolutely . . . frantic!

MAGS. I hate it when you do this.

FANNY. I'm just trying to get you to face the facts around here.

MAGS. There's nothing wrong with him! He's just as sane as the next man. Even saner, if you ask me.

FANNY. You know what he's doing now? You couldn't guess in a million years! . . . He's writing criticism! Daddy! (*She laughs.*) Can you believe it? The man doesn't have one analytic bone in his body. His mind is a complete jumble and always has been! (*There's a loud crash from* GARDNER'S *study.*)

GARDNER. (*Offstage.*) SHIT!

MAGS. He's abstracted . . . That's the way he is.

FANNY. He doesn't spend any time with me anymore. He just holes up in that filthy study with Toots. God, I hate that bird! Though actually they're quite cunning together. Daddy's teaching him Grey's Elegy. You ought to see them in there, Toots perched on top of Daddy's head, spouting out verse after verse . . . Daddy, tap tap tapping away on his typewriter. They're quite a pair.

GARDNER. (*Pokes his head back in.*) Have you seen that Stevens' poem I was reading before?

FANNY. (*Long suffering.*) NO, I HAVEN'T SEEN THAT
STEVENS' POEM YOU WERE READING BEFORE . . . !
Things are getting very tight around here, in case you haven't
noticed. Daddy's last Pulitzer didn't even cover our real estate
tax, and now that he's too doddery to give readings anymore,
that income is gone . . . (*Suddenly handing* MAGS *the sugar
bowl she'd been wrapping.*) Mags, *do* take this sugar bowl. You
can use it to serve tea to your students at that wretched art
school of yours . . .

MAGS. It's called Pratt! The Pratt Institute.

FANNY. Pratt, Platt, whatever . . .

MAGS. And I don't serve tea to my students, I teach them
how to paint.

FANNY. Well, I'm sure none of them has ever seen a sugar
bowl as handsome as this before.

GARDNER. (*Reappearing again.*) You're sure you haven't
seen it . . . ?

FANNY. (*Loud and angry.*) YES, I'M SURE I HAVEN'T
SEEN IT! I JUST TOLD YOU I HAVEN'T SEEN IT!

GARDNER. (*Retreating.*) Right you are, right you are. (*He
exits.*)

FANNY. God! (*Silence.*)

MAGS. What do you have to yell at him like that for?

FANNY. Because the poor thing's as deaf as an adder! (MAGS
sighs deeply; silence.)

FANNY. (*Suddenly exuberant, leads her over to a lamp.*) Come,
I want to show you something.

MAGS. (*Looking at it.*) What is it?

FANNY. Something I made. (MAGS *is about to turn it on.*)
WAIT, DON'T TURN IT ON YET! It's got to be dark to get
the full effect. (*She rushes to the windows and pulls down the
shades.*)

MAGS. What *are* you doing . . . ?

FANNY. Hold your horses a minute. You'll see . . . (*As the
room gets darker and darker.*) Poor me, you wouldn't believe
the lengths I go to to amuse myself these days . . .

MAGS. (*Touching the lamp shade.*) What is this? It looks like
a scene of some sort.

FANNY. It's an invention I made . . . a kind of magic lantern.

MAGS. Gee . . . it's amazing . . .

FANNY. What I did was buy an old engraving of the Grand
Canal . . .

MAGS. You *made* this?

FANNY. . . . and then color it in with crayons. Next, I got out

my sewing scissors and cut out all the street lamps and windows
. . . anything that light would shine through. Then I pasted it
over a plain lampshade, put the shade on this old horror of a
lamp, turned on the switch and . . . (*She turns it on.*) . . .
VOILA . . . VENICE TWINKLING AT DUSK! It's quite
effective, don't you think . . . ?

MAGS. (*Walking around it.*) Jeez . . .

FANNY. And see, I poked out all the little lights on the
gondolas with a straight pin.

MAGS. Where on earth did you get the idea?

FANNY. Well you know, idle minds . . . (FANNY *spins the
shade, making the lights whirl.*)

MAGS. It's really amazing.
I mean, you could sell this
in a store!

GARDNER. (*Enters.*) HERE
IT IS. IT WAS RIGHT ON
TOP OF MY DESK THE
WHOLE TIME. (*He crashes
into a table.*) OOOOOWW-
WWW!

FANNY. LOOK OUT, LOOK OUT!

MAGS. (*Rushes over to him.*)
Oh, Daddy, are you all right!

FANNY. WATCH WHERE
YOU'RE GOING, WATCH
WHERE YOU'RE GOING!

GARDNER. (*Hopping up and down on one leg.*) GOD-
DAMNIT! . . . I HIT MY SHIN!

FANNY. I was just showing Mags my lamp . . .

GARDNER. (*Limping over to it.*) Oh yes, isn't that something? Mum is awfully clever with that kind of thing . . . It was
all her idea, the whole thing. Buying the engraving, coloring it
in, cutting out all those little dots.

FANNY. Not "dots" . . . lights and windows, lights and
windows!

GARDNER. Right, right . . . lights and windows.

FANNY. Well, we'd better get some light back in here before
someone breaks their neck. (*She zaps the shades back up.*)

GARDNER. (*Puts his arm around* MAGS.) Gee, it's good to
have you back.

MAGS. It's good to be back.

GARDNER. And I like that new red hair of yours. It's very
becoming.

MAGS. But I told you, I hardly touched it . . .

GARDNER. Well, something's different. You've got a glow.
So . . . how do you want us to pose for this grand portrait of
yours . . . ? (*He poses self-consciously.*)

MAGS. Oh Daddy, setting up a portrait takes a lot of time

and thought. You've got to figure out the background, the lighting, what to wear, the sort of mood you want to . . .

FANNY. OOOOH, LET'S DRESS UP, LET'S DRESS UP! (*She grabs a packing blanket, drapes it around herself and links arms with* GARDNER, *striking an elegant pose.*) This *is* going to be fun. She was absolutely right! Come on, Gar, look distinguished!

MAGS. Mummy please, it's not a game!

FANNY. (*More and more excited.*) You still have your tuxedo, don't you? And I'll wear my marvelous long black dress that makes me look like that fascinating woman in the Sargeant painting! (*She strikes the famous profile pose.*)

MAGS. MUMMY . . . ?!

FANNY. I'm sorry, we'll behave, just tell us what to do. (*They settle down next to each other.*)

GARDNER. That's right, you're the boss.

FANNY. Yes, you're the boss.

MAGS. But I'm not ready yet, I haven't set anything up.

FANNY. Relax, darling, we just want to get the hang of it . . . (*They stare straight ahead, trying to look like suitable subjects, but they can't hold still. They keep making faces; lifting an eyebrow, wriggling a nose, twitching a lip, nothing grotesque, just flickering little changes; a half smile here, a self-important frown there. They steal glances at each other every so often.*)

GARDNER. How am I doing, Fan?

FANNY. Brilliantly, absolutely brilliantly!

MAGS. But you're making faces.

FANNY. *I'm* not making faces, (*Turning to* GARDNER *and making a face.*) are *you* making faces, Gar?

GARDNER. (*Instantly making one.*) Certainly not! I'm the picture of restraint! (*Without meaning to, they get sillier and sillier. They start giggling, then laughing.*)

MAGS. (*Can't help but join in.*) You two are impossible . . . completely impossible! I was crazy to think I could ever pull this off! (*Laughing away.*) Look at you . . . just . . . look at you!

BLACKOUT

SCENE 2

Two days later, around five in the afternoon. Half of the Churchs' household has been dragged into the living room for packing. Overflowing cartons are everywhere. They're filled with pots and pans, dishes and glasses, and the entire contents of two linen closets. MAGS *has placed a stepladder under one of the windows. A pile of tablecloths and curtains is flung beneath it. Two side chairs are in readiness for the eventual pose.*

MAGS. (*Has just pulled a large crimson tablecloth out of a carton. She unfurls it with one shimmering toss.*) PERFECT . . . PERFECT . . . !

FANNY. (*Seated on the sofa, clutches an old pair of galoshes to her chest.*) Look at these old horrors, half the rubber is rotted away and the fasteners are falling to pieces . . . GARDNER . . . ? OH GARRRRRRRRRDNERRRRR . . . ?

MAGS. (*Rippling out the tablecloth with shorter snapping motions.*) Have you ever seen such a color . . . ?

FANNY. I'VE FOUND YOUR OLD SLEDDING GALOSHES IN WITH THE POTS AND PANS. DO YOU STILL WANT THEM?

MAGS. It's like something out of a Rubens . . . ! (*She slings it over a chair and then sits on a foot stool to finish the Sara Lee banana cake she started. As she eats, she looks at the tablecloth, making happy grunting sounds.*)

FANNY. (*Lovingly puts the galoshes on over her shoes and wiggles her feet.*) God, these bring back memories! There were real snow storms in the old days. Not these pathetic little two-inch droppings we have now. After a particularly heavy one, Daddy and I used to go sledding on the Common. This was way before you were born . . . God, it was a hundred years ago . . . ! Daddy would stop writing early, put on these galoshes and come looking for me, jingling the fasteners like castanets. It was a kind of mating call, almost . . . (*She jingles them.*) The Common was always deserted after a storm, we had the whole place to ourselves. It was so romantic . . . We'd haul the sled up Beacon Street, stop under the State House, and aim it straight down to the Park Street Church, which was much further away in those days . . . Then Daddy would lie down on the sled, I'd lower myself on top of him, we'd rock back and forth a few times to gain momentum and then . . . WHOOOOO OOOSSSSSSSSHHHHH . . . down we'd plunge like a pair of eagles locked in a spasm of love making. God, it was wonderful! . . . The city whizzing past us at ninety miles an hour . . . the cold . . . the darkness . . . Daddy's hair in my mouth . . . GAR . . . REMEMBER HOW WE USED TO GO SLEDDING IN THE OLD DAYS . . . ? Sometimes he'd lie on top of me. That was fun. I liked that even more. (*In her foghorn voice.*) GARRRRRRRRRRRDNERRRRR . . . ?

MAGS. Didn't he say he was going out this afternoon?

FANNY. Why, so he did! I completely forgot. (*She takes off the galoshes.*) I'm getting just as bad as him. (*She drops them into a different carton.*) Gar's galoshes, Cotuit. (*A pause.*)

MAGS. (*Picks up the tablecloth again, holds it high over her head.*) Isn't this fabulous . . . ? (*She then wraps FANNY in it.*) It's the perfect backdrop. Look what it does to your skin.

FANNY. Mags, what *are* you doing?

MAGS. It makes you glow like a pomegranate . . . (*She whips it off her.*) Now all I need is a hammer and nails . . . (*She finds them.*) YES! (*She climbs up the stepladder and starts hammering a corner of the cloth into the molding of one of the windows.*) This is going to look so great . . . ! I've never seen such a color!

FANNY. Darling, what is going on . . . ?

MAGS. Rembrandt, eat your heart out! You Seventeenth Century Dutch has-been, you. (*She hammers more furiously.*)

FANNY. MARGARET, THIS IS NOT A CONSTRUCTION SITE . . . PLEASE . . . STOP IT . . . YOO HOOOOO . . . DO YOU HEAR ME . . . ?

(GARDNER *suddenly appears, dressed in a raincoat.*)

FANNY. MARGARET, WILL YOU PLEASE STOP THAT RACKET?!

GARDNER. YES, DEAR, HERE I AM. I JUST STEPPED OUT FOR A WALK DOWN CHESTNUT STREET. BEAUTIFUL AFTERNOON, ABSOLUTELY BEAUTIFUL!

FANNY. (*To* MAGS.) YOU'RE GOING TO RUIN THE WALLS TO SAY NOTHING OF MAMA'S BEST TABLECLOTH . . . MAGS, DO YOU HEAR ME? . . . YOO HOO . . . !

MAGS. (*Is done, she stops.*) There!

GARDNER. WHY THAT LOOKS VERY NICE, MAGS, very nice indeed . . .

FANNY. DARLING, I MUST INSIST you stop that dreadful . . .

MAGS. (*Steps down, stands back and looks at it.*) That's it. That's *IT!*

FANNY. (*To* GARDNER, *worried.*) Where have you been?

(MAGS *kisses her fingers at the backdrop and settles back into her banana cake.*)

GARDNER. (*To* FANNY.) You'll never guess who I ran into on Chestnut Street . . . Pate Baldwin! (*He takes his coat off and drops it on the floor. He then sits in one of the posing chairs* MAGS *has pulled over by the window.*)

MAGS. (*Mouth full of cake.*) Oh Daddy, I'm nowhere near ready for you yet.

FANNY. (*Picks up his coat and hands it to him.*) Darling, coats do *not* go on the floor.

GARDNER. (*Rises, but forgets where he's supposed to go.*) He was in terrible shape. I hardly recognized him. Well, it's the Parkinson's disease . . .

FANNY. You mean, Hodgkin's disease . . .

GARDNER. Hodgkin's disease . . . ?

MAGS. (*Leaves her cake and returns to the tablecloth.*) Now to figure out exactly how to use this gorgeous light . . .

FANNY. Yes, Pate has Hodgkin's disease, not Parkinson's disease. Sammy Bishop has Parkinson's disease. In the closet . . . your coat goes . . . in the closet!

GARDNER. You're absolutely right! Pate has Hodgkin's disease. (*He stands motionless, the coat over his arm.*)

FANNY. . . . and Goat Davis has Addison's disease.

GARDNER. I always get them confused.

FANNY. (*Pointing towards the closet.*) That way . . . (GARDNER *exits to the closet;* FANNY *calling after him.*) GRACE PHELPS HAS IT TOO, I THINK. Or, it might be Hodgkin's, like Pate. I can't remember.

GARDNER. (*Returns with a hanger.*) Doesn't the Goat have Parkinson's disease?

FANNY. No, that's Sammy Bishop.

GARDNER. God, I haven't seen the Goat in ages! (*The coat still over his arm, he hands* FANNY *the hanger.*

FANNY. He hasn't been well.

GARDNER. Didn't Heppy . . . *die?!*

FANNY. What are you giving me this for? . . . Oh, Heppy's been dead for years. She died on the same day as Luster Bright, don't you remember?

GARDNER. I always liked her.

FANNY. (*Gives him back the hanger.*) Here, I don't want this.

GARDNER. She was awfully attractive.

FANNY. Who?

GARDNER. Heppy!

FANNY. Oh yes, Heppy had real charm.

MAGS. (*Keeps experimenting with draping the tablecloth.*) Better . . . better . . .

GARDNER. . . . which is something the Goat is short on, if you ask me. He has Hodgkin's disease, doesn't he? (*Puts his raincoat back on and sits down.*)

FANNY. Darling, what *are* you doing? I thought you wanted to hang up your coat!

GARDNER. (*After a pause.*) OH YES, THAT'S RIGHT! (*He goes back to the closet; a pause.*)

FANNY. Where were we?

GARDNER. (*Returns with yet another hanger.*) Let's see . . .

FANNY. (*Takes both hangers from him.*) FOR GOD'S SAKE, GAR, PAY ATTENTION!

GARDNER. It was something about the Goat . . .

FANNY. (*Takes the coat from* GARDNER.) HERE, LET ME DO IT . . . ! (*Under her breath to* MAGS.) See what I mean about him? You don't know the half of it! (*She hangs it up in the closet.*) Not the half.

MAGS. (*Still tinkering with the backdrop.*) Almost . . . almost . . .

GARDNER. (*Sitting back down on one of the posing chairs.*) Oh Fan, did I tell you, I ran into Pate Baldwin just now. I'm afraid he's not long for this world.

FANNY. (*Returning.*) Well, it's that Hodgkin's disease . . . (*She sits in the posing chair next to him.*)

GARDNER. God, I'd hate to see him go. He's one of the great editors of our times. I couldn't have done it without him. He gave me everything, everything!

MAGS. (*Makes a final adjustment.*) Yes, that's it! (*She stands back and gazes at them.*) You look wonderful . . . !

FANNY. Isn't it getting to be . . . (*She taps at an imaginary watch on her wrist and drains an imaginary glass.*) . . . cocktail time?!

GARDNER. (*Looks at his watch.*) On the button, on the button! (*He rises.*)

FANNY. I'll have the usual, please. Do join us, Mags! Daddy bought some Dubonnet especially for you!

MAGS. Hey. I was just getting some ideas.

GARDNER. (*To* MAGS *as he exits for the bar.*) How about a little . . . *Dubonnet* to wet your whistle?

FANNY. Oh Mags, it's like old times having you back with us like this!

GARDNER. (*Offstage.*) THE USUAL FOR YOU, FAN?

FANNY. I wish we saw more of you . . . PLEASE! . . . Isn't he darling? Have you ever known anyone more darling than Daddy . . . ?

GARDNER. (*Offstage; singing from the bar.*) "You Made Me Love You,"* etc. MAGS, HOW ABOUT YOU? . . . A LIT-TLE . . . DUBONNET . . . ?

FANNY. Oh, *do* join us!   MAGS. (*To* GARDNER.) No, nothing, thanks!

FANNY. Well, what do you think of your aged parents picking up and moving to Cotuit year round? Pretty crazy, eh what? . . . Just the gulls, oysters and us!

GARDNER. (*Returns with* FANNY's *drink.*) Here you go . . .

FANNY. Why thank you, Gar. (*To* MAGS.) You sure you won't join us?

GARDNER. (*Lifts his glass towards* FANNY *and* MAGS.) Cheers! (GARDNER *and* FANNY *take that first life-saving gulp.*)

FANNY. Aaaaahhhhh!   GARDNER. Hits the spot, hits the spot!

MAGS. Well, I certainly can't do you like that!

FANNY. Why not? I think we look very . . . *comme il faut!* (*She slouches into a rummy pose,* GARDNER *joins her.*) WAIT . . . I'VE GOT IT! I'VE GOT IT! (*She whispers excitedly to* GARDNER.)

MAGS. Come on, let's not start this again!

GARDNER. What's that? . . . Oh yes . . . yes, yes . . . I know the one you mean. Yes, right, right . . . of course. (*A pause.*)

FANNY. How's . . . *this* . . . ?! (FANNY *grabs a large serving fork and they fly into an imitation of Grant Wood's "American Gothic."*)

MAGS. . . . and I wonder why it's taken me all these years to get you to pose for me. You just don't take me seriously! Poor old Mags and her ridiculous portraits . . .

FANNY. Oh darling, your portraits aren't *ridiculous!* They may not be all that one *hopes* for, but they're certainly not . . .

MAGS. Remember how you behaved at my first group show in Soho? . . . Oh, come on, you remember. It was a real circus! Think back . . . It was about six years ago . . . Daddy had just been awarded some presidential medal of achievement and you insisted he wear it around his neck on a bright red ribbon, and you wore this . . . *huge* feathered hat to match! I'll never forget it! It was the size of a giant pizza with twenty-inch red turkey feathers shooting straight up into the air . . . Oh come on, you remember, don't you . . . ?

*Note: This song is still under copyright protection. Permission to use it in productions of *Painting Churches* ought to be procured from the copyright owner.

FANNY. (*Leaping to her feet.*) HOLD EVERYTHING! THIS IS IT! THIS IS REALLY IT! Forgive me for interrupting, Mags darling, it'll just take a minute. (*She whispers excitedly to* GARDNER.)

MAGS. I had about eight portraits in the show, mostly of friends of mine, except for this old one I'd done of Mrs. Crowninshield.

GARDNER. All right, all right . . . let's give it a whirl. (*A pause, then they mime Michelangelo's "Pieta" with* GARDNER *lying across* FANNY'S *lap as the dead Christ.*)

MAGS. (*Depressed.*) "The Pieta." Terrific!

FANNY. (*Jabbing* GARDNER *in the ribs.*) Hey, we're getting good at this.

GARDNER. Of course it would help if we didn't have all these modern clothes on.

MAGS. AS I WAS SAYING . . .

FANNY. Sorry, Mags . . . sorry . . . (*Huffing and creaking with the physical exertion of it all, they return to their seats.*)

MAGS. . . . As soon as you stepped foot in the gallery you spotted it and cried out, "MY GOD, WHAT'S MILLICENT CROWNINSHIELD DOING HERE?" Everyone looked up, what with Daddy's clanking medal and your amazing hat which I was sure would take off and start flying around the room. A crowd gathered . . . Through some utter fluke, you latched on to *the* most important critic in the city, I mean . . . Mr. Modern Art himself, and you hauled him over to the painting, trumpeting out for all to hear, "THAT'S MILLICENT CROWNINSHIELD! I GREW UP WITH HER. SHE LIVES RIGHT DOWN THE STEET FROM US IN BOSTON. BUT IT'S A VERY POOR LIKENESS, IF YOU ASK ME! HER NOSE ISN'T NEARLY THAT LARGE AND SHE DOESN'T HAVE SOMETHING QUEER GROWING OUT OF HERE CHIN! THE CROWNINSHIELDS ARE REALLY QUITE GOOD LOOKING, STUFFY, BUT GOOD LOOKING NONETHE-LESS!"

GARDNER. (*Suddenly jumps up, ablaze.*) WAIT, WAIT . . . IF IT'S MICHAELANGELO YOU WANT . . . I'm sorry, Mags . . . One more . . . just one more . . . please?

MAGS. Sure, why not? Be my guest.

GARDNER. *Fanny, prepare yourself!* (*He whispers into her ear.*)

FANNY. THE BEST! . . . IT'S THE BEST! OH MY DEAR-EST, YOU'RE A GENIUS, AN ABSOLUTE GENIUS! (*More whispering.*) But I think *you* should be God.

GARDNER. Me? . . . Really?

FANNY. Yes, it's much more appropriate.

GARDNER. Well, if you say so . . . (FANNY *and* GARDNER *ease down to the floor with some difficulty and lie on their sides,* FANNY *as Adam,* GARDNER *as God, their fingers inching closer and closer in the attitude of Michelangelo's "The Creation." Finally, they touch.*)

MAGS. (*Cheers, whistles, applauds.*) THREE CHEERS . . . VERY GOOD . . . NICELY DONE, NICELY DONE! (*They hold the pose a moment more, flushed with pleasure, then rise, dust themselves off and grope back to their chairs.*) So, there we were . . .

FANNY. Yes, *do* go on . . . !

MAGS. . . . huddled around Millicent Crowninshield, when you whipped into your pocketbook and suddenly announced, "HOLD EVERYTHING! I'VE GOT A PHOTOGRAPH OF HER RIGHT HERE, THEN YOU CAN SEE WHAT SHE REALLY LOOKS LIKE!" . . . You then proceeded to crouch down to the floor and dump everything out of your bag, and I mean . . . *everything!* . . . Leaking packets of sequins and gummed stars, sea shells, odd pieces of fur, crochet hooks, a Monarch butterfly embedded in plastic, dental floss, antique glass buttons, small jingling bells, lace . . . I thought I'd die! Just sink to the floor and quietly die! . . . You couldn't find it, you see. I mean, you spent the rest of the afternoon on your hands and knees crawling through this ocean of junk muttering, "It's *got* to be here somewhere, I know I had it with me!" . . . Then Daddy pulled me into the thick of it all and said, "By the way, have you met our daughter Mags yet? She's the one who did all these pictures . . . paintings . . . portraits . . . whatever you call them." (*She drops to her hands and knees and begins crawling out of the room.*) By this time, Mum had somehow crawled out of the gallery and was lost on another floor. She began calling for me . . . "YOO HOO, MAGS . . . WHERE ARE YOU? . . . OH MAGS, DARLING . . . HELLO . . . ? ARE YOU THERE . . . ?" (*She re-enters and faces them.*) This was at my *first* show.

BLACKOUT

SCENE 3

Twenty-four hours later. The impact of the impending move has struck with hurricane force. FANNY *has lugged all their clothing into the room and dumped it in various cartons. There*

are coats, jackets, shoes, skirts, suits, hats, sweaters, dresses, the
works. She and GARDNER *are seated on the sofa, going through*
it all.

FANNY. (*Wearing a different hat and dress, holds up a ratty*
overcoat.) What about this gruesome old thing?

GARDNER. (*Is wearing several sweaters and vests, a Hawaiian*
holiday shirt, and a variety of scarves and ties around his neck.
He holds up a pair of shoes.) God . . . remember these shoes?
Pound gave them to me when he came back from Italy. I
remember it vividly.

FANNY. *Do* let me give it to the Thrift Shop! (*She stuffs the*
coat into the appropriate carton.)

GARDNER. He bought them for me in Rome. Said he couldn't
resist, bought himself a pair too since we both wore the same
size. God, I miss him! (*Pause.*) HEY, WHAT ARE YOU
DOING WITH MY OVERCOAT?!

FANNY. Darling, it's threadbare!

GARDNER. But that's my overcoat! (*He grabs it out of the*
carton.) I've been wearing it every day for the past thirty-five
years!

FANNY. That's just my point: it's had it.

GARDNER. (*Puts it on over everything else.*) There's nothing
wrong with this coat!

FANNY. I trust you remember that the cottage is an eighth
the size of this place and you simply won't have room for half
this stuff! (*She holds up a sports jacket.*) This dreary old jacket,
for instance. You've had it since Hector was a pup!

GARDNER. (*Grabs it and puts it on over his coat.*) Oh no you
don't . . .

FANNY. . . . and this God-awful hat . . .

GARDNER. Let me see that. (*He stands next to her and they*
fall into a lovely frieze.)

MAGS. (*Suddenly pops out from behind a wardrobe carton*
with a flash camera and takes a picture of them.) PERFECT!

FANNY. (*Hands flying to her*   GARDNER. (*Hands flying to*
face.*) GOOD GOD, WHAT   his heart.*) JESUS CHRIST,
WAS THAT . . . ?   I'VE BEEN SHOT!

MAGS. (*Walks to the center of the room, advancing the film.*)
That was terrific. See if you can do it again.

FANNY. What *are* you doing . . . ?

GARDNER. (*Feeling his chest.*) Is there blood?

FANNY. I see lace everywhere . . .

MAGS. It's all right, I was just taking a picture of you. I often
use a Polaroid at this stage.

FANNY. (*Rubbing her eyes.*) Really Mags, you might have given us some warning!

MAGS. But that's the whole point: to catch you unawares!

GARDNER. (*Rubbing his eyes.*) It's the damndest thing . . . I see lace everywhere.

FANNY. Yes, so do I . . .

GARDNER. It's rather nice, actually. It looks as if you're wearing a veil.

FANNY. I *am* wearing a veil! (*The camera spits out the photograph.*)

MAGS. OH GOODY, HERE COMES THE PICTURE!

FANNY. (*Grabs the partially developed print out of her hands.*) Let me see, let me see . . .

GARDNER. Yes, let's have a look. (*They have another quiet moment together looking at the photograph.*)

MAGS. (*Tiptoes away from them and takes another picture.*) YES!

FANNY. NOT AGAIN! PLEASE, DARLING!	GARDNER. WHAT WAS THAT . . . ? WHAT HAP-PENED . . . ?

(*They stagger towards each other.*)

MAGS. I'm sorry, I just couldn't resist. You looked so . . .

FANNY. WHAT ARE YOU TRYING TO DO . . . *BLIND* US?!

GARDNER. Really, Mags, enough is enough . . . (GARDNER *and* FANNY *keep stumbling about, kiddingly.*)

FANNY. Are you still there, Gar?

GARDNER. Right as rain, right as rain!

MAGS. I'm sorry, I didn't mean to scare you. It's just a photograph can show you things you weren't aware of. Here, have a look. (*She gives them to* FANNY.) Well, I'm going out to the kitchen to get something to eat. Anybody want anything? (*She exits.*)

FANNY. (*Looking at the photos, half amused, half horrified.*) Oh, Gardner, have you ever . . . ?

GARDNER. (*Looks at them and laughs.*) Good grief . . .

MAGS. (*Offstage from the kitchen.*) IS IT ALL RIGHT IF I TAKE THE REST OF THIS TAPIOCA FROM LAST NIGHT?

FANNY. IT'S ALL RIGHT WITH ME. How about you, Gar?

GARDNER. Sure, go right ahead. I've never been that crazy about tapioca.

FANNY. What are you talking about, tapioca is one of your favorites.

MAGS. (*Enters, slurping from a large bowl.*) Mmmmmm-mm . . .

FANNY. Really, Mags, I've never seen anyone eat as much as you.

MAGS. (*Takes the photos back.*) It's strange. I only do this when I come home.

FANNY. What's the matter, don't I feed you enough?

GARDNER. Gee, it's hot in here! (*Starts taking off his coat.*)

FANNY. God knows, you didn't eat anything as a child! I've never seen such a fussy eater. Gar, what *are* you doing?

GARDNER. Taking off some of these clothes. It's hotter than Tofit in here! (*Shedding clothes to the floor.*)

MAGS. (*Looking at her photos.*) Yes, I like you looking at each other like that . . .

FANNY. (*To* GARDNER.) Please watch where you're dropping things, I'm trying to keep some order around here.

GARDNER. (*Picks up what he dropped, dropping even more in the process.*) Right, right . . .

MAGS. Now all I've got to do is figure out what you should wear.

FANNY. Well, I'm going to wear my long black dress, and you'd be a fool not to do Daddy in his tuxedo. He looks so distinguished in it, just like a banker!

MAGS. I haven't really decided yet.

FANNY. Just because you walk around looking like something the cat dragged in, doesn't mean Daddy and I want to, do we, Gar? (GARDNER *is making a worse and worse tangle of his clothes.*) HELLO . . . ?

GARDNER. (*Looks up at* FANNY.) Oh yes, awfully attractive, awfully attractive!

FANNY. (*To* MAGS.) If you don't mind me saying so, I've never seen you looking so forlorn. You'll never catch a husband looking that way. Those peculiar clothes, that God-awful hair . . . Really, Mags, it's very distressing!

MAGS. I don't think my hair's so bad, not that it's terrific or anything . . .

FANNY. Well, I don't see other girls walking around like you. I mean, girls from your background. What would Lyman Wigglesworth think if he saw you in the street?

MAGS. Lyman Wigglesworth?! . . . Uuuuuuughhhhhhh! (*She shudders.*)

FANNY. Alright then, that brilliant Cabot boy . . . what *is* his name?

GARDNER. Sammy.

FANNY. No, not Sammy . . .

GARDNER. Stephen.

FANNY. Oh, for God's sake, Gardner . . .

GARDNER. Stephen . . . Stanley . . . Stuart . . . Sheldon . . . Sherlock . . . It's Sherlock!

MAGS. Spence!

FANNY. SPENCE, THAT'S IT! HIS NAME IS SPENCE! 　GARDNER. THAT'S IT . . . SPENCE! SPENCE CABOT!

FANNY. Spence Cabot was first in his class at Harvard.

MAGS. Mum, he has no facial hair.

FANNY. He has his own law firm on Arlington Street.

MAGS. Spence Cabot has six fingers on his right hand!

FANNY. So, he isn't the best-looking thing in the world. Looks isn't everything. He can't help it if he has extra fingers. Have a little sympathy!

MAGS. But the extra one has this weird nail on it that looks like a talon . . . it's long and black and— (She shudders.)

FANNY. No one's perfect, darling. He has lovely handwriting and an absolutely saintly mother. Also, he's as rich as Croesus! He's a lot more promising than some of those creatures you've dragged home. What was the name of that dreadful Frenchman who smelled like sweaty socks? . . . Jean Duke of Scripto?

MAGS. (Laughing.) Jean-Luc Zichot!

FANNY. . . . And that peculiar little Oriental fellow with all the teeth! Really, Mags, he could have been put on display at the circus!

MAGS. Oh yes, Tsu Chin. He was strange, but very sexy . . .

FANNY. (Shudders.) He had such tiny . . . feet! Really, Mags, you've got to bear down. You're not getting any younger. Before you know it, all the nice young men will be taken and then where will you be? . . . All by yourself in that grim little apartment of yours with those peculiar clothes and that bright red hair . . .

MAGS. MY HAIR IS NOT BRIGHT RED!

FANNY. I only want what's best for you, you know that. You seem to go out of your way to look wanting. I don't understand it . . . Gar, what are you putting your coat on for? . . . You look like some derelict out on the street. We don't wear coats in the house. (She helps him out of it.) That's the way . . . I'll just put this in the carton along with everything else . . . (She drops it into the carton, then pauses.) Isn't it about time for . . . cocktails!

GARDNER. What's that? (FANNY taps her wrist and mimes

drinking. GARDNER *looks at his watch.*) Right you are, right you are! (*Exits to the bar.*) THE USUAL . . . ?

FANNY. *Please!*

GARDNER. (*Offstage.*) HOW ABOUT SOMETHING FOR YOU, MAGS?

MAGS. SURE WHY NOT . . . ? LET 'ER RIP!

FANNY. SHE SAID YES.   MAGS. I'LL HAVE SOME
SHE SAID YES!   DUBONNET!

GARDNER. (*Poking his head back in.*) How about a little Dubonnet?

FANNY. That's just what she said . . . she'd like some . . . Dubonnet!

GARDNER. (*Goes back to the bar and sings a Jolson tune.*) GEE, IT'S GREAT HAVING YOU BACK LIKE THIS, MAGS . . . IT'S JUST GREAT! (*More singing.*)

FANNY. (*Leaning closer to* MAGS.) You have such *potential,* darling! It breaks my heart to see how you've let yourself go. If Lyman Wigglesworth . . .

MAGS. Amazing as it may seem, I don't *care* about Lyman Wigglesworth!

FANNY. From what I've heard, he's quite a lady-killer!

MAGS. But with whom? . . . Don't think I haven't heard about his fling with . . . Hopie Stonewall!

FANNY. (*Begins to laugh.*) Oh God, let's not get started on Hopie Stonewall again . . . ten feet tall with spots on her neck . . . (*To* GARDNER.) OH DARLING, DO HURRY BACK! WE'RE TALKING ABOUT PATHETIC HOPIE STONE-WALL!

MAG. It's not so much her incredible height and spotted skin, it's those tiny pointed teeth and the size 11 shoes!

FANNY. I love it when you're like this!

(MAGS *starts clomping around the room making tiny pointed teeth nibbling sounds.*)

FANNY. GARDNER . . . YOU'RE MISSING EVERY-THING! (*Still laughing.*) Why is it Boston girls are always so . . . tall?

MAGS. Hopie Stonewall isn't a Boston girl, she's a giraffe. (*She prances around the room with an imaginary dwarf-sized Lyman.*) She's perfect for Lyman Wigglesworth!

GARDNER. (*Returns with* FANNY's *drink which he hands her.*) Now, where were we . . . ?

FANNY. (*Trying not to laugh.*) HOPIE STONEWALL! . . .

GARDNER. Oh yes, she's the very tall one, isn't she? (FANNY *and* MAGS *burst out laughing.*)

MAGS. The only hope for us . . . "Boston girls" is to get as far away from our kind as possible.

FANNY. She always asks after you, darling. She's very fond of you, you know.

MAGS. Please, I don't want to hear!

FANNY. Your old friends are *always* asking after you.

MAGS. It's not so much how creepy they all are, as how much they remind me of myself!

FANNY. But you're not "creepy," darling . . . just . . . shabby!

MAGS. I mean, give me a few more inches and some brown splotches here and there, and Hopie and I could be sisters!

FANNY. (*In a whisper to* GARDNER.) Don't you love it when Mags is like this? I could listen to her forever!

MAGS. I mean . . . look at me!

FANNY. (*Gasping.*) Don't stop, don't stop!

MAGS. Awkward . . . plain . . . I don't know how to dress, I don't know how to talk. When people find out Daddy's my father, they're always amazed . . . "Gardner Church is YOUR father?! Aw come on, you're kidding?!"

FANNY. (*In a whisper.*) Isn't she divine . . . ?

MAGS. Sometimes I don't even tell them. I pretend I grew up in the Midwest somewhere . . . farming people . . . we work with our hands.

GARDNER. (*To* MAGS.) Well, how about a little refill . . . ?

MAGS. No, no more thanks. (*Pause.*)

FANNY. What did you have to go and interrupt her for? She was just getting up a head of steam . . . ?

MAGS. (*Walking over to her easel.*) The great thing about being a portrait painter you see is, it's the *other* guy that's exposed, you're safely hidden behind the canvas and easel. (*Standing behind it.*) You can be as plain as a pitchfork, as inarticulate as mud, but it doesn't matter because you're completely concealed: your body, your face, your intentions. Just as you make your most intimate move, throw open your soul . . . they stretch and yawn, remembering the dog has to be let out at five . . . To be so invisible while so enthralled . . . it takes your breath away!

GARDNER. Well put, Mags. Awfully well put!

MAGS. That's why I've always wanted to paint you, to see if I'm up to it. It's quite a risk. Remember what I went through as a child with my great masterpiece . . . ?

FANNY. You painted a masterpiece when you were a child . . . ?

MAGS. Well, it was a masterpiece to me.

FANNY. I had no idea you were precocious as a child. Gardner, do you remember Mags painting a masterpiece as a child?

MAGS. I didn't paint it. It was something I made!

FANNY. Well, this is all news to me! Gar, *do* get me another drink! I haven't had this much fun in years! (*She hands him her glass and reaches for* MAGS'.) Come on, darling, join me . . .

MAGS. No, no more, thanks. I don't really like the taste.

FANNY. Oh come on, kick up your heels for once!

MAGS. No, nothing . . . really.

FANNY. Please? Pretty please . . . ? To keep me company?!

MAGS. (*Hands* GARDNER *her glass*.) Oh, all right, what the hell . . .

FANNY. That's a good girl! GARDNER. (*Exiting*.) Coming right up, coming right up!

FANNY. (*Yelling after him*.) DON'T GIVE ME TOO MUCH NOW. THE LAST ONE WAS AWFULLY STRONG . . . AND HURRY BACK SO YOU DON'T MISS ANYTHING . . . ! Daddy's so cunning, I don't know what I'd do without him. If anything should happen to him, I'd just . . .

MAGS. Mummy, nothing's going to happen to him . . . !

FANNY. Well, wait 'til you're our age, it's no garden party. Now . . . where were we . . . ?

MAGS. My first masterpiece . . .

FANNY. Oh yes, but *do* wait til Daddy gets back so he can hear it too . . . YOO HOOOO . . . GARRRRRRRD-NERRRRRR? . . . ARE YOU COMING . . . ? (*Silence*.) Go and check on him, will you?

GARDNER. (*Enters with both drinks; he's shaken*.) I couldn't find the ice.

FANNY. Well, *finally!*

GARDNER. It just up and disappeared . . . (*Hands* FANNY *her drink*.) There you go. (FANNY *kisses her fingers and takes a hefty swig*.) Mags. (*Hands her hers*.)

MAGS. Thanks, Daddy.

GARDNER. Sorry about the ice.

MAGS. No problem, no problem. (GARDNER *sits down; silence*.)

FANNY. (*To* MAGS.) Well, drink up, drink up! (MAGS *downs it in one gulp*.) GOOD GIRL! . . . Now, what's all this about a masterpiece . . . ?

MAGS. I did it during that winter you sent me away from the dinner table. I was about nine years old.

FANNY. We sent you from the dinner table?

MAGS. I was banished for six months.

FANNY. You *were* . . . ? How extraordinary!

MAGS. Yes, it *was* rather extraordinary!

FANNY. But why?

MAGS. Because I played with my food.

FANNY. You did?

MAGS. I used to squirt it out between my front teeth.

FANNY. Oh, I remember that! God, it used to drive me crazy, absolutely . . . crazy! (*Pause.*) "MARGARET, STOP THAT OOZING RIGHT THIS MINUTE, YOU ARE *NOT* A TUBE OF TOOTHPASTE!"

GARDNER. Oh yes . . .

FANNY. It was perfectly disgusting!

GARDNER. I remember. She used to lean over her plate and squirt it out in long runny ribbons . . .

FANNY. That's enough dear.

GARDNER. They were quite colorful, actually; decorative almost. She made the most intricate designs. They looked rather like small, moist Oriental rugs . . .

FANNY. (*To* MAGS.) But why, darling? What on earth possessed you to do it?

MAGS. I couldn't swallow anything. My throat just closed up. I don't know, I must have been afraid of choking or something.

GARDNER. I remember one in particular. We'd had chicken fricassee and spinach . . . She made the most extraordinary . . .

FANNY. (*To* GARDNER.) WILL YOU PLEASE SHUT UP?! (*Pause.*) Mags, what *are* you talking about? You never choked in your entire life! This is the most distressing conversation I've ever had. Don't you think it's distressing, Gar?

GARDNER. Well, that's not quite the word I'd use.

FANNY. What word *would* you use, then?

GARDNER. I don't know right off the bat, I'd have to think about it.

FANNY. THEN, THINK ABOUT IT! (*Silence.*)

MAGS. I guess I was afraid of making a mess. I don't know, you were awfully strict about table manners. I was always afraid of losing control. What if I started to choke and began spitting up over everything . . . ?

FANNY. Alright, dear, that's enough.

MAGS. No, I was really terrified about making a mess, you always got so mad whenever I spilled. If I just got rid of everything in neat little curly-cues beforehand, you see . . .

FANNY. I SAID: THAT'S ENOUGH! (*Silence.*)

MAGS. *I* thought it was quite ingenious, but you didn't see it that way. You finally sent me from the table with, "When you're ready to eat like a human being, you can come back and join us!" . . . So, it was off to my room with a tray. But I couldn't seem to eat there either. I mean, it was so strange settling down to dinner in my *bedroom* . . . So I just flushed everything down the toilet and sat on my bed listening to you: clinkity clink, clatter, clatter, slurp slurp . . . but that got pretty boring after a while, so I looked around for something to do. It was wintertime because I noticed I'd left some crayons on top of my radiator and they'd melted down into these beautiful shimmering globs, like spilled jello, trembling and pulsing . . .

GARDNER. (*Eyes closed.*) "This luscious and impeccable fruit of life
Falls, it appears, of its own weight to earth . . ."

MAGS. Naturally, I wanted to try it myself, so I grabbed a red one and pressed it down against the hissing lid. It oozed and bubbled like raspberry jam!

GARDNER. "When you were Eve, its acrid juice was sweet, Untasted, in its heavenly, orchard air . . ."

MAGS. I mean, that radiator was really hot! It took incredible willpower not to let go, but I held on, whispering, "Mags, if you let go of this crayon, you'll be run over by a truck on Newberry Street, so help you God!" . . . So I pressed down harder, my fingers steaming and blistering . . .

FANNY. I had no idea about any of this, did you, Gar?

MAGS. Once I'd melted one, I was hooked! I finished off my entire supply in one night, mixing color over color until my head swam . . . ! The heat, the smell, the brilliance that sank and rose . . . I'd never felt such exhilaration! . . . Every week I spent my allowance on crayons. I must have cleared out every box of Crayolas in the city!

GARDNER. (*Gazing at* MAGS.) You know, I don't think I've ever seen you looking prettier! You're awfully attractive when you get going!

FANNY. Why, what a lovely thing to say.

MAGS. AFTER THREE MONTHS THAT RADIATOR WAS . . . SPECTACULAR! I MEAN, IT LOOKED LIKE SOME COLOSSAL FRUIT CAKE, FIVE FEET TALL . . . !

FANNY. It sounds perfectly hideous.

MAGS. It was a knockout; shimmering with pinks and blues, lavenders and maroons, turquoise and golds, oranges and creams . . . For every color, I imagined a taste . . . YELLOW: lemon curls dipped in sugar . . . RED: glazed cherries laced with rum

. . . GREEN: tiny peppermint leaves veined with chocolate
. . . PURPLE: . . .

FANNY. That's quite enough!

MAGS. And then the frosting . . . ahhhh, the frosting! A
satiny mix of white and silver . . . I kept it hidden under
blankets during the day . . . My huge . . . (*She starts laughing.*)
. . . looming . . . teetering sweet . . .

FANNY. I ASKED YOU TO STOP! GARDNER, WILL
YOU PLEASE GET HER TO STOP!

GARDNER. See here, Mags, Mum asked you to . . .

MAGS. I was so . . . *hungry* . . . losing weight every week. I
looked like a scarecrow what with the bags under my eyes and
bits of crayon wrapper leaking out of my clothes. It's a wonder
you didn't notice. But finally you came to my rescue . . . if you
call what happened a rescue. It was more like a rout!

FANNY. Darling . . . *please!*   GARDNER. Now look, young
                                                        lady . . .

MAGS. The winter was almost over . . . It was very late
at night . . . I must have been having a nightmare because
suddenly you and Daddy were at my bed, shaking me . . . I
quickly glanced towards the radiator to see if it was covered
. . . *It wasn't!* It glittered and towered in the moonlight like
some . . . gigantic Viennese pastry! You followed my gaze and
saw it. Mummy screamed . . . "WHAT HAVE YOU GOT IN
HERE? . . . MAGS, WHAT HAVE YOU BEEN DOING?"
. . . She crept forward and touched it, and then jumped back.
"IT'S FOOD!" she cried . . . "IT'S ALL THE FOOD SHE'S
BEEN SPITTING OUT! OH, GARDNER, IT'S A MOUN-
TAIN OF ROTTING GARBAGE!"

FANNY. (*Softly.*) Yes . . . it's coming back . . . it's coming
back . . .

MAGS. Daddy exited as usual, left the premises. He fainted,
just keeled over onto the floor . . .

GARDNER. Gosh, I don't remember any of this . . .

MAGS. My heart stopped! I mean, I knew it was all over. My
lovely creation didn't have a chance. Sure enough . . . Out
came the blowtorch. Well, it couldn't have *really* been a blowtorch, I mean, where would you have ever gotten a blowtorch . . . ? I just have this very strong memory of you standing
over my bed, your hair streaming around your face, aiming this
. . . flame thrower at my confection . . . my cake . . . my tart
. . . my strudel . . . "IT'S GOT TO BE DESTROYED IMME-
DIATELY! THE THING'S ALIVE WITH VERMIN! . . .
JUST LOOK AT IT! . . . IT'S PRACTICALLY CRAWLING

ACROSS THE ROOM!" . . . Of course in a sense you were
right. It *was* a monument of my cast-off dinners, only I hadn't
built it with food . . . I found my own materials. I was languishing
with hunger, but oh, dear Mother . . . I FOUND MY OWN
MATERIALS . . . !

FANNY. Darling . . . *please?!*

MAGS. I tried to stop you, but you wouldn't listen . . . OUT
SHOT THE FLAME! . . . I remember these waves of wax
rolling across the room and Daddy coming to, wondering what
on earth was going on . . . Well, what did you know about my
abilities . . . ? You see, I had . . . I mean, I *have* abilities . . .
(*Struggling to say it.*) I have abilities. I have . . . strong abilities. I have . . . very strong abilities. They are very strong . . .
very very strong . . . (*She rises and runs out of the room
overcome as* FANNY *and* GARDNER *watch, speechless.*)

THE CURTAIN FALLS

ACT TWO

SCENE 1

Three days later. Miracles have been accomplished. Almost all of the Churchs' furniture has been moved out and the cartons of dishes and clothing are gone. All that remains are odds and ends. MAGS' tableau looms, impregnable. FANNY and GARDNER are dressed in their formal evening clothes, frozen in their pose. They hold absolutely still. MAGES stands at her easel, her hands covering her eyes.

FANNY. All right, you can look now.

MAGS. (*Removes her hands.*) Yes . . . ! I told you you could trust me on the pose.

FANNY. Well, thank God you let us dress up. It makes all the difference. Now we really look like something.

MAGS. (*Starts to sketch them.*) I'll say . . . (*A silence as she sketches.*)

GARDNER. (*Recites Yeats' "The Song of Wandering Aengus" in a wonderfully resonant voice as they pose.*)
"I went out to the hazel wood,
Because a fire was in my head,
And cut and peeled a hazel wand,
And hooked a berry to a thread,
And when white moths were on the wing,
And moth-like stars were flickering out,
I dropped the berry in a stream
And caught a little silver trout.

When I had laid it on the floor
I went to blow the fire a-flame,
But something rustled on the floor,
And someone called me by my name:
It had become a glimmering girl
With apple blossoms in her hair
Who called me by my name and ran

389

And faded through the brightening air.

Though I am old with wandering
Through hollow lands and hilly lands,
I will find out where she has gone,
And kiss her lips and take her hands;
And walk among long dappled grass,
And pluck till time and times are done,
The silver apples of the moon,
The golden applies of the sun."
(*Silence.*)

FANNY. That's lovely, dear. Just lovely. Is it one of yours?

GARDNER. No, no, it's Yeats. I'm using it in my book.

FANNY. Well, you recited it beautifully, but then you've always recited beautifully. That's how you wooed me, in case you've forgotten . . . You must have memorized every love poem in the English language! There was no stopping you when you got going . . . your Shakespeare, Byron, and Shelley . . . you were shameless . . . *shameless!*

GARDNER. (*Eyes closed.*)
"I will find out where she has gone,
And kiss her lips and take her hands . . ."

FANNY. And then there was your own poetry to do battle with; your sonnets and quatrains. When you got going with them, there was nothing left of me! You could have had your pick of any girl in Boston! Why you chose me, I'll never understand. I had no looks to speak of and nothing much in the brains department . . . Well, what did you know about women and the world . . . ? What did any of us know . . . ? (*Silence.*) GOD, MAGS, HOW LONG ARE WE SUPPOSED TO SIT LIKE THIS . . . IT'S AGONY!

MAGS. (*Working away.*) You're doing fine . . . just fine . . .

FANNY. (*Breaking her pose.*) It's so . . . boring!

MAGS. Come on, don't move. You can have a break soon.

FANNY. I had no idea it would be so boring!

GARDNER. Gee, I'm enjoying it.

FANNY. You would . . . ! (*A pause.*)

GARDNER. (*Begins reciting more Yeats, almost singing it.*)
"He stood among a crowd at Drumahair;
His heart hung all upon a silken dress,
And he had known at last some tenderness,
Before earth made of him her sleepy care;
But when a man poured fish into a pile,
It seemed they raised their little silver heads . . ."

FANNY. Gar . . . PLEASE! (*She lurches out of her seat.*)
God, I can't take this anymore!

MAGS. (*Keeps sketching* GARDNER) I know it's tedious at
first, but it gets easier . . .

FANNY. It's like a Chinese water torture! . . . (*Crosses to*
MAGS *and looks at* GARDNER *posing.*) Oh darling, you look
marvelous, absolutely marvelous! Why don't you just do Daddy!?

MAGS. Because you look marvelous too. I want to do you
both!

FANNY. Please . . . ! I have one foot in the grave and you
know it! Also, we're way behind in our packing. There's still
one room left which everyone seems to have forgotten about!

GARDNER. Which one is that?

FANNY. You know perfectly well which one it is!

GARDNER. I do . . . ?

FANNY. Yes, you do!

GARDNER. Well, it's news to me.

FANNY. I'll give you a hint. It's in . . . *that* direction. (*She
points.*)

GARDNER. The dining room.

FANNY. No.

GARDNER. The bedroom.

FANNY. No.

GARDNER. Mags' room.

FANNY. No.

GARDNER. The kitchen.

FANNY. *Gar . . . ?!*

GARDNER. The guest room?

FANNY. Your God awful study!

GARDNER. Oh, shit!

FANNY. That's right, "oh shit!" It's books and papers up to
the ceiling! If you ask me, we should just forget it's there and
quietly tiptoe away . . .

GARDNER. My study . . . !

FANNY. Let the new owners dispose of everything . . .

GARDNER. (*Gets out of his posing chair.*) Now, just one
minute . . .

FANNY. You never look at half the stuff in there!

GARDNER. I don't want you touching those books! They're
mine!

FANNY. Darling, we've moving to a cottage the size of a
handkerchief! Where, pray tell, is there room for all your
books?

GARDNER. I don't know. We'll just have to make room!

MAGS. (*Sketching away.*) RATS!

FANNY. I don't know what we're doing fooling around with Mags like this when there's still so much to do . . .

GARDNER. (*Sits back down, overwhelmed.*) My study . . . !

FANNY. You can stay with her if you'd like, but one of us has got to tackle those books! (*She exits to his study.*)

GARDNER. I'm not up to this.

MAGS. Oh good, you're staying!

GARDNER. There's a lifetime of work in there . . .

MAGS. Don't worry, I'll help. Mum and I will be able to pack everything up in no time.

GARDNER. God . . .

MAGS. It won't be so bad . . .

GARDNER. I'm just not up to it.

MAGS. We'll all pitch in . . .

(GARDNER *sighs, speechless. A silence as* MAGS *keeps sketching him.* FANNY *comes staggering in with an armload of book which she drops to the floor with a crash.*)

GARDNER. WHAT   MAGS. GOOD GRIEF!
WAS THAT . . . ?!

FANNY. (*Sheepish.*) Sorry, sorry . . . (*She exits for more.*)

GARDNER. I don't know if I can take this . . .

MAGS. Moving is awful . . . I know . . .

GARDNER. (*Settling back into his pose.*) Ever since Mum began tearing the house apart, I've been having these dreams . . . I'm a child again back at 16 Louisberg Square . . . and this stream of moving men is carrying furniture into our house . . . van after van of tables and chairs, sofas and loveseats, desks and bureaus . . . rugs, bathtubs, mirrors, chiming clocks, pianos, ice boxes, china cabinets . . . but what's amazing is that all of it is familiar . . . (FANNY *comes in with another load which she drops on the floor. She exits for more.*) No matter how many items appear, I've seen every one of them before. Since my mother is standing in the midst of it directing traffic, I ask her where it's all coming from, but she doesn't hear me because of the racket . . . so finally I just scream out . . . "WHERE IS ALL THIS FURNITURE COMING FROM?" . . . Just as a mover man is carrying Toots into the room, she looks at me and says, "Why, from the land of Skye!" . . . The next thing I know, *people* are being carried in along with it . . . (FANNY *enters with her next load, drops it and exits.*) . . . people I've never seen before are sitting around our dining room table. A group of foreigners is going through my books, chattering in a language I've never heard before. A man is playing a Chopin Polonaise on Aunt Alice's piano. Several children are taking baths in our tubs from Cotuit . . .

MAGS. It sounds marvelous.

GARDNER. Well, it isn't marvelous at all because all of these perfect strangers have taken over our things . . . (FANNY enters, hurls down another load and exits.)

MAGS. How odd . . .

GARDNER. Well, it *is* odd, but then something even odder happens . . .

MAGS. (Sketching away.) Tell me, tell me!

GARDNER. Well, our beds are carried in. They're all made up with sheets and everything, but instead of all these strange people in them, *we're* in them . . . !

MAGS. What's so odd about that . . . ?

GARDNER. Well, you and Mum are brought in, both sleeping like angels . . . Mum snoring away to beat the band . . .

MAGS. Yes . . . (FANNY enters with an other load, lets if fall.)

GARDNER. But there's no one in mine. It's completely empty, never even been slept in! It's as if I were dead or had never even existed . . . (FANNY exits.) "HEY . . . WAIT UP!" I yell to the moving men . . . "THAT'S MY BED YOU'VE GOT THERE!" but they don't stop, they don't even acknowledge me . . . "HEY, COME BACK HERE . . . I WANT TO GET INTO MY BED!" I cry again and I start running after them . . . down the hall, through the dining room, past the library . . . Finally I catch up to them and hurl myself right into the center of the pillow. Just as I'm about to land, the bed suddenly vanishes and I go crashing down to the floor like some insect that's been hit by a fly swatter!

FANNY. (Staggers in with her final load, drops it with a crash and then collapses in her posing chair.) THAT'S IT FOR ME! I'M DEAD! (Silence.) Come on, Mags, how about you doing a little work around here.

MAGS. That's all I've been doing! This is the first free moment you've given me!

FANNY. You should see all the books in there . . . and papers! There are enough loose papers to sink a ship!

GARDNER. Why is it we're moving, again . . . ?

FANNY. Because life is getting too complicated here.

GARDNER. (Remembering.) Oh yes . . .

FANNY. And we can't afford it anymore.

GARDNER. That's right, that's right . . .

FANNY. We don't have the . . . *income* we used to!

GARDNER. Oh yes . . . *income!*

FANNY. (*Assuming her pose again.*) Of course we have our savings and various trust funds, but I wouldn't dream of touching those!

GARDNER. No, no, you must never dip into capital!

FANNY. I told Daddy I'd be perfectly happy to buy a gun and put a bullet through our heads so we could avoid all this, but he wouldn't hear of it!

MAGS. (*Sketching away.*) No, I shouldn't think so. (*Pause.*)

FANNY. I've always admired people who kill themselves when they get to our stage of life. Well, no one can touch my Uncle Edmond in that department . . .

MAGS. I know, I know . . .

FANNY. The day before his seventieth birthday he climbed to the top of the Old North Church and hurled himself face down into Salem Street! They had to scrape him up with a spatula! God, he was a remarkable man . . . state senator, President of Harvard . . .

GARDNER. (*Rises and wanders over to his books.*) Well, I guess I'm going to have to do something about all of these . . .

FANNY. Come on, Mags, help Daddy! Why don't you start bringing in his papers . . . (GARDNER *sits on the floor, picks up a book and soon is engrossed in it.* MAGS *keeps sketching, oblivious. Silence. To* MAGS. Darling . . . ? HELLO . . . ? (*They both ignore her.*) God, you two are impossible! Just look at you . . . heads in the clouds! No one would ever know we've got to be out of here in two days. If it weren't for me, nothing would get done around here . . . (*She starts stacking* GARD-NER'S *books into piles.*) There! That's all the maroon ones!

GARDNER. (*Looks up.*) What do you mean, *maroon* ones . . . ?!

FANNY. All your books that are maroon are in *this* pile . . . and your books that are green in *that* pile . . . ! I'm trying to bring some order into your life for once. This will make unpacking so much easier.

GARDNER. But my dear Fanny, it's not the color of a book that distinguishes it, but what's *inside* it!

FANNY. This will be a great help, you'll see. Now what about this awful striped thing? (*She picks up a slim, aged volume.*) Can't it go . . . ?

GARDNER. No!

FANNY. But it's as queer as Dick's hatband! There are no others like it.

GARDNER. Open it and read. Go on . . . open it!

FANNY. We'll get nowhere at this rate.

GARDNER. I said . . READ!

FANNY. Really, Gar, I . . .

GARDNER. Read the dedication!

FANNY. (*Opens and reads.*) "To Gardner Church, you led the way. With gratitude and affection. Robert Frost." (*She closes it and hands it to him.*)

GARDNER. It was published the same year as my "Salem Gardens."

FANNY. (*Picking up a very dirty book.*) Well, what about this dreadful thing? It's filthy. (*She blows off a cloud of dust.*)

GARDNER. Please . . . *please?!*

FANNY. (*Looking through it.*) It's all in French.

GARDNER. (*Snatching it away from her.*) Andre Malraux gave me that . . . !

FANNY. I'm just trying to help.

GARDNER. It's a first edition of Baudelaire's "Fleurs du Mal."

FANNY. (*Giving it back.*) Well, pardon me for living!

GARDNER. Why do you have to drag everything in here in the first place . . ?

FANNY. Because there's no room in your study. You ought to see the mess in there! . . . WAKE UP, MAGS, ARE YOU GOING TO PITCH IN OR NOT . . . ?!

GARDNER. I'm not up to this.

FANNY. Well, you'd better be unless you want to be left behind!

MAGS. (*Stops her sketching.*) Alright, alright . . . I just hope you'll give me some more time later this evening.

FANNY. (*To* MAGS.) Since you're young and in the best shape, why don't you bring in the books and I'll cope with the papers. (*She exits to the study.*)

GARDNER. Now just a minute . . .

FANNY. (*Offstage.*) WE NEED A STEAM SHOVEL FOR THIS!

MAGS. O.K., what do you want me to do?

GARDNER. Look, I don't want you messing around with my . . . (FANNY *enters with an armful of papers which she drops into an empty carton.*) HEY, WHAT'S GOING ON HERE . . . ?

FANNY. I'm packing up your papers. COME ON, MAGS, LET'S GET CRACKING! (*She exits for more papers.*)

GARDNER. (*Plucks several papers out of the carton.*) What is this . . . ?

MAGS. (*Exits into his study.*) GOOD LORD, WHAT HAVE YOU DONE IN HERE . . . ?!

GARDNER. (*Reading.*) This is my manuscript. (FANNY *enters with another batch which she tosses on top of the others.*) What *are* you doing . . . ?!

FANNY. Packing, darling . . . PACKING! (*She exits for more.*)

GARDNER. SEE HERE. YOU CAN'T MANHANDLE MY THINGS THIS WAY! (MAGS *enters, staggering under a load of books which she sets down on the floor.*) I PACK MY MANU-SCRIPT! I KNOW WHERE EVERYTHING IS!

FANNY. (*Offstage.*) IF IT WERE UP TO YOU, WE'D NEVER GET OUT OF HERE! WE'RE UNDER A TIME LIMIT, GARDNER. KITTY'S PICKING US UP IN TWO DAYS . . . TWO . . . DAYS! (*She enters with a larger batch of papers and heads for the carton.*)

GARDNER. (*Grabbing* FANNY'S *wrist.*) NOW, HOLD IT . . . ! JUST . . . HOLD IT RIGHT THERE . . . !

FANNY. OOOOOWWWWWWWWWW!

GARDNER. *I* PACK MY THINGS . . . !

FANNY. LET GO, YOU'RE HURTING ME!

GARDNER. THAT'S MY MANUSCRIPT! GIVE IT TO ME!

FANNY. (*Lifting the papers high over her head.*) I'M IN CHARGE OF THIS MOVE, GARDNER! WE'VE GOT TO GET CRACKING!

GARDNER. I said . . . GIVE IT TO ME!

MAGS. Come on, Mum, let him have it. (*They struggle.*)

GARDNER. (*Finally wrenches the pages from her.*) LET . . . ME . . . HAVE IT . . . ! THAT'S MORE LIKE IT . . . !

FANNY. (*Soft and weepy.*) You see what he's like . . . ? I try and help with his packing and what does he do . . . ?

GARDNER. (*Rescues the rest of his papers from the carton.*) YOU DON'T JUST THROW EVERYTHING INTO A BOX LIKE A PILE OF GARBAGE! THIS IS A BOOK, FANNY. SOMETHING I'VE BEEN WORKING ON FOR TWO YEARS . . . ! (*Trying to assemble his papers, but only making things worse, dropping them all over the place.*) You show a little respect for my things . . . you don't just throw them around every which way . . . It's tricky trying to make sense of poetry, it's much easier to write the stuff . . . that is, if you've still got it in you . . .

MAGS. Here, let me help . . . (*Taking some of the papers.*)

GARDNER. Criticism is tough sledding. You can't just dash off a few images here, a few rhymes there . . .

MAGS. Do you have these pages numbered in any way?

FANNY. (*Returning to her posing chair.*) HA!

GARDNER. This is just the introduction.

MAGS. I don't see any numbers on these.

GARDNER. (*Exiting to his study.*) The important stuff is in my study . . .

FANNY. (*To* MAGS) You don't know the half of it . . . *Not the half . . .* !

GARDNER. (*Offstage; thumping around.*) HAVE YOU SEEN THOSE YEATS POEMS I JUST HAD . . . ?

MAGS. (*Reading over several pages.*) What is this . . . ? It doesn't make sense. It's just fragments . . . pieces of poems.

FANNY. That's it, honey! That's his book. His great critical study! Now that he can't write his own poetry, he's trying to explain other people's. The only problem is, he can't get beyond typing them out. The poor lamb doesn't have the stamina to get beyond the opening stanzas, let alone trying to make sense of them.

GARDNER. (*Thundering back with more papers which keep falling.*) GOD DAMNIT, FANNY, WHAT DID YOU DO IN THERE! I CAN'T FIND ANYTHING!

FANNY. I just took the papers that were on your desk.

GARDNER. Well, the entire beginning is gone. (*He exits.*)

FANNY. I'M TRYING TO HELP YOU, DARLING!

GARDNER. (*Returning with another armload.*) SEE THAT . . . ? NO SIGN OF CHAPTER ONE OR TWO . . . (*He flings it all down to the floor.*)

FANNY. Gardner . . . PLEASE?!

GARDNER. (*Kicking through the mess.*) I TURN MY BACK FOR ONE MINUTE AND WHAT HAPPENS . . . ? MY ENTIRE STUDY IS TORN APART! (*He exits.*)

MAGS. Oh Daddy . . . don't . . . please . . . Daddy . . . please?!

GARDNER. (*Returns with a new batch of papers which he tosses up into the air.*) THROWN OUT . . . ! THE BEST PART IS THROWN OUT! . . . LOST . . . (*He starts to exit again.*)

MAGS. (*Reads one of the fragments to steady herself.*)
"I have known the inexorable sadness of pencils
Neat in their boxes, dolor of pad and paper-weight,
All the misery of manila folders and mucilage . . ."

They're beautiful . . . just beautiful.

GARDNER. (*Stops.*) Hey, what's that you've got there?

FANNY. It's your manuscript, darling. You see, it's right where you left it.

GARDNER. (*To* MAGS.) Read that again.

MAGS.

"I have known the inexorable sadness of pencils,
Neat in their boxes, dolor of pad and paper-weight,
All the misery of manila folders and mucilage . . ."

GARDNER. Well, well, what do you know . . .

FANNY. (*Hands him several random papers.*) You see . . . no
one lost anything. Everything's here, still intact.

GARDNER. (*Reads.*)

"I knew a woman, lovely in her bones,
When small birds sighed, she would sigh back at them;
Ah, when she moved, she moved more ways than one:
The shapes a bright container can contain! . . ."

FANNY. (*Hands him another.*) And . . .

GARDNER. Ah, yes, Frost . . . (*Reads.*)

"Some say the world will end in fire,
Some say ice.
From what I've tasted of desire
I hold with those who favor fire."

FANNY. (*Under her breath to* MAGS.) He can't give up the
words. It's the best he can do. (*Handing him another.*) Here
you go, here's more.

GARDNER.

"Farm boys wild to couple
With anything   with soft-wooded trees
With mounds of earth   mounds
Of pinestraw   will keep themselves off
Animals by legends of their own . . ."

MAGS. (*Eyes shut.*) Oh Daddy, I can't bear it . . . I . . .

FANNY. Of course no one will ever publish this.

GARDNER. Oh, here's a marvelous one. Listen to this!

"There came a Wind like a Bugle—
It quivered through the Grass
And a Green Chill upon the Heat
So ominous did pass
We barred the Windows and the Doors
As from an Emerald Ghost—

The Doom's electric Moccasin . . ."

SHIT, WHERE DID THE REST OF IT GO . . . ?

FANNY. Well, don't ask *me*.

GARDNER. It just stopped in midair!

FANNY. Then go look for the original.

GARDNER. Good idea, good idea! (*He exits to his study.*)

FANNY. (*To* MAGS.) He's incontinent now too. He wets his pants, in case you haven't noticed. (*She starts laughing.*) You're not laughing. Don't you think it's funny? Daddy needs diapers . . . I don't know about you, but I could use a drink! GAR . . . WILL YOU GET ME A SPLASH WHILE YOU'RE OUT THERE . . . ?

MAGS. STOP IT!

FANNY. It means we can't go out anymore. I mean, what would people say . . . ?

MAGS. Stop it. Just stop it.

FANNY. My poet laureate can't hold it in! (*She laughs harder.*)

MAGS. That's enough . . . STOP IT . . . Mummy . . . I beg of you . . . *please stop it!*

GARDNER. (*Enters with a book and indeed a large stain has blossomed on his trousers. He plucks it away from his leg.*) Here we go . . . I found it . . .

FANNY. (*Pointing at it.*) See that? See . . . ? He just did it again! (*Goes off into a shower of laughter.*)

MAGS. (*Looks, turns away.*) SHUT . . . UP . . . ! (*Building to a howl.*) WILL YOU PLEASE JUST . . . SHUT . . . UP!

FANNY. (*To* GARDNER.) Hey, what about that drink?

GARDNER. Oh yes . . . sorry, sorry . . . (*He heads towards the bar.*)

FANNY. Never mind, I'll get it, I'll get it. (*She exits, convulsed. Silence.*)

GARDNER. Well, where were we . . . ?

MAGS. (*Near tears.*) Your poem.

GARDNER. Oh yes . . . the Dickinson. (*He shuts his eyes, reciting from memory, holding the book against his chest.*) "There came a Wind like a Bugle—
It quivered through the Grass
And a Green Chill upon the Heat
So ominous did pass
We barred the Windows and the Doors
As from an Emerald Ghost—"
(*Opens the book and starts riffling through it.*) Let's see now, where's the rest . . . ? (*He finally finds it.*) Ahhh, here we go . . . !

FANNY. (*Re-enters, drink in hand.*) I'm back! (*Takes one look at* GARDNER *and bursts out laughing again.*)

MAGS. I don't believe you! How you can laugh at him . . . ?!

FANNY. I'm sorry, I wish I could stop, but there's really nothing else to do. Look at him . . . just . . . look at him . . . !

MAGS. (*This is all simultaneous as* MAGS *gets angrier and angrier.*) It's so cruel . . . you're so . . . incredibly cruel to him . . . I mean, YOUR DISDAIN REALLY TAKES MY BREATH AWAY! YOU'RE IN A CLASS BY YOURSELF WHEN IT COMES TO HUMILIATION . . . !

GARDNER. (*Reading.*)
"The Doom's electric Moccasin
That very instant passed—
On a strange Mob of panting Trees
And Fences fled away
And Rivers where the Houses ran
Those looked that lived—that Day—
The Bell within the steeple wild
The flying tidings told—
How much can come
And much can go,
And yet abide the World!"
(*He shuts the book with a bang, pauses and looks around the room, confused.*) Now, where was I . . . ?

FANNY. Safe and sound in the middle of the living room with Mags and me.

GARDNER. But I was looking for something, wasn't I . . . ?

FANNY. Your manuscript.

GARDNER. THAT'S RIGHT! MY MANUSCRIPT! My manuscript!

FANNY. And here it is all over the floor. See, you're standing on it.

GARDNER. (*Picks up a few pages and looks at them.*) Why, so I am . . .

FANNY. Now all we have to do is get it up off the floor and packed neatly into these cartons!

GARDNER. Yes, yes, that's right. Into the cartons.

FANNY. (*Kicks a carton over to him.*) Here, you use this one and I'll start over here . . . (*She starts dropping papers into a carton nearby.*) . . . BOMBS AWAY . . . ! Hey . . . this is fun . . . !

GARDNER. (*Picks up his own pile, lifts it high over his head and flings it down into the carton.*) BOMBS AWAY . . . This *is* fun . . . !

FANNY. I told you! The whole thing is to figure out a system!

GARDNER. I don't know what I'd do without you, Fan. I thought I'd lost everything.

FANNY. (*Makes dive-bomber noises and machine-gun explo-*

sions as she wheels more and more papers into the carton.)
TAKE THAT AND THAT AND THAT . . . !

GARDNER. (*Joins in the fun, outdoing her with dips, dives and blastings of his own.*) BLAM BLAM BLAM BLAM! . . . ZZZZZZZZRAAAAAAAA FOOM! . . . BLATTY DE BLATTY DE BLATTY DE KABOOOOOOOOM . . . ! WHA-AAAAAA . . . DA DAT DAT DAT DAT . . . WHEEE-EEEEEAAAAAAAAAAAA . . . FOOOOOO . . . (*They get louder and louder as papers fly every which way.*)

FANNY. (*Mimes getting hit with a bomb.*) AEEEEEEII-IIIIIIIIIIII! YOU GOT ME RIGHT IN THE GIZZARD! (*She collapses on the floor and starts going through death throes, having an absolute ball.*)

GARDNER. TAKE THAT AND THAT AND THAT AND THAT . . . (*A series of explosions follow.*)

MAGS. (*Furious.*) This is how you help him . . . ? THIS IS HOW YOU PACK HIS THINGS . . . ?

FANNY. I keep him company. I get involved . . . which is a hell of a lot more than you do!

MAGS. (*Wild with rage.*) BUT YOU'RE MAKING A MOCK-ERY OF HIM . . . YOU TREAT HIM LIKE A CHILD OR SOME DIM-WITTED SERVING BOY. HE'S JUST AN AMUSEMENT TO YOU . . . !

FANNY. (*Fatigue has finally overtaken her. She's calm to the point of serenity.*) . . . and to you who see him once a year, if that . . . What is he to *you*? . . . I mean, what do you give him from yourself that costs you something . . . ? Hmmmmmm . . . ? (*Imitating her.*) "Oh, hi Daddy, it's great to see you again. How have you been? . . . Gee, I love your hair. It's gotten so . . . *white!*" . . . What color do you expect it to get when he's this age . . . ? I mean, if you care so much how he looks, why don't you come and see him once in a while? . . . But oh no . . . you have your paintings to do and your shows to put on. You just come and see us when the whim strikes. (*Imitating her.*) "Hey, you know what would be really great? . . . To do a portrait of you! I've always wanted to paint you, you're such great subjects!" . . . *Paint* us . . . ?! What about opening your eyes and really *seeing* us . . . ? Noticing what's going on around here for a change! It's all over Daddy and me. This is it! "Finita la commedia!" . . . All I'm trying to do is exit with a little flourish, have some fun . . . What's so terrible about that? . . . It can get pretty grim around here, in case you haven't noticed . . . Daddy, tap, tap tapping out his nonsense all day; me traipsing around to the thrift shops trying to amuse myself . . . He never keeps me company anymore, never takes me out anywhere . . . I'd put a bullet through my head in a minute, but then who'd look after him? . . . What do you think we're moving to the cottage for . . . ? So I can watch him like a hawk and make sure he doesn't get lost. Do you think that's anything to look forward to? . . . Being Daddy's nursemaid out in the middle of nowhere? I'd much rather stay here in Boston with the few friends I have left, but you can't always do what you want in this world! "L'homme propose, Dieu dispose!" . . . If you want to paint us so badly, you ought to paint us as we really are. There's your picture . . . ! (*She points to* GARDNER *who's quietly playing with a paper glider.*) . . . Daddy spread out on the floor with all his toys and me hovering over him to make sure he doesn't hurt himself! (*She goes over to him.*) YOO HOO . . . GAR . . . ? . . . HELLO? . . .

GARDNER. (*Looks up at her.*) Oh, hi there, Fan. What's up?

FANNY. How's the packing coming . . . ?

GARDNER. Packing . . . ?

FANNY. Yes, you were packing your manuscript, remember? (*She lifts up a page and lets it fall into a carton.*)

GARDNER. Oh yes . . .

FANNY. Here's your picture, Mags. Face over this way . . . turn your easel over here . . . (*She lets a few more papers fall.*) Up, up . . . and away . . .

BLACKOUT

SCENE 2

The last day. All the books and boxes are gone. The room is completely empty except for MAG'S *backdrop. Late afternoon light dapples the walls; it changes from pale peach to deeper violet. The finished portrait sits on the easel covered with a cloth.* MAGS *is taking down the backdrop.*)

FANNY. (*Offstage to* GARDNER.) DON'T FORGET TOOTS!

GARDNER. (*Offstage from another part of the house.*) WHAT'S THAT . . . ?

FANNY. (*Offstage.*) I SAID: DON'T FORGET TOOTS! HIS CAGE IS SITTING IN THE MIDDLE OF YOUR STUDY! (*Silence.*)

FANNY. (*Offstage.*)	GARDNER. (*Offstage.*)
HELLO . . . ? ARE YOU THERE?	I'LL BE RIGHT WITH YOU, I'M JUST GETTING TOOTS!

GARDNER. (*Offstage.*) WHAT'S WHAT? I CAN'T HEAR YOU?

FANNY. (*Offstage.*) I'M GOING THROUGH THE ROOMS ONE MORE TIME TO MAKE SURE WE DIDN'T FORGET ANYTHING . . . KITTY'S PICKING US UP IN FIFTEEN MINUTES, SO PLEASE BE READY . . . SHE'S DROP-PING MAGS OFF AT THE STATION AND THEN IT'S OUT TO ROUTE 3 AND THE CAPE HIGHWAY . . .

GARDNER. (*Enters, carrying Toots in his cage.*) Well, this is it. The big moment has finally come, eh what, Toots? (*He sees* MAGS.) Oh hi there, Mags, I didn't see you . . .

MAGS. Hi, daddy. I'm just taking this down . . . (*She does and walks over to Toots.*) Oh Toots, I'll miss you. (*She makes little chattering noises into his cage.*)

GARDNER. Come on, recite a little Grey's Elegy for Mags before we go.

MAGS. Yes, Mum said he was really good at it now.

GARDNER. Well, the whole thing is to keep at it every day. (*Slowly to Toots.*)
"The curfew tolls the knell of parting day,
The lowing herd wind slowly o'er the lea . . ."
Come on, show Mags your stuff!
(*Slower.*)
"The curfew tolls the knell of parting day,
The lowing herd wind slowly o'er the lea."
(*Silence; he makes little chattering sounds.*) Come on, Toots, old boy . . .

MAGS. How does it go?

GARDNER. (*To* MAGS.)
"The curfew tolls the knell of parting day,
The lowing herd wind slowly o'er the lea . . ."

MAGS. (*Slowly to Toots.*)
"The curfew tolls for you and me,
As quietly the herd winds down . . ."

GARDNER. No, no, it's: "The curfew tolls the knell of parting *day* . . . !

MAGS. (*Repeating after him.*) "The curfew tolls the knell of parting day . . ."

GARDNER. . . . . "The lowing herd wind slowly o'er the lea . . ."

MAGS. (*With a deep breath.*)
"The curfew tolls at parting day,
The herd low slowly down the lea . . . no, *knell!*
They come winding down the *knell* . . . !"

GARDNER. Listen, Mags . . . *listen!* (*A pause.*)

TOOTS. (*Loud and clear with* GARDNER's *inflection*)
"The curfew tolls the knell of parting day,
The lowing herd wind slowly o'er the lea,
The ploughman homeward plods his weary way,
And leaves the world to darkness and to me."

MAGS. HE SAID IT . . . HE SAID IT! . . . AND IN YOUR
VOICE! . . . OH DADDY, THAT'S AMAZING!

GARDNER. Well, Toots is very smart, which is more than I
can say for a lot of people I know . . .

MAGS. (*To* TOOTS.) "Polly want a cracker? Polly want a
cracker?"

GARDNER. You can teach a parakeet to say anything, all you
need is patience . . .

MAG. But *poetry* . . . that's so hard . . .

FANNY. (*Enters carrying a suitcase and* GARDNER's *typewriter
in its case. She's dressed in her traveling suit wearing a hat to
match.*) WELL, THERE YOU ARE! I THOUGHT YOU'D
DIED!

MAGS. (*To* FANNY.) He said it! I finally heart Toots recite
Grey's Elegy. (*Leaning close to the cage.*) "Polly want a cracker?
Polly want a cracker?"

FANNY. Isn't it uncanny how much he sounds like Daddy?
Sometimes when I'm alone here with him, I've actually thought
he *was* Daddy and started talking to him. Oh yes, Toots and I
have had quite a few meaty conversations together! (FANNY
wolf whistles into the cage, then draws back. GARDNER *covers
the cage with a traveling cloth. Silence.*)

FANNY. (*Looks around the room.*) God, the place looks so
bare.

MAGS. I still can't believe it . . . Cotuit, year round. I wonder if there'll be any phosphorus when you get there?

FANNY. What on earth are you talking about? (*Spies the
backdrop on the floor, carries it out to the hall.*)

MAGS. Remember that summer when the ocean was full of
phosphorus?

GARDNER. (*Carrying Toots out into the hall.*) Oh yes . . .

MAGS. It was a great mystery where it came from or why it
settled in Cotuit. But one evening when Daddy and I were
taking a swim, suddenly it was there!

GARDNER. (*Returns.*) I remember.

MAGS. I don't know where Mum was . . .

FANNY. (*Re-enters.*) Probably doing the dishes!

MAGS. (*To* GARDNER.) As you dove into the water, this
shower of silvery-green sparks erupted all around you. It was

incredible! I thought you were turning into a saint or something, but then you told me to jump in too and the same thing
happened to me . . .

GARDNER. Oh yes, I remember that . . . the water smelled
all queer.

MAGS. What *is* phosphorus, anyway?

GARDNER. Chemicals, chemicals . . .

FANNY. No, it isn't. Phosphorus is a green liquid inside
insects. Fireflies have it. When you see sparks in the water it
means insects are swimming around . . .

GARDNER. Where on earth did you get that idea . . . ?

FANNY. If you're bitten by one of them, it's fatal!

MAGS. . . . and the next morning it was still there . . .

GARDNER. It was the damndest stuff to get off! We'd have to
stay in the shower a good ten minutes. It comes from chemical
waste, you see . . .

MAGS. Our bodies looked like mercury as we swam around . . .

GARDNER. It stained all the towels a strange yellow-green.

MAGS. I was in heaven, and so were you for that matter.
You'd finished your day's poetry and would turn somersaults
like some happy dolphin . . .

FANNY. Damned dishes . . . why didn't I see any of this . . . ?!

MAGS. I remember one night in particular . . . We sensed
the phosphorus was about to desert us, blow off to another
town. We were chasing each other under water. At one point
I lost you, the brilliance was so intense . . . but finally
your foot appeared . . . then your leg. I grabbed it! . . . I
remember wishing the moment would hold forever, that we
could just be fixed there, laughing and iridescent . . . Then
I began to get panicky because I knew it would pass, it
was passing already. You were slipping from my grasp. The
summer was almost over. I'd be going back to art school,
you'd be going back to Boston . . . Even as I was reaching
for you, you were gone. We'd never be like that again.
(*Silence.*)

FANNY. (*Spies* MAGS' *portrait covered on the easel.*) What's
that over there? Don't tell me we forgot something!

MAGS. It's your portrait. I finished it.

FANNY. You finished it? How on earth did you manage that?

MAGS. I stayed up all night.

FANNY. You did? . . . *I* didn't hear you, did you hear her,
Gar . . . ?

GARDNER. Not a peep, not a peep!

MAGS. Well, I wanted to get it done before you left.

You know, see what you thought. It's not bad, considering
. . . I mean, I did it almost completely from memory. The
light was terrible and I was trying to be quiet so I wouldn't
wake you. It was hardly an ideal situation . . . I mean, you
weren't the most cooperative models . . . (*She suddenly panics
and snatches the painting off the easel. She hugs it to her chest
and starts dancing around the room with it.*) Oh God, you're
going to hate it! You're going to hate it! How did I ever get
into this? . . . Listen, you don't really want to see it . . .
it's nothing . . . just a few dabs here and there . . . It was
awfully late when I finished it. The light was really impossible
and my eyes were hurting like crazy . . . Look, why don't
we just go out to the sidewalk and wait for Kitty so she
doesn't have to honk . . .

GARDNER. (*Snatches the painting out from under her.*)
WOULD YOU JUST SHUT UP A MINUTE AND LET US
SEE IT . . . ?

MAGS. (*Laughing and crying.*) But it's nothing, Daddy . . .
really! . . . I've done better with my eyes closed! It was so late I
could hardly see anything and then I spilled a whole bottle of
thinner into my palette . . .

GARDNER. (*Sets it down on the easel and stands back to look
at it.*) THERE!

MAGS. (*Dancing around them in a panic.*) Listen, it's just a
quick sketch . . . It's still wet . . . I didn't have enough time
. . . It takes at least forty hours to do a decent portrait . . .

(*Suddenly it's very quiet as* FANNY *and* GARDNER *stand back to
look at it.*)

MAGS. (*More and more beside herself, keeps leaping around
the room wrapping her arms around herself, making little whimpering sounds.*) Please don't . . . no . . . don't . . . oh please!
. . . Come on, don't look . . . Oh God, don't . . . please . . .
(*An eternity passes as* FANNY *and* GARDNER *gaze at it.*)

GARDNER. Well . . .

FANNY. Well . . . (*More silence.*)

FANNY. I think it's perfectly   GARDNER. Awfully clever,
dreadful!   awfully clever!

FANNY. What on earth did you do to my face . . . ?

GARDNER. I particularly like Mum!

FANNY. Since when do I have purple skin . . . ?!

MAGS. I told you it was nothing, just a silly . . .

GARDNER. She looks like a million dollars!

FANNY. AND WILL YOU LOOK AT MY HAIR . . . IT'S BRIGHT ORANGE!

GARDNER. (*Views it from another angle.*) It's really very good!

FANNY. (*Pointing.*) That doesn't look anything like me!

GARDNER. . . . first rate!

FANNY. Since when do I have purple skin and bright orange hair . . . ?!

MAGS. (*Trying to snatch it off the easel.*) Listen, you don't have to worry about my feelings . . . really . . . I . . .

GARDNER. (*Blocking her way.*) NOT SO FAST . . .

FANNY. . . . and look at how I'm sitting! I've never sat like that in my life!

GARDNER. (*Moving closer to it.*) Yes, yes, it's awfully clever . . .

FANNY. I HAVE NO FEET!

GARDNER. The whole thing is quite remarkable!

FANNY. And what happened to my legs, pray tell? . . . They just vanish below the knees! . . . At least my dress is presentable. I've always loved that dress.

GARDNER. It sparkles somehow . . .

FANNY. (*To* GARDNER.) Don't you think it's becoming?

GARDNER. Yes, very becoming, awfully becoming . . .

FANNY. (*Examining it at close range.*) Yes, she got the dress very well, how it shows off what's left of my figure . . . My smile is nice too.

GARDNER. Good and wide . . .

FANNY. I love how the corners of my mouth turn up . . .

GARDNER. It's very clever . . .

FANNY. They're almost quivering . . .

GARDNER. Good lighting effects!

FANNY. Actually, I look quite . . . *young*, don't you think?

GARDNER. (*To* MAGS.) You're awfully good with those highlights.

FANNY. (*Looking at it from different angles.*) And *you* look darling . . . !

GARDNER. Well, I don't know about that . . .

FANNY. No, you look absolutely darling. Good enough to eat!

MAGS. (*In a whisper.*) They like it . . . They like it! (*A silence as* FANNY *and* GARDNER *keep gazing at it.*)

FANNY. You know what it is? The wispy brush strokes make us look like a couple in a French Impressionist painting.

GARDNER. Yes, I see what you mean . . .

FANNY. . . . a Manet or Renoir . . .

GARDNER. It's very evocative.

FANNY. There's something about the light . . . (*They back up to survey it from a distance.*) You know those Renoir café scenes . . . ?

GARDNER. She doesn't lay on the paint with a trowel, it's just touches here and there . . .

MAGS. They *like* it . . . !

FANNY. You know the one with the couple dancing . . . ? Not that we're dancing. There's just something similar in the mood . . . a kind of gaity, almost . . . The man has his back to you and he's swinging the woman around . . . OH GAR, YOU'VE SEEN IT A MILLION TIMES! IT'S HANGING IN THE MUSEUM OF FINE ARTS! . . . They're dancing like this . . . (*She goes up to him and puts an arm on his shoulder.*)

MAGS. They like it . . . they like it!

FANNY. She's got on this wonderful flowered dress with ruffles at the neck and he's holding her like this . . . that's right . . . and she's got the most rhapsodic expression on her face : . .

GARDNER. (*Getting into the spirit of it, takes FANNY in his arms and slowly begins to dance around the room.*) Oh yes . . . I know the one you mean . . . They're in a sort of haze . . . and isn't there a little band playing off to one side . . . ?

FANNY. Yes, that's it!

(*Kitty's horn honks outside.*)

MAGS. (*Is the only one who hears it.*) There's Kitty! (*She's torn and keeps looking towards the door, but finally can't take her eyes off their stolen dance.*)

FANNY. . . . and there's a man in a dark suit playing the violin and someone's conducting, I think . . . And aren't Japanese lanterns strung up . . . ? (*They pick up speed, dipping and whirling around the room. Strains of a faraway Chopin waltz are heard.*)

GARDNER. Oh yes! There are all these little lights twinkling in the trees . . .

FANNY. . . . and doesn't the woman have a hat on . . . ? A bit red hat . . . ?

GARDNER. . . . and lights all over the dancers too. Every-

thing shimmers with this marvelous glow. Yes, yes . . . I can
see it perfectly! The whole thing is absolutely extraordinary!
(*The lights become dreamy and dappled as they dance around
the room.* MAGS *watches them, moved to tears and . . .*)

THE CURTAIN FALLS

MA RAINEY'S BLACK BOTTOM

A DRAMA IN TWO ACTS

by
August Wilson

For my mother

They tore the railroad down
so the Sunshine Special can't run
I'm going away baby
build me a railroad of my own

—Blind Lemon Jefferson

413

Ma Rainey's Black Bottom opened on April 6, 1984, at the Yale Repertory Theater in New Haven, Connecticut, with the following cast:

STURDYVANT	*Richard M. Davidson*
IRVIN	*Lou Criscuolo*
CUTLER	*Joe Seneca*
TOLEDO	*Robert Judd*
SLOW DRAG	*Leonard Jackson*
LEVEE	*Charles S. Dutton*
MA RAINEY	*Theresa Merritt*
POLICEMAN	*David Wayne Nelson*
DUSSIE MAE	*Sharon Mitchell*
SYLVESTER	*Steven R. Blye*

Director: Lloyd Richards
Settings: Charles Henry McClennahan
Costumes: Daphne Pascucci
Lighting: Peter Maradudin
Music Director: Dwight Andrews

Ma Rainey's Black Bottom opened on October 11, 1984, at the Cort Theater on Broadway in New York City, with the following cast:

STURDYVANT	*John Carpenter*
IRVIN	*Lou Criscuolo*
CUTLER	*Joe Seneca*
TOLEDO	*Robert Judd*
SLOW DRAG	*Leonard Jackson*
LEVEE	*Charles S. Dutton*
MA RAINEY	*Theresa Merritt*
POLICEMAN	*Christopher Loomis*
DUSSIE MAE	*Aleta Mitchell*
SYLVESTER	*Scott Davenport-Richards*

Director: Lloyd Richards
Settings: Charles Henry McClennahan
Costumes: Daphne Pascucci
Lighting: Peter Maradudin
Music Director: Dwight Andrews

THE SETTING

There are two playing areas: what is called the "band room," and the recording studio. The band room is at stage left and is in the basement of the building. It is entered through a door up left. There are benches and chairs scattered about, a piano, a row of lockers, and miscellaneous paraphernalia stacked in a corner and long since forgotten. A mirror hangs on a wall with various posters.

The studio is upstairs at stage right, and resembles a recording studio of the late 1920s. The entrance is from a hall on the right wall. A small control booth is at the rear and its access is gained by means of a spiral staircase. Against one wall there is a line of chairs, and a horn through which the control room communicates with the performers. A door in the rear wall allows access to the band room.

THE PLAY

It is early March in Chicago, 1927. There is a bit of a chill in the air. Winter has broken but the wind coming off the lake does not carry the promise of spring. The people of the city are bundled and brisk in their defense against such misfortunes as the weather, and the business of the city proceeds largely undisturbed.

Chicago in 1927 is a rough city, a bruising city, a city of millionares and derelicts, gangsters and roughhouse dandies, whores and Irish grandmothers who move through its streets fingering long black rosaries. Somewhere a man is wrestling with the taste of a woman in his cheek. Somewhere a dog is barking. Somewhere the moon has fallen through a window and broken into thirty pieces of silver.

It is one o'clock in the afternoon. Secretaries are returning from their lunch, the noon Mass at St. Anthony's is over, and the priest is mumbling over his vestments while the altar boys practice their Latin. The procession of cattle cars through the stockyards continues unabated. The busboys in Mac's Place are cleaning away the last of the corned beef and cabbage, and on the city's Southside, sleepy-eyed negroes move lazily toward their small cold-water flats and rented rooms to await the onslaught of night, which will find them crowded in the bars and juke joints both dazed and dazzling in their rapport with life. It is with these negroes that our concern lies most heavily: their values, their attitudes, and particularly their music.

It is hard to define this music. Suffice it to say that it is music that breathes and touches. That connects. That is in itself a way of being, separate and distinct from any other. This music is called blues. Whether this music came from Alabama or Mississippi or other parts of the South doesn't matter anymore. The men and women who make this music have learned it from the narrow crooked streets of East St. Louis, or the streets of the city's Southside, and the Alabama or Mississippi roots have been strangled by the northern manners and customs of free men of definite and sincere worth, men for whom this music often lies at the forefront of their conscience and concerns. Thus they are laid open to be consumed by it; its warmth and redress, its braggadocio and roughly poignant comments, its vision and prayer, which would instruct and allow them to reconnect, to reassemble and gird up for the next battle in which they would be both victim and the ten thousand slain.

ACT ONE

The lights come up in the studio. IRVIN *enters, carrying a microphone. He is a tall, fleshy man who prides himself on his knowledge of blacks and his ability to deal with them. He hooks up the microphone, blows into it, taps it, etc. He crosses over to the piano, opens it, and fingers a few keys.* STURDYVANT *is visible in the control booth. Preoccupied with money, he is insensitive to black performers and prefers to deal with them at arm's length. He puts on a pair of earphones.*

STURDYVANT. (*Over speaker.*) Irv . . . let's crack that mike, huh? Let's do a check on it.

IRVIN. (*Crosses to mike, speaks into it.*) Testing . . . one . . . two . . . three . . . (*There is a loud feedback.* STURDYVANT *fiddles with the dials.*) Testing . . . one . . . two . . . three . . . testing. How's that, Mel? (STURDYVANT *doesn't respond.*) Testing . . . one . . . two . . .

STURDYVANT. (*Taking off earphones.*) Okay . . . that checks. We got a good reading. (*Pause.*) You got that list, Irv?

IRVIN. Yeah . . . yeah, I got it. Don't worry about nothing.

STURDYVANT. Listen, Irv . . . you keep her in line, okay? I'm holding you responsible for her . . . If she starts any of her . . .

IRVIN. Mel, what's with the goddamn horn? You wanna talk to me . . . okay! I can't talk to you over the goddamn horn . . . Christ!

STURDYVANT. I'm not putting up with any shenanigans. You hear, Irv? (IRVIN *crosses over to the piano and mindlessly runs his fingers over the keys.*) I'm not just gonna stand for it. I want you to keep her in line. Irv? (STURDYVANT *enters from the control booth.*) Listen, Irv . . . you're her manager . . . she's your responsibility . . .

IRVIN. Okay, okay, Mel . . . let me handle it.

STURDYVANT. She's your responsibility. I'm not putting up with any Royal Highness . . . Queen of the Blues bullshit!

IRVIN. Mother of the Blues, Mel. Mother of the Blues.

STURDYVANT. I don't care what she calls herself. I'm not putting up with it. I just want to get her in here . . . record those songs on that list . . . and get her out. Just like clockwork, huh?

IRVIN. Like clockwork, Mel. You just stay out of the way and let me handle it.

STURDYVANT. Yeah . . . yeah . . . you handled it last time. Remember? She marches in here like she owns the damn place . . . doesn't like the songs we picked out . . . says her throat is sore . . . doesn't want to do more than one take . . .

IRVIN. Okay . . . okay . . . I was here! I know all about it.

STURDYVANT. Complains about the building being cold . . . and then . . . trips over the mike wire and threatens to sue me. That's taking care of it?

IRVIN. I've got it all worked out this time. I talked with her last night. Her throat is fine . . . We went over the songs together . . . I got everything straight, Mel.

STURDYVANT. Irv, that horn player . . . the one who gave me those songs . . . is he gonna be here today? Good. I want to hear more of that sound. Times are changing. This is a tricky business now. We've got to jazz it up . . . put in something different. You know, something wild . . . with a lot of rhythm. (*Pause.*) You know what we put out last time, Irv? We put out garbage last time. It was garbage. I don't even know why I bother with this anymore.

IRVIN. You did all right last time, Mel. Not as good as you did before, but you did all right.

STURDYVANT. You know how many records we sold in New York? You wanna see the sheet? And you know what's in New York, Irv? Harlem. Harlem's in New York, Irv.

IRVIN. Okay, so they didn't sell in New York. But look at Memphis . . . Birmingham . . . Atlanta. Christ, you made a bundle.

STURDYVANT. It's not the money, Irv. You know I couldn't sleep last night? This business is bad for my nerves. My wife is after me to slow down and take a vacation. Two more years and I'm gonna get out . . . get into something respectable. Textiles. That's a respectable business. You know what you could do with a shipload of textiles from Ireland?

(*A buzzer is heard offstage.*)

IRVIN. Why don't you go upstairs and let me handle it, Mel?

STURDYVANT. Remember . . . you're responsible for her.

(STURDYVANT *exits to the control booth.* IRVIN *crosses to get the door.* CUTLER, SLOW DRAG, *and* TOLEDO *enter.* CUTLER *is in his mid-fifties, as are most of the others. He plays guitar and trombone and is the leader of the group, possibly because he is the most sensible. His playing is solid and almost totally unembellished. His understanding of his music is limited to the chord he is playing at the time he is playing it. He has all the qualities of a loner except the introspection.* SLOW DRAG, *the bass player, is perhaps the one most bored by life. He resembles* CUTLER, *but lacks* CUTLER's *energy. He is deceptively intelligent, though, as his name implies, he appears to be slow. He is a rather large man with a wicked smile. Innate African rhythms underlie everything he plays, and he plays with an ease that is at times startling.* TOLEDO *is the piano player. In control of his instrument, he understands and recognizes that its limitations are an extension of himself. He is the only one in the group who can read. He is self-taught but misunderstands and misapplies his knowledge, though he is quick to penetrate to the core of a situation and his insights are thought-provoking. All of the men are dressed in a style of clothing befitting the members of a successful band of the era.*)

IRVIN. How you boys doing, Cutler? Come on in. (*Pause.*) Where's Ma? Is she with you?

CUTLER. I don't know, Mr. Irvin. She told us to be here at one o'clock. That's all I know.

IRVIN. Where's . . . huh . . . the horn player? Is he coming with Ma?

CUTLER. Levee's supposed to be here same as we is. I reckon he'll be here in a minute. I can't rightly say.

IRVIN. Well, come on . . . I'll show you to the band room, let you get set up and rehearsed. You boys hungry? I'll call over to the deli and get some sandwiches. Get you fed and ready to make some music. Cutler . . . here's the list of songs we're gonna record.

STURDYVANT. (*Over speaker.*) Irvin, what's happening? Where's Ma?

IRVIN. Everything under control, Mel. I got it under control.

STURDYVANT. Where's Ma? How come she isn't with the band?

IRVIN. She'll be here in a minute, Mel. Let me get these fellows down to the band room, huh? (*They exit the studio. The lights go down in the studio and up in the band room.* IRVIN *opens the door and allows them to pass as they enter.*) You boys go ahead and rehearse. I'll let you know when Ma comes. (IRVIN *exits.* CUTLER *hands* TOLEDO *the list of songs.*)

CUTLER. What we got here, Toledo?

TOLEDO. (*Reading.*) We got ... "Prove It on Me" ... "Hear Me Talking to You ... "Ma Rainey's Black Bottom" ... and "Moonshine Blues."

CUTLER. Where Mr. Irvin go? Them ain't the songs Ma told me.

SLOW DRAG. I wouldn't worry about it if I were you, Cutler. They'll get it straightened out. Ma will get it straightened out.

CUTLER. I just don't want no trouble about these songs, that's all. Ma ain't told me them songs. She told me something else.

SLOW DRAG. What she tell you?

CUTLER. This "Moonshine Blues" wasn't in it. That's one of Bessie's songs.

TOLEDO. Slow Drag's right ... I wouldn't worry about it. Let them straighten it up.

CUTLER. Levee know what time he supposed to be here?

SLOW DRAG. Levee gone out to spend your four dollars. He left the hotel this morning talking about he was gonna go buy some shoes. Say it's the first time he ever beat you shooting craps.

CUTLER. Do he know what time he supposed to be here? That's what I wanna know. I ain't thinking about no four dollars.

SLOW DRAG. Levee sure was thinking about it. That four dollars liked to burn a hole in his pocket.

CUTLER. Well, he's supposed to be here at one o'clock. That's what time Ma said. That nigger get out in the streets with that four dollars and ain't no telling when he's liable to show. You ought to have seen him at the club last night, Toledo. Trying to talk to some gal Ma had with her.

TOLEDO. You ain't got to tell me. I know how Levee do.

(*Buzzer is heard offstage.*)

SLOW DRAG. Levee tried to talk to that gal and got his feelings hurt. She didn't want no part of him. She told Levee he'd have to turn his money green before he could talk with her.

CUTLER. She out for what she can get. Anybody could see that.

SLOW DRAG. That's why Levee run out to buy some shoes. He's looking to make an impression on that girl.

CUTLER. What the hell she gonna do with his shoes? She can't do nothing with the nigger's shoes.

(SLOW DRAG takes out a pint bottle and drinks.)

TOLEDO. Let me hit that, Slow Drag.

SLOW DRAG. (*Handing him the bottle.*) This some of that good Chicago bourbon!

(*The door opens and* LEVEE *enters, carrying a shoe box. In his early thirties,* LEVEE *is younger than the other men. His flamboyance is sometimes subtle and sneaks up on you. His temper is rakish and bright. He lacks fuel for himself and is somewhat of a buffoon. But it is an intelligent buffoonery, clearly calculated to shift control of the situation to where he can grasp it. He plays trumpet. His voice is strident and totally dependent on his manipulation of breath. He plays wrong notes frequently. He often gets his skill and talent confused with each other.*)

CUTLER. Levee . . . where Mr. Irvin go?

LEVEE. Hell, I don't know. I ain't none of his keeper.

SLOW DRAG. What you got there, Levee?

LEVEE. Look here, Cutler . . . I got me some shoes!

CUTLER. Nigger, I ain't studying you.

(LEVEE *takes the shoes out of the box and starts to put them on.*)

TOLEDO. How much you pay for something like that, Levee?

LEVEE. Eleven dollars. Four dollars of it belong to Cutler.

SLOW DRAG. Levee say if it wasn't for Cutler . . . he wouldn't have no new shoes.

CUTLER. I ain't thinking about Levee or his shoes. Come on . . . let's get ready to rehearse.

SLOW DRAG. I'm with you on that score, Cutler. I wanna get out of here. I don't want to be around here all night. When it comes time to go up there and record them songs . . . I just wanna go up there and do it. Last time it took us all day and half the night.

TOLEDO. Ain't but four songs on the list. Last time we recorded six songs.

SLOW DRAG. It felt like it was sixteen!

LEVEE. (*Finishes with his shoes.*) Yeah! Now I'm ready! I can play some good music now! (*He goes to put up his old shoes and looks around the room.*) Damn! They done changed things around. Don't never leave well enough alone.

TOLEDO. Everything changing all the time. Even the air you breathing change. You got, monoxide, hydrogen . . . changing all the time. Skin changing . . . different molecules and everything.

LEVEE. Nigger, what is you talking about? I'm talking about the room. I ain't talking about no skin and air. I'm talking about something I can see! Last time the band room was upstairs. This time it's downstairs. Next time it be over there. I'm talking about what I can see. I ain't talking about no molecules or nothing.

TOLEDO. Hell, I know what you talking about. I just said everything changin'. I know what you talking about, but you don't know what I'm talking about.

LEVEE. That door! Nigger, you see that door? That's what I'm talking about. That door wasn't there before.

CUTLER. Levee, you wouldn't know your right from your left. This is where they used to keep the recording horns and things . . . and damn if that door wasn't there. How in hell else you gonna get in here? Now, if you talking about they done switched rooms, you right. But don't go telling me that damn door wasn't there!

SLOW DRAG. Damn the door and let's get set up. I wanna get out of here.

LEVEE. Toledo started all that about the door. I'm just saying that things change.

TOLEDO. What the hell you think I was saying? Things change. The air and everything. Now you gonna say you was saying it. You gonna fit two propositions on the same track . . . run them into each other, and because they crash, you gonna say it's the same train.

LEVEE. Now this nigger talking about trains! We done went from the air to the skin to the door . . . and now trains. Toledo, I'd just like to be inside your head for five minutes. Just to see how you think. You done got more shit piled up and mixed up in there than the devil got sinners. You been reading too many goddamn books.

TOLEDO. What you care about how much I read? I'm gonna ignore you 'cause you ignorant.

(LEVEE *takes off his coat and hangs it in the locker.*)

SLOW DRAG. Come on, let's rehearse the music.

LEVEE. You ain't gotta rehearse that . . . ain't nothing but old jug-band music. They need one of them jug bands for this.

SLOW DRAG. Don't make me no difference. Long as we get paid.

LEVEE. That ain't what I'm talking about, nigger. I'm talking about art!

SLOW DRAG. What's drawing got to do with it?

LEVEE. Where you get this nigger from, Cutler? He sound like one of them Alabama niggers.

CUTLER. Slow Drag's all right. It's you talking all that weird shit about art. Just play the piece, nigger. You wanna be one of them . . . what you call . . . virtuoso or something, you in the wrong place. You ain't no Buddy Bolden or King Oliver . . . you just an old trumpet player come a dime a dozen. Talking about art.

LEVEE. What is you? I don't see your name in lights.

CUTLER. I just play the piece. Whatever they want. I don't go talking about art and criticizing other people's music.

LEVEE. I ain't like you, Cutler. I got talent! Me and this horn . . . we's tight. If my daddy knowed I was gonna turn out like this, he would've named me Gabriel. I'm gonna get me a band and make me some records. I done give Mr. Sturdyvant some of my songs I wrote and he say he's gonna let me record them when I get my band together. (*Takes some papers out of his pocket.*) I just gotta finish the last part of this song. And Mr. Sturdyvant want me to write another part to this song.

SLOW DRAG. How you learn to write music, Levee?

LEVEE. I just picked it up . . . like you pick up anything. Miss Eula used to play the piano . . . she learned me a lot. I knows how to play *real* music . . . not this old jug-band shit. I got style!

TOLEDO. Everybody got style. Style ain't nothing but keeping the same idea from beginning to end. Everybody got it.

LEVEE. But everybody can't play like I do. Everybody can't have their own band.

CUTLER. Well, until you get your own band where you can play what you want, you just play the piece and stop complaining. I told you when you came on here, this ain't none of them hot bands. This is an accompaniment band. You play Ma's music when you here.

LEVEE. I got sense enough to know that. Hell, I can look at you all and see what kind of band it is. I can look at Toledo and see what kind of band it is.

TOLEDO. Toledo ain't said nothing to you now. Don't let Toledo get started. You can't even spell music, much less play it.

LEVEE. What you talking about? I can spell music. I got a dollar say I can spell it! Put your dollar up. Where your dollar? (TOLEDO *waves him away.*) Now come on. Put your dollar up. Talking about I can't spell music. (LEVEE *peels a dollar off his roll and slams it down on the bench beside* TOLEDO.)

TOLEDO. All right, I'm gonna show you, Cutler. Slow Drag. You hear this? The nigger betting me a dollar he can spell music. I don't want no shit now! (TOLEDO *lays a dollar down beside* LEVEE's.) All right. Go ahead. Spell it.

LEVEE. It's a bet then. Talking about I can't spell music.

TOLEDO. Go ahead, then. Spell it. Music. Spell it.

LEVEE. I can spell it, nigger! M-U-S-I-K. There! (*He reaches for the money.*)

TOLEDO. Naw! Naw! Leave that money alone! You ain't spelled it.

LEVEE. What you mean I ain't spelled it? I said M-U-S-I-K!

TOLEDO. That ain't how you spell it! That ain't how you spell it! It's M-U-S-I-C! C, nigger. Not K! C! M-U-S-I-C!

LEVEE. What you mean, C? Who say it's C?

TOLEDO. Cutler. Slow Drag. Tell this fool. (*They look at each other and then away.*) Well, I'll be a monkey's uncle! (TOLEDO *picks up the money and hands* LEVEE *his dollar back.*) Here's your dollar back, Levee. I done won it, you understand. I done won the dollar. But if don't nobody know but me, how am I gonna prove it to you?

LEVEE. You just mad 'cause I spelled it.

TOLEDO. Spelled what! M-U-S-I-K don't spell nothing. I just wish there was some way I could show you the right and wrong of it. How you gonna know something if the other fellow don't know if you're right or not? Now I can't even be sure that I'm spelling it right.

LEVEE. That's what I'm talking about. You don't know it. Talking about C. You ought to give me that dollar I won from you.

TOLEDO. All right. All right. I'm gonna show you how ridiculous you sound. You know the Lord's Prayer?

LEVEE. Why? You wanna bet a dollar on that?

TOLEDO. Just answer the question. Do you know the Lord's Prayer or don't you?

LEVEE. Yeah, I know it. What of it?

TOLEDO. Cutler?

CUTLER. What you Cutlering me for? I ain't got nothing to do with it.

TOLEDO. I just want to show the man how ridiculous he is.

CUTLER. Both of you all sound like damn fools. Arguing about something silly. Yeah, I know the Lord's Prayer. My daddy was a deacon in the church. Come asking me if I know the Lord's Prayer. Yeah, I know it.

TOLEDO. Slow Drag?

SLOW DRAG. Yeah.

TOLEDO. All right. Now I'm gonna tell you a story to show just how ridiculous he sound. There was these two fellows, see. So, the one of them go up to this church and commence to taking up the church learning. The other fellow see him out on the road and he say, "I done heard you taking up the church learning," say, "Is you learning anything up there?" The other one say, "Yeah, I done take up the church learning and I's learning all kinds of things about the Bible and what it say and all. Why you be asking?" The other one say, "Well, do you know the Lord's Prayer?" And he say, "Why, sure I know the Lord's Prayer, I'm taking up learning at the church ain't I? I know the Lord's Prayer backwards and forwards." And the other fellow says, "I bet you five dollars you don't know the Lord's Prayer, 'cause I don't think you knows it. I think you be going up to the church 'cause the Widow Jenkins be going up there and you just wanna be sitting in the same room with her when she cross them big, fine, pretty legs she got." And the other one say, "Well, I'm gonna prove you wrong and I'm gonna bet you that five dollars." So he say, "Well, go on and say it then." So he commenced to saying the Lord's Prayer. He say, "Now I lay me down to sleep, I pray the Lord my soul to keep." The other one say, "Here's your five dollars. I didn't think you knew it." (*They all laugh.*) Now, that's just how ridiculous Levee sound. Only 'cause I knowed how to spell music, I still got my dollar.

LEVEE. That don't prove nothing. What's that supposed to prove.

TOLEDO. (*Takes a newspaper out of his back pocket and begins to read.*) I'm through with it.

SLOW DRAG. Is you all gonna rehearse this music or ain't you?

(CUTLER *takes out some papers and starts to roll a reefer.*)

LEVEE. How many times you done played them songs? What you gotta rehearse for?

SLOW DRAG. This a recording session. I wanna get it right the first time and get on out of here.

CUTLER. Slow Drag's right. Let's go on and rehearse and get it over with.

LEVEE. You all go and rehearse, then. I got to finish this song for Mr. Sturdyvant.

CUTLER. Come on, Levee . . . I don't want no shit now. You rehearse like everybody else. You in the band like everybody else. Mr. Sturdyvant just gonna have to wait. You got to do that on your own time. This is the band's time.

LEVEE. Well, what is you doing? You sitting there rolling a reefer talking about let's rehearse. Toledo reading a newspaper. Hell, I'm ready if you wanna rehearse. I just say there ain't no point in it. Ma ain't here. What's the point in it?

CUTLER. Nigger, why you gotta complain all the time?

TOLEDO. Levee would complain if a gal ain't laid across his bed just right.

CUTLER. That's what I know. That's why I try to tell him just play the music and forget about it. It ain't no big thing.

TOLEDO. Levee ain't got an eye for that. He wants to tie on to some abstract component and sit down on the elemental.

LEVEE. This is get-on-Levee time, huh? Levee ain't said nothing except this some old jug-band music.

TOLEDO. Under the right circumstances you'd play anything. If you know music, then you play it. Straight on or off to the side. Ain't nothing abstract about it.

LEVEE. Toledo, you sound like you got a mouth full of marbles. You the only cracker-talking nigger I know.

TOLEDO. You ought to have learned yourself to read . . . then you'd understand the basic understanding of everything.

SLOW DRAG. Both of you all gonna drive me crazy with that philosophy bullshit. Cutler, give me a reefer.

CUTLER. Ain't you got some reefer? Where's your reefer? Why you all the time asking me?

SLOW DRAG. Cutler, how long I done known you? How long we been together? Twenty-two years. We been doing this together for twenty-two years. All up and down the back roads, the side roads, the front roads . . . We done played the juke joints, the whorehouses, the barn dances, and city sit-downs . . . I done lied for you and lied with you . . . We done laughed together, fought together, slept in the same bed together, done sucked on the same titty . . . and now you don't wanna give me no reefer.

CUTLER. You see this nigger trying to talk me out of my reefer, Toledo? Running all that about how long he done knowed me and how we done sucked on the same titty. Nigger, you *still* ain't getting none of my reefer!

TOLEDO. That's African.

SLOW DRAG. What? What you talking about? What's African?

LEVEE. I know he ain't talking about me. You don't see me running around in no jungle with no bone between my nose.

TOLEDO. Levee, you worse than ignorant. You ignorant without a premise. (*Pauses.*) Now, what I was saying is what Slow Drag was doing is African. That's what you call an African conceptualization. That's when you name the gods or call on the ancestors to achieve whatever your desires are.

SLOW DRAG. Nigger, I ain't no African! I ain't doing no African nothing!

TOLEDO. Naming all those things you and Cutler done together is like trying to solicit some reefer based on a bond of kinship. That's African. An ancestral retention. Only you forgot the name of the gods.

SLOW DRAG. I ain't forgot nothing. I was telling the nigger how cheap he is. Don't come talking that African nonsense to me.

TOLEDO. You just like Levee. No eye for taking an abstract and fixing it to a specific. There's so much that goes on around you and you can't even see it.

CUTLER. Wait a minute . . . wait a minute. Toledo, now when this nigger . . . when an African do all them things you say and name all the gods and whatnot . . . then what happens?

TOLEDO. Depends on if the gods is sympathetic with his cause for which he is calling them with the right names. Then his success comes with the right proportion of his naming. That's the way that go.

CUTLER. (*Taking out a reefer.*) Here, Slow Drag. Here's a reefer. You done talked yourself up on that one.

SLOW DRAG. Thank you. You ought to have done that in the first place and saved me all the aggravation.

CUTLER. What I wants to know is . . . what's the same titty we done sucked on. That's what I want to know.

SLOW DRAG. Oh, I just threw that in there to make it sound good. (*They all laugh.*)

CUTLER. Nigger, you ain't right.

SLOW DRAG. I knows it.

CUTLER. Well, come on . . . let's get it rehearsed. Time's wasting. (*The musicians pick up their instruments.*) Let's do it. "Ma Rainey's Black Bottom." One . . . two . . . You know what to do.

(*They begin to play.* LEVEE *is playing something different. He stops.*)

LEVEE. Naw! Naw! We ain't doing it that way. (TOLEDO *stops playing, then* SLOW DRAG.) We doing my version. It say so right there on that piece of paper you got. Ask Toledo. That's what Mr. Irvin told me . . . say it's on the list he gave you.

CUTLER. Let me worry about what's on the list and what ain't on the list. How you gonna tell me what's on the list?

LEVEE. 'Cause I know what Mr. Irvin told me! Ask Toledo!

CUTLER. Let me worry about what's on the list. You just play the song I say.

LEVEE. What kind of sense it make to rehearse the wrong version of the song? That's what I wanna know. Why you wanna rehearse that version?

SLOW DRAG. You supposed to rehearse what you gonna play. That's the way they taught me. Now, *whatever* version we gonna play . . . let's go on and rehearse it.

LEVEE. That's what I'm trying to tell the man.

CUTLER. You trying to tell me what we is and ain't gonna play. And that ain't none of your business. Your business is to play what I say.

LEVEE. Oh, I see now. You done got jealous cause Mr. Irvin using my version. You don't got jealous cause I proved I know something about music.

CUTLER. What the hell . . . nigger, you talk like a fool! What the hell I got to be jealous of you about? The day I get jealous of you I may as well lay down and die.

TOLEDO. Levee started all that 'cause he too lazy to rehearse. (*To* LEVEE.) You ought to just go on and play the song . . . What difference does it make?

LEVEE. Where's the paper? Look at the paper! Get the paper and look at it! See what it say. Gonna tell me I'm too lazy to rehearse.

CUTLER. We ain't talking about the paper. We talking about you understanding where you fit in when you around here. You just play what I say.

LEVEE. Look . . . I don't care what you play! All right? It don't matter to me. Mr. Irvin gonna straighten it up! I don't care what you play.

CUTLER. Thank you. (*Pauses.*) Let's play this "Hear Me Talking to You" till we find out what's happening with the "Black Bottom." Slow Drag, you sing Ma's part. (*Pauses.*) "Hear Me Talking to You." Let's do it. One . . . Two . . . You know what to do.

(*They play.*)

SLOW DRAG. (*Singing.*)
Rambling man makes no change in me
I'm gonna ramble back to my used-to-be
Ah, you hear me talking to you
I don't bite my tongue

You wants to be my man
You got to fetch it with you when you come.

Eve and Adam in the garden taking a chance
Adam didn't take time to get his pants
Ah, you hear me talking to you
I don't bite my tongue
You wants to be my man
You got to fetch it with you when you come.

Our old cat swallowed a ball of yarn
When the kittens were born they had sweaters on
Ah, you hear me talking to you
I don't bite my tongue
You wants to be my man
You got to fetch it with you when you come.

(IRVIN *enters. The musicians stop playing.*)

IRVIN. Any of you boys know what's keeping Ma?

CUTLER. Can't say, Mr. Irvin. She'll be along directly, I reckon. I talked to her this morning, she say she'll be here in time to rehearse.

IRVIN. Well, you boys go ahead. (*He starts to exit.*)

CUTLER. Mr. Irvin, about these songs . . . Levee say . . .

IRVIN. Whatever's on the list, Cutler. You got that list I gave you?

CUTLER. Yessir, I got it right here.

IRVIN. Whatever's on there. Whatever that says.

CUTLER. I'm asking about this "Black Bottom" piece . . . Levee say . . .

IRVIN. Oh, it's on the list. "Ma Rainey's Black Bottom" on the list.

CUTLER. I know it's on the list. I wanna know what version. We got two versions of that song.

IRVIN. Oh. Levee's arrangement. We're using Levee's arrangement.

CUTLER. OK. I got that straight. Now, this "Moonshine Blues" . . .

IRVIN. We'll work it out with Ma, Cutler. Just rehearse whatever's on the list and use Levee's arrangement on that "Black Bottom" piece. (*He exits.*)

LEVEE. See, I told you! It don't mean nothing when I say it. You got to wait for Mr. Irvin to say it. Well, I told you the way it is.

CUTLER. Levee, the sooner you understand it ain't what you say, or what Mr. Irvin say . . . it's what Ma say that counts.

SLOW DRAG. Don't nobody say when it come to Ma. She's gonna do what she wants to do. Ma says what happens with her.

LEVEE. Hell, the man's the one putting out the record! He's gonna put out what he wanna put out!

SLOW DRAG. He's gonna put out what Ma want him to put out.

LEVEE. You heard what the man told you . . . "Ma Rainey's Black Bottom," Levee's arrangement. There you go! That's what he told you.

SLOW DRAG. What you gonna do, Cutler?

CUTLER. Ma ain't told me what version. Let's go and play it Levee's way.

TOLEDO. See, now . . . I'll tell you something. As long as the colored man look to white folks to put the crown on what he say . . . as long as he looks to white folks for approval . . . then he ain't never gonna find out who he is and what he's about. He's just gonna be about what white folks want him to be about. That's one sure thing.

LEVEE. I'm just trying to show Cutler where he's wrong.

CUTLER. Cutler don't need you to show him nothing.

SLOW DRAG. (*Irritated.*) Come on, let's get this shit rehearsed! You all can bicker afterward!

CUTLER. Levee's confused about who the boss is. He don't know Ma's the boss.

LEVEE. Ma's the boss on the road! We at a recording session. Mr. Sturdyvant and Mr. Irvin say what's gonna be here! We's in Chicago, we ain't in Memphis! I don't know why you all wanna pick me about it, shit! I'm with Slow Drag . . . Let's go on and get it rehearsed.

CUTLER. All right. All right. I know how to solve this. "Ma Rainey's Black Bottom." Levee's version. Let's do it. Come on.

TOLEDO. How that first part go again, Levee?

LEVEE. It go like this. (*He plays.*) That's to get the people's attention to the song. That's when you and Slow Drag come in with the rhythm part. Me and Cutler play on the breaks. (*Becoming animated.*) Now we gonna dance it . . . but we ain't gonna countrify it. This ain't no barn dance. We gonna play it like . . .

CUTLER. The man ask you how the first part go. He don't wanna hear all that. Just tell him how the piece go.

TOLEDO. I got it. I got it. Let's go. I know how to do it.

CUTLER. "Ma Rainey's Black Bottom." One . . . two . . .
You know what to do.

(*They begin to play.* LEVEE *stops.*)

LEVEE. You all got to keep up now. You playing in the
wrong time. Ma come in over the top. She got to find her own
way in.

CUTLER. Nigger, will you let us play this song? When you get
your own band . . . then you tell them that nonsense. We know
how to play the piece. I was playing music before you was born.
Gonna tell me how to play . . . All right. Let's try it again.

SLOW DRAG. Cutler, wait till I fix this. This string started to
unravel. (*Playfully.*) And you know I want to play Levee's
music right.

LEVEE. If you was any kind of musician, you'd take care of
your instrument. Keep it in tip-top order. If you was any kind
of musician, I'd let you be in my band.

SLOW DRAG. Shhheeeeet! (*He crosses to get his string and
steps on* LEVEE'S *shoes.*)

LEVEE. Damn, Slow Drag! Watch them big-ass shoes you
got.

SLOW DRAG. Boy, ain't nobody done anything to you.

LEVEE. You done stepped on my shoes.

SLOW DRAG. Move them the hell out the way, then. You was
in my way . . . I wasn't in your way. (CUTLER *lights up another
reefer.* SLOW DRAG *rummages around in his belongings for a
string.* LEVEE *takes out a rag and begins to shine his shoes.*)
You can shine these when you get done, Levee.

CUTLER. If I had them shoes Levee got, I could buy me a
whole suit of clothes.

LEVEE. What kind of difference it make what kind of shoes I
got? Ain't nothing wrong with having nice shoes. I ain't said
nothing about your shoes. Why you wanna talk about me and
my Florsheims?

CUTLER. Any man who takes a whole week's pay and puts it
on some shoes—you understand what I mean, what you walk
around on the ground with—is a fool! And I don't mind telling
you.

LEVEE. (*Irritated.*) What difference it make to you, Cutler?

SLOW DRAG. The man ain't said nothing about your shoes.
Ain't nothing wrong with having nice shoes. Look at Toledo.

TOLEDO. What about Toledo?

SLOW DRAG. I said ain't nothing wrong with having nice
shoes.

LEVEE. Nigger got them clodhoppers! Old brogans! He ain't nothing but a sharecropper.

TOLEDO. You can make all the fun you want. It don't mean nothing. I'm satisfied with them and that's what counts.

LEVEE. Nigger, why don't you get some decent shoes? Got nerve to put on a suit and tie with them farming boots.

CUTLER. What you just tell me? It don't make no difference about the man's shoes. That's what you told me.

LEVEE. Aw, hell, I don't care what the nigger wear. I'll be honest with you. I don't care if he went barefoot. (SLOW DRAG *has put his string on the bass and is tuning it.*) Play something for me, Slow Drag. (SLOW DRAG *plays.*) A man got to have some shoes to dance like this! You can't dance like this with them clodhoppers Toledo got. (LEVEE *sings.*)

Hello Central give me Doctor Jazz
He's got just what I need I'll say he has
When the world goes wrong and I have got the blues
He's the man who makes me get on my dancing shoes.

TOLEDO. That's the trouble with colored folks . . . always wanna have a good time. Good times done got more niggers killed than God got ways to count. What the hell having a good time mean? That's what I wanna know.

LEVEE. Hell, nigger . . . it don't need explaining. Ain't you never had no good time before?

TOLEDO. The more niggers get killed having a good time, the more good times niggers wanna have. (SLOW DRAG *stops playing.*) There's more to life than having a good time. If there ain't, then this is a piss-poor life we're having . . . if that's all there is to be got out of it.

SLOW DRAG. Toledo, just 'cause you like to read them books and study and whatnot . . . that's your good time. People get other things they likes to do to have a good time. Ain't no need you picking them about it.

CUTLER. Niggers been having a good time before you was born, and they gonna keep having a good time after you gone.

TOLEDO. Yeah, but what else they gonna do? Ain't nobody talking about making the lot of the colored man better for him here in America.

LEVEE. Now you gonna be Booker T. Washington.

TOLEDO. Everybody worried about having a good time. Ain't nobody thinking about what kind of world they gonna leave their youngens. "Just give me the good time, that's all I want." It just makes me sick.

SLOW DRAG. Well, the colored man's gonna be all right. He

got through slavery, and he'll get through whatever else the white man put on him. I ain't worried about that. Good times is what makes life worth living. Now, you take the white man . . . The white man don't know how to have a good time. That's why he's troubled all the time. He don't know how to have a good time. He don't know how to laugh at life.

LEVEE. That's what the problem is with Toledo . . . reading all them books and things. He done got to the point where he forgot how to laugh and have a good time. Just like the white man.

TOLEDO. I know how to have a good time as well as the next man. I said, there's got to be more to life than having a good time. I said the colored man ought to be doing more than just trying to have a good time all the time.

LEVEE. Well, what is you doing, nigger? Talking all them highfalutin ideas about making a better world for the colored man. What is you doing to make it better? You playing the music and looking for your next piece of pussy same as we is. What is you doing? That's what I wanna know. Tell him, Cutler.

CUTLER. You all leave Cutler out of this. Cutler ain't got nothing to do with it.

TOLEDO. Levee, you just about the most ignorant nigger I know. Sometimes I wonder why I ever bother to try and talk with you.

LEVEE. Well, what is you doing? Talking that shit to me about I'm ignorant! What is you doing? You just a whole lot of mouth. A great big windbag. Thinking you smarter than everybody else. What is you doing, huh?

TOLEDO. It ain't just me, fool! It's everybody! What you think . . . I'm gonna solve the colored man's problems by myself? I said, we. You understand that? We. That's every living colored man in the world got to do his share. Got to do his part. I ain't talking about what I'm gonna do . . . or what you or Cutler or Slow Drag or anybody else. I'm talking about all of us together. What all of us is gonna do. That's what I'm talking about, nigger!

LEVEE. Well, why didn't you say that, then?

CUTLER. Toledo, I don't know why you waste time on this fool.

TOLEDO. That's what I'm trying to figure out.

LEVEE. Now there go Cutler with his shit. Calling me a fool. You wasn't even in the conversation. Now you gonna take sides and call me a fool.

CUTLER. Hell, I was listening to the man. I got sense enough to know what he was saying. I could tell it straight back to you.

LEVEE. Well, you go on with it. But I'll tell you this . . . I ain't gonna be too many more of your fools. I'll tell you that. Now you put that in your pipe and smoke it.

CUTLER. Boy, ain't nobody studying you. Telling me what to put in my pipe. Who's you to tell me what to do?

LEVEE. All right, I ain't nobody. Don't pay me no mind. I ain't nobody.

TOLEDO. Levee, you ain't nothing but the devil.

LEVEE. There you go! That's who I am. I'm the devil. I ain't nothing but the devil.

CUTLER. I can see that. That's something you know about. You know all about the devil.

LEVEE. I ain't saying what I know. I know plenty. What you know about the devil? Telling me what I know. What you know?

SLOW DRAG. I know a man sold his soul to the devil.

LEVEE. There you go! That's the only thing I ask about the devil . . . to see him coming so I can sell him this one I got. 'Cause if there's a god up there, he done went to sleep.

SLOW DRAG. Sold his soul to the devil himself. Name of Eliza Cottor. Lived in Tuscaloosa County, Alabama. The devil came by and he done upped and sold him his soul.

CUTLER. How you know the man done sold his soul to the devil, nigger? You talking that old-woman foolishness.

SLOW DRAG. Everybody know. It wasn't no secret. He went around working for the devil and everybody knowed it. Carried him a bag . . . one of them carpetbags. Folks say he carried the devil's papers and whatnot where he put your fingerprint on the paper with blood.

LEVEE. Where he at now? That's what I want to know. He can put my whole handprint if he want to!

CUTLER. That's the damnedest thing I ever heard! Folks kill me with that talk.

TOLEDO. Oh, that's real enough, all right. Some folks go arm in arm with the devil, shoulder to shoulder, and talk to him all the time. That's real, ain't nothing wrong in believing that.

SLOW DRAG. That's what I'm saying. Eliza Cotter is one of them. All right. The man living up in an old shack on Ben Foster's place, shoeing mules and horses, making them charms and things in secret. He done hooked up with the devil, showed up one day all fancied out with just the finest clothes you ever seen on a colored man . . . dressed just like one of them crackers . . . and carrying this bag with them papers and things. All right. Had a pocketful of money, just living the life of a rich man. Ain't done no more work or nothing. Just had him a string of women he run around with and throw his money away on. Bought him a big fine house . . . Well, it wasn't all that big, but it did have one of them white picket fences around it. Used to hire a man once a week just to paint that fence. Messed around there and one of the fellows of them gals he was messing with got fixed on him wrong and Eliza killed him. And he laughed about it. Sheriff come and arrest him, and then let him go. And he went around in that town laughing about killing this fellow. Trial come up, and the judge cut him loose. He must have been in converse with the devil too . . . 'cause he cut him loose and give him a bottle of whiskey! Folks ask what done happened to make him change, and he'd tell them straight out he done sold his soul to the devil and ask them if they wanted to sell theirs 'cause he could arrange it for them. Preacher see him coming, used to cross on the other side of the road. He'd just stand there and laugh at the preacher and call him a fool to his face.

CUTLER. Well, whatever happened to this fellow? What come of him? A man who, as you say, done sold his soul to the devil is bound to come to a bad end.

TOLEDO. I don't know about that. The devil's strong. The devil ain't no pushover.

SLOW DRAG. Oh, the devil had him under his wing, all right. Took good care of him. He ain't wanted for nothing.

CUTLER. What happened to him? That's what I want to know.

SLOW DRAG. Last I heard, he headed north with that bag of his, handing out hundred-dollar bills on the spot to whoever wanted to sign on with the devil. That's what I hear tell of him.

CUTLER. That's a bunch of fool talk. I don't know how you fix your mouth to tell that story. I don't believe that.

SLOW DRAG. I ain't asking you to believe it. I'm just telling you the facts of it.

LEVEE: I sure wish I knew where he went. He wouldn't have to convince me long. Hell, I'd even help him sign people up.

CUTLER. Nigger, God's gonna strike you down with that blasphemy you talking.

LEVEE. Oh, shit! God don't mean nothing to me. Let him strike me! Here I am, standing right here. What you talking about he's gonna strike me? Here I am! Let him strike me! I ain't scared of him. Talking that stuff to me.

CUTLER. All right. You gonna be sorry. You gonna fix yourself to have bad luck. Ain't nothing gonna work for you.

(*Buzzer sounds offstage.*)

LEVEE. Bad luck? What I care about some bad luck? You talking simple. I ain't knowed nothing but bad luck all my life. Couldn't get no worse. What the hell I care about some bad luck? Hell, I eat it everyday for breakfast! You dumber than I thought you was . . . talking about bad luck.

CUTLER. All right, nigger, you'll see! Can't tell a fool nothing. You'll see!

IRVIN. (*Enters the studio, checks his watch, and calls down the stairs.*) Cutler . . . you boys' sandwiches are up here . . . Cutler?

CUTLER. Yessir, Mr. Irvin . . . be right there.

TOLEDO. I'll walk up there and get them.

(TOLEDO *exits. The lights go down in the band room and up in the studio.* IRVIN *paces back and forth in an agitated manner.* STURDYVANT *enters.*)

STURDYVANT. Irv, what's happening? Is she here yet? Was that her?

IRVIN. It's the sandwiches, Mel. I told you . . . I'll let you know when she comes, huh?

STURDYVANT. What's keeping her? Do you know what time it is? Have you looked at the clock? You told me she'd be here. You told me you'd take care of it.

IRVIN. Mel, for Chrissakes! What do you want from me? What do you want me to do?

STURDYVANT. Look what time it is, Irv. You told me she'd be here.

IRVIN. She'll be here, okay? I don't know what's keeping her. You know they're always late, Mel.

STURDYVANT. You should have went by the hotel and made sure she was on time. You should have taken care of this. That's what you told me, huh? "I'll take care of it."

IRVIN. Okay! Okay! I didn't go by the hotel! What do you want me to do? She'll be here, okay? The band's here . . . she'll be here.

STURDYVANT. Okay, Irv. I'll take your word. But if she doesn't come . . . if she doesn't come . . . (STURDYVANT *exits to the control booth as* TOLEDO *enters.*)

TOLEDO. Mr. Irvin . . . I come up to get the sandwiches.

IRVIN. Say . . . uh . . . look . . . one o'clock, right? She said one o'clock.

TOLEDO. That's what time she told us. Say be here at one o'clock.

IRVIN. Do you know what's keeping her? Do you know why she ain't here?

TOLEDO. I can't say, Mr. Irvin. Told us one o'clock.

(The buzzer sounds. IRVIN goes to the door. There is a flurry of commotion as MA RAINEY enters, followed closely by the POLICEMAN, DUSSIE MAE, and SYLVESTER. MA RAINEY is a short, heavy woman. She is dressed in a full-length fur coat with matching hat, an emerald-green dress, and several strands of pearls of varying lengths. Her hair is secured by a headband that matches her dress. Her manner is simple and direct, and she carries herself in a royal fashion. DUSSIE MAE is a young, dark-skinned woman whose greatest asset is the sensual energy which seems to flow from her. She is dressed in a fur jacket and a tight-fitting canary-yellow dress. SYLVESTER is an Arkansas country boy, the size of a fullback. He wears a new suit and coat, in which he is obviously uncomfortable. Most of the time, he stutters when he speaks.)

MA RAINEY. Irvin . . . you better tell this man who I am! You better get him straight!

IRVIN. Ma, do you know what time it is? Do you have any idea? We've been waiting . . .

DUSSIE MAE. (To SYLVESTER.) If you was watching where you was going . . .

SYLVESTER. I was watching . . . What you mean?

IRVIN. (Notices POLICEMAN.) What's going on here? Officer, what's the matter?

MA RAINEY. Tell the men who he's messing with!

POLICEMAN. Do you know this lady?

MA RAINEY. Just tell the man who I am! That's all you gotta do.

POLICEMAN. Lady, will you let me talk, huh?

MA RAINEY. Tell the man who I am!

IRVIN. Wait a minute . . . wait a minute! Let me handle it. Ma, will you let me handle it?

MA RAINEY. Tell him who he's messing with!

IRVIN. Okay! Okay! Give me a chance! Officer, this is one of our recording artists . . . Ma Rainey.

MA RAINEY. Madame Rainey! Get it straight! Madame Rainey! Talking about taking me to jail!

IRVIN. Look, Ma . . . give me a chance, okay? Here . . . sit down. I'll take care of it. Officer, what's the problem?

DUSSIE MAE. (To SYLVESTER.) It's all your fault.

SYLVESTER. I ain't done nothing . . . Ask Ma.

POLICEMAN. Well . . . when I walked up on the incident . . .

DUSSIE MAE. Sylvester wrecked Ma's car.

SYLVESTER. I d-d-did not! The m-m-man ran into me!

POLICEMAN. (*To* IRVIN.) Look, buddy . . . if you want it in a nutshell, we got her charged with assault and battery.

MA RAINEY. Assault and what for what!

DUSSIE MAE. See . . . we was trying to get a cab . . . and so Ma . . .

MA RAINEY. Wait a minute! I'll tell you if you wanna know what happened. (*She points to* SYLVESTER.) Now, that's Sylvester. That's my nephew. He was driving my car . . .

POLICEMAN. Lady, we don't know whose car he was driving.

MA RAINEY. That's my car!

DUSSIE MAE and SYLVESTER. That's Ma's car!

MA RAINEY. What you mean you don't know whose car it is? I bought and paid for that car.

POLICEMAN. That's what you say, lady . . . We still gotta check. (*To* IRVIN.) They hit a car on Market Street. The guy said the kid ran a stoplight.

SYLVESTER. What you mean? The man c-c-come around the corner and hit m-m-me!

POLICEMAN. While I was calling a paddy wagon to haul them to the station, they try to hop into a parked cab. The cabbie said he was waiting on a fare . . .

MA RAINEY. The man was just sitting there. Wasn't waiting for nobody. I don't know why he wanna tell that lie.

POLICEMAN. Look, lady . . . will you let me tell the story?

MA RAINEY. Go ahead and tell it then. But tell it right!

POLICEMAN. Like I say . . . she tries to get in this cab. The cabbie's waiting on a fare. She starts creating a disturbance. The cabbie gets out to try and explain the situation to her . . . and she knocks him down.

DUSSIE MAE. She ain't hit him! He just fell!

SYLVESTER. He just s-s-s-slipped!

POLICEMAN. He claims she knocked him down. We got her charged with assault and battery.

MA RAINEY. If that don't beat all to hell. I ain't touched the man! The man was trying to reach around me to keep his car door closed. I opened the door and it hit him and he fell down. I ain't touched the man!

IRVIN. Okay. Okay . . . I got it straight now, Ma. You didn't touch him. All right? Officer, can I see you for a minute?

DUSSIE MAE. Ma was just trying to open the door.

SYLVESTER. He j-j-just got in t-t-the way!

MA RAINEY. Said he wasn't gonna haul no colored folks . . .
if you want to know the truth of it.

IRVIN. Okay, Ma . . . I got it straight now. Officer? (IRVIN
pulls the POLICEMAN *off to the side.*)

MA RAINEY. (*Noticing* TOLEDO.) Toledo, Cutler and everybody here?

TOLEDO. Yeah, they down in the band room. What happened to your car?

STURDYVANT. (*Entering.*) Irv, what's the problem? What's
going on? Officer . . .

IRVIN. Mel, let me take care of it. I can handle it.

STURDYVANT. What's happening? What the hell's going on?

IRVIN. Let me handle it, Mel, huh?

STURDYVANT. (*Crosses over to* MA RAINEY.) What's going
on, Ma. What'd you do?

MA RAINEY. Sturdyvant, get on away from me! That's the
last thing I need . . . to go through some of your shit!

IRVIN. Mel, I'll take care of it. I'll explain it all to you. Let
me handle it, huh? (STURDYVANT *reluctantly returns to the
control booth.*)

POLICEMAN. Look, buddy, like I say . . . we got her charged
with assault and battery . . and the kid with threatening the
cabbie.

SYLVESTER. I ain't done n-n-nothing!

MA RAINEY. You leave the boy out of it. He ain't done
nothing. What's he supposed to have done?

POLICEMAN. He threatened the cabbie, lady! You just can't
go around threatening people.

SYLVESTER. I ain't done nothing to him! He's the one talking
about he g-g-gonna get a b-b-baseball bat on me! I just told
him what I'd do with it. But I ain't done nothing 'cause he
didn't get the b-b-bat!

IRVIN. (*Pulling the* POLICEMAN *aside.*) Officer . . . look
here . . .

POLICEMAN. We was on our way down to the precinct . . .
but I figured I'd do you a favor and bring her by here. I mean,
if she's as important as she says she is . . .

IRVIN. (*Slides a bill from his pocket.*) Look, Officer . . . I'm
Madame Rainey's manager . . . It's good to meet you. (*He
shakes the* POLICEMAN'*s hand and passes him the bill.*) As soon
as we're finished with the recording session, I'll personally stop
by the precinct house and straighten up this misunderstanding.

POLICEMAN. Well . . . I guess that's all right. As long as

someone is responsible for them. (*He pockets the bill and winks at* IRVIN.) No need to come down . . . I'll take care of it myself. Of course, we wouldn't want nothing like this to happen again.

IRVIN. Don't worry, Officer . . . I'll take care of everything. Thanks for your help. (IRVIN *escorts the* POLICEMAN *to the door and returns. He crosses over to* MA RAINEY.) Here, Ma . . . let me take your coat. (*To* SYLVESTER.) I don't believe I know you.

MA RAINEY. That's my nephew, Sylvester.

IRVIN. I'm very pleased to meet you. Here . . . you can give me your coat.

MA RAINEY. That there is Dussie Mae.

IRVIN. Hello . . . (DUSSIE MAE *hands* IRVIN *her coat.*) Listen, Ma, just sit there and relax. The boys are in the bandroom rehearsing. You just sit and relax a minute.

MA RAINEY. I ain't for no sitting. I ain't never heard of such. Talking about taking me to jail. Irvin, call down there and see about my car.

IRVIN. Okay, Ma . . . I'll take care of it. You just relax. (IRVIN *exits with the coats.*)

MA RAINEY. Why you all keep it so cold in here? Sturdyvant try and pinch every penny he can. You all wanna make some records, you better put some heat on in here or give me back my coat.

IRVIN. (*Entering.*) We got the heat turned up, Ma. It's warming up. It'll be warm in a minute.

DUSSIE MAE. (*Whispering to* MA RAINEY.) Where's the bathroom?

MA RAINEY. It's in the back. Down the hall next to Sturdyvant's office. Come on, I'll show you where it is. Irvin, call down there and see about my car. I want my car fixed today.

IRVIN. I'll take care of everything, Ma. (*He notices* TOLEDO.) Say . . . uh . . . uh . . .

TOLEDO. Toledo.

IRVIN. Yeah . . . Toledo. I got the sandwiches, you can take down to the rest of the boys. We'll be ready to go in a minute. Give you boys a chance to eat and then we'll be ready to go.

(IRVIN *and* TOLEDO *exit. The lights go down in the studio and come up in the band room.*)

LEVEE. Slow Drag, you ever been to New Orleans?

SLOW DRAG. What's in New Orleans that I want?

LEVEE. How you call yourself a musician and ain't never been to New Orleans.

SLOW DRAG. You ever been to Fat Back, Arkansas? (*Pauses.*) All right, then. Ain't never been nothing in New Orleans that I couldn't get in Fat Back.

LEVEE. That's why you backwards. You just an old country boy talking about Fat Back, Arkansas, and New Orleans in the same breath.

CUTLER. I been to New Orleans. What about it?

LEVEE. You ever been to Lula White's?

CUTLER. Lula White's? I ain't never heard of it.

LEVEE. Man, they got some gals in there just won't wait! I seen a man get killed in there once. Got drunk and grabbed one of the gals wrong . . . I don't know what the matter of it was. But he grabbed her and she stuck a knife in him all the way up to the hilt. He ain't even fell. He just stood there and choked on his own blood. I was just asking Slow Drag 'cause I was gonna take him to Lula White's when we get down to New Orleans and show him a good time. Introduce him to one of them gals I know down there.

CUTLER. Slow Drag don't need you to find him no pussy. He can take care of his own self. Fact is . . . you better watch your gal when Slow Drag's around. They don't call him Slow Drag for nothing. (*He laughs.*) Tell him how you got your name Slow Drag.

SLOW DRAG. I ain't thinking about Levee.

CUTLER. Slow Drag break a woman's back when he dance. They had this contest one time in this little town called Bolingbroke about a hundred miles outside of Macon. We was playing for this dance and they was giving twenty dollars to the best slow draggers. Slow Drag looked over the competition, got down off the bandstand, grabbed hold of one of them gals, and stuck to her like a fly to jelly. Like wood to glue. Man had that gal whooping and hollering so . . . everybody stopped to watch. This fellow come in . . . this gal's fellow . . . and pulled a knife a foot long on Slow Drag. 'Member that, Slow Drag?

SLOW DRAG. Boy that mama was hot! The front of her dress was wet as a dishrag!

LEVEE. So what happened? What the man do?

CUTLER. Slow Drag ain't missed a stroke. The gal, she just look at her man with that sweet dizzy look in her eye. She ain't about to stop! Folks was clearing out, ducking and hiding under tables, figuring there's gonna be a fight. Slow Drag just looked over the gal's shoulder at the man and said, "Mister, if you'd quit hollering and wait a minute . . . you'll see I'm doing you a favor. I'm helping this gal win ten dollars so she can buy you a gold watch." The man just stood there and looked at him, all the while stroking that knife. Told Slow Drag, say, "All right, then, nigger. You just better make damn sure you win." That's when folks started calling him Slow Drag. The women got to hanging around him so bad after that, them fellows in that town ran us out of there.

(TOLEDO *enters, carrying a small cardboard box with the sandwiches.*)

LEVEE. Yeah . . . well, them gals in Lula White's will put a harness on his ass.

TOLEDO. Ma's up there. Some kind of commotion with the police.

CUTLER. Police? What the police up there for?

TOLEDO. I couldn't get it straight. Something about her car. They gone now . . . she's all right. Mr. Irvin sent some sandwiches.

LEVEE. (*Springs across the room.*) Yeah, all right. What we got here? (*He takes two sandwiches out of the box.*)

TOLEDO. What you doing grabbing two? There ain't but five in there . . . How you figure you get two?

LEVEE. 'Cause I grabbed them first. There's enough for everybody . . . What you talking about? It ain't like I'm taking food out of nobody's mouth.

CUTLER. That's all right. He can have mine too. I don't want none.

(LEVEE *starts toward the box to get another sandwich.*)

TOLEDO. Nigger, you better get out of here. Slow Drag, you want this?

SLOW DRAG. Naw, you can have it.

TOLEDO. With Levee around, you don't have to worry about no leftovers. I can see that.

LEVEE. What's the matter with you? Ain't you eating two sandwiches? Then why you wanna talk about me? Talking about there won't be no leftovers with Levee around. Look at your own self before you look at me.

TOLEDO. That's what you is. That's what we all is. A leftover from history. You see now, I'll show you.

LEVEE. Aw, shit . . . I done got the nigger started now.

TOLEDO. Now, I'm gonna show you how this goes . . . where you just a leftover from history. Everybody come from different places in Africa, right? Come from different tribes and things. Soonawhile they began to make one big stew. You had the carrots, the peas, and potatoes and whatnot over here. And over there you had the meat, the nuts, the okra, corn . . . and then you mix it up and let it cook right through to get the flavors flowing together . . . then you got one thing. You got a stew.

Now you take and eat the stew. You take and make your history with that stew. All right. Now it's over. Your history's over and you done ate the stew. But you look around and you see some carrots over here, some potatoes over there. That stew's still there. You done made your history and it's still there. You can't eat it all. So what you got? You got some leftovers. That's what it is. You got leftovers and you can't do nothing with it. You already making you another history . . . cooking you another meal, and you don't need them leftovers no more. What to do?

See, we's the leftovers. The colored man is the leftovers. Now, what's the colored man gonna do with himself? That's what we waiting to find out. But first we gotta know we the leftovers. Now, who knows that? You find me a nigger that knows that and I'll turn any whichaway you want me to. I'll bend over for you. You ain't gonna find that. And that's what the problem is. The problem ain't with the white man. The white man knows you-just a leftover. 'Cause he the one who done the eating and he know what he done ate. But we don't know that we been took and made history out of. Done went and filled the white man's belly and now he's full and tired and wants you to get out the way and let him be by himself. Now, I know what I'm talking about. And if you wanna find out, you just ask Mr. Irvin what he had for supper yesterday. And if he's an honest white man . . . which is asking for a whole heap of a lot . . . he'll tell you he done ate your black ass and if you please I'm full up with you . . . so go on and get off the plate and let me eat something else.

SLOW DRAG. What that mean? What's eating got to do with how the white man treat you? He don't treat you no different according to what he ate.

TOLEDO. I ain't said it had nothing to do with how he treat you.

CUTLER. The man's trying to tell you something, fool!

SLOW DRAG. What he trying to tell me? Ain't you here. Why

you say he was trying to tell *me* something? Wasn't he trying to tell you too?

LEVEE. He was trying all right. He was trying a whole heap. I'll say that for him. But trying ain't worth a damn. I got lost right there trying to figure out who puts nuts in their stew.

SLOW DRAG. I knowed that before. My grandpappy used to put nuts in his stew. He and my grandmama both. That ain't nothing new.

TOLEDO. They put nuts in their stew all over Africa. But the stew they eat, and the stew your grandpappy made, and all the stew that you and me eat, and the stew Mr. Irvin eats . . . ain't in no way the same stew. That's the way that go. I'm through with it. That's the last you know me to ever try and explain something to you.

CUTLER. (*After a pause.*) Well, time's getting along . . . Come on, let's finish rehearsing.

LEVEE. (*Stretching out on a bench.*) I don't feel like rehearsing. I ain't nothing but a leftover. You go and rehearse with Toledo . . . He's gonna teach you how to make a stew.

SLOW DRAG. Cutler, what you gonna do? I don't want to be around here all day.

LEVEE. I know my part. You all go on and rehearse your part. You all need some rehearsal.

CUTLER. Come on, Levee, get up off your ass and rehearse the songs.

LEVEE. I already know them songs . . . What I wanna rehearse them for?

SLOW DRAG. You in the band, ain't you? You supposed to rehearse when the band rehearse.

TOLEDO. Levee think he the king of the barnyard. He thinks he's the only rooster know how to crow.

LEVEE. All right! All right! Come on, I'm gonna show you I know them songs. Come on, let's rehearse. I bet you the first one mess be Toledo. Come on . . . I wanna see if he know how to crow.

CUTLER. "Ma Rainey's Black Bottom," Levee's version. Let's do it.

(*They begin to rehearse. The lights go down in the band room and up in the studio. MA RAINEY sits and takes off her shoe, rubs her feet. DUSSIE MAE wanders about looking at the studio. SYLVESTER is over by the piano.*)

MA RAINEY. (*Singing to herself.*)
Oh, Lord, these dogs of mine
They sure do worry me all the time
The reason why I don't know
Lord, I beg to be excused
I can't wear me no sharp-toed shoes.
I went for a walk
I stopped to talk
Oh, how my corns did bark.

DUSSIE MAE. It feels kinda spooky in here. I ain't never been in no recording studio before. Where's the band at?

MA RAINEY. They off somewhere rehearsing. I don't know where Irvin went to. All this hurry up and he goes off back there with Sturdyvant. I know he better come on 'cause Ma ain't gonna be waiting. Come here . . . let me see that dress. (DUSSIE MAE *crosses over.* MA RAINEY *tugs at the dress around the waist, appraising the fit.*) That dress looks nice. I'm gonna take you tomorrow and get you some more things before I take you down to Memphis. They got clothes up here you can't get in Memphis. I want you to look nice for me. If you gonna travel with the show you got to look nice.

DUSSIE MAE. I need me some more shoes. These hurt my feet.

MA RAINEY. You get you some shoes that fit your feet. Don't you be messing around with no shoes that pinch your feet. Ma know something about bad feet. Hand me my slippers out my bag over yonder.

DUSSIE MAE. (*Brings the slippers.*) I just want to get a pair of them yellow ones. About a half-size bigger.

MA RAINEY. We'll get you whatever you need. Sylvester, too . . . I'm gonna get him some more clothes. Sylvester, tuck your clothes in. Straighten them up and look nice. Look like a gentleman.

DUSSIE MAE. Look at Sylvester with that hat on.

MA RAINEY. Sylvester, take your hat off inside. Act like your mama taught you something. I know she taught you better than that. (SYLVESTER *bangs on the piano.*) Come on over here and leave that piano alone.

SYLVESTER. I ain't d-d-doing nothing to the p-p-piano. I'm just l-l-looking at it.

MA RAINEY. Well. Come on over here and sit down. As soon as Mr. Irvin comes back, I'll have him take you down and introduce you to the band. (SYLVESTER *comes over.*) He's gonna take you down there and introduce you in a minute . . .

have Cutler show you how your part go. And when you get your money, you gonna send some of it home to your mama. Let her know you doing all right. Make her feel good to know you doing all right in the world.

(DUSSIE MAE *wanders about the studio and opens the door leading to the band room. The strains of* LEVEE's *version of "Ma Rainey's Black Bottom" can be heard.* IRVIN *enters.*)

IRVIN. Ma, I called down to the garage and checked on your car. It's just a scratch. They'll have it ready for you this afternoon. They're gonna send it over with one of their fellows.

MA RAINEY. They better have my car fixed right too. I ain't going for that. Brand-new car . . . they better fix it like new.

IRVIN. It was just a scratch on the fender, Ma . . . They'll take care of it . . . don't worry . . . they'll have it like new.

MA RAINEY. Irvin, what is that I hear? What is that the band's rehearsing? I know they ain't rehearsing Levee's "Black Bottom." I know I ain't hearing that?

IRVIN. Ma, listen . . . that's what I wanted to talk to you about. Levee's version of that song . . . it's got a nice arrangement . . . a nice horn intro . . . It really picks it up . . .

MA RAINEY. I ain't studying Levee nothing. I know what he done to that song and I don't like to sing it that way. I'm doing it the old way. That's why I brought my nephew to do the voice intro.

IRVIN. Ma, that's what the people want now. They want something they can dance to. Times are changing. Levee's arrangement gives the people what they want. It gets them excited . . . makes them forget about their troubles.

MA RAINEY. I don't care what you say, Irvin. Levee ain't messing up my song. If he got what the people want, let him take it somewhere else. I'm singing Ma Rainey's song. I ain't singing Levee's song. Now that's all there is to it. Carry my nephew on down there and introduce him to the band. I promised my sister I'd look out for him and he's gonna do the voice intro on the song my way.

IRVIN. Ma, we just figured that . . .

MA RAINEY. Who's this "we"? What you mean "we"? I ain't studying Levee nothing. Come talking this "we" stuff. Who's "we"?

IRVIN. Me and Sturdyvant. We decided that it would . . .

MA RAINEY. You decided, huh? I'm just a bump on the

log. I'm gonna go which ever way the river drift. Is that it?
You and Sturdyvant decided.

IRVIN. Ma, it was just that we thought it would be better.

MA RAINEY. I ain't got good sense. I don't know nothing
about music. I don't know what's a good song and what ain't.
You know more about my fans than I do.

IRVIN. It's not that, Ma. It would just be easier to do. It's
more what the people want.

MA RAINEY. I'm gonna tell you something, Irvin . . . and
you go on up there and tell Sturdyvant. What you all say don't
count with me. You understand? Ma listens to her heart. Ma
listens to the voice inside her. That's what counts with Ma.
Now, you carry my nephew on down there . . . tell Cutler he's
gonna do the voice intro on that "Black Bottom" song and that
Levee ain't messing up my song with none of his music shit.
Now, if that don't set right with you and Sturdyvant . . . then I
can carry my black bottom on back down South to my tour,
'cause I don't like it up here no ways.

IRVIN. Okay, Ma . . . I don't care. I just thought . . .

MA RAINEY. Damn what you thought! What you look like
telling me how to sing my song? This Levee and Sturdyvant
nonsense . . . I ain't going for it! Sylvester, go on down there
and introduce yourself. I'm through playing with Irvin.

SYLVESTER. Which way you go? Where they at?

MA RAINEY. Here . . . I'll carry you down there myself.

DUSSIE MAE. Can I go? I wanna see the band.

MA RAINEY. You stay your behind up here. Ain't no cause
in you being down there. Come on, Sylvester.

IRVIN. Okay, Ma. Have it your way. We'll be ready to go in
fifteen minutes.

MA RAINEY. We'll be ready to go when Madame says we're
ready. That's the way it goes around here. (MA RAINEY *and*
SYLVESTER *exit. The lights go down in the studio and up in the
band room.* MA RAINEY *enters with* SYLVESTER.) Cutler, this
here is my nephew Sylvester. He's gonna do that voice intro on
the "Black Bottom" song using the old version.

LEVEE. What you talking about? Mr. Irvin says he's using my
version. What you talking about?

MA RAINEY. Levee, I ain't studying you or Mr. Irvin. Cutler,
get him straightened out on how to do his part. I ain't thinking
about Levee. These folks done messed with the wrong person
this day. Sylvester, Cutler gonna teach you your part. You go
ahead and get it straight. Don't worry about what nobody else
say. (MA RAINEY *exits.*)

CUTLER. Well, come on in, boy. I'm Cutler. You got Slow Drag . . . Levee . . . and that's Toledo over there. Sylvester, huh?

SYLVESTER. Sylvester Brown.

LEVEE. I done wrote a version of that song what picks it up and sets it down in the people's lap! Now she come talking this! You don't need that old circus bullshit! I know what I'm talking about. You gonna mess up the song Cutler and you know it.

CUTLER. I ain't gonna mess up nothing. Ma say . . .

LEVEE. I don't care what Ma say! I'm talking about what the intro gonna do to the song. The peoples in the North ain't gonna buy all that tent-show nonsense. They wanna hear some music!

CUTLER. Nigger, I done told you time and again . . . you just in the band. You plays the piece . . . whatever they want! Ma says what to play! Not you! You ain't here to be doing no creating. Your job is to play whatever Ma says!

LEVEE. I might not play nothing! I might quit!

CUTLER. Nigger, don't nobody care if you quit. Whose heart you gonna break?

TOLEDO. Levee ain't gonna quit. He got to make some money to keep him in shoe polish.

LEVEE. I done told you all . . . you all don't know me. You don't know what I'll do.

CUTLER. I don't think nobody too much give a damn! Sylvester, here's the way your part go. The band plays the intro . . . I'll tell you where to come in. The band plays the intro and then you say, "All right, boys, you done seen the rest . . . Now I'm gonna show you the best. Ma Rainey's gonna show you her black bottom." You got that? (SYLVESTER *nods.*) Let me hear you say it one time.

SYLVESTER. "All right, boys, you done s-s-seen the rest n-n-now I'm gonna show you the best. M-m-m-m-m-m-ma Rainey's gonna s-s-show you her black b-b-bottom."

LEVEE. What kind of . . . All right, Cutler! Let me see you fix that! You straighten that out! You hear that shit, Slow Drag? How in the hell the boy gonna do the part and he can't even talk!

SYLVESTER. W-w-w-who's you to tell me what to do, nigger! This ain't your band! Ma tell me to d-d-d-do it and I'm gonna do it. You can go to hell, n-n-n-nigger!

LEVEE. B-b-b-boy, ain't nobody studying you. You go on and fix that one, Cutler. You fix that one and I'll . . . I'll shine your shoes for you. You go on and fix that one!

TOLEDO. You say you Ma's nephew, huh?

SYLVESTER. Yeah. So w-w-what that mean?

TOLEDO. Oh, I ain't meant nothing . . . I was just asking.

SLOW DRAG. Well, come on and let's rehearse so the boy can get it right.

LEVEE. I ain't rehearsing nothing! You just wait till I get my band. I'm gonna record that song and show you how it supposed to go!

CUTLER. We can do it without Levee. Let him sit on over there. Sylvester, you remember your part?

SYLVESTER. I remember it pretty g-g-g-good.

CUTLER. Well, come on, let's do it, then.

(*The band begins to play.* LEVEE *sits and pouts.* STURDYVANT *enters the band room.*)

STURDYVANT. Good . . . you boys are rehearsing, I see.

LEVEE. (*Jumping up.*) Yessir! We rehearsing. We know them songs real good.

STURDYVANT. Good! Say, Levee, did you finish that song?

LEVEE. Yessir, Mr. Sturdyvant. I got it right here. I wrote that other part just like you say. It go like:

You can shake it, you can break it
You can dance at any hall

You can slide across the floor
You'll never have to stall
My jelly, my roll,
Sweet Mama, don't you let it fall.

Then I put that part in there for the people to dance, like you say, for them to forget about their troubles.

STURDYVANT. Good! Good! I'll just take this. I wanna see you about your songs as soon as I get the chance.

LEVEE. Yessir! As soon as you get the chance, Mr. Sturdyvant.

(STURDYVANT *exits.*)

CUTLER. You hear, Levee? You hear this nigger? "Yessuh, we's rehearsing, boss."

SLOW DRAG. I heard him. Seen him too. Shuffling them feet.

TOLEDO. Aw, Levee can't help it none. He's like all of us. Spooked up with the white men.

LEVEE. I'm spooked up with him, all right. You let one of

them crackers fix on me wrong. I'll show you how spooked up I am with him.

TOLEDO. That's the trouble of it. You wouldn't know if he was fixed on you wrong or not. You so spooked up by him you ain't had the time to study him.

LEVEE. I studies the white man. I got him studied good. The first time one fixes on me wrong, I'm gonna let him know just how much I studied. Come telling me I'm spooked up with the white man. You let one of them mess with me, I'll show you how spooked up I am.

CUTLER. You talking out your hat. The man come in here, call you a boy, tell you to get up off your ass and rehearse, and you ain't had nothing to say to him, except "Yessir!"

LEVEE. I can say "yessir" to whoever I please. What you got to do with it? I know how to handle white folks. I been handling them for thirty-two years, and now you gonna tell me how to do it. Just 'cause I say "yessir" don't mean I'm spooked up with him. I know what I'm doing. Let me handle him my way.

CUTLER. Well, go on and handle it, then.

LEVEE. Toledo, you always messing with somebody! Always agitating somebody with that old philosophy bullshit you be talking. You stay out of my way about what I do and say. I'm my own person. Just let me alone.

TOLEDO. You right, Levee. I apologize. It ain't none of my business that you spooked up by the white man.

LEVEE. All right! See! That's the shit I'm talking about. You all back up and leave Levee alone.

SLOW DRAG. Aw, Levee, we was all just having fun. Toledo ain't said nothing about you he ain't said about me. You just taking it all wrong.

TOLEDO. I ain't meant nothing by it, Levee. (*Pauses.*) Cutler, you ready to rehearse?

LEVEE. Levee got to be Levee! And he don't need nobody messing with him about the white man—cause you don't know nothing about me. You don't know Levee. You don't know nothing about what kind of blood I got! What kind of heart I got beating here! (*He pounds his chest.*) I was eight years old when I watched a gang of white mens come into my daddy's house and have to do with my mama any way they wanted. (*Pauses.*) We was living in Jefferson County, about eighty miles outside of Natchez. My daddy's name was Memphis . . . Memphis Lee Green . . . had him near fifty acres of good farming land. I'm talking about good land! Grow anything you want!

He done gone off of shares and bought this land from Mr. Hallie's widow woman after he done passed on. Folks called him an uppity nigger 'cause he done saved and borrowed to where he could buy this land and be independent. (*Pauses.*)

It was coming on planting time and my daddy went into Natchez to get him some seed and fertilizer. Called me, say, "Levee you the man of the house now. Take care of your mama while I'm gone." I wasn't but a little boy, eight years old. (*Pauses.*)

My mama was frying up some chicken when them mens come in that house. Must have been eight or nine of them. She standing there frying that chicken and them mens come and took hold of her just like you take hold of a mule and make him do what you want. (*Pauses.*)

There was my mama with a gang of white mens. She tried to fight them off, but I could see where it wasn't gonna do her any good. I didn't know what they were doing to her . . . but I figured whatever it was they may as well do to me too. My daddy had a knife that he kept around there for hunting and working and whatnot. I knew where he kept it and I went and got it.

I'm gonna show you how spooked up I was by the white man. I tried my damnedest to cut one of them's throat! I hit him on the shoulder with it. He reached back and grabbed hold of that knife and whacked me across the chest with it. (LEVEE *raises his shirt to show a long ugly scar.*)

That's what made them stop. They was scared I was gonna bleed to death. My mama wrapped a sheet around me and carried me two miles down to the Furlow place and they drove me up to Doc Albans. He was waiting on a calf to be born, and say he ain't had time to see me. They carried me up to Miss Etta, the midwife, and she fixed me up.

My daddy came back and acted like he done accepted the facts of what happened. But he got the names of them mens from mama. He found out who they was and then we announced we was moving out of that county. Said good-bye to everybody . . . all the neighbors. My daddy went and smiled in the face of one of them crackers who had been with my mama. Smiled in his face and sold him our land. We moved over with relations in Caldwell. He got us settled in and them he took off one day. I ain't never seen him since. He sneaked back, hiding up in the woods, laying to get them eight or nine men. (*Pauses.*)

He got four of them before they got him. They tracked him

down in the woods. Caught up with him and hung him and set him afire. (*Pauses.*)

My daddy wasn't spooked up by the white man. Nosir! And that taught me how to handle them. I seen my daddy go up and grin in this cracker's face . . . smile in his face and sell him his land. All the while he's planning how he's gonna get him and what he's gonna to do him. That taught me how to handle them. So you all just back up and leave Levee alone about the white man. I can smile and say yessir to whoever I please. I got time coming to me. You all just leave Levee alone about the white man.

(*There is a long pause.* SLOW DRAG *begins playing on the bass and sings.*)

SLOW DRAG. (*Singing.*)
If I had my way
If I had my way
If I had my way
I would tear this old building down.

BLACKOUT

ACT TWO

(The lights come up in the studio. The musicians are setting up their instruments. Ma Rainey walks about shoeless, singing softly to herself. Levee stands near Dussie Mae who hikes up her dress and crosses her leg. Cutler speaks to Irvin off to the side.)

CUTLER. Mr. Irvin, I don't know what you gonna do. I ain't got nothing to do with it, but the boy can't do the part. He stutters. He can't get it right. He stutters right through it every time.

IRVIN. Christ! Okay. We'll . . . Shit! We'll just do it like we planned. We'll do Levee's version. I'll handle it, Cutler. Come on, let's go. I'll think of something. *(He exits to the control booth.)*

MA RAINEY. *(Calling Cutler over.)* Levee's got his eyes in the wrong place. You better school him, Cutler.

CUTLER. Come on, Levee . . . let's get ready to play! Get your mind on your work!

IRVIN. *(Over speaker.)* Okay, boys, we're gonna do "Moonshine Blues" first. "Moonshine Blues," Ma.

MA RAINEY. I ain't doing no "Moonshine" nothing. I'm doing the "Black Bottom" first. Come on, Sylvester. *(To Irvin.)* Where's Sylvester's mike? You need a mike for Sylvester. Irvin . . . get him a mike.

IRVIN. Uh . . . Ma, the boys say he can't do it. We'll have to do Levee's version.

MA RAINEY. What you mean he can't do it? Who say he can't do it? What boys say he can't do it?

IRVIN. The band, Ma . . . the boys in the band.

MA RAINEY. What band? The band work for me! I say what goes! Cutler, what's he talking about? Levee, this some of your shit?

IRVIN. He stutters, Ma. They say he stutters.

MA RAINEY. I don't care if he do. I promised the boy he

454

could do the part . . . and he's gonna do it! That's all there is to it. He don't stutter all the time. Get a microphone down here for him.

IRVIN. Ma, we don't have time. We can't . . .

MA RAINEY. If you wanna make a record, you gonna find time. I ain't playing with you, Irvin. I can walk out of here and go back to my tour. I got plenty fans. I don't need to go through all of this. Just go and get the boy a microphone.

(IRVIN *and* STURDYVANT *consult in the booth,* IRVIN *exits.*)

STURDYVANT. All right, Ma . . . we'll get him a microphone. But if he messes up . . . He's only getting one chance . . . The cost . . .

MA RAINEY. Damn the cost. You always talking about the cost. I make more money for this outfit than anybody else you got put together. If he messes up he'll just do it till he gets it right. Levee, I know you had something to do with this. You better watch yourself.

LEVEE. It was Cutler!

SYLVESTER. It was you! You the only one m-m-mad about it.

LEVEE. The boy stutter. He can't do the part. Everybody see that. I don't know why you want the boy to do the part no ways.

MA RAINEY. Well, can or can't . . . he's gonna do it! You ain't got nothing to do with it!

LEVEE. I don't care what you do! He can sing the whole goddamned song for all I care!

MA RAINEY. Well, all right. Thank you.

(IRVIN *enters with a microphone and hooks it up. He exits to the control booth.*)

MA RAINEY. Come on, Sylvester. You just stand here and hold your hands like I told you. Just remember the words and say them . . . That's all there is to it. Don't worry about messing up. If you mess up, we'll do it again. Now, let me hear you say it. Play for him, Cutler.

CUTLER. One . . . two . . . you know what to do.

(*The band begins to play and* SYLVESTER *curls his fingers and clasps his hands together in front of his chest, pulling in opposite directions as he says his lines.*)

SYLVESTER. "All right, boys, you d-d-d-done s-s-s-seen the best . . . (LEVEE *stops playing*.) Now I'm g-g-g-gonna show you the rest . . . Ma R-r-rainey's gonna show you her b-b-b-black b-b-b-bottom." (*The rest of the band stops playing*.)

MA RAINEY. That's all right. That's real good. You take your time, you'll get it right.

STURDYVANT. (*Over speaker*.) Listen, Ma . . . now, when you come in, don't wait so long to come in. Don't take so long on the intro, huh?

MA RAINEY. Sturdyvant, don't you go trying to tell me how to sing. You just take care of that up there and let me take care of this down here. Where's my Coke?

IRVIN. Okay, Ma. We're all set up to go up here. "Ma Rainey's Black Bottom," boys.

MA RAINEY. Where's my Coke? I need a Coke. You ain't got no Coke down here? Where's my Coke?

IRVIN. What's the matter, Ma? What's . . .

MA RAINEY. Where's my Coke? I need a Coca-Cola.

IRVIN. Uh . . . Ma, look, I forgot the Coke, huh? Let's do it without it, huh? Just this one song. What say, boys?

MA RAINEY. Damn what the band say! You know I don't sing nothing without my Coca-Cola!

STURDYVANT. We don't have any, Ma. There's no Coca-Cola here. We're all set up and we'll just go ahead and . . .

MA RAINEY. You supposed to have Coca-Cola. Irvin knew that. I ain't singing nothing without my Coca-Cola! (*She walks away from the mike, singing to herself.* STURDYVANT *enters from the control booth.*)

STURDYVANT. Now, just a minute here, Ma. You come in an hour late . . . we're way behind schedule as it is . . . the band is set up and ready to go . . . I'm burning my lights . . . I've turned up the heat . . . We're ready to make a record and what? You decide you want a Coca-Cola?

MA RAINEY. Sturdyvant, get out of my face. (IRVIN *enters*.) Irvin . . . I told you keep away from me.

IRVIN. Mel, I'll handle it.

STURDYVANT. I'm tired of her nonsense, Irv. I'm not gonna put up with this!

IRVIN. Let me handle it, Mel. I know how to handle her. (IRVIN *to* MA RAINEY.) Look, Ma . . . I'll call down to the deli and get you a Coke. But let's get started, huh? Sylvester's standing there ready to go . . . the band's set up . . . let's do this one song, huh?

MA RAINEY. If you too cheap to buy me a Coke, I'll buy my

own. Slow Drag! Sylvester, go with Slow Drag and get me a Coca-Cola. (SLOW DRAG *comes over*.) Slow Drag, walk down to that store on the corner and get me three bottles of Coca-Cola. Get out my face, Irvin. You all just wait until I get my Coke. It ain't gonna kill you.

IRVIN. Okay, Ma. Get your Coke, for Chrissakes! Get your coke!

(IRVIN *and* STURDYVANT *exit into the hallway followed by* SLOW DRAG *and* SYLVESTER. TOLEDO, CUTLER, *and* LEVEE *head for the band room*.)

MA RAINEY. Cutler, come here a minute. I want to talk to you. (*Cutler crosses over somewhat reluctantly*.) What's all this about "the boys in the band say"? I tells you what to do. I says what the matter is with the band. I say who can and can't do what.

CUTLER. We just say 'cause the boy stutter . . .

MA RAINEY. I know he stutters. Don't you think I know he stutters. This is what's gonna help him.

CUTLER. Well, how can he do the part if he stutters? You want him to stutter through it? We just thought it be easier to go on and let Levee do it like we planned.

MA RAINEY. I don't care if he stutters or not! He's doing the part and I don't wanna hear any more of this shit about what the band says. And I want you to find somebody to replace Levee when we get to Memphis. Levee ain't nothing but trouble.

CUTLER. Levee's all right. He plays good music when he puts his mind to it. He knows how to write music too.

MA RAINEY. I don't care what he know. He ain't nothing but bad news. Find somebody else. I know it was his idea about who to say who can do what. (DUSSIE MAE *wanders over to where they are sitting*.) Dussie Mae, go sit your behind down somewhere and quit flaunting yourself around.

DUSSIE MAE. I ain't doing nothing.

MA RAINEY. Well, just go on somewhere and stay out of the way.

CUTLER. I been meaning to ask you, Ma . . . about these songs. This "Moonshine Blues" . . . that's one of them songs Bessie Smith sang, I believes.

MA RAINEY. Bessie what? Ain't nobody thinking about Bessie. I taught Bessie. She ain't doing nothing but imitating me. What I care about Bessie? I don't care if she sell a million

records. She got her people and I got mine. I don't care what
nobody else do. Ma was the *first* and don't you forget it!

CUTLER. Ain't nobody said nothing about that. I just said
that's the same song she sang.

MA RAINEY. I been doing this a long time. Ever since I was a
little girl. I don't care what nobody else do. That's what gets me
so mad with Irvin. White folks try to be put out with you all the
time. Too cheap to buy me a Coca-Cola. I lets them know it,
though. Ma don't stand for no shit. Wanna take my voice and
trap it in them fancy boxes with all them buttons and dials
. . . and then too cheap to buy me a Coca-Cola. And it don't
cost but a nickle a bottle.

CUTLER. I knows what you mean about that.

MA RAINEY. They don't care nothing about me. All they
want is my voice. Well, I done learned that, and they gonna
treat me like I want to be treated no matter how much it hurt
them. They back there now calling me all kinds of names . . .
calling me everything but a child of god. But they can't do
nothing else. They ain't got what they wanted yet. As soon as
they get my voice down on them recording machines, then it's
just like if I'd be some whore and they roll over and put their
pants on. Ain't got no use for me then. I know what I'm talking
about. You watch. Irvin right there with the rest of them. He
don't care nothing about me either. He's been my manager for
six years, always talking about sticking together, and the only
time he had me in his house was to sing for some of his friends.

CUTLER. I know how they do.

MA RAINEY. If you colored and can make them some money,
then you all right with them. Otherwise, you just a dog in the
alley. I done made this company more money from my records
than all the other recording artists they got put together. And
they wanna balk about how much this session is costing them.

CUTLER. I don't see where it's costing them all what they say.

MA RAINEY. It ain't! I don't pay that kind of talk no mind.

(*The lights go down on the studio and come up on the band
room.* TOLEDO *sits reading a newspaper.* LEVEE *sings and
hums his song.*)

LEVEE. (*Singing.*)
You can shake it, you can break it
You can dance at any hall
You can slide across the floor
You'll never have to stall

My jelly, my roll,
Sweet Mama, don't you let it fall.

Wait till Sturdyvant hear me play that! I'm talking about some real music, Toledo! I'm talking about *real* music! (*The door opens and* DUSSIE MAE *enters.*) Hey, mama! Come on in.

DUSSIE MAE. Oh, hi! I just wanted to see what it looks like down here.

LEVEE. Well, come on in . . . I don't bite.

DUSSIE MAE. I didn't know you could really write music. I thought you was just jiving me at the club last night.

LEVEE. Naw, baby . . . I knows how to write music. I done give Mr. Sturdyvant some of my songs and he says he's gonna let me record them. Ask Toledo. I'm gonna have my own band! Toledo, ain't I give Mr. Sturdyvant some of my songs I wrote?

TOLEDO. Don't get Toledo mixed up in nothing. (*He exits.*)

DUSSIE MAE. You gonna get your own band sure enough?

LEVEE. That's right! Levee Green and his Footstompers.

DUSSIE MAE. That's real nice.

LEVEE. That's what I was trying to tell you last night. A man what's gonna get his own band need to have a woman like you.

DUSSIE MAE. A woman like me wants somebody to bring it and put it in my hand. I don't need nobody wanna get something for nothing and leave me standing in my door.

LEVEE. That ain't Levee's style, sugar. I got more style than that. I knows how to treat a woman. Buy her presents and things . . . treat her like she wants to be treated.

DUSSIE MAE. That's what they all say . . . till it come time to be buying the presents.

LEVEE. When we get down to Memphis, I'm gonna show you what I'm talking about. I'm gonna take you out and show you a good time. Show you Levee knows how to treat a woman.

DUSSIE MAE. When you getting your own band?

LEVEE. (*Moves closer to slip his arm around her.*) Soon as Mr. Sturdyvant say. I done got my fellows already picked out. Getting me some good fellows know how to play real sweet music.

DUSSIE MAE. (*Moves away.*) Go on now, I don't go for all that pawing and stuff. When you get your own band, maybe we can see about this stuff you talking.

LEVEE. (*Moving toward her.*) I just wanna show you I know what the women like. They don't call me Sweet Lemonade for nothing. (LEVEE *takes her in his arms and attempts to kiss her.*)

DUSSIE MAE. Stop it now. Somebody's gonna come in here.

LEVEE. Naw they ain't. Look here, sugar . . . what I wanna know is . . . can I introduce my red rooster to your brown hen?

DUSSIE MAE. You get your band then we'll see if that rooster know how to crow.

LEVEE. (*Grinds up against her and feels her buttocks.*) Now I know why my grandpappy sat on the back porch with his straight razor when grandma hung out the wash.

DUSSIE MAE. Nigger, you crazy!

LEVEE. I bet you sound like the midnight train from Alabama when it crosses the Mason-Dixon line.

DUSSIE MAE. How's you get so crazy?

LEVEE. It's women like you . . . drives me that way. (*He moves to kiss her as the lights go down in the band room and up in the studio.* MA RAINEY *sits with* CUTLER *and* TOLEDO.)

MA RAINEY. It sure done got quiet in here. I never could stand no silence. I always got to have some music going on in my head somewhere. It keeps things balanced. Music will do that. It fills things up. The more music you got in the world, the fuller it is.

CUTLER. I can agree with that. I got to have my music too.

MA RAINEY. White folks don't understand about the blues. They hear it come out, but they don't know how it got there. They don't understand that's life's way of talking. You don't sing to feel better. You sing 'cause that's a way of understanding life.

CUTLER. That's right. You get that understanding and you done got a grip on life to where you can hold your head up and go on to see what else life got to offer.

MA RAINEY. The blues help you get out of bed in the morning. You get up knowing you ain't alone. There's something else in the world. Something's been added by that song. This be an empty world without the blues. I take that emptiness and try to fill it up with something.

TOLEDO. You fill it up with something the people can't be without, Ma. That's why they call you the Mother of the Blues. You fill up that emptiness in a way ain't nobody ever thought of doing before. And now they can't be without it.

MA RAINEY. I ain't started the blues way of singing. The blues always been here.

CUTLER. In the church sometimes you find that way of singing. They got blues in the church.

MA RAINEY. They say I started it . . . but I didn't. I just helped it out. Filled up that empty space a little bit. That's all. But if they wanna call me the Mother of the Blues, that's all right with me. It don't hurt none. (SLOW DRAG and SYLVESTER *enter with the Cokes.*) It sure took you long enough. That store ain't but on the corner.

SLOW DRAG. That one was closed. We had to find another one.

MA RAINEY. Sylvester, go and find Mr. Irvin and tell him we ready to go.

(SYLVESTER *exits. The lights in the band room come up while the lights in the studio stay on.* LEVEE *and* DUSSIE MAE *are kissing.* SLOW DRAG *enters. They break their embrace.* DUSSIE MAE *straightens up her clothes.*)

SLOW DRAG. Cold out. I just wanted to warm up with a little sip. (*He goes to his locker, takes out his bottle and drinks.*) Ma got her Coke, Levee. We about ready to start. (SLOW DRAG *exits.* LEVEE *attempts to kiss* DUSSIE MAE *again.*)

DUSSIE MAE. No . . . come on! I got to go. You gonna get me in trouble. (*She pulls away and exits up the stairs.*)

LEVEE. (*Watches after her.*) Good God! Happy birthday to the lady with the cakes!

(*The lights go down in the band room and come up in the studio.* MA RAINEY *drinks her Coke.* LEVEE *enters from the band room. The musicians take their places.* SYLVESTER *stands by his mike.* IRVIN *and* STURDYVANT *look on from the control booth.*)

IRVIN. We're all set up here, Ma. We're all set to go. You ready down there?

MA RAINEY. Sylvester you just remember your part and say it. That's all there is to it. (*To* IRVIN.) Yeah, we ready.

IRVIN. Okay, boys. "Ma Rainey's Black Bottom." Take one.

CUTLER. One . . . two . . . You know what to do.

(*The band plays.*)

SYLVESTER. All right boys, you d-d-d-done s-s-seen the rest . . .

IRVIN. Hold it! (*The band stops.* STURDYVANT *changes the recording disk and nods to* IRVIN.) Okay. Take two.

CUTLER. One . . . two . . . You know what to do.

(*The band plays.*)

SYLVESTER. All right, boys, you done seen the rest . . . now I'm gonna show you the best. Ma Rainey's g-g-g-gonna s-s-show you her b-b-black bottom.

IRVIN. Hold it! Hold it! (*The band stops.* STURDYVANT *changes the recording disk.*) Okay. Take Three. Ma, let's do it without the intro, huh? No voice intro . . . you just come in singing.

MA RAINEY. Irvin, I done told you . . . the boy's gonna do the part. He don't stutter all the time. Just give him a chance. Sylvester, hold your hands like I told you and just relax. Just relax and concentrate.

IRVIN. All right. Take three.

CUTLER. One . . . Two . . . You know what to do.

(*The band plays.*)

SYLVESTER. All right, boys, you done seen the rest . . . now, I'm gonna show you the best. Ma Rainey's gonna show you her black bottom.

MA RAINEY. (*Singing.*)
Way down south in Alabama
I got a friend they call dancing Sammy
Who's crazy about all the latest dances
Black Bottom stomping, two babies prancing

The other night at a swell affair
As soon as the boys found out that I was there
They said, come on, Ma, let's go to the cabaret.
When I got there, you ought to hear them say,

I want to see the dance you call the black bottom
I want to learn that dance
I want to see the dance you call your big black bottom
It'll put you in a trance.

All the boys in the neighborhood
They say your black bottom is really good
Come on and show me your black bottom
I want to learn that dance

I want to see the dance you call the black bottom
I want to learn that dance
Come on and show the dance you call your big black bottom
It puts you in a trance.

Early last morning about the break of day
Grandpa told my grandma, I heard him say,
Get up and show your old man your black bottom
I want to learn that dance

(*Instrumental break.*)
I done showed you all my black bottom
You ought to learn that dance.

IRVIN. Okay, that's good, Ma. That sounded great! Good job, boys!

MA RAINEY. (*To* SYLVESTER.) See! I told you. I knew you could do it. You just have to put your mind to it. Didn't he do good, Cutler? Sound real good. I told him he could do it.

CUTLER. He sure did. He did better than I thought he was gonna do.

IRVIN. (*Entering to remove* SYLVESTER's *mike.*) Okay, boys . . . Ma . . . let's do "Moonshine Blues" next, huh? "Moonshine Blues," boys.

STURDYVANT. (*Over speaker.*) Irv! Something's wrong down there. We don't have it right.

IRVIN. What? What's the matter, Mel . . .

STURDYVANT. We don't have it right. Something happened. We don't have the goddamn song recorded!

IRVIN. What's the matter? Mel, what happened? You sure you don't have nothing?

STURDYVANT. Check that mike, huh, Irv. It's the kid's mike. Something's wrong with the mike. We've got everything all screwed up here.

IRVIN. Christ almighty! Ma, we got to do it again. We don't have it. We didn't record the song.

MA RAINEY. What you mean you didn't record it? What was you and Sturdyvant doing up there?

IRVIN. (*Following the mike wire.*) Here . . . Levee must have kicked the plug out.

LEVEE. I ain't done nothing: I ain't kicked nothing!

SLOW DRAG. If Levee had his mind on what he's doing . . .

MA RAINEY. Levee, if it ain't one thing, it's another. You better straighten yourself up!

LEVEE. Hell . . . it ain't my fault. I ain't done nothing!

STURDYVANT. What's the matter with that mike, Irv? What's the problem?

IRVIN. It's the cord, Mel. The cord's all chewed up. We need another cord.

MA RAINEY. This is the most disorganized . . . Irvin, I'm going home! Come on. Come on, Dussie. (MA RAINEY *walks past* STURDYVANT *as he enters from the control booth. She exits offstage to get her coat.*)

STURDYVANT. (*To* IRVIN.) Where's she going?

IRVIN. She said she's going home.

STURDYVANT. Irvin, you get her! If she walks out of here . . .

(MA RAINEY *enters carrying her and* DUSSIE MAE'S *coat.*)

MA RAINEY. Come on, Sylvester.

IRVIN. (*Helping her with her coat.*) Ma . . . Ma . . . listen. Fifteen minutes! All I ask is fifteen minutes!

MA RAINEY. Come on, Sylvester, get your coat.

STURDYVANT. Ma, if you walk out of this studio . . .

IRVIN. Fifteen minutes, Ma!

STURDYVANT. You'll be through . . . washed up! If you walk out on me . . .

IRVIN. Mel, for Chrissakes, shut up and let me handle it! (*He goes after* MA RAINEY, *who has started for the door.*) Ma, listen. These records are gonna be hits! They're gonna sell like crazy! Hell, even Sylvester will be a star. Fifteen minutes. That's all, I'm asking! Fifteen minutes.

MA RAINEY. (*Crosses to a chair and sits with her coat on.*) Fifteen minutes! You hear me, Irvin? Fifteen minutes . . . and then I'm gonna take my black bottom on back down to Georgia. Fifteen minutes. Then Madame Rainey is leaving!

IRVIN. (*Kisses her.*) All right, Ma . . . fifteen minutes. I promise. (*To the band.*) You boys go ahead and take a break. Fifteen minutes and we'll be ready to go.

CUTLER. Slow Drag, you got any of that bourbon left?

SLOW DRAG. Yeah, there's some down there.

CUTLER. I could use a little nip.

(CUTLER *and* SLOW DRAG *exit to the band room, followed by* LEVEE *and* TOLEDO. *The lights go down in the studio and up in the band room.*)

SLOW DRAG. Don't make me no difference if she leave or not. I was kinda hoping she would leave.

CUTLER. I'm like Mr. Irvin . . . After all this time we done put in here, it's best to go ahead and get something out of it.

TOLEDO. Ma gonna do what she wanna do, that's for sure. If I was Mr. Irvin, I'd best go and get them cords and things hooked up right. And I wouldn't take no longer than fifteen minutes doing it.

CUTLER. If Levee had his mind on his work, we wouldn't be in this fix. We'd be up there finishing up. Now we got to go back and see if that boy get that part right. Ain't no telling if he ever get that right again in his life.

LEVEE. Hey, Levee ain't done nothing!

SLOW DRAG. Levee up there got one eye on the gal and the other on his trumpet.

CUTLER. Nigger, don't you know that's Ma's gal?

LEVEE. I don't care whose gal it is. I ain't done nothing to her. I just talk to her like I talk to anybody else.

CUTLER. Well, that being Ma's gal, and that being that boy's gal, is one and two different things. The boy is liable to kill you . . . but you' ass gonna be out there scraping the concrete looking for a job if you messing with Ma's gal.

LEVEE. How am I messing with her? I ain't done nothing to the gal. I just asked her her name. Now, if you telling me I can't do that, then Ma will just have to go to hell.

CUTLER. All I can do is warn you.

SLOW DRAG. Let him hang himself, Cutler. Let him string his neck out.

LEVEE. I ain't done nothing to the gal! You all talk like I done went and done something to her. Leave me go with my business.

CUTLER. I'm through with it. Try and talk to a fool . . .

TOLEDO. Some mens got it worse than others . . . this foolishness I'm talking about. Some mens is excited to be fools. That excitement is something else. I know about it. I done experienced it. It makes you feel good to be a fool. But it don't last long. It's over in a minute. Then you got to tend with the consequences. You got to tend with what comes after. That's when you wish you had learned something about it.

LEVEE. That's the best sense you made all day. Talking about being a fool. That's the only sensible thing you said today. Admitting you was a fool.

TOLEDO. I admits it, all right. Ain't nothing wrong with it. I done been a little bit of everything.

LEVEE. Now you're talking. You's as big a fool as they make.

TOLEDO. Gonna be a bit more things before I'm finished with it. Gonna be foolish again. But I ain't never been the same fool twice. It might be a different kind of fool, but I ain't gonna be the same fool twice. That's where we parts ways.

SLOW DRAG. Toledo, you done been a fool about a woman?

TOLEDO. Sure. Sure I have. Same as everybody.

SLOW DRAG. Hell, I ain't never seen you mess with no woman. I thought them books was your woman.

TOLEDO. Sure I messed with them. Done messed with a whole heap of them. And gonna mess with some more. But I ain't gonna be no fool about them. What you think? I done come in the world full-grown, with my head in a book? I done been young. Married. Got kids. I done been around and I done loved women to where you shake in your shoes just at the sight of them. Feel it all up and down your spine.

SLOW DRAG. I didn't know you was married.

TOLEDO. Sure. Legally. I been married legally. Got the paper and all. I done been through life. Made my marks. Followed some signs on the road. Ignored some others. I done been all through it. I touched and been touched by it. But I ain't never been the same fool twice. That's what I can say.

LEVEE. But you been a fool. That's what counts. Talking about I'm a fool for asking the gal her name and here you is one yourself.

TOLEDO. Now, I married a woman. A good woman. To this day I can't say she wasn't a good woman. I can't say nothing bad about her. I married that woman with all the good graces and intentions of being hooked up and bound to her for the rest of my life. I was looking for her to put me in my grave. But, you see . . . it ain't all the time what you' intentions and wishes are. She went out and joined the church. All right. There ain't nothing wrong with that. A good Christian woman going to church and wanna do right by her god. There ain't nothing wrong with that. But she got up there, got to seeing them good Christian mens and wondering why I ain't like that. Soon she figure she got a heathen on her hands. She figured she couldn't live like that. The church was more important than I was. So she left. Packed up one day and moved out. To this day I ain't never said another word to her. Come home one day and my house was empty! And I sat down and figured out that I was a fool not to see that she needed something that I wasn't giving her. Else she wouldn't have been up there at the church in the first place. I ain't blaming her. I just said it wasn't gonna happen to me again. So, yeah, Toledo been a fool about a woman. That's part of making life.

CUTLER. Well, yeah, I been a fool too. Everybody done been a fool once or twice. But, you see, Toledo, what you call a fool and what I call a fool is two different things. I can't see where you was being a fool for that. You ain't done nothing foolish.

You can't help what happened, and I wouldn't call you a fool for it. A fool is responsible for what happens to him. A fool cause it to happen. Like Levee . . . if he keeps messing with Ma's gal and his feet be out there scraping the ground. That's a fool.

LEVEE. Ain't nothing gonna happen to Levee. Levee ain't gonna let nothing happen to him. Now, I'm gonna say it again. I asked the gal her name. That's all I done. And if that's being a fool, then you looking at the biggest fool in the world . . . 'cause I sure as hell asked her.

SLOW DRAG. You just better not let Ma see you ask her. That's what the man's trying to tell you.

LEVEE. I don't need nobody to tell me nothing.

CUTLER. Well, Toledo, all I gots to say is that from the looks of it . . . from your story . . . I don't think life did you fair.

TOLEDO. Oh, life is fair. It's just in the taking what it gives you.

LEVEE. Life ain't shit. You can put it in a paper bag and carry it around with you. It ain't got no balls. Now, death . . . death got some style! Death will kick your ass and make you wish you never been born! That's how bad death is! But you can rule over life. Life ain't nothing.

TOLEDO. Cutler, how's your brother doing?

CUTLER. Who, Nevada? Oh, he's doing all right. Staying in St. Louis. Got a bunch of kids, last I heard.

TOLEDO. Me and him was all right with each other. Done a lot of farming together down in Plattsville.

CUTLER. Yeah, I know you all was tight. He in St. Louis now. Running an elevator, last I hear about it.

SLOW DRAG. That's better than stepping in muleshit.

TOLEDO. Oh, I don't know now. I liked farming. Get out there in the sun . . . smell that dirt. Be out there by yourself . . . nice and peaceful. Yeah, farming was all right by me. Sometimes I think I'd like to get me a little old place . . . but I done got too old to be following behind one of them balky mules now.

LEVEE. Nigger talking about life is fair. And ain't got a pot to piss in.

TOLEDO. See, now, I'm gonna tell you something. A nigger gonna be dissatisfied no matter what. Give a nigger some bread and butter . . . and he'll cry 'cause he ain't got no jelly. Give him some jelly, and he'll cry 'cause he ain't got no knife to put it on with. If there's one thing I done learned in this life, it's that you can't satisfy a nigger no matter what you do. A nigger's gonna make his own dissatisfaction.

LEVEE. Niggers got a right to be dissatisfied. Is you gonna be satisfied with a bone somebody done throwed you when you see them eating the whole hog?

TOLEDO. You lucky they let you be an entertainer. They ain't got to accept your way of entertaining. You lucky and don't even know it. You's entertaining and the rest of the people is hauling wood. That's the only kind of job for the colored man.

SLOW DRAG. Ain't nothing wrong with hauling wood. I done hauled plenty wood. My daddy used to haul wood. Ain't nothing wrong with that. That's honest work.

LEVEE. That ain't what I'm talking about. I ain't talking about hauling no wood. I'm talking about being satisfied with a bone somebody done throwed you. That's what's the matter with you all. You satisfied sitting in one place. You got to move on down the road from where you sitting . . . and all the time you got to keep an eye out for that devil who's looking to buy up souls. And hope you get lucky and find him!

CUTLER. I done told you about that blasphemy. Taking about selling your soul to the devil.

TOLEDO. We done the same thing, Cutler. There ain't no difference. We done sold Africa for the price of tomatoes. We done sold ourselves to the white man in order to be like him. Look at the way you dressed . . . That ain't African. That's the white man. We trying to be just like him. We done sold who we are in order to become someone else. We's imitation white men.

CUTLER. What else we gonna be, living over here?

LEVEE. I'm Levee. Just me. I ain't no imitation nothing!

SLOW DRAG. You can't change who you are by how you dress. That's what I got to say.

TOLEDO. It ain't all how you dress. It's how you act, how you see the world. It's how you follow life.

LEVEE. It don't matter what you talking about. I ain't no imitation white man. And I don't want to be no white man. As soon as I get my band together and make them records like Mr. Sturdyvant done told me I can make, I'm gonna be like Ma and tell the white man just what he can do. Ma tell Mr. Irvin she gonna leave . . . and Mr. Irvin get down on his knees and beg her to stay! That's the way I'm gonna be! Make the white man respect me!

CUTLER. The white man don't care nothing about Ma. The

colored folks made Ma a star. White folks don't care nothing about who she is . . . what kind of music she make.

SLOW DRAG. That's the truth about that. You let her go down to one of them white-folks hotels and see how big she is.

CUTLER. Hell, she ain't got to do that. She can't even get a cab up here in the North. I'm gonna tell you something. Reverend Gates . . . you know Reverend Gates? . . . Slow Drag know who I'm talking about. Reverend Gates . . . now I'm gonna show you how this go where the white man don't care a thing about who you is. Reverend Gates was coming from Tallahassee to Atlanta, going to see his sister, who was sick at that time with the consumption. The train come up through Thomasville, then past Moultrie, and stopped in this little town called Sigsbee . . .

LEVEE. You can stop telling that right there! That train don't stop in Sigsbee. I know what train you talking about. That train got four stops before it reach Macon to go on to Atlanta. One in Thomasville, one in Moultrie, one in Cordele . . . and it stop in Centerville.

CUTLER. Nigger, I know what I'm talking about. You gonna tell me where the train stop?

LEVEE. Hell, yeah, if you talking about it stop in Sigsbee. I'm gonna tell you the truth.

CUTLER. I'm talking about *this* train! I don't know what train you been riding. I'm talking about *this* train!

LEVEE. Ain't but one train. Ain't but one train come out of Tallahassee heading north to Atlanta, and it don't stop at Sigsbee. Tell him, Toledo . . . that train don't stop at Sigsbee. The only train that stops at Sigsbee is the Yazoo Delta, and you have to transfer at Moultrie to get it!

CUTLER. Well, hell, maybe that what he done! I don't know. I'm just telling you the man got off the train at Sigsbee . . .

LEVEE. All right . . . you telling it. Tell it your way. Just make up anything.

SLOW DRAG. Levee, leave the man alone and let him finish.

CUTLER. I ain't paying Levee no never mind.

LEVEE. Go on and tell it your way.

CUTLER. Anyway . . . Reverend Gates got off this train in Sigsbee. The train done stopped there and he figured he'd get off and check the schedule to be sure he arrive in time for somebody to pick him up. All right. While he's there checking the schedule, it come upon him that he had to go to the bathroom. Now, they ain't had no colored rest rooms at the station. The only colored rest room is an outhouse they got sitting way back two hundred yards or so from the station. All right. He in the outhouse and the train go off and leave him there. He don't know nothing about this town. Ain't never been there before—in fact, ain't never even heard of it before.

LEVEE. I heard of it! I know just where it's at . . . and he ain't got off no train coming out of Tallahassee in Sigsbee!

CUTLER. The man standing there, trying to figure out what he's gonna do . . . where this train done left him in this strange town. It started getting dark. He see where the sun's getting low in the sky and he's trying to figure out what he's gonna do, when he noticed a couple of white fellows standing across the street from this station. Just standing there, watching him. And then two or three more come up and joined the other one. He look around, ain't seen no colored folks nowhere. He didn't know what was getting in these here fellows' minds, so he commence to walking. He ain't knowed where he was going. He just walking down the railroad tracks when he hear them call him. "Hey, nigger!" See, just like that. "Hey, nigger!" He kept on walking. They called him some more and he just keep walking. Just going down the tracks. And then he heard a gunshot where somebody done fired a gun in the air. He stopped then, you know.

TOLEDO. You don't even have to tell me no more. I know the facts of it. I done heard the same story a hundred times. It happened to me too. Same thing.

CUTLER. Naw, I'm gonna show you how the white folks don't care nothing about who or what you is. They crowded around him. These gang of mens made a circle around him. Now, he's standing there, you understand . . . got his cross around his neck like them preachers wear. Had his little Bible with him what he carry all the time. So they crowd on around him and one of them ask who he is. He told them he was Reverend Gates and that he was going to see his sister who was sick and the train left without him. And they said, "Yeah, nigger . . . but can you dance?" He looked at them and commenced to dancing. One of them reached up and tore his cross off his neck. Said he was committing a heresy by dancing with a cross and Bible. Took his Bible and tore it up and had him dancing till they got tired of watching him.

SLOW DRAG. White folks ain't never had no respect for the colored minister.

CUTLER. That's the only way he got out of there alive . . . was to dance. Ain't even had no respect for a man of God! Wanna make him into a clown. Reverend Gates sat right in my house and told me that story from his own mouth. So . . . the white folks don't care nothing about Ma Rainey. She's just another nigger who they can use to make some money.

LEVEE. What I wants to know is . . . if he's a man of God, then where the hell was God when all of this was going on? Why wasn't God looking out for him? Why didn't God strike down them crackers with some of this lightning you talk about to me?

CUTLER. Levee, you gonna burn in hell.

LEVEE. What I care about burning in hell? You talk like a fool . . . burning in hell. Why didn't God strike some of them crackers down. Tell me that! That's the question! Don't come telling me this burning-in-hell shit! He a man of God . . . why didn't God strike some of them crackers down? I'll tell you why? I'll tell you the truth! It's sitting out there as plain as day! 'Cause he a white man's God. That's why! God ain't never listened to no nigger's prayers. God take a nigger's prayers and throw them in the garbage. God don't pay niggers no mind. In fact . . . God hate niggers! Hate them with all the fury in his heart. Jesus don't love you, nigger! Jesus hate your black ass! Come talking that shit to me. Talking about burning in hell! God can kiss my ass.

(CUTLER *can stand no more. He jumps up and punches* LEVEE *in the mouth. The force of the blow knocks* LEVEE *down and* CUTLER *jumps on him.*)

CUTLER. You worthless . . . That's my God! That's my God! That's my God! You wanna blaspheme my God!

(TOLEDO *and* SLOW DRAG *grab* CUTLER *and try to pull him off* LEVEE.)

SLOW DRAG. Come on, Cutler . . . let it go! It don't mean nothing!

CUTLER. (*Has* LEVEE *down on the floor and pounds on him with a fury.*) Wanna blaspheme my God! You worthless . . . talking about my God!

(TOLEDO *and* SLOW DRAG *succeed in pulling* CUTLER *off* LEVEE, *who is bleeding at the nose and mouth.*)

LEVEE. Naw, let him go! Let him go! (*He pulls out a knife.*) That's your God, huh? That's your God, huh? Is that right?

Your God, huh? All right. I'm gonna give your God a chance. I'm gonna give your God a chance. I'm gonna give him a chance to save your black ass. (LEVEE *circles* CUTLER *with the knife.* CUTLER *picks up a chair to protect himself.*)

TOLEDO. Come on, Levee . . . put the knife up!

LEVEE. Stay out of this, Toledo!

TOLEDO. That ain't no way to solve anything.

LEVEE. (*Alternately swipes at* CUTLER *during the following.*) I'm calling Cutler's God! I'm talking to Cutler's God! You hear me? Cutler's God! I'm calling Cutler's God. Come on and save this nigger! Strike me down before I cut his throat!

SLOW DRAG. Watch him, Cutler! Put that knife up, Levee!

LEVEE. (*To* CUTLER.) I'm calling your God! I'm gonna give him a chance to save you! I'm calling your God! We gonna find out whose God he is!

CUTLER. You gonna burn in hell, nigger!

LEVEE. Cutler's God! Come on and save this nigger! Come on and save him like you did my mama! Save him like you did my mama! I heard her when she called you! I heard her when she said, "Lord, have mercy! Jesus, help me! Please, God, have mercy on me, Lord Jesus, help me!" And did you turn your back? Did you turn your back, motherfucker? Did you turn your back? (LEVEE *becomes so caught up in his dialogue with God that he forgets about* CUTLER *and begins to stab upward in the air, trying to reach God.*) Come on! Come on and turn your back on me! Turn your back on me! Come on! Where is you? Come on and turn your back on me! Turn your back on me, motherfucker! I'll cut your heart out! Come on, turn your back on me! Come on! What's the matter? Where is you? Come on and turn your back on me! Come on, what you scared of? Turn your back on me! Come on! Coward, motherfucker! (LEVEE *folds his knife and stands triumphantly.*) Your God ain't shit, Cutler.

(*The lights fade to black.*)

MA RAINEY. (*Singing.*)
Ah, you hear me talking to you
I don't bite my tongue
You wants to be my man
You got to fetch it with you when you come.

(*Lights come up in the studio. The last bars of the last song of the session are dying out.*)

IRVIN. (*Over speaker.*) Good! Wonderful! We have that, boys. Good session. That's great, Ma. We've got ourselves some winners.

TOLEDO. Well, I'm glad that's over.

MA RAINEY. Slow Drag, where you learn to play the bass at? You had it singing! I heard you! Had that bass jumping all over the place.

SLOW DRAG. I was following Toledo. Nigger got them long fingers striding all over the piano. I was trying to keep up with him.

TOLEDO. That's what you supposed to do, ain't it? Play the music. Ain't nothing abstract about it.

MA RAINEY. Cutler, you hear Slow Drag on that bass? He make it do what he want it to do! Spank it just like you spank a baby.

CUTLER. Don't be telling him that. Nigger's head get so big his hat won't fit him.

SLOW DRAG. If Cutler tune that guitar up, we would really have something!

CUTLER. You wouldn't know what a tuned-up guitar sounded like if you heard one.

TOLEDO. Cutler was talking. I heard him moaning. He was all up in it.

MA RAINEY. Levee . . . what is that you doing? Why you playing all them notes? You play ten notes for every one you supposed to play. It don't call for that.

LEVEE. You supposed to improvise on the theme. That's what I was doing.

MA RAINEY. You supposed to play the song the way I sing it. The way everybody else play it. You ain't supposed to go off by yourself and play what you want.

LEVEE. I was playing the song. I was playing it the way I felt it.

MA RAINEY. I couldn't keep up with what was going on. I'm trying to sing the song and you up there messing up my ear. That's what you was doing. Call yourself playing music.

LEVEE. Hey . . . I know what I'm doing. I know what I'm doing, all right. I know how to play music. You all back up and leave me alone about my music.

CUTLER. I done told you . . . it ain't about *your* music. It's about *Ma's* music.

MA RAINEY. That's all right, Cutler. I done told you what to do.

LEVEE. I don't care what you do. You supposed to improvise

on the theme. Not play note for note the same thing over and over again.

MA RAINEY. You just better watch yourself. You hear me?

LEVEE. What I care what you or Cutler do? Come telling me to watch myself. What's that supposed to mean?

MA RAINEY. All right . . . you gonna find out what it means.

LEVEE. Go ahead and fire me. I don't care. I'm gonna get my own band anyway.

MA RAINEY. You keep messing with me.

LEVEE. Ain't nobody studying you. You ain't gonna do nothing to me. Ain't nobody gonna do nothing to Levee.

MA RAINEY. All right, nigger . . . you fired!

LEVEE. You think I care about being fired? I don't care nothing about that. You doing me a favor.

MA RAINEY. Cutler, Levee's out! He don't play in my band no more.

LEVEE. I'm fired . . . Good! Best thing that ever happened to me. I don't need this shit! (LEVEE *exits to the band room.* IRVIN *enters from the control booth.*)

MA RAINEY. Cutler, I'll see you back at the hotel.

IRVIN. Okay, boys . . . you can pack up. I'll get your money for you.

CUTLER. That's cash money, Mr. Irvin. I don't want no check.

IRVIN. I'll see what I can do. I can't promise you nothing.

CUTLER. As long as it ain't no check. I ain't got no use for a check.

IRVIN. I'll see what I can do, Cutler. (CUTLER, TOLEDO, *and* SLOW DRAG *exit to the band room.*) Oh, Ma, listen . . . I talked to Sturdyvant, and he said . . . Now, I tried to talk him out of it . . . He said the best he can do is to take your twenty-five dollars of your money and give it to Sylvester.

MA RAINEY. Take what and do what? If I wanted the boy to have twenty-five dollars of my money, I'd give it to him. He supposed to get his own money. He supposed to get paid like everybody else.

IRVIN. Ma, I talked to him . . . He said . . .

MA RAINEY. Go talk to him again! Tell him if he don't pay that boy, he'll never make another record of mine again. Tell him that. You supposed to be my manager. All this talk about sticking together. Start sticking! Go on up there and get that boy his money!

IRVIN. Okay, Ma . . . I'll talk to him again. I'll see what I can do.

MA RAINEY. Ain't no see about it! You bring that boy's money back here!

(IRVIN *exits. The lights stay on in the studio and come up in the band room. The men have their instruments packed and sit waiting for* IRVIN *to come and pay them.* SLOW DRAG *has a pack of cards.*)

SLOW DRAG. Come on, Levee, let me show you a card trick.

LEVEE. I don't want to see no card trick. What you wanna show me for? Why you wanna bother me with that?

SLOW DRAG. I was just trying to be nice.

LEVEE. I don't need you to be nice to me. What I need you to be nice to me for? I ain't gonna be nice to you. I ain't even gonna let you be in my band no more.

SLOW DRAG. Toledo, let me show you a card trick

CUTLER. I just hope Mr. Irvin don't bring no check down here. What the hell I'm gonna do with a check?

SLOW DRAG. All right now . . . pick a card. Any card . . . go on . . . take any of them. I'm gonna show you something.

TOLEDO. I agrees with you, Cutler. I don't want no check either.

CUTLER. It don't make no sense to give a nigger a check.

SLOW DRAG. Okay, now. Remember your card. Remember which one you got. Now . . . put it back in the deck. Anywhere you want. I'm gonna show you something. (TOLEDO *puts the card in the deck.*) You remember your card? All right. Now I'm gonna shuffle the deck. Now . . . I'm gonna show you what card you picked. Don't say nothing now. I'm gonna tell you what card you picked.

CUTLER. Slow Drag, that trick is as old as my mama.

SLOW DRAG. Naw, naw . . . wait a minute! I'm gonna show him his card . . . There it go! The six of diamonds. Ain't that your card? Ain't that it?

TOLEDO. Yeah, that's it . . . the six of diamonds.

SLOW DRAG. Told you! Told you I'd show him what it was!

(*The lights fade in the band room and come up full on the studio.* STURDYVANT *enters with* IRVIN.)

STURDYVANT. Ma, is there something wrong? Is there a problem?

MA RAINEY. Sturdyvant, I want you to pay that boy his money.

STURDYVANT. Sure, Ma. I got it right here. Two hundred for you and twenty-five for the kid, right? (STURDYVANT *hands the money to* IRVIN, *who hands it to* MA RAINEY *and* SYLVESTER.) Irvin misunderstood me. It was all a mistake. Irv made a mistake.

MA RAINEY. A mistake, huh?

IRVIN. Sure, Ma. I made a mistake. He's paid, right? I straightened it out.

MA RAINEY. The only mistake was when you found out I hadn't signed the release forms. That was the mistake. Come on, Sylvester. (*She starts to exit.*)

STURDYVANT. Hey, Ma . . . come on, sign the forms, huh?

IRVIN. Ma . . . come on now.

MA RAINEY. Get your coat, Sylvester. Irvin, where's my car?

IRVIN. It's right out front, Ma. Here . . . I got the keys right here. Come on, sign the forms, huh?

MA RAINEY. Irvin, give me my car keys!

IRVIN. Sure, Ma . . . just sign the forms, huh? (*He gives her the keys, expecting a trade-off.*)

MA RAINEY. Send them to my address and I'll get around to them.

IRVIN. Come on, Ma . . . I took care of everything, right? I straightened everything out.

MA RAINEY. Give me the pen, Irvin. (*She signs the forms.*) You tell Sturdyvant . . . one more mistake like that and I can make my records someplace else. (*She turns to exit.*) Sylvester, straighten up your clothes. Come on, Dussie Mae.

(*She exits, followed by* DUSSIE MAE *and* SYLVESTER. *The lights go down in the studio and come up on the band room.*)

CUTLER. I know what's keeping him so long. He up there writing out checks. You watch. I ain't gonna stand for it. He ain't gonna bring me no check down here. If he do, he's gonna take it right back upstairs and get some cash.

TOLEDO. Don't get yourself all worked up about it. Wait and see. Think positive.

CUTLER. I am thinking positive. He positively gonna give me some cash. Man give me a check last time . . . you remember . . . we went all over Chicago trying to get it cashed. See a nigger with a check, the first thing they think is he done stole it someplace.

LEVEE. I ain't had no trouble cashing mine.

CUTLER. I don't visit no whorehouses.

LEVEE. You don't know about my business. So don't start nothing. I'm tired of you as it is. I ain't but two seconds off your ass no way.

TOLEDO. Don't you all start nothing now.

CUTLER. What the hell I care what you tired of. I wasn't even talking to you. I was talking to this man right here.

(IRVIN *and* STURDYVANT *enter.*)

IRVIN. Okay boys. Mr. Sturdyvant has your pay.

CUTLER. As long as it's cash money, Mr. Sturdyvant. 'Cause I have too much trouble trying to cash a check.

STURDYVANT. Oh, yes . . . I'm aware of that. Mr. Irvin told me you boys prefer cash, and that's what I have for you. (*He starts handing out the money.*) That was a good session you boys put in . . . That's twenty-five for you. Yessir, you boys really know your business and we are going to . . . Twenty-five for you . . . We are going to get you back in here real soon . . . twenty-five . . . and have another session so you can make some more money . . . and twenty-five for you. Okay, thank you, boys. You can get your things together and Mr. Irvin will make sure you find your way out.

IRVIN. I'll be out front when you get your things together, Cutler. (IRVIN *exits.* STURDYVANT *starts to follow.*)

LEVEE. Mr. Sturdyvant, sir. About them songs I give you? . . .

STURDYVANT. Oh, yes, . . . uh . . . Levee. About them songs you gave me. I've thought about it and I just don't think the people will buy them. They're not the type of songs we're looking for.

LEVEE. Mr. Sturdyvant, sir . . . I don't got my band picked out and they's real good fellows. They knows how to play real good. I know if the peoples hear the music, they'll buy it.

STURDYVANT. Well, Levee, I'll be fair with you . . . but they're just not the right songs.

LEVEE. Mr. Sturdyvant, you got to understand about that music. That music is what the people is looking for. They's tired of jug-band music. They wants something that excites them. Something with some fire to it.

STURDYVANT. Okay, Levee. I'll tell you what I'll do. I'll give you five dollars apiece for them. Now that's the best I can do.

LEVEE. I don't want no five dollars, Mr. Sturdyvant. I wants to record them songs, like you say.

STURDYVANT. Well, Levee, like I say . . . they just aren't the kind of songs we're looking for.

LEVEE. Mr. Sturdyvant, you asked me to write them songs. Now, why didn't you tell me that before when I first give them to you? You told me you was gonna let me record them. What's the difference between then and now?

STURDYVANT. Well, look . . . I'll pay for your trouble . . .

LEVEE. What's the difference, Mr. Sturdyvant? That's what I wanna know.

STURDYVANT. I had my fellows play your songs, and when I heard them, they just didn't sound like the kind of songs I'm looking for right now.

LEVEE. You got to hear *me* play them, Mr. Sturdyvant! You ain't heard *me* play them. That's what's gonna make them sound right.

STURDYVANT. Well, Levee, I don't doubt that really. It's just that . . . well, I don't think they'd sell like Ma's records. But I'll take them off your hands for you.

LEVEE. The people's tired of jug-band music, Mr. Sturdyvant. They wants something that's gonna excite them! They wants something with some fire! I don't know what fellows you had playing them songs . . . but if I could play them! I'd set them down in the people's lap! Now you told me I could record them songs!

STURDYVANT. Well, there's nothing I can do about that. Like I say, it's five dollars apiece. That's what I'll give you. I'm doing you a favor. Now, if you write any more, I'll help you out and take them off your hands. The price is five dollars apiece. Just like now. (*He attempts to hand* LEVEE *the money, finally shoves it in* LEVEE's *coat pocket and is gone in a flash.* LEVEE *follows him to the door and it slams in his face. He takes the money from his pocket, balls it up and throws it on the floor. The other musicians silently gather up their belongings.* TOLEDO *walks past* LEVEE *and steps on his shoe.*)

LEVEE. Hey! Watch it . . . Shit Toledo! You stepped on my shoe!

TOLEDO. Excuse me there, Levee.

LEVEE. Look at that! Look at that! Nigger, you stepped on my shoe. What you do that for?

TOLEDO. I said I'm sorry.

LEVEE. Nigger gonna step on my goddamn shoe! You done fucked up my shoe! Look at that! Look at what you done to my shoe, nigger! I ain't stepped on your shoe! What you wanna step on my shoe for?

CUTLER. The man said he's sorry.

LEVEE. Sorry! How the hell he gonna be sorry after he gone

ruint my shoe? Come talking about sorry! (*Turns his attention back to* TOLEDO.) Nigger, you stepped on my shoe! You know that! (LEVEE *snatches his shoe off his foot and holds it up for* TOLEDO *to see*.) See what you done done?

TOLEDO. What you want me to do about it? It's done now. I said excuse me.

LEVEE. Wanna go and fuck up my shoe like that. I ain't done nothing to your shoe. Look at this! (TOLEDO *turns and continues to gather up his things*. LEVEE *spins him around by his shoulder*.) Naw . . . naw . . . look what you done! (*He shoves the shoe in* TOLEDO's *face*.) Look at that! That's my shoe! Look at that! You did it! You did it! You fucked up my shoe! You stepped on my shoe with them raggedy-ass clodhoppers!

TOLEDO. Nigger, ain't nobody studying you and your shoe! I said excuse me. If you can't accept that, then the hell with it. What you want me to do?

(LEVEE *is in a near rage, breathing hard. He is trying to get a grip on himself, as even he senses, or perhaps only he senses, he is about to lose control. He looks around, uncertain of what to do.* TOLEDO *has gone back to packing, as have* CUTLER *and* SLOW DRAG. *They purposefully avoid looking at* LEVEE *in hopes he'll calm down if he doesn't have an audience. All the weight in the world suddenly falls on* LEVEE *and he rushes at* TOLEDO *with his knife in his hand.*)

LEVEE. Nigger, you stepped on my shoe! (*He plunges the knife into* TOLEDO's *back up to the hilt.* TOLEDO *lets out a sound of surprise and agony.* CUTLER *and* SLOW DRAG *freeze.* TOLEDO *falls backward with* LEVEE, *his hand still on the knife, holding him up.* LEVEE *is suddenly faced with the realization of what he has done. He shoves* TOLEDO *forward and takes a step back.* TOLEDO *slumps to the floor.*) He . . . he stepped on my shoe. He did. Honest, Cutler, he stepped on my shoe. What he do that for? Toledo, what you do that for? Cutler, help me. He stepped on my shoe, Cutler. (*He turns his attention to* TOLEDO.) Toledo! Toledo, get up. (*He crosses to* TOLEDO *and tries to pick him up.*) It's okay, Toledo. Come on . . . I'll help you. Come on, stand up now. Levee'll help you. (TOLEDO *is limp and heavy and awkward. He slumps back to the floor.* LEVEE *gets mad at him.*) Don't look at me like that! Toledo! Nigger, don't look at me like that! I'm warning you, nigger! Close your eyes! Don't you look at me like that! (*He turns to* CUTLER.) Tell him to close his eyes. Cutler. Tell him don't look at me like that.

CUTLER. Slow Drag, get Mr. Irvin down here.

(*The sound of a trumpet is heard,* LEVEE's *trumpet, a muted trumpet struggling for the highest of possibilities and blowing pain and warning.*)

BLACKOUT

ABOUT THE EDITOR

BROOKS McNAMARA is Professor of Performance Studies in the Tisch School of the Arts at New York University and Director of the Schubert Archive, which he founded in 1976. A contributing editor to *The Drama Review*, he has designed stage settings for Cafe La Mama, The Performance Company and the New York Cultural Center.